SWORDS OF SOUL & SHADOW

GATE CHRONICLES BOOK III

SWORDS OF SOUL & SHADOW

GATE CHRONICLES BOOK III

ALLI EARNEST

DRAGON PAGE
ENTERTAINMENT

THE GATE CHRONICLES

Cities of Smoke & Starlight

Realms of Wrath & Ruin

Swords of Soul & Shadow

Contents

THE GATE CHRONICLES...1

PART I: CITIES I

PROLOGUE 1

CHAPTER 1 15

CHAPTER 2.. 33

CHAPTER 3.. 42

CHAPTER 4 47

CHAPTER 5..67

CHAPTER 6 81

CHAPTER 7 99

CHAPTER 8..106

CHAPTER 9 119

CHAPTER 10...128

CHAPTER 11...137

CHAPTER 12 146

CHAPTER 13 166

CHAPTER 14...176

PART II: REALMS.. 191

INTERLUDE I 192

CHAPTER 15 193

CHAPTER 16..209

CHAPTER 17 220

CHAPTER 18..232

CHAPTER 19..240

CHAPTER 20 261

CHAPTER 21..268

CHAPTER 22 289

CHAPTER 23 303

CHAPTER 24..320

CHAPTER 25 335

CHAPTER 26 340

CHAPTER 27 350

CHAPTER 28 354

CHAPTER 29..367

CHAPTER 30 375

CHAPTER 31..392

CHAPTER 32..408

CHAPTER 33 411

CHAPTER 34..448

CHAPTER 35 460

CHAPTER 36 471

CHAPTER 37 491

PART III: SWORDS..511

INTERLUDE II 512

CHAPTER 38 513

CHAPTER 39 516

CHAPTER 40 535

CHAPTER 41 547

CHAPTER 42 554

CHAPTER 43 570

CHAPTER 44 583

CHAPTER 45 592

CHAPTER 46 605

CHAPTER 47 621

CHAPTER 48 637

CHAPTER 49 641

CHAPTER 50 652

CHAPTER 51 679

CHAPTER 52 693

CHAPTER 53 709

EPILOGUE 717

LOVE THIS BOOK? 728

ACKNOWLEDGMENTS 729

GLOSSARY 731

ABOUT THE AUTHOR 735

KAVOST PEAKS
Tev Rubika
SUNKEN CITY
Jayde
RUNE BAY
Cerulene
NARDEN PASS
LENARA CANYON
ACHILLES
STONESET
KYVENA
SOL ADRID
CRYSTALFELL
FOREST OF GÂLAN
Silver Coast
THE WORLD OF
Yalvara
JOSEI OCEAN
BAY OF STORMS
VATN WOOD
Tasava
SALI BOG
VARANI MOUNTAINS
HADDON'S PASS
MYRRAI
DRAGONAE LANDS
VADRI WASTES
CAPITAL CITY
VILLAGE/CITY
FORT
BORDER

For Kase & Hallie, you've earned this dedication three times over—even if you only live in my head

PART I: CITIES

PROLOGUE

BROTHER

50 Years Ago

TWELVE WAS MUCH TOO YOUNG an age to have blood under one's nails.

It was also much too young to be working in the Zuprium mines, but the boy didn't have a choice.

He longed for fresh air, not the sort he breathed now...stale, like water left in the summer heat. The scent didn't match the mines themselves. More experienced miners told him he'd get used to it, that it would cling to him like sweat soon enough. If they meant to reassure, they failed miserably.

Uneven, jagged scraps of rock bit through the soles of his secondhand boots. He had to wrap both hands around the handle of his pa's old pickax so he could swing it hard enough to harvest the crystal in front of him. His fingertips barely touched one another.

The crystal sang to him in its ethereal way, the only beauty down in mountain depths. In the lantern light, it glittered and grinned like the summer sun.

It knew it was to be harvested. It knew the boy only did this to keep food on the table. It knew he wanted to be anywhere but covered in Zuprium dust and sweat.

He did not know how. It just did. Its song told him so.

But its music wasn't the only thing hollering in this hole; pain raised its voice with every swing of his pickax, complaints lodged by the bruises on his arms.

They would take a few weeks to disappear. First red as a mountain hornet, then purple, then green, and yellow. They always faded that way. The only difference was the boy could now pretend the mines had made them.

Even with Ma's poultices, Pa's mind was going too fast...and with it, his restraint. None of the herbs in Ma's garden could fix the brain. James Hale needed help only doctors in Kyvena could provide, but when your only lot in life was a pickax and a handful of Zuprium dust, you couldn't afford to reach that help...or pay the hefty price for it.

Instead, you simply went insane.

The dust ate at your mind and body until it couldn't no longer. It got into every mountain cottage nook and cranny. Most mountain folk died at the ripe old age of forty—if they were lucky.

The boy hated it all.

He hated the mountains. He despised the way the dirt floor of his family's one-room cottage smelled when rain leaked through the roof. He loathed the haggard miners who traipsed through the door that wouldn't stay shut, begging Ma for poultices to ease the pain. It was the most they could hope for somewhere as far removed as Ravenhelm.

Their larger sister village, Stoneset, also boasted fruitful Zuprium mines. Maybe they had the ability to avoid what was known round those parts as the Fogs; maybe they didn't. Maybe the capital ignored them all the same, so long as they met their Zuprium load for the month.

The pickax handle scraped his palms and fingertips, leaving splinters behind if he wasn't careful. But careful wouldn't carve these crystals out of the wall; swinging the pickax took nearly all his strength.

Most didn't enter the mines sooner than sixteen, but with Pa getting worse by the month—the week—the *day*, the Hale family had no choice...they needed to eat, and most miners only had stale bread or nearly rotten potatoes to trade, no money. Not enough to pay Ma what her poultices were worth. At ten, the boy's younger brother, Michael, had figured out what herbs he could collect from the garden and nearby forest to make the potatoes taste nearly edible. It wasn't enough.

The thought of his brother's bright blue eyes and blond hair that never laid flat tightened his hold on the pickax. He threw his whole weight behind the next strike.

The crystal was about the size of his fist and emitted a faint glow in the lantern light. To the untrained eye, it might look like gold, but it was something more valuable than any jewelry. Its veins ran deep within these mountains; it told the story of the planet itself. Some said it was magic. The boy said it was a way to live and a way to die.

The pickax struck true. A sharp cloud of dust floated out of the small crack left behind. Beautiful as it sparkled in the light, but a slow death to those breathing it in. A flashpistol bullet to the head would be quicker, but the boy would do anything to keep his brother out of the mines, even if it meant the boy lost his own mind by the time he was thirty.

It was funny to think that three months before, he'd been playing groggon in the field behind the tiny schoolhouse with his brother and friends. He'd been faster and stronger than boys even three years his senior. He'd dreamed the sport was his way of leaving, his ticket to fame and the capital. On that particular day in June, he'd scored the winning goal and had basked in the light of victory. He'd gone home a champion.

Pa snapped that very same day.

Ten months later, the boy slammed the pickax again, his grunt echoing in the dim, roughly hewn corridor. The gas lantern above was a necessary evil so deep within the mountain. Hit the crystal wrong, and tatters of flesh would be all that was left when the miners dug you out.

It'd been six months since the last explosion. A record.

One he didn't feel like breaking.

The boy wiped sweat off his forehead and coughed. He would get some herbs from Ma when he returned home. They slowed the process slightly, which was why his father was one of the *lucky few* who dodged the worst of the symptoms until they were older.

Lucky, too, that he'd only begun working in the mines after Cerl mercenaries killed his own father. Before that, James Hale had been a baker's son, breathing in nothing more dangerous than flour.

The boy's muscles ached. Soon, the call to end the day would go round, and he could go home and pray his father was asleep. He wouldn't have to tiptoe around anything that might set Pa off.

A few of the miners nearby laughed at a crude joke the boy barely understood. The chuckles turned into hacking coughs.

He swung his pickax again.

At the same moment the tip connected with the crystal, the floor shook under his feet. The gas lantern swung on its hook so violently that it fell and shattered.

The boy blinked in the false twilight. Softly glowing crystals and another lantern further up the corridor were the only illumination. Shouts echoed all around him.

Mine explosion.

The boy's heart hammered as the other miners sprinted toward the entrance, but all he could do was stare down at the dim outline of his pickax. No one he liked was down in the mines. His mother and brother were safe in the cottage. He was the only one in real danger, and even at twelve, he found he didn't care.

If he died down here, Ma and Michael would starve without the pittance he received every week. They'd get along for a bit with scraps handed to them by neighbors for a while, but after that...

He gritted his teeth.

Then again, he wasn't in the deepest part of the mountain where the more dangerous tunnels were dug. The mine supervisor had taken pity on the boy. He'd known his father before the Fogs had worked its way to his brain. The supervisor wanted him to be a messenger runner. The boy insisted on mining. It paid more.

And it would pay nothing if he ran out empty-handed.

Rage flowing through his veins, he swung the pickax and nailed the stone next to the cluster.

He laughed as rock shards bit his cheeks and exposed skin. The little stings were nothing compared to the pain in his chest. He hit the rock again and again, loosening the crystal bit by bit. His fingers bled worse than before. Blood ran down his hand and wrists from the busted blisters, but it almost made him feel better.

Maybe the Fogs had emerged early for him. That'd be just his luck.

Another rumble shook the cavern, and he paused again. He didn't care, it didn't matter…but two in one day, after six months of nothing? That seemed odd.

"Brother!"

The boy stopped his mad swinging and turned. He breathed heavily, blood still leaking from his hands like water from a cracked pot.

"Brother!"

Michael?

What was Michael doing in the mines?

The boy gripped his pickax hard, pain lancing through his palm like lightning. He grimaced. The pain kept him focused. He trudged toward the tunnel entrance. The remaining gas lanterns hanging from the interspersed beams down the main corridor flickered. Only a third or so had survived the explosions.

The boy steadied himself on the wall.

He should've been terrified. He should've run to the entrance when the other miners had. He should've felt something other than rage. Any more explosions, and the entire thing would collapse with the boy inside.

But the only thing that frightened him right now was the sight of a small figure wobbling at the tunnel's entrance.

"Brother!" Now that Michael was closer, fear and pain coated the syllables like sludge.

He probably ran to the mines soon as the village felt the first explosion. His brother had always cared more.

"It's okay! I'm here!" The boy ran up the last slope. "What are you—"

Michael collapsed, his arms cradling his stomach.

Now the boy was afraid.

The boy threw his pickax aside and fell beside his

brother, grabbing his narrow shoulders. "What happened?"

Something rusty and strange speckled his brother's pale face. Splotches of the stuff coated his blond hair. "Soldiers— they—and Ma—" Michael sobbed, tears coursing down his face. The rusty freckles all over his face began to run like rivulets, brightening rust to a more recognizable red.

Blood.

Had Michael been inside the mines when the explosion happened? He should've been at the schoolhouse, or maybe even home helping Ma.

"Michael." The boy's own bloody hands gripped his brother's shoulders tighter. The red fingerprints left behind were barely noticeable against his brother's ragged homespun cotton shirt. "Slow down. What's going on?"

"Soldiers."

His brother's crying sharpened into shallow, panicky breaths, like he couldn't quite expand his lungs big enough. The boy pulled him into a tight hug. "What soldiers?"

The word was nearly lost in the sobs as Michael's body shuddered. "Cerls."

Relief and terror warred in his veins. Relief that the mines wouldn't collapse and terror it wasn't exploding crystals; terror, to hear that word outside of his father's old stories.

Living on the border always came with its dangers, but Cerls had not attacked Ravenhelm in his lifetime. The last skirmish had orphaned his father and forced him into the mines, but that had been sixteen years ago.

The boy pulled back. "How many?"

But all Michael could do was cry. He made an odd choking sound as blood dribbled from his mouth.

The boy froze. "Are you hurt?"

Michael finally removed his hands from his stomach, revealing a growing stain on his dirty wool shirt.

Not rusty. Not dried or speckled or small.

Red. So much red.

The boy's heart leapt into his throat. "Where's Ma?"

"Told me to run." Michael coughed, more blood sliding from his lips to his chin as he shook his head. The boy wiped it with his shirtsleeve. The scarlet streak stood out against the Zuprium dust coating it.

No.

He couldn't worry about her. He couldn't worry about the piece of his soul that just ripped away and died with the knowledge that...no, he couldn't even admit it. He could grieve later. Michael needed him.

The boy blinked back the stinging tears in his own eyes as the sobs overtook Michael again; he stood and grabbed his pickax, gritting his teeth. "I'll be back."

"No, Brother!" Michael's voice broke on the last word. "They're still out there!"

He was only ten, for stars' sake.

The boy shook his head. "You need a medic."

He'd heard there was one in Stoneset, a woman who could heal almost anything. He'd also heard she was going mad, but she was Michael's only chance. His mother had treated a few gut wounds over the years without success. All she could do was ease the passing.

A kindness she probably hadn't been given herself.

He looked around. This would be the safest place for his brother to hide, away from the town, but if he didn't get him to the woman in Stoneset...

No. No. No. He *needed* Michael. Without him, the boy didn't know what would become of himself. He'd be a shell.

He'd have *nothing*.

The Cerls were looking for anything that could make them a quick hunder. Ridiculous they thought they could find that here. Of course, there were those who believed the Zuprium they mined could do more than make decent blades and flashpistols, but they were the real crazy ones.

The boy tossed his pickax aside and grunted as he picked up Michael, trying not to jostle him too much. His brother whimpered. The boy's already aching arms protested, but he would not leave his brother here to die alone in the mines. Not if there was a chance the Stoneset woman could save him. Gossip said she was Yalven, but he didn't believe such slop. They were just a bedtime story told to keep naughty children in line.

He left his pickax and trekked up the tunnel. There, new sounds met his ears: screams and wails, guttural noises he couldn't place. He froze, pressing himself against the wall. Michael moaned at the sudden movement.

"Broth—Brother..."

"Hold on." The boy couldn't mask the fear in his voice.

It was tight and precise, like it'd been squeezed from his throat. "I'll fix this."

His brother's life leaked from his side, and by the time the boy figured out how to get to Stoneset, it'd be too late.

But the boy would try anyway.

As gently as he could, the boy lowered his brother to the ground. "I'll come back, I swear." He arranged Michael against the wall in the most comfortable position he could think of. "I just need to find something, or someone...I'll be back with help, and you'll be fine."

As if he could make it so simply by saying it.

"No, no..." Michael sobbed. He reached, but his arms were too weak; they dropped without finding the boy. "Don't go!"

The boy wiped away his brother's tears and stood, the blood clinging to his skin and clothing as if it were his own. He willed courage into his limbs and strode forward, turning at the mine entrance, the sun blazing and hot on his pale face. "I love you, Michael."

And then the boy was off. The morning had been crisp, but the late April day had turned into one of heat and the promise of summer beauty. How horrifying the contrast. The shouts had died down, and the ground no longer shook, but the destruction around the last bend in the tree-lined path made the serene spring day feel like a mockery.

Soldiers. Blue jackets. Triple diamond tattoos everywhere he looked.

Cerls.

The fear in his veins ran cold like the mountain snows, like his family's tiny cottage when the fire went out in the dead of winter. The blacksmith's arm lay at a grotesque angle, a Cerl above him wiping blood from a sword. He sprawled at the edge of the village in the middle of the road. Sickness rose up in the boy's throat and choked any scream he might've let loose.

He flung himself back into the trees and hid behind the largest one. His breaths came in squeaks and wheezes. Why were they here? What had his people done to justify this? The previous attack had happened because the marauding bandits needed supplies, and Ravenhelm just happened to be closest.

Those men were not bandits. They were soldiers; *Trips,*

as everyone called them, or *thrice-blasted Trips* if his father got to ranting.

The boy needed a plan. Even if he hadn't left his pickax behind, it wouldn't have done him any good against a Cerl's sword. He needed a horse and cart to get Michael to Stoneset fast as possible. It was nearly a full day's walk with a clear sky and no soldiers at your back.

The boy forced himself to look around the tree again, bracing for the death and destruction. He scanned the village for the enemy, purposefully avoiding looking directly at the dead littering the roads and alleys he'd known his entire life.

But his eyes caught on one of the mine guards closest to the tree line. Red hair. Too many freckles. Only a handful of years older than the boy himself. His crossbow lay halfway underneath his body where he'd fallen. Blood stained the grass.

The boy could use the crossbow. It would be lighter than the pickax. He was just strong enough to use it properly.

The boy looked back toward the village. He spotted a few of his fellow miners among the dead, their bodies lining one of the alleyways closest to him that ran between the tavern and village hall.

Only a few soldiers remained. Two of them sat atop horses. Smoke and flames licked the rooftops of most cottages. The two with horses seemed to be looking for something.

If the boy could grab the crossbow and bolts and make his way to the edge of the last cottage, he could ambush them. He'd hit them with the bolts and steal their horses. He'd run down anyone else who tried to stop him.

Then he'd hitch them both to a wagon and carry his brother to safety. A rudimentary plan, but it was the only one he had, and the only one he'd get.

He didn't have time to try for a better one.

Holding his breath, the boy crept to the dead mine guard and slid the crossbow and quiver from his limp grasp. The wood clung to his hands, sticky with congealing blood.

Swallowing the bile in his throat, the boy wrapped one hand around the crossbow and grabbed three bolts from the quiver.

"May you find your place among the stars," the boy whispered as he left the guard's body and snuck to the nearest cottage. His heart pounded in his ears so loudly he couldn't hear or feel anything but the incessant beating.

Thump-thump. Thump-thump.

He pressed against the cottage wall and willed his heart to calm enough to make his hands stop trembling. He could do this. Kill the two soldiers. Steal their horses. Get Michael to Stoneset.

He'd never killed anyone before. He'd thought about it when his father flew into one of his rages, but he'd never acted on that instinct.

Thump-thump.

He didn't know how close the soldiers were. He could only hear his heart. He leaned forward and around the corner of the cottage.

The soldiers were closer now, but the boy couldn't understand what they said. The school mistress didn't teach Cerleze. Why learn the language of the enemy? That thinking was probably the reason why the village had been destroyed in the first place.

Where were the troops from Achilles? Sure, Ravenhelm hadn't warranted much of a military presence, and no one sane wanted a station out in some byway mountain village, but there'd always been a few soldiers who rotated in and out every few months to keep the peace. Those with the Fogs tended to get rowdy, and of course, the Cerls had always been a looming but unlikely threat.

Where were those soldiers now? Had they perished? Or had they run at the first sign of trouble?

The boy fitted one of the bolts into the crossbow with fumbling fingers. He managed to slide it into the groove at last, pulling it back, swallowing the grunt of effort that tried to escape.

He needed those horses. A mule and the boy's faulty footsteps would be too slow. The horses looked mountain-hardy and surefooted...they'd made it here in the first place, hadn't they?

He looked to the Cerls next.

He'd been hunting before, but those had been animals, and he'd needed to eat. It was one of the only good memories he had of his father before the Fogs had coated them in pain. But killing squirrels and the occasional deer wasn't anything like slaying a person.

Michael's pale face and blood-soaked shirt flashed in his mind.

The Cerls hadn't hesitated before hurting Michael. The boy couldn't hesitate either. Not when he was the only one left to save his brother.

The clop of horse hooves and the bray of nervous whinnies came closer. The boy sucked in a few more breaths. His finger hovered over the trigger.

If he distracted the left soldier with a bolt through the one on the right's chest, he'd have time to load another and shoot the final soldier. He could do it. He *would* do it.

For Michael.

He counted down in his head. *Three...*

Indecipherable words exchanged between the soldiers. *Two...*

They would die. The boy would kill them. *One...*

The boy leapt out, swinging the crossbow out and aiming. The soldiers startled, the horses spooking at the boy's sudden appearance.

The man on the right yelled something to the other. He wore a pristine blue coat, colorful badges decorating the right breast. The boy focused on one of those badges and let the crossbow bolt loose.

The recoil nearly made the boy lose his footing, but the bolt hit home, nailing the soldier in the chest. Blood spurted, staining those pretty badges; the soldier's hand flew to the puncture as he gasped, falling forward onto his horse.

Someone shouted behind him, but the boy was too busy scrambling to load another bolt. The other soldier was faster, taller, younger than the first—yet his presence was commanding. His night-dark hair was only slightly disheveled, a glittering earring in one ear. He grabbed his own crossbow and leveled it at the boy. Without thinking, the boy leapt sideways, collapsing onto the dirt road, skidding shoulder-first through a puddle of drying blood from one of his schoolmates, only recognizable by the star-shaped birthmark on the back of his hand. A shooting star, now that blood had smeared a trail behind it.

He didn't feel any pain. But he heard the *thunk* of the bolt landing true.

"Brother?"

No.

The bolt had missed him by a hair's breadth. But it hadn't *missed* entirely.

The first wounded soldier slid off his mount and onto the body-littered street below. The boy scrambled for his loose crossbow, but he couldn't reach it in time.

Instead, his eyes met Michael's—then fell, finding where blood leaked from beneath the Cerl's bolt, lodged deep in Michael's chest.

"*No!*" The boy forgot about the living soldier and stumbled to his feet, grasping and pulling himself over another dead body to make it to his brother's side. "No, no, *no!*"

The Cerl didn't fire on him. The shouts and another horn sounded closer, but the boy no longer cared what happened. He scooped his brother into his arms. He was so light, much lighter than he'd been in the mine. Was it only the boy's imagination? Was he losing it already? The Fogs?

Michael stared ahead, gaze soft and hazy, more blood gushing out his lips with each bubbling, fluid-filled breath.

"Why, why didn't you stay—" The boy had lost himself to his anguish and rage. "I was going to save you. I was going to—"

More hooves thundered, and the boy looked up to see the Jaydian banner flying high above the lead rider. The sacred tree inside the sun. Life and Light.

Yet everything in the boy's life had gone dark.

They'd gotten here too late.

The boy held his brother close and just caught the words wheezing out with another bubble of blood. "I didn't—I didn't...want to be...alone..."

And then he was gone, his eyes fixed listlessly on the sky above. The sunset had begun, the red streaks bathing his brother's too-pale face in its angry light.

The boy sobbed against his brother's hair once more before closing his eyes with unsteady fingers. He laid him down in the muck. The Cerl soldiers were gone, chased off by the Jaydian troops. His brother was dead.

The boy took slow steps forward, standing over the soldier he'd killed. He stared into the Cerl's lifeless face.

It wasn't too different from Michael's. Maybe in death, differences weren't so apparent. Or maybe the boy was simply numb. The soldier's eyes were lined with age and golden like the dying sun. He hated the color.

He unsheathed the soldier's sword and inspected the hilt. Some sort of writing decorated the blade itself; the metal was almost white, but it still shone with the tell-tale bronze glint of Zuprium. The tip was jagged, broken—or maybe it had been made that way. The pommel was unadorned except for a startlingly blue jewel that shone like a star.

"You're safe, now," a deep voice said from behind him.

The boy didn't even flinch, only turned slightly to see a Jaydian soldier behind him. The man was tall and broad-shouldered, his uniform coated in dust; they must've ridden hard to get here. The boy guessed someone had finally alerted them. Maybe one of the soldiers stationed in the village had gone. All he knew was they were too late.

The man walked closer, his hands out to show he meant no harm, but there wasn't anything he could do to make the boy feel any better or worse.

"What happened, son?" the man asked.

A few other soldiers inspected the bodies; a few others ran through the town looking for survivors. The boy's voice was as lifeless as the bodies around him. "They're all dead."

"Your parents?"

The boy was silent. But silence was enough to answer.

What did this man want? Why badger him? Why act like he'd been saved?

Maybe if he attacked the man with the strange sword, he could go out with the rest of his home, his family. That would surely end with a flashpistol to the head, and the boy would welcome it happily.

His hand clenched harder around the sword grip. He could do it. He'd just killed one man. What was one more? The Jaydian deserved it. He hadn't arrived in time to save Michael. Not even the Yalven woman in Stoneset could do anything now.

The Jaydian man barked out a few orders to his men. Some sort of officer or commander, then. Definitely a flashpistol to the head if the boy killed him.

The boy finally looked up into his eyes and loosened his grip on the sword.

His eyes were soft green, not that devilish golden-brown. The man removed his cap and held it to his chest, bowing slightly. "I'm Colonel Carleton Shackley. I'll make sure you're taken care of, son." He gestured with his hat toward the boy. "You've been through a lot today, I imagine. What's your name?"

The boy clenched his teeth together so hard it hurt. Who was he now without a mother, a father, and a brother? Who was he without the village he'd lived in for the entirety of his twelve years on this planet? He wasn't sure he still had a soul.

He shut his eyes only to find the dead soldier's and his dead brother's staring back at him.

Who was he now?

"Son?"

The boy swallowed his hatred best he could and opened his eyes. "Harlan…Harlan Hale."

C H A P T E R   1

UNDONE

Hallie

THE FLASH PORTRAIT WAS ONLY eight years old. But to Hallie Walker, those eight years might as well have been a lifetime.

The day she'd purchased it was frozen in her memory like a portrait itself; the mountains had finally welcomed summer like a childhood sweetheart, the snows melting on all but the highest mountain peaks. Thanks to the thaw, traders and peddlers of all sorts made their way to the cleared Narden Pass, wagons weighed down with all sorts of baubles, sweets, and gadgets from Kyvena.

The Summer Market days were the only time Hallie could almost imagine leaving the close and quaint village she'd known all her life. The promise of adventure had hung thick in the air like the spicy perfume coming from one wagon, singing as sweetly as Stoneset's resident bard with his soft, soulful tenor.

Though her family always had food on the table, she could never afford anything too fancy from the dust-swept merchants. Instead, she'd trailed her fingers over soft leather book spines and tested all the latest trinkets and vowed that one day, when she was owner of the inn, she would allocate enough to buy at least one book a year.

It was a good dream; she was certain the people of Stoneset would appreciate a little library to use that didn't belong to the schoolmistress. Mistress Jules would lend out her books from time to time, but she was from the capital and came from money. Marrying one of the miners had helped, but general mountain suspicion wouldn't allow complete trust in an outsider.

That day was different, though. Papa had given her and Jack spending money and told them to use it wisely. Jack's version of *wisely* was to buy a bag bursting with crinkly-wrapped peppermint sweets. Instead of a coveted copy of *Little Women* by Louisa May Alcott, Hallie had chosen a flash portrait for Papa—it was his birthday, after all. The peddler had complimented her on being such a sweet, thoughtful girl. How wrong he was.

Hallie had only remembered the occasion at all because Mama had declined to join them at the market in favor of baking a cake. So Hallie had wrangled her brother for the flash portrait and forced him to smile. What the peddler hadn't captured was Jack's teasing insults under his breath or Hallie pinching his side in retribution after the flash.

Eight years, a lifetime—yet she remembered it as if it were yesterday. Though she'd longed for the book back then, she was thankful now that she'd chosen the portrait, gazing at it as she adjusted the gas lamp in her father's tent.

If only she could return to that balmy summer day, sweat clinging to her brow and the world at her feet. Instead, she shivered in the chill of the present-day hidden cavern. Even with the days lengthening and the snows melting, her father's old tent didn't offer much warmth. Neither did the cot in the corner, nor did Kase's stolen military jacket slung around her shoulders.

She grabbed the framed portrait from the nearby crate, her best attempt at a bedside table, wishing the memory alone could chase the cold out.

The chill ran down to her very bones; the heat that had nearly killed her days earlier was gone. On the one hand, it was a blessing. When she'd bid Kase and her father goodbye, she'd been certain it was final. What limited control she'd gained over her newfound power was tenuous, after all. But once Kase left her with his goggles and the memory of his kiss, that power had fallen away, draining into her core and disappearing entirely.

She was empty.

She didn't understand it one bit, and the journals her father had given her—penned by her great-grandmother—had been mostly useless. Sure, they had hinted at a way to Myrrai, and the lingering scrap of the Lord Elder in the power that had once thrummed in Hallie's veins had confirmed it, but other than that, the tale they told made little sense.

After Navara had made it to Stoneset, she had fallen in love with the blacksmith and become the town medic. If Hallie hadn't known Navara's lineage, her life's tale would have seemed no less ordinary than any of the women Hallie had grown up with in Stoneset.

The remaining journals were dominated by logs of Navara's patients and their ailments. A few pages here and there detailed her day-to-day feelings. A few included her hopes and dreams—the wish that her son and his wife would decide to have children soon made frequent appearances.

But the final journal was written in Yalven, and Hallie had only been able to translate half of the first page. The dialect was odd. However, what little she'd translated proved to be rather grim.

Navara's son had contracted what was colloquially known in the Nardens as *The Fogs*. The disease was common among Zuprium miners, a deterioration of the mind that worsened the more one was exposed to the raw metal. Leading medical professionals in Kyvena had theories about why this was so, but none of them seemed substantial.

Though Stoneset's medic had treated several cases of it in Hallie's childhood—or managed them, rather, seeing as there was no cure—since Navara's time, the disease had decreased slightly thanks to new regulations. Every male was still required to do some work in the mines, but on rotations. Niels had decided to volunteer before his assigned time because his family had needed the money.

Jack had never worked the mines, but he'd still died in one.

Regardless, Navara's final journal read like a descent into madness, even if she hadn't worked the mines and contracted The Fogs herself. Maybe treating it so long had affected her somehow, and the final straw had been her son succumbing to the disease—Hallie's grandfather, a man she'd never met.

Perhaps that proximal madness was why Navara hadn't been successful in finding a cure.

Hallie looked back at the flash portrait once more before setting it back on the crate. Half the reason her parents had saved so fastidiously for years was so that Jack would never have to do time in the mines. Hallie would've gotten married young to Niels and prayed he deteriorated slowly enough for them to have a long and comfortable life together. It affected everyone differently, after all; some would not fall prey to it for decades, while others would succumb in weeks. It was a game of chance; a horrid one, but a reality of the life they lived.

Hallie eyed her pack, where the journals were tucked away. Papa had told her that the end of Navara's life hadn't been pretty. From what she could tell, he'd been right.

Her great-grandmother was supposed to inherit this power, not Hallie. She hadn't had a choice—she'd been forced to take it from the Lord Elder. Like the miners didn't have a choice but to poison themselves to protect their families.

Was this her version of The Fogs, her mind deteriorating thanks to something she hadn't chosen? Had running from her fate only made the ending of her life so much worse?

Either way, Hallie had been holed up in Papa's tent for three days with only her past, her thoughts, and a dead woman's inked ramblings for company. If she wasn't mad already, it couldn't be far off.

"Hal?"

And Niels' nagging brought that madness ever closer. He was trying to be kind, she knew, but he wasn't getting the hint.

Hallie rolled back onto the cot as softly as she could, trying not to let it creak as she pulled Kase's jacket more tightly around her shoulders. If she were quiet enough, she could feign sleep, a near-foolproof way to avoid the man she'd been meant to marry a lifetime ago.

"Hal? I know you're in there."

Well, of course he would know that. He'd moved his own tent next to hers. Whatever reservations he'd had before must've evaporated, much to her chagrin. If he would only leave her alone, she might be able to hear herself think well enough to finally figure things out.

Instead of answering, Hallie rolled to face the tent wall. She'd managed to avoid any serious conversations with him so far. The only words she'd spoken were *thank you* when he'd brought her food from Ms. Vella's cookpot. He had regular patrol duty for the first half of the day, so at least she could avoid him during breakfast and lunch.

Ms. Vella had always had a soft spot for both Hallie and Jack. She and her husband had lost their own son in the Great War, so she'd called them the grandchildren she never had. For the past two mornings, while Niels was safely occupied elsewhere, Hallie had gone to sit with her and eat breakfast. The woman had no one else—her husband had died in the Cerl attack. That news had thrown a punch into Hallie's gut, but she'd taken the blow well enough; it was a feeling she'd grown too accustomed to the past few months.

"Ms. Vella made chicken and dumplings." Niels' shadow bent down, a bowl clattering as he set it at the tent's entrance. "Guy's also promised to tell a few stories."

Guy had been the resident bard before the attack. Now, he'd stepped into the role of village leader. All the old ones were dead, and her father had left for the capital.

"Then they're gonna talk about going back," Niels added. "Thought you might be interested in that conversation, at least."

Now that Achilles had been neutralized, some of the villagers felt safe to return to their homes. Others believed the caverns still offered protection from anything else that might come their way. They didn't realize Hallie was the reason the fort fell. The story was that something within the fort detonated and destroyed it. Hallie hadn't corrected them.

But if Correa was dead, then what leader did they have? Had King Filip survived the attack, or did they really expect the village bard to play that part with this terrifying world as his stage?

Hallie shut her eyes and pretended—wished—she really was asleep. If she closed her eyes long enough, maybe she could pretend well enough to make it real.

Not that her dreams were much of an escape. Most of the time, Kase was there…sometimes kissing her, sometimes disintegrating beneath her fingertips. Before Achilles, her dreams had been riddled with the trauma of the *Eudora Jayde* journey, but since the fort's destruction, the nightmares had shifted, worsened. They almost felt more real than her waking hours.

In the nightmares, fire raced in her blood, and the air smelled of ash as Kase's skin fell away. His scream still pierced her ears when she woke up.

Screams, because she'd failed to take on the Essence over and over again. Screams because Correa had tortured him.

Lightning, fire, screaming, ash.

Hallie clenched every muscle at once, willing the memories away.

"I'll just leave your food here." Niels paused. "Hope you decide to join us."

I'm safe. We're not in Achilles. I'm safe. Kase is safe.

Slowly, Hallie relaxed her tight muscles and took deep breaths as his footsteps faded away. The other survivors chatted amicably, likely preparing the evening meal for their families or heading to wherever Guy had decided to tell his stories that night. But how could Hallie join something so normal when the world around them was so wrong? She couldn't help them decide whether or not to return to the village proper—she couldn't even decide what to stare at.

Just to make her own point, she rolled over and inspected the portrait once more. The life in Jack's eyes struck her to the core.

If her brother hadn't died, would he have been roped into this as well? If he'd been here, would he have been the one to take on the power, to allow Hallie to live her life in ignorant bliss?

Was it wrong to wish that he had?

Of course, if he had survived, she would've never met Kase.

Stars, her chest ached. She just wanted him to be there. She wanted him to tell her it was going to be all right, that they would find a way through whatever horrors awaited them.

She blinked away the moisture pooling in her eyes. No use wishing for things that would never be. She could only do what Kase needed her to do...for herself and for Yalvara.

She took a deep breath. The sooner she found the Passage, the sooner she could find a way back to Kase.

If her power allowed it.

Finally, she made up her mind and pulled the latest journal out of her pack. She had a job to do, and she didn't have the luxury of pretending the world outside the cavern walls didn't exist.

She slid her fingers over the worn leather and hooked them underneath the cover. Running the pads of her fingertips over the edges, she found the place where she'd left off. But when she went to turn to the next page, a pinprick of pain bit the tip of her pointer finger. Parchment cut.

She cursed softly and sucked on it. In her time at University, she'd gotten used to the sensation; once, she'd even sliced herself with parchment three times in one sitting. Not her proudest moment. Someone had once told her parchment cuts only stung so badly because they ripped skin instead of cleanly cutting it.

She didn't know if she believed that, but her stupid finger throbbed regardless.

Inspecting the page once more, Hallie ran her finger over the messy jargon on the page. This shouldn't have been so difficult—she was a Yalven scholar, for stars' sake. Did that not mean anything?

She pulled out her sketchbook and made a few notes. A few of these words could be translated in a few different ways. She would need to decipher what the woman was trying to say by guessing at context she didn't have...which could, of course, render the entire thing entirely unhelpful.

But she had little choice. Not when—

Heat throbbed in her center. With it came a flash, a picture that made her gasp: the archway again, flickering through her mind like a flame.

It was the first time in three days she'd felt it. Seen it.

Hallie put a hand to her stomach as the heat died down and turned to ice once more. She looked at the page before her and noticed a small, infinitesimal streak of brown. Her blood—the parchment cut. The rusty smear struck through one of the first lines of script.

A coincidence, surely.

She leaned closer, analyzing the symbols there. It did seem to say something about a portal of some sort...in a certain context. She made a hasty note in her sketchbook.

A coincidence...but maybe not.

The door to the Gate Chamber had opened because of her Yalven ancestry; her blood had been the key. Could it open the door to her power, too?

She tapped her cut finger and her thumb together.

Only one way to find out.

She'd still be under her record of three papercuts in one sitting. Besides, this was for science's sake.

Clenching her teeth against the pain to come, she set her middle finger against the parchment edge and sliced it.

"Blast, blast, blast, that hurts," she hissed to herself. Inspecting her finger, she willed blood to appear. "Please don't make me slice it again."

A few more moments of pinching and pleading, and blood finally peeked out of the slender, stinging cut. She touched her finger to the edge of the page, then pulled back and inspected the faint, wavy imprint of her fingertip.

Nothing extraordinary.

She blew softly on the page, like stirring the dying embers of a fire. Maybe it needed a moment to work. Maybe she'd well and truly lost it.

Waiting, waiting...

Nothing.

Yep. I've lost it.

Laughter echoed through the cavern—Guy's doing, most likely. She was surprised the bard had stayed here as long as he had; bards weren't exactly known for settling in one place, after all. But she was glad, this once, to be proven wrong.

It turned out the qualities of a skilled bard and the qualities of a skilled leader had plenty of overlap: both required an abundance of charisma, a talent for public speaking, the ability to inspire particular emotions in their audience, and the kind of shrewd insight that anticipated trouble before it arrived. And he'd certainly proven his courage by stepping up after the attack to help keep the survivors alive.

Joining the others at the fire would've been easy. If she only put down the journal and left her father's tent, she could pretend she wasn't an Essence wielder for the night. She could pretend she hadn't spent the last few years among the upper echelons of society. She could fall back into the mountain accent she'd tried so hard to suppress. Easy.

Nothing was ever easy.

Hallie no longer belonged among the people she'd known her entire life. She was different; not above them, not better than them, just not the same. She'd lived a lifetime away from the sleepy little village of her birth, and no one could rewind time.

Some might say she'd lost herself. But *some* would be wrong. In fact, she had found herself in a messy-haired, cocky pilot with a heart of stardust and a penchant for dusty tomes

Maybe it wasn't too late; maybe she could find her way back to Myrrai. Find her way back to Kase.

She inspected her two parchment cuts. If her power stopped responding, she wouldn't be able to make it to the Yalven city, but she *could* make it to Kyvena. There'd not be any danger of succumbing to the power she didn't understand or control.

But would that mean she'd failed?

She'd convinced Kase, her father, and Niels she could do it. The Lord Elder had given her the vision of the passage for a reason, surely...yet he'd gone silent in the days since.

Perhaps she'd proven herself incompetent or unworthy somehow. Or perhaps she was simply tired and should trade fruitless daydreams for actual sleep.

She looked down at the spiky, inconsistent Yalven characters below.

Maybe failure wouldn't be so bad.

No one was forcing her to do this. If her power had disappeared, that was fine; it meant she wouldn't have to worry about the world or Jagamot or anything at all. She could just...be.

But there was that voice at the back of her head, the one that always waited until her lowest moments to sow that seed of doubt in her naysaying. A voice that very much sounded like reason.

If she wanted Kase to live a long and full life, she needed to solve this. He deserved better than her hesitation and doubt.

He deserved the world. And she wouldn't stop until she gave it to him.

Without stopping to consider the consequences, she turned off the lantern and smashed it onto the stone below. The laughter outside cut off sharply, but Hallie didn't care. She grabbed the largest glass shard from the casing and sliced it across her palm. She gritted her teeth against the burning ache. Blood bubbled from the jagged wound, slithering to her wrist.

She pressed it onto the parchment. She was mad. Absolutely mad. It hurt like burning suns.

Blood soaked the page. The journal was ruined, and Hallie only had a second to feel bad about that fact.

Heat leapt from her core, blazing a fiery trail up her chest and to her fingers and toes, a detonation that knocked her to her knees. She stuffed a hand in her mouth to keep herself from screaming. Sweat ran down her face, joining the blood on the page below her.

The cavern disappeared. Darkness crushed her chest. Her knees pressed into the stone floor she could no longer see.

Too much, too much—it might kill her. The weight might grind her to dust. She couldn't move.

She screamed, but something stole the sound away as soon as it met her lips. The fire inside her burned so violently, yet it shed no light.

The Lord Elder had said his power would burn through her. She'd expected that burning to devour her slowly, a spark chewing through a log; she hadn't expected it to consume her like chaff, a flash of light with nothing left behind.

Panic choked Hallie, but no sound came out. It was as if she'd found herself in the vastness of space, only able to focus on the fact she couldn't breathe. She curled into a ball and willed it to end.

"He's too young. Father could heal him."

The voice came from the darkness. Hallie blinked, but she remained blind. Where was the woman? She sounded...familiar. Her words came soft but clear, iced with slightly elongated vowels. It reminded her of her own voice.

"Ara, you'll kill yourself tryin'. He don't want that." The second voice was deeper, male. The gravely edge to his tone suggested he'd done time in the mines, though that gave no hints as to his age; it was always hard to tell whether miners had been working there forty years or ten. The grit took early and overstayed its welcome.

Some force shoved her forward. More shouting, more screaming—hers? Someone else's? The force yanked her back. She still couldn't breathe.

Hallie's skin tingled, shuddered—then caught fire.

She collapsed, her body caught up in the inferno. The void beyond swallowed her screams.

Her stomach lurched up into her throat, but she couldn't retch. There was no air.

Then, as suddenly as the phantasmal fire had come upon her, it extinguished.

Air flooded her lungs; she coughed, sucking down oxygen in great gasping breaths as she forced herself to blink. Tears stung her eyes as they alighted on the canvas ceiling of her father's tent.

What in the blasted suns and stars had just happened?

Once her lungs stopped aching from lack of air, she pushed herself to her knees. Chills wracked her body. She shivered violently. She grounded herself by firmly pressing her fingertips into the rocky floor below.

Breathe in. Breathe out.

She spent several minutes repeating the mantra to herself. After the sweat dried upon her skin, and her stomach stopped rebelling, she sat back on her heels. She pressed her stray hair back into its messy braid.

She was okay. Everything was okay.

The corner of the offending journal caught her eye. She must have flung it aside in the throes of…whatever that state had been.

Internally, she cringed at her carelessness. The Hallie she'd known did not mistreat books like that. But this new Hallie was something else.

She inspected her hands, where power still tingled like pinpricks upon her skin. No visible wounds except where she'd cut herself with the glass shard, and even that had scabbed over already. Nothing to represent whatever power she'd unwittingly unleashed.

Madness. There could be no doubt.

With shaking hands, she fetched the journal and opened it to the page she'd coated in her blood. The paper was clean; no trace of scarlet stained it. But the tingling didn't stop.

She snapped the journal shut and stuffed it back into her pack. She would deal with it after she ate something. An empty stomach was the last thing she needed on top of crazed visions or cuts that healed in seconds.

She stood and stepped toward the entrance, but her legs sagged, threatening to fail. She staggered a little, catching herself on her cot.

Steady. Steady. Loss of blood, perhaps... or a loss of power. It was hard to tell. Both ideas made her feel a little woozy.

Especially since she hadn't lost all that much blood.

The chicken and dumplings waiting outside the tent made for a perfect distraction. She sat back down with the crude stone bowl and spoon, both carved from the same stone that made up the cavern.

The townsfolk of Stoneset were certainly resourceful. Guy had put a system in place: if you wanted to eat, you had to work. Some people oversaw the gathering of food from the gardens or hunting for meat. Another group washed and mended clothes. A third prepared food. The last patrolled the surrounding areas. The children were tasked with more menial chores, of course, such as fetching water from the underground river or the nearest well. Others ran messages between the busy adults.

Hallie had yet to be assigned a job at all, but Guy had told her he'd give her a few days to recover first, and then they would talk.

Hallie would be long gone before that time came. Hopefully.

She ate her dinner, which was delicious and perfectly savory, if a little lukewarm. But that was her own fault.

She tapped the spoon on the side of the bowl. Maybe going out and joining the others by the fire *would* be nice. She could manage thanking Ms. Vella for the meal and probably avoid having any meaningful conversation with Niels. Some of the younger girls even wanted Hallie to tell them about the capital. They'd come around twice to ask her about it, and—

Thunder boomed outside the tent.

Not thunder—the blast of a flashpistol.

The sound ricocheted through the caves, followed by screams. Hallie slapped her free hand to her ear, the other pressed into her shoulder.

Shouting. More flashpistol blasts.

She didn't hear the bowl as it hit the stone floor, nor did she bother with the food that splattered on the canvas wall.

The screaming. It was exactly, *exactly* like what she'd heard before coming out of whatever trance she'd gone into earlier—the one with the voices and the darkness.

It didn't end within a matter of seconds.

Instead, the screams grew louder and more frantic. Running, pounding footsteps. More pistol fire. They all rose to a deafening cacophony as they echoed off the cavern walls.

Hallie ripped open the tent flap to meet Niels. His frame took up the entire entrance, blond hair mussed, eyes panicked. He had a pack on his back and a flashpistol in hand.

"What's happening?" Her irritation with him couldn't drown out the relief that he was okay.

"Cerls."

The word poured ice water into her veins. "Soldiers?"

He pushed her back into the tent. "Grab your pack. We're leaving."

"But what about the others?"

"Blast it, Hallie," Niels growled, grabbing her pack. "Let's go."

But if it was Correa, she could do something. She could fight. "I can help."

Niels shoved the last of her effects into her pack, including the portrait of her and Jack, and pushed the bag against her chest. He eyed her. "No, you can't."

Smoke from the flashpistol blasts scalded her nose. She dug her fingernails into her palms. Her cheeks flushed, and frustration bubbled in her blood. How dare he discount her. She threw her pack aside and snatched a shard of glass. She wasn't sure if she was going to use it as a shiv or make herself bleed to harness whatever power she'd just awoken, but she was going to fight.

The noise in the cavern made her head ring. Between the pistol fire and screams, she could barely concentrate on what was before her.

Niels grabbed her shoulders. "I promised your Pa I'd take care of you."

"The Cerls are looking for me." She tried to shove past him, but he was a boulder in her path. "For *me*. People are going to die because I'm here."

She didn't know it for certain, but it was entirely too coincidental that soldiers had found them here only now, *months* after the Stoneset survivors had settled in the cavern. Hallie was the reason they were here. She was certain of it.

She wouldn't let Niels or anyone else stop her from trying to make it right.

He squeezed her shoulders hard. Hallie kicked his right shin. He swore loudly and grabbed his leg. "What did you—Hallie!"

Hallie twisted away, breaking his grip. She lunged toward the tent entrance, but she wasn't built for speed or fighting or—well, anything, really. Not as she was.

Niels grabbed her forearm and pulled her back. He looked her straight in the eyes as she tugged. "If they really want you, they're going to have to fight their way through me."

They wouldn't get the chance. She'd fight him first. "Unhand me!"

She could do this—she could do *something*. She'd brought the whole fort down on their heads at Achilles, for stars' sake.

All she had to do was spill enough of her blood.

Niels looped her pack's strap over her shoulder this time, his hand still clenching her forearm. It was beginning to hurt. She twisted and yanked, but he held firm. "Stop it and listen to me. We'll take the tunnel toward Ravenhelm, then circle back."

Something hot and searing and *awful* tore through her middle. She doubled over, shoving her own hand into her mouth to muffle her cry. Niels yanked his flashpistol from where he'd stuffed it into the back of his trousers and whipped it toward the tent entrance. "What? Where are you hit? Did they—"

"I'm not hurt." Hallie clutched her stomach, bracing herself until the heat abated some. She wasn't sure what had triggered it, but *something* was trying to get her attention. It felt just like before, when the Lord Elder had given her the image of the archway, but...stronger. Much stronger. A tidal wave, not a ripple in a tide pool.

Ravenhelm. She needed to go to Ravenhelm.

But the soldiers were attacking here. She needed to fight *here*.

"What's wrong?" Niels asked, his voice slightly frantic. "Don't lie to me, Hal—"

A tall, barrel-chested man ripped back the tent flap. The canvas screeched as it tore. The pistol in his hand leaked blue smoke, the muzzle poised and ready to fire directly into Hallie's skull.

Everything froze. The only movement came from the sparks popping and fizzing in her peripheral vision, though she could not say where they were coming from—only that they were there. Maybe she'd been hit after all, only by an electropistol, not a flashpistol.

The intruder's uniform was dark blue and filthy. Ragged holes, streaks of dirt, and dark, blotchy stains decorated the front.

Blood. Enough that the uniform must have been stolen off a dead man. Nobody could have survived after losing that much blood, nobody could have survived...

Survived what Hallie had done to the fort.

Oh stars. Nausea turned her skin clammy, chilled with guilt, even if the man in front of her was clearly alive—and threatening her with a Cerl pistol, besides.

He hadn't moved. Hadn't shot. She stared at the unfeeling metal ring pointed at her forehead.

"Looking for a *shilka* who looks just like you." He held the weapon steady, aimed straight between her eyes.

Hallie's heartbeat thudded behind her forehead, pounding like a drum. She wasn't sure what to do, what to say.

It was her fault. Her fault. Hers. The screams, the uniform, the *blood*...all her fault.

The fire in her core rose. The sparks clouded her vision.

She could do something. She could make him fall apart like she had done with the fort. She didn't know how she knew she could do that, only that she could.

But ability did not make it the right choice. She hadn't meant to kill anyone at Achilles. If she ruined this man the way she'd ruined the fort, she *would* know. She would be the reason he didn't go home to his family.

Even a hearty lungful of Zuprium dust wouldn't be enough to fog *that* out of her head.

All this she had time to consider, because the man still hadn't pulled the trigger. He just stood in front of them, watching, blue smoke lazily leaking from the barrel of his strange gun. Niels shifted to block her from the line of fire. The man traced his movements with the weapon.

"Why?" Hallie managed to get out, though she'd much rather keep quiet. "Why do you need me?"

Half an hour prior, she'd been quietly deciphering the convoluted writings of her dead ancestor, thinking back to birthday gifts and books and the brother she'd lost. Now there was a very good chance she was about to be blown to bits. She would never see her parents again. Not Petra. Not Masie and Nole. Not anyone who mattered to her.

Not Kase.

The power within her raged at that thought of never seeing him again. Like Kase held a spark to the waiting fuse.

The soldier's finger twitched on the trigger, but Hallie was faster.

Later, she wouldn't be able to describe exactly what she'd done. All she knew was that she could not bear the thought of never seeing Kase again, that everything inside her rebelled against it, that she shoved the possibility away with all her might.

And the sparks that had nearly blinded her surged toward the soldier instead.

Niels ducked.

The Cerl bullet froze in midair, its blue fire crackling like ice—then retraced its path back into the barrel.

The power didn't stop there. It bubbled and eddied. It languished upon its prey, drinking in the man's very being. The weapon in the man's hand unraveled like a skein of yarn. Then the hand itself followed suit.

The man's skin and sinew turned to ash as it dropped to the rocky floor. Hallie's jaw dropped with them, horror freezing her in place.

For all the rest of her days, Hallie would never forget how loudly the man screamed as he came undone before her eyes.

The unraveling didn't stop. It wound up his arm, his

shoulder, across his collarbone, untangling his neck like an impatient seamstress with a knot in her thread. His sounds of anguish reached a fever pitch before his throat scattered into filaments of flesh, then crumbled to dust. Not a man any longer, but a knotty and tired sweater, its loose strands caught on a nail intent on tugging the weaving free.

Niels shouted at Hallie, but she could only stare, wide-eyed, as the soldier disappeared before her very eyes. No blood. No bones. As if he had ceased to be.

Blood pulsed in her face. Her throat squeezed tightly. Frigid air came in and out in squeaks. She fell to the ground, scrabbling at the smoke that had once been the man before her. She needed to fix this. She hadn't meant to do that. She hadn't meant to—to do—oh, stars—

Another soldier shouldered in just in time to see the last of the man's body disappear in a wisp of smoke. The air was rancid, smelling like Yalvar fuel.

Before the newcomer had any chance to do anything at all, Niels fired his pistol, hitting the man square in the chest. He pulled Hallie up by the strap of her pack, practically throwing her toward the back of the tent. "Go!"

She wrenched the canvas up and stumbled forward, slinging the pack further over her shoulder. Her hands tingled so furiously they burned; she swayed, but Niels caught her before she could fall. "Don't fall apart now. If they can't find you here, they'll leave."

"But what if they don't? What if they hurt them anyway?" Hallie was surprised she could still find the words as she wound past screaming children and the people trying to hide them.

Niels yanked her down as blue fire zinged overhead. He shot his flashpistol in the direction it had come from and shoved her behind a trunk-like stalagmite jutting up from the cavern floor. Blue fire raged around them. More screams.

Niels rifled through his pack and pulled out an electropistol. He shoved it in her hand. "Don't argue. Just run."

"But what if we can't—what about—" Stars, she couldn't even get a sentence out.

He dragged her along. "The tunnel is just ahead."

"But—"

A hand reached out and grabbed her wrist, yanking her

out of Niels' grip. Without thinking, she shoved her pent-up energy into them.

She didn't turn around to see if they'd unraveled just like the first soldier. She didn't want to know—and the sight ahead of her held her attention too tightly, anyway.

Niels must have slowed to look back for her—he'd been surrounded by soldiers. His wide eyes found her over their heads.

Run. He didn't have to say it again. She knew what he wanted.

The ground shook. Pistols fired. Blood ran down the stone. Hallie fell against the wall. Her hand stung.

The ground moved again, shaking hard and fierce.

By the time her brain registered that it was an earthquake—by the time she realized the force of it had knocked the soldiers surrounding Niels to the ground—it was over.

Niels tugged her up. They sprinted toward the tunnel, leaping over bodies trying to rise. Hallie's knees rattled, her bones clacking together as she ran for her life.

Blue fire zinged behind them, ricocheting off the walls and floor and everywhere. Blood sprayed her face.

Niels went down, hand to his shoulder.

"No!" Hallie screamed, but he was up before she could help.

"We need to get to...get to the tunnel," he panted. "It's just a graze. Keep moving."

They made it to the edge of the cavern and turned down the tunnel that would lead them to the ruins of Ravenhelm.

Something moved behind them. Hallie didn't think— only thrust what little power she had left into the rock. The sparks in her vision dissipated.

And then everything finally went silent.

CHAPTER 2

SOMETHING SPIRITUAL

Kase

KASE SHACKLEY DIDN'T THINK HIS father would execute him on the spot...emphasis on the word *think*. But he had been wrong before.

His stomach twisted, instinct screaming for him not to go to Kyvena, but he had no choice. Not really. If he wanted to make anything right, if he wanted Jayde to have a chance of winning this war, he needed to face his past. And that included his father.

Out of the two Walkers, he would have preferred Hallie's company over her father's. She was much more amenable than the bald man with the fatherly girth guiding him through the dank, dark mountain passages. He'd met other fathers—Jove would become one soon—but the only one he'd spent any notable time with had been his own.

How did one even make conversation with a father?

He'd only ever known his father's disparaging corrections or his silence. Kase had always assumed that lack of warmth came from his father's time in the military—that any love had been beaten out of him by a particularly strict sergeant. The same kind of command he'd instated over his household and his sons.

But if the military was to blame, Kase's late brother Zeke would have been just like Harlan. Cold. Angry. And Zeke had been neither.

So maybe Harlan had simply been born that way. It didn't really matter why he was the way he was—he just *was*.

Even in his own head, he couldn't stop his thoughts from going in circles, which wasn't helpful when he was trying his best not to make as terrible an impression on Hallie's father as he had Hallie herself when they'd first met. There was more at stake now, and Kase didn't think an adventure to the lost continent of Tasava was in their future to give them time to clear up any miscommunications.

In the twisting tunnels underneath the mountains, Stowe Walker was even more intimidating—especially when he stood like he did now, sipping from a canteen and staring off into the darkness ahead, waiting in silence for Kase to be ready to move on.

Stowe stood nearly as tall as Kase, but had at least fifty pounds on him—not an ideal boxing foe if any disagreement came to blows. Hallie clearly got her height from him, as she had at least an inch or three above most women in Kyvena's high society.

Shocks, Kase missed her. It'd only been three days.

"We should make good ground today if nothing's caved in," Stowe said, his soft voice as dead and dull as the stone around them.

"Then what?" They'd passed a few offshoots that had been blocked up by stone and broken beams as they'd traveled, but nothing promising. "Will we need to turn around?"

Kase didn't fancy facing whatever awaited them in the Pass. He didn't know just how many people had survived Fort Achilles' collapse. He barely understood what had destroyed it in the first place, because flash bombs certainly couldn't have done it. According to Niels, those had taken sizable chunks out of the gates and caused a small ruckus, but that was it.

Kase had a feeling it had something to do with Hallie

and General Correa, but he wasn't sure what; and if he was honest with himself, he didn't truly want to know. Power on that scale was something out of storybooks. Seeing Hallie's face moments before the entire fort imploded...those were memories he'd rather not dwell on. Ever. Magic was only supposed to exist in storybooks, yet Kase had felt it when Correa had placed a finger on his cheek. He'd seen it with the Yalvs. The Gate had been brimming with it. And he didn't like it one bit.

Kase ran a hand through his hair as Stowe answered, "We'll decide that when we get there, son."

Not helpful.

Stowe started off. Kase stood, swung his pack on his back, and followed behind in silence. The walls closed in like a coffin—hopefully not a harbinger of the fate awaiting him in the capital. He didn't understand how the miners could stand going into tunnels such as these every single day, hacking away at the stone in near-absolute dark just to find bits and pieces of a metal that they wouldn't even use.

Instead, the Zuprium would be sent off to Kyvena for refining and use in the construction of whatever the Jaydian Councils thought important—whether that be a next-generation hover like the *Eudora Jayde* or reinforced electric gate doors to the upper city.

But society relied heavily on the mystical metal. Without it, Jayde would collapse—so someone had to mine it.

Kase would have hated it. He hated *this*, traveling through a maze of gloom without any indication of what was happening above, ahead, or behind them. They traveled deeper and deeper into abject darkness with only a gas lantern to light the way.

Twist after twist, step after step, beam after beam, they wound their way into oblivion. He didn't care what awaited them once they got out; he just needed to be out of this hole only meant for the dead. He just needed sunlight.

His boots slid in a streak of slime, and he caught himself on the wall, clinging to it as they rounded the next corner—and finally, light appeared.

It was faint, like a waning candle on a moonless night, peeking shyly around the tunnel's next curve—but once he realized it wasn't a cluster of the pale, spider-like cave crickets he'd have nightmares about for the rest of his life, hope poured energy back into his body. Light meant escape; light meant the end of their journey through moist, leering darkness.

Kase had wished for sunshine, and it waited around the bend.

But it wasn't alone. Cold, heavy dread swept away his excitement. If they neared the end of the caverns, that only meant *his* end crept ever closer. The caves might be kinder than whatever awaited him in Kyvena.

"Is that sunlight?" Kase asked, the words brittle, breathy.

"No," Stowe whispered.

He couldn't decide if he was relieved or not. "Then what is it?"

Stowe's voice was thinner than the edge of a knife as he turned his lantern down to its lowest setting, the light now barely brighter than the one that awaited them. "You got that pistol of yours?"

Kase pulled the weapon from his pack. Hair stood straight up on the back of his neck as his fingers found the grip of the cool metal. The memories of the blood he'd cleaned from it made him want to chuck it clear down one of the offshoot mining tunnels they'd passed.

If I hadn't attacked that soldier, I'd be dead. Hallie would be imprisoned.

Zeke's coping mechanism for Battle Fright was something Kase relied on too much as of late. He tightened his grip on the pistol, the old grief resurfacing.

Zeke made his own choice.

Deep breath in. Deep breath out. In and out. In. Out.

Stowe shifted from one foot to the other.

"Could it be Hallie's mother?" Kase whispered, leaning toward the older man.

Stowe held up his freckled hand lined with valleys and crept forward. The light hadn't grown; its flickering stayed weak, withdrawn. If someone was in the caves, they must have decided to use a candle instead of a lantern, though that was a ridiculous idea. Clearly whoever stood around the bend wasn't used to being deep in the heart of the Nardens...though Kase wasn't either, and even he would've told them that wouldn't work for long.

Maybe it was someone trapped without any way out

because they didn't know the tunnels like Stowe. Maybe they'd gotten lost and had run out of everything but a solitary candle. They might've been stuck for days, afraid to move on and lose what little strength they had left.

Kase resisted the urge to run a hand through his hair. A Cerl soldier might very well be awaiting them as soon as they turned the corner, and here he was, daydreaming about the fictional survival stories he'd read in the library at Shackley Manor.

He turned to his right to tell Hallie, knowing she'd appreciate his gallows humor—but all he found waiting for him was darkness.

Kase shook his head and followed Hallie's father forward.

As they approached the bend, Stowe retrieved the machete attached to his pack. He held it loosely in his right hand. Kase cocked his electropistol, sparks flickering to life at the end of the barrel.

Anxiety clawed further up his throat. I'm using this weapon to defend myself. If I don't, I could be hurt.

The tightness eased slightly.

"I'll go first, but make sure you fire true if it's one of them blasted Trips." Stowe's voice was as cold as ice.

Trips. A nickname coined by the mountain folk for those marked with the triple interwoven diamond tattoos on the necks of Cerl soldiers. Kase had seen the symbol too frequently as of late.

Not only had he fought Cerls on Tasava, the Yalven continent, and in the battle of Myrrai where they'd killed Zeke with their fiery, near-magical blue bullets; but only days earlier, he and Hallie had been betrayed by Yarrow, the trapper who'd been hiding his identity at the behest of General Marcus Correa. He'd been a Cerl soldier working against them the entire time, all to save a brother who was already dead.

A Cerl himself...yet Yarrow met his end at the hands of the Cerl king and Essence-wielder, King Filip.

Kase gripped his pistol tighter.

Stowe slipped around the corner, his machete held out, ready to swing at any attacker. Kase flew behind him, finger poised on the trigger.

Kase halted. The light wasn't a Cerl.

It wasn't even a wayward traveler or a pack of crickets or the sunlight.

A large rock formation sprouted from the stone below and fanned out in a glittering, glowing cluster. Each crystal jutted out from the center base and narrowed to a point that could pierce the thickest hover hull. The cluster pulsed with soft golden light, but swirls of darkness fluttered through each crystal, making it flicker. The entire thing was nearly as tall as Kase.

Above it, the cavern ceiling reached so high Kase couldn't see the top. The walls and floor were just as craggy and unkempt as the tunnels behind, but it was the gem cluster in the room's center that commanded both Kase and Stowe's attention.

"What is that?" Kase whispered, still not relaxing his grip on the electropistol.

Stowe hooked his machete through the reinforced leather loop and turned up his lantern.

"It's raw Zuprium. Biggest chunk I ever seen. But it ain't supposed to glow like that."

Kase uncocked his electropistol. "What do you mean, it's not supposed to glow like that?"

Stowe lowered the lantern to the floor and stepped forward, closing in on the cluster. "Looks diseased."

"I'd say lethal. Wouldn't want that aimed at my head."

Stowe shrugged, and Kase groaned inwardly. If he'd stayed with Hallie, she would've laughed—even out of pity— or swiped back with a quip. Instead, he'd left her behind to wander the mountains with a farm boy.

Shocks. Kase was terrible at this relationship thing, if he could even call it that. No wonder his fling with Lavinia Richter had ended before it even started...and now she was dead, killed by the Cerls.

He'd merely thought Lavinia was a means to an end. What would the consequence be for loving Hallie?

Kase attempted to relax his coiled back muscles. I cannot control others' actions. *I can only take responsibility for my own.*

He clenched his jaw tightly before unclenching it again. I cannot control others' actions. *I can only take responsibility for my own.*

"You okay, son?" Stowe's voice interrupted Kase's growing anxiety.

He blinked. "I'm fine."

"Legend says they blind you right before they burst." Hallie's father stretched a hand toward the cluster. If he tripped, the closest spike would impale it. Kase held his breath as Stowe continued, "I didn't feel hopeless until we saw it. The thing is corrupted, but I don't know how I know that."

Kase tilted his head. Hopeless. Yes, that was exactly what he felt. The hair on the back of his neck stood erect once more. "It's just a mineral. A mineral that's refined into the most valuable metal on all Yalvara, but only that."

Stowe looked back, his golden eyes shining amidst the shadows of his face. "You ain't never worked the mines. There's something spiritual about it that connects you to the planet itself."

"I thought you were an innkeeper. What do you know about mining?"

"Almost every man does time in the mines."

With that, Stowe reached out and touched the nearest spike. As soon as his finger made contact with it, he sucked in a sharp breath, jerking his hand back. "Blasted sharp."

On the end of the spike in question, a scarlet trail slithered down the long protrusion and into the base of the cluster. Kase furrowed his brow. Stowe had barely touched the cluster. That was too much blood.

The cluster pulsed brightly. Kase threw up his hands to shield himself, staggering back. He shut his stinging eyes against the powerful glow, stumbling back, tripping over his own feet and crashing to the ground. Luckily, his pack cushioned him from the worst of the blow.

Something rumbled through the cave. The glow lessened against his eyelids; he blinked just as a crack resounded.

Before him, Stowe stared at the cluster. What had once been small black rivulets threading through the soft glow had swollen into rivers, twisting and writhing like angry snakes.

Another crack. Heavy clods of dirt and small stones rained upon Kase's head and jacket.

He looked up as more debris dislodged. The cluster of Zuprium seemed to swell and grow. A jagged, bone-rattling splintering shook the air above them.

"Stowe!" Kase shouted as a large chunk fell, narrowly missing the older man. Hallie's father didn't move, didn't even flinch. He simply stared at the Zuprium cluster as if entranced.

Kase looked up again. The next crack reverberated off the walls, louder than the last. He stopped thinking and barreled forward, grasping the man's collar and yanking him toward the other end of the room.

"Gotta get out..." Kase grunted, tugging Stowe harder, but the man barely moved. He seemed transfixed with the furious Zuprium crystal.

So Kase stopped tugging and pulled out his electropistol instead. He cocked, aimed, and fired three times at the cluster; the balls of electricity slammed into it and enveloped it in sparks. More black tendrils joined the others, raging at being disturbed.

A large chunk of the ceiling fell directly toward Stowe's head. Kase dove, flinging his pistol aside.

An invisible hand yanked him into the air.

He sputtered. Everything in the small cavern floated a few inches above the floor—the rocks, Stowe's lantern, the packs, and both men. Kase blinked hard. Maybe he'd been hit too hard by falling debris.

"What—what—" He couldn't form the question.

Stowe shouted—*now* he decided to snap out of it—and scrambled for the ground below. The toes of his boots barely scuffed the stone. Kase looked back toward the crystal. Electric sparks still played along its surface, but the black tendrils had retreated slightly, as if it had been appeased by their distress.

"Infusing Zuprium with electricity makes the hovers work," Kase whispered. This was what his uncle had discovered. It was the only explanation he had.

"I hate those blasted flying death traps," Stowe grunted as he grabbed for one of the rocks jutting from the wall and pulled himself to the floor.

Kase looked up at the floating debris. "Dunno how long this'll last. We should get out of—"

The sparks on the crystal faded, and the black tendrils returned to their previous ferocity. Kase's stomach flew into his throat as he smashed back to the ground. He knocked his right elbow and knees hard on the floor, but he saved his chin and face from taking the brunt. He scrambled to his feet, turning to find Stowe, only to see a newly dislodged rock hurtling toward the man.

Kase dove toward him once more, and this time, he made contact. Something burned along his right cheek, and pain spiked in his head.

Everything went dark.

CHAPTER 3

DOWNPOUR

AIR WHOOSHED FROM JOVE SHACKLEY'S lungs as he leaped over the ruins of the wall surrounding his childhood home. Whether it had been hit by a dragon or taken out with some sort of massive weapon, he didn't know; he only knew it hadn't been short enough to leap over before.

Smoke and screams and orange fire painted the sky. A loud rumble knocked him off his feet, the impact wrenching his hurt shoulder. He pulled himself back to his feet, hissing through his teeth when his shoulder protested.

Ben Reiss and his dragon's destruction of Kyvena hadn't fully processed in Jove's mind. One World had joined forces with the Cerls. As an intelligence agent, Jove had known they were connected, but he'd never dreamed they'd be able to pull off something on this scale.

Small demonstrations, a little violence, several arrests? That was closer to what Jove had anticipated. Why would he have ever thought otherwise? The Jaydian Hover Crews were the best in the world.

He looked back at the burning city below him just as an enemy hover dropped something from its cargo hold.

"*Get down!*" Harlan Shackley shouted.

Jove and the Yalven emissary beside him, Saldr, hit the cobblestone so hard, Jove's bones ached. The ground shook and rattled them further. He couldn't hear anything over the screams and other commotions throughout the city.

Holy shocks, they were bombing the city.

His father had already recovered and sprinted for the manor's entrance. Jove might've kept pace had he not been shot only minutes before. Instead, he stumbled to his feet only to fall again.

Blasted shoulder. Blasted bombs. Blasted everything.

Saldr helped him to his feet. "Are you all right, Master Shackley?"

No part of this was all right.

More violent, swearing shouts from Harlan; he was cursing at the looters trying to force their way into the manor. Jove retrieved the stolen Cerl pistol from the ground, hitting the hammer too hard with his thumb. Its stinging pain was more like an annoying wasp buzzing in Jove's head. He squeezed the slick trigger. Fiery blue bullets joined his father's own shots into the crowd of criminals. Jove stumbled from the recoil.

They shouted. One man screamed as blood soaked the back of his light-colored jacket. He fell in a crumpled heap. Jove's chest heaved painfully as if something was sucking the lifeblood from his heart. He fired again. Another wrenching sensation. The bullet hit the side of the manor and ricocheted into another looter.

The rest scattered, running away from more blue bullets coming from Harlan's weapon. Jove should have been up there with him, should have been at his side as he stormed the manor's entrance, but...

Fire tore through Shackley Manor's roof and busted out windows along the top floor. Chaos reigned everywhere he looked. If he broke into his home and found his family dead...

No. He could not do it. He could not go into that house and find his wife...his *son*—

The worn and weary cobblestones dug into his knees before he knew he'd fallen again. Not pain this time, but despair.

How could he have left his family? He was supposed to protect them, and he'd just...left.

The alcohol couldn't shield him from this. The evening's horrors had burned it out of him. The understanding of what he'd done pierced deeper than any bullet.

I left them.

I left them.

I left—

Enough.

He placed his hands upon the cobblestones, wary of the glass, and pushed himself to his feet. His stomach felt hollow yet full of lead at the same time. Bile waited at the back of his throat.

But he owed it to Clara to face what he'd done. If she was alive, he had to protect her. If she was not...

He couldn't think about that. Not if he wanted to keep his feet moving.

By the time he got to his father's side, Harlan had already kicked down the door, shouting "Celeste!" into the darkness beyond.

No response.

Jove stumbled into the foyer. The elegant family portrait on the wall hadn't been touched. Nothing had been—yet. The looters would be back.

The figures immortalized in brush strokes stared back at him in the dim firelight filtering through the open front door. Jove had felt important that day. He'd helped wrangle his younger siblings just enough to sit still for it. Zeke was the only one who'd smiled.

Jove hated the painting. It was nothing but a pretty lie.

Harlan thundered up the stairs, Cerl pistol in one hand, sword in the other. Jove didn't follow. He trudged down the corridor to the chamber where he and Clara had been staying since Samuel had been born. Hope bubbled in his chest when he realized the lower floor seemed untouched. The fire raging through the upper levels hadn't spread here yet.

But the unnerving quiet scared him into a sprint.

They're all right. They aren't hurt. Clara probably took Samuel and hid down one of the servants' passages.

She wouldn't have known about the Catacombs beneath their feet—a maze of tunnels and hollowed-out caverns that had been Jayde's answer and preparation for another conflict on the scale of the Great War. Jove had been sworn to secrecy about their existence. Now he wished he'd broken that vow.

For how badly he'd struggled to force himself in, now his feet couldn't go fast enough. He nearly stumbled over himself as he rushed into the bed chamber, the door banging against the wall. "Clara!"

The room was tidy and undisturbed. The aged bassinet still sat next to the large four-poster bed, the drapes flung wide. The bed overflowed with tasseled and embroidered pillows. A sheaf of parchment lay on the bedside table.

With heavy footfalls, Jove trudged over to the bassinet, guilt and dread filling his chest.

Thunder rumbled in the distance. He wasn't certain if it was another bomb drop or the dragon or merely an early spring thunderstorm on the horizon. He didn't care which.

When he grasped the letter in his war-soiled fingers, crusted flakes of blood fell upon the script crafted in his wife's careful handwriting.

Jove,

We've gone to Crystalfell. Don't come until you're ready.

Clara

Jove let his head fall in his hands, his brow brushing the parchment.

Relief struck him first: they weren't here. They'd left, hopefully before the city erupted into chaos.

Fear came next: if they hadn't left soon enough, they might've been caught up in the riots or incinerated by the dragon flying through the city skies. They could be dead after all, and he'd never know.

Jove crushed the note in his fist and chucked it at the wall.

"They're not here." His father's voice was hard and echoed in the empty room. "We need to go."

"No." The word came out slightly mangled. Even if Clara wasn't dead or injured, she'd taken their son with her and fled.

He'd left them, so she had left him. Because he was a cancer infecting those around him with his grief until they could no longer function.

Harlan stepped lightly into the room. "With the fire on the upper floors, the Manor isn't stable. We'll keep looking, but they aren't here. There's no reason to stay."

Jove heard the words as if they were spoken from the opposite end of a tunnel, but he got up and followed anyway. Harlan already thought him weak. He wouldn't give him an excuse to confirm it.

As they rejoined an armed and unnaturally pale Saldr outside, Jove looked back one last time on his childhood home.

It hadn't really been home for some time now, but watching destruction close in on it still hurt. His mother's library would be ash soon, as would the odd pairs of socks he'd not brought with him to the townhouse when he'd married. The countless family portraits wouldn't survive. Odds and ends that had once belonged to Zeke, to Kase...even to Ana.

Yet, Jove's soul was numb, and he couldn't bring himself to care even as the first raindrops fell from the sky and soaked his bloodstained coat.

Don't come until you're ready.

Ready to...what? What could he do, what could he become that would make all of this right again?

The rain turned into a downpour. It might wash some of the ruin away, but it couldn't cleanse what had been sullied in him.

His father led them back over the ruined wall and into the city of chaos.

Jove didn't look back as the manor burned.

CHAPTER 4

SHE WAS FIRE

Hallie

HALLIE'S BREATHS CAME HEAVY, AND her pack dug into her shoulders. No other sounds followed them down the tunnel or the stilted mountain path to the ruined village. She had no idea if anything was left of the cavern or the soldiers or anything at all.

The soldiers were dead. Hallie had killed them.

Somehow.

She refused to look at her hands. If she didn't look at the blood, she could pretend it wasn't there.

The memory of undoing that soldier thread by thread was harder to ignore.

"You did what you had to do," Niels said as they rounded the last bend of the overgrown trail through the trees. He'd wrapped his upper right arm with a bandage and a few herbs he'd kept from her father's stores. The bullet had only grazed him in the tunnel, like he'd said, but he still winced every time he jostled it. "Once you've calmed down, we'll go back and help."

Calmed down. Like she'd lost her temper, not taken a body apart without a weapon. "I'm fine."

Niels was the seasoned fighter. He'd been patrolling and conducting sneak attacks on the Cerls for months. This was Hallie's first time doing anything of the sort. She didn't count the battle in Myrrai when Zeke died; she'd really only run then. This time, she had *killed* someone. She felt dirty, like her hands were stained with something worse than blood, like they would never be clean no matter how hard she scrubbed them.

Helping had been her idea, but…she'd killed those people. If she went back, she might have to kill more.

"They were after me." Her words were measured. She couldn't afford anger or frustration or crippling guilt. Not now. "It's better if we keep going. We'll probably lead them away from the others."

"And why exactly are we leading them to Ravenhelm?" Niels looked warily at the ruins beyond the trees.

Ravenhelm was something of a legend in the Nardens, a ghost story one told around the dinner fire. Though only a half-day's ride away on a very sturdy horse or a mule, very few visited. The burned-out homes and overgrown town square served as a warning of how quickly a town could be wiped out if they were caught unaware.

Legend said the only survivor of the attack that had razed Ravenhelm was a young boy who managed to kill the Cerl commander with some sort of weapon. Some claimed it had been a simple crossbow, others a flashpistol; several of the older folk who'd lived in Stoneset at the time swore the boy took him out with only a pickaxe. Stoneset's bard rarely told his version, but it was quite fanciful—complete with a glimmering sword. To hear it told, the boy could have been King Arthur, drawing Excalibur from the stone.

Stories often outgrew their britches in the mountains.

Hallie never knew which version to believe, if any. The only record of the attack lay in oral tradition. Sure, there was probably a military record somewhere, but the attack had been more of an embarrassment for Jayde. It was also one of the many precursors to the Great War years later.

Sticking her hand in her pocket, she found Kase's goggles and squeezed them, soaking in renewed strength from that small piece of him. She could do this. "That's where the Passage is."

Apparently, she'd left facts, logic, and reasoning behind and entered the realm of 'follow the magical visions in your head.' The scholarly side of her brain called herself a stars-idiot.

"Passage?" Niels asked skeptically.

"It's how my great-grandmother got to Jayde."

"Passage," he repeated. "Like a...door?"

Always with that doubt.

"An archway," she corrected. "I think. Not sure what it'll look like now, as it's been several decades."

She squinted at the village. It could hold the archway as it had appeared in Hallie's mind, but the likelihood of that was slim. Many homes were empty husks, aged with time and withered vines. Some were missing entire walls or roofs—as if some vengeful god had smashed it with a fist. The cobblestones below were so overgrown with moss, only a few determined ones poked through the hardy foliage.

She couldn't tell what Niels was thinking, but he must've thought her mad. *She* certainly did, after all.

Niels paused and rechecked his pistol for bullets. He loaded three more into the chamber. "Hope I don't need to use this again."

Hallie looked down at her weapon. The electropistol was easy enough to use. It had one step: pull the trigger. She just needed to aim and pray she hit close to her target. She just didn't want to think of what her target might be. But was it any better than using her Essence power?

She wasn't sure.

Throwing her shoulders back, she led the way into the village. "Just let me know if you think anything feels off."

Niels' footsteps followed shortly after. She didn't look back to see what sort of face he made, but she could imagine. It probably rivaled the one he used to wear whenever Jack made him do something particularly dangerous.

Jack.

The flash of memories tasted bitter, like cheap wine left in the sun all day. Each and every memory from her childhood felt that way, even like it belonged to someone else.

Hallie chewed her lip and pressed on, running her

fingers along the first home she came to. The roof was missing—either destroyed in the attack or with the passage of time. Cracks riddled the foundation like blood vessels. Dead vines crawled up the wall. The pads of her fingers scraped against the rough and crumbling mortar between the eroding bricks.

The last time Hallie entered an abandoned village, she'd gotten herself kidnapped. Whatever drug they'd given her had muddled the few memories she'd retained of the incident. All she really remembered was leaving Kase outside the inn. Then she'd woken in a leaky dungeon cell without him.

Kase had done his best to save her, had even concocted an entire plan to rescue her with Niels' help...only for it to go terribly awry.

Heat traveled from her chest to her fingertips once more. She curled her hands into fists and gritted her teeth.

No way to save me this time.

That was, if she didn't figure out a way to separate the Essence power from the wielder. If she didn't, she knew she couldn't hold the power forever. It would drain her, little by little, until there was nothing left of her. The inevitability of it all made her sick.

On paper, Ravenhelm was much smaller than Stoneset, but with the debris still littering the ground fifty years after its downfall, it felt much bigger. There were more nooks and crannies to check. More walls to hide behind. More mysteries and whispers on the wind she couldn't pick out.

They searched everywhere. Niels was particularly handy when she needed to lift a chunk of crumbling debris in front of a blacksmith's cottage. The forge lay just behind a caved-in roof, the bellows tossed aside and smothered with detritus.

It was all for naught, but the scholarly side of her brain switched on anyway as they wove through the past. What an interesting tableau of Jaydian history. Only a smattering of years prior, society had relied on livestock to go anywhere— horses, oxen, or mules being the best choice in the mountains. No wonder the Jaydian forces hadn't arrived in time to save the village on their fanciful ponies.

The mountain had reclaimed most of Ravenhelm by now. In the summer, it was probably rife with mountain flora and fauna, an oddly beautiful portrait of such a tragic scene. Now, though, the snow was midway through melting, and it seemed stark, less picturesque, better suiting the history.

With each step she took through the tangled maze, she wished she hadn't. Half-melted brown slush squelched as they checked a little nook in one of the toppled houses near the front of the village. Another winding side street allowed for moonlight to reflect upon the silver patches of snow that had survived the day's spring sunlight.

Hallie wasn't sure if it was the village's aura or the threat of someone else following them, but she felt unsteady. They hadn't seen or heard anyone since the caverns, but her neck prickled with anticipation. With each step she took, her heart ticked up in fervor. The morbid side of her wondered if she was walking over graves. She hadn't done much research into the attack in the past. She'd nearly forgotten about it when she'd been at University and had the resources to do some digging. She'd simply assumed that the Jaydian forces had cleaned up the bodies afterward and sent the souls to the stars.

But if they'd done that much, why not clear away the rubble? Why not let nature fully reclaim the area?

The moss-covered streets might've hidden the worst of the massacre, but what if the crunching sound she heard every so often was the sound of still-decaying bones snapping under her feet?

She turned a corner and heat flared in her body—not painful this time, just an almost-comforting pulse, like fire on a bitter winter night. She stopped, Niels barely catching himself as he ran into her, his lantern swinging.

"This way," she whispered. She took a step forward, and a pleasant tingling began—soft at first, but with each step, it grew. She tried not to think; instead, she let instinct guide her as she wandered over upturned cobblestone and slushy snow. The mountain wind painted her cheeks with pain, stinging her uncovered face and tangling her messy braid as it whistled through the alleyway.

The image of the archway flashed in her mind, fuzzy and glowing around the edges like light gathered in a tangled, fraying rope.

The archway wasn't made of stone, she realized. It was of light and...time.

How she knew that, she couldn't say.

On the other side of the alleyway, a rotting carriage lay toppled on its side. Most of the wood had decayed away. The leather leads were buried beneath snow patches and the fallen wall from the next cottage over.

The tingling disappeared.

Bone-chilling cold soaked her body. She gasped.

Niels put a hand on her shoulder. "Hal, what—"

A blazing blue fire zinged above Hallie's head, blasting out the remnants of the broken window on the decrepit home beside them. Before she could process anything, Niels dove on top of her. He pressed her against the aging wood of the home next door. The wood groaned with the impact, threatening to splinter.

Niels' heart pounded against her back. She recoiled as he growled and turned, firing the flashpistol in the direction of the blue fire and pushing her out of the way with his good arm, the other one working to keep his aim as steady as possible.

All of it happened in less than three seconds, but time seemed to slow as Hallie pulled herself off the door. She looked toward their attackers.

No. No. No.

While hard to tell specifics with only the moonlight and a discarded, broken lantern, she knew General Correa's eyes, even with that crazed look. His uniform was torn and dirty like those of the soldiers that had attacked the cavern.

He'd survived Achilles.

And he would never let her free.

Just looking at him now made her body explode with phantom pain. She fought her body's response. He hadn't touched her. She wouldn't let him torture her again. She had the power now. She could make *him* suffer.

In the scuffle, Hallie had dropped the electropistol. Niels retrieved it and fired bolts in Correa's direction. He wasn't used to the lack of recoil; he missed by several feet. Correa fired his Cerl pistol back. Hallie and Niels dodged just in time as the blue fire raced past, striking some other bit of the ruined house beside them.

Niels went to fire the flashpistol once more. Nothing happened. "Blast!"

In a moment of insanity, he tossed it aside. The pistol

skidded across the mossy cobblestones and under the overturned carriage. Ice-cold fear thrummed in Hallie's veins. The weapon was merely jammed, presumably, and he'd just—*thrown* it without a care.

Regardless, she scrambled after the discarded weapon as Correa skirted behind the half-wall of the home across the street. Some of the roof had caved in, and most of the front wall was missing. Golden light from Secondmoon glinted on the dirty window in the nearly intact front door. Correa fired again, but his aim went even more awry.

"I only need the girl!" he shouted as he fired once more. This time, his aim was better. Niels lunged in time to avoid it, barely, but landed on his injured shoulder.

He let out a scream through clenched teeth as he pulled himself back up. "Run!"

Hallie grasped the handle of the flashpistol, trying to cock it, but like she suspected, the mechanism didn't budge. Jammed. She peeked around the side of the carriage as Niels edged around the doorway and shot an electrobolt at Correa. It hit the cottage door. Sparks engulfed the entire thing, jumping out and catching on the drying overgrowth.

A small flame budded where the spark had hit. Surely it wouldn't grow. Not with the lingering snow. Surely not. Nothing was dry enough.

But maybe they'd get lucky.

Heat flared inside her chest when that flame did indeed leap to life. As the fire climbed, so did her power, rising higher and pushing harder and growing more and more unbearable by the second.

Hallie whimpered involuntarily as she pushed the heat into the jammed pistol in her hands, unsure what else to do with the power begging for release.

Fire ravaged her veins and flooded into the metal weapon. Someone screamed—it might have been her.

In a blink of an eye, the feeling abated, but her hands tingled. She looked down at the flashpistol.

Despite the discomfort in her fingers, she cocked it with ease, no longer jammed.

Holy blasting stars.

She leaned out from behind the carriage and aimed toward Correa's hiding place. She hovered her finger over the trigger, breathing deeply to calm her racing heart.

She could do this. She could—

Tingling pain lanced through her hand, releasing her grip on the pistol.

Being old technology and not as reliable, it fired. The bullet nailed an upturned cobblestone, blasting it apart, and ricocheted sideways, hitting Niels in the leg. He shouted and fell against the wall. He slid to the ground, blood smearing on the moss and staining the sludgy snow.

"No!" she shouted. Her hand ached. She stumbled toward him where he tried to fire at Correa. His face was drawn into a pained grimace, his aim wilder than before.

She fell beside him, dodging a bullet. An orange glow grew on the other side of the street, but all she could really see was the blood soaking Niels' trousers. She fumbled around for her pack, for anything that could help as his shaking, uninjured arm kept the electropistol trained on where they'd last seen Correa.

"I don't know if—I'm sorry—I just—" She couldn't find the words as she leaned back onto the threshold. Her good hand touched something that felt like fire.

She hissed and pulled it back. One of the bricks, the one she'd touched, wasn't covered in moss or decay. It shone with a bronze glow, a soft light glimmering from its surface.

Hallie pressed both hands to the Zuprium brick. Fire raced through her fingers, into her hands, and up through her arms.

The Passage. It had to be. It didn't look like the archway in her mind, but the power was convincing enough.

She reached for her power again, closing her eyes and drowning out the sounds of the firefight. She needed to focus. She needed to hone this, to tame it into whatever it needed to be to get them out.

Her power moved stubbornly as sweat poured down her face and chilled in the mountain air. Tendrils of golden light in her mind's eye coiled and spun, but each time she tried to force them into the brick, they escaped her grasp.

The brick still burned the pads of her fingers. She could feel it—but the power wouldn't obey.

"I'm not sure what you are attempting to do, but I'd say bargaining with us is a better bet," a voice murmured above her.

Two hands found her shoulders and squeezed. Cold like

ice flowed through her veins, dousing her power like a match tossed into a snowbank.

The night was silent save for the crackling flames nearby. She opened her eyes and tore herself from the brick. The hands didn't leave her shoulders.

A gurgling noise.

She looked up to find a pair of golden eyes amidst a perfectly proportioned face and framed with silky golden hair. Unkempt at the moment, but still shimmering in the soft moonlight.

King Filip was beautiful, even in such a bedraggled state. The days since Achilles had been unkind to him. She'd only heard horror stories about the king who allowed his people to starve so that he could live in luxury. It was hard to reconcile this Adonis of a man with the greedy, greasy king she'd imagined in her University courses.

Worse, he was an Essence wielder.

Hallie's heart sputtered weakly, and she swayed on her feet. It was three against two, and Niels was bleeding from a pistol shot she'd unwittingly inflicted upon him.

They were both going to die, and it was her fault.

King Filip held Niels under his chin. The newest bloodstain on his knee grew like a puddle of spilled ink on his trousers. He clawed at Filip's fingers with one hand, but the harder he tried, the more King Filip's grip tightened.

Another voice spoke in her ear. Female, with a rasping lull to it. "Come with us, and your friend lives."

Lies.

Hallie wanted to scream, but she couldn't find her voice. She'd been in this situation before...except this time, it wouldn't be the Yalvs who rescued them in the ruins of the old city on Tasava. Yarrow's final moments and death-scream echoed in her ears.

This time, it would be Niels.

No.

Hallie tried to stoke her power, but nothing pulsed or flared. The tendrils, though merely evasive moments before, had disappeared completely.

No!

The voice spoke again, power zinging through each word and tingling up Hallie's spine. She caught a glimpse of long, dark hair. "You have little choice."

It was the woman. The one from Achilles, the other half of King Filip's Essence power.

Hallie abandoned her pursuit of her magic and eyed the discarded flashpistol instead. She must have used the last of the power she'd regained fixing it. Or maybe it just liked to rebel against her whenever it could, like it had a mind of its own.

She had no control. She needed someone to teach her. She needed to get to Myrrai and find a way to rid herself of this curse.

She needed to find her way back to Kase. She would not die here.

Hallie straightened in the woman's grip and looked King Filip in the eye. "Why should I believe you now?"

"We both work for the same goal."

Hallie shook her head. "Then why the demonstration at Achilles? Correa tortured me, and you—you're threatening my guide even now!"

King Filip loosened his grip, and Niels collapsed to the ground in a heap, gasping for breath. The moon paled the crimson blood leaking from his wound to scarlet. His face was too pale. Held fast, Hallie couldn't help him.

"My uncle and I both harbor hatred toward your people," King Filip said. He wore simple clothes very much like what the Jaydian elite would wear daily—a button-down shirt, blue vest, trousers, and a leather traveler's jacket. He was only missing a bowler hat. Judging by the dirt and occasional rip, the clothes had seen better days. Hardly appropriate for a fight. "It is not easy to keep in check."

At that moment, Hallie couldn't recall what he'd worn at Achilles. A sneaking suspicion told her he'd stolen the clothes from somewhere. Stoneset, more than likely. The horror might have struck her harder had she not been trapped between two Cerls, Niels bleeding out on the cratered ground, Correa still battling the flames on the other side of the lane.

"Hate us for *what*?" Hallie choked.

King Filip snapped his fingers. A light bloomed above them as if the air had caught fire. It solidified into a ball and floated just beside his head. "A question I won't dignify with an answer. We want you alive, but your guide is not necessary. We can take you drugged and bound and leave him to die, or you can come willingly, and your reward will be his life. It's your choice."

Choice. That was no *choice.*

Niels had stopped moving now except for the shallow rise and fall of his chest. Unconscious. If she didn't decide soon, blood loss would decide for her.

Even if they kept their word, it would only be to use Niels against her later. Was that worse or better than dying here, from a wound *Hallie* had dealt him?

She didn't know that answer…but she knew hers. She'd lost too many people. She refused to lose one more.

If she agreed to work with them, she could help Niels. Maybe they would unwittingly teach her how to use her power, or maybe she could trick them into it somehow. It was the only reason she was valuable in the first place; they would need her capable of using it if they wanted to do anything with her.

But Correa.

She couldn't become his prisoner again. She could still feel the lightning pain as it coursed through her body.

She chewed on her lip so hard she drew blood.

But she *had* done something to him at Achilles. She could do so again. If she could convince them to let her go to Myrrai, they might even help her find what she needed. They might even help her with the Passage.

She just needed a story good enough to convince them.

"We're trying to get to Myrrai." The words were thick, but she said them with as much confidence as she could. "If you heal my guide and get us there, I will help you."

Better to stick with calling Niels her guide, not her friend. The less he mattered to her, the less they would try to use him against her…she hoped.

The memory of Kase's screams as she tried over and over to convince the Lord Elder to pass on his power would live with her forever. She'd made the mistake of letting Correa see how much he meant to her. She wouldn't make that mistake with Niels.

Filip smiled, banal, oddly plain for a man so beautiful, so hateful. "Is that all?"

She had to word this precisely right. Wetting her chapped lips, she answered, "You have the Essence power?"

"In the moments before my mother died, she passed her

Essence down to me." King Filip cracked his neck as if the conversation strained it in some way. "A feat the assassins were only able to pull off at all because she was without her vessel. She only had the strength left to pass her power onto me. Fate knows how long the Essence power would have been lost if she hadn't." He looked back at the flames. "My uncle would not approve, but alas, Fate has chosen this moment for me."

The calm way he spoke about his mother's death unnerved her. But then, being the king of Cerulene meant he couldn't show weakness. And to many men, emotion was weakness. What could be hiding underneath the icy yet beautiful façade?

Hallie had lost greatly, and it had sent her halfway across the world to avoid her past. But she'd been on the cusp of adulthood when Jack died. Still horrible, but not the same as a child watching assassins murder her mother.

Not to mention taking on the power of a god in the same moment.

No wonder rumors swirled through the realms about his cruelty and iron fist. Hallie wasn't sure if she would've fared better. Not that it excused his actions, but she could understand how he'd turned into this, if only a little.

"You claim we're working toward the same goal. If that's true, prove it. I'll work with you...if you teach me how to use my power."

King Filip's smile had yet to leave his lips. "Excellent." He gestured to Niels. "Heal him."

Hallie didn't understand at first. "What?"

The king repeated his command. "Heal him." He crouched beside Niels. "Or we could build him a pyre, if you prefer. Your first test could be lighting it."

Hallie's heart lurched. She tugged against the woman's grip, but she held Hallie fast. "I don't know how. I can't control it. I could kill him!"

"He's already dying," King Filip pointed out. "Whether you stop it or send him off, you'll still learn something, won't you?"

The woman pushed her forward. Hallie was prepared for the rush of power that time. She gritted her teeth against the inferno waiting on the other side of the dam. It raged within her, begging to be released, angry at being restrained.

Her hold was tenuous, like a stray thread. One tug, and the entire thing might unravel.

She tried not to think about the man who had done exactly that when she'd touched him.

She walked stiffly and knelt, every movement making her skin burn worse. She clenched her teeth against the pain, but it did little to stem it. The chilled ground bit into her knees, but she barely felt it. Niels was too pale.

"It hurts," she said, the words coming out in spurts. "I don't know how to let it out without—"

"You're focusing too much on the flow," King Filip said, his voice steady as he hesitantly took her hand and laid it on Niels' knee. "Find a single strand and grasp it. Hold it tight. Focus only on that strand."

Sweat stung her eyes. She was so distracted by the power raging within her that she could barely tell she was now covered in Niels' blood. She tried to follow King Filip's directions. The toll of the last few days weighed heavily on her. She'd nearly died several times, said goodbye to Kase and her father, killed soldiers, and now she was at the mercy of the Cerl king.

The power writhed in her body, and it took all her willpower to find anything to focus on at all. In her mind's eye, it was like a bonfire, blindingly bright. The undulating flames snarled and snapped, crackled and leapt. It burned so badly, she nearly begged for the woman to take it away once more.

"Can't...can't..." she sputtered.

"Essence powers need to be tamed. If you let them roam freely within you, they will devour you," the woman said.

Hallie breathed best she could against the crushing weight in her chest. It felt like her lungs were carved from marble. She willed them to accept the oxygen, prying her airways open with sheer force of will.

In, two, three. Out, two, three, four.

The weight only lessened slightly. The air couldn't blow the fire out.

"Again," King Filip said. "Focus."

In, two, three. Out, two, three, four.

A little less pressure.

In, two, three. Out, two, three, four.

The blaze dimmed, yet sharpened, coming into focus in

her mind's eye. It no longer blinded her. Each flame was a strand, and with each breathing cycle she completed, the strands became clearer.

In and out. Pause. In and out.

One flame strand fluttered more softly than the others, pliable, swaying to music only it could hear.

"Good," King Filip said, his voice lower yet closer. "Don't lose it. Keep it within your grasp."

Hallie nodded, afraid to do more than that. "Now what? How do I heal him?"

"Each Essence power is unique, and the Lord Elder held the power for centuries." The king spoke lazily, almost as if he'd suddenly lost interest in the conversation. "I can only teach you control."

Without losing her grip on the strand, she opened one eye. Still not sure what she was doing, she coaxed the power into him slowly, focusing on the single flame. The heat flowed from her and into him. His jagged breathing hitched...then smoothed.

With each pulse of her power as it entered Niels, the strain on her mind lessened. The heat abated, dimming to a soft, comforting burn. Not too hot. Just enough to remind her it was there.

She could still feel the power working in Niels. It repaired the ruptured blood vessels from both wounds, replaced the chipped bone shards from the one she'd inflicted, and resealed the skin—almost like she'd rewound time. Except nothing around them changed. Only Niels.

What were the repercussions of a power like that? Could she affect more than just a single person? Stories she'd read about time magic flashed in her mind. Would saving Niels here only cause a worse outcome in the future? Would there be a price to pay for saving him?

Her blood ran cold as the fire extinguished.

She collapsed, spots gathering in her sight. She blinked them away, her hands and arms tingling, almost numb.

Warm fingers encircled her wrist and pressed heat into her. The spots cleared from Hallie's vision. The prickling sensation in her limbs slowly faded.

"We will work on your control. You focused too hard on the one strand and allowed the rest of your power to leak," the woman said, her hand still around Hallie's wrist, heat like fire on a cold winter's night entering her bloodstream. It stung, but it wasn't unbearable.

Hallie blinked, trying to stay her shaking hand. "What?"

"I can only give you enough Soul to keep you stable for now," the woman clarified as she let go of Hallie. The cold in her body had improved, though she wouldn't say she was warm. She hesitantly reached for her power, for the heat, but it had retreated behind a wall again. "Using your power often in small doses will keep you from overextending yourself due to build-up."

She didn't trust this woman, but she had to admit there seemed to be some truth to it. She didn't feel as terrible as she had after Achilles.

But what was Soul?

King Filip knelt beside them and checked Niels. "His pulse is very weak."

He then put a hand to Niels' cheek, a glow emanating from his fingers. Hallie scrambled toward him. "No! Please!"

So much for not overreacting.

The woman grabbed Hallie, keeping her from leaping forward. She looked to the king. "Do not overburden yourself."

Filip took his hand back. Niels' face was still pale in the wan light, but he was no longer the same color as the snow patches beneath his bloodstained trousers.

He'd…had he helped Niels?

"What did you do?" she demanded.

"He is no longer in immediate danger of succumbing to injuries, but it is a temporary solution. You did well up to the end." King Filip stood and straightened, looking back as the fire on the other side of the lane abated. "I merely allowed his body to take a portion of Soul to aid his natural healing. But with the bullet still in there, it will be painful to walk."

Guilt slammed into Hallie like an avalanche. "Will I be able to fix it once I can…" She didn't know exactly how to ask, but the King seemed to understand.

"I am unsure, but it would be unwise for you to attempt it again now. You need more control, and we cannot risk the Essence power you wield being reborn."

"Why?"

Boots crunching through the snow and debris interrupted them. Correa appeared behind the King. Dark smudges streaked across his cheeks, his hair mussed and unkempt. He walked with a pronounced limp. The lines at the corners of his eyes deepened as he squinted. "Because Jagamot is here now."

Hallie recoiled, stumbling back involuntarily. It had been too much to hope the fire would kill Correa. The sparks only had so much kindling to devour with the melting snows.

The woman caught her, but it wasn't her touch that made Hallie's blood run cold. She shivered as she met Correa's eyes. Before the recent firefight, he'd ordered her to kill Kase with her own power. He'd tortured them both before Hallie had been able to take the Essence. He was a monster.

"Excellent work, Your Majesty," Correa said, a small dip of his head. It was an odd scene, knowing what she knew now—that Filip was his nephew. She briefly wondered if it bothered Correa to bow to someone so much younger. "But I would argue that your methods are still too tame for the task ahead of us."

"I am your sovereign." Filip's drawl was lazy and bored—different than it had been moments before. "My methods are not yours to argue."

Correa turned his gaze upon her. "Where are her restraints?"

"The Lady Fely is more than her match, General." The last word had a bit of a bite to it, but it was so subtle she wasn't sure if anyone else would catch it. "She can barely keep her feet as it is. No need to be excessive."

Correa's fingers twitched, as if he longed to use his power against his nephew. A small spark leapt from his pointer finger to his thumb so fast Hallie barely glimpsed it. But it was enough.

She tried to swallow, but it was as if her fear had solidified in her throat. Her chest squeezed. She couldn't breathe. The pain branched like lightning in her veins.

A light touch at her elbow brought a small pulse of heat. The woman, Lady Fely. The heat was gone as quickly as it appeared, but Hallie was able to breathe.

What had Filip said? That he'd given Niels a little bit of *Soul*? What did that mean? Was it actually someone's spirit? Their own, perhaps, or one of the lives they'd collected? Like Yarrow's?

Hallie's stomach roiled as Correa holstered his pistol. "Leave him and let's go."

"No," the King replied.

That same bored voice.

Hallie waited with bated breath. Correa's glare turned deadly. "This is not the time to be careless. We must find the final Essence. Asa has been unsuccessful at locating him and the secondary Gate."

"My brother might have been successful if you hadn't ordered the city burned."

A pause. "Were we not in agreement?"

"Are kings not allowed to change their minds?" King Filip crossed his arms. "I am sorry, Uncle, but I don't see the value in us both going to the capital to search for a man who, by all accounts, is centuries old. Asa should be able to find him just fine with your help." The King crossed his arms and stood to his full height. He was still shorter than Correa, but only by a hairsbreadth. "I shall meet you in the Yalven city."

Correa cursed. "Like the stars you will."

"I will take the Essence of Time to Myrrai and await you there."

They stared at one another. Hallie barely understood what they spoke about, but she could gather that she was the Essence of Time...and that whoever Asa was, he was important. She hadn't done a whole lot of research into the Cerls, but she didn't recall a younger prince. He was quite possibly illegitimate. The royal families of First Earth had also been obsessed with bloodlines. Stars-ridiculous, if you asked Hallie, but she'd had the privilege of growing up in Jayde. The government had its issues, but it allowed for the general populace to have a say in who made the decisions that affected everyone.

The two men continued to face off until, finally, Correa sighed. "Find Kainadr. Await my orders. We only have one chance to make this work."

Filip nodded his head. "Good luck, Uncle. Tell Asa I will see him soon."

Hallie itched to grab Kase's goggles in her pocket to ground herself, but they might think she was reaching for a weapon.

Where had she gone wrong? What had she done to end up here? Her hands shook. She couldn't help it.

This was different. This time, she was willingly putting herself in their clutches. She was making a deal with them. She would work with them.

She didn't know if that made it better or worse.

She no longer felt like herself, but this deal was the only way she could do anything to help her country, her parents, and Kase.

Heat tingled at her fingertips once more. She didn't think it was fear this time.

Correa paced a moment before turning back to her. "Regrettably, I was here in this little village nearly fifty years prior, looking for evidence of a Passage. Our intelligence suggested someone was looking for a way to the holy city."

He paused. The heat rose up her arms slowly as the threads untangled. Fifty years...was that why they'd attacked? Had Navara been the reason the homes were burned out and overgrown?

Hallie thought back to the journal and her experience inside it—the darkness and the conversation. If someone had been looking for a way to Myrrai, had it been Navara? Had she tried to go back to her homeland to save whoever they'd been discussing in the...memory?

Correa prompted, "Is that why you are here, Miss Walker?"

Hallie squeezed her hands tightly and used the pain in her palms to ground herself. The answer was right in front of her. It had to be. She glanced subtly at the brick in question. She was certain that was the key. But if Navara had been unsuccessful in opening the Passage back up, could Hallie open it herself? The Lord Elder had created it, and Hallie now had his power.

The image of the glowing archway flashed in her mind insistently.

"It is," she said with as much confidence as she could muster. "I believe a Passage lies here, though if you weren't able to find it all those years ago, it might be that it has disappeared."

The woman shifted behind her, and Hallie flinched without meaning to. "Weren't you trying to do something with that brick there?"

Hallie hesitated. Her heart drummed loudly. She gave in and stuck her hand in her pocket, her fingers gripping the edge of Kase's goggles as hard as she could. They gave her strength, and neither of her captors stopped her. She took a moment to breathe. The heat in her arms had reached her shoulders, but as she grasped the goggles, it receded slightly. "I'm not exactly sure."

Correa stepped forward around Niels and looked down at the brick in question. "Fate works quite mysteriously."

He bent down and brushed a hand on it. Sparks leapt from his fingers. He scoffed. "Of course, the maker of this particular Passage didn't want it found by anyone. Only those who needed it. It seems as if we were not in need in the past. I'd blame General Ormond, but it bodes ill to speak of the dead…" he paused and looked over his shoulder toward something only he could see. "Especially in the place of his passing."

"What?" Hallie asked.

Correa stood and shook out the arm that had touched the brick. "There are three ways to get to the holy city. The first is by traversing the sea above it or on it—a lengthy journey and nearly impossible until recently. The second is through the Gates. The final one is through smaller Passages created by the Essence of Time. This side of Yalvara used to have many of these Passages, but between the wars and the actions of the misguided peoples of Yalvara, most are now closed." He gestured to Hallie and pointed at the brick. "But you can open this one."

Without taking her eyes from Correa, Hallie stepped forward, trying her best to hide the shaking in her knees.

She knelt next to the brick and placed her fingers upon it, regrettably letting go of the goggles. The heat returned to her arms in full force, and with her fingers on the brick, they burned just like they had minutes earlier.

She closed her eyes against the heat and pain. She envisioned the fire and its spiraling, uncontrollable tendrils. Focusing hard, she grasped one and pushed it through her fingers into the brick. She closed her eyes and braced for…whatever would happen.

Her heart raced. Her power writhed harder, strands vying for control, fighting for her to release her hold on the one she'd chosen. She shut them out as best she could. Sweat poured down her face, dripping down her nose and onto the ground below.

She clenched her teeth as the power warred within her, begging to be released. It was as if the floodgates had opened once she searched for a piece of it. Like a living entity, the power wanted to be used. It wanted to wreak havoc, to destroy, to unleash itself upon the world. But Hallie held on. Her jaw ached from clenching it so hard. She pressed the one tendril into the bricks with all the strength she had left.

Nothing.

She ripped her hands away, and the cold early morning froze the sweat on her face. She shivered.

"Let the flames loose," King Filip said from nearby. "It's contrary, I know, but in some circumstances, your power needs to be uncontrolled. Keep hold of the one strand to keep you grounded. Let the others flow into the brick. Visualize your outcome."

Well, he'd been mostly right before when she'd tried healing Niels. Hallie breathed heavily and shivered some more. With hesitancy, she pressed her hands to the brick again. Heat immediately radiated out from the place she touched. Her power responded with vicious desire. She grabbed at one of the strands and held onto it, but she allowed the madness pressing against her skin and soul to flow out through her fingers instead. She screamed. It burned. It scalded and flowed like a river into the brick below.

Light exploded behind her eyelids, and she nearly lost control of everything. She was on fire. She *was* fire. She clung to the strand, but it was like clasping a hand in a raging storm.

"Hallie!" someone screamed. Niels? Or was it Kase? Someone else?

She couldn't let go of the brick. She lost hold of her one strand of power. The light grew brighter. The pain increased.

She fell straight through the shining portal.

C H A P T E R   5

BLASTED DEATH TRAPS

Kase

KASE AWOKE TO COLD WETNESS on the side of his face.

He flinched and batted whatever was causing the sensation. The cold stung, but he wasn't sure why. He hit another hand, forcing his lids open. It was Hallie. It had to be. He'd been dreaming of her, and now she was here, poking at him to irritate him into waking up. He smiled and blinked away the rest of his sleep.

Stowe bent over him, rag in hand. He squinted down at Kase. "Quit smilin' at me like that."

Wrong Walker. Kase bent his smile back out of shape and sat up. Pain radiated through his skull, and he slapped a hand to it…which, of course, caused more pain. Something else leaked onto his hand.

He pulled away. Dark blood mixed with flakes smeared across his palm.

"Don't move just yet, son," Stowe said a little more kindly, sitting back and digging through his pack.

"What happened?" Kase looked around the room, trying

his best not to move his neck much, hoping that Stowe would stop the blood pouring from the side of his face. The pounding in his head only lessened somewhat.

The space was only lit with electropistol sparks, but Kase could see enough. They sat in the tunnel just adjacent to the Zuprium crystal, which was visible through an opening in the rocks blocking them from going back. At the top was a crack big enough for someone very slim to crawl through. To the left was only darkness.

They had no way to go except forward. Kase didn't fancy another battle with the crystal anyway.

Stowe handed him a vial of brown liquid. "A rock clipped your head pretty good, but you're a tough'n. Lucky my pack wasn't buried too deep, and this was cushioned quite nice like."

Kase took it from him as Stowe continued, "Don't have none of that fancy medicine you inject into your skin like they do in the capital, but this'll dull the pain until we can get you checked out proper."

Kase downed the vial in one gulp. It tasted like dirt. He grimaced and squeezed his eyes shut as the liquid tingled its way to his stomach. Ugh. Hopefully he didn't throw it up. "Thanks."

Stowe tied up his pack. "It's the least I could do after you...well, thank you, son."

Kase gave a small laugh. "Guess my luck is changing, then."

Stowe helped Kase stand as well. "From what little Niels told me about you, I owe you much more than a simple numbing medicine."

"Oh, yeah? And what did he say about me?" Kase rolled his bruised shoulder and winced at the pain. Guess whatever it was he'd drunk hadn't taken effect yet.

"That you're arrogant and rich and don't know nothin' about mountain life, but you've put yourself in harm's way to save my daughter more times than he could count, so there's that."

Annoyance flared in Kase's cheeks as he furrowed his brow. "It's what anyone would've done."

"It's not, and for that, I owe you a mighty debt." Stowe handed Kase his pack. It was rather dusty and ripped in a few places, but it was mostly intact. Gingerly, he tugged it onto his shoulder. He took the electropistol from Stowe as well. The lantern wasn't anywhere in sight. Lovely.

Kase shook his head. "You don't owe me anything."

Stowe gave him a look that said differently, but he dusted off his trousers and looked back at the rock fall. "Rather get away from here fast like. Sometimes one cave-in'll cause others. Miracle I didn't lose Hallie in that one back when Jack..." He coughed. "Sorry. Bein' in the mines just...reminds me of...things."

Kase eyed the wall of debris. He didn't know what exactly happened back there, but he hoped they didn't stumble across another one. He didn't think he would get lucky a second time.

He ignored the slight tilt as he stepped forward and put a hesitant hand on Stowe's shoulder. "I'm sorry for your loss, Mr. Walker."

"It just hits me sometimes outta nowhere." Stowe put his own hand on Kase's shoulder. "That concoction will take a few minutes to work, but we need to get on now."

He looked into Kase's eyes for so long that Kase almost felt uncomfortable. After a moment, Stowe looked away. "Might have a concussion, but without a good light, I can't tell if your pupils are dilatin' proper or not."

The pounding in Kase's head eased a little. It still hurt, but it no longer felt as if a knife stabbed him in the temple repeatedly. "I'll be fine."

"Sure you will," Stowe chuckled, patting Kase's arm as he walked off.

Kase let him get a few paces ahead before muttering to himself, "I'm not *arrogant*."

Several hours, three twists, eight forks, and ten collapsed side tunnels later, the midday sunshine made Kase's eyes burn. But the pain in his head stayed under control thanks to continued shots of Stowe's numbing concoction, and they were now in the Jaydian foothills, blessedly out of the tunnels. He'd nearly lost count of the collapsed ones.

The hike down the mountain would still be quite the beast to slay, with its uneven pathways through the thick trees, but at least they weren't in the dark.

Part of him hoped to stop in Nar and steal any hover that had survived Hallie's sabotage—shocks, he was still proud of her for that—or one that had been called to the town once they'd realized they couldn't catch the criminals in their own ships.

Hard to believe he and Hallie were the criminals in question. Harder to believe Hallie had gone from grumpy bookshop attendant to one of Jayde's most wanted in a matter of months. Quite impressive. He wondered if she also had a terribly drawn wanted poster outside the tavern. The artist probably wouldn't mess up *her* nose.

If he had, blast the consequences. Kase would track the bloke down himself and clock him.

"There should be a carriage for hire in Nar, which'll be comin up soon," Stowe huffed from beside him. He paused and put his hand on a nearby tree to catch his breath. Kase stopped and looked back, fighting the urge to run a hand through his hair. "Good thing too, cause I ain't gettin' in a hover."

"Can we reconsider that stance? A hover would be quickest, and I'm...well..." He shifted his weight to his other foot. "I used to be a pilot."

Stowe cast a doubtful look over him. "You got that kind of money?"

"Well, no." He hadn't thought he'd have to spell this out. "We'll probably have to steal one."

Stowe furrowed his brow. "Son, I'm a good, law-abiding citizen."

"Well, your daughter blew up the hangar, so even if we had the money, the only hovers available will be the ones used to ferry military personnel. Law-abiding citizens won't be getting any rides."

Stowe's mouth dropped open. He shook his head and blinked. "You must be talkin' bout a different Hallie Walker."

"You raised quite a woman, let me tell you," Kase said with a small smile. "If we can't find a carriage or a hover to steal, we may be able to use my...reputation to secure one. But that's a last resort."

The absolute last resort, because it would mean getting arrested and sent to Kyvena in chains. It wasn't ideal, but it would work.

"I don't like the sound of your reputation...especially if you've turned my daughter into some criminal."

Kase shrugged. "Just get her to tell you the story once she joins us in Kyvena."

Stowe only stared at him for a moment more before trudging past him, shaking his head.

It took about twenty minutes to weave through the trees...twenty minutes too long, if one were to ask Kase. Mostly because of the birdsong ringing through the branches, so joyful it grated on Kase's ears. Even worse, one of the calls sounded too much like a human voice, and he kept almost snapping his neck checking over his shoulder for someone in pursuit.

He didn't fancy a fight amongst the trees. It would be easier to hide, but harder to get a clear shot.

At the edge of the woods, across a field of freshly turned dirt ready for planting, Nar finally came into view. Kase scanned the city outskirts for any lonesome hovers. When he'd left Nar in the middle of a rainstorm, he'd thought he'd never see it again.

He was not completely wrong.

No one seemed to be walking around the city, even though it was only early evening, the sun still hanging half a thumb's length above the horizon. People should be out and about socializing, shopping, maybe even heading to the taverns for an early dinner.

But that didn't mean the city was deserted.

In place of people, blue-tinged hovers patrolled the streets, zooming along ten feet above the ground.

Kase froze in his tracks. Those hovers didn't belong to Jayde. When Jove had explained the mission to Tasava all those months ago, he'd said the Cerls were after more Zuprium. He'd implied that it was the Cerls who'd compromised the Jaydian mines.

Kase didn't know for sure, but by the look of those hovers, that assumption was correct. They looked a little like Jaydian airships, but not enough, and the sheen...

There was something unsettling about the blueness of them. It was like they'd taken Zuprium and infused it with the hottest part of a fire.

These were sleeker than Kase's old standard hover. The noses were more pointed, the wings more aerodynamic and tucked closer to the hover's side. Kase wiped his sweaty hands on his trousers. These looked more like old fighter jets out of books Kase had read about warfare on First Earth. He didn't think he wanted to know what sort of firepower these had. It couldn't be good.

Kase briefly wondered if that had been the next step in his uncle's research before he died, or if the advancement was a natural evolution from the secrets about infusing electricity with the metal he sold to them.

He wished he'd been old enough to remember more than a few fleeting glimpses of the man and his cousins. Jove remembered a little more, being nearly five years older. He'd always said he'd liked how his older cousins would let him play cricket with them in the courtyard. Not exactly helpful information, unless the Cerls were gearing up for a tournament.

"There's a small cabin in the woods that way." Kase retrieved his electropistol and handed off his pack to the older man before pointing to the thick trees about a mile to their right. "The man's name is Ossie. Stay with him. If I'm not back in an hour, you'll have to figure out another way to get to the capital. Find Jove Shackley."

If he's still alive.

Stowe slung the pack onto his free shoulder. "Don't need to worry about me."

Kase scratched at the healing cut on his cheek. "Hallie would."

The man shrugged. "Somehow I don't think you'll be finding a motorcoach for hire."

Kase hoped the guilt didn't spill onto his face. "No." He squirmed a second under the man's steady gaze, then turned away, pointing to where the treeline ended near the other edge of the town. "Would it make you feel better to know I'm stealing a hover from people who want to kill us?"

Stowe's features didn't budge.

Kase continued, "Listen, it's the only way we're getting to Kyvena in a reasonable amount of time, and with the Cerls here...well, my brother needs to know what's going on. It's life or death." Kase hoped he looked more confident than he felt. "I'll do a quick scout of the airfields."

Stowe handed back Kase's pack and pulled a flashpistol from his own pack. "I ain't hiding away while you run off risking your neck."

Kase stared at the weapon for a second, feeling like his brain was going to burst. Why hadn't Stowe used that in the cave when they'd thought they'd come across a Cerl? He'd chosen a machete instead, the absolute madman. "You've had that the *whole time*?"

Stowe fished a few bullets from his pocket and loaded them into the revolving chamber. "Aye." He shifted the chamber back into place with a loud click. "But it's more dangerous to us in the caves. Ricochet and the like. Coulda ended up hitting us. Out here, it'll find Cerl flesh just fine."

He then fetched the machete and held it in the other hand like he was John Silver.

Kase still didn't back down. "I appreciate the thought, but I'll be much better off scouting by myself."

"You've seen a lot, son, but you weren't there when the Trips took Stoneset."

Apparently stubbornness ran in the Walker bloodline.

Kase finally nodded. "Fine. But if we run into trouble..."

This was a terrible idea. Stowe couldn't run quickly, and while he'd survived the attack on Stoneset, he didn't have any skills that would improve their odds of evading Cerl soldiers. Kase would just have to make sure he didn't do anything completely stupid.

"...Make sure you shoot straight," he finished reluctantly.

With that, the duo skirted along the tree line, quietly making their way toward the airfields. Kase was intensely curious to see what Hallie had made of it with her crash.

The Jaydian military might have cleaned it up prior to the Cerls arriving, but if not...

His pride twisted into dread.

What if Nar was easily overtaken because Hallie had destroyed the airfields? Because they couldn't mount a better response thanks to the hovers in the hangar being mangled into heaps of metal?

Kase vowed he would do anything to make sure she didn't suffer the consequences of her actions if they both survived this war. How could she have known that her actions would've led to the Cerl takeover?

Of course, it would have been a crime regardless, and Kase might not be...available...to defend her in court if it came to it.

He didn't know whether he'd prefer the firing squad to hanging. Firing squad was probably quicker. Maybe. That would depend on how much the shooters wanted him to suffer.

It wouldn't do to dwell on the possibilities. He could only focus on getting himself to Kyvena and warning them of the danger to come—if it wasn't too late. It was better to own up to his mistakes than to run from them. The universe had taught him *that* lesson loud and clear.

If he hadn't run, Hallie might still be here with him.

That is...if she would've still wanted him. The adventure to Stoneset had only brought them closer. Without that shared trauma, would they still be what they were—whatever they were?

Kase tripped on an exposed root and cursed. *Blast it. Focus, you dulkop.*

"You all right up there?" Stowe asked.

Kase nodded and waved him off.

Nope, but I'm not telling you about my hypothetical scenarios involving your daughter because I've discovered I'm rather insecure about it all. You're at my back with a machete and a flashpistol.

This wasn't at all how he'd imagined getting to know his future father-in-law. That is, if...well, now Kase might be getting ahead of himself.

A few more minutes, trees, and intrusive thoughts later, a line of blue hovers—about five—came into view. To their right was a heap of metal that took up most of the right side of the area. Someone had begun to clear the debris, but something must have interrupted the progress.

The hangar. He muttered another curse. At least this one was softer.

Kase could barely tell the structure had been a building once, not a grotesque pile of ruins. What in the blazes had done that? Had that really been Hallie?

His blood chilled. He prayed it wasn't solely Hallie's doing. Because if so, his fear of her actions crippling any palpable response to an attacking Cerl Airforce was very much valid.

Kase gripped his pistol harder. Stowe shifted beside him, his thoughts probably running along the same lines. He shouldn't have told her father what she'd done.

Her only saving grace might be that the Cerls had probably killed anyone who would be able to identify Hallie as the one to blame for the catastrophic defeat.

Soldiers in dark blue uniforms waited on the outer perimeter, spaced at regular intervals amid the ruins. Kase looked back toward the town once more, looking for any sign of life, but all he could see were structures that used to be homes and shops—now marred with blackened stone and gutted streets.

Kase's stomach turned. He swallowed down the bile that threatened to rise. Maybe they ought to shift the plan—keep going on foot, steal a hover or motorcoach from the next town, and avoid Nar entirely. There was nothing he could do to help these people now, if there were any survivors at all.

But walking might take weeks—weeks Kyvena didn't have.

Shocks.

He scratched the patches of beard along his jaw. He needed to think this through. The reality was, stealing a Cerl hover was his best option. Not the safest or the smartest, but the best.

Still, not only would he need to get one of those hovers and figure out how it worked in a matter of minutes—seconds, more likely—but he also had to keep Stowe alive. His palms went slick with sweat despite the slight chill in the air.

But he was Kase Shackley, the best stars-blasted pilot in the realm. If anyone could pull it off, he could.

Bravado had proved it could get him most anywhere. Hopefully it wouldn't fail him today.

Bravado, he thought firmly, wishing he could say it to Niels' face. *Not arrogance.*

He inspected the airfield's defenses once more. The soldiers weren't going to be as gullible as the dragon in the forest, but if he shot something on the other side of the airfields...no, that wasn't going to be enough. They might be jumpy but they *had* taken out an entire Jaydian unit to conquer Nar, with or without Hallie's unwitting help.

Kase's head hurt from chasing after a plan that might work. He stared out at the hangar ruins. If Hallie was here, she'd already have a plan—a brilliant, if deadly and foolhardy, plan.

Some sort of insect buzzed near his ear. He swatted at it.

What would Hallie do?

Before he could answer the question, leaves and underbrush crunched behind him. He glanced back, ready to berate Stowe for being so careless, but just past Hallie's father, another figure waited amongst the trees.

A ragged old man stood there, hair a mess, pipe hanging from his lips. His beard was even more unkempt than his hair, and he seemed to be missing several teeth.

"Never thought I'd see yer skinny hide no more," the man growled. He reminded Kase of a bear—especially in his voluminous furs, though it wasn't nearly cold enough to justify them. Even his eyes had a feral look about them.

Gone was the odd but jolly old man Kase had met only a few weeks before. Kase had appreciated his help avoiding the Jaydian soldiers last time, and the furs he and Hallie had used as makeshift beds had been quite comfortable. Ossie had even pretended to have a cat to avoid suspicion and was taken in for questioning.

Kase glanced toward the airfields and patrols. They were far enough away to have not heard the man, but Kase didn't know if soldiers were in the woods. He needed to get the man quiet or on his way quickly. He smiled, the gesture irritating his healing cut, and reached to shake the man's hand. "Good to see you again."

He still held the electropistol loosely at his side with his other hand, keeping one eye on the airfields.

Ossie merely looked at his hand and sniffed. His voice was loud enough to wake the dead. "You cost me a pretty sum to get outta there, ya know."

Stowe didn't say anything, only watched, his eyes wary. Kase felt the tension in the air more than the slight chill. He looked closer at Ossie. The edges of his eyes were rimmed red, and sweat beaded in the folds of his mature skin above his scraggly beard.

Too much sweat, even with the furs.

Hadn't Yarrow mentioned something about keeping Ossie stocked with moonshine? And with Yarrow gone...well, he assumed the drink had probably begun to run out.

Kase renewed the grip on his weapon. He didn't know what Ossie was like normally—whether sober or drunk. Kase had figured he'd been overloaded on drink last time they'd met, but now, he didn't know what to think. Ossie was clearly going through withdrawal. With the Cerl attack, he probably couldn't get anything from Nar anyway, even if he'd dared trek down.

Kase stepped back, retracting his hand and setting it on

Stowe's forearm. He smiled again at Ossie.

"Sorry about that." Kase hoped his voice was placating enough. "I appreciate all you did to help us, really."

"Except you done killed Yarrow," Ossie continued, voice raising to a full shout. He pulled something from his pocket. The blade was about as long as Kase's palm, and the numerous rust spots running along the edge spoke of its age and lack of care.

Well, shocks.

Even if Kase managed to avoid a killing blow, just a scratch would probably give him some violently aggressive disease. Couldn't think of one at that moment, but whatever it was, it would be painful.

The electropistol in Kase's hand sparked as he pointed the barrel at Ossie's chest. "He was a Cerl soldier. He deserved to die."

Maybe not in the way he had, but his betrayal still stung.

The man yelled something unintelligible, and Kase's finger hesitated on the trigger. Except Ossie swung the dagger straight at Stowe. Stowe spun, ducking underneath Ossie's wild stab. Out of the corner of his eye, he saw soldiers begin to move their way.

Kase squeezed the trigger.

A bolt of electricity rocketed from the barrel, sending a bolt of pain through Kase's bruised shoulder. Kase missed the flailing man's chest, but the shot nailed Ossie in the side. The man crumpled with a gurgling scream, and Kase glanced toward the airfields. The soldiers were running now, their own weapons out.

He yanked Stowe up by the jacket. "Come on!"

Through the trees, they sprinted from the soldiers and the still-screaming Ossie. Kase didn't have time to feel anything but pure panic, but his thoughts were shockingly clear. If they circled around to the right, then maybe they could use the hangar ruins as cover. Then they could steal a hover.

Shocks, he'd needed a distraction, and Ossie had delivered. He just hoped Ossie recovered once Kase was well away from there, even if the old man had wanted to gut him. Kase knew a thing or two about withdrawals; he couldn't fully blame him. The man was already going through it. Hopefully, he'd get to the other end alive.

Stowe's breathing grew softer. Kase glanced over his shoulder to see the older man falling behind. Kase slowed and grabbed him by the jacket once more. "If we don't make it onto a hover, they'll kill—"

The branch in the tree to their left exploded with blue fire. Kase cursed, and Stowe heaved himself forward. They sprinted toward the Cerl hovers on the airfields. Breaking through the last of the trees, Kase fired his electropistol at random. Shouts and other blasts followed, but none hit their intended target.

Kase raced up the ladder of the nearest blue-tinged hover. He sliced his hand on something, but he barely felt the sting. Throwing himself over the side and into the cockpit, he slammed the butt of his pistol against the Cerl pilot's head. The man slumped in his chair. Kase pushed him out the other side before turning back and wrenching Stowe up the last rung. He ignored the nausea rising in his chest as the Cerl's body smacked the edge of the wing before hitting the ground below.

"Strap in, and fire at anything that moves!" Kase didn't look to see if Stowe obeyed as he buckled himself into the safety harness. He assumed the second chair beside him was for a weapons' specialist, but he couldn't focus on anything other than the flashing buttons in front of him. He reached up and slammed the windshield down. His own blood dripped onto the steering control. He could bandage his hand later. It wouldn't kill him.

He read the Cerleze marking the different buttons and knobs. Never had he ever been more thankful for his expensive schooling. The previous pilot had prepped the craft well enough, seeing as the machine hummed with power.

Kase had to get it in the air. Three seconds ago.

He swayed in the seat with each bullet ricocheting off the side of the ship. Another clanged on the underbelly.

"One of 'em has a cannon!" Stowe shouted over the commotion.

Kase glanced up to see a Cerl with the weapon slung on his shoulder, blue smoke leaking out the end, the barrel squared up with Kase's face.

"Hope you're strapped, Stowe!" he yelled over his shoulder.

"What?"

He smashed the 'Lift' button, blood splattering the console. Forget trying to figure anything out. They were dead if they sat there any longer. He'd have to learn in the air.

The engine roared, and Kase fell forward with the power suddenly surging through the craft. He caught himself on the steering control and fumbling around with his right foot, whooping when he found some sort of pedal. He pressed it to the floor.

The hover shot forward like a bolt, and Kase's lungs protested. He clenched his jaw and as many muscles as he could. He yanked the steering control up, and the craft followed. The skin on his face strained against his skull, chafing against the bone like it was about to slide off. Kase tensed further as blackness crowded at the edge of his vision. He didn't know how Hallie's father would fare with the gravitational pull. Kase felt as if he'd taken on five times his weight as he swung the craft around, but he forced himself to focus and pressed the button on the steering control for what he assumed were the front guns.

Fiery blue bullets sprayed the ground and people below, including the soldier holding the deadly cannon. He fell, but not before his own weapon went off. What was left of Kase's stomach flew into his throat as he slammed the accelerator and executed a standing barrel roll, avoiding the blast.

Other hovers made it into the air as Kase blinked away the blurriness from the blood rushing to his head. He'd wasted too much time. He pressed the pedal again and shot forward, rocketing toward the sky before leveling out.

Only one of the Cerls was able to follow. Kase didn't have enough brain space or time to be impressed.

"Stowe! Fire on them now!"

No answer.

Blast it. The man must have lost consciousness. *Lose your tail, and then you can panic.*

He raced toward the road to Kyvena. He didn't think he could outrun them. They knew what all the controls did; he was guessing at everything. But maybe he could out-maneuver them.

Kase's body pressed into the seat as the speed ramped up. Blue fire shot past him. One rocked the ship. Kase nearly bit through his tongue.

He yanked the steering control toward his chest and didn't let go. In the blink of an eye, he back-flipped his hover over, the other ship was beneath him, above his head. It'd worked with Ike the last time he was in Nar, but this time he didn't have Hallie to impress with his loops—only her father to save.

He leveled out, clenching everything to stop himself from blacking out. He pressed the weapon trigger once more and sprayed the hover directly in front of him.

The ship exploded.

Kase yanked the steering control up and to the right, but the fiery cloud still engulfed him. The echoes of screams blared in his ears. The flames were no longer surrounding him in the hover cockpit. For a split second, he held his dying sister in his arms, and—

No. That day is over. It isn't happening now. Ana is dead. She made her own choice, and I choose not to die today.

With the heat sensors blaring in his ears, the hover smashed through the last of the inferno. In the next half second, the wide-open road cleared before him.

"Ha ha!" Kase whooped and looked back toward the destruction.

Nothing but the flames sat on the rapidly shrinking horizon. No other hovers were coming.

He glanced over at Stowe to find him frozen, but alive. Awake, too. "You all right?"

The man's mouth opened and closed repeatedly, but he finally nodded. Kase pushed a button on the dash to allow more oxygen to the cockpit. "Sorry about that."

Stowe shook his head. "It's okay. Just need to—"

He turned green.

Kase looked for something to help, but Stowe scavenged through his pack and drank one of his vials. After a few moments, his face returned to its normal color. "Hate these blasted death traps, but thanks."

Kase's heart surged. He'd done it. Without thinking about the ridiculousness of the gesture, Kase patted the hover dash. "Excellent work, my boy. Now let's really fly."

HUMAN AGAIN

Hallie

HALLIE COULDN'T SEE.

Nausea bloomed in her stomach, waves of dizziness loosening her tentative grasp on the strange reality she'd fallen into.

What in the blazes...

She couldn't finish the thought. Her brain wouldn't let her. It ached, as did the rest of her body, but it was...dull. Not quite real. Like the pain belonged to a bystander, and she just happened to be close enough to feel some of it. Detached from her body, yet aware of everything.

Tingling mixed with the nausea. The riotous pinpricks were confined to her hands, like a hoard of bees peppering her with gentle stings. People spoke above her and around her, but she couldn't tell if they were even speaking Common. They could've been conversing in the Queen's Rubikan, and she wouldn't even know.

Another wave of nausea hit, and she retched, her

stomach twisting. Nothing came up. Pain spiked in her head. At least she could feel that.

More frantic words. She could understand the tone, if not the language.

Why couldn't she see anything? She hadn't passed out. The pain made her want to, but it vanished as soon as she stepped through the Passage into the awaiting dark. Had she done something wrong?

Was this what dying felt like? Storybooks had always told her there would be lights at the end of dark tunnels and portions of her life flashing before her eyes. There was no light here, no flashes, not even a dark tunnel. It was just...nothing.

She couldn't grasp at the edges to pull her back. Her hands wouldn't work. Nothing worked.

Maybe she could make her own flashes. If this was the end, she needed to think of something that would make her happy, that would make her last moments on this stars-forsaken planet worthwhile. Maybe her parents, or going to the theater in Kyvena. Maybe The *Odyssey*. Maybe...maybe...

All she could think about was Kase and his laugh, his smirk when he'd said something particularly irritating only because he knew he could, and his steadying hands as he held her that last time.

The *last* time.

Her eyes watered, tears leaking from beneath the lids like liquid fire.

"More. She needs more, my love," King Filip said softly.

At least words were making sense again.

Someone's cold fingers found her own. She whimpered. Each touch cut like knives.

"It's best if you step aside," King Filip said, a little further away—maybe speaking over his shoulder. "The Lady Fely has kept her alive and will continue to feed her the Soul she needs."

She took a deep breath but cut it short when her lungs seared.

Hallie could barely concentrate on anything except for the tingling inside her body as it crawled up her arms. It made the rest of her feel hollow and burnt. A buzzing began in her ears.

The fingers left her hand. The knives stopped stabbing

her, but everything still hurt.

More warmth bubbled up from where someone else had put a hand on her shoulder. It wasn't painful. It was nice. A soothing sensation that her body drank in.

With each passing moment, the tingling receded. It was still there in the background, but it no longer dominated her thoughts. She became more and more aware of her surroundings, though she hadn't opened her eyes. The dark fog lifted slightly, slowly dissipating. The warmth continued to flow into her, and her breaths deepened. She swallowed. She blinked.

The world was fuzzy and mostly dark, but she was no longer blind. Some sort of glowing orb floated above her. Whether it was a star or the sun or something of her own imagination, Hallie didn't know. She blinked again, the edges of her vision clarifying.

Three people waited above her, their faces cast in half shadow, the only light in the room a floating ball of fire—small and round.

The tingling faded, just a shadow of what it had been moments ago. A hand behind her back helped her sit up, and Hallie winced with the movement. She swayed. Her head felt as if someone had bludgeoned it with a brick. Another wave of nausea washed over her, but it vanished soon as she steadied herself. The pain lingered, drawing tears to her eyes, but she could take it.

"Blessed be Fate." King Filip pushed back the golden hair that had escaped its tie. He moved the glowing orb closer to Hallie with a wave of his hand. "We can still defeat the Darkness."

"Hal?" Niels asked from beside her. He looked peaky, his face ashy and wan. "Are you all right?"

His voice was terse, but whether that was from his injury or their companions, she didn't know.

"What happened?" Her own was scratchy and brittle, but she was able to speak.

"You really do not know how to use your gift, do you?" Lady Fely said from somewhere behind her. With another touch of her shoulder, warmth blossomed through her again, and the tingling and pain vanished completely.

"How could I? Correa forced it upon me." Hallie regretted the words almost as soon as they left her lips.

But neither Lady Fely nor King Filip acknowledged she'd said anything at all.

They were in a small chamber, lit only by the floating fireball. In the corner lay a small brick carved with symbols and emitting a faint light. It was very similar to the one in Ravenhelm.

Had she brought them to Myrrai? Had she done it?

As if to answer her unspoken question, King Filip closed his eyes and snapped his fingers. A small spark appeared just above them; with a few murmured words, the light grew bigger and brighter until it matched the other one floating just a few feet away. He pushed the newest light away from him and unholstered his pistol. "I will inspect the corridor. Please stay here and recover your strength." He nodded to Lady Fely, then narrowed his eyes at Hallie and Niels. "I will return shortly."

While Hallie knew she was too valuable to kill, she heard the unspoken threat. She might have made a deal with them, but it didn't mean they were friends. It didn't mean she was free. They could still kill Niels if she didn't cooperate...and just because they couldn't *kill* her didn't mean they wouldn't *hurt* her.

She closed her eyes briefly to push away the memories of Correa's power running through her body. When she opened them again, Filip was gone, and Lady Fely sat between the Passage brick and the crude doorway the Cerl king had just exited.

Niels grimaced as he adjusted his position against the wall closest to Hallie. The woman didn't say anything. Instead, she inspected her fingernails, her knees pulled to her chest. A ready pistol lay on her other side.

Hallie whispered, "I'm sorry. I wasn't able to finish the...whatever I was doing. I think the bullet is still lodged in your leg, and..." She had to take a few breaths. Her strength still wasn't what it should be. "I did something wrong."

"You lost your focus." Lady Fely didn't even look up as she said it. "Trying to do something that advanced so early wasn't a good idea."

Her accent was different from Filip's or Correa's. Hallie couldn't pinpoint what it was exactly. It just didn't seem to fit.

"It wasn't *my* idea," she pointed out.

"It's all right," Niels said, pushing himself further up the wall. He winced as the movement jostled his leg. His other injury—the upper arm from the Stoneset cavern didn't seem to be bothering him. "I'm no longer in danger of bleeding out."

"Externally, maybe." Lady Fely still hadn't looked up from her nails.

Hallie refused to take the bait. Clenching her teeth, she said, "I'm sorry, Niels. I really am. As soon as I've recovered enough, I'll try again."

"Another healing so soon might kill you," Lady Fely corrected, "and because you've already attempted once and failed, you likely made it more complicated, so it would *definitely* kill you. And as frustrating as it is, we need you to stay alive for the time being."

Hallie ignored the woman. "I'll try anyway. It's my fault."

Niels shook his head, and for some reason a small grin whispered across his face. "I vowed to never let you fix me up again after I tried to teach you how to bake Ma's apple streusel cake."

She hadn't expected him to make a joke, and a choked, disbelieving laugh bubbled up from her chest. "I didn't *intend* to grab the cordial."

"And you didn't *intend* to spill it, neither."

Hallie glanced toward the woman, but she didn't act like she listened or even cared. Hallie looked back at Niels. He was smiling, looking at her. But instead of making her feel happy or nostalgic for time past, it frustrated her. She'd spilled the cordial on his shirt, and had been so startled she'd dropped the bottle. The cleanup led to an afternoon filled with laughter, a slipshod bandaging of his cut finger, and a few kisses.

It was a lifetime ago...and it had happened to a different Hallie.

She pulled her knees to her chest and rested her forehead against them. The memory wasn't a bad one, but why bring it up now?

For one, it established the fact that they had a past, which the Cerl King and his...whatever she was...could use against them. Secondly, it was a little out of the blue. And last, it felt like a desperate attempt on his part, but for what reason she wasn't sure. There wasn't anything there but just that—a past.

He'd been cautious and distant since they'd been reunited, though he'd made sure she had food. He'd helped fight off the soldiers and then Correa. She'd shot him with the flashpistol for his trouble.

This was merely a tenuous friendship based on memories. Nothing about their interactions should have signalled any possibility of anything else, so why was he spouting off something so personal? In front of the enemy, no less?

Niels had always had a good head on his shoulders. He'd gone along with her and Jack's schemes, but usually he'd been the voice of reason keeping them from doing something too dangerous. Mostly.

Something was off. That was the only explanation. But she didn't know what.

Niels moved a little, as if to push himself to his feet, but he hissed through his teeth and sat back down with a grimace.

"What?" Hallie asked. Lady Fely looked over at last.

Niels shook his head. "Fetch another roll of bandages from my pack, will you?"

Apparently his shoulder wasn't fixed, either. Shame and guilt warmed her face. Not only had she failed to heal his knee, she hadn't even tried to help with his shoulder. She glanced toward Lady Fely, asking the silent question; the woman merely nodded, allowing Hallie to crawl closer and help Niels untangle the pack strap from his unhurt shoulder.

Even after the chaos of the last day, the contents were still packed relatively neatly. He'd brought rations, another pistol, a light wool shirt, and bandages. She pulled out one roll and helped him work it around his injured arm, fingers fumbling as she tied it off. She tried her best not to touch him any more than required.

He adjusted the sling a little as she sat back on her heels. He winced with the movement, but his face quickly calmed. He gave her a small smile. "Thanks. That's a tad better. Ma would be impressed."

His mother, the daughter of a sailor who'd retired to the mountains, was clever with knots. She helped the miners with all sorts of ropes and pulls when needed. And she would *not* be impressed with Hallie's work here.

"How's your Ma doing?" she asked, not sure what else to

say. "I'm sorry I didn't get to catch up with her."

Not that she'd had the chance, as she hadn't actually seen Mrs. Metzinger at all. That wasn't entirely strange, since she'd rarely left her tent, but knowing his mother, it was odd that she hadn't come to see Hallie.

Niels took a moment too long to answer.

An uneasy feeling began in her gut. "Niels?"

Niels' jaw feathered, the shadows deeper in the flickering light from the floating fireball.

Unease sharpened to horror.

No.

"Nadia? Andre? Your pa?" she choked.

"I'm the only one."

"During the attack? The first one?"

"Yes."

His voice was so quiet, but in the stillness, the single word clanged like the University's clock tower bells. His sister, Nadia, couldn't have been older than ten.

Sweat immediately beaded across her forehead and hairline, heat gnawing at her insides as her power throbbed. She wobbled, pressing one hand against the stone floor to steady herself.

The Cerls would pay. She would do everything she could to find what she needed in Myrrai…then she would have her own vengeance.

"I am sorry for your loss," Lady Fely said from the door. Hallie blinked, surprised—not that she'd been listening, but that she'd offered something other than hatred.

The woman smirked. Her beauty was evident even in the dim lighting with the dirt smudged on her cheek and her hair in a tangled braid. "While I am betrothed to the King, I am not of Cerulene."

When neither Hallie nor Niels responded, she sighed. "I am of the Isles. They chose me because of my lineage."

Hallie's heartbeat ticked up at the information. The Isles were a Rubikan city-state. They'd been one of the supporters of the old queen during the civil war, if she remembered her history correctly. She quickly dampened her surprise.

She didn't want to feel any sympathy for the woman who was helping her enemy. This could be Fely's way of trying to lure her into complacency. She would work with them, but she wouldn't allow herself to fall into their trap.

She would never trust them.

Niels grunted as he pushed himself to his feet. His grimace gave away how much effort it took. The light revealed a sheen on his face, but he stayed standing, though he hadn't removed his hand from the wall.

"Do you know where we are?" he asked, as if the last conversation hadn't even happened.

"Somewhere in Myrrai." She hoped, anyway. It was unlikely to be anywhere else, right? She wanted to fish out her grandmother's journal and try to work her magic again, but she didn't want Fely to know what she could do. The journal might not even be useful here.

Pinpricks buzzed in Hallie's chest, and she stuck her hand into her pocket to grab Kase's goggles. The cool metal would soothe her sore fingertips; they still felt scalded, almost, like she'd set her hand on a hot stove.

Instead, rough fabric lining scratched the pads of her fingers.

Empty.

The goggles were gone.

"Where...?" She searched her pocket again. She searched the other. Nothing. She glanced at the floor around her. No goggles. She crawled to her pack and tore through it. Not there.

"Hal, what's wrong?"

She stopped her frantic search, righting her satchel and pack from where she'd dumped out the contents from both. "I can't find Kase's—my pilot's goggles." She ran her hands among the scant items. She'd only had *Frankenstein*, her sketchpad, and a few pencils in her satchel. The pack she'd picked up from her childhood home held a few of her mother's old blouses and trousers, as the ones she'd brought with her had been destroyed in the Pass. The goggles were nowhere. "They were in my pocket."

Niels' lips thinned, but he dropped his pack at her feet. "I don't believe I have them, but you can look."

Hallie shook her head. "No, I just dug through there for the bandages. I would have seen them."

"These?" Fely said from her post near the doorway. "Nearly left them in the ruins. Figured they might be your Relic."

Hallie cricked her neck looking over at the woman, who

did in fact have the familiar goggles in her hands, undamaged except for a small crack in one of the lenses. Rubbing her sore neck, Hallie unsteadily pushed herself to her feet and retrieved them. "Thank you."

Fely arched a dark brow. "In the beginning, it's best if you hold your Relic while using your power." She fished out a necklace from beneath her rugged blouse. "It's probably why you couldn't complete the healing, and why the Passage drained you so badly."

Hallie clutched the goggles to her chest. The tightness in her chest loosening with each second that passed. She felt a little foolish to be so worked up over them, but she couldn't help it. "Correa said something about them in Achilles, but he said my pocket watch was my Relic."

"Do you have the watch?"

Hallie shook her head and retreated to where her belongings were still strewn about the cavern floor. "No, I lost it when...well, you know...the fort collapsed."

Fely tapped her lips thoughtfully. "Was the watch valuable to you?"

Hallie nodded. "It was my brother's."

"Made of the holy metal?"

That phrase took Hallie aback. She'd only heard Yalvs use that specific terminology. If Fely had some sort of Essence power, she had to have some Yalven blood. She guessed it made sense, but something about that line of thinking irked her. She just couldn't put a finger on what exactly.

"Yes," she answered finally. "It was made out of Zuprium."

"A Relic must be something crafted of the holy metal and have specific meaning to the wielder. However, it is unfortunate if the Relic was indeed the watch." Fely played with the locket she'd unearthed from her blouse. "But that may depend on the Essence power you possess." She closed her fingers around the locket. "This is the reason I am able to keep myself sane though I am but a vessel."

Kneeling, Hallie finished repacking both her satchel and pack. She carefully laid the goggles in her pack, then thought better of it, untying her maiden belt and looping the goggles through it instead. She double-knotted the belt just to be safe.

"If you have lost your first relic, it might be difficult to replace it." Fely rose to her feet. She peered into the corridor beyond. "I must ask the King, but we may very well be unable to teach you full control over your power without it."

Hallie stood. "Then we'd best find what we need before it's too late."

She tried to inject as much confidence and nonchalance as she could into the words, but judging by the doubtful glance Niels gave her, she hadn't succeeded. Hallie handed his pack to him before slinging her own onto her shoulder.

"We will wait for the King," Fely said as Hallie approached.

"He's been gone too long to just be checking the corridor," Hallie protested. "He's either continued on without us, or he's encountered something dangerous. If we don't catch up, he might not come back."

Her point landed true. Unease flashed across Fely's face. She hesitated only a moment before lurching to her feet, pistol in hand.

Hallie sucked in a breath, and Niels lunged forward like he intended to shield her; but Fely only waved impatiently with her other hand. "Believe me, if I wanted to hurt you, this would not be my weapon of choice." She ran her thumb over the grip. "Besides, we're allies, at least for now. So killing you would be counterintuitive, would it not?"

Hallie and Niels exchanged uncertain looks.

This might be their best chance to run, while Fely was alone. But even if they got away from their captors, Niels would never be able to outrun them; he couldn't even walk without leaning on the wall.

She would have to dispose of them, then, if it came down to it. She'd unraveled the soldier in the cavern. Physically speaking, she could probably figure out how to do it again, but emotionally? That was different.

In any case, they couldn't try it now. Not with her power mostly drained and Niels in so much pain. Plus, she had no idea how she'd get around Fely's ability to neutralize her power.

So instead of planning an ill-advised escape, she distracted herself by inspecting the mural on the wall as they passed. Judging by the state of it—the paint peeling or faded, some of it worn all the way down to the stone—it had to be ancient.

Five dark-haired people—Yalvs, she guessed—reached toward a brilliant sphere in the sky that likely represented the sun. Simple, but beautiful. It didn't ring a bell as far as the Yalven legends and stories she knew, but as she'd discovered on her visit to Myrrai in the late autumn, what Jaydians knew about the Yalvs barely scratched the surface.

She edged closer, careful not to touch it. A flaw in the mural caught her eye: a divot in the heart of the sun, like a piece had fallen out.

She looked around as she drew out her sketchbook, but didn't see anything that looked like it might fit inside.

"What are you doing?" Fely asked. She'd paused further down the hallway, Neils a few paces behind.

"Sketching a copy." A rough one, but better than nothing. "Do you mind?"

When Fely shrugged, Hallie opened to a new page and jotted down a description of what she saw alongside a small, rough sketch. It was times like these she wished she had a flash portrait device. Her fingers were still clumsy, and drawing just felt wrong.

Fely stepped up beside her. "Many of our ancestors were quite gifted in the arts. The ability to create beauty out of the mundane was a prized quality in their culture."

Hallie blinked. She, of course, knew that from being a Yalven scholar at the University, but she hadn't expected it from Fely. "Were you also a scholar in the Isles?"

The woman shook her head. "Not formally, but my family has kept our traditions alive. We chose to stay in our ancestral home when many of our fellow countrymen fled to Tasava before the Passages closed."

Excitement sparked. Hallie tightened her grip on her sketchbook. "I didn't realize there were many people on our side of the world who would..."

The ground shook so hard that Hallie pitched forward into the wall. She turned just fast enough for her pack to catch the brunt of the impact, but her neck still strained with the quick motion.

It was over as quickly as it began. She rubbed her smarting neck as she turned to look at Niels; he was clutching his leg, but otherwise unscathed. "What was that?" he panted.

"I don't know." The fireball still floated like a ghost above them. It hadn't been affected at all.

Fely was slowly pushing herself up from the ground. Blood trickled down her face from a vicious cut near her hairline; she swayed as soon as she found her feet, and Niels caught her with his good arm. He helped her sit back down, pain spiriting across his own features.

Now was her chance. She could leave Fely here, take Niels, and—

And they would probably run into Filip on the way out, and they'd lose the modicum of freedom he'd let them keep. All for nothing.

She hesitated only a bit longer before kneeling in front of Fely. "Let me see."

Fely shakily wiped blood from her brow; even wounded, her features were striking. Some people had all the luck.

"It's not deep," Hallie observed. "Head wounds tend to bleed a lot regardless of the injury. But we should..." She looked to Niels. "Let's wrap her head in that last roll of bandages."

He slipped the pack off his shoulder and handed it off. Hallie fished out the roll tucked near the bottom and got to work.

Fely flinched, but allowed Hallie to help. "It's nothing. We need to find the King."

"That wasn't a natural quake," Niels said, eyes on the darkness beyond them. She didn't ask how he knew.

"We had several near-misses on the way to Myrrai the first time," Hallie said, unwrapping the bandage with swift fingers. "In retrospect, I think much of what we faced might have been set up by the Yalvs to discourage visitors."

She reached the end of the long gauze...and something small and shiny fell out. She caught it on instinct, then opened her hand.

Nestled in her palm was a dainty metal ring.

She held it out to Niels. The band bore no engravings, and the sapphire in the middle was barely a chip. "What's this?"

"Ma's." He grabbed it and held it between his index and thumb.

"Oh."

She should have had more to say in memory of a woman she'd known most of her life. Had anyone asked, she would have told them whenever a Rubikan trader brought cinnamon from the far islands, Mrs. Metzinger made a batch of fresh cinnamon rolls, and she never failed to share some with Hallie and Jack. She would have told them she'd never heard Mrs. Metzinger say an unkind word about anyone, nor had she ever heard an unkind word said about her. She would have said...

Well, it didn't matter what she would have said, because no one had asked. They didn't have time for spontaneous eulogies, anyway.

Instead, Hallie made quick work of wrapping the woman's head, then got to her feet. "Let's keep moving."

Niels nodded, tucking the ring into his pocket; Fely stood up again, and this time stayed standing. "Thank you."

"Of course." Hallie gave her a hesitant smile. "Are you okay to keep going?"

"I will be fine." The words were confident; the way Fely leaned into the wall as she walked, not so much. She was still faster than Niels, but not by much.

If the library was still standing after being laid waste by Ben Reiss and the dragon he'd brought through the Gate, she'd try and find something more about the mural. For now, she forced herself to leave it behind, though dread pooled in her stomach the further they walked up the corridor. What they'd find at the end, she could only imagine.

Judging by the subtle burn in her calves, the incline had begun to subtly increase. She hadn't thoroughly explored the Gate Temple on her first visit, so that didn't mean they weren't somewhere in the mountain, but the caverns and the distant dripping noises made her think they were somewhere below ground.

Between Niels and Fely, they traveled much more slowly than Hallie would have liked; the fireball floated along with them, casting just enough light to see their next couple steps by. They found no sign of Filip, or anything that might have kept him from coming back. The corridors snaked like a cat's tail, unpredictable and sudden.

"You probably think I'm silly for keeping Ma's ring," Niels murmured, breaking the silence.

"I kept Jack's pocket watch." Hallie stopped in front of another mural—this one depicting the Gate chamber, though it looked different than she remembered it. She didn't think she'd seen yawning cathedral windows with elaborate swirled traceries in the chamber. A mystery to be solved another day. "I don't think it's silly at all."

Niels' lips quirked into a lopsided smile. "He loved that thing." He adjusted his sling. "Always trying to tinker with it and make it work."

A small laugh bubbled up in Hallie's throat. It almost choked out her reply. "Yeah."

Losing that watch for the second time had felt like mourning him all over again. And knowing that loss might keep her from ever mastering this power of hers only made it worse.

Fely played with the chain holding the locket around her neck, eyes on the mural. "Having a little piece of someone we love with us when they can't be makes us feel human again."

Hallie clutched Kase's goggles tightly, anchoring herself. The memory of their last kiss replayed in her head, and for a moment, she nearly threw caution to the wind and raced back to the portal brick. If Niels could have kept up, or if she'd known Correa wasn't waiting on the other side, she might have done it. "Is your Relic...is the locket special to you?"

Fely's gaze chilled. She turned away from the mural. "If we don't find any trace soon, we'll turn back and see if Filip has returned. Maybe he found a different way."

Hallie risked a small glance with Niels before taking the lead again.

They wound their way onward, climbing up around the corner where the stone walls bled into Zuprium bricks. A wave of heat billowed over them like a rolling sea.

Hallie clutched the wall, preparing for another quake, but it never came.

"What in the blazes was that?" Niels asked.

Nausea crept up her throat, but she couldn't explain why. Something just felt...off.

She looked back at Fely. The woman's face was too pale, but Hallie didn't know if it was due to the blood loss or something else.

"Niels, do you still have your electropistol?" Hallie asked, keeping one hand on the wall just in case.

"No," Niels said at the same time Fely reminded her, "The King took it with him."

Hallie moved away a couple paces. She only had a theory, no concrete guess, but...

"Hallie," Niels prompted, "I know that look. What was that?"

It'd been too long for him to still know her that well. She fought not to scowl as she pointed to the bricks breaking up the monotonous stone, blending in and multiplying further down the corridor. "It's the Zuprium."

Niels frowned. "I don't think I understand."

Neither did she. All she knew was that the Yalvs had done something to make sure that those with 'sparking magic' couldn't harm them. Clearly, they hadn't planned for their own magic to be turned against them with the Cerls and Ben. It was the only explanation Hallie could conjure.

"When the First Earthers landed, all their fancy technology went dark," Hallie explained.

"Yeah, it was a new planet. They didn't realize the laws of nature would be different here." Niels' breathing was still labored.

That was the story some believed. Hallie knew better.

"Not exactly," Fely said, clearly following the same train of thought.

Hallie squinted up ahead, trying to make out anything waiting for them in the darkness. Dim light sifted through and reflected dully off the Zuprium bricks ahead, and it had to be coming from somewhere—maybe a gap in the stone. It couldn't be coming from their fireball; the light playing on the bricks shone the color of gray mist, whereas the light from their orb was a soft gold.

With careful feet and a hand along the wall, she walked toward it.

"What do you mean, not exactly?" Niels asked as both he and Fely's footsteps scuffled along behind her.

Hallie blew a strand of hair out of her face. "To the Yalvs, our technology was destructive. They used Zuprium to subdue the electricity...or, as they called it, 'sparking magic.' The slow disappearance of the Yalvs from our side of the world reduced the potency of their wards. However, on Tasava, the wards are still intact."

Niels was silent for a beat, save for the clop of his boots on the metal floor. "And you learned this all from a book?"

"No."

Another few beats of silence. "So…you learned it in a lecture?"

Hallie didn't like thinking back to the *Eudora Jayde* mission. Every time she did, she felt the pain in her hand all over again, saw Ebba crumple, heard Kase's unhinged pounding on the Gate Temple door.

"We must turn around," Fely insisted from behind.

"I think we're almost out of here," Hallie said, putting as much confidence in her voice as she could. The light was growing brighter, the gray of a murky dawn. She didn't know if the Passage somehow manipulated time, but she was surprised she hadn't fallen over from exhaustion if she had indeed been up the entire night. Adrenaline was a funny thing.

"Hallie…" Niels prompted.

"Not now. We're so—"

"Hallie."

Hallie chanced a quick glare over her shoulder; instead of Niels, she found Fely. The woman's breathing was labored, and sweat beaded on her brow.

Niels wasn't trying to stop her; he was telling her to wait. Hallie slowed. "Sorry."

Fely took deep breaths and lowered herself to the floor. "Something is wrong. I just don't—" She cut herself off with a gasp. "We have to go *back*."

Hallie doubled back and knelt beside her. The bandage was spotted with browning blood, but it wasn't soaked. "Does anything hurt? Is it your head?"

Fely shook her head, grimacing. "No."

She didn't really know what else to ask. Jack had been the one who knew all that stuff. She looked at Niels. "Stay with her. I'll check ahead, and then we'll turn back."

She didn't even believe herself that time.

"Tell me what's going on," Niels demanded.

She couldn't, even if she'd wanted to. Fely might have a concussion, but she claimed the pain hadn't worsened. She seemed pale, but the bleeding had mostly stopped.

Something in her gut told her it was much worse than a concussion; that it had something to do with Fely's power.

Like most things lately, it was just a guess. But the longer the thought weighed on her mind, the more sure of it she became.

They had to be in Myrrai. The Zupirum bricks and the wave of warmth confirmed it.

Niels grabbed her arm. Hallie jumped. He'd gone pale, too, bathed in the pre-morning light coming from around the corner. She still couldn't tell if it was a window or door. "Don't."

She yanked her arm out of his grasp. "I'll just be a moment."

"We don't know what's up there."

"I'll be fine."

"Hallie..."

Irritation crawled up her throat. She clenched her teeth to keep it contained. "I'll be back in a moment."

Niels looked back down at Fely. Her eyes had closed, her head tipped back against the wall. He strode past Hallie, jaw clenched, gait unsteady. "I'm coming with you."

She scrambled after him, checking to make sure Fely wasn't stirring; she had a Cerl pistol, after all, and the Zuprium wouldn't affect it the way it did electropistols.

Luckily, Fely didn't stir.

"I can take care of myself," Hallie hissed as she caught up with him.

"Then tell me what's going on." Niels caught her arm again. "And tell me why we aren't trying to run now that she's out!"

Hallie's nails bit into her palms. "Now isn't the time."

"Now's the only time!"

Heat pulsed within her core, the frustration building up like bricks. She wasn't even sure what they were arguing about. "I don't know what you're asking me. We're going to run, I just have to see—"

"Would you tell Kase if he was here?"

Well yes, she thought, but Kase wouldn't have to ask in the first place. He'd just know. "What is this actually about, Niels?"

Niels hesitated before running a hand along his jaw. "Nothing. I shouldn't have said anything."

Giving him a look, she turned the corner, Niels a wall of silence behind her. A doorway glowing with the early light of morning waited beyond...

And just on the other side, a body crowned in golden hair lay prone under a pile of rock and metal.

"Oh, stars," Hallie breathed.

"Oh, stars," Hallie breathed.

NOT HIGHER THAN A GRASSHOPPER

Kase

"YOU'RE STARTING TO DRIFT A little, son."

The words jolted Kase out of his thoughts. He winced, steadying the craft with a brush of his palm over the wheel.

So many hours flying at top speed in this strange hover had taken its toll. His head ached like someone had taken a hammer to the inside of his skull and attempted to crack the bone.

No Cerls on the horizon behind or ahead of them. At the height and speed they were flying, Kase doubted anyone could match them.

Pain spiked in his head, and blackness spread across his vision.

"Steady, steady!" Stowe yelled as Kase's eyesight came back.

Towering trees appeared out of nowhere. They'd lost altitude.

Kase whipped the steering control up. His stomach followed. Déjà vu made his head swirl even worse; at least he hadn't hit any Yalven columns that time.

"I'm going to land," Kase gritted out. The pressure in his head ground his teeth against each other. His stomach rebelled, but it'd have to wait. He could throw up when they were on the ground.

Faster than he would've thought possible, Kase landed at the edge of a meadow, the trees he almost crashed into standing unscathed behind him.

Stomach in his throat, he shut down the craft, and the ship went dark. He popped the windshield and pushed it up.

He unbuckled himself with shaking fingers. Stowe was talking, but Kase couldn't hear a word. If he didn't get out of the machine soon, anything he'd eaten in the last day would be all over the dashboard. Finally, freed of his safety restraints, he scrambled out of the cockpit and down the hover wing—

And then he promptly heaved up the contents of his stomach onto the mottled brown and green grass.

He put his hand on the side of the hover to steady himself as he dry-heaved. The metal warmed under his fingers.

Stowe came up behind him, his footfalls crunching. "Let's sit you against one of those trees there once you finish up."

Kase couldn't answer. Nothing was left in his stomach. His bones ached. It was like he had the latest strain of influenza that had passed through the capital a year back. Kase had been laid out for a week.

This time, he didn't have soup to settle his stomach or books to read while he convalesced. Shocks, just thinking of it now brought on a whole new wave of nostalgia…and a little shame.

Maybe Bookshop Attendant Hallie had been correct about him. He'd been rather pampered, sure…but if he had the chance, he would go back to that in a heartbeat.

He tried to relax his muscles, but even as exhausted as he was, he couldn't get the tension to release.

Was this his punishment for what happened in Nar? Was his body finally catching up with his actions? He'd shot Ossie. He didn't think he'd killed him or the Cerl pilot, but he'd never know for sure.

Another wave of sick washed over him, and a third left his throat burning. He wiped his mouth, though nothing but spit and acid had come up.

If I hadn't done anything, I would be dead. Stowe would be dead. I did what I had to do.

His heart skittered weakly. He squeezed his eyes shut, forcing himself to keep using Zeke's method of dealing with Battle Fright.

If they'd figured out who I was, they would have imprisoned me and used me as leverage. They would've killed Stowe. I had no choice.

There was no Hallie to save with his name now.

An arm went around his shoulder. "Come on."

A few beads of sweat dripped down the back of Kase's neck and into his already damp collar. He steadied himself and tried pushing off from the older man. "Thanks."

"Stop wriggling, boy, I got you." Stowe didn't let go of his upper arm until he'd walked Kase over to one of the trees and eased him down to the ground.

Kase's body felt like it was about to fall apart at the seams. He leaned his head back against the tree, the bark scratching at his head and catching on his hair. He didn't care. It was nice to just *be,* if only for a few moments. His eyelids scraped like sandpaper as he shut his eyes.

Stowe climbed back up into the hover. After a few minutes of shuffling, the man said, "I got something that'll perk you right up, but I'd rather you rest a spell first."

Kase didn't even bother opening his eyes. "I'll be okay."

A few more moments with only a light breeze and the sounds of shuffling for company, Stowe's footfalls crunched closer. "Drink some water."

Kase could barely lift his head off the tree trunk. "I don't think...I don't think I can even swallow."

If he hadn't been so tired, that might have scared him more. What in the blazes was happening to him?

A hand supported the back of his neck. Wincing, he cracked open his eyes to see a canteen being brought to his lips and Hallie's father looming above him. "Hydrate first. Then sleep. I'll help."

Kase let him, because he didn't have enough energy to argue.

For the next hour, Stowe took the time and care to make sure he drank the entire canteen. He also supported him as he heaved one more time, then gave him more water.

The next thing he knew, a sharp, stabbing neck pain woke him from a dreamless sleep.

His eyes flew open, but they no longer hurt. He reached for his pistol, ready to fire.

But he let his hand fall when he found only the outline of his stolen Cerl hover and Stowe propped up against his packs, using the scarce moonlight to read some book with a leafy plant on the cover. A small, soft voice inside him wanted to ask if he could borrow it when the other man finished.

He didn't. Mostly because he wasn't sure if he could hold the book long enough to read without his arms giving out.

Kase grumbled as he brought his hand up to rub his neck, but it caught on a thick blanket over his legs. He couldn't see much in the waning gold of Secondmoon's light, but the wool blanket glittered a soft blue color where the moonlight hit it. Like something had been woven into it.

Setting aside his read, Stowe looked up. Kase winced as the book met the ground. If Hallie had gotten her love of reading from her father, she must have gotten her respect for books from someone else; she would never commit such a heinous act as placing a perfectly good book on damp grass.

"Found blankets in that tiny cargo hold." Stowe opened his pack and pulled out a few items. "Not real good with maps, but I figure we're probably 'bout halfway to the capital."

Kase shook his head, wincing at the crick in his neck. He rubbed it harder and gritted his teeth against the sharp pain. When he slept next, he dearly hoped it wasn't sitting upright against a tree. However, the rest *had* taken the edge off his exhaustion. Parts of his bones still felt like they'd been formed from mazelberry jam, but he felt fit enough to fly again. He no longer felt like emptying the contents of his stomach, at least.

"There's no way we're halfway to the capital. That kind of trip would take us nearly a week." Kase couldn't tell exactly what Stowe was mixing inside the small vial he held, but he didn't think it would help whatever ailed him. There was something wrong with that ship. Unfortunately, it was their only way to get anywhere without having to walk unless they could commandeer something else, and he didn't feel like risking another hover-jacking like that.

Stowe stood with his vial and grabbed a folded sheet of parchment. "I never even left the mountains before this, but I'm pretty sure we passed Settler's Barrows. Looked mighty like the little picture on the map."

Kase extricated himself from the blanket and forced himself to stand, using the burly maple trunk for support. Without the blanket covering him, the crisp early morning air penetrated every exposed bit of skin and worked its way into his bones. He glanced back down at the blanket and its glittering fibers. "You said you found those on the hover?"

Stowe handed him the vial he'd been carrying. Kase took it, but he didn't drink. Stowe didn't comment further, only retrieved the blanket. He folded it over one arm and shrugged. "Felt warm, and you looked awful cold."

Kase tapped the stopper on the vial. "What's in this?"

"Pick Up tonic with coffee shavings. Gotta be careful with 'em; I could only get a bag of roasted beans from Rubikan traders once a year. Coffee don't grow up in the mountains."

Kase threw back the contents. He didn't think it'd help his predicament, but it wouldn't hurt either. He grimaced at the chilled concoction. "Definitely better hot."

Stowe let out a barking laugh and handed Kase the map. "Would've warmed it if I thought banking a fire was wise."

Kase handed back the empty vial and opened the map. It had to be an older version, because it still featured a unified Tev Rubika, but it was better than nothing. "Where'd you get this from?"

Stowe tied up his pack. "We've had it a while. Still has Ravenhelm on it."

"Niels said something about that place. Not sure what it is, though."

Stowe grabbed both packs and the strange blanket. "Ruins, mainly. Before this last winter's attack, Ravenhelm's was the worst in mountain history. Leveled the whole place. Killed everyone except a little boy not higher than a grasshopper. Killed the commander with a well-placed crossbolt, some stories say. Heard some crazier ones, but fifty years will grow a story good, and I wasn't but a wee lad myself."

Something about the story tickled at the back of Kase's mind, but with so much else whirling through it, he couldn't quite get his hands around the thought.

He looked back at the map instead, trying to ignore the odd feeling about the ruined town.

Stowe stuck a finger at Settlers' Barrows. "Passed that a little ways back, I tell ya."

Kase rubbed his jaw. The short beard that had begun growing in the last few weeks or so prickled his fingers. He briefly wondered if Hallie would approve of the longer style. Would she like it if Niels grew one?

Blast it.

He shook his head to clear the thought of the two of them together on the other side of the mountains. He needed to concentrate. He squinted at the map once more and traced a finger along the route he was sure they'd taken. He hadn't thought much of concealing their route—his only worry had been to get away as quickly as possible, and the Cerl hover had certainly delivered.

But if all Cerl hovers were like this one, why hadn't anyone caught up to them? How hadn't they caught up or overtaken the *Eudora Jayde* back in the autumn?

Unless they were purposefully following them for some reason.

Ben. He was the reason.

"You're right," Kase admitted, tamping down the knife twist of betrayal he felt at that thought. He remembered passing the Barrows, vaguely. He didn't know for sure how far they'd gotten after, but no matter what, they *had* made excellent time. If they kept on the same pace, they could possibly hit the capital in the next day or so, depending on just how far they'd gone past the Barrows, how long Kase was willing to fly for the day...and if their fuel held out.

He peeked over at the strange hover once more. What *was* fueling it, anyway?

He folded up the map and handed it back to Stowe before scrambling up the hover wing. Stowe followed close behind, throwing up the packs and blanket. Kase caught them. Warmth spread from where his fingers and palms met the rough-spun blanket fibers. Kase stuffed the thing down beside his chair. Might come in handy. Whatever the Cerls had done with it, Kase wished he'd had it back in the mountain cavern with Hallie in the Pass, though he wasn't sure he would have traded her sleeping snuggled against his back for warmth instead.

The engine hummed faintly when Kase revved it up. Dried blood smeared the label on the button; it flaked off when Kase scratched it with a fingernail. He rubbed at the other stain on the steering control before gripping it.

A deep chill filled his veins and arteries. He eyed the blanket. Maybe he should lay it over his knees.

No; he would be fine. The blanket would only make it awkward to fly, and doubly difficult to evade any who wished them harm. He had a job to do.

With a breath in and out, Kase pulled up on the steering control and eased his foot onto the accelerator. Gritting his teeth against the lingering cold, he flew into the early dawn light crawling over the horizon.

C H A P T E R 8

NOT IDEAL

Niels

NIELS METZINGER HAD ALWAYS BEEN the strong one.

He never crumbled under pressure. The flashpistol graze in his shoulder and the bullet lodged in his lower thigh didn't come close to the time he'd taken a pickax to the leg while training Guy's youngest son in the mines. Or that day in late July when Hallie had walked out of his life without saying goodbye.

She'd been hurting; he knew that. But he'd been hurting, too; he'd lost his best friend in that accident. It'd been a stars-reckless ridiculous thing to do, exploring the mines for no good reason. Stupid. They should've known better than that.

Niels should've known better than that.

He'd gone over those last moments a million times in the last three years. The quaking rumble of stone was one he knew all too well. He'd been warned to either run for the exit or say his own final rites depending on where he stood in the mountain tunnels. Not even the Fogs could keep survival instincts like that at bay.

But survival instincts or not, if he could go back, he'd save Jack and sacrifice himself.

Jack had always been one for adventure. His plan had been to head off to the University of Jayde that coming summer and become a medic: the first small step on Jack's grandiose path to fame and fortune.

He'd been certain the tunnel held the answers to the universe…or at least to how they could *all* strike it rich and dine on fine food and drink in the capital. If you asked Niels, he would have said it was Jack's well-meaning way of trying to take them with him when he left. To not to feel guilty that he was leaving in the first place.

Niels had never wanted all that. Once Jack had left, Niels would've asked Hallie to marry him. Eighteen would've been rather young if they'd grown up anywhere besides Stoneset, but what else could Niels do? With his job in the mines, he didn't have the luxury of growing old with someone. His mother had been endlessly angry that he'd doomed himself to the Fogs, but she'd also known they didn't have a choice. His older brother's trapping business had flopped, landing him with a pickaxe in hand himself, and his father's farm had barely sustained them through the winter. They'd been poor…too poor to save enough money to send him to University with Jack. Few families in Stoneset could.

How ironic that none of it mattered in the end. Not one bit.

Jack had died. Hallie had taken his place in Kyvena. The Cerls had killed Niels' family. Being in the mines had saved his life that day; his mother hadn't lived to appreciate the irony in that.

And now, as he sat in the shadows of some ancient temple and stared at the King of Cerulene's rubble-strewn body, all he could think was that he'd give anything to be back in those mines. He'd give anything for the girl standing beside him to look at him with anything other than distrust. He played with the ring in his pocket to calm his nerves.

Hallie fell to her knees beside the prone Cerl King. His golden hair splayed on the cracked stone and metal bricks. A beam had fallen, pinning his lower body in place. Hallie clutched her stomach as if she was going to be sick.

The sun was only beginning to peek over the horizon,

casting a shroud of ethereal beauty across the ruined temple. It contrasted mightily with the grotesque sight before him.

Niels dropped his pack and lowered himself next to the man who'd ordered his family's deaths. Pain lanced through his arm and leg, nearly dropping him on his seat, but he gritted his teeth and lowered himself slowly instead, his bad leg outstretched.

Fingers shaking, Niels searched the king's wrist for a pulse. His skin was like ice, but whether that was due to shock, blood loss, or simply the chilly morning, Niels didn't know. The king's pulse fluttered weakly. Soft, struggling breaths whistled through the man's open mouth.

"We gotta help him," he muttered, unsure why he'd said it, or why he believed it. The man deserved to die a thousand times over. The Cerls hated them; had it been Niels under that beam, the King would have almost definitely left him to his fate.

But Niels was not a Cerl. He was a man of the Nardens, and he wouldn't leave someone to die if there was a chance he could save them, no matter who they might be.

Hallie didn't speak. He inched himself closer, breathing carefully through the pain. Hallie might've been the one who'd let the errant bullet loose, but the only one Niels could truly blame was himself. He knew better than to toss a pistol like that.

In the heat of the moment, all he'd thought to do was keep firing, and worry about the consequences later.

He hadn't thought a half-functioning leg would be the consequence.

Still quite a sight better than the Cerl King's situation. At least the bullet had only gone in one leg.

"If we can get this beam off..." Niels pulled his hand back. He couldn't see any blood pooling underneath the body, but it could be hidden by the rubble. He chose to take that as a good sign. "If we can lift this, we might be able to...might be able to..."

Might be able to what? Even if Filip lived, his legs had been crushed to smithereens; he might never walk again. Niels and Hallie weren't medics, and they were stuck stars-knew-where without any way of getting help.

He looked back at Hallie, who stood, staring at the King with fear in her eyes—fear and something else, something dark as the yawning mouth of a mineshaft. She opened and closed her mouth, but no sound emerged.

Nerves chattered his teeth. "Hallie…"

"No," Hallie finally managed to croak out. "You were right; we need to run. He's good as gone, and Fely's injured. It won't be easy for her to follow us, and even if she does, she'll stop to help him. This is our chance." She inspected the surroundings. "I think we're in the old ruins, so we only need to hike the mountain to the city. It'll be slow going with your leg, but we can make it."

Niels blinked at her. He wasn't sure he'd heard her correctly. "But he's still alive."

Hallie shook her head. "Not for long. I know it sounds bad, but…"

His mouth dropped a little at the shock of her callousness. "I'm only up and walking because he helped you heal me."

"He only did that because he needs something from me."

"He already had you. He coulda let me die, and he didn't. I ain't paying that back like this!"

He grabbed his pack and looked for anything he thought could help, but he knew it was worthless. Nothing in his pack would fix crushed bone.

Hallie's pallor contrasted heavily with the freckles across her nose and cheeks. "He allowed Correa to torture me and Kase."

When she put it that way…maybe Niels was being too kind. But that didn't sound like the Hallie he knew. What had happened to the Hallie who wept when his family's lamb had died after breaking its leg too badly to be fixed? What had happened to the Hallie who'd cried over a book with a cracked spine like most folk wept at funerals? What had happened to the Hallie who'd—

"Niels," she snapped, interrupting his worries. "What are you waiting for?"

He chewed on the edge of his tongue and looked back at the King.

Correa had tortured her, not the King. The King might have ordered Niels' family killed, but he hadn't done the deed.

There were always consequences, intended and not,

when you had that much power. If the Cerl King had been looking in his family's faces when he'd ordered them killed, would he have still given the order? A faceless enemy was much easier to harm, to hate, than one you had to look in the eye.

A scream came from the corridor they'd just exited. Fely had caught up quick enough after all; she stumbled forward, face bloodless and pale as a new star. "Heal him! Heal him now!"

Hallie moved out of the way just as Fely fell on her knees at the Cerl King's head. "I can't. I don't...I failed earlier. I don't have the right—"

"Use this!" She thrust her locket into Hallie's hands. "He can't die, he can't, he...he can't. Heal him."

Hallie simply shook her head this time.

"Without him, we *all* die, do you understand?" Fely looked up, angry now, cheeks wet with tears. "Do it!"

Hallie clutched the locket in her fist. Niels put his fingers to the King's wrist again. His vision swam; the pain in his head increased with each passing second. He blinked away the darkness at the edge of his vision. He couldn't succumb to the migraine now. He had to fight it. Blasted Fogs.

The pulse beneath his fingers was erratic, weaker than before. He was no medic, but he guessed they only had minutes, if that. "Hurry, Hal."

He didn't know what to expect, seeing as he'd been unconscious at the time, but he had her to thank in part for his leg being mostly whole. She could do it again; he knew it.

After another moment of hesitation, Hallie knelt beside the woman. "I don't know what I'm doing."

Only a little relief broke through his dread. They still had a long way to go, even if she was willing to try.

"Use the stored Soul in the locket," Fely breathed. "Don't lose your grip on your tether. And *feel*."

The instructions were clear as mud. But Hallie seemed to get it. "And if I'm not able to do it?"

"Then we all die." Fely's hand glowed a soft yellow in the morning light as she set it on the King's neck. "We don't have the sword. We don't have all the Essences. If he dies now, then Jagamot will never be defeated."

"But you said I won't be able to control anything without the watch." Hallie still clutched the locket. Her hair fluttered in the soft wind swirling around them. Niels shivered.

"Try the goggles, try anything," Fely pleaded. "Just don't let him die."

For all she said about the King's death meaning they would all die, he didn't think that was the whole of it. The Cerl King clearly meant something to her, something more than the other half of an arranged marriage. He recognized her panic; he'd felt it the day Jack died, when Hallie had nearly been crushed in the collapse.

He would never forget the adrenaline thrumming through his veins at breakneck speed. The rough threads of her jacket clutched in his fingers as he pulled her out of the falling beam's path. Her warmth tucked against his chest as the stone and dirt rained down around them. The relief that it was Jack beneath the rubble and not her. The horror and guilt that he'd been relieved his best friend was dead.

His head spiked with pain.

He reached into his pocket once more, but this time he took out the ring. He slipped it onto his pinky. It wasn't much comfort, but it was something. He rubbed his temples with one hand.

Hallie crouched beside Fely, placing a hand on the King's shoulder. She murmured words under her breath, too quiet for Niels to hear. Kase's goggles and Fely's locket dangled from her other hand.

The ring's sapphire dug into his palm as he tightened his grip, nearly breaking the skin.

He didn't know what to expect. He'd seen the blackout in the caverns, and he'd watched her unravel a man before his eyes, but the shock of white-gold light trickling from her fingers now wasn't as potent as it had been then.

He wished he could do something, anything to help. But with his limbs riddled with injuries and no power thrumming through his veins, he couldn't do anything but sit there and keep his headache from worsening.

He did make an effort to keep an eye on their surroundings. Without any knowledge of the area, he wasn't sure what might be lurking past his field of vision. He wished he had his pistol, but he wasn't sure where that had gone, and he didn't see the Cerl weapon on Fely, either. Maybe she'd dropped it during her strange episode in the tunnel corridor.

The ruined building's ceiling was missing in places, and

the crumbling brown columns held up fragments of carved reliefs. If he closed his eyes, he could almost imagine what it might have looked like in its prime.

Two moss-covered statues stood tall on the far side of the giant room. He couldn't tell much about them with the overgrowth, only that both held swords. Most of the ground was jagged with upended cobblestones. Dirt, dead grass, and remnants of the past filled in the cracks and crevices.

It was like something out of the storybooks Hallie used to let him borrow before they were together. He'd enjoyed them well enough, but honestly, he'd only read them so he'd have something to talk to Hallie about. Even though she was his best friend's sister, he'd wanted her to notice him.

He *still* wanted her to notice him—to notice how he ached to brush the stray hair from her face as she bent over the King's prone form. To notice that he'd somehow fallen more in love with her in her absence. To notice he was here, and Kase wasn't, and for it to matter.

But he shouldn't want any of that.

It should have bothered him to watch her hands glow with otherworldly power; it should have separated her fully from the Hallie he'd known. But it felt right, somehow. Like she'd finally gotten to live out the stories she loved so much.

The light enveloping her hand pulsed. He swallowed around the fear lodging itself in his throat, trying not to think about a soldier coming apart before his eyes when that light touched him.

He watched her closely as she worked. Her hands were the same, though power flickered around them.

Kase would've figured out a way to help her. Niels had only known him a short amount of time, but he'd seen enough to know the man was quite resourceful and brilliant. Blast him.

It really was a shame he liked Kase Shackley. The man had offered himself up on a gilded plate to the Cerl general and emerged victorious—all for Hallie.

Niels would've done the same if it would've made a difference. However, unlike Kase, he wasn't the son of one of the most powerful men on Yalvara. He was the son of a dead man.

Hallie swayed a little, her hand falling from the King's shoulder. Niels caught her. "Hallie!"

She shook her head, pushing off of him and pushing her palm against the King. "Almost had it."

Niels chewed on the inside of his cheek and tried to focus on anything else but Hallie losing herself to whatever power hid beneath her skin. The only sounds were Hallie's quiet murmuring, Fely's muffled breathing, and the morning birds calling to one another.

Hallie's breathing hitched, and Niels crouched beside her. "Hal?"

Her eyes were closed, the power flowing out through her fingers. "Don't."

He stood again. He hated that she wouldn't let him help. Stowe had trusted him to take care of her. He could do that. He could prove to her he was still the same Niels she'd been in love with before Jack died.

But she wasn't the same Hallie. He would never understand just what she'd gone through at Achilles, nor would he comprehend what she could do. He didn't know what it would take to get her to see him again.

Convincing her would take time. But it was time worth spending, if it helped her find her way back to herself. He would be the foundation she needed to find her way home.

He just had three years of separation to erase between them. Easy.

She collapsed.

Blast his leg, he fell to his knees and pulled her face to him. "Hallie!"

Her face had drained of color, scrunched against unseen pain. Her freckles stood out like stars in the night sky. She blinked, slivers of gold peeking out beneath her eyelids. "Did it work?"

Fely didn't remove the hand still pressing golden light into the King's skin. "I'm not sure, but he doesn't feel as...absent."

Hallie sat up, swayed a little, but caught herself before Niels could. He sat back, embarrassment licking his cheeks. Why wouldn't she let him help her?

Niels swallowed his conflicting emotions and crawled forward best he could, feeling for the King's pulse instead. The *thump-thump* definitely felt stronger than before. "If we can free him, I think he'll be all right."

Easier said than done. The beam looked ancient and

immovable. It was a miracle the King had survived at all.

"If we had a saw…" he began, then stopped, because there was no point sharing ideas they couldn't use. "We gotta be careful not to move him too much until we know if Hallie did him any good."

The offended glance she shot him pierced like another bullet. He coughed. "It's just that you're still weak, and you don't know how to use your power yet." Another glare. He had to get his foot out of his mouth. "What I'm trying to say is—"

"You're saying we have to get this beam off and hope for the best." Hallie's voice was calm, but colder than the mountain snows. Her breathing was still a little labored. "But I think I'm getting the hang of this now. I might be able to do something if…" She inspected the locket. It wasn't glowing any longer. "Is there a way you can add more…?"

Fely held out her hand impatiently. "Give it here."

Niels rubbed the back of his neck as Fely poured more golden light into the locket. It wasn't nearly as bright as Hallie's; it wasn't even as bright as when Fely had used it earlier. Pouring it into the locket seemed to deplete her own strength somehow.

After a minute, Fely handed the locket back to Hallie. Hallie clutched it in her fist. "Be ready to move him. He should be stable enough, though I'm not sure if he'll be able to walk any time soon."

Fely positioned her arms underneath the King's arms, ready to pull when told. Hallie turned to Niels. Her eyes betrayed no emotion, only command. "I'm going to attempt to…" she paused, as if trying to find the right word, "…do something to the beam, but I don't think I can do it for long. Will you help pull the King out?"

He nodded and joined Fely, sliding his hand under the King's right shoulder and wrapping his good arm around the man's chest.

This felt like a horrible idea.

"Maybe we should try to leverage the beam first," he ventured. There was plenty of rubble around. Surely there would be something they could use.

"None of us have the strength for that," Hallie said matter-of-factly. She climbed over a pile of rubble and placed one hand on the beam, the other still clutching the locket.

"But you might not have the strength to—Hallie!"

If Niels hadn't seen it himself, he wouldn't have believed what happened. It took several seconds, but as the glow over her hands intensified in a blinding flash, the beam lifted off the King. Only by an inch or two, but it was enough.

It didn't move like something was lifting it. It moved like time itself was flowing backwards; the entire thing sparkled as if sprinkled with a thousand tiny stars, lifting back toward the spot where it used to stand.

Niels set the King down as soon as he was clear of the rubble. The beam crashed back down with a clatter, but it didn't shake the ground like he expected it to. That must not have been the quake they'd felt earlier, then.

Hallie crashed, too, collapsing facefirst into the rubble. But by the time he crawled to her, calling her name, she was moving once more on her own.

Niels' heart pounded in his chest. "Are you all right?"

She rubbed her hand across her lip; her fingers came away bloody. It wasn't bleeding terribly—probably just scraped by the rubble, or maybe she'd bitten it. She pushed herself up on her elbows, the locket still clenched in her hand. She looked down at it, a curious expression on her face.

"Oh, thank the stars and fate," Fely gasped from behind him. Niels looked over his shoulder to see the King grimacing as Fely adjusted him into a more comfortable position.

Niels wouldn't have believed it if he hadn't seen it for himself. "You did it."

Hallie pushed herself shakily to her feet and stumbled forward, the locket swinging in her fist. Niels jumped up to help, but Hallie waved him off. "I'm fine."

"You don't look fine," Niels murmured under his breath, but he joined her.

If she'd heard him, she didn't act like it. She just handed the locket back over to Fely, who quickly reattached it around her neck.

Niels ran a hand through his hair. He would figure this out. He just needed to be patient. Normally that wasn't hard for him, but the Fogs had begun chipping away at that.

Just the thought made his headache flare again. He clenched his teeth against the pain. No one noticed as the King's eyes opened fully.

"I cannot feel…I cannot feel my legs." He didn't sound regal anymore. His usual silky voice was rugged and raspy. "I need to walk. I need to find…my uncle needs me at the chamber. What happened?"

"You almost died," Hallie said frankly.

Filip blinked, looking at Hallie. "Did you…?"

She shrugged. "Good thing you showed me what to do."

Fely smoothed back his hair. "She used my relic's reserve—not entirely her own power."

The King was silent for a moment, his eyes closed, his face strained. After a moment, a soft golden glow enveloped his body. Both Hallie and Niels flinched, but Fely stayed steady.

It was over as quickly as it had begun. The King opened his eyes once more, his breathing labored, his skin cloudy. "I might be able to supplement with my own, but it will not be an easy feat, nor a quick one." His jaw worked. "If I can't find the sword, all of this will have been for naught."

If the King was putting on a show, Niels had to admit he was an excellent actor. The distress in his voice seemed real enough.

Niels didn't know if that made him feel better or not, but as a man, he could sympathize. As a man, you needed to be the strongest, the best, the one to have all the answers. When you didn't, you felt useless. He barely understood what the task was. He'd only agreed to come along with Hallie because she needed him, whether she knew it or not.

Though he was beginning to doubt that now. He'd been completely useless the entirety of their journey thus far. He'd only gotten in the way. He was the reason she'd nearly burnt out from using her power; if he hadn't been hurt, if she hadn't tried to heal him, she would've had enough power to open the portal with no problem.

"Where are we, exactly?" Niels asked, interrupting the King and Fely's conversation.

Hallie patted her lip once more, but it had stopped bleeding. She fetched a canteen from her pack and took a sip. "I think this is the old city."

He leveraged himself to his feet, using the nearby stone pile for assistance. His hand slipped, scraping his palm. He sucked air through his teeth.

Hallie set aside her canteen. "You need a medic."

Niels pressed his tongue to the roof of his mouth to try to relieve some of the headache that roared when he'd slipped. It didn't help much. "I think we both know we ain't gonna find one of those out here."

She gave him a skeptical look and pulled her pack onto her back. "If we're lucky, we'll find some medicines in the healing wing of the palace. The only problem is, we'll have to hike to get there."

Fely finally pulled her hand back, panting heavily; she wiped her wrapped brow awkwardly. The bandage wasn't soaked, but a few fresh spots of blood had appeared near where she'd been injured. "We can't go anywhere yet. We need the sword."

"What sword?" Hallie asked, packing the canteen back into her pack and standing. "You keep mentioning it."

Fely and the King exchanged glances. With a subtle nod, Fely looked back at Hallie. "Kainadr's Shadow, an ancient blade forged with the power of a god. It is the Myrrai Gate's guardian."

Niels blinked. He had no idea what any of that meant. Hallie looked equally confused.

"But that's just a fairy tale." Hallie played with the straps of her pack. "All the scholars say so. Even if the story is based upon truth, the legend has expanded so much it's unrecognizable—like King Arthur and Excalibur from First Earth."

Fely shook her head. "Your scholars are wrong. Asa was supposed to control the Gate and acquire the sword when he was in Myrrai, but something went awry." She pushed herself to her feet, a little wobbly. King Filip looked like he wanted to help, but his jaw only clenched harder. "There is another sword, but that one may be lost forever. We pray Asa is successful in his own mission. We must be successful in ours."

Niels reached out to help her and winced at the pain spiking in his shoulder. Fely held up a hand. "I am well enough." She took a few steadying breaths and looked Hallie directly in the eye. "I do not know if Filip's body will accept the healing, and his Essence power must go into the sword before all Yalvara is lost. I cannot risk moving him. I need you to find Kainadr's Shadow and return here."

"That doesn't explain what you need the sword to do," Hallie countered.

"It explains everything." She looked over at the statues at the other end of the ruins. She wiped a shaky hand across her brow once more. "It's their legacy, and the reason we are here to deal with the consequences nearly three thousand years later."

Hallie seemed to hesitate for a moment, but then she nodded. "All I need to do is get to the Gate Chamber and ask it for a sword?"

If Fely detected the disbelief in her statement, she didn't show it. "I am unsure it will be that simple. But as an Essence wielder, you should be able to sense the Shadow." She rubbed at her wounded head. "This is not ideal, but it is all we can do."

"You should go," Filip rasped. "They might—"

"I am not leaving you." Fely glared between Hallie and Niels. "They will go and come back with the sword."

He couldn't tell if she was asking or threatening.

Hallie nodded stiffly, then turned to Niels. "Then let's go. We have a hike ahead of us."

She walked away. He'd not seen that look in her eyes in a long, long time. Something was wrong, and he wasn't sure he wanted to figure it out.

With one last look toward the Cerls, Niels hurried to follow, the unease in his stomach simmering with each staggering limp. He just needed to give Hallie time. He'd earn her trust back soon...or he would die trying.

C H A P T E R   9

IN THESE MOUNTAINS

32 Years Ago

HARLAN HALE SHACKLEY THOUGHT IT ironic that eighteen years removed from mine work, he still had blood under his nails. His past haunted him no matter where he went. Yet this time, the blood was not his own.

He rubbed his hand on his military-grade trousers. Not that it helped anything other than his mental well-being. He didn't think he'd ever wash out the last few years of life on the front and dying men out of his uniform no matter how hard he scrubbed.

It was a testament how dire the last decade had been that, when he was about to perform a complicated surgery on a dying man, his only thought was *At least it's not my blood.*

Regardless, Harlan knew all too well people didn't survive long in the mountains unless they'd been born and raised there. For all their immense beauty, the towering shadows hid secrets better left in the dark. Harlan was one of those secrets.

He rifled through his dwindling supplies in his medic

pack. Amputating a leg was not the way Harlan had figured his military career would progress. He also never thought he'd end up back in the mountains he'd left all those years ago. Such was his luck.

He'd only joined the military to please his adoptive father, though it turned out that Harlan had a gift for war. He'd been top of his class in the military academy. Too bad he'd been relegated to the medical legion. He figured Carleton had some say in that.

Lord Carleton Shackley was an honest man, not anything like his true father, the one who would've died before Harlan's fourteenth summer even if the Cerls hadn't killed him. No, Carleton wasn't James Hale. Carleton never hit him. Carleton never screamed obscenities at him. Carleton never told him how worthless he was. Instead, he only knew his adoptive father as Carleton.

The dying man in front of him groaned as Harlan found a pot of salve. It wouldn't do much to numb the pain in his leg, but it would do enough that the man wouldn't flail while Harlan finished the procedure. He would need to restock soon.

He disinfected his hands and applied the salve just above the wound, rubbing it all the way around.

The man's jerking fell away once the salve took effect. A harsh mountain wind blew through, rustling the tent flap—the promise of winter. He hoped it wasn't some kind of omen, considering this part of the surgery might end up killing the man despite him living through the initial pistol shot.

The flap opened again, this time deliberately. A tall, reedy man entered. "The fire's hot enough, and the cleaver is heating up. You're good to cauterize as needed, but one day, I'll fix up something that'll work much better than the side of a hot cleaver."

Harlan pulled the long bandage tight midway down the man's thigh. He could tourniquet limbs in his sleep at this point. He tied off the knot with a grunt and grabbed a discarded arrow shaft pulled out of another man's chest. They had to adapt fast out here; it'd been cleaned enough, and resources were scarce. Lucky some Cerls still used arrows instead of the newest iteration of flashpistols.

Well, lucky was relative. Lucky that Harlan didn't have

to go out and find a sturdy stick to tourniquet a man's leg. Not so lucky for the man who'd taken the arrow to his chest in the first place.

Harlan looked over at his medic partner. "Prepare to cauterize. If he survives the cut, we'll need to work fast."

He was unsure if he should even try, but if it worked, then the soldier might just pull out a close one. He refused to get his hopes up, though.

"I mean to knock that pessimism right out of you soon as our shift is done," his partner said, his blue eyes alight.

Harlan rolled his own eyes and cleaned his saw with carbolic acid, though disease was the least of the man's worries at the moment. "You forget, Major Fairchild, we're in the middle of a war, though the higher-ups don't like to call it what it is."

"It's times like these when your mountain accent is thickest, my friend."

Harlan gritted his teeth. "I'm trying."

"It's not a bad thing." A hand squeezed his shoulder. "No shame in being who you are."

Except Ezekiel Fairchild knew just how much Harlan wished to hide his past. Harlan finished cleaning his instruments and gestured to his waiting patient. "Make yourself useful and strap this man down."

Ezekiel walked to the man's other side. "Make it quick. All three of our newest arrivals have been triaged and are stable, but I think one of them has some sort of disease in his lungs. Not bronchitis. Sounds worse. I'm thinking pneumonia; worst case of it I've ever heard."

"You do your work well, Major Fairchild."

"It helps that I upgraded my triage equipment."

Ever the tinkerer, Ezekiel was always trying to improve life on the front. Such optimism was dangerous, but important; he kept Harlan from sinking into the darkest parts of himself.

Fetching the straps from underneath the cot, Ezekiel pulled them tight and secured the buckle at the man's chest and another at his hips. He then settled closer to the soldier's right leg and disinfected his hands. "I hate how formal you get when you work. These men would think we're merely acquaintances instead of friends."

"You mean the man currently under our poor excuse for

general anesthesia?" Harlan grunted. They'd been forced to use alcohol, since their opium stores had gone dry.

Ezekiel just scoffed, but he held the man steady. Harlan positioned himself appropriately above, one hand on the table, one on the saw. He placed the serrated blade just below the tourniquet. He would have only minutes to sever the man's leg before he cauterized it. If he was off by even a few seconds, the man could bleed out. He'd already lost too much blood. He took a deep breath and visualized the process in his mind, making sure he could foresee every potential outcome.

Though he was but a medic, he was the best the Jaydian military had. Of course, he wouldn't be half as effective if not for Ezekiel Fairchild and his inventions, but Harlan had no time to think upon those things. The soldier's life needed saving. Though he despised it, surgery was something he could do well.

He lost himself to the bloody process and hoped for a better tomorrow.

HOURS LATER, SITTING ON A rocky outcropping, Harlan's fingernails were finally free of blood.

"That was some good work." Ezekiel took a swig from his flask and passed it to Harlan.

He swirled the contents before imbibing. The mountain whiskey burned his throat all the way down, but it helped rid his body of the tension of the last few hours. While the man had survived the amputation, it was still unlikely he'd last the week. Not Harlan's fault. Just the way life was, he guessed. The fever had set in too fast.

He'd done what he could. The surgery had been successful. That was the only good thing there was to say.

He coughed a little to clear his throat of the alcohol's aftermath. He passed the flask back. "Not good enough."

Ezekiel took another sip and grimaced, ruffling the dark curls that had begun to grow back after his latest military shave. He'd need to cut it again before returning to the capital. "Shocks, you mountain people don't mess around with your libations." He replaced the cap and tucked the flask back into his jacket pocket. "It's not your fault if the man dies.

It's the soldiers who brought him in. They didn't get him to you in time to prevent the infection from setting in."

Harlan didn't look at his friend. His only friend. Only Ezekiel would be able to tell just how much this affected him. He would notice the hatred in his eyes.

The papers claimed these were just rogue bands of Cerls attacking the countryside, but it was more than that. The Cerls were looking for something, using the attacks as a front. If anyone knew the difference, it was Harlan.

He'd lived the first twelve years of his life in these mountains. The Nardens were still in his blood, and he knew that if he ever got to kill a Cerl himself, he would do so without hesitation. If he could only get out of this medical legion, he could make a difference. With a full-blown war on the horizon, they would soon be too deep to do anything to stop it. But Harlan could. If they let him.

"When I've served my time, I'm going to leave and invent something that'll save men like him," Ezekiel said, his voice soft.

Red clouds painted the sky as the sun kissed the horizon. Some would say it was a sign of good luck. Harlan disagreed. "In this life, it's better not to dream."

Ezekiel laughed. "I did say I'd knock the pessimism out of you this evening, right?"

Harlan allowed himself a small, crooked smile. "Afraid it's lodged so deep that even a few hits wouldn't do anything."

"Not to mention you're still undefeated in the sparring ring," Ezekiel huffed. "But regardless, I do think you could stand to lighten up."

"And as I've said before, we don't have the luxury. We're soldiers."

"Medics."

"In the middle of a war."

The sun fell below the horizon casting them into twilight. Ezekiel stood and stretched. "Don't let the papers hear you say that. They wouldn't want to report the truth."

Harlan pushed himself to his feet and straightened his jacket. Ezekiel started for the encampment, Harlan following. The day and the swigs of whiskey caught up with him on the way. Each footstep weighed a thousand pounds. He needed sleep, though he knew it would evade him for hours yet. He needed to clean his uniform and flashpistol, though the latter hardly saw any action.

"We get leave in a few weeks, I believe?" Ezekiel asked, turning a little to see Harlan.

He nodded. "My mother's asked me to come home for at least a week of it. As if there's anywhere else I'd like to see."

Aurelia Shackley wasn't his real mother, but she insisted he call her as such. He supposed it was nice.

Ezekiel paused, waiting for him to catch up. He slung an arm around his shoulder. "What if you come round for dinner at the townhouse? Get away from that stuffy old manor for a bit?"

"I don't need your pity."

"Course you don't, but Rose dearly wants to meet the man who's kept me sane the last few years. I might even persuade Lessie to join us. She'd be coming to the capital soon anyway with winter upon us. I'm determined to see to it that she finds some suitor to put up with her at last. 'Twas old Pa's dying wish, may his soul rest among the stars. I could use some assistance in that endeavor." Ezekiel shot Harlan a quick glance before letting his arm fall back to his side. "Besides, this is the first time we've earned leave at the same time. Humor me."

According to his friend, the Lady Celeste Fairchild was rather opinionated and scholarly, two traits which had put off two betrothals in kind. Harlan was unsure how his presence was supposed to solve either of those issues.

Judging by the stories he'd heard, he had an inkling that the Lady Celeste was running off potential suitors on purpose. But that didn't mean he wanted to be her next target.

Still, he owed his friend at least a cordial acceptance. Surely he could figure a way out of it before the time came.

What else did he have to do on his leave? Sit in Shackley Manor with his adoptive mother and avoid all conversation relating to the daily life of a military surgeon? That left them with precious little to talk about.

"Fine. But none of your silly card games after dinner. I refuse to trounce you in front of your wife. It'd be rude."

Ezekiel just laughed. "No worries about that. She destroys me at Stars and Blasts every chance she can."

"Merciless."

"It's why I married her. And bless her, but she hasn't lost

any of her skill in the years since."

Ezekiel dug in his pocket and pulled out a small leather wallet, flashing the tiny portrait of his sleeping twin boys as if he hadn't shown them to Harlan a dozen times before. "Still can't believe they're nearly five now."

His voice took on that melancholy tone that came over him whenever the influence of drink and talk about his family mixed. Harlan coughed to fill the awkward space and put a hand on his friend's shoulder. "Didn't you get to see them last year around the holidays?"

Ezekiel put away the portrait. "No amount of leave can make up for the fact that I'm missing them grow up."

"Well, then, it's a good thing you only have a year of service left, isn't it?"

His friend smiled, his good humor returning. "And then maybe I'll get around to making your life easier out here."

"I'd expect no less."

The camp came into view. The rows of tents were like wayward autumn leaves. No wonder the Cerls were gaining ground. The military had grown lax in recent years, drunk on their victories and false peace. Harlan focused on finding his own tent. He might be able to sleep a little if he kept his mind fixed on their upcoming leave, not on the events of the day. Amputations always stayed with him a little longer.

Ezekiel bid him goodnight before heading to his own tent another scattered row over. As Harlan entered his nearly barren living space, he focused firmly on the future.

It would truly be nice to get away from the stench of death and blood for three weeks. It was the longest stretch of leave he'd earned at once since he'd joined up nearly thirteen years prior. Part of him worried Major Gibbons wouldn't be up to the task of managing the patients without him, but Harlan forced himself not to dwell on that. That was not his problem. Yet.

Harlan loosened the buttons on his jacket, spent a quarter-hour cleaning the stains on the sleeves that had been exposed over his apron, and laid it neatly across his trunk. The whiskey still buzzed in his veins, and his stomach swam as he settled on his cot, staring up at the blank canvas above him. He'd take a quick break, then get to cleaning his weapons.

Three whole weeks in the capital. He'd be glad to eat

fresh food that didn't taste like tree bark. His mother would make sure he ate a few meals consisting of chicken pot pie, a favorite of his. It'd been too long since he'd had a good one. Of course, he had a small apartment in the nicer part of the lower city that afforded him a little comfort, but it was rather sparse. He was hardly ever home. No time to accumulate unnecessary knick-knacks and baubles just to decorate a dusty, rarely seen shelf.

Part of him was jealous of Ezekiel. He had a family to go home to, even if it was difficult to be away from them. It was different for Harlan.

Maybe if he'd married, he would want to go home. In a society that prided itself in marrying young, he was an oddity. At thirty years of age, he had yet to have any interest in that aspect of life. Carleton hadn't drawn up a customary betrothal contract when he'd become of age on account of his military career; he'd always said Harlan would have his pick later.

Harlan didn't feel inclined to pick at all. He was a good soldier, a good medic. Why add any distractions when he could make a name for himself without feeling like he needed to hold back for the sake of a wife and kids? Why would he willingly sign up for the burden Ezekiel carried every day?

Harlan was free.

So why didn't he feel better about that?

He smoothed the mustache he'd begun to grow the last week. The whiskers were rough under his fingers. His real father had always worn a long, full beard—a commonality in Ravenhelm. Life was too short for miners, so why waste the time on shaving?

His heart twinged. The Cerls had taken that all away.

Shocks, he shouldn't have drunk any of that blasted whiskey. It made him feel things.

If only he could be out on the battlefield fighting, he could find a way to get rid of the guilt plaguing him once and for all—whether that be in death or in victory. Through the buzz, he felt a headache coming on, a reminder of his time in the mines. The Fogs could force him out of service early if the condition progressed too rapidly. It might mean an early death like it had for so many of those he'd known.

But even if it struck in full force tomorrow, how could

he leave Ezekiel behind?

Harlan shut his eyes and pushed out a sigh. Ezekiel was the greatest friend any man could have, yet for some reason he'd chosen Harlan to follow around the last few years, but that's not what bothered him.

Harlan had no family, and the family he'd had way back when had been the kind where no one really loved each other at all. Michael had been the only one he'd truly cared about.

Harlan's chest ached again. Michael. He tried his best not to think of his brother, of his last few moments here on Yalvara. He'd been ten. Ten years old. A child.

Stars, what kind of man would he have been today? Who would Harlan have been? Completely mad from the Fogs? Or…or…

He forced himself to rise and finish cleaning the uniform before moving to the weapons. The monotony kept his hands busy. If he concentrated enough on the task at hand, he could will away the alcohol and the feelings that accompanied it. His headache never grew worse, only waited at the edges. A small mercy.

After he finished his chores, he fell heavily onto his cot and turned off the gas lantern.

As the darkness grew, the only light coming from nearby tents or an odd cookfire painting the side of the canvas wall, he forced himself to relax and focus on anything but his past.

C H A P T E R   1 0

LEFT BEHIND

Jove

THE TUNNELS BENEATH THE CITY were one of the many secrets Jove had kept once he'd been appointed High Guardsman. He'd never imagined he would have to use them. How naive he'd been, looking through the lens of someone too young to have that much power.

The main reason the High Council kept such things need-to-know was because policing the tunnels would have taken up too much funding. They were the perfect hideout for seedier characters with less-than-savory intentions.

They were also a health hazard. The nearby sewers gave the damp air a sour odor. If people were hiding down here, they'd have to figure out the Cerl problem quickly if they were to avoid a plague. He knew the last completed project in the Catacombs had been digging wells, but that wasn't a guarantee against disease when the tunnels would be overrun with refugees.

The Catacombs didn't house the dead, but one of the

architects had nicknamed them that when they'd been designed at the end of the Great War. Ironic. Jaydians burned their dead, sending the departed spirits to journey among the stars; yet if Cerulene had their way, all the Kyvena survivors would die beneath the ground.

Regardless, the Catacombs resembled the city streets above with their square grid; the architects had even included a small bay for hoverships, though its entrance was hidden out in the hills a mile or two away. It would be useless if they didn't figure out how to reinstate the electricity, and Jove didn't know if that was possible. He didn't understand what Loffler had done.

How anyone could neutralize the electricity of an entire city, he didn't understand. It was terrifying. No wonder Jove's Jaydian ancestors had forced a treaty to keep the Yalven Essence powers under control.

And Anderson. Who knew what was happening to him now. Jove couldn't waste time guessing; he could do nothing but wander aimlessly under a ruined city, searching for his wife and child, agonizingly aware that he'd run off to drown himself in alcohol while they fought for their lives.

Jove trailed behind his father and Saldr as the tunnel widened, the voices of those now trapped below the surface of Yalvara echoing off the stone. The fingers of Jove's right hand twitched. Out of habit, he felt around in his pocket, but it was empty. He'd lost his cigarettes somewhere along the way.

Blast.

As they entered the throng of people setting up camp and trying to find family and friends, Jove searched each face for Clara's. Every minute that passed without finding her and Samuel, his hand twitched for cigarettes, even when he knew there were none. He didn't think he'd easily find a pint of ale, either.

His racing thoughts grew louder and more insistent the further they walked. His eyes darted from person to person without really seeing anything. His feet kept trudging along without questioning his path.

"It's Harlan Shackley!" a voice shouted from up ahead, interrupting Jove's spiral.

Jove looked up. Others had blocked the corridor. Saldr's hand went to his pouch, though Jove knew it to be empty.

The individual people in the crowd varied—mostly Jaydians in various states of dishevelment, though he did spot a few Yalven men towering over the rest. Several had minor injuries. Some looked on the brink of death.

Dark braids caught the corner of his eye. He whipped his head toward a corridor branching off the one he was in. A woman strode in the other direction—the same stature, the same smooth gait as his missing wife.

"Clara!" Jove shouted, stumbling and pushing past a few refugees who stood in his path. She didn't look back.

He couldn't blame her. But he had to see her. He just had to know she and Samuel were all right.

"Clara!" Jove couldn't go much faster with each step shooting knives into his injured shoulder.

She still didn't stop—but Jove did. The parchment crinkled in his jacket pocket, mocking him.

Clara wasn't cruel. She would answer if she heard him calling. It couldn't be her.

Had his wife and son perished in the attack after all? Had they died not realizing how sorry he was?

People moved around him like fish in a stream. Some muttered curses at him for standing still amidst the flow. Shouting echoed off the tunnel walls from behind him. He brought a hand to his eyes.

He couldn't live without Clara, just like he wasn't living without Zeke.

"Jove!"

That voice.

He dropped his hand and turned wildly about. Behind him. It came from behind him. His eyes searched the refugees, the faces all blurring together with his tears and panic.

He knew that voice.

A woman in her late fifties sprinted for him, her dark hair threaded with silver; outside of her usual bun, the curls were as unruly as Kase's. Dirt streaked one of her cheeks. Rips decorated the demure yet elegant gown she'd worn hours earlier to her husband's sentencing.

"Mother," Jove choked. His mother was alive. Alive. And if she'd made it—

He took three steps toward her before the ground rumbled. Most people clung to the edges of the tunnel. Jove did not. He reached for his mother.

He pitched forward as the ground beneath him was ripped inexplicably skyward. He flew through the air and landed hard on his bad shoulder. He screamed. Hands encircled his other, but his vision blurred in and out. The pain—it was like when his father had shoved him into the desk when Kase and Ana had tried to run away, and Jove's arm had snapped.

And then he was falling.

Clara

CLARA SHACKLEY WAS NOT IMMUNE to anguish and sorrow. She'd dealt with both in spades. She painted in part to relieve those feelings, to process, to analyze, and finally lay them to rest. However, with a heavy pack on her back, a newborn in her arms, and the metallic smell of blood in the thick underground air, she didn't think she'd be able to paint away her grief over the sight before her.

Some might have called the brick walls and torch-lined tunnels claustrophobic and eerie, but with her artist's eye, she appreciated the beauty of the weathered and beaten dirt floor contrasting with the shape of the brick archways leading to other parts of what the soldiers called the Catacombs. Yet nothing could have prepared anyone for the wails echoing off the walls.

Samuel's mouth yawned wide, his own cries joining those mourning loved ones lost in the fires and fighting.

Clara couldn't fall apart like those around her. But each of Samuel's mewing cries was another arrow in her chest.

That night, she had just reached the outer gates when the city went dark. While arguing with the soldiers stationed there, screams had erupted behind her. She'd turned to find a beast out of legend flying overhead, an inferno they had not seen since the fire of Kyvena gushing from its jagged maw. At the sight of it, the soldiers had ushered her down into the Catacombs, and she hadn't fought them. Even if she'd wanted to, shock had ravaged her body with such deep, dark cold she could hardly move without being led.

A female officer had stayed with her, organizing the

streams of refugees who followed them. Clara could only sit and pray someone would arrive and announce they'd all been hallucinating.

A dragon.

A real, live dragon.

It still didn't feel real. She'd painted several of the mythical creatures over the years, in swaths of beautiful, bright colors with striking poses suggesting elegance and intelligence that went beyond human atrocity to something wiser than they were, but they'd only been studies in preparation for Les' figurines.

This monster soaring on wings of golden fire was nothing but a nightmare.

Here, safe in the Catacombs, she cooed at Samuel, her sleepy hushes and soft bounces doing so little against his cries, it was a wonder he started to quiet at all. He laid in her arms, tiny and fragile—perhaps as fragile as herself. Her body ached, still recovering from the birth. She felt every pull and uncomfortable stretch on her skin, the discomfort of sitting on a hard brick seat, the tears stinging her eyes, the ache of wishing for Jove to be there.

Not the Jove she'd known recently. She wanted her husband from before, her betrothed who stole her heart and made her believe their union, while motivated by their parents and ultimately political, would be something beautiful. Colorful. The stuff of dreams.

She wanted to escape into her paintings again. The morbid urge to paint the beast crept through her, but the better part of herself kept her frozen on the stone floor, her back pressed against the brick wall behind her, cradling her infant son in her arms. The grit dug into her back. At least it felt real. It felt familiar.

She was stone, not glass, not the fickle wind. Stone.

Repeating that kept her sane until Samuel finally fell asleep in her arms.

Hours had passed, and her husband had yet to come through the doorway. The Catacombs, while expansive, brimmed with terrified city residents in varying states of injury, shock, or dress. Some had come in nightgowns, others in sequined yet bedraggled evening gowns, swept from the middle of a play or an elegant evening with friends and family in their stuffy, comfortable homes and thrust into the middle of a war. Now they were flecked with blood, sitting on a bare brick floor like her.

A few soldiers shouted about setting up an infirmary in one of the eastern caverns. Another group attempted to organize the influx, taking down the names of missing family members.

Jove. Jove Shackley. Yes, that Jove Shackley. Light-skinned. Blue eyes. Short, dark hair. Tall. Husband. Father. Missing.

Left behind.

Other than to describe her husband, she hadn't spoken to anyone since the attack had begun; whatever words she might've had turned to smoke as soon as she tried to speak them. Instead, her emotions poured out in her tears, an unceasing flood.

Had he found that note? The one that she'd left on the side table?

Was that why he hadn't come to find them?

No. He wouldn't abandon them to this, no matter what she'd said. She pressed her hand to the wall behind her and eased herself to her feet, one inch at a time so as not to disturb her baby or her aching body. Maybe if she kept moving, she'd find him. Or Les. Her father-in-law probably hadn't made it out of the cells.

She didn't know how she felt about that.

Deep breath in. Deep breath out.

She was okay. She was alive.

Don't wake the baby.

She cuddled Samuel closer, hoping her swaying gait would keep him unaware of the chaos his new world had devolved into.

When her husband hadn't returned with Les after the sentencing, she'd made her decision. She knew he'd gone out drinking. He'd promised to stop, but he'd given her enough broken promises to fill the near-empty Davey Estate.

She closed her eyes against the ache in her chest. She prayed hard, but heavy tears were her only answer.

Between One World, the Cerls, and the dragon, an inebriated Jove wouldn't make it far—especially if they discovered who he was.

She would never get to say goodbye or tell him just how much she loved him. She'd feigned sleep when he'd kissed her temple before he'd left for the courts, and now...

It might be the last kiss he ever gave her.

Her heart throbbed again.

Pain threaded through her ankle as she twisted it on a loose rock. She bit her lip to keep from losing what weak grip she had on her emotions. Thankfully, she hadn't dropped her son, though the jostling had woken him. Limping to the next clear space of wall beside an offshoot tunnel, she slid to the ground, her pack grinding and scratching against the brick.

She laid her head back and pushed down her pain, trying to focus on what to do next now that the world had shattered into a thousand glass shards. Samuel's cries pierced the roaring tide of sound. No amount of shushing did anything. She didn't remember when she'd last fed him. It could've been an hour or seven, but she just couldn't think straight. His cries rose in pitch.

She needed to feed him. She needed to find Jove. She needed—she needed—

"Here, let me help you, hon. I've got a spot away from the ruckus where you can feed your babe," a soft, aged feminine voice said from above.

Clara opened her eyes to see a white woman, probably in her forties, with dark but mostly gray hair pulled back into a smooth bun. Her eyes were peridot green and full of concern. Clara opened her mouth to speak, but nothing came out. Instead, tears slid down her face.

I am a Davey. I am strong.

But the old mantra didn't work. So she tried a new one.

I am stone. Not glass. Not wind. Stone.

She simply nodded at the woman, who helped her to her feet and whispered a gentle "Right this way," before leading her a short way down the offshoot where a few families sat huddled on the floor, arms wrapped around each other. They looked cold, and scared—but then, who didn't down in the Catacombs? Their darting eyes looked up fearfully as the two women approached, but once they recognized the older woman and saw Clara holding a baby, they settled back down.

The woman helped Clara to a small alcove, the flickering torch above casting a slight shadow into the space. She undid the leather ties on Clara's rucksack and pulled out a dove-gray knitted blanket, handing it over.

Careful of her sore ankle and the knot in her throat,

Clara settled herself on the rough ground. Samuel squirmed in her arms. She set the blanket on her shoulders and worked to calm and feed Samuel. Once his cries quieted, the woman sat beside her, pulling out a few hard crackers, one of which she handed to Clara.

Trying not to disturb Samuel, Clara took the cracker with a shaking hand and nibbled a bit of the edge. It reminded her of the fare soldiers took on their missions, something that didn't spoil easily and tasted mostly of salt. Clara broke off another chunk with her teeth and chewed. Not her favorite, but the saltiness reminded her of the seaside she'd grown up beside.

"Sorry I don't have much else to offer, but that'll keep you satiated for an hour or two." The woman finished off her own fare before dusting her fingers on her worn brown trousers.

Clara cleared her throat, and finally, her words began working again, though her voice still came out thick and muddled. "Thank you."

She didn't know what else to say. What else was there?

The woman fished out knitting needles and golden yarn and gave a small smile that didn't reach her eyes. "After birthing two of my own children, I cannot imagine trying to navigate postpartum while hiding in an underground bunker."

Clara gave her a watery smile. "It's not been a month."

She didn't mention the fact that not only had the time since been full of raging hormones and lost hours of sleep, her father-in-law had gone on trial and been sentenced to death. Clara nearly laughed at the absurdity of it all.

The woman smiled encouragingly. "I'm Zelda, and I'll be glad to help you out until we find your family. Didn't expect to arrive at the capital for the first time in the middle of an attack."

"You just got here?"

"This morning."

Clara nodded, glad to feel sorry for someone else for once. "I'm Clara. This is Samuel."

She couldn't say anything more, for anything else would make her crumble. Instead, she and Zelda sat there in companionable silence. Samuel finished and fell back asleep. Zelda knitted. Before long, Clara found herself drifting away against the wall.

She jerked awake, but Zelda readjusted the coverlet. "Hold your baby tight, and I'll keep an eye out. We'll figure this all out soon."

She wanted to argue, to say that she didn't need sleep. She needed Jove. But her eyelids drooped, the adrenaline from everything fading at last, and she found she didn't have any fight left to give.

C H A P T E R   1 1

NEVER WANTED TO LEAVE

Niels

IF YOU'D ASKED NIELS A day ago whether or not he was in good shape, he'd have answered yes. He'd done five years in the mines, and besides the slow onset of the Fogs, he would've said he could hike a mountain without any trouble. But with two injuries, one being a bullet still lodged in his leg...well, that would've made him a liar.

If he could've walked straight on while leaning on the branch he'd fashioned as a walking stick before they started hiking, he would have suffered only stiffness and a slight ache. But a mountain wasn't something to be conquered like a road in the plains. Each step up the incline, he had to bite the inside of his cheek to keep from crying out. The pain would calm after a minute, but shortly after, he'd repeat the process once more.

It was agony.

He was determined to keep the worst of it from Hallie. She had enough on her mind, and with the Cerl King waiting for them to return with some sword, he didn't want to add yet another burden to her plate. If she did know, she would only blame herself for failing to heal him all the way.

What kind of world had Niels woken up in? He'd seen the Essence power used multiple times now, yet each time he was almost convinced he'd dreamt it.

His lungs burned a little from the changing altitude, but as a son of the mountains, he adjusted easily. He briefly wondered if Hallie would come down with a bout of high-altitude sickness. He hoped not; she'd seemed fine back in the caverns and in Achilles, but judging by the strain on his own lungs, this mountain path would take them much higher than the altitude even he was used to.

But they had more pressing problems.

Niels barely watched where he was walking. He only concentrated on not throwing up, keeping his leg as steady as possible, and *not* focusing on the girl walking in front of him, her red braid swaying as they climbed.

He lost track of just how long they climbed, but it was well past midday, bordering on golden hour, when they approached the immense gates made from what could only be Zuprium—a metal in which he was nearly an expert. He took deep, controlled breaths, aware of the slick sweat coating every inch of him, and tried not to topple back down the mountain.

The crisp air did feel nice after the hike, but it did nothing for his leg.

On the outside, the gates, towers and wall looked as if they hadn't been touched with anything but the rich, waning sunlight in quite a while.

"Should we call out? I don't want to add *crossbow bolt to the stomach* to my list of injuries." Niels limped forward, shielding Hallie from the nearest window. No one appeared in it or on the walkway, but he didn't want to risk it.

He was naked without a weapon of his own. All he had was a girl with some sort of power he couldn't explain and she couldn't control. He was useless as anything but a shield.

Hallie strode forward. "There's no one."

He caught her jacket. "Hal."

She turned and shook her head. "Just trust me."

Her eyes were as heavy as the rain laden clouds at their back. He swallowed and cleared his throat. "I'll follow."

If she thought his behavior strange, she didn't let on.

Instead, she threw her shoulders back and marched toward the gates.

The towering gatehouse and doors that could swallow his childhood home held a history he didn't understand. They were made of Zuprium, but someone had taken a graver to it and created a scene that reminded him of the one displayed in the tunnels beneath the other city. A bright and shining sun lay between two doors. People danced around it, but as Niels got closer, he realized an archway was tucked away within the sun. It was barely visible in the fading sunlight; he couldn't tell if that had been done intentionally or caused by weathering and time. Maybe the pain clouding his mind was also messing with his eyesight.

With their combined strength, they were able to push the left door open. The metal scraped and screeched against the stone beneath their feet. Niels tripped when they stopped, but he caught himself on the cold metal door. White-hot fire zinged up his leg. He couldn't stop himself from crying out. Hallie twisted to look at him, alarm clearing the clouds from her eyes. "Niels?"

"It's all right," Niels said, pushing his hair back and tucking the stray strands behind his ear. He gritted his teeth and willed himself to hold on a little longer. He could do that. He'd been through worse.

Well, he hadn't. But lying to himself made it easier to bear.

"You can stay here in the gate house if you'd like," Hallie offered, pointing to the shadowed archway that was visible now that they had opened one of the doors. "I'll go find what we need, and then we can go back."

"No. I'm not leaving you to wander around by yourself."

Her nostrils flared; her jaw stiffened. "I know what I'm doing."

She was under a lot of stress. They both were. But how many times were they going to have this argument? He straightened and readjusted his grip on his makeshift staff. "I'd rather not split up."

"And I'd rather you not ruin your leg any further."

Ah. She felt guilty. But this wasn't her fault, not really. "I'll be fine. I have to get used to it anyway. Not like the bullet's going anywhere."

Her face darkened. That was the absolute wrong thing

to say, but it was true. His leg ached, and his lungs still burned from the more difficult hike; if he wanted to keep up, he'd have to adapt.

Hallie looked away. Her hair was falling out of her braid. The sweat coating her face and the exertion it took to climb the mountain had given way to a pink flush across her cheeks and fine, fiery wisps curling at her temples.

Stars, she was beautiful.

As soon as he thought it, the image of her kissing Kase in the cavern came back to him and sobered him quickly.

Blast everything.

He looked past her and up at the city at last.

The buildings here were made from Zuprium, the roofs impossibly slim and pointed. The structure jutting out above the rest nearest the mountainside must have been a palace by the smattering of towers and turrets. In the golden light, the city glowed like radiant starlight. But an emptiness and sense of loss hung heavy in the crisp evening air. The wind sang a mournful song through the trees at his back and freed the hair he'd tucked behind his ear.

"Welcome to Myrrai," Hallie whispered.

Niels stepped forward and slid an arm around her shoulders. It was a little difficult with her pack, but he pulled her close. "I'm sorry."

He wasn't entirely sure what he was sorry for, but this place meant something to her, and he ached to figure out what had happened. Now was not the time to ask.

She shrugged him off and started up the winding lane, avoiding a dark, yawning stain upon the stone.

How was he supposed to show her he cared if she wouldn't even meet him halfway? He was doing all the right things, but she was stubborn as a stone lodged in a mountain stream.

He'd agreed to come along to keep her safe. He hadn't realized he'd have to fight her every step of the way to do it.

Niels gripped his stick harder and followed after her. He'd get to the bottom of it, but he didn't know how much longer he could be patient. An ache had begun behind his right eye. He'd only had a small respite between headaches this time.

Niels followed slowly, his head on a swivel. What had happened? Why was it seemingly abandoned? According to everyone else, this place held answers, but if there wasn't anyone to answer them, what was the purpose? He didn't think that whatever sword the Cerl King wanted would just be lying out in the open. That wasn't the way the stories worked, and the line between real life and fantastical had blurred in recent days.

He hadn't read much since Hallie had left.

The quicker they figured out how to get back home, the better. He didn't have much hope for that either. That thought should have filled him with dread, but he was here with Hallie, and she was all he needed.

A rattling sound echoed through a nearby alley. Niels jerked and spun toward it. Immediately, he regretted that choice. His leg exploded with heat and pain. He couldn't stifle the hissing gasp that escaped his lips. He fell against the cottage beside him. The wall groaned at the impact.

"Niels!"

If Niels hadn't been in so much pain, he would've made a note of the fear in her voice. Instead, all he could hear was his pounding heart as his blood leaked out of the wound at a blistering pace.

Niels pressed a hand to his knee. Fresh blood oozed over his fingers.

How? How had that happened? Hadn't Hallie fixed it? Had the bullet ruptured something?

"You're bleeding again. Did you—" Hallie knelt next to his leg and looked toward the alleyway where he'd heard the noise. "Did something hit you?"

"No, nothing."

She hesitated. "May I?"

He nodded, and she leaned forward, her fingers prodding a little.

He grunted at the fresh onslaught of pain. His head felt a little lighter. Not a good sign.

She pulled back, face falling. "It's reopened." She glanced around as if looking for the answer among the ghosts. "I must not have...whatever I did back in Ravenhelm didn't work. Or it didn't hold. Or..." She worried her lip with her teeth. "I'm not sure what to do."

Nausea ate away at his stomach, and his headache only grew. "I need to rest. Then we can bandage it properly."

"I'm not Jack."

"Thank the stars for that," Niels mumbled as Hallie slung his arm around her shoulder and helped him limp in the direction of what he'd assumed was a palace when he'd spotted it below. "You're much prettier."

It would've sounded more romantic if he hadn't ground it out through the pain.

Hallie's breath came heavier and faster as they finally reached the archway. "Much prettier, yes, but you need a medic's touch, not a pretty face." She paused. "Maybe I should go get Fely."

"Rest first."

A wave of heat rolled over them, like the one in the tunnels beneath the ruined statue temple in the valley below. Hallie didn't seem to notice; she kept tugging him forward until they reached a giant foyer and turned right.

"Can you make it much further? The healer's wing is too far, but the kitchens are through the corridor there. They'll have water taps and a place to boil it."

Her skin had gone white as goat's milk. Her golden eyes were no longer dark and sorrowful, but brimming with fear. He gave a curt nod. "I can make it."

Even though he felt anything but capable of that. He couldn't show weakness. Not in front of her.

She helped him down the corridor, and he'd never been more grateful. If she hadn't been holding him up, he knew he would've collapsed. He hoped it wasn't obvious just how much he leaned on her.

Right, painful limp left, right, excruciating limp left.

He repeated the steps in his head to remind himself to keep going, to focus on walking instead of the fire that was now his leg. Stars, he'd never had an injury that had hurt this badly. It was hard to think past the next step ahead. He clenched his teeth until they ached.

How had it reopened? Had her power truly failed? The wound felt as fresh as when he'd first been hit.

His head still felt lighter than a feather, and a storm raged in his stomach.

When they rounded the corner, the turn jostled his leg. The pain erupted into a firestorm. His good leg gave out, and he collapsed, Hallie with him. She shouted as she fell right on top of him.

His leg screamed. An involuntary, strangled cry escaped

his hold. He would not yield more than that. He would pass out before he let that happen.

Hallie rolled off him. "Niels, what happened? Can you...did something else...is it just your leg? Oh stars, oh stars. It's my fault."

He was able to summon a choked chuckle. "It's okay. 'Tis but a simple flesh wound."

Seemed he could remember how to speak all proper-like when he was in pain. Or maybe he was simply descending into madness. As if in answer, his Fogs headache flared; blackness flickered in and out, so swiftly he wasn't sure how much time he lost.

When he blinked, Hallie was flinging aside shirts and pants and anything else in her pack. Niels barely saw her through the haze distorting his vision, one that told him the next blackout might be permanent. Her panicked words were now garbled nonsense in his ears.

Hiking the mountain had been too ambitious. His leg had always been a ticking time bomb, and now his time was up.

His vision went in and out. One second Hallie was ripping things out of his pack and hers, the next her panicked eyes floated above his. "I don't have time to go down the mountain and back. I don't have time—"

"I'll be...fine..."

He didn't think she heard him. He wasn't even sure he'd spoken out loud.

White-hot pain bit into his leg and radiated down to his toes before bouncing up into his chest, climbing all the way to his neck. He clenched his eyes shut, a few searing tears escaping. A few seconds later, cold air pierced the heat like a dagger. It didn't last long before the heat returned.

Fingers, hot and inquisitive, poked his wound.

It took everything in his power to keep the scream from ripping through his throat at the stinging pain that lit through his leg over the next few seconds. Light blazed against his lids.

The tension left his body, but the headache stayed. The pain in his leg receded to a mild sting, like he'd been stung by a mountain hornet. His breathing still came in gasps, and sweat ran in rivulets down his face, but he was able to open his eyes.

It wasn't bright in the corridor. The sun had dipped

below the horizon, and the light floating through the window above them was a dull, fading gold, streaked with red. Firstmoon would be rising soon.

"Niels? Can you hear me?"

Hallie sounded oddly breathless, like she had run a marathon before speaking. He turned his head to find her crouched near his injured leg. His trousers were missing below his knee, the stiff material slashed and frayed. She'd cut it off. Blood coated the floor beneath his leg and the knees of Hallie's trousers.

"Yes," he croaked. She looked worse than he felt, like she was about to pass out herself. "What did you do?"

She shifted back on her heels, swaying a little with the motion. She clutched those stupid goggles in her right hand. She wiped her brow before holding out her hand, a bullet sitting in the center of her palm.

He blinked. "What—did you take—how did you—Fely said that it would kill you!"

"It was close to the surface." She looked away. "I had to."

"But why? Why would you put your life at risk to even try?"

Niels scanned the floor for a knife, a pair of shears, anything that she might've used to extract it. Because she couldn't have been so stars-blasted stupid as to use her power again when Fely had said it would probably kill her.

Yet there she sat, armed with nothing but her own hands, breathing heavily and wiping her brow of sweat again and again. He shifted a little; his leg protested with the movement, but it wasn't nearly as bad as it had been earlier. It was even better than the first time she'd tried to heal him.

Hallie fiddled with her hands in her lap. "Because I couldn't let you die."

Niels sat forward, taking one of her hands. She didn't resist, but she still wouldn't look at him. "Hallie." He rubbed her fingers until she looked up. "Thank you."

She smiled as she slipped her fingers from his. "It'll probably open up again, but at least you're not in too much pain."

He stared at her hard. She was still the same Hallie he'd known. Same stubborn hair refusing to be tamed even though she'd rebraided it before hiking the mountain. Same dusting of freckles across her nose. Same perfect lips.

But her eyes.

She'd always been spirited and unafraid to berate you for misquoting part of her favorite passages from *The Odyssey*. The fire that burned in her eyes now wasn't spirited. Those eyes could have incinerated with one glare, shaded by her brow with her back to the dimly lit corridor.

He didn't know what had changed that. It made her even more the woman he wanted to spend the rest of his life with. He would help her heal from whatever had made her eyes that way. She would always be his Hallie.

And he thought he'd figure out a way to get over her. Stupid.

He grabbed her hand and pulled her to him, catching her lips with his.

No matter how hard he tried not to, he'd imagined this moment for nearly three years. Whether the daydream was about her returning home to him or him going to the capital, it ended the same way every single time—him kissing her like she'd never left him standing there in middle of a dust-ridden mountain road.

Like she'd never wanted to leave.

Her lips were slightly chapped and stiff. She didn't move or respond until a second later, when—

When she pulled back, she pushed herself to her feet and grabbed her pack.

"Hallie…"

She didn't say anything, nothing at all, only walked down the corridor and around the corner.

The joy and relief evaporated as quickly as they had come upon him. He tried to get up, but his leg was still weak. She'd only reset it to where it had been a few hours ago.

Why had she left? Why was she always leaving?

A coldness seeped into his chest as he stared at the corner she'd disappeared around. He'd pushed it. He'd acted on instinct, not by any scientific measure or calculated move. He followed his heart instead of his mind, and now, he might have ruined any good grace he'd gained.

"I'm such a stars-idiot," he muttered as he hit his head repeatedly on the metal wall behind him.

C H A P T E R 1 2

CHOCOLATES

32 Years Ago

THE CAPITAL HADN'T CHANGED IN the year since Harlan's last extended leave. Since then, he'd only been given the odd day or two off. That alone should have indicated to anyone paying attention that the fighting in the mountains was more than mere skirmishes. However, no one important listened to Harlan, and no one seemed to be paying attention.

Having received another promotion, Carleton Shackley had taken over the security and well-being of those in Kyvena. Some naysayers scoffed that it wasn't a promotion at all, that the Commander was losing his touch and had been quietly sent home where he only had to deal with minor inconveniences like petty theft or the like.

Harlan knew differently. The ones keeping your family safe should be the people you trusted implicitly. The fact that the Lord Kapitan saw fit to move Carleton to the capital only showed that he might be seeing what Harlan was seeing on the ground. He could foresee the storm coming and wanted to make sure those at home were prepared for the worst of it.

Carleton was the best man for that job.

Despite the grim horizon, his adopted father's promotion gave him a little hope, which was why he had set up appointments with both Carleton and the Lord Kapitan for Thursday morning. It was the only time he could get both in a meeting together. Of course, he was only able to do so with the help of his family name.

Funny that something like a surname could take you far in a world such as this. The name 'Hale' had done nothing but force him into the mines at too young an age. 'Shackley' could change the world.

Regardless, he would make his case about needing someone else to lead the battalion at Fort Achilles to stop this needless game of cat and mouse with the Cerls. It was a decent idea. More than decent. He was certain a new direction was what they needed. Going on the offensive was the only way to keep the enemy at bay—striking them where it hurt was the only effective strategy.

He just hoped that the supposed gift of being adopted into one of the most prodigious families in all of Jayde, perhaps even Yalvara, would pay off.

The carriage bumped along the cobblestone streets, worsening Harlan's headache with every bob and dip on the short trip to the Fairchild Townhome. He should've just walked. He should've done many a thing, and yet, here he was back in Kyvena, dressed in dinner tails in the back of what most would consider a nice carriage with only the best horse pulling it. His adoptive mother, Aurelia, had forced him into it. He didn't care for the extra plush cushions on the seats nor the painted ceiling meant to inspire awe in the less fortunate, but she'd insisted he make an impression.

No matter how far he climbed in Jaydian society, he would always be a boy born in the mountains forced to make choices no twelve-year-old should have made. He believed Michael would've enjoyed living in the capital. For one, he would've liked all the sweet shoppes and bakeries boasting the best chocolate delicacies in all the world.

Harlan's headache intensified, as it was wont to do when he thought of his brother. He rubbed his right temple with one hand. It'd been at least a month since his last migraine. He guessed that the lack of dying men requiring complicated surgeries had broken whatever dam had been holding them back in the interim.

He tried not to dwell on the fact that headaches such as this were the first sign of the Fogs, or—as Harlan had learned in the years since—*Zuprium Neurotoxitosis*, as those trained in modern medical practices called it. He could only hope that the advanced symptoms never made an appearance. Sure, if he'd stayed in Ravenhelm and kept working in the mines, he'd be much worse off than he was at thirty, but this proved that any time spent in the mines at all was dangerous.

But Jayde still required Zuprium, and now Stoneset and a few other outlying villages even smaller than Ravenhelm were being crushed under the demand for more and more.

He just hoped this episode was short-lived, as he was due at the Fairchild's in half an hour for dinner, cigars, and—if Ezekiel followed through with his threat—a few rounds of cards.

Why had Harlan agreed to the charade, again? His friend clearly thought too much of him. How could he be expected to make nice with Ezekiel's wife and sister—a sister Harlan was supposed to believe was a good match for him—after so long with no one but dying men and Ezekiel himself for company?

Ridiculous. Especially since Harlan never planned on marrying, much to Aurelia's dismay.

He only felt moderately bad about it, and only because Aurelia Shackley was barren. She and Carleton had no children of their own.

It was up to Harlan to continue the line he wasn't a member of by blood, yet he had no urge to do so. Bringing children into such a world would be a disservice to them. They would only face a world rife with war, disease, and suffering.

He smoothed his hand over his mustache again. At tea with his mother that afternoon, she'd said the newest facial hair fashion only made him more handsome, that it was probably good he decided to wear it, that it would make him even more appealing to the marriageable ladies of high society.

He wasn't sure how he felt about her approval. It was nice, he guessed. But at thirty, did he really care what she thought? He should. She'd raised him in a loving home since he was twelve. Still, he'd almost shaved before leaving.

Another three turns, several bumps, and an intensifying headache later, Harlan arrived at his friend's modest residence. A façade, really. The Fairchild family was one of the oldest and wealthiest families in all of Jayde—even older than the Shackleys. Both families had estates out in the country, but Aurelia said the Shackleys had decided to make Kyvena their main residence. The Fairchilds had chosen to spend most of their time and money on a sprawling mansion outside of Crystalfell. Ezekiel had spoken highly of the extensive grounds of his childhood home—something about the perfect place to hunt.

However, Ezekiel's Kyvena home had been his inheritance from his father. While not as extravagant as the city manors, the townhome was sequestered in one of the more picturesque lanes in the upper city. Sitting on a winding lane dotted with benches and mature oak trees, the home had a serenity about it that immediately put Harlan at ease.

The carriage pulled to a soft stop courtesy of a highly trained mare. After a moment, a liveried footman appeared and opened the carriage door with a bow.

"Lieutenant Colonel Shackley, it is an honor."

Grabbing his top hat from the seat beside him, Harlan exited the carriage and followed a second footman up the front steps. They'd been crafted from the finest white stone—probably from out west in the Lenara canyon. Lacy filigree decorated the panes in the gas lanterns hanging from hooks on either side of a cheerful red door.

A butler greeted him with a short bow as he opened it after the footman's knock. "Welcome to Fairlight House, Lieutenant Colonel. Mister Plinth will take your hat and outer coat."

The footman held out his hand as Harlan gave him his effects. Childlike laughter echoed in the foyer, and the butler smiled and strode off toward the noise.

Harlan followed the man through an archway under the stairs, passing a painting of a sunset in the Nardens. He wanted to inspect it further, but the butler hadn't stopped, and Harlan didn't want to be rude.

A moment later, the butler gestured Harlan to the parlor. The room was smaller than the one at Shackley Manor, but tall portraits of breathtaking scenery along the nearest wall and floor-to-ceiling windows overlooking the rest of the city on the far side compensated for its size. Stylized gas lanterns hung from the ceiling in the place of a standard chandelier.

Two boys with dark curly hair ran amuck, chasing one another around the settee. A plump woman with hair like spun gold laughed as they ran by her place on said settee. The Lady Fairchild, Harlan guessed. Her pale blue eyes and rosy cheeks made her look as if she had a vivaciousness for life that Harlan lacked.

Ezekiel swirled a scotch glass in one hand and argued good-naturedly with a woman sitting in one of the green upholstered chairs. Facing away from the door, the woman in question threw up her hands in exasperation. "I'm perfectly capable of running the estate, and you know it."

Taking a drink, Ezekiel held his silence for a moment. He seemed to be buying time to come up with a response when he spotted Harlan standing in the doorway. He coughed and sputtered, the drink going down the wrong way, and set his glass aside.

The twin boys stopped their chase and looked up, as did their mother. Ezekiel's face broke into a smile. "So glad you've made it, my friend."

Striding forward, he shook Harlan's hand vigorously and pulled him in to clasp his shoulder. He looked striking in his own dinner tails, like a man born to wear them...unlike Harlan, who felt like an imposter. Ezekiel's grin never left his face as he said, "I'm impressed you didn't come in your uniform."

Harlan fought the urge to roll his eyes. "You invited me to dinner, not to battle."

The darkness in his friend's eyes was fleeting. "Of course, you might think differently by the end of the night." He let go of Harlan's shoulder and hand and turned. "Boys, please come and shake the gentleman's hand."

The two chaotic beings that were Ezekiel's twin sons fought each other for precedence, but after a waspish look from their mother as she rose from the settee, the taller one stepped forward, having won the honor.

Ezekiel beamed as the boy stuck out his hand. Harlan gave it a quick shake. The boy nodded. "Randall Fairchild, my lord."

He spoke it with such an air of elegance that Harlan nearly questioned whether or not he had imagined the children running feral only moments before. However, the other one took one look at Harlan's outstretched hand and crossed his arms instead. He harrumphed for good measure.

"Sullivan Ezra Fairchild!" his mother hissed.

Harlan tensed, unsure of what to expect. When he'd been that young, he'd regularly received a beating for any perceived mischievous behavior. Instead, Ezekiel put a hand on his son's raucous curls and mussed them. "I know you want to keep playing, but it's important that young men greet guests upon their entrance to a room. I expect you to be courteous to anyone who walks into this parlor no matter how you might feel about the situation." He squatted next to the boy. "Now, please introduce yourself properly to our guest."

The boy's nostrils flared, but with an elbow from his twin, he grabbed Harlan's hand and muttered. "Sullivan."

"Thank you," Ezekiel said as he rose. He held his sons with a firm gaze for a moment longer before smiling at someone else who'd just entered the room behind Harlan. "Now, you go on and get to bed, you wild sprogs."

Both groaned, but at a look from their father, they relented and filed out the door with someone Harlan assumed to be their nanny. Ezekiel turned back to him, grabbing his shoulder once more and leading him to the two women.

"Sorry about that. Manners are something we've yet to master, but I was even more of a terror when I was that age, if you can believe it."

"No matter," Harlan gave him a small smile. "I've been greeted with much worse."

The twinkle in his friend's eye told him he recalled one of the patients who'd spat in Harlan's face when he'd attempted to triage him after one particularly nasty skirmish a few months back.

The blond woman stood and held out her hand as Ezekiel said, "This is my wife, Lady Rose. Rose, this is Lieutenant Colonel Harlan Shackley."

Harlan gave the woman a soft peck on her hand and let it drop. "A pleasure, my lady."

Ezekiel gestured to the other woman in the chair, the

one he'd been arguing with upon their arrival. She had a book in her lap and hadn't bothered to look up at all during the previous commotion.

"And this is my sister, Lady Celeste—" He sighed. "Lessie, look, I know you're mad at me, but you don't have to pull out the book."

"I'm unsure of what you're referring to," the woman replied as she turned the page with an air of superiority only a queen could hope to achieve. "If you believe me so incapable of running the estate myself, then of course, I could not possibly possess the skills to host a dinner party, let alone greet a guest."

Ezekiel's charming demeanor melted at last. He retrieved his drink and took a measured sip before whispering harshly to his sister.

Rose hid a smile behind her hand as she nodded to the servant in the corner of the room. "May we offer you a drink, Master Shackley?"

Harlan cleared his throat. "Brandy will be fine."

"Of course," she said, gesturing to the highbacked wing chair beside her. "Please, do have a seat. I have been eager to meet you after hearing so much about you from Ezekiel."

Harlan took the round glass from the manservant with a small nod of thanks. He took a sip before responding, "I don't know if I would trust everything he says about me."

He hadn't meant it as a joke necessarily, but Rose's laugh rang like a bell. Some of the tension in his shoulders eased.

"My husband does like to embellish," she whispered conspiratorially before taking a sip of her martini. "To hear him talk, you'd think we'd invited the Rubikan Queen to dinner tonight."

"She would have appreciated the invitation, I'm sure." Harlan said dryly. From what he knew, the woman had recently come into power upon the death of her uncle, who had no children of his own. However, the dowager Queen-Consort had a few children from a previous marriage. Supposedly, the eldest son planned to wage a query in the courts over succession rights.

Whether or not Lady Rose was aware of the political climate, she laughed all the same. "Wouldn't that be a turn."

That reaction caught the attention of Ezekiel and the woman—Celeste, he'd put together, though she still had yet to be properly introduced—whose furious whispered argument hushed for a moment as they searched for the source of the interruption. Harlan met the woman's eyes, and the hand with his brandy glass paused on the way to his lips.

Her large eyes were the color of dusk. He thought they might've sparkled like the night sky had she been laughing, but at that moment, her glare could have swallowed the stars. Long, thin fingers played with the chain of a Zuprium locket hanging from her neck. Her face was framed by the same unruly dark curls as her brother, though hers were arranged in the latest fashion, pulled back from her face in a loose knot, a deep blue ribbon tied around it and fluttering to her shoulder. The style only accentuated her high cheekbones. Her rosy lips were pursed, but she'd finally closed the book, which sat on her lap. He couldn't see the title.

"So you're the famous Harlan Shackley," Celeste said. She didn't bother with his rank or even his title as a gentleman of the realm. She simply raised a dark eyebrow and turned away, cracking her book back open. "Absolutely not."

Harlan's face flushed, but whether it was embarrassment or the prelude to losing his temper, he didn't know. How could she dismiss him so quickly? He ran a hand over his mustache. Aurelia had been wrong. Though he was unsure why he even cared. Marriage to *anyone* wasn't in the plan, much less marriage to a shrew. He'd walked in here knowing his friend was playing matchmaker, but to be dismissed within seconds of meeting the woman in question? It was a little insulting.

"Pardon me?" Harlan rested the brandy on his knee.

Ezekiel ran a hand down his face before turning back to his sister. "It's my duty as your guardian to see you taken care of, yet you are bent on running off any potential suitor. Why?"

"I'm twenty-seven. I need no guardian."

"Father wished to see you settled."

"Father's wishes are no longer relevant, are they?" The woman's nostrils flared, but she turned her waspish glare back to Harlan once her brother turned away, draining his glass of alcohol, all illusions of propriety apparently dismissed. "Let me ask you, Harlan Shackley. Would you allow your unwed sister to manage the estate you do not have any plans on ever returning to? Seeing as she is both willing and capable and has requested to do so repeatedly over the past five years?

Harlan chewed on the inside of his cheek and swirled the contents of his glass. He glanced briefly at Ezekiel, but the other man pressed the pads of his thumb and forefinger into his eyes. Seemed his friend also had a headache, though from a different source.

It took a lot to work Ezekiel up, and while Harlan might sympathize, a part of him couldn't help being amused by Ezekiel's ire. It helped curtail his irritation over the woman's dismissal. Shrew she might be, but at least she had a mind of her own. She might eventually find a husband that would put up with her free thinking. She was certainly attractive enough.

He tapped a finger on the side of the glass. "That entirely depends on the situation at hand."

The woman narrowed her eyes at him. "A diplomatic answer to cover your belief that women are merely porcelain dolls to be kept on a shelf?"

"Lessie..." Ezekiel started. Rose took another sip of her own drink and smoothed her gown.

Lady Celeste held up a hand. "No, no. I'd like to know what our guest really thinks."

He wasn't sure if the shift from using his name to calling him their *guest* was an improvement or another insult. He suspected the latter. Her skill at turning a statement that should've been kind and hospitable into something acerbic was unmatched. Only half an hour spent in her company, and she'd proven herself a force to be reckoned with.

He took another moment to think through his response, sipping his brandy. The oak-and-cardamom taste washed over his tongue, calming his nerves and his headache. Though both still gnawed at him, the alcohol acted as a balm. "I meant just what I said—it depends. Whose perspective would you prefer to analyze?"

"I daresay yours, Master Shackley."

Ezekiel threw back the rest of his second drink. His wife took his empty glass before the servant could refill it once more.

Harlan tapped the side of his glass again to give himself time to think. "Groups of people are not monoliths, and to consider them so is an injustice."

"Monoliths they may not be, but society slots them into predetermined roles regardless." She set her book aside and clasped her hands upon her crossed knees.

"Expectations keep society afloat. Order is important for survival, but that doesn't mean women are only valuable tucked away on a shelf."

She raised an eyebrow at that. "Interesting point, Master Shackley. Care to expand on it?"

"Someone's worth is determined by what they do with the life they're given, not by how society labels them." He set his brandy on the side table with a soft *chink.* "However, you can also argue those labels hold some truth. A home needs running. It needs protecting—whether that be physically or financially—and the people best suited to performing those tasks should take them in hand. Whether those roles are fulfilled by the lady of the house, the lord, or even a butler ought to be decided between the parties involved, not an outsider looking in."

Ezekiel and his wife whispered in the corner; the younger Lady Fairchild's gaze sharpened, with surprise this time rather than hostility. "Your opinions don't align with those of your contemporaries, which I find odd for a man of your station."

"Men of my station, as you say, usually cling to their birthright and don't dare venture any ideas that lead away from it."

"And you do not cling to yours?"

He didn't answer, only picked up his glass once more and took a drink. The butler reappeared just when he needed him to. "Dinner is ready, my lord."

Ezekiel offered his elbow to his wife before looking at Harlan and his sister. "Shall we?"

He'd seemingly decided to ignore his sister's attitude. Harlan gave his glass to the servant and made to follow the couple.

"I will allow you to escort me to the dining hall," Celeste said breezily, rising from the chair with her book in hand.

Harlan raised his brows, but he held out his arm. He wasn't sure if it was a test or not, and he was unsure if he wanted to pass it.

With her book tucked under her arm, she slid her other

hand into the crook of his arm. For all her mighty temper, that hand looked dainty and porcelain-like against the black of his dinner jacket. "This means nothing other than the fact you have managed to intrigue me, Master Shackley."

Ezekiel looked back with a small smirk playing at his mouth. Lady Celeste didn't see it. Harlan wished he hadn't.

Harlan led Celeste into the dining hall. "And the book?"

"I said you intrigued me." She moved toward the seat pulled back by one of the servants. "Yet intrigue can wax and wane. You could very well prove to be a banal dining companion."

"Thus, the book?"

"Thus, the book."

He could not imagine he would prove such a poor dinner companion as to be bested by a book, but then, he had yet to catch the title.

Dinner was a fine affair. The courses were timely and the food of the highest quality. He would have sworn it was the best he'd ever tasted, though that might have been a year of military rations talking. The conversation stayed light and comforting as well. It seemed the siblings had agreed to disagree until after dinner.

They did bicker over a few childhood experiences both had different recollections of, and Lady Rose interjected to give her objective truth. Rose's family and the Fairchilds had neighboring estates outside of Crystalfell, the second largest city in Jayde.

Harlan didn't say much. He didn't need to. With each bout of laughter and lighthearted banter, the more his headache melted away. It was a nice feeling and one he hadn't felt in many years.

Dinners at Shackley Manor weren't unpleasant, but they lacked a sense of home, though Aurelia tried hard to make it so. The dinner table was never without Harlan's favorite dessert, chocolate mousse. A fire always burned inside the hearth in the winter, and every table boasted artfully arranged bouquets of wildflowers in the spring. But Aurelia could not fabricate what truly made a place home.

"Well then, Lieutenant Colonel, seeing as you have more advanced opinions than your peers...how do you feel about the University allowing women to apply? Do you see it as a stain on society like so many others?" Lady Celeste asked as they finished the main course of braised lamb and roasted, candied brussels sprouts.

Another test, it seemed. Harlan dabbed the corner of his mouth with his napkin and allowed the servant to take away his plate. He shrugged. "I don't really have an opinion."

"Another diplomatic answer." She smirked. "You should run for Stradat."

That got a smile from him. "I have no desire to run the country."

"But your father is in one of the highest positions in the city. Surely you'd want to follow in his footsteps?"

Harlan swirled his wine a little before taking a sip. "I only want Cerulene to leave us be, which is best accomplished where I am."

More or less. He hoped he made a little progress in the meeting Thursday morning.

Ezekiel nodded as the footmen brought the dessert course into the dining hall. "Harlan has a good head on his shoulders. Our unit is easily the best managed with him at the helm."

A man set a small bowl of decadent chocolate mousse in front of him. Ezekiel's doing, no doubt. Garnished with mazelberries and some sort of herb, it looked expensive, but all the same, it would taste delicious. "He flatters me. The men in our unit are the best we could ask for."

"So you would agree that women at the University is an atrocity?" she pressed, clearly unwilling to be coaxed from her course of questioning.

Harlan picked up his dessert spoon. "Because I praised my men? Or are you merely miffed I refused to give a polarizing answer the first time?"

Ezekiel and Rose hid smiles behind their hands as Lady Celeste bristled. "Well, if you'd given me *any* answer at all, I might have continued the conversation and argued the benefits, but alas, you chose to be political. So I can only assume you land with your peers and wouldn't allow women to attend the University if given the choice."

Harlan didn't look at her as he dipped the spoon in the dessert. "I said I didn't have an opinion, because I do not. My mother was an untrained herbalist, yet she was the best at what she did. Attending the University or not doesn't impact a woman's worth. I wouldn't call it a necessity, nor an atrocity."

When he looked up, Celeste's eyebrows had scrunched together. "I didn't realize Lady Shackley was an herbalist."

Harlan's spoon froze on the way to his mouth. He eyed Ezekiel across the table. His friend dabbed the corner of his mouth with his napkin and shook his head.

Very few people knew of Harlan's origins. Ezekiel was the only one outside the Shackley family who knew the details. He'd not passed them on, clearly, which Harlan was grateful for, so he only had himself to blame for the slip-up.

Harlan set the spoon down and took a longer draw of wine before picking the utensil back up. "The Commander and Lady Shackley adopted me after my parents passed."

Celeste's pretty mouth dropped slightly in a soft gasp. "Oh stars, I apologize. I didn't realize..."

Harlan took a small bite of the dessert at last. It was certainly as decadent as the delicacy could get—rich, smooth, and flavorful. The mazelberries were a nice touch. He swallowed and gave her a small, encouraging smile. "An honest mistake. Few people know, and I do favor the Commander somewhat, though it's only a funny coincidence. Most people who are aware I was adopted assume I am the product of some untoward affair."

Lady Celeste gave him a polite smile, her fiery tongue doused with the revelation. "I hadn't heard that rumor."

Ezekiel set aside his glass bowl and napkin, muttering, "Because you refuse to leave the country estate."

Harlan used the distraction to take another bite of dessert. It helped ease the tension that had started accumulating at the base of his skull.

"And you refuse to return to it," she shot back at her brother.

Rose finished off her dessert and gestured with her spoon to her sister-in-law. "I do think you'd enjoy the city, Les. There are several bookshops, and the theater is newly renovated. Our box is quite elegant, and they've booked some very talented troupes as of late."

"And the boys would dearly love to spend more time with their aunt." Ezekiel sat back in his chair, hands folded over his middle.

It was nice seeing him so relaxed. He and Harlan rarely had the opportunity to simply *be*. His friend deserved to be at home with his family—not out fighting a shadow war that seemingly would never end.

Les brightened at the mention of her nephews. "I do love doting on them."

Rose let out a soft snort. "Though Sullivan does not need any more chocolates from the confectionary."

"It's a shame he couldn't enjoy this mousse with us tonight," Lady Celeste said, taking a heaping spoonful. "We do both love chocolate."

Ezekiel and Rose laughed before Ezekiel said, "I asked Reg to make it special. It's Harlan's favorite."

Lady Celeste looked across the table at him. "Truly?"

Harlan dabbed the corner of his mouth with his cloth napkin. "It is, though I only ever eat it when I'm home on leave."

She allowed herself a small smile, the first directed at him. His heart thumped a bit off-kilter. She said, "Then I must insist that you try the one at the Dantes on Haviland Lane. It is a heavenly experience."

Maybe it was the alcohol, or maybe the fact that he felt more at home than he had in ages, but he gave her a small smile back.

Ezekiel finished off his dessert, seemingly unaware of his friend and sister striking a silent truce. "She's right, though I would recommend their mazelberry rum sundae. It's exquisite enough to make a grown man weep." He mimed brushing a tear. "I'm feeling emotional just thinking about it."

His sister tore her eyes away from Harlan's and burst into laughter. "Or maybe you're a sad drinker."

"I'd say you need coffee instead of scotch when we retire to the parlor, dear." Lady Rose said, setting aside her spoon and gesturing for the footmen to clear the table.

The siblings laughed together as Harlan finished his dessert. Ezekiel then invited everyone back to the parlor where they could enjoy said coffees, heeding his wife's advice.

It was customary for the men to enjoy a cigar away from the ladies after dinner, but Harlan found he liked the break in tradition.

The conversation stayed light and didn't devolve into arguments, though Lady Celeste and Ezekiel continued to pick at each other good-naturedly. The camaraderie between the two siblings was entertaining, but it wasn't entirely easy to watch. Even if Michael had lived, Harlan didn't believe they would have been so close. Neither Ezekiel nor Lady Celeste had been forced to deal with the same hardships as Harlan.

After a few minutes, his headache crept back in, a throbbing that even the coffee and conversation couldn't dim. He quietly excused himself to the lavatory, leaving his drink on the settee and exiting the room.

A servant closed the door quietly behind him. But instead of finding the lavatory, he leaned against the wall, his head resting against it, his eyes closed.

The pain radiated from the front of his skull to the back, then to the front again. He pinched the bridge of his nose, but it only offered fleeting relief.

He should see a medic about the headaches while he was in the capital. They had access to medicines and knowledge he didn't have at the front. Headaches were simple compared to lodged shrapnel and amputation, after all—why waste resources on something inconsequential?

He pushed himself off the wall and wandered down the hallway a little. Standing still was only making his headache worse, though moving around might not help either. The reprieve for an hour or so had been nice, but fleeting.

He found himself back at the painting of the Nardens he'd glimpsed earlier. He'd spent his first twelve years nestled in the peaks in a one-room cottage with a dirt floor and spent nearly twenty years trying to escape them, only to return to defend them. They were a part of his blood and his bones, no matter what his surname might be.

"My brother says that painting doesn't reveal the majesty of the mountains," a soft voice said from his right.

He glanced aside to find Lady Celeste walking toward him, her deep blue evening gown swishing with her steps. She was tall for a woman; when she halted beside him, the top of her head was level with his chin. She nodded to the landscape. "I'd love to see them up close one day. We can only see their shadows from the estate."

Harlan smoothed his mustache, debating what to say. Despite her prickles, he didn't wish to upset her with his biased opinions of the mountains. He settled on something innocuous. "The sunrise crawling over the peaks in the morning can be breathtaking."

She nodded, as if she knew exactly what he meant; then her eyes narrowed. "I was under the impression you spent most of your time on the eastern side of the range. The sunrise wouldn't be over the peak."

"You have knowledge of troop movements?" Harlan asked, neatly dodging the question hidden there.

She shook her head. "Not directly. I read a lot." She held up her book. "That includes newspaper articles. They don't say much, but the news we do get is rather vague and useless—unless you can read between the lines like me." She glanced back toward the parlor. "Rose and I are both eager for Ezekiel to finish his term and return home. These aren't a few isolated incidents, am I correct?"

Harlan opened his mouth, but nothing came out of it. She'd proven herself astute already, but to deduce such information through research and watered-down news articles, with no firsthand experience being on the front lines?

And *reading between the lines*...what did that mean? He needed to look more closely at the news he'd scorned. If someone was leaking information, perhaps with some kind of code or otherwise...

He'd think on it later. For now, he turned back to the landscape. "Ezekiel has been a great asset to the medical corps, and it will be a dark day when he's discharged." He paused and tried to subtly rub at his aching temple. "He's a light in the midst of a brewing storm."

Hesitantly, she laid a hand on his upper arm. A very personal touch for someone so adamantly against him in the beginning. They were also alone without a chaperone. She seemed to realize as much after a moment and pulled back her gloved hand. "Thank you. Perhaps you're not as hopeless as you look."

Then she went back to the parlor, leaving Harlan a little confused, a little insulted...and more than a little intrigued. He didn't know what the future held, but maybe it wasn't as dark as he'd assumed.

Clara

FOR TWO DAYS, PRAYER HAD been Clara's constant companion. She'd prayed for peace, for strength, and for her heart to keep beating.

Everything hurt. Her feet, her back, her shoulders, her very soul. Samuel's hunger was constant. Even with Zelda's help, she barely slept at night. Her dreams were full of screams and fire and a dark hole she would never be able to climb out of.

Most of the last two nights had been closing her eyes and hoping her pitiful pleas for peace would be enough.

She just needed to be *enough*.

It was the missive clutched in her hand that had finally given her a surge of strength. It wasn't until she'd read the words on the parchment—the ink dark like night itself had formed into words and summoned her—that she had begun to believe everything would be okay.

Her father-in-law was alive. His sins were reprehensible, but he'd been spared like her. Who was she to say he wasn't deserving of a second chance if she was? She tucked Samuel closer to her chest. Harlan would know where to find Jove, Les…maybe even her mother.

She prayed harder.

Masses of people fought to get to the tent, and overworked, bedraggled soldiers pushed them back. The discordant, echoing shouts woke Samuel. Clara smoothed his hair and kissed it, but he didn't calm at all. Some people shouted vile things at the tent. A man with crazed eyes threw mud. A soldier arrested the latter. Her own escorts formed a tighter ring around her.

"Enter the tent, Lady Shackley. Hurry," one said gruffly, all but pushing her through the flap.

The canvas walls did little to block out the sounds from outside, but at least it was calmer inside. A few mismatched chairs sat in the middle, a small cot pushed to the other side. Two men stood conversing near the chairs. The Yalven man was tall and willowy with raven-black hair done in a braid. The other was the Stradat Lord Kapitan, his cheeks slightly sunken.

He'd lost weight since Clara had last seen him—which, other than the flash portraits in the paper, had been nearly a week ago. The last true interaction she'd had with him was before Samuel's birth. Jove had told her that he'd visited the night Kase ran away and had met Samuel while she was asleep, but that was it.

He'd aged nearly ten years in a week.

She wanted to hate him. She wanted to spit in his face and walk right back out, but she couldn't. Not until she knew where her husband was. Not until she knew why he'd been spared.

"Lady Clara Shackley," one of her soldier escorts announced.

Harlan stopped speaking with the Yalven man; he turned his haunted eyes on her immediately, an unexpected warmth rippling across them when he spotted Samuel in her arms. That flicker of life went out as quickly as it had come upon him, however. He bowed stiffly and gestured for her to take one of the chairs. "I am relieved to find you well and whole."

The Stradat Lord Kapitan had never been outright rude or cruel to her, but the sentiment still took her off guard. She gave him a small smile. "I am grateful as well."

She had a thousand questions, but she didn't want to push him. Taking a seat, she adjusted Samuel in her arms, shushing him softly. He clasped one of his hands around her finger and squeezed. Soon, he breathed easily.

The sound outside the tent never changed.

Harlan took one of the other seats, and the Yalven man followed. Harlan gestured to the other man. "This is Lord Saldr of Myrrai, the Yalven emissary who returned with Kase and Miss Walker a few months ago." He crossed his arms, holding them close to his chest. "Lady Clara is Jove's wife, and this is their son, Samuel."

Clara nodded. "Good to meet you, Lord Saldr."

He bowed his head, suddenly appearing nervous, though Clara wasn't certain as to why.

She took a second to breathe before asking, "Have you seen Jove? Or Lady Les? My own searches have proved fruitless."

Harlan smoothed his mustache, looking at his scuffed and muddy boots. The silence was quickly filled with Clara's pounding heartbeat. With each second that passed without an answer, the sound thundered in her ears.

It drowned out the people's shouts just outside, railing against the man who sat before her.

Give me strength.

"Jove survived the attack on the city, but upon arriving at the Catacombs, we believe he fell into one of the chasms that have begun opening up." Harlan's words were stiff like a forgotten paintbrush. "We have not found Lady Les. I fear she may have...perished before she could reach the tunnels."

Strength.

Clara's chest collapsed in on itself as the burning tears in her eyes slipped down her face and sprinkled her baby's blanket.

It was the other man, Lord Saldr, who spoke next. "Lord Jove fought bravely in the fight for the city, and we hope to search for him soon as we are able. My people and any spare soldiers are trying to find a way down into the depths of Yalvara to search, but it may be best to prepare your heart for the worst. I am sorry, Lady Shackley."

Clara could barely comprehend the words coming from the man's mouth. All she could think was of her husband and the pain he was probably in, if he was even alive to feel it. She was here, safe, and he was either suffering or...or...

She took several shaky breaths, trying to calm the storm raging within her. "So all is not lost? There is some hope he may have survived?"

Harlan cleared his throat and smoothed his mustache again. "We believe so, but without electricity, we must find the right equipment and personnel to search, which isn't a priority at the moment because of the crisis on our hands." He leaned forward and ran a hand through his hair, mussing it in a way Clara had never seen. "As for Les, we have not been able to interview enough survivors who may know her fate. Our reconnaissance to the Manor only showed Thoreau and Zuri did not survive the initial attack." Clara gasped; he paused after naming the butler and the maid, allowing her a moment to recompose herself before he added, "But we found no evidence to suggest Les had also been killed. She may have been kidnapped, particularly if the Cerls were aware of who she was, but we must not rush to conclusions just yet, not until all avenues have been trod."

Clara closed her eyes against the tears that continued to fall. If she hadn't been at the gates, if she had waited or had been on her way, she might have suffered the same fate.

"It is a great relief to have found you, Clara," Harlan said, gruffly. "And once we are able to assess our current situation, I will do everything in my power to find them both. Until then, I will assign a rotation of guards to secure your location and person. You may go about as you have done, working in the ward and helping out where needed, but please do not put yourself into harm's way."

She wiped away her tears and sniffed. "And my mother? I've been told she was outside the city when the gates were closed."

"I have a lead, and I will bring her to you if we do indeed find her." Harlan rose from his chair and offered his hand. "I apologize for how little information I have to give you, but I would not lie to you, for that would be a much greater disservice."

She stared at his offered hand, uncertain, before taking it and rising as well. "Thank you."

He let go of her hand and cupped the back of Samuel's head. "Stay safe."

And then he turned away.

Clara left after that, her guards escorting her through the masses once more. She was numb from the information he'd heaped upon her, and she didn't know what the next day held, but her father-in-law's behavior distracted her from those worries.

He'd been indifferent in the past, but this was almost kind—especially in the face of such terrible news.

Everything happened for a reason, and while she hated that it had taken the destruction of the capital to wake Harlan Shackley up, she was grateful *something* had. If it truly had.

If that was the case, she prayed it worked—for his sake, for Samuel's, and for Jove's.

C H A P T E R   1 3

IN DIFFERENT WAYS

Kase

AFTER ANOTHER DAY OF FLYING until Kase physically couldn't continue, they stopped for the night and made camp, after which Kase fell asleep the second his head touched his pack. He dreamed of the towns he'd bypassed for fear that the Cerls had overtaken them, too; dreams of bodies strewn in the streets and of buildings decimated by bombs. He relived his dogfight at Nar, except this time he was the one who went up in flames.

The dawn rays burned his lids, and the acrid smell of smoking meat wafted past his nose. Kase jolted awake, wiping dried spittle from his chin with a grimace and clawing around for his electropistol.

"Whoa, there. We're fine, son," came Stowe's voice from a few paces away.

Kase stopped rummaging through his pack and looked up to find Hallie's father roasting some sort of fish on a spit.

The fire was small, and with the early sunlight, the smoke wouldn't be as noticeable. His breathing slowed.

He pushed himself up and dusted off his trousers. They'd accumulated a collection of dry grass and leaves in the night. "Didn't know there were fish nearby. I'm starving."

And he was. Whatever energy he'd gained via the hardtack he'd consumed the day before had dried up with his night of fitful sleep.

Stowe tested the fish with his fingertips. "There's a small creek in the woods right through there, not too far. Kept you in sight while I set up a line." He removed the fish from the fire and inspected the meat once more. After a second or two, he nodded and handed the spit over to Kase. "Yep, should be roasted right good."

"Thanks."

Stowe took a swig from his canteen. "No good spices on hand, course, but it'll hold you over. Filled up your water, too. I'm looking forward to a good meal once we make it to the capital. Heard stories about the fine cuisine."

Kase bit into the roasted fish, which was really a whole bunch of juicy, slightly charred nothing. He didn't have the heart to say how much he hated fish. He didn't think it was the taste, necessarily, but rather the smell...and the fact that while Stowe had removed the fins and the skin, the dead thing still had eyeballs looking at him. Clearly Hallie had inherited her lack of cooking skills from her father.

He choked it down regardless and prayed he didn't chuck it up later. Stowe might take his criticism just as well as his daughter had.

"You must be dead on your feet," Kase said after swallowing another disgusting mouthful. His lack of grimace at that one could've earned him a place in the theater. "I would've taken over watch."

Stowe rubbed his bald head, the morning sunlight glinting off the sun-reddened skin there. "I'll get some shut-eye soon as we're in that flying contraption. I ain't seen no one fall over dead asleep as fast as you did last night."

A small blush warmed the back of Kase's neck. He coughed through another unsavory bite of fish. "Where'd you get the fishing line?"

Stowe looked back toward the hover. "Say what you want about those Trip soldiers, but they know how to prepare for a journey or two. Found one of them pistols, too. Thing feels evil, though. Left that in the compartment."

Kase finished off the fish and set the spit and remains aside. It felt like an accomplishment. "The ship is different than what I usually fly. Seems almost like it's…"

Alive.

Stowe looked toward the craft. "Don't like the sound of it much, but that might be me being an old curmudgeon of a mountain man." He glanced back at Kase with a small smile on his face. "You're a pretty decent pilot, though. If I were to fly with anyone else, don't think I'd make it very far without leaping off fast as I was able."

Kase couldn't help the snort that came from him. "Thanks."

Too bad his own father didn't share that sentiment. Hallie was blasted lucky.

Kase rubbed his tongue over his teeth, looking for any stray fish meat stuck there. "I'm more worried about why flying is wiping me out so badly. I don't think it's just adrenaline wearing off or anything. And it flies much smoother and faster than our hovers."

Stowe fished out his caffeine concoction and mixed up a shot for Kase. "Narden legend says the Trips gave themselves over to the black gods of their home planet. Dunno if I believe in the occult or gods, but nothing good ever comes out Cerulene. Even living on the border of all three realms, I've never met a Rubikan or Jaydian trader who wants to do business with them, but the Cerls pay well for any sort of Zuprium."

Kase knocked back the shot and grimaced as the lukewarm mixture went down his throat.

Stowe stood. "They tell some awful tales of what happens when any Cerl upsets King Filip." He spat to the side and stood. "And then there's those rogue Trip bands looking to stir up trouble in the mountains. That's what we thought the attack was last winter—but it was that Correa. He and his soldiers massacred the villagers. Didn't use no bombs or the like, just went in and used them pistols and swords. Took us months of cleaning up. Only could do it at night." He went silent, looking over toward the rising sun's pink rays peeking over the horizon. They painted the bottom of the cotton-like clouds like blood.

Kase didn't say anything. The destruction of Nar and the thought of what awaited them in Kyvena was enough to still his tongue.

Stowe rubbed his head again and looked back at Kase, his eyes a little misty. "Zelda and I were visiting...well, visiting the Burning site when it happened. We do that from time to time, because it's..."

Kase's chest squeezed. He understood what he was trying to say. Kase would sometimes rub the frame of Ana's portrait in the corridor of Shackley Manor.

"If you hadn't been, Hallie would've lost you both," Kase said.

Stowe gave a wry chuckle. "She's not been the same since Jack. None of us have."

Kase's fingers caught in the even messier strands of his curls as he ran a hand through. He really needed to clean up soon. "I've lost a brother and a sister in the last few years—my brother only a few months back." He was glad his voice didn't choke. He shoved his hands into his pockets, but he didn't break eye contact with Stowe. He didn't want to betray Hallie's trust. "It took Hallie knocking some sense into me, but before I met her, I was a mess."

Stowe didn't say anything, and Kase reached out and hesitantly put his hand on Stowe's shoulder as a sign of comfort. "We all deal with grief in different ways, but Hallie taught me that running away isn't the answer. I think she'd want you to know that."

Stowe looked thoughtful for a moment—then, without warning, he turned to Kase and pulled him into a hug.

At first, Kase stiffened. He barely knew this man, and he was a bear compared to Kase's thinner frame. But after a second, Kase relaxed and hugged him back, blinking mist out of his eyes. It was odd to be hugged by a father. He wasn't certain Harlan even knew the word.

After another moment, Stowe pulled back, wiping his own eyes. "You'll take good care of her, son."

Kase's smile was the first genuine one he'd had since leaving Hallie behind. He held out his hand for the other man to shake. "Only if she'll let me."

Stowe took his offered hand and chuckled. "Gets that from her mama."

Hallie

NIELS HAD KISSED HER.

Cold. Hallie's entire body felt cold. The power was still there, but it had turned to the darkest of ice. She couldn't tug it loose; she couldn't push it to her fingers.

She couldn't ask what was happening to it, because the only people who might know were a mile or two away, near the place Ebba died. Returning there would only weaken her hold on reality even further. Besides, going back to finding Fely and Filip would have required passing Niels again.

At least his leg was better off.

She didn't know how she'd done it. She'd clutched her power tether as hard as she possibly could and pushed the rest into Niels.

It hadn't been easy. She'd nearly lost hold twice. And she'd drained herself even further.

She should be dead.

But somehow she wasn't.

And something in the back of her mind told her it was only because she'd been here in the palace, surrounded by Zuprium, that she'd been able to heal him.

If she truly had healed him. It was possible this one would fail just as the first had. Was he going to be forced to relive his pain every few hours until Hallie could no longer fix him? Would Saldr know what to do if they ever got back to Kyvena?

She'd much rather think of a plan to help him than...than that kiss.

Her boots tapped along the corridor in time with her heart. It drowned out the silence and the memories of the last time she walked across these floors, of Kase and Zeke. Of Saldr. Of the multitude of Yalvs whose footsteps no longer echoed with hers.

She didn't know how far she'd walked or even where she was going, but somehow she'd ended up in front of the quarters she, Kase, and Zeke had shared. It was like her subconscious mind knew she needed to see something familiar.

She entered the room. Her eyes adjusted to the dark enough even though the early beams of moonlight shining through the window weren't terribly bright. A part of her registered that the silence she'd ignored on the way here should have been eerie, that most of the people who roamed these corridors were dead. Only a small remnant had made it to Kyvena. The Lord Elder was gone, his power given to Hallie in a dank dungeon room that lay beneath rubble.

She fell onto the sofa where she and Kase had spent one of their nights in the palace reading books. Those were scattered across the shelves, a few upon the floor.

All she could do was stare at them and wish it were months ago. She'd lived an eternity in the interim, and everything was only going to get worse.

And yet, here she was, bringing a shaking hand to her cold lips.

Niels had *kissed* her.

Dread filled her stomach.

But not for the reason she would've thought. She'd felt...nothing. No spark. No forgotten desire. There had been a small part of her worried that she might feel something more. They had a past, after all. Once upon a time, they'd wanted to marry. But if the last few months felt like a lifetime, then that time in Hallie's life had been eons ago.

She'd grown up. She'd realized her worth, her passion. And now she knew for certain that Niels could only offer something adequate, not something extraordinary. If she went back to him, she would be settling.

The relief was mixed with sadness.

She would have to break his heart. Again.

It was odd. She didn't know what she had expected. She'd spent years running from her feelings, hiding behind the walls of the University and her studies to avoid thinking about the things she'd left unsaid, about the perfectly good life she'd left behind.

But the longer she'd been away, she'd realized that that life was no longer what she wanted. There was so much more she could do in the world. Hallie no longer wanted the safe life, the one where she knew what lay around the next bend.

She wielded an Essence power, and that dictated unpredictability. While Kase was nowhere near perfect, he was the rock that held her steady. He might be rough around the edges, but that was what she needed.

Pulling his pilot goggles from her pocket, she ran her thumb over the frames, her lips tugging into a sad smile.

Hallie didn't believe in soulmates. The impossibility of it was too much, and life was too disorganized for something like that. Choosing someone every day, no matter their flaws—that was true love.

Even so, with Kase, it almost felt like fate. She rubbed her thumb across the goggle lens again. If she could only see him once more, she'd tell him she loved him, tell him that she would always love him, and maybe...just maybe, she did believe in soulmates, even if her logical side said it was improbable. With Kase, everything just felt right.

But how could she explain that to Niels in a way that didn't shatter him? He'd lost his entire family and had come on this adventure to keep a promise to her father.

Then again, it was clear now he'd also made that choice for his own reasons.

She couldn't help resenting him a little for the timing, of all things. She had the world on her shoulders, and now she had to figure out how to let him down gently—especially after she'd just run away from him again. At least she hadn't run halfway across the country this time.

No, he was an adult. He knew she and Kase were together now. This was his own fault. She hadn't given him any indication that she would've been receptive to a kiss...had she?

She rubbed her eyes. This is why she'd avoided any entanglements after entering the University. They only distracted her from the real task at hand.

Her power. She needed to focus on that. She could figure out Niels later.

Stepping up to the bookshelf, she picked up some of the scattered tomes, straightening them and setting them to rights, She ran her fingers across the spines. They were cold, but the embossed words welcomed her touch. In her mind, she could hear Kase's voice as he read from the only one written in Common—the biography of a dragonar tamer. She pulled that book from the shelf and sat on the sofa. It was a soft comfort in such a place.

One thing that would never change about her: she never could resist a book. Simply holding it calmed her anxious spirit. What she wouldn't give to be back in that time, Kase beside her.

Would she make the same choices if given the chance to relive those days? Would she still end up back here, alone?

Would she still choose to take on this power, knowing what it would cost her?

If she could control time, she was indeed the most powerful Essence of them all. Correa would never let her go, and she could understand why. But what did her power have to do with Jagamot? And what did it have to do with the legend of the two swords?

Navara was supposed to take the power from the Lord Elder. She'd been chosen to do so, but she'd run from her responsibility. She'd fallen in love and married on the complete other side of the world...and then her son had gotten the Fogs.

Maybe there were more answers in the journal, and she just hadn't found them yet. It seemed the least Navara owed her.

Setting aside the dragonar book, Hallie pulled out the last journal and opened to the page where she'd pressed her bloodied hand to find it...empty.

Empty.

No blood. No ink.

"What in the blazes..." she whispered under her breath. She nearly ripped the page trying to turn it. The next was full of her great grandmother's muddled Yalven.

The back of her head ached. She was missing something. Words didn't just get up and walk away.

Unless something had *un*written them.

Hallie flipped through the journal quickly. Nothing she could translate on the spot said anything about using Essence power. But Navara was Yalven. Saldr wasn't an Essence, yet he could do certain things with that dust, the Vasa. He could pop in and out of existence, transporting himself when needed. It was like he bent time in those moments, not that Hallie quite understood the science or magic behind that. Maybe Navara could do something similar? Maybe she could manipulate...

Wait.

Hallie walked over to the window with Firstmoon's light starting to poke through. If she held the book at an angle...

A soft sparkling poured across the pages, revealed by the light.

Zuprium. It had to be. Navara had lived in a mining village. The dust would've been everywhere.

And the Yalvs used the metal to heal, fight, and more.

Navara had mixed Zuprium dust with the ink to write her journals, or at least part of them. A smile played across Hallie's lips. She could use this.

She unwrapped her hand, gritting her teeth against the pain of ripping the bandage off, some of the scab coming off with it. She pressed her fingers around the reopened cut and coaxed blood to the surface.

Once she had enough blood pooling in the creases of her palm, she turned to the next page and pressed her hand to it.

Within seconds, the chamber in Myrrai disappeared, replaced by impenetrable darkness. It was silent for a beat before the previous voices returned.

Quiet sobs rang through the void. "I can't. I can't do it. If only there is another way to...there has to be...I need Raern to fix him." The woman's voice.

The male one responded, "You left your people, and you did everything you could for Jack. Adrienne will need you to help with the birth. Jack said they're going to name him Stowe if he's a boy, and Ara after you if she's a girl."

"The Passage has to open again."

"There is no cure for the Fogs. I've accepted it, and Jack has too."

The ground shook, rocketing Hallie back to reality. The newly replaced books clamored, bumped, and fell off the shelves. Her bones rattled. She slammed the diary shut and stuffed it back into her satchel. Out the window, black smoke rose from the lower part of the city.

Another earthquake. This one was probably aftershock, but it felt just as powerful as the previous. It reminded her of when she'd been in the forest with Kase and they'd stumbled across a dragon.

But it was the smoke that gave her pause. She squinted. It wasn't really moving like smoke. It floated in the air lazily, but it didn't dissipate. It reached a certain height and then just...floated, the wind making it wave like tree branches.

Something was very wrong.

Stuffing the book in her pack as well, she left the chamber. She'd come to Myrrai to find answers, and while not ideal, her answers were now going to come in the form of a sword and the King of Cerulene.

C H A P T E R   1 4

GONE

Kase

NOW THAT KASE AND STOWE were out of the foothills, the landscape stayed flat, full of fields and farms being prepared for late spring planting. Every so often, they'd pass someone along the road, either walking or riding a horse—but with the stolen hover's speed, Kase couldn't tell if they were Jaydian or not. He could only hope the Cerls had left the country folk alone. The absence of motorcoaches was odd, but then again, he'd grown up in the capital, where people could afford to pay for the Yalvar fuel to run them. The main methods of travel outside the larger cities were livestock and carriages.

They'd only passed one carriage-for-hire. Kase didn't know whether to take that as a good or bad sign. On the one hand, it could mean that Nar's fall was an anomaly. On the other, maybe it was the only carriage that had survived some attack.

By the time Kase had worked through those thoughts,

the carriage was already a mile back. He shrugged off the unease and pulled the Cerl blanket into his lap. He'd given up on trying to fly without it; the thing seemed to be infused with something to help with the chill that seized him every time he flew. It wasn't simply that he stopped shivering when he put the blanket over his knees; it warmed him to his very soul.

A rather odd sensation—a feeling he could only compare to when Hallie kissed him in that dungeon. Full of sadness and hope and fire. He could almost feel her lips on his now, feel the burning deep within him and the passion that had simmered beneath the surface.

What was she doing now? Was she missing him as much as he missed her? Was she eating enough? Was she cold? Hot? Hurt? Sick? Would he ever see her again?

Would she still want him after spending so much time with Niels?

Blasting terrible that Kase liked the man. He thrummed his fingers on the steering control and peeked at Stowe. He wasn't asleep, only gazing out at the flashing fields. Clearly, Hallie's bubbly personality had *not* come from her father.

Kase cleared his throat. "So, Niels. He's a good guy?"

Something on the dash flashed weakly. Irritation flared, and he pressed it quickly. It flashed brighter in response. Nothing else happened.

Blasted contraption.

Stowe readjusted his sitting position. The leather creaked in response. "Known him since he was born. Good family. Should've made the Cerls pay more for what they done to 'em."

Kase gripped the steering control harder. The same light blinked again, faster. Kase opened his mouth, but movement on the horizon stole any words he might've said. Another traveler on the road; he could only tell because they'd been flying low in case he passed out again. Better to crash low than crash high.

So far, they'd been ignored by everyone they'd passed. So when the passerby turned and aimed a pistol at the hover, Kase had to wrench the steering control to try and get out of its range.

The hover veered sharply left, avoiding the man. The blanket fell off Kase's lap.

Something smacked against the hover's hull as Kase yanked it around, ready to fire on the assailant—only to find that he recognized the man holding the flashpistol.

It was the stupid blond who'd danced with Hallie at Laurent. Cornhead. His hair was white in the midday sun.

Sure, it was a Cerl hover, but what made the stars-idiot think a flashpistol would do anything besides irritate the pilot?

Maybe the name Cornhead was too generous.

As if in response to his thoughts, something on the hover dash beeped loudly and sprayed Kase with some sort of blue fluid. Kase slammed the hover brakes and sputtered through the thin liquid dripping off his eyelashes and nose.

Did—what—what just happened?

He quickly wiped his face and found Cornhead pointing the pistol back at the hover. He landed in a hurry and waved his arms at the man. "Wait!"

Not sure what Cornhead had expected, but that was not it. He let the pistol fall to his side. Kase released the windshield and stood, hands raised in the air. "You're from Laurent, aren't you?"

Of course, he already knew the answer, but he figured that was the best way to begin. No Cerl would've known about Laurent, being as small as it was.

When Cornhead didn't reload the pistol and fire, Kase took a fuller breath and climbed over the side of the cockpit.

Cornhead's hand twitched, and Kase threw himself down just before the pistol went off. His chin pounded the dirt, and his jaw ached; one moment later, and the bullet would've been in his head. He felt around his teeth with his tongue. None missing or knocked out of place.

He peeked up, spitting blood. He'd definitely bitten his tongue, but nothing seemed to be gushing. "Stop! I'm a Jaydian hover pilot, you—"

He stopped himself. Insulting the stars-idiot holding a pistol would not be his best plan.

"Stole this from Nar," he gritted out instead. "We've met, if you remember."

Shocks, his jaw hurt like the blazes.

Cornhead held the flashpistol loosely at his side and didn't raise it again. Kase took that as a good sign and pushed himself to his feet.

Cornhead narrowed his eyes. "You talk like one of them capital people."

Interesting—a mountain dialect. Maybe that was why Hallie had danced with him. Kase resisted the urge to fire an electrobolt at him just for the wave of jealousy the memory brought on.

"My name's Kase Shackley, and yes, I'm from Kyvena. My friend and I are on our way there." Kase looked back at Stowe, who hadn't left the hover cockpit—instead, he watched with a hesitant expression on his face, ready to duck. *Helpful.* Kase continued, "The Cerls are coming this way, and we need to warn the capital."

Cornhead paled. "More are coming?"

"More?"

Cornhead nodded. "Been flying over a few times a day for a week now. Never more than one or two at once, and when I saw your hover, I just got plumb tired of it."

The breath froze in Kase's chest.

Kase whipped his head back at Stowe. "We need to go." He turned back to Cornhead. "They've already taken Nar, and even if they don't use their hovers, most of you don't stand a chance. I'd stock up on supplies and electropistols if you can. Any hover pilots nearby should be able to fight, and—"

Cornhead shook his head. "That's the thing. The electricity ain't working. Hasn't been for days now."

Kase didn't wait for further explanation. He merely turned, scrambled up the hover's wing, and leapt into the cockpit.

"Let's fly."

AT THAT POINT, KASE DIDN'T care how cold or dizzy he felt. He didn't question the use of the blanket at all as he wrapped it around his shoulders and pushed the hover to its full capacity. The craft didn't question Kase's need to fly faster, it only obeyed.

It was almost like it *was* Kase, in a weird way.

Of course, he fully realized that idea was absolutely stars-ridiculous. Except the hover really did seem to know what he wanted; the more desperately Kase wanted to get to the capital, the faster the hover flew. The more Kase envisioned the city drowning in flames and enemy hoverships, the more he pushed the craft, and it responded in kind. The lights flared brighter and brighter until Kase was sure they'd blind him, but he didn't stop.

He *couldn't* stop.

Stowe hadn't said anything since Cornhead's revelation about the electricity. He understood the need to get to the capital quickly. His wife had supposedly been making her way to Kyvena for weeks, but whether by foot or by carriage, it was hard to say if she'd gotten there in time. Stowe kept a wary eye out for her, but he didn't stop Kase's mad dash. The Cerls had been planning this for a while, and while Kase wasn't sure exactly how they'd done it, he simply knew they had, and his father wouldn't have been expecting it.

Had they had help? A Yalv? Was Saldr's willingness to go with him and Hallie to Jayde after the mission simply the desire to make things right? Or was there a more sinister reason?

The threat of what Eravin might have done when Kase rejected his offer also haunted him. What if One World was working with the Cerls? If Eravin had spread that Kase was the one who'd started the fire over three years ago, what would be waiting for him in the city? Would the High Council be able to control the fallout? Was everything that happened Kase's fault? Had Kase destroyed the capital for a second time?

After the assassination of Forrest Richter and his household, knowing the Stradat Lord Kapitan had used his status and family name to keep his son from facing the consequences of his actions would only detonate the powder keg ready to spark.

What a mess. And that was an understatement.

Kase tried hard to think back to his time with Correa. The Cerl Commander was an Essence-wielder, as was King Filip...and Hallie. There were others. Skibs. Was there another they hadn't accounted for? Kase wished he could remember more, but the strain from flying with little to no rest was catching up with him.

He tipped back another one of Stowe's caffeine concoctions. Some splashed on his cheek. He handed back the vial and wiped the offending droplet away with the sleeve of his jacket.

"Should be there soon," Kase croaked. His throat was raw. He couldn't pinpoint why, exactly, as it'd only been a few hours since they'd left Cornhead outside Laurent.

Stowe didn't answer. He was probably just as nauseated as Kase waiting for the capital city to appear on the horizon.

Kase's mother, brother, and pregnant sister-in-law were still in the city. Their faces burned bright in his mind, and the hover surged again. He hoped Clara hadn't had the baby yet. He hoped his mother was safe.

He didn't care about Harlan.

Kyvena's main defense was their superior air force and electropistols. That was half the reason why Ezekiel Fairchild's betrayal had been so devastating. On one hand, his uncle had given the Cerls a weapon; on the other, his mother still locked herself in her library every year on the anniversary of his death.

As the hero who led Jayde to victory in the war, Harlan had been the one to order the execution of his brother-in-law and Ezekiel's two sons...barely men, but just as guilty, according to the death declarations. They'd been twenty-two at the time.

Kase's fingers gripped the steering control harder, and the engine revved in response. If the Cerls had any advantage now, it was likely because of his uncle.

Was Ezekiel the reason the Cerl hover felt more like an extension of Kase than anything else? Was he the reason electricity in Kyvena and the surrounding villages had ceased to work?

A smudge appeared on the horizon, and Kase's stomach dropped. The hover sped up. With each passing second, the once-glittering capital city nestled in the hills of Jayde grew larger.

The Jayde Center's glass dome was gone. An air of ruin hung over the city like a specter. The once-majestic stone of the outer wall lay in heaps, and the great doors hung off their hinges. Kase pushed the hover harder, pulling up to clear the top of a severely damaged section of the wall.

He didn't register most of the city's destruction as he skimmed the rooftops of the lower city. He didn't want to risk flying any higher for fear that the Cerls were waiting somewhere nearby. He needed to climb the hill to the upper city and find his mother.

Many city mansions showed some sort of damage, but as most of them were constructed of the finest stone, they stood mostly intact. Some were worse off than others. Several were missing parts or the entirety of their roofs.

Like the gate at the wall, the one at Shackley Manor hadn't been a deterrent to anyone who wanted to enter the estate. One of the swirling iron-rod doors hung at a grotesque angle, the other flung to the side without a care.

What in the stars would've done something like that?

Heart pounding, Kase set the Cerl hover down in the front courtyard.

Most of the Manor's upper floor was missing, as if something large had taken a bite out of it. The windows were broken, the stone blackened with soot. He knew the look of a building devoured by fire, but it hadn't consumed the entire manor.

He popped the windshield up and scrambled out of the hover. He hit the ground hard, his knees nearly giving out. He sliced his hand on something.

"Son!"

Kase could barely hear Stowe's voice, and he didn't care. He needed to find his mother. The door hung wide open, the lock busted. He flew inside.

Someone had thrown paint across the family portrait dominating the entrance hall. A streak of red dripped down Harlan's stone-like features. A jagged slash marred Kase's own.

Lead filled his stomach. He'd always hated the portrait, hated it for what it represented, for the memories it evoked. It only served as a reminder of everything he'd lost.

But seeing it destroyed only drove the knife deeper—it made him want to give up completely.

He took several deep breaths, willing the tension in his jaw to ease.

"I cannot control others' actions. I can only take responsibility for my own," he whispered under his breath. He turned away and eyed the grand staircase.

The looters couldn't do much to the stone stairs, but paint that looked too much like blood had dried in dark russet patches on a scattered few.

"Take these." Stowe came up beside him and handed

him the electropistol and Cerl weapon he'd left in the hover. Kase watched himself take the pistol, not entirely present in his own body. He cocked the weapon, but no sparks sputtered to life at the end.

The electricity. Gone.

Cornhead was right.

He handed it back to Stowe and hit the hammer on the Cerl pistol. Instead of sparks jumping from the end, a wave of cold swept over him like every time he started up the Cerl hover. The metal was the same blue hue.

For a split second, Kase wished he'd taken the time to rest instead of running in without thinking. He'd forgotten he'd cut his hand. Fresh blood smeared on the pistol's textured grip.

But if his mother...if she was...

Kase couldn't think past the terror. He couldn't let himself think about the worst-case scenario; if he thought it, he feared it would become real.

So without thinking, he searched the first floor. Stowe followed behind, his flashpistol ready to fire. Most of it had been looted, burned, or defaced. The family crest, complete with swords, was still intact in the dining room—*ironic*—even if it was now covered in the same brown stains as the stairs. Seemed that whoever had broken in with the intent of stealing all the finer things—including the silver spoons kept in the sideboard at the end of the dining hall—hadn't wanted or couldn't pry the crest off the wall.

Kase thundered up to the second floor. "Mother!"

He hadn't expected an answer, but he'd hoped for it. And when he didn't find her in her library or her bedroom, both of which had been ransacked, it got much harder not to think about the worst.

"Mother!" he shouted again. Only his echo replied.

They wouldn't have just killed her. She'd be a perfect prisoner, someone to hold for ransom. They'd have to be stars-idiots to kill her. She was important.

Kase didn't know which was worse—death or capture. His stomach and chest coiled so tightly, he thought he might burst.

His parents' bed chamber still had its high, arched ceilings with ornate trim and molding that matched the rest of the manor's more elegant rooms. The towering four-poster bed's curtains had been slashed. Red-soaked feathers littered the ground and the eviscerated covers and pillows.

Kase's vision blurred. *No.* He couldn't lose it now. He needed to find survivors. He needed to find his family.

If he had a family left to find.

A hand on his shoulder shook him out of his thousand-yard stare. "Son, we need to go."

He clenched his still aching jaw. How long had it been since his run-in with Cornhead? An hour? Two? The pain cleared his head as nausea swirled in his stomach. Pain brought the task before him back into focus, even if he was unsure of exactly what that task was.

He just needed to do something. Anything.

As he skimmed the room one last time, a heap of brown fabric crumpled beside his mother's wardrobe caught his eye. The door had been ripped off and hacked to pieces. Her various necklaces, which once hung on hooks inside the door, were nowhere to be found. Mirror and glass shards mixed on the floor like a macabre mosaic, light painting each piece in fiery sunset hues. Glass shards crunched beneath his boots as he stumbled over to the material, gathering it in his hands.

Shaking off glass shards, Kase held up his pilot's jacket.

And he lost the very last shred of self-control he had left.

His mother must have gone into his room and taken this from his wardrobe. She'd kept it here, close to her. A slash ran through it from mid-chest to the hem.

His fingers dug into the leather as a tear escaped. His nostrils flared.

My only wish is for you to be happy, to be safe, to be loved, she'd written in her last letter, stowed in his pack. *You'll always have a home here with me.*

He might never get to say sorry.

And out of all the regrets he had in his life, that one was probably one of the biggest.

His throat closed up, and his hands shook.

I cannot control others' actions. I can only control my own.

Except this was his fault. This was all his fault.

Another tear escaped his collapsing hold, finding its way down his cheek, over his healing cut, and finally to his chin.

"I'm sorry," Stowe whispered.

Kase wiped his eyes with his sleeve and sniffed loudly. "I don't want..."

He couldn't finish the sentence. He couldn't, because Stowe was only being kind, and he didn't deserve Kase's ire.

Stowe hadn't done anything. He hadn't hurt anyone. He hadn't been the one to burn the manor or destroy his family's possessions. He wasn't the reason the city was empty, the only evidence people had once lived here was the bits of life they'd left behind.

Like shattered glass. Family portraits. A simple leather jacket.

Wiping his eyes once more and forcing false confidence into his voice, he said, "Let's go."

He balled up his jacket, tucked it underneath his arm, and pushed past Stowe out into the dark corridor.

He couldn't keep the emotions from bubbling up and overflowing onto his cheeks. It was impossible. He had lived the worst years of his life stalking the halls of the ancient Shackley estate. He'd hated this home and everything it had stood for. It held only wretched memories, hadn't it?

His throat bobbed as he came around the corner and found himself at the top of the grand staircase. He and Ana used to stand at the top of the staircase when they were young and roll the cricket ball down to a waiting Jove and Zeke. The cricket ball would wiggle and jaggedly make its way to the waiting team, making a game of catching it.

Ana, for all her seven years, had always been crafty. She always came up with new ways to make their older brothers work for the catch. Kase, on the other hand, usually just wanted to make Jove fall.

The game always inevitably ended in an argument or their mother giving them a lecture about the priceless antiques they'd destroyed. Even the most uneventful rounds always produced at least one shattered vase.

Kase started down the stairs. Nobody waited at the bottom to catch him.

He was halfway down, trying not to think of anything else that would widen the hole in his chest, when something like a roar rattled the walls. He slipped and barely caught himself on the railing, his jacket falling and landing with an invisible thump as another roar ripped the air.

Fumbling to grab the Cerl pistol from the back of his pants, Kase retrieved his jacket and dashed down the rest of the stairs.

That sound.

Another roar. This one crackled like lightning. Familiar.

Hiding behind the ruined door, he peeked outside. The estate across the way was blackened with soot, as well. Kase could just see it beyond the Shackley gate and the ruined wall. The Cerl hover waited just a few feet away, the rolling sunset clouds reflecting off its wings.

He didn't see whatever had made that unearthly sound, but he knew what it was.

Dragon.

There was no question. It sounded exactly like the two he had seen on Tasava last autumn. The question was how it had gotten *here*—and where was it now?

He ventured a little further out the door, Stowe's footsteps clomping behind him.

A distant tremor shook his bones. The rumble grew louder and more piercing, like the air itself crackled. That sound was even more familiar to him than the dragon's roar.

Seconds later, hovers sped overhead, their blue bellies shining as they zoomed at top speed above the manor. The grass and trees that had survived the initial attack bowed to the speed of the Cerl hovers.

The city was destroyed. Surely they wouldn't continue to...no, no, no.

They were headed straight for the airfields.

Kase sprinted from his childhood home, not caring if anyone saw him. He didn't know what in the blazes had happened, but if they took out the airfields, there was no chance they'd recover. He scrambled up the wing, the metal cold and hard underneath his hands.

He had just thrown his pilot's jacket into the cockpit when the first bomb fell.

His shout was buried by the next one. And the next. And the next.

Each one shook him to his core, to his bones, to his soul.

All he could do was gape at the plumes rising above the city wall.

Gone.

Gone.

The airfields were gone. Just like that.

He swayed on his feet. He couldn't catch his breath. He wracked his brain for the words—but there were none.

Despite the evidence staring him directly in the face, he had hoped to find someone at the airfields who would be willing to help. He'd known the electricity was out. He'd known thousands were dead. He'd known it was a lost cause, but he'd still had that stars-blasted hope.

Wind thrust him forward, nearly knocking him from the hover. Stowe, who'd climbed up the wing shortly after him, barely caught himself on the dash.

Kase looked up, his chest heavy, still breathing erratically—and found a sight he'd hoped he'd never see again.

The serpentine body was covered in glittering gold scales. Its maw was as big as a hover, and its body the length of at least three. The wings stretched wide as it soared above, its eyes searching for...for something. On his back sat a figure, a man with blond hair. Kase couldn't make out details, but instinctively he knew the man's features would be fox-like.

Skibs.

It wasn't over. The attack wasn't over.

Blood drained from Kase's face. He hit the deck, grabbing Stowe on his way down. They hunkered in the too-tight foot space. If only they could disappear.

The hover responded with a soft beeping. Kase bit a curse at it from under his breath.

Another great beating of wings shook the windshield hinge and snapped the whole thing shut. It was a miracle it didn't break.

Another roar.

THUD.

The ground quaked. Kase nearly hit his head on the acceleration pedal, but caught himself just in time. His teeth rattled from the impact, and his jaw still ached from dodging Cornhead's bullet earlier.

The memory of facing the dragon in the Yalven hunt came back to him. He'd fought one before, but there were two differences now. Firstly, he didn't have trained Yalven hunters with him to take down the beast when he inevitably failed. Secondly, this one had wings.

For several seconds, everything was quiet. Maybe the dragon hadn't landed as close as he'd feared it would. If so, the beast had to be even more impressive than he'd originally thought if its landing could affect him this far away.

Or was it still out there, sizing them up? They were in a Cerl hover, which might have given it pause. Was Skibs still astride it?

So many questions. Hallie would've had twelve more.

Holding his breath, Kase raised his head just enough. If nothing else, maybe he could get a good glimpse of the dragon, even from afar, so he could tell Hallie about it later. She'd wanted to sketch it so badly in the forest.

A glittering golden eye gazed directly at him.

That answered one question. The dragon had definitely *not* landed far away.

Kase ducked his head once more and waited for the teeth to come. Stowe's face was so pale, he could've been a ghost. Kase just shook his head, knowing anything he said or did wouldn't project the confidence he needed.

Think.

He needed to do something. Maybe if he could figure out a distraction, he could fly them out of here. The Cerl hover had the speed.

Clearly he had a death wish, because he braved another peek above the dash. But the dragon was no longer looking at him. Instead, it watched the horizon, smoke leaking from its nostrils. Its neck stretched and craned toward the sky, its shining scales proud in sunset light. Probably not a good sign.

A second later, its rider slid down the gigantic foreleg.

Kase stopped breathing.

Skibs looked a little different than the last time Kase had seen him. His hair was longer, his chin coated in red scruff. His blue eyes stood out against the tanned skin of his face. Wearing armor that glowed a soft blue, not unlike the hover, he looked like a hero out of some sprawling epic.

"This home is off-limits." Skibs' voice was just as Kase remembered, strong and commanding when he meant something, a tone that brokered no arguments. His old friend stopped a few feet from the hover. He didn't look directly at Kase, which probably saved him; instead he looked past him, at the Shackley estate.

Kase's fingernails bit so hard into his palms, they broke the skin. The stinging pain kept his head clear—kept him from doing something incredibly stupid.

Skibs crossed his arms. "The General will have your head if you're out here looting. Return to your station at once, or I'll personally dole out your punishment."

Kase nodded, praying his old friend wouldn't look directly at him. Skibs stood there another moment, still watching the estate, before climbing back up the wing and mounting his dragon. Kase recoiled as the beast's head faced him head-on, certain all over again he was about to get eaten—

And with a great leap and thrust of wings, Skibs and the dragon took to the sky.

The air slammed into the Cerl hover, and Kase banged his head on the dashboard for real that time. He cursed, rubbing his forehead and looking up as the dragon flew toward the distant forest.

Holy blasting stars.

Forget a sketch. He could give Hallie enough detail for a portrait if she wanted to try her hand at it.

Even though Hallie had helped him remember what had happened in the Gate chamber with Skibs, Kase still couldn't quite believe it. Even when Saldr had revealed Skibs had been the one to bring a dragon through the Gate and destroy Myrrai, he still hadn't been able to line up the man he'd known with the one Skibs had become.

Skibs had been his best friend, the only person to care about Kase after Ana died—after Eravin abandoned him. The Cerls had killed Skibs' parents and kidnapped his brother. Only Skibs had survived; he'd made his way to Kyvena on his own. Skibs had spoken callously of his life before, telling tales that made Harlan seem like a saint. Skibs had seen the Cerl attack on his small border village as an escape.

Had that all been a lie? Was Kase simply a terrible judge of character?

He strapped himself into his chair. "We need to find my brother."

If he was still alive.

If anyone in the government had survived the initial attack or even the ones afterward, they would be holed up in a bunker somewhere. Maybe. The airfields had one underneath the Hover Colonel's complex, but that was probably a ruined heap of burning rubble by now.

He started up the engine to the hover. To the Jayde Center, then. Hopefully he could find something there— anything at all—that could lead him to his family and a way to save whatever survivors they could find.

PART II: REALMS

Interlude I

NAVARA

The end never goes quietly, whether for gods or man. It comes in a rushing of fate and a gnashing of teeth.

C H A P T E R 1 5

A DOOMSDAY NOVEL

Kase

BY THE TIME KASE FOUND a copse of trees to hide the Cerl hover in and made a plan, night had fallen. Kase's breath puffed out in front of him, and Firstmoon hung in the sky like a lost king of old. Its glow laced the rubble and debris and sank into the shadowed alleyways. Oddly, Kase still hadn't seen any bodies.

Not that he was complaining, but an attack on this scale would've been catastrophic. There should have been casualties. An attack that left the city inhabited by ghosts should've left more than just scattered refuse. Instead, it reminded him of Stoneset with its empty lanes and clean, crooked byways.

He turned to Stowe and whispered, "What happened to the bodies of those you lost in the Stoneset attack?"

Stowe took in the scene warily. He scratched his bearded

chin. "Burned."

"You burned them?" That was incredibly risky. If the Cerls had seen the smoke—

Stowe shook his head. "The Cerls did. We just cleaned up the rubble left behind."

Fury rose within him...mixed with curiosity. Why go out of the way to take care of the enemy bodies? To give them a proper send-off, more or less? He didn't know if it was a kindness or some kind of additional insult. He suspected the latter.

Stowe hesitated a moment before saying, "A few of our scouts noted that the Cerls in charge of the burnings said rites over the pyres."

"Interesting." Kase tugged his jacket collar higher. It was nice to be back in his old leather even if it hung a little strange with the rip in the back. He would figure out how to mend it later. "I can't imagine how long that would've taken here if they did the same."

He didn't know if his anger bled into his words, but Hallie's father didn't say anything about it. He probably felt the same. Kase couldn't allow even a little respect to enter his mind where the Cerls were concerned. Besides, the rites could've very well been curses.

But at least Kase didn't have to step over bodies to climb the steps of the Jayde Center.

With only Firstmoon to light their trek, Kase kept the Cerl pistol cocked and ready in his grip. The frostbitten tingle in his fingers was a comfort; even with no electricity, this weapon would work.

The night itself was beautiful without all the electric lights. Kase could see the stars for what they were, sparkling gems sewn into an inky tapestry. It reminded him of the nights spent out on the *Eudora* mission or with Hallie on their way to Stoneset. Both times had been times of trial and stress, but the night sky had been a constant companion through it all.

Tonight, the stars watched with bated breath. They judged him. Each sparkle condemned him, reminded him of his wrongs.

Stowe held his silence as they entered the building proper. The door sat heavy and ominous, no one there to deny or grant them entry. Kase never thought he'd wish someone was there to stand in his way.

Truthfully, Kase wasn't the biggest fan of the government. Sure, he'd fly a hover into battle against their enemies, but it wasn't out of blind devotion. At best, he'd been neutral about the buildings in which the government had been housed.

Until that exact moment.

The Jayde Center's atrium had been pristine the last time Kase had graced its threshold. The marble floors had been polished, the Jaydian emblems hung with pride. Government workers and aides had crawled through the corridors and traversed up and down the stairs, light streaming through the glass dome, drawing rainbows on the walls.

Now it was a scene from a doomsday novel.

Moonlight stretched through the gaping hole where the glass dome had sat upon the central tower, lording the wealth and engineering prowess of its makers over the city. Now it chilled him like the sight of any corpse would, its remains only highlighting the destruction before him.

No matter how high you climbed, how strong you were, how prepared you were for the inevitable...you could still fall.

If Kase had thought the destruction at the Manor had been bad, it was nothing compared to the Jayde Center. There might not have been bodies lying in disarray or in varying states of decay like he'd expected, but uneven bulbous brown splotches and streams now marred the once-polished marble floors. The banners that had proudly displayed the Jaydian emblem lay shredded or burned, trampled and thrown in corners. The ground glittered with pulverized glass, shimmering like the sneering stars outside.

Funny, how he hadn't quite believed the city conquered until that moment. He'd seen his razed childhood home, taken in the general destruction of the city, and watched as they bombed the airfields. But to see its heart torn out and destroyed like this...

There was no more Jayde.

And he hadn't been there. He hadn't been home to defend it, to make sure his mother got out safely. All that was left of them was an empty Manor, a marred portrait, broken glass, and Kase's ripped leather jacket.

Breathe. Just breathe.

He took a breath in, counting to three, and let it out in four beats. He repeated the rhythm with three successive breaths. He pressed his feet into the ground below.

He couldn't change what had already happened. He could only move forward.

A hand on his shoulder brought him out of his thoughts. "There will be survivors. They would've prepared for something like this. We just have to find them."

Kase cleared his throat. "Yes, the bunker. I'm certain there's an entrance we can get to. They had one at the airfields, but...well...there should be one here. Probably check my father's office."

"Lead the way, then."

If Stowe felt anything at all, he was hiding it well. But then, this hadn't been his home.

Kase could barely keep his thoughts straight. All he was good for was flying hovers—not collapsed governments and tracking down survivors. Maybe he should just leave, run for Tev Rubika—or heck, even Myrrai. He could meet up with Hallie.

His heart leapt. With the Cerl hover's speed, he could make it there in record time. He wouldn't need to deal with the Bay of Storms or any of the other dangers they'd faced in the autumn.

"Son?"

Kase blinked away the daydream. "Right. Sorry. This way."

He couldn't entertain that option until he'd exhausted all possibilities to find his family. He couldn't run again. He'd run before, and look what had happened.

He'd known that turning Eravin down and fleeing would cause issues. He'd known that his father would have to deal with the fallout. Kase just wasn't sure if that fallout was what had collapsed Jayde's defenses.

The corridor was so dark he couldn't see where he was walking, the only light shining from the end of the narrow hallway. Stowe paused beside him.

"There's light coming from the door at the end," Stowe whispered close to Kase's ear.

For the third time that evening, Kase had to be pulled from his thoughts. He needed to do so much, but he wanted to be anywhere else.

He took another moment to get his thoughts and breathing under control.

A great crash echoed from the corridor behind them. Both Kase and Stowe somehow caught themselves on the wall beside them. Kase slid down the wall and covered his head. Stowe followed.

As quickly as the quake came upon them, it ceased. A dust cloud met them, and Kase pulled his shirt over his mouth.

Once the dust settled, Kase peeked up. He kept his mouth and nose covered, which muffled his voice. "What was that?"

"Felt like a mine collapse, but there are no mines here, are there?" Stowe kept his own shirt over his mouth and nose and stood shakily. He looked back the way they'd come. "Guessing our way back is blocked."

Kase swallowed the fear vying for his attention. "It might've been another bombing run. Close, too."

But why were they targeting an empty city?

Unless they knew about the bunkers.

The thought chilled Kase to the core.

With his racing thoughts under control for the moment, Kase nodded to Stowe, and they continued down the corridor. He kept the lower part of his face covered and the pistol gripped in his hand. He headed toward the light. It was probably just an open window allowing the moonlight to seep underneath the door, but it might be a survivor. A stupid one, if they were using a light, which would only serve as a beacon for anyone looking up at the Jayde Center—especially with the rest of the city blanketed in darkness—but one that might at least be able to give him a hint about his family's whereabouts.

As they crept closer, Kase heard low voices coming from beyond the door; he stopped and cocked his pistol, Stowe nearly stepping on the backs of his boots.

Kase pulled his pistol closer to his body and pointed the barrel skyward, his muscles tense. He nodded at Stowe before creeping closer.

The nondescript door bore a simple plaque—some secretary's office. His father's was just around the corner, if he remembered correctly. It'd been a while since he'd visited him at the Jayde Center.

He didn't press his ear to the wood, but he put it so close to the crack that he could hear the muffled argument within. The first man spoke with the elongated 's' sounds of a Cerl.

Kase gripped his pistol tighter and prepared to swerve aside, aiming for his father's office instead. If Cerl soldiers were here, he'd rather avoid a fight. He could take them, but he was more worried about Stowe.

But then another man spoke. A voice as familiar to Kase as his own.

I know where to find that pretty redhead you stumble around after, that voice had said one of the last times he'd heard it.

Fire caught in Kase's blood. Without thinking much further than his rage, he kicked in the door. It slammed against the wall, the plaque clattering to the floor.

Both men inside looked up, hands flying to pistols at their sides. The Cerl drew his faster, aiming the barrel at Kase's head.

Kase didn't hesitate. He swung his own pistol at the Cerl soldier and fired.

Not even a Cerl was fast enough to dodge this close. But outside of a hover, Kase didn't have the most consistent aim—the fiery blue bullet hit the man's shoulder instead of his chest. He collapsed against the heavy desk sitting in the middle of the room, his pistol skittering across the floor and hitting the opposite wall. Blood-sprayed papers and maps and loose fountain pens skidded across the surface. The only item to avoid the destruction was the gas lantern closer to where Eravin Gray stood, blinking at Kase like he was bored.

Kase was milliseconds away from shooting that smug look off Eravin's face when the man took his own pistol, put the barrel to the Cerl's forehead, and pulled the trigger.

Kase flinched from the sound, shutting his eyes tight. Nausea flooded his system; he had to grit his teeth on a gag. *Not in front of Eravin.*

"You're late," Eravin said calmly, as if he hadn't just executed a man at point-blank range.

Kase held up his pistol with a shaking hand, the adrenaline of pure survival instinct draining away, shock replacing it with a shiver. He didn't look at the dead Cerl. The body slid off the desk and thumped onto the floor.

Stowe started forward, but Kase caught him with his free

hand, holding him back; he didn't take his eyes or weapon off Eravin. His jaw hurt from clenching it so hard. All he heard in his head was the scream of the Cerl as Kase had shot him. All he could feel was the rage and triumph and guilt of his own actions, and then the horror of Eravin's.

I cannot lose myself here.

He shoved his conscious mind through, pressing his feet against the floor to ground himself, but that floor was marred by a pool of blood seeping closer to Kase's dusty boots. He breathed as deeply as he could through his nose, but his lungs weren't working properly. They ached. He smelled iron.

Eravin tilted his head. "I was trying to pry him for information, but it seems you still can't keep your temper."

Stowe spoke up. "He's still breathing. I might could..."

Eravin brought up his pistol and pointed it at Stowe. Kase jumped in front of him, arms spread as he blurted, "I thought One World was working with the Cerls."

Not letting the pistol drop, Eravin said, "Usually." When Kase didn't back down, he sighed and lowered the weapon. "If you have information I can sell, I'll let you live. Even if that might not be for very long."

The pistol cooled in Kase's hand. He could shoot him. He could take care of any future issues right then. This man had gone off the deep end and blackmailed him. He was dangerous.

Except, once upon a time, he'd been one of Kase's closest friends.

He chewed on the inside of his cheek. Could he use Eravin? If the man had any connection to the Cerls at all, Kase could leverage what he learned to buy his own freedom if need be. However, was it moral to use someone for the present, only to betray them later...even in the name of the greater good? Would that make him just as bad as Eravin?

Maybe Eravin had been forced to make the same choice. Maybe he was only a product of his circumstances, not of his own choices.

Kase's anxiety knocked at the door, and he gripped his pistol harder, resisting the urge to run a hand through his hair. If it would save Hallie in the long run, he would do it. He didn't have a choice. Kase could be condemned for all eternity—he didn't care, not if it spared her.

Kase spoke as confidently as he could, though he felt

anything but. "I have information about General Marcus Correa for my brother's ears only, but I'll put in a good word for you if you help us."

Eravin laughed and holstered his pistol. "What makes you think your word is worth anything now? All Kyvena wants you dead. Well, anyone that's left."

Kase didn't put his pistol away. Stowe cleared his throat. "If I may…"

Eravin scoffed. "*You may* put the man out of his misery, if you like, though he doesn't deserve it."

Kase glanced back to Stowe with a question in his gaze. Stowe nodded toward the Cerl, whose rattling breaths were barely audible. Kase clenched his jaw. His heart thumped too loudly as Stowe stepped around him and a leather chair to reach the soldier. Eravin leaned his hip against the desk, inspecting his fingernails.

Kase shook his head. "No one deserves to be executed that way."

"Actually," Eravin raised an eyebrow, "considering he was half the reason Kyvena went up in flames for a second time, I'd say he did."

Kase's jaw ached with tension. "What?"

Eravin went back to his blood-crusted nails. Kase didn't want to know who that blood belonged to. Eravin shrugged. "That man was the one who brought One World in to aid in the city takeover. Went ahead and cut me at the knees. I had my own plans, but alas, he riled up the people even more than they were after you rejected our invitation. So he deserved my bullet—even more poetic that it was a weapon from his own kingdom. It's not my usual bloody smile on the neck, but it's quite effective."

Kase's stomach twinged, but he kept his eyes trained on the man in front of him.

I cannot lose myself here.

Stowe finished mixing a few liquids together and tipped the liquid into what was left of the man's mouth. The death rattles ceased.

Kase didn't know whether to be relieved or not. He still couldn't look at the man's face. Instead, he turned back to Eravin. "We need to find my brother."

Eravin pulled a messenger cap out of his back pocket, depositing it onto his head. Kase could barely see his eyes between the dim lighting and the shadow cast by the cap's brim, but they still seemed to glow as he smiled. "It's a good thing I know the way into the tunnels and the Cerl doesn't, then, isn't it?"

"Tunnels?"

Eravin raised a brow. "You don't know? Ah, well, if you had joined our little group earlier, you would've learned that once the Great War ended, the High Council signed an initiative to construct underground tunnels for the populace to hide in if there was ever an attack on the capital. Ingenious, really, except *the populace* didn't know a thing about it." He paused and shrugged one shoulder, a slim grin still painted across his face. "You people think One World is the bad guy. That's yet another reason I'd disagree."

Kase didn't really know how to respond. On one hand, it made sense the leaders of Jayde would prepare for an eventual war with Cerulene. The Great War had been a rather convoluted mess, and though he didn't quite remember the specifics about how it started or anything other than how his own family was intimately involved, he could see why the tunnels were constructed—that was, if Eravin was telling the truth. But it was the last part of Eravin's explanation that gave him pause. Why hadn't the people been made aware? If the tunnels were built for their potential protection, wouldn't it be vital for people to know they existed?

When Kase failed to respond, Eravin knocked a pattern on the side of the desk he leaned upon. After a moment, a crack echoed through the room, and the paneling of the desk popped open like a door.

Eravin squatted down and pulled it open, revealing flickering torchlight and a gaping hole down into the earth below. "After you."

THE SCENT OF DAMP EARTH was thick in Kase's nose as he dropped from the ladder into the tunnels. The air pressed in on him as he straightened and tucked his pistol in the back of his trousers. Good thing his jacket was still ripped in case he needed to reach for his weapon, though he hoped he wouldn't have to do so among his own people.

Unless, of course, they decided to get retribution for

what Kase had done to their neighbors, their mothers, fathers, brothers, sisters...if Eravin had indeed spread the information that Kase had gotten off for the fires without being punished by Jaydian law.

He kept his hand close to his pistol.

None of those people realized that the consequences he'd faced had been just as bad, if not worse. He couldn't go one day without seeing his sister in the shadows, only to turn on the light and find them empty. They didn't know the cruelty and disappointment of his father. They didn't know Kase's shame.

But he also couldn't blame them. They deserved to be angry. He'd been careless, and that had cost lives.

Kase took a deep breath and put a hand to the tunnel wall. The brick was structural, keeping the tunnels from collapse with the weight of the city above, but Kase didn't know if they'd had the funds to finish out the project with the Rubikan refugees flooding into the city over the last few years. Would these tunnels be simply that—unfinished tunnels that were no good to anyone? Or would there be more developed caverns where people could safely hide?

He suspected the former. But he wouldn't mind, just this once, if Eravin ended up being right. Not if his family had made it here, too.

Hushed murmurs and flickering gas lanterns wait along the tunnel they'd entered. Ahead, he could just make out the chaotic tapestry of slipshod shelters, crafted from whatever building materials those fleeing the capital's destruction had been able to find—blankets, discarded crates, coats. Some even leaned against each other for warmth. But plenty of people huddled against the walls alone, without anything to their name other than the clothes on their back.

Kase tapped his fingers along the strap of his pack. Nothing inside it could really do any good for these people. And even if he gave them everything he had, it would never be enough.

Eravin nodded to the guard a few feet away. The woman looked as if she'd had an hour or two of sleep in the last week. Her messy braid hid under the collar of her carelessly buttoned Jaydian uniform. Rips and burns decorated much of the jacket in other places. She looked up when Kase, Eravin, and Stowe climbed down, but she didn't move from her position.

Kase wasn't one to say anything, but if his father caught this guard shirking her duties, then it wouldn't end well for her.

She nodded to them. "Don't get handsy. Don't look at anybody wrong." She pointed down the tunnel past the makeshift city. "Hospital ward is that way if you need attention, but last I heard, the wait is a few hours at best." She pointed in the other direction. "If you don't need a medic, consult with the team in the central cavern. They'll get you assigned to duty rotation."

Duty rotation. That was a good sign. Some kind of organization had been put into place, even if the state of the people around him made it seem otherwise.

Stowe knelt and rummaged through his pack, whipping out his special caffeine concoction. He handed it to the soldier. "You look dead on your feet."

She took it and eyed the contents. Then she glanced back at Stowe. "Why do you care?"

Stowe shouldered his pack once more. "It's the least I could do to thank you for your service, lass."

She snorted, but she still uncorked the vial and knocked back the dark liquid. Shaking her head, she handed it back. "Thanks. Welcome to the Catacombs."

With that, Kase gestured for Eravin to lead the way toward the central cavern. He'd rather follow than get a well-placed bullet in the back, tentative truce or none. Ironic how things changed over the years. Five years ago, Kase wouldn't have anyone else watching his back.

The number of people lining the tunnels and alcoves was impressive. In the cramped space, it might be easy to mentally inflate the number of survivors, but they still gave Kase hope. If so many from the lower city were gathered here, surely his mother must have made it out.

That was what he kept telling himself, anyway.

He scanned the faces for her blue eyes and dark hair streaked with glittering gray. He didn't linger too long, lest they look back at him and realize just who *he* was.

With any luck, they'd all mistake him for a greenie hover pilot on his way to report to his Lead, though his poor jacket had seen much better days. His pack covered some of the biggest rips, at least. Maybe that was why the soldier on guard had let them pass without any trouble—they looked as roughed-up as any other refugee, and their weapons weren't visible.

Or maybe she'd just been that grateful for Stowe's caffeinated gift. Good thing Harlan wasn't around to see it— he probably would have accused the guard of taking bribes.

Eravin wound his way through the labyrinth like he'd lived in it his whole life. The guard hadn't mentioned that there were so many tunnel branches weaving and winding like the veins of some reptilian creature from First Earth...a *snake*. Or maybe something from Greek mythology, like the Hydra. Yes, that fit.

Hallie would've seen the similarity, too.

Of course, it could be in the same blueprint of the city above, but without landmarks like the public squares, it was hard to navigate.

Soon, raised voices echoed off the tunnel, replacing the pall of whimpers and murmurs. Kase resisted the urge to grab his pistol, but he pushed back his jacket to make it easier to reach just in case.

Many people clogged the next tunnel, all vying to see what lay ahead. Eravin, who'd been quietly leading the party, elbowed his way through the crowd. Kase let his jacket fall back into place and followed, murmuring apologies as he wove after Eravin. With an inch or two of height on most of the people gathered, he could see some of what lay ahead, but not much. All he could make out was a dark expanse and someone shouting at the void below.

They reached the edge of the crowd to find a part of the tunnel floor had collapsed. Kase turned to the person next to him, a man with soft brown eyes and brown skin leathered with age. "What happened?"

The man pointed. "Been cave-ins all over. People getting swallowed up left and right. Someone even said one of the Stradats' sons fell into one a few days ago."

All the air left Kase's lungs. "Son...which one?"

The man wasn't necessarily talking about Jove. Kase thought he remembered Stradat Loffler or Sarson having a son, though he hadn't bothered to learn about them or speak to them at any of the state functions he'd gone to as a child, or even as an adult. Lavinia Richter had been the only child of a Stradat he'd cared to talk to.

"Harlan Shackley's son. The only decent one left to him. Pity he paid for the sins of the father, but…" The man sneered, calling Harlan a rather foul name and spitting on the ground before adding, "Serves him right after what he done. Gives him a taste of what some of us went through in that fire three years ago. Shame he was the only Stradat to survive."

Kase didn't realize he'd moved until he stumbled into someone—Stowe.

"Let's get a little air, son," he said, his hand on Kase's chest. It was hard to tell if Stowe was holding him back or keeping him upright. He wasn't really sure which he required himself.

Eravin only watched with a detached interest before he peeked over the edge of the chasm again. Kase's vision shrank to a pinpoint of light as Stowe dragged him backward. Only Stowe's shoulder, propped against his, kept him upright as they pushed their way through the throng of people.

The only Stradat to survive.

Only decent one left…shame…

Before Kase knew it, they were in a nearly deserted corridor off the main branch. Stowe finally let go and propped him against a wall. He fetched his canteen and forced Kase to take a swig.

The water was lukewarm and had a slight humid taste to it, like it'd been sitting out in the sun just long enough to start evaporating. For a second, Kase wished he was back in the Narden Pass, surrounded by snow.

These people hated his father enough to wish his children dead. They claimed Jove was already gone. And Kase…

The man hadn't recognized him. More than ever, he counted it as a blessing how heavily he favored his mother with her curls and blue eyes. Jove was much the same. Zeke had taken after Harlan the most. Ana had been something else entirely, with her blonde hair and pale blue eyes. Many a rumor had circulated about her parentage a few years before her death, but both Kase and Jove worked hard to quiet them. Only their methods had differed.

Kase's method may or may not have involved busted knuckles and a few trips to the headmaster's office. Justified, of course.

"Looks like we have a bit of a dilemma, haven't we?"

Eravin turned the corner and joined them in the corridor. "If you're trying not to get recognized or have people connect you with Harlan, that little display of yours was about the worst way to go about it."

He smirked, and Kase wanted nothing more than to smack it right off his face. However, the tunnel wall was currently all that was holding Kase up. Any sudden movements wouldn't be wise. "I didn't ask for your opinion."

The words sounded weak even to Kase's ears. Stowe stepped up, putting a hand on Eravin's shoulder. The man flinched, but he recovered quickly, stepping back. Stowe looked down the sparsely populated corridor, then—golden eyes as hard as stone—looked back at Eravin. "I don't care what all happened between the two of you, you need to quit sniping at each other and get to looking for someone who can make use of what we have. Jayde is more important than whatever grudge you're holding."

Whatever else you could say about Stowe, you couldn't say he was a coward. The man had witnessed Eravin shoot someone point blank and still stepped up between him and Kase without flinching.

Eravin's smirk didn't leave his face. "Well, then, we'd best be on our way, don't you think?"

Stowe watched him for another moment before helping Kase stand straight. "I'm sorry about your brother, son. But if he's out of reach, we'll have to find someone else."

Kase ran his hand over his face, trying to breathe. Maybe the man had been mistaken. Maybe it'd been a different Stradat's son, but somewhere along the chain, it'd gotten mixed up. Especially if these people were hoping for Harlan to experience a reckoning.

Jove could be fine. And even if he *had* fallen, it didn't mean he was dead. Kase had just...overreacted.

He didn't know if he could take another death.

Not for the first time—nor for the last—he desperately wished he had Hallie by his side. He hadn't realized just how much he depended on her strength until he no longer had her to lean on.

He straightened up to his full height. "I'm good. Let's go."

Kase pulled his collar up to help obscure his face as he led the other two down the corridor. Odds were they were all connected at several points. It wouldn't make sense for everything to branch out and go on for eternity. They passed several hollowed-out rooms full of people. These rooms looked a little more developed, and the people inside them—though their clothing was dirty and torn—looked familiar. He couldn't be certain, but it looked as if many of the upper-class survivors had taken these rooms. One had little alcoves with what looked like beds.

Must've been nice.

Did they feel any guilt for living in relative comfort when just fifteen feet down the way, someone lay on the bare ground, huddled beneath a threadbare cloak?

Kase clenched his teeth and kept walking. Part of him wondered when he started to care about things like that. He'd never really noticed the people on the side of the lower-city streets in the past—not out of malice or even superiority, just naivety. Now he couldn't tear his attention away.

After several minutes of walking with only the odd gas lantern hanging from the wall to light their way, the corridor became more and more populated. It was good to know they were probably heading in the right direction. They passed a few more of those rooms, but besides cursory glances about for his mother, he didn't dwell on them too long. The people staying there were more likely to know his face.

The scene here was much the same as the spot where they'd first descended into this subterranean nightmare. The scrap houses made for a colorful palette that no one would deem art. Kase didn't look too long in anyone's face and tugged his collar higher.

"Hey!" A man jumped up from where he sat with at least three daggers in ornate leather sheaths strapped about his waist. Kase couldn't place him, but he looked familiar. His pulse ticked faster.

When Kase turned his head aside and kept walking, the man grabbed his pack and yanked him back. Kase went for his pistol instinctively, his fingers finding the icy metal. The man let go of his pack and narrowed his eyes.

"It *is* you. Kase Shackley."

Then he pulled back his arm and punched Kase in the stomach.

Sharp pain radiated out from the impact, and Kase gasped, hunching over against the pain, the pistol falling from his grasp.

Blasted shocks, that hurt. At least he didn't go for the daggers.

He cradled his aching middle with one hand and held up the other to stop the next blow as the man pulled his fist back again.

Stowe yanked the man back before he could swing again, but it wasn't enough to keep everyone else in the dingy corridor from hearing Kase's name. Kase bent against the wall as the hushed murmurs rose to a cacophony of shouts.

Stowe tried to hold the crowd back, but with the limited space, Kase couldn't defend himself properly. Someone kicked the pistol against his foot. Someone else grabbed hold of his jacket. Kase wrenched out of their grip and squatted down, curling around himself. Static rose in his ears, drowning out everything—even the ache in his stomach. He cursed, but the words were lost in the tumultuous crowd. His bruised abdomen screamed in protest as he desperately scrabbled for the Cerl pistol, his only thought to stop them from dragging him off and—

"*Silence!*" someone shouted above the din.

Kase looked up. The crowd parted, and Kase's blood ran cold.

Harlan Shackley, the Stradat Lord Kapitan himself—and his own father—strode toward him with an expression chiseled from stone.

C H A P T E R   1 6

THE HOLY METAL

Jove

"JOVE."

His eyelids were entirely too heavy. Most everything ached. What little didn't ache throbbed with a piercing pain instead, but his head was the worst, only rivaled by his shoulder. Weakness spread through his limbs, and his stomach roiled.

"Jove?"

With great effort, he moved his head to the side—and promptly vomited.

A ripping sound. The kiss of silk against his mouth was nearly as painful as the heaving had been.

Gentle fingers felt his forehead and smoothed his hair.

Clara?

He tried to open his eyes, but it hurt. He tried to say her name, but he couldn't get his mouth to move.

"It's okay. You're going to be okay. I'm here."

He blinked harder. It was nearly as dark as it was with

his eyes closed, but a little light filtered down through something above. The shape was jagged and small and impossibly far. A star, maybe?

No...no, he was underground. The Catacombs. He, Harlan, and Saldr had made it to the safe houses underneath Kyvena. He'd been looking for Clara. He'd seen Clara—or so he'd thought. But then...

He scrunched his face against the pounding in his head. The sour tang of vomit was too close, too pungent. It nearly made him empty his stomach a second time.

He turned his head to the opposite side to get away from the smell, though he was certain there was some sick on his shirt. A face loomed there in the near-darkness. Besides the light coming from the star or hole above—Jove still hadn't figured out which—another soft glow came from someplace nearer. Golden. Flickering.

His mother's face came into focus, gold and red annealing into light and blood.

Blood. It carved paths down her face from a wound near her hairline. She sat at an odd angle, as if trying to keep weight off one of her ankles. Jove tried to sit up, to no avail. His body simply wouldn't respond.

"Mother. What happened? Did we...how did...?"

He wasn't sure how he'd survived such a long fall, if that indeed was a hole above. He could remember only bits and pieces of what had happened. One moment he'd been running toward his mother—the next, he'd been falling.

He looked up again at the speck of light. How far had they fallen?

His mother brought a shaky hand up and wiped her tears, but that only smeared blood across her cheek. She sniffled a little. "Holes have been opening up all over these tunnels. I'm guessing one took us, but I didn't see...I just saw you running to me, and then we were falling. We must've slid most of the way down, because...well, I think we're alive. This isn't the sort of heaven I'd ever read about. Far from it, in fact."

Jove wasn't so sure. If he was dead, he wouldn't expect to wake anywhere close to heaven. Clara was the one who believed in all that, and Jove would never reach the same saintly goodness as her. If anything, this hole seemed fitting.

But his mother wasn't guilty of the same things he was.

So...alive. Probably.

He groaned. "Can we climb out?"

His mother chewed on the inside of her cheek and fidgeted with the ring on her finger. It was her engagement ring—a Zuprium band with a matching crystal. He'd given Clara a similar one, but his mother's crystal was much larger. "I'm not sure we're fit for climbing. My ankle is a bit swollen, but I believe it's only a sprain. I don't know if we should move you. With all that blood—I thought—" Her words choked off in a small sob. "I'm so relieved you're awake."

Now that he'd been conscious for a few minutes, Jove was able to separate the different pains in his body. Most of him was incredibly sore, which was to be expected if he'd truly tumbled down some hole and landed on solid rock. His shoulder was probably done for unless he saw a medic sometime soon, or Saldr with his magic dust stuff. His head ached the worst after that—with the vomiting, he probably had a concussion. Maybe.

Zeke had always been the one who could diagnose conditions like that; Jove had just made a good practice patient. Still, he'd picked some things up through experience. Pain lanced up his side with every breath—a bruised or cracked rib—and he was pretty sure he'd done something to a few of his fingers. He didn't have the courage to lift up his hand and inspect them.

He'd rather delay seeing them bent at gnarled, unnatural angles.

He was still alive. His mother wouldn't lose another child, yet. That was what mattered for now.

At least, he hoped she hadn't lost another child. But who in the stars could say where Kase was?

"Will you help me sit up?" Jove tried to shove himself up using his only working arm, but the strain of his muscles pulling at all his broken parts made his eyes tear up.

His mother cupped his face with one hand. "You need to stay still, baby. Moving might make things worse."

Pre-fatherhood Jove would've balked at the endearment, but with Samuel still missing, he didn't bother correcting her. He understood too well. If they all survived this, he'd never let Samuel leave the house until he was at least forty-five.

And if he was honest, even at Jove's very mature age of

nearly twenty-six...for a moment, it was nice to be taken care of by his mother.

"We have to find a way out of here," he groaned. "Can't do that lying down."

She folded her hands in her lap. "I'm sure they'll send someone to fetch us soon." She looked around the cavern. Jove couldn't see where the other light was coming from. It was odd. But a new wave of pain set his leg twitching, forcing him to close his eyes against it. After a moment, the wave dissipated.

She was right. He couldn't move another inch. Not until some of the pain subsided.

"I know a few cave plants and mosses that might help your pain and speed your healing if I can find them," his mother said from somewhere above him.

Jove's eyes popped open. "But your ankle—"

"—Will feel better once I put some *prunella vulgaris* on it." She smoothed his hair once more. "Don't worry about me."

Prunella what?

Jove gave in. He wasn't in any state to argue, let alone stop her from going and finding whatever she needed. Had he not been in so much pain, he might've insisted he do the foraging—but then again, Jove had never cared much about plant life. He'd probably pick something lethal by accident.

He couldn't see her anymore. Every now and then, he'd hear a small grumble, but he couldn't quite make out what she was saying.

The longer he lay there staring up at the hole, his pain pulsing with the beat of his heart, he couldn't help but wonder how he'd even gotten here in the first place.

How far he had fallen...literally. He'd somehow been promoted to High Guardsman not even a year ago, and now he found himself in a cavern deep within the planet, unable to move without vomiting or nearly blacking out, letting his mother fuss over him and wander around a potentially hazardous space alone.

He couldn't see well enough to tell what lay around him...and on second thought, he wasn't sure if he wanted to know. He and his mother couldn't be the only ones down here. She'd mentioned multiple cave-ins.

Though it hadn't *felt* like a cave-in. In the moments

leading up to the accident, he recalled the ground beneath him flying up into the sky, like a rug ripped out from under him by some vengeful beast. How that was even possible, Jove didn't know.

Maybe it wasn't. Maybe his mind was going after everything he'd been through in the last twenty-four hours. Maybe he'd finally leapt off the brink into insanity.

He didn't *feel* insane, though. His mind was sound, and he felt very much the pain his body was in. Granted, he didn't think people with unstable minds thought they were unstable. But what other explanation was there?

Chunks of the planet didn't just soar into the sky.

"Oh, dear!" his mother exclaimed in a panic, interrupting his thoughts. Jove tried to turn his head in her direction, but the pain nearly made him black out. He heard a scuffling sound, still far away. "Here, I'll give you some of this. It'll stop the bleeding and—"

Another raspy, low voice replied, "Just...the dust...my pouch...sprinkle it on my face and chest."

The accent. Yalven. A man, Jove was sure, though he still didn't quite trust his ears...or any of his senses, really. But he sounded so much like Saldr, if younger.

Someone else was down here, after all.

A few heartbeats later, the Yalv began to sing softly. Jove couldn't even begin to translate the words. He knew enough to read some of the more modern dialect, but the spoken word was something else entirely.

A brilliant glow lit the chamber as the man's song died off. Jove closed his eyes against the light, but that only made his head spin harder.

His mother gasped. "So it *is* true!"

"We praise Toro for his swift answer," said the Yalv, his voice stronger now. "Allow me to heal your injuries, Miss."

"If you would, could you attend to my son first? I'm afraid his wounds are much worse."

A few seconds of shuffling and footsteps later, Jove squinted through the pain pounding in his head to make out the dim outline of the Yalven man. He had a short beard and familiar dark hair, though instead of a slick braid, the man's was rather unkempt. A gift from the fall, no doubt. His eyes were dark gold, closer to topaz than the brighter honey-like tones Jove was used to seeing.

"This is Kainadr," his mother introduced. "He's going to help you."

"Your mother gave her name as Shackley." Kainadr's face floated above him like a specter in the night, looking entirely too thrilled given the situation they found themselves in. "You are the Jaydian that Lord Saldr has spoken highly of?"

Jove didn't know exactly what he would have given Saldr to speak highly about. He'd only been doing his job, and not very well at that. He'd only met with the quiet Yalv twice over the time he'd been in the city.

"Sure?" The words came out a little choked—not from emotion, but because his throat had begun to hurt, too. Now that he was conscious, the pain just kept building the longer he lay still. The fall hadn't killed him outright, but maybe it was just taking its time.

The Yalven man's eyes widened. Immediately, he dug into the pouch at his waist and sprinkled Jove with dust. Jove shut his eyes, blinking against the grit when some of the grains landed in his eyes. The man sang softly once again, no easier to translate despite being closer now.

Light burned against and underneath his eyelids. The dust glowed. Jove fought against the burning, its claws like a fire charring his flesh. His eyes throbbed. The light was so bright it blinded him. He could no longer hear the man's words.

Then it all fell away at once, as if someone had dunked Jove in ice water.

His pain wasn't gone, but all that was left was a dull ache that might easily be forgotten if Jove wasn't focused on it. He blinked into the darkness. For a moment, he feared that he might have gone blind after all, but then his mother's face appeared above him, her eyes glistening with tears.

She stroked his temple and looked to the Yalv. "He'll be okay? What about his shoulder?"

The Yalv, Kainadr, breathed heavily. "Toro has answered swiftly once more, all praises be. He will recover fully once his body finishes accepting the Vasa. Most of his minor injuries have been healed, and the Vasa has sped up the healing process of the more grievous wounds. I would not call myself fortunate for falling deep within Yalvara's depths, but perhaps it is you who are the fortunate ones that I am here."

Jove groaned. Apparently speaking in too many words was a common trait among the Yalvs. Kainadr looked him over once more. "Is there some other injury I have failed to ask Toro to heal?"

"I'm fine." No need to insult the man who might have very well saved his life. Jove clenched his teeth and pushed himself into a sitting position. It was possible, but each movement felt a little foreign, like his body had never performed them before. He nodded to his mother. "Will you please heal her next?"

Kainadr squinted at him in the faint light. "You do not have the curled hair Lord Saldr described, but the eyes, yes. Are you kin to the Master Shackley?"

Ah. He was talking about Kase. That made...well, about as little sense, if Jove was being honest.

Les gave him a soft, knowing smile. "I believe you might mean my youngest, Kase."

Kainadr focused his attention on Jove's mother. "Lord Saldr had the highest praise for two Jaydians—this Kase, possibly, and another. A woman with red hair and golden eyes. She helped many of my brethren find jobs within the city, but then one day, she simply stopped coming. We feared something terrible befell them. No one has seen either of them here in the tunnels, but with the chaos this evening, it's hard to say..." He smeared some of his dust upon Les' ankle and paused to sing under his breath. The dust glowed, and his mother gasped.

When the light faded, she smiled and stretched her ankle. "Thank you, Master Kainadr. It feels even better than it did before."

Kainadr dipped his head in response before coating his fingers with his dust and singing a word or two. It was hard to tell with his accent and Jove's aching head. In response, the dust seemed to catch fire on his fingertips before coalescing into a ball the size of Jove's thumbnail. It then rose into the air just above the Yalv.

"I need to conserve the holy metal, but this helps, yes?" Kainadr said, pointing at the floating fireball above his shoulder.

It was small, but it did flare brightly. Jove just caught sight of a trouser leg over to his right. He couldn't see past the person's knee. A mound of rocks interrupted the sight.

Jove looked away quickly. "Have you checked for other survivors?"

"I could not move until your mother helped me reach the dust. I will see to the others," Kainadr said, standing up. He waved at his fireball, and it followed him.

Jove didn't watch. He couldn't. Being so close to death for the second or third or even fourth time in the last day had taken too much out of him.

He'd been High Guardsman. He should have helped. Instead, he found himself staring at his hands while his mother sat beside him, her arm around his shoulder.

It was some time before Kainadr returned, shaking his head. "If anyone survived the initial fall, they succumbed to their injuries in the time since. I am sorry." He squatted down beside Jove and held out his hand. "However, around that corner there—" he pointed to where the subtle glow was, off to the right, "—I believe we will find a cluster of holy metal. Many times, the larger ones grow near streams, and if we are not to be rescued in the next few hours, it will be vital we have clean water."

Neither Les nor Jove offered any argument. For Jove's part, he didn't have the energy or the will. His entire body ached, but everything inside felt numb. He could only watch where his feet trod as they made their way toward the other light.

The only sounds were their own footfalls and the echoing drip from somewhere beyond them. It was eerie, something out of nightmares, but he supposed it was better than being in the city above, where the houses were burning and bodies littered the streets.

And he still hadn't found Clara and Samuel.

At last, they made it to the turn. The light was coming from the other end of the short tunnel, and now that they were closer, Jove could tell it was flickering. It ended in a cavern not much larger than the foyer of Shackley Manor. Near its center stood a large crystalline structure; it looked very much like the top of a fir tree, its branches fanning out and growing upward toward the ceiling. It glowed a soft golden color, though black tentacles thrashed softly within each branch.

"May Toro have mercy on our souls," Kainadr

whispered, coming to a stop.

"I believe that is a Zuprium crystal?" His mother asked, inching forward to inspect it, but Jove caught her elbow.

"There's something wrong with it." He had no reason to know that, but a sense of malevolence crawled through his skin when he looked at it. He turned to Kainadr. "Do you know?"

Kainadr seemed very much in shock; Jove wasn't sure if the man had even blinked again. He just stared, his little fireball guide wavering before flickering out. "This is why Yalvara is angry."

Jove cocked his head. "I'm sorry. What?"

His mother turned back toward them. "The reason the tunnel collapsed? This crystal caused it?"

Kainadr pointed to the other side of the crystal. "See there? The rockslide? The corruption of the holy metal means Jagamot is returning, which is making Yalvara unstable."

His mother turned back to the crystal and walked around it. "I do think it feels off, though I haven't studied many texts concerning Zuprium in years."

It probably brought up bad memories for her. Uncle Ezekiel had become famous from his work with the metal. "But we should still be able to find water, at least? "

His question was answered by his mother's gasp. Jove looked up just in time to see her dive forward; he lunged toward her, but his leg gave out. He cried out and fell hard on his knee. Kainadr ran forward and muttered what sounded like a curse in his language.

Jove managed to hobble back to his feet and painfully inch forward. "What? What is it? What happened?"

Neither his mother nor Kainadr seemed to be injured in any way. The Zuprium crystal hadn't done anything or moved or speared anyone with one of those branches. But his mother was fixated on something regardless; she darted forward again, and when Jove finally made it to the other side of the crystal, it was easy to see why.

Anderson Enright lay sprawled upon the floor, eyes closed.

Jove went cold and nearly collapsed again. His mother bent next to the man, feeling the corner of his jaw, eyes scanning the rest of the man's body. "He's got a pulse, and he's breathing, but both are too faint. I don't see any injuries, do you?"

None of his limbs bent at an odd angle. Nothing seemed to be bleeding. Nothing about him suggested he should be comatose at the bottom of some chasm...except the last time Jove had seen him was when Loffler had been dragging him through the cells, claiming he had the power to make all the electricity go dark.

Jove still had only an elementary grasp on all of it. The power of the Essences wasn't supposed to exist. The Yalvs had signed the Treaty hundreds of years ago...then had broken it.

And Kase had lied about it upon his return from Tasava with Zeke's body in tow.

Staying angry at his brother was something he didn't have the time nor strength for. Though Kase definitely deserved his ire, it could be dealt with later.

Once he knew Kase was still alive for him to be angry at.

As softly as he could without straining his still-healing shoulder, he knelt beside Anderson. Kainadr dug in his pouch and sprinkled dust over the man, whispering in a singsong.

Anderson's body glowed brighter than the cluster now at Jove's back. He raised a hand to block the light. It burned his eyes, though not as badly as when he was healed.

Once it faded, he lowered his hand. Anderson seemed to be breathing a little smoother, if he assessed it generously.

Les held Anderson's wrist again and checked his pulse. "Stronger, but I'm not sure if whatever you did was enough."

Hesitantly, Kainadr knelt as well and took out a pinch of dust, sprinkling it on Anderson's face. He sang a little, but instead of the blinding light, the dust rose from Anderson's skin and formed symbols above his head.

Kainadr inspected each one, tapping his lips in thought. "I am unable to perform more intricate diagnostics, but from what this here is indicating," he pointed at a symbol that resembled what Jove thought looked like an eye, "I would say that this man is in perfect health."

He moved his hands a little, and the symbols reconfigured themselves. "However, this here is telling me that he has something internal that is bleeding. And this other one here," he pointed again to an eye symbol, "directly contradicts that."

"So you don't know?" Jove asked flatly. Why did Kainadr

seem determined to give the longest possible answer to every question?

"I was named after the greatest warrior of our people and was even given a holy sword, but I was Called to heal after preparing my entire life to fight," he said, not really answering the question. "My parents were quite distraught."

Jove vaguely remembered Saldr saying something about Called in that breakfast meeting, but he couldn't remember specifics. He didn't need backstory. He just needed to know if the man could help. "What does that have to do with—"

"You should be able to help, you mean," his mother interrupted, giving him a glare that shut his mouth, "but you can't?"

"Indeed. Lord Saldr or Healer Jera would be able to perform more complicated diagnostics if we are ever recovered from these dark depths," Kainadr replied, wiping sweat from his brow. "However, I will watch him closely until that time comes and endeavor to make sure he doesn't fall toward the darkness. His condition seems to have reached an equilibrium, at least."

Jove didn't understand half of what the man said, but he could gather enough to understand that Anderson was healed enough that he was no longer in danger. And if that was the case, all Jove really wanted right then was to rest.

His mother left Anderson's side and inspected the rest of the small cavern, where water slid down the walls and pooled into a narrow cistern-like basin among the rocks. "We have water, and with a little foraging, we could likely find something edible." She dusted off her gown. "If we stay put, our likelihood of being found swiftly goes up quite a bit. We'll be rescued soon."

Jove could appreciate her optimistic outlook, but he had to look at the harsh reality: they'd fallen into a hole during the middle of an attack on the city. They had water, yes...and a giant corrupted Zuprium crystal that was supposedly causing cave-ins. If anything, this was where they would probably die. No one would come looking for them.

And Jove wasn't even sure if he wanted them to try.

C H A P T E R   1 7

ANSWER ME

Kase

SITTING IN HIS FATHER'S TENT didn't feel much different than waiting for his punishment in the Manor's study. No matter where he waited to take the brunt of his father's fury, he still felt small.

Between the confined quarters and the bedraggled furniture, his father had little room to pace, as was his usual habit in Kase's company. The sporadic quiver of his father's feet told him he wanted to, but resisted. Kase refused to look anywhere but at Harlan's worn and muddy boots.

Never in his life had he seen his father so unkempt. In the small glimpses he chanced, days of salt-and-pepper stubble decorated his father's cheeks—more salt than pepper. Kase couldn't remember a time when he'd worn anything but a perfectly trimmed mustache. The only thing that was normal was the hair smoothed back from his face and his hard stare. Kase quickly dropped his eyes back to the mud-speckled boots.

"Where have you been?" Harlan asked, his voice cold,

not betraying the anger and frustration smoldering beneath the surface.

But Kase wasn't cowed completely. He wouldn't just sit there and allow himself to be trod upon.

"Where's Jove?" The words came out filled with disdain. He knew that tone would lead to an argument—it always had in the past—but it was just a reflex, a way to defend himself against the man before him.

A flinch of Harlan's left foot. Kase thought one of the mud smudges reminded him of a Zuprium crystal. His father's rough hand grabbed him by the chin and thrust his face up. Kase gritted his teeth, but he didn't resist.

"Do not change the subject," Harlan ground out, dragging Kase a little closer. "Answer me. Now."

He couldn't yell here—not if he wanted to keep their conversation mostly private. Guards stood on the other side of the tent walls. Kase wasn't sure where Stowe had gone, nor was he aware of Eravin's whereabouts. He was stuck with the man he hated most in the world, though Correa ran a close second.

But he'd faced down torture at the hands of the latter. If he could do that, he could handle his father.

Kase grabbed Harlan's wrist and pushed it away. He stared his father directly in his eyes, the ones that reminded him so much of Zeke.

For the first time in months, he didn't have to repeat his mantra when he thought about his middle brother. He knew Zeke had made a choice, and Kase would never have taken that away from him. Unwavering, he held his father's gaze. "Tell me where Jove is."

Harlan's nostrils flared, not unlike Jove's did when he argued with Kase. He waited a minute before responding. "A section of the tunnels collapsed a week ago. We believe Jove fell in, but we aren't certain how far."

Kase's skin went hot, then cold. It was true. He'd fallen. If Kase hadn't been sitting, he might've lost feeling in his legs and fallen himself. "No."

"We have a crew searching, but without our technology, it's been fruitless," Harlan said, no emotion leaking into his voice, not even anger or concern. As if they were discussing the recent weather changes instead of the potential death of his eldest son. But he continued, "Now answer my question.

Where have you been?"

The words didn't quite reach Kase's ears.

His thoughts still hadn't caught up to the conversation at hand. His head swam like he was drowning, the water pouring into his lungs and filling him up. He worked his mouth, trying to say anything, but nothing came out.

He tried to suck in a breath, but everything had stopped working. Kase was barely aware of his father moving about. Kase could only focus on the reality that he was the only Shackley child left. On how unfair it was that, out of all of them, he'd been chosen to survive.

He'd needed Jove to be there, to take control. Jove would know what to do—he always knew what to do.

Jove had a wife relying on him. Kase relied on him. He couldn't be *gone*.

He had no one now. He had to be the leader. But how could a drowning man lead anyone anywhere but the bottom of the sea?

His vision narrowed. He needed to breathe, but his lungs felt too full and too empty at the same time.

Someone waved what looked like a stuffed tea bag in front of his nose. Kase shivered, and that woke his lungs. He took a short, tight breath and breathed in *something*.

It smelled rich and deep...a hint of ripened fruit, of family holidays on the Silver Coast. It was mixed with a soft floral musk, dry and sweet as the last bloom of autumn. The scent warmed the cold in his core.

With slightly shaking fingers, Kase took the sachet, blinking until he could focus.

"What..." His voice sounded hoarse, even though he hadn't been screaming. It was as if his throat was figuring out how to function in the right way again after disuse, even though the episode had been short. "What is this?"

It truly did look like a tea bag, but bulbous and overstuffed. His vision cleared up with each new inhale of whatever lay inside. Impossibly tiny stitches held the top closed.

Harlan stepped back, and Kase took another whiff of the tea bag. It relaxed his tense muscles even more.

Surely his father couldn't have helped him. He looked back toward the tent flap, looking to see if someone else had entered. But it hung still, undisturbed. Only the background noise of a crowded cavern just beyond the canvas walls met his ears. He turned back to his father and held up the tea bag. "What is this?"

Harlan had clearly given it to him. But how had he known it would help the panic that kept seizing Kase out of the blue? And *why* had he given it to him?

Harlan Shackley never did anything altruistically. He never did anything to *help* Kase. And if for some reason he had, it would most definitely come with a cost.

"Something that will keep your emotions in check while you answer my questions." Harlan folded his arms across his chest. "Now answer me. *Where have you been?*"

Moment of kindness over, apparently. If it had ever started.

Even with his heart still skittering and his skin still clammy from his reaction to Jove's likely death, anger flushed Kase's features. But whatever was in the little teabag allowed air to flow to his lungs with each breath. It tempered the anger at Harlan's dismissal.

"I came back to help." The words were tinged with the bitterness Kase couldn't keep in check even with the strange bag's help.

Harlan stepped back, his fist clenching, but he didn't strike. Not yet. "To help? Help what? The current state of the city is your fault."

"And how do you figure that?" If he played dumb, he might get just get by. Even if part of him knew he'd only said it to get under Harlan's skin.

"Because the entire city rioted for a week straight *before* the Cerls arrived. Because you told someone you started that fire. And when the Cerls attacked, we had no support. It was a miracle so many are here in the tunnels."

"I didn't tell anyone." Recently. Besides Hallie. Eravin had already known.

"Then how did the entire city find out?"

Kase's stomach turned violently. He knew *exactly* how. However, would it behoove him to betray the tentative truce he had with Eravin? He ought to for his own sake, but this was Harlan. The retaliation wouldn't be mild.

Would he execute Eravin? Throw him in one of the gaping tunnel holes? Set him in front of a firing squad?

The leader of One World deserved it. He'd killed that

Cerl without any remorse back at the Jayde Center. He'd threatened Kase more than once.

But Eravin had once been his friend. And it was Kase's fault Eravin's mother was dead.

Kase ran his tongue along the edge of his upper teeth. If he wanted to earn penance for Eravin's mother's death, saving her son was his best chance.

"I can't answer that," he hedged, "but I do have information. The Cerls need the last Essence for some ritual. It's why they attacked the city."

Harlan went still. If Kase hadn't been so on edge, he might've marveled at catching his father off guard. Harlan recovered quickly, his scowl finding its place on his face once more. "How do you know that?"

"Doesn't matter."

"Don't play with me." Harlan fisted his right hand. "You've already lied to the High Council, and that charge is probably the least of your worries."

Kase's nostrils flared. He'd lived through a nightmare in the last month. Nothing his father nor the High Council could do scared him anymore. The entire government and city were in shambles.

He stood, the sachet dropping to the ground. He was taller than his father. Not by much, but the inch felt like a mile. Kase feared nothing. "Correa took Achilles. All our people are dead."

It was Harlan's turn to be silent. He didn't even move. After a few tense seconds he said, low and slow, "I don't believe you."

Kase rubbed his own unshaven cheek. The puckered and healing cut interrupted his short beard—a physical representation of the scarring no one else could see. "I think they had inside help. The only Jaydian survivors are Stoneset villagers holed up in the mountain caverns. Not sure how much longer they can hide."

His father cursed loudly and kicked the pebbles beneath his boot, adding yet another scuff.

Kase gazed steadily at his father as the older man took it all in. He remembered the last conversation he'd had with Harlan—the one that had ended with a busted lip. He traced his tongue along the inside of his lip, tasting phantom blood.

"You can believe me or not, but it's true." Kase crossed

his arms, growing more confident with each passing moment. "I watched it happen; nearly died at Correa's hands myself."

It was Kase's curse—to survive against the odds.

Harlan swallowed, his gaze still as frozen as ice. He remembered. He remembered what he'd said to Kase. The slight feathering of his jaw said so, but Kase couldn't tell if it was of regret or irritation. Either way, his father didn't rise to the bait. "The Cerls seek the Spark Essence."

Cold shock coursed through Kase's body at the words. *"How do you know that?"*

He'd come all this way to give Harlan that information. He'd left Hallie—and his father had already known. He clenched his fists against his sides, his arms still folded.

"I was unsuccessful in keeping the Essence wielder from wreaking havoc on our world. For once, I and the Cerls are aligned on that front." It was his turn to rub a hand down his face. More lines had grown around his eyes and crossed his forehead in Kase's brief time away. Vaguely, Kase wondered if he'd been the cause. He hoped so.

Harlan continued, "I've even been meeting with Cerl defectors, and all of it was for naught."

What?

"How long?" Kase uncrossed his arms.

"Doesn't matter. I had a good contact in Nar particularly. Dead now." Harlan grabbed a rock he'd been using as a paperweight on the makeshift desk. He gripped it in his hands. Kase knew he wanted to throw it, but his father reined in his temper and set the rock back down, his hands shaking slightly.

The longer Kase stood there, the more the words sank in. He lowered himself into the chair and put his face in his hands. His father had been missing on multiple occasions during the months after Kase had returned from Tasava. Vicious rumors of an affair had circulated quickly in a society so obsessed with decorum. Kase himself had believed them. Harlan had never done much to dispute it.

Cerl defectors. The affair rumors had been a great cover, Kase loathed to admit. Still, it didn't excuse Harlan's other sins.

Pressing the heels of his palms against his eyes, Kase muttered, "Correa needs all the Essence powers in order to defeat something called Jagamot. Not sure what that is."

"*All* of them? Where did you get that information?"

"*I told you*, I nearly *died* at their hands." Kase sat back, blinked away the wavy lines in his eyes, and twisted Ana's ring around his finger. "The Cerls kidnapped Hallie, and I…I turned myself in to save her."

Harlan's eyebrows rose a little at the mention of Hallie. They fell by the end of Kase's sentence. "Ridiculous. You could've been—if I had—"

Kase leaned forward, elbows on his knees. "I did what I had to do." He steeled himself to deliver the next bit of news. "They're systematically working their way through the countryside." After seeing Nar, he guessed that the blue markers he'd memorized on the map in Correa's office must've coordinated with the places they'd taken over or had planned to do so—maybe even with One World's help.

"Nar?"

"Overrun."

Harlan turned his back to Kase, a hand rubbing down his face. For once, his frustration wasn't aimed at his youngest son, not entirely. His father spoke to the back of the tent. "Have they collected all the Essence powers, sans Loffler?"

Kase shook his head to clear it. Surely, he'd heard wrong. Loffler was half-dead and useless. "What does that old coot have to do with this?"

Harlan let out a disbelieving chuckle. "Everything, apparently." He folded his arms across his chest. His jacket was missing all his accolades. The only thing decorating it was the Jaydian emblem on the breast. Harlan smoothed his mustache, taming the few wayward strands. "So Correa has found them all, except him?"

And Hallie. Kase ground his teeth. "No."

"No?"

Kase hid his face in his hands once more. What would his father do if he knew about Hallie? Send someone to fetch her? Imprison her? Force her to use that power no matter what it might do to her?

For a moment, the tent disappeared, overcome by fire licking stone as the fort crumbled around him.

"Answer me." His father's voice was hard, but it lacked its usual bite.

Kase ground the heels of his palms into his eyes once

more. *What to say...what to say...*

"Kase Michael Shackley, if you withhold information that could win us this war, I will not hesitate to throw you in a cell."

That would be difficult, since the only cells Harlan could throw him in were now a pile of rubble on top of Kyvena's tallest hill. His writhing emotions kept the retort twisted up inside.

Besides, to his great displeasure, his father was right. If he didn't tell him all he knew, they might as well surrender; they wouldn't stand a chance against the Cerl forces, much less the end of the world. He apologized to Hallie silently as he muttered, "Hallie Walker took the Essence power from the Lord Elder."

Kase still didn't look up, but Harlan's sharp intake of breath told him everything he needed to know.

"She's not here," he said quickly.

"Then where is she?"

Kase dropped his hands and met his father's gaze. "Myrrai."

"Why?"

"She believes there's something there that'll help us." Kase took a shallow breath. He hoped his father didn't notice just how shaky it was—or how uncertain he was about everything beyond what he'd already said.

He couldn't be sure exactly what they were facing. Correa could be some unhinged fanatic, his rambling about Jagamot nothing but religious drivel. But Hallie had done *something* at Achilles. Massive forts didn't just come apart at the seams.

Harlan turned away from him, looking toward the back of his tent once more. Kase was silent. He wasn't sure what else he could say to help. He'd delivered the message—that was as far as he'd planned.

The tent flap opened; the subtle breeze it delivered felt cold on Kase's neck.

One of the guards said, "I apologize for the interruption, Stradat Lord Kapitan. But Lord Stephenson needs to speak with you."

"Not now."

"He says it's urgent."

Harlan let out a frustrated sigh. "Tell him I will see him

in five minutes."

The tent flap closed, and Kase stood. "I'll just go...go find somewhere to sleep for the night."

"You're under house arrest."

"Father—"

Harlan let out a growl of frustration, voice lowering dangerously. "The city wants you to hang. And with the continued flyovers, everyone is already on edge. Your presence here is a bomb waiting to detonate."

"But our hovers...what's keeping us from fighting back?"

Kase already suspected the answer, and he wasn't sure if he wanted it confirmed. The airfields likely hadn't survived the bombing he'd witnessed. But what about before that? What had happened during the attack?

Harlan cleared his throat. "The Jaydian hovers were not operational during the initial assault, courtesy of Abram Loffler. That is why knowing Essence wielders were still at large ahead of time would have been helpful."

Kase's face grew hot once more. "We were only trying to protect...I..."

He couldn't find his words. What if he implied something about Hallie? What if Kase came clean, and his father retaliated against her if she returned?

If.

"What's done is done. We must find a way to fight back without the Crews."

"I stole a Cerl hover in Nar," Kase said.

Harlan froze, but only for a moment. A sardonic sneer blossomed on his face. "Of course you did."

"I can fly it. I can take care of the flyovers."

Harlan threw his hands in the air. "You can't do anything against an entire fleet. Besides, you aren't going anywhere. Not now."

"But—"

"You've done enough."

Kase threw his shoulders back, standing tall, ready to fight. "I'm the best pilot you have. You can't afford to keep me grounded."

Harlan poked him in the chest. "You're the *only* pilot we have, so no, I'm not risking your life just because you have an overinflated ego."

All the air left Kase's lungs. "What do you mean, *only*?"

Harlan stared into his soul. The hazel color shifted depending on the day, the lighting, and his father's mood. Today, dark brown streaks stood out against the green. Danger. "It's my understanding the Hover Colonel called in all pilots to fight the Cerls that night. Except the electricity died. The hovers and their pilots on the airfield strip were sitting ducks. The others fell out of the sky. Those who survived were killed by the Cerls or One World."

"Your *understanding*? Wouldn't you know, being the Lord Kapitan?"

The muscle in his father's jaw jumped again. "I took the fall when the secret about the Kyvena fire got out. While you were off turning yourself over to the Cerl commander."

Kase blinked. "I don't understand."

The father Kase had known would've never done that. It was almost...noble.

"You ran, and the city wanted blood." Harlan's anger drained away, leaving him looking so tired in that moment that Kase could scarcely believe his father and the man in front of him were one and the same. Harlan leaned heavily on the scuffed table. "If the Cerls hadn't attacked, I wouldn't be here now."

Kase said nothing. He wasn't sure what that meant, exactly. Something in the back of his mind told him he should be thanking his father, but he couldn't. The man in front of him didn't deserve that kindness. Giving Kase a tea bag full of herbs and taking the fall, whatever that meant, wasn't enough to erase past hurts or garner his respect.

Harlan clasped his hands behind his back. "However, when we surveyed a few of the refugees gathered here, we discovered that both Millicent Sarson and Heddie Koppen perished." His voice was hard and flinty, like he didn't quite believe the words he'd just said. "The remaining City Council members and I are rationing food supplies and keeping the peace between the refugees while we figure out a way to mount a resistance against the Cerls, but if the cave-ins keep happening, we're going to have to send people back to the surface soon. It's hardly safer down here than up there."

Kase couldn't help the quiver in his voice. "And there's no way we can fight back? Are we certain all the pilots are dead?"

"Without the Hover Colonel, I've been forced to rely on

word of mouth and three traumatized greenies not yet called up, but the gaping holes in the airfields and wreckage of other hovers on the city outskirts do not leave much hope."

Kase fell back into the small chair. Dead. Every last person. "And the ones on missions elsewhere?"

"We can't be sure, but it seems you saw enough in Nar to guess."

Kase worked his jaw, trying to tamper his grief. All the names and faces of those he knew flashed in his mind, but he couldn't pause to think on any of them. Otherwise he might fall apart. "Greenies can fly well enough."

Harlan sighed. "We can't force them to fly. It's practically suicide. One is Laurence Hixon, if that tells you anything."

Kase winced. Hixon was the greenie that he'd fought in the duel all those months ago. So three greenies...but all untried washouts.

"Then you have no choice but to use me. The Cerl hover isn't anything like I've flown before." Kase pushed past his shock about the Crews. "It's almost intuitive. The Cerls won't realize I'm the one flying until it's too late."

"Absolutely not."

Kase stood again. He gestured wildly with his hands. "It's what I was trained to do, and if it helps turn the tide even a little, it's worth it. I could do short flyovers, take a few out at a time, and—"

"No."

"But—"

Harlan grabbed his shoulders, gripping them so hard Kase winced. "I will *not* lose another son."

Jove. He was ashamed he'd nearly forgotten. How cruel that Kase was the son Harlan hated most, yet he might be the only one left to continue his legacy.

Kase swallowed. "Why are the caves collapsing?"

"We can't be sure, but we assume it's because too many people are in the tunnels, and the infrastructure cannot withstand the influx. That's why we're looking to move people out as soon as we can." He released Kase.

Kase swallowed and searched for the tea bag, discarded at his feet. "Where's Mother? How's she taking it?"

He looked around, half expecting her to appear and give him the lecture of his life for scaring her.

Harlan was silent. He looked toward the corner of the tent, then back at Kase.

He'd never seen Harlan's face wear this kind of tension before. His eyes gleamed, but not with anger or hatred. If Kase didn't know better, he might have said his father was...emotional. Yet, his voice shook only on the final word. "We haven't been able to locate her. I believe she may have perished during the attack."

Numb. Kase was numb.

Harlan stepped past him toward the entrance. "I'll arrange for your own tent and a few guards to keep you safe from the masses. By order of the High Council and the Stradat Lord Kapitan, your house arrest begins now."

CHAPTER 18

AS IT SHOULD

Kase

IT'D BEEN HOURS SINCE KASE had been moved to a new tent, and he'd received no word on Jove or his mother. Nothing at all. He'd paced the floor until his feet hurt. No one came to visit. No one had told him anything at all.

The initial attack had happened only a week ago, so his mother could still very well be among the refugees in the tunnels or even hiding somewhere in the city. Kase refused to believe she was dead. His mother was too tough to die.

If he didn't keep believing that, he would lose his mind.

Covering his eyes with his leather-clad arm, he fell heavily onto the cot and laid back. The more developed cavern his prison tent was in allowed for the conversations and any sound to echo around him like a discordant symphony. There was no way he'd be able to sleep with the racket. He was set up just down the tunnel from the larger cavern where his father's tent and other important officials had congregated—still loud. While the smaller cavern chamber might offer a less complicated escape, it would also make it easier for someone to slit his throat.

He briefly wondered if the elevated voices had anything to do with him. Maybe his father hadn't been able to control the population after they'd realized he had finally returned.

The two soldiers guarding his tent wouldn't be much good against a determined mob.

His mother and brother were missing. He was trapped in a tent. He might never see Hallie again. And all of it was for nothing.

Harlan had already known most of the information Kase had to offer thanks to his defectors. In the end, Kase had been the one with horrible news dumped in his lap—Jove and his mother missing, likely dead; the city having fallen to riots before the Cerls ever showed up, thanks to him; the Crews decimated, *dead*, except for a handful of incompetent greenies...and Kase himself. And he couldn't do anything to make his own survival worthwhile, because he was stuck in this *blasted tent*.

He clenched his hands into fists. Being up in the sky was the only way to calm his racing thoughts, but he had nothing above him but canvas and rock.

After another half hour or so, a few words from outside had him sitting up. He had no idea how much time had passed, but it no longer mattered.

Amidst the annoying, indiscernible chatter, someone approached his tent and spoke with the guards, voice soft and feminine. "The Stradat Lord Kapitan has given me permission to speak with Master Kase Shackley."

Kase's heart leapt into his throat.

Clara. With everything that had happened, he'd forgotten about her. How thoughtless of him. Relief shoved him to his feet, giving him the energy to straighten his spine and smooth his rumpled clothing.

Clara might have information about what happened to Jove or his mother. She wouldn't keep it from him—he could trust her to be honest. She might even help Kase get out of this tent so he could do something. *Anything.*

Whipping the tent flap back, Kase took in his sister-in-law. She looked like herself, though a little worse for wear. Her blouse and skirt were wrinkled. She probably hadn't grabbed anything else when fleeing the townhouse. Bags hung like specters underneath her dark eyes—they probably rivaled Kase's own. But she gave him a small smile, and Kase immediately felt at ease. She was still the Clara he remembered.

The bundle of blankets in her arms began to squirm.

Shocks. Is that...?

He took a cursory glance at her stomach. In his initial assessment, he'd failed to notice the size of it. The roundness had receded considerably, which had to mean the squirming bundle was Kase's...

Oh stars. Oh shocks. If Jove was never found, did that mean Kase had to take over fatherly duties?

He'd told his brother no. But was that why Clara was here now?

Dread, nearly heavier than the revelations he'd received in the Stradat Lord Kapitan's tent, filled his stomach. Kase opened and closed his mouth repeatedly. "Clara, you...is that...when did you have the baby?"

With the thick bundle of blankets, Kase couldn't tell much—not even if the baby was a boy or girl.

"A few weeks ago." Clara gave him another sad smile. "We need to talk."

No, we don't. We don't, because Jove will be fine. We don't, because I can't be a father figure. I'm under house arrest and will probably be executed at some point. The baby can't lose two fathers so young in life.

"Of course," Kase said instead, moving out of the way so she could enter his canvas prison chamber. She moved past him, and the bundled baby in her arms opened its eyes.

They were blue as the sky on a clear day.

Kase froze. Those were Jove's eyes. Kase's eyes.

He let the flap fall. "Clara, I..."

She held up her free hand. "I know Jove is missing. I know your mother...hasn't been found yet." She took a moment to compose herself, wiping the stray tear that bubbled over. She swallowed. "I don't need an explanation of where you've been. I just wanted to make sure you're okay."

Kase blinked away the burning in his eyes, relief and shame mixing. Here he was, panicking because he thought he was going to have to take responsibility for the child in her arms, the child that Jove wanted to entrust to his brother if anything should ever happen to him...and his sister-in-law was only here to make sure he was okay.

Kase was most definitely a screw-up.

Clara perched herself on the edge of the cot and gestured for him to sit beside her. Silently, he did. She took a shaky breath and said, "I don't know the details about what happened three years ago. I've heard the rumors by way of the papers and eavesdropped conversations since I've been here, but I don't care."

Kase didn't look at her as he said, "It's true. I started the fire."

Best to just come out with it. Better she hear the absolute truth from him.

Admitting it to Hallie had been hard enough, and it hadn't gotten any easier. Clara's family lived outside the city. Her friends were all upper-class and had avoided the worst of the blaze, but she'd also lost Ana. Kase was the reason she no longer had a sister, either. Ana had been so excited to have another girl in the family.

Clara's hand found his forearm. "I know. But I also know you. You wouldn't have done that on purpose. There is more to the story, and I want to hear it."

Kase's throat wasn't working properly. Ana had been his best friend first and his sister second. She'd been right beside him and Eravin on countless adventures. Kase deserved this house arrest.

Clara added, "But I don't need to know, if you don't wish to tell me. I trust you. Jove trusts you."

Kase pinched the bridge of his nose. "They don't even know where he is."

With how many goodbyes he'd had to say lately and all the losses he'd suffered, the pain and shock should've gotten easier. It hadn't.

Hallie would've told him that it shouldn't get better, that it was normal to feel that way. But Hallie wasn't here. And Kase might very well lose her too.

"They'll find Jove," Clara said firmly. "Or he will find his way to us."

So optimistic. Kase wished he could feel the same. "How did it happen? The Stradat Lord Kapitan didn't really elaborate."

"I don't know. I wasn't...I wasn't there." Her voice sounded far away for a moment. She cleared her throat. "I know everything will be all right, because all things work together for good, even if we might not realize the goodness in the moment. I have faith."

Kase looked up, still blinking the prickling in the corners of his eyes away. "I don't understand."

All Kase knew was that he couldn't win. It was as if fate itself stood against him.

"You will. One day." Clara took a deep breath and shifted the bundle of blankets in her arms. "Until then, it's high time you meet your nephew."

Kase didn't know if his barely contained emotions would hold up against that. Plus, the baby was tiny. Only weeks old. What if he wasn't gentle enough? What if it was the first step to him agreeing to take on a fatherly role?

He put up his hands. "I don't...I mean, it's not like...what if I drop him?"

That seemed the safest way to reject her without hurting her feelings.

Clara smirked through the tears budding in her own eyes. "You won't."

Oh, shocks, not the tears. One minute. He'd hold him for one minute, just to keep her from crying, then give him straight back.

She held out the bundle, the blanket slipping a little more. Trying to still the trembling in his hands, Kase took the baby from her.

"His name is Samuel. Samuel Lee Shackley."

Kase swallowed. The baby was asleep again, his familiar blue eyes hidden behind tawny lids and thick lashes. He hadn't realized babies could be born with such thick lashes. They dusted his plump, light brown cheeks smushed by the hands curled beneath his chin. He squirmed, a small grunt spilling from his impossibly tiny pink lips.

"Samuel," Kase whispered. His heart fluttered a little as he stared at the little boy. Almost the instant his nephew's soft weight pressed against him, all his worries faded.

Kase was an uncle. All he could think was that this baby was so small, yet weighed a thousand pounds. This little life belonged to Clara and Jove, but somehow, he also belonged to Kase. It was not the feeling he'd been expecting at all. It almost made him believe he could step into whatever role Samuel required. How odd that just holding Samuel would be the balm he needed.

A few tears escaped his hold. "He's perfect."

Warmth laced Clara's voice. "*That's* how I know this all will work out as it should."

Kase didn't say what he knew: that it wouldn't, that everything was crumbling around him. He wished he could have her faith, but it had let him down in the past more times than he could count. "I don't know."

"I do," she said softly, so softly that Kase barely heard her over the echoed tunnel noise. "I know because I am not in control, and if I'm not in control, I can't change what's to come, and that, Kase, is true freedom. I can only do my best with the time left to me. These past few weeks have taught me that like nothing else could, and I nearly broke, but beauty is born from the ashes."

Kase didn't say anything. How could he crush that beautiful hope of hers?

Maybe if he kept his beliefs to himself, he could find a way to pretend Clara was right. That there was some higher purpose to what had happened in his life. He just needed to be patient.

Clara pulled a small bag onto her lap. He hadn't even noticed she'd been carrying anything. He'd been too focused on his new nephew and his anxieties. She pulled out a notebook about the size of his old copy of the Odyssey and a plain pencil. She set it on the cot. "I don't have the capacity to go into why right now, not with everything going on." She patted her hand on the notebook. "But I haven't been able to paint or do anything creative as of late, so this notebook is only going to waste. It also feels a little pretentious, carrying around something that isn't helpful to our situation here." She gave Kase a small smile. "I thought you could use it to write out your thoughts, or send me messages if you need anything. Your father's orders were clear, but he didn't say you couldn't write letters."

"Thank you," Kase said.

The notebook wasn't fancy, but it was bound in expensive dark brown leather. He could use it to send a note to Stowe, too, if needed. A little bit of the tension in his muscles melted away. It was a step in the right direction.

Kase's arm tingled beneath Samuel's weight. He adjusted his grip, moving as slowly as he could so as not to wake up the sleeping babe. That maneuver failed spectacularly; Samuel's face scrunched with the movement, and his mouth opened to let out a frustrated cry. Without thinking about what he was doing, he shushed him and stroked his finger down his nephew's silky cheek. "It's okay, little buddy."

Samuel's face slowly relaxed. He wrapped his entire tiny hand around Kase's finger, squeezing as he fell back to sleep.

It was a shot right to the heart.

How could something so small make such an impact on him, and so quickly? He let out a breath of relief. "That was easier than I thought."

He couldn't move his finger now. Samuel had a death grip on it. Kase couldn't help grinning.

Clara chuckled softly. "You're a natural."

Kase shook his head. "Not so sure about that, but I'll have to rub it in Jove's—"

He went silent. Clara placed a hand on his shoulder. "They'll find him."

"But what if..." He couldn't even get out the words. He'd thought them plenty, feared them, but to say them...

Kase's jaw wobbled a little.

Clara pulled him into a side hug. "Then we will deal with that when it comes, but in the meantime, rest and write out your thoughts. Journaling has always helped me process things." She let him go and stood, stretching. "I have a shift at the hospital ward soon, so I need to go, but I'll come visit tomorrow with Samuel. Send a note if you need anything before then, okay?"

Kase rose slowly, trying not to jostle Samuel too much. "Who's watching him?"

"My mother. She made it to the city before...everything. Between me, her, and a new friend of mine, Samuel's been spoiled pretty handsomely." She smiled as Kase handed her son back. Samuel cried a little bit, but Clara bounced him softly. "He's going to be hungry soon, too."

Kase stuck his hands in his pockets. "Thank you for stopping by. I'm glad you're okay. And Samuel. And...just...thank you. For everything. You didn't have to."

"Of course I did," Clara said, her brow furrowing. "We're family, Kase. It's what we do."

Her family, maybe, but not his. His family let him fend

for himself. But Kase didn't argue with her. He only nodded. "See you soon, then."

She left with a word of thanks to the guards, but her words lingered in her wake. Kase picked up the journal and pencil. It reminded him painfully of Hallie.

Chewing on his lip, he opened up the book. He'd write a quick note to Stowe to let him know what had happened. He also wanted to know if he'd found Hallie's mother.

When he finished scrawling a few lines and a hasty signature, he handed it off to one of the guards with instructions on who to give it to. The man assured him he'd get it to where it needed to go, though he did so gruffly. Kase didn't care. He went back to his cot and forced himself back into a fitful sleep.

CHAPTER 19

IN EVERY WAY

Hallie

HALLIE TURNED THE FINAL CORNER in the undamaged palace and found herself back at Niels' abandoned pack. She ground her teeth. Here he was in an unfamiliar, dangerous city, and he thought it was just fine to wander off without anyone knowing where he went.

She couldn't deny the thin rivulet of relief that trickled in, because his absence meant she wouldn't have to face him right away. She rubbed her eyes. What a horrible thing to think. They were wandering in an abandoned city with the world on the edge of possible destruction, and all she could think was about how fortuitous it was she didn't have to break his heart for a second time just yet.

Shame fluttered in her cheeks.

She really needed to get her priorities straight. She let out a frustrated sigh. Maybe she should just go to the library on her own. Let him stew or do whatever he needed until she found something that she thought would help them. Maybe she'd even find him there.

She walked back through the palace, distracting herself by making a plan. Once she found the information on Jagamot and the Essences, she would find Niels. Once she found Niels, she would somehow figure out a way back to Kyvena. Maybe she could use her power to open up one of the Passages in the Gate Temple. She could probably handle that. She'd healed Niels, after all.

Oh stars, what if her healing had reverted like it had the first time? What if he was actually bleeding out somewhere, and she was too selfish to try looking for him?

A wave of warmth greeted her as she stepped through the archway at the palace entrance and entered the city once more.

Dread, heavy and black, filled her stomach. With the city's empty, scorched lanes surrounding untouched Zuprium-roofed homes, it felt like entering an empty tomb, eerie and pregnant with anticipation.

Power gathered in her core and tingled in her fingertips. With her more frequent usage, she could now tell the difference between the onslaught her Essence power had been and the gently flickering candle it was now. She knew she could tug more out and turn that candle into a respectable campfire or even a controlled blaze, but if she wasn't careful, she'd lose control and create an inferno. She didn't think she could finesse it in a way that would light that little fireball like King Filip had. With her, it was all or nothing. The King could probably teach her how to control it, but he was currently at the bottom of the mountain in a bad state.

Hallie was going to leave him there, and she told herself he deserved it. All her life, she'd known that the Cerl King cared little for his people. He'd had his military attack Jayde in small bands for years and years after the Great War. He was a despot. He was a monster.

That was what she'd always been told. That was what all the traders had said. She'd seen what the Cerls could do on the *Eudora Jayde* mission. She remembered Rodr and the way they'd used him to gain access to the Gate Temple by cutting off his arm.

But the look on Fely's face when they'd found the King comatose, trapped under the beam, would stay with Hallie forever. It was the look of horror she'd worn on her own face the day her brother died. She'd seen it in the mirror for days after.

It was the same sort of anguish she'd felt when Correa had tried to make her kill Kase.

The heat of her power flooded her with vengeance. She paused, hand on the palace wall, teeth clenched against the pain.

Find a tendril, hold on.

The power was elusive. The ground beneath her came too fast, but she caught herself before she could bust her face. She lost control, channeling the power directly into the Zuprium bricks beneath her splayed fingers.

She squeezed her eyes shut against the pain, moaning, still searching for that tendril. She grappled for it. Her breaths came too fast.

She reached far into herself until finally, her mental fingers caught the tail of one tendril and grabbed hold. Crushing it in her grip, she couldn't hear anything, couldn't see anything. She just held on.

Breathing heavily, she pushed herself to her knees.

Mentally, she built a wall to hold the simmering power back. She didn't let go of her tendril—not until the wall was secure. With each brick laid, the tension eased in her shoulders. Her fingers fumbled to find Kase's goggles at her waist. She squeezed them until the edges bit into her palm.

She was going to be okay. For now.

She slowly pushed herself to her feet. Outside the palace, the city was just as bleak as it had been the previous day. The acrid stench of charred wood, melted metal, and, oddly, Yalvar fuel filled the air, mingling with the suffocating smoke that hung like a shroud over the ruins. Had it only been a few months since she'd been standing here with Kase and Zeke, praying that they could make it to the Gate temple in time to protect it from whatever scheme the Cerls had?

She picked up the electropistol from where she'd dropped it and held it in her other hand. The smell of smoke grew stronger the more breaths she took.

Wait.

She took in her surroundings. Why was there smoke? She hadn't set any fires. Maybe the earthquake?

Maybe it was stupid to come out here at this time. She wouldn't be able to find anything now. She could use a torch or something like that to search, but that would be tedious.

Panic replaced her relief, and the fire licked at the wall she'd constructed.

The smell of smoke grew stronger, but there was no telltale glow. Almost too soft to hear, a subtle rumbling and a *thump-thump* echoed in the night.

A trail of cold wound its way down her spine. Something was very, very wrong. Her mind might have been playing tricks on her. It made sense that she was hearing things, but there was something within her that told her she wasn't imagining the sensations and the smell. It was a sign, as if the power itself was trying to tell her something.

It was much like the warm pulses she'd gotten after Achilles that told her to go find the Passage...except this time, there weren't any images flashing in her head. She looked back toward the palace, all quiet and dark.

She'd just started walking back toward the palace to find a torch when the strange *thump-thump*, like a heartbeat, started again. She paused. It wasn't her own heart. Hers fluttered a little and sped up at the unease settling in her blood. This one was low and slow. It was how she imagined a dragon's heartbeat might sound.

She quickened her pace toward the palace. Dragons— or, as the Yalvs called them, dragonars—roamed freely on this side of the world. Hallie would rather not relive her experience with the one in the forest. She didn't have Kase to outwit it this time.

Stars, where was Niels?

Thump-thump.

The pulse reverberated in her bones. It burned like acid, like layers of bone and muscle were peeling away. Her legs nearly gave out, but she caught herself when she stumbled. "What in the—"

Thump-thump.

By the time the next one struck, she'd reached the palace. She caught herself on the palace archway, digging her fingernails into it as she held back a scream.

When the sound ripped through her body again, her power met it. The sensation struck the heat and puddled there, simmering, but it didn't hurt nearly as badly. She fumbled for Kase's goggles and gripped them.

When the next phantom heartbeat tried to shatter

through her, it hurt even less; the Essence power within her seemed to be tempering it. An image of the Gate flashed in her mind. She looked up toward the mountain temple.

Finally, something.

She was probably being a stars-idiot, but she pushed herself toward it without a light to guide her. She wasn't sure what she was going to find inside, but it didn't matter. She had to go.

The Essence inside her wanted her to go. It needed her to do...something. It was what led her to Myrrai in the first place with the Passage, and that instinct hadn't dimmed. She would rather go to the library and figure out what her next steps were, but that could wait. It was like the Gate inside the temple was a lantern, and she the moth drawn to its light.

Her boots scuffed along the lane as she headed toward the temple, the cobblestones stained with ash, blood, and debris she tried to ignore. Memories flashed in her mind, of Ebba's chest lit with a golden glow as the bullet struck her, of Kase shielding her from a Cerl bullet, of the Cerls using Rodr's blood to force open the temple door.

She inspected the doorway itself. Deep claw marks raked across the metal and stone, splintering it in jagged lines. Something large had burst through, leaving the door bent and misshapen, hanging at a grotesque angle from torn, rusted hinges. She blinked. Zuprium didn't rust. Maybe...that was...wait...

She shuffled closer, looking at the nearest hinge closely. That wasn't rust.

It was old blood.

Her stomach churned, and she stepped back, willing the nausea to abate. But she made the mistake of looking down.

The stain streaked down the door, the rusty reminder pooling beneath her feet. Time and weather had reduced it to nothing but pigment, but...

This was where Zeke had died.

She gripped Kase's goggles, willing the grief and power bubbling up from her stomach to subside.

Squatting down and running her hand on the stone below her, she whispered the words of leaving as if they would make a difference now, even though they'd burned him a few months before.

"May you find your place amongst the stars."

It wasn't enough. It would never be enough, but it was all she could do for now. She would defeat the Cerls, make them pay for what they'd done—to Zeke, to Kase, to her.

She'd do it for Stoneset, for Jayde.

Thump-thump.

She winced against the pain, but her power responded quickly, countering whatever it was. Thank the stars. It was the first time her power had spared her from pain. After another second or two of silence, she opened her eyes and stood.

Soft threads of golden smoke drifted like snakes in an invisible wind. They leaked from the doorway and the temple beyond. She could barely see them, which was probably why she hadn't noticed them before. The tendrils seemed to beckon her, leading her into the temple.

It curled and twisted around her ankles, over the place where Zeke had died, and out into the city.

The old Hallie woke with a vengeance, and her fingers twitched, overcome with the urge to draw the strange phenomena.

Where was it coming from? What was it? The smoke had a slightly luminescent quality about it, but being so faint, it didn't give off much light. She peeked around the massive door.

Whatever had destroyed it hadn't merely been trying to leave the temple—it had been enraged. The stone threshold was stained dark, and beneath the scent of smoke, there was the faint, sickly-sweet odor of decay.

The dragon Ben had brought through. It must have done this.

Where was it now? Was it lying in wait for her inside? Was that its heart she heard?

She clenched her hands. She would solve this mystery, then go home. She needed to be there. With Kase. With Petra, Ellis, and everyone at University she loved. She even spared a thought for the librarian who hated her guts.

The last thought brought a small smile to her face for only a moment. What would the old hag say when she discovered it was Hallie who'd returned to save her and the thousands of books in the library?

She took a few fortifying breaths. She would see what waited inside this temple, then go back to the palace to find

Niels. He had to be there somewhere. It had been stupid of her to leave the palace, but now that she had, she couldn't turn back. She needed to know what lay inside, what called to her.

She turned only briefly, looking down into the city of ghosts, where shadows shifted like the restless spirits of the fallen. Moonlight on scorched cottage roofs glinted off shattered glass and twisted metal. It would be worse inside the temple.

Another heartbeat gave her pause, but it was over in a moment, even if it did rattle her bones. Nothing else moved. Not even the door hanging by a thread. So incredibly odd.

Hallie stepped over the ruined threshold and into the temple. Her fingers flared with heat as she ran them along the door frame's broken stones. She hadn't paused to inspect the stones last time she'd been here.

It almost felt like coming home. Yet it scared her.

Not only was there the possibility of failure and being stranded there, but something about the smoke and the Gate and everything here felt like a warning. She was out of her element and unprepared for the future to come.

Yet these bricks, this Zuprium contradicted those feelings as long as she ran her fingers over them. She looked down at the goggles. They were sparse on Zuprium, but it was there in the frames, holding the lenses in. She ran her thumb over the small crack in the right one.

Had that feeling always been there? Had she simply ignored it up until now? Stoneset had been rife with Zuprium dust. Had that made a difference? She let her fingers fall from the bricks and immediately felt the loss. She hadn't ruled out the idea that she might simply be losing it, not just yet. With all the stress of the last few months, it wasn't such a bizarre theory.

She wished Navara had written more about her people and the life she'd led here. Instead, she'd unraveled into raving at the end, trying to find a way back to Myrrai. She hadn't been successful.

The Gate's image flashed in her mind again, urging her to continue. She turned away from the threshold and followed the smoke. She could deal with thoughts of Navara and her near-useless journals later.

In the stone corridors, the warm pulses intensified,

though she was able to stay standing. The smoke curls grew denser and brighter. With each step, she walked beside an echo of Kase in her memory, stumbling beside her as they trailed the cart carrying Zeke's body.

Steadying herself on the wall, she took a deep breath. It felt like yesterday, but at the same time, everything she'd gone through since made it feel as if she'd lived three lifetimes. If she were to measure that in novels, she'd estimate it as two rather large ones filled with fantastical worlds and domineering kings ruling with iron fists. She wished her last few months had been but ink on paper, for if it had, she could very well write herself a happy ending.

But that wasn't reality...at least, not the one she found herself in.

Taking a few more moments to breathe, she finally pushed off the wall and strode forward, following the smoke.

The temple was a maze of murals and corridors. Even in the faint light, she discerned the difference between the wall paintings and those that hid underneath the ruined city in the valley below. These told of more modern times, particularly when the First Earthers landed. She wished she'd paid more attention to these the last time she'd visited, though at the time, she and Kase had just witnessed Zeke's death and were attempting to protect the Gate from the Cerls.

Several nerve-jangling disconnected heartbeats later, she found herself in a very familiar corridor. Debris and rubble lay strewn about, but she'd kissed Kase on the cheek just there, beneath the empty sconce that hung at an odd angle. It was where he'd almost kissed her for the first time, though they'd been interrupted.

Now, she was glad for that interruption. Their first kiss was worth the wait...though she hadn't chosen the most romantic of settings, unless you were into the dank and dreary dungeon thing.

The heart in her chest gave a painful throb. Stars, if this was what it was like to truly love someone, to miss them with each waking moment when apart, was it worth it?

She knew it was, even as her eyes stung, her vision blurring. Just like she knew Kase felt the same. The look in his eyes when they'd said goodbye had told her that. She swallowed the lump in her throat. She'd never felt that with

Niels, no matter what eighteen-year-old Hallie had believed. Leaving him hadn't felt like tearing her heart out and leaving it behind with someone else.

Thump-thump.

This one crashed through Hallie like an ocean wave, and her power surged. The smoke throbbed with the heartbeat.

Just a little further. I'll see what this is, then I'll find Niels, and we'll go back to Jayde.

But what about Fely and King Filip? What about the sword?

She shook those thoughts away. She couldn't let guilt command her decisions.

The phantom heartbeats and the smoke meant something. The Gate was around the corner, and if the front door of the temple was in such terrible shape, she could assume this one would be the same. She closed her eyes for a second and stretched her hearing as far as she could. She didn't want to walk into a trap.

No growls or roars, so probably no dragons. She couldn't hear anyone inside. But that didn't make her feel safer. She could be mistaken; worse, she could be hallucinating. She might've very well hit her head in the palace, and this was all something she'd made up in her mind.

She wasn't sure that would be a bad thing. If she woke right now, it might be better.

Her power hadn't abated after the last heartbeat, and it burned through her body as if she were an eternal flame, never burning out. It stung, but she kept hold of Kase's goggles. Her brother's pocket watch might have tempered the pain completely, but the goggles helped a little.

The only real sound was a light crackling, like a bonfire, which would explain the smoke. But the better question was how and when a fire had started in the first place, and what kind of fire produced glowing smoke.

All the more evidence in favor of all this taking place completely in her head.

An urgency tugged at her, one she couldn't quite put into words. It begged her to round the corner. It pleaded for her not to turn aside now.

And as the reckless Hallie that had been born as of the last year, she marched right around the corner and into the Gate chamber.

Blackened walls riddled with gouges matching the temple entrance scoured the floor. Rocks and bricks and Zuprium littered the floor, and in the center of it all stood the glowing Gate.

Thick twists and coils of her smoke guide wafted from the glowing center of the archway. Images no longer flashed. Instead, all that remained was a simple black sword with a ruby in the pommel. It was as if the sword was caught in a stream, the smoke from the Gate flowing over it like water.

Her skin crawled, like a thousand tiny beetles scurrying up her body.

The Gate was angry.

The ground shook with its fury, tossing her aside like chaff in the wind. She curled into a ball and huddled against the ruined door frame. Shouts echoed in the corridor, but she couldn't tell if they were her own or the screams of vengeful ghosts.

"Hal..." A hand brushed her back.

Niels.

How did he get here? Had he been in the temple the entire time? The quaking had stopped, but the tremors still rattled in her bones. She uncurled herself.

"Was that you shouting?" His face was whiter than snow.

She made a cursory glance at his leg. It was still bloody, but the stain was brown and beginning to fade. Old blood. He didn't seem to be favoring it. Her healing hadn't reverted. Yet.

"No," Hallie answered, getting to her feet. She shrugged off his offer of help and dusted her trousers. "I don't think so."

His face visibly relaxed. "I saw you head up this way, but I wasn't sure if you still needed time...I'm sorry. I just—I just—"

Hallie shook her head. While she might've begun her quest into the city earlier to find and talk with him about that, this wasn't the time or the place. Not when sudden cold filled her entire being and grew with each step she took into the Gate chamber. The quaking was gone, but the fury still radiated from the Gate.

THUMP-THUMP.

Hallie screamed as pain drenched her body. The Gate— the heartbeat was coming from the *Gate.* She fell backward against the wall, her pack cushioning her.

"Hallie!" Niels bent down to her level, catching her by her shoulders. "What hurts?"

Why hadn't her power stopped it that time? Why did it hurt so badly?

Niels didn't look as if he was hit with anything. He just looked worried...and a little sweaty. How had he found her so quickly? Why hadn't he caught up with her earlier?

She shook her head. "I...I think that's the sword. Kainadr's Shadow."

Not one scholar believed the old Yalven folk tales were true...but the Cerl King did. And sure enough, a sword waited in the Gate.

Whether or not that was *the* sword wasn't clear. But at this point, it would seem odder to Hallie if it wasn't.

She knew from her last experience with the Gate that it would take in Yalvs and somehow transform them into swords. She wasn't sure why, and it was one thing she'd like to research further in the library, though she hadn't been able to find anything in the week after Zeke died. She and Kase had gone to research and read every single day and had found nothing.

But having a sword would only help her position. She knew nothing about sword fighting, but having any weapon was better than having none at all. Maybe she'd get lucky, and any opponent they came across *also* wouldn't have a clue.

When she got back to Kyvena, she would ask Saldr about it.

She walked a little closer. The sword was dark as night with a nondescript cross guard. A vivid red gem sat in the pommel—a ruby. At the moment, Hallie couldn't remember what gemstone Rodr's had. She didn't think this was the same sword. For one, Rodr's sword had been made of Zuprium. This one looked like it'd been forged from ink.

It hung in the middle of the archway. Her ears rang as she stared at it. She could have sworn it was singing her name.

She thought back to the legend of Kainadr and Xera, of the statues in the ruined valley temple. Could it really be? The stories never described the swords themselves, only that Xera and Kainadr gave themselves over to become swords to help Toro defeat Jagamot.

No scholar knew what happened to the swords

afterward. It was the main reason many scholars put it down to a nice myth.

But this sword beckoned to her, like it was a part of her.

Without waiting to second-guess herself, she reached for the sword. Her hand went through the odd golden water that didn't feel like water, just like Ben had done back in the late autumn, just like her satchel with her copy of *The Odyssey* and sketchbook full of notes from her first journey to Tasava.

A torrent of invisible fire raced up her arm from where she stuck her hand into the Gate, grasping for the sword—but no matter how hard she pushed, she just couldn't reach it. The ground shook once more, but she gripped the bricks on one side of the Gate and refused to let her hand move. She screamed at the anguish eating away at her flesh as her power responded and flooded the archway in a great whoosh.

Her fingers found the sword grip. She pulled. The sword came loose from whatever held it captive, and she stumbled backward. Niels caught her. She stiffened and tugged out of his hold as quickly as she could.

"Thanks," she muttered as she inspected the weapon in her hand. The pain fell away like summer rain off the inn's roof, and soon it was gone completely.

"What is that?"

The sword seemed to drink in the light from the Gate instead of reflecting it. It wasn't too heavy. It felt just right in her hands.

"A myth," Hallie whispered.

"I don't understand."

Hallie didn't respond. The sword was cold, and her power responded only in the places where her skin touched the metal. She observed the Gate. The sense of wrong was still there. Her palm began to ache from where she held the sword. She switched it to the other hand. The first grew cold; the one holding the weapon, hot.

She held it out to Niels. "Tell me what you feel."

He hesitated, his mouth opening as if to say something, but he closed it sharply and took the weapon. He held it awkwardly as if afraid it would attack. He shrugged. "Just feels like a sword, not that I ever held one before." He handed it back. "Listen, Hal, I know this isn't the best of times, but we gotta talk about what happened."

Hallie's power responded to the sword once it was back

in her hands. It wasn't painful, only uncomfortable.

Niels waited. If she made eye contact, they'd have to have the conversation. She didn't want to. Not yet. Not when she had a mystery in her grasp and the world to save. Maybe it was cowardly of her, but she only had so much bravery. Even though she knew she had to break his heart. It was only fair. Fair to him, her, Kase. Everyone. If only he hadn't kissed her.

"Not now, Niels," she pled.

"You know I only want you to be happy."

Hallie closed her eyes for a moment, the outline of the sword painted on the back of her eyelids. She gripped it tightly to keep herself grounded.

Niels didn't pick up on the hint. "Can we please just talk about it?"

Hallie didn't loosen her grip on the sword, but she looked up at last. His eyes, ones she knew better than her own, were soft and pleading. Regret flooded her veins. No matter what had happened three years ago, she was the one who had left. She was the one who had made them near-strangers. That part wasn't his fault. She worried her lip a second before she whispered, "I'm sorry."

He took a step forward, his hand finding her upper arm. He held it lightly and bent to look in her eyes. She didn't move out of his grip, but she avoided his gaze.

"Look...I tried, all right? I thought I was able to move on, but after these last few months of horror I've been through...and then you show up and get kidnapped by the Cerls, and I thought...I can't help it, Hal. I will always love you."

Hallie swallowed, taking a small step back. Niels' hand fell back to his side. She shook her head and finally looked him back in the eyes once more. He had lines around his eyes that hadn't been there when she'd left three years ago. A few scars peppered his brow; another snaked out from the corner of his lip. That one had been courtesy of Jack. All three of them had been throwing snowballs, and a rock got balled up in one of them. Jack had felt terrible. Hallie had ripped a bit of cloth from her skirt to help stop the bleeding. Hallie's mother hadn't been impressed with the added mending to her already full basket.

The ones on his brow could've been from the mines, or

maybe they were from the years she hadn't been home. She would never know, and that was okay. She had survived a few scrapes of her own since that she might never tell him about.

Stars, she'd gone on a whole death-defying mission in the fall that had gifted her a whole litany of new scars she'd rather not dwell on. There was only one person who could understand who she was now, who she'd become.

That man was not Niels Metzinger, no matter how much he wanted it to be.

Her thumb traced the sword pommel. A flush crept up her neck and onto her cheeks. "I...I can't do this. Not now."

"You keep saying that."

"Niels, we've grown up. I'm not the Hallie you knew. I'll never be her again."

There. She'd said something, at least.

"Kase doesn't know you like I do." Niels rubbed the heel of his palm against the side of his head, almost as if he had a headache. He found her eyes once again. "He couldn't protect you, but I can. I would've never let the Cerls kidnap you."

Hallie's mouth fell open, heat pounding against the wall. Niels had no idea. Absolutely no idea. He didn't even realize how clueless he was. "I don't need protecting."

"Correa tortured you, forced those powers upon you. I wouldn't have let it happen."

"He would've killed you."

Niels stepped closer, his face too close to hers. She couldn't go back any further. "And I would've happily died if that meant you were safe."

If this were a romance novel, Hallie knew the heroine would've grabbed him by the shirt and kissed him senseless. But this wasn't some fantasy romance. This was reality. This was gritty and real and nothing like a book.

Hallie had something real, and it wasn't anything bought with cheap flowers and over-the-top confessions of love. She slid sideways away from him. "Kase nearly did." Despite her best effort, her words came out choked, but that didn't stop her. "He's my match in every way, and he sees me for my strengths, for my flaws, for everything I am. He challenges me. Encourages me. Drives me to be better than I am instead of wishing I'd go back to being the same old Hallie."

"I never said that! I just...you've never even given me the chance to show you..." Niels took in a breath. "I'd been saving money. Enough to go to Kyvena. To find you."

Shock radiated through her. She turned, her mouth dropping open slightly. "What?"

"Took me a few years, but I finally had enough. And then the attack happened."

Her heart fluctuated between shock, fear, and anger. The latter won out. "And why do you think showing up in the capital would've changed anything?"

She spit the words as if they were acid. They burned her tongue and her throat. Everything, every word, touch, look, every feeling she'd bottled up until now finally caught flame. Niels' eyes reflected her rage, though his was controlled, bridled.

"I would've moved mountains for you, and don't you try to deny your feelings. Don't you say you feel nothing at all for me." Niels jammed his hand into his pocket and pulled out that Zuprium band. "I saved this ring for you. And only you. We had planned a life before you left, or have you forgotten?"

Hallie stared at his mother's ring. The one he'd saved before her Burning.

"Look at me, Hal," he pled. "You're the only family I have left."

The anger coursed through her at his words, at his guilting. He might have full-heartedly believed he was making sense and showing her the side of him that he thought she wanted, but...

This entire time, he'd thought she could simply forget his past—*their* past—and move on. But she couldn't. Her power wavered, straining against the wall she'd built earlier. Tears fell down her face like rain.

She needed to just say it. It was the only way he'd understand.

"We killed Jack. You and I. And no matter what we do, that will always be our history. I can never separate you from that."

She brushed her hand over her eyes, hoping to stem the flow, but she only cried harder, her words coming out in gasps. "I've tried to move on. I've tried—I've *tried* to replace what was there, but nothing worked. I'm no longer the Hallie Walker you knew. I've grown up and changed. And that's *okay*."

That hurt. The look of defeat in his eyes pierced her, and she realized how cruel she'd been. She hadn't meant to be, but she'd still done it.

Hallie turned away, looking back at the Gate.

"At least you made the last part easy for me," a deep and craggy voice spoke from the doorway.

A leaden knot coalesced just beneath her ribs.

Hallie whipped her head up and dragged the sword into a defensive position. It still felt odd where her skin touched it, but it was bearable for now. Niels grabbed a pistol from the back of his pants and aimed it toward the entrance.

Hallie was confused for a second as he shouldn't have had a weapon on him, but then she recognized it not as his flashpistol, but one of Yalven make. He must've picked it up when she couldn't find him.

An ancient man stood in the doorway, and Hallie found him terribly familiar, though she couldn't quite place him. His beard was white and long, his skin wrinkled. His eyes were bright and golden brown.

"I know you," Hallie said quietly. Her memory was foggy, but it tried to work through where she'd seen this man before, because it had been relatively recently. Had he been in the room in Achilles? No. No, it wasn't that. From before. From Kyvena.

And then it clicked.

"Abram Loffler." Hallie lowered her sword. "I mean, Stradat Loffler. Why...how...um, sorry to be rude, but how did you get here?" Her brain could not put together how this old man had crossed an ocean and half a continent all by himself. "Sir."

She added the last belatedly, but she couldn't remember if she should call him *sir* or *my lord* or something else. Maybe he was like the Stradat Lord Kapitan and wanted to be called by his title at all times.

"Oh, I don't think that matters a bit, do you?" The gleam in his eyes unnerved her a little. "Now be a dear and hand over that sword."

The last Hallie remembered of the man was when she'd been helping the Yalvs on the night of their arrival. She hadn't thought much of him then, only that he was a little out of it. So much had happened since that she couldn't recall much else. What confused her was what he was doing *here* of all places. He was part of Jayde's ruling body...yet here he was, thousands of miles away, looking rather younger than she remembered.

Something wasn't adding up. Hallie glanced down at the sword again, renewing her grip. She edged backward. "Why?"

Filip and Fely needed this sword. And now Loffler wanted it. Out of the three of them, Loffler should have been the one she trusted. He was a Stradat, for stars-sake.

But there was something about his eyes that told her otherwise. Maybe the rumors were true, and he had gone mad. Nothing was making sense.

"What's a Stradat doing out here?" Niels asked, shifting in front of Hallie.

Loffler took a wearied step in their direction. "And you are?"

"Niels Metzinger of Stoneset." Niels cocked the Yalven pistol, but that was entirely the wrong move.

Before Hallie could even blink, Loffler thrust his hands out. Something dark yet bright at the same time leapt from his fingers. Both Hallie and Niels dropped to the ground as what looked like black lightning flashed over her head. No, not black—it was purple, so dark it looked black, except for a moment right before it clashed with the Gate. The archway shook, and the ground beneath Hallie's aching body shuddered.

Earthquake.

There was only one reason someone would have that sort of power.

"Essence," Hallie gasped. "You're an Essence wielder."

"Indeed," Loffler replied, throwing out a hand. Hallie flinched, but no power shot at her. Loffler stepped forward. "And you are as well. I can sense it. Not that I need it, but I can help you rid yourself of it. It hurts, doesn't it?"

Hallie breathed heavily. "Why are you here?"

Loffler laughed. "For the sword, of course. Or were you not listening earlier?"

Scooping up the sword, she edged backward, matching the old man step for step. She needed to keep him talking until she could figure something out. She'd pushed Ben through the Gate. Would that work this time?

She glanced back without meaning to. The Gate's golden smoke was now streaked with darkness like the man's powers.

Not good.

She'd read enough books to know that was very much not the ideal situation. She just wished she could be reading about this now instead of living it out.

"Do...not...give it...to him," an exhausted voice spat from the chamber door.

In the ruined doorway, King Filip leaned heavily on Fely. The bandage on her head was soaked with new blood. Filip was sweating, looking as though he'd just stood up from his deathbed. His eyes were ringed in red. Somehow, they'd hiked the mountain in record time. Fely's hand clenching his other side glowed faintly. But just how much power was she giving him? Hallie hadn't been able to heal his legs completely.

Loffler turned. "Ah, Your Majesty. You've certainly looked better."

Hallie used the distraction to back closer to the Gate and to Niels. They needed to plan.

"You're the one who's doing this, aren't you?" Filip said, still barely getting the words out. He took a shaky step forward, one arm over Fely's shoulder, the other pressing into the crumbling wall. "You're the reason we even need to go through with my uncle's plan. Don't deny it."

"I've waited nearly five hundred years for this moment, and Jagamot is not a kind master. He's planned his revenge since the Dawn, and I will bring it to fruition."

"And you've corrupted enough crystals, haven't you? My uncle said that would happen. The earthquakes?" Filip took more lumbering slow steps forward until they were mere feet away from Loffler. Fely's hand kept glowing, but she glanced at Hallie.

Unadulterated fear, worse than when Filip had nearly been crushed by the beam, waited in her eyes. Nothing could have prepared Hallie for it.

What was she supposed to do now? Could she open a portal here and escape? She prodded her power, but she wasn't sure it would be enough—not after the earlier healings. When she'd created the Passage earlier, it'd been using the existing brick from the first Passage created by the Lord Elder. Without it, she didn't know if it would work.

Maybe she could use the Gate? It held many timelines; surely there was one that included Kyvena in the present day.

She tried to think back to what she'd read in the book *The Gate of Time*, but she had trouble recalling anything. The black strings of Loffler's power threaded through the golden smoke still, and something told her not to touch it. Could she trust the uncontaminated part of the power left? It might be enough to do something. But she didn't understand what to do.

Without Fely and Filip, she was shooting in the dark. They were her enemies, but they did know a little more about her power than she did. They might help her like they did earlier. But they needed to neutralize Loffler somehow first.

She thought back to her last visit here. She just needed to distract him enough for the plan to work, but she didn't have Ebba's slingshot or stone this time.

Hallie leaned as close to Niels as she could and whispered, "I don't know what's about to happen, but we need to get him in front of the Gate. Got it?"

"Your plan?"

"Just follow my lead."

And pray for the best.

The muscles of her upper and lower arms knotted beneath her skin as she forced her power into the weapon. She bit her lip hard to keep herself from crying out against the flare of heat threatening to boil her from within. Hallie met Fely's gaze, then looked down at the sword. Fely followed her line of sight, then just barely dipped her chin.

Clenching her teeth against the lingering pain, Hallie gripped the sword in both hands and stood as quickly and quietly as she could, but her old boots creaked with the movement. Loffler twisted and thrust out his hands. Hallie didn't think, only flung the sword at him while ducking out of the way.

Lightning hit the Gate again, and Loffler dodged the sword. Not that she was the strongest person in the room, nor did she have very precise aim, but he'd leapt out of the way far too easily—*how* was he so spry for his age? Was it the Essence power thrumming through his veins? Did that allow him to cheat time? The Lord Elder hadn't looked older than forty, and he'd been her great-great grandfather.

But Hallie had little time to dwell on that because she'd just realized she'd made a mistake.

She'd meant to throw the sword to Fely. Instead, she'd

unwittingly given Loffler exactly what he wanted.

The old man retrieved the weapon in a flash and thrust it into King Filip's chest.

Fely screamed and dropped Filip, stumbling out of reach of the next swipe of the sword. Niels leapt at Loffler, tackling him to the ground.

Hallie could only stare in horror at the blood bubbling out of the King's chest. Niels wrestled the man, but the sword was still in Filip's chest.

Fely scrambled over, trying to wrench the sword out, but Loffler threw off Niels and lunged, grabbing the hilt. He hefted it and swung it at Fely, who leapt away, just narrowly missing the swipe.

Niels picked himself up and nailed Loffler square in the chest with a powerful kick. Loffler thrust out with his hand, lightning zinging out, but Niels dodged it.

He didn't see the sword.

It arced as Loffler fell backward into the Gate. The sword caught on Niels' wrist. Blood spurted from where it cut deeply into the flesh. Niels screamed, but it was drowned by the entire room shaking.

Fely scrambled over and picked up the sword as a giant crack began at the corner of the room. "The crystals! He's setting off the crystals!"

Hallie still had no idea what it meant, but she lunged for both Niels and Fely. "We need to leave! What do I do without the Passage brick?"

She tried to stop the bleeding in Niels' wrist, but the cut was too deep. She could see the bone.

Fely stopped her, strapping the sword to Hallie's pack, hooking in the little loop on the side. "Take your power and thrust it into the ground. All of it. Keep hold of one tendril and use the Yalven words of power to create it. The Gate's power should help you."

"What? What words of power?"

"Just do it!"

The Gate roared. The crack in the wall opened further and further. They were going to fall into the chasm if Hallie didn't create the Passage immediately. She let go of Niels' arm and pressed her hands into the blood-soaked ground.

Filip's body slid into the chasm, tumbling head over feet into oblivion.

"*Now!*" Fely screamed.

Hallie stopped thinking, only poured every single bit of heat she possessed into the stone below. Fely and a bleeding Niels held onto her arms.

"*Vreali amarel hilao* Kyvena!" Hallie yelled, but nothing happened. She'd chosen the words because they were Yalven for *Passage open now.*

Fely began sliding into the chasm, pulling Hallie with her. Niels tried to hold them, but the blood loss was only making him weaker.

No, no, no, no. She would not die today. She needed to see Kase. She needed to hold him one last time. She lost hold of her power tendril, pushing it into her hands and screamed, "*KYVENA VREALI TORO!*"

Golden light erupted.

CHAPTER 20

SOMETHING HONORABLE

32 Years Ago

NOT ONLY WAS IT IRRESPONSIBLE to celebrate on the front in such a manner, it was also costly. Celebrations meant libations and one too many drunken fools cutting themselves on their sword while stumbling back to their tent. With Harlan's failed meeting with both the Stradat Lord Kapitan and Carleton during his leave six months ago, he'd been forced to continue patching up soldiers where no one believed the war would escalate.

Harlan didn't know if it would be this year, the next, or within the next five years, but it would happen. The Cerl king grew restless behind his borders and hungry for more Zuprium if the reports were to be believed—for weapons most likely.

Either the Lord Kapitan was blind to the Cerl king's ambitions, or he didn't care.

Both bothered Harlan.

"Come on, H, just relax," Ezekiel said, clapping him on

the shoulder and handing him an ale. Light from Firstmoon warred with the campfires across the dull side of the wooden tankard. Foam sloshed over the edge and dampened the cuff of Harlan's wool uniform. He bit back a frustrated sigh. At least that stain wouldn't be blood.

"We've won a single battle, with limited casualties, yes, but we've not won the war," Harlan said quietly, taking a sip— lukewarm and coarse like barley topped with burnt honey. It was the best the military had to offer on the edge of the mountains. Better than the moonshine some resorted to.

Ezekiel frowned but sat beside him on the log outside Harlan's tent. "Don't borrow tomorrow's sorrow." He stretched his long legs out in front of him, taking another sip of his own mug. The fire crackled softly, soothingly, too, if Harlan hadn't been on edge. "Not terrible considering."

Someone nearby struck up a reedy tune. The fiddle was a rare commodity in a place such as this and more rarely used. It wove between the bouts of jagged laughter and drunken congratulations, filling in the gaps with a jovial noise and unpracticed flare.

A battle limited to five deaths was quite a feat, commendable even, except the men shouldn't have died at all. In Harlan's opinion, if the Lord Kapitan took these border skirmishes seriously, he would realize the only way to stop them was to go on the offensive.

But even Harlan had to admit that a rogue band of trained soldiers was no good against a host of Jaydians. They needed an army; a focused, diligent unit trained and hardened for war. They needed to strike where it would hurt the worst, where it would discourage any retaliation.

They needed to send the Cerl king a message, and attacking his guerrilla warriors would do nothing but prolong the conflict.

"I'm a realist," Harlan said, taking another sip and setting the drink aside. He stared up at the peaks surrounding them, their towering night-dark silhouettes a soft comfort. "We'll be worse off once this all really begins."

Ezekiel crossed his ankles and shook his head. "You know you're right. I've been tinkering with a few things that might help us in the long run, but with your failure to engage the uppers...I'm worried that no matter what I present, it would be knocked aside and discarded."

"Well, you've not long until release. Surely you could do something when you're out?" Harlan asked, smoothing his mustache. He didn't like to think of Ezekiel leaving him. It was better—especially since his friend had received a letter a few months after they returned to the front. His wife, Rose, was pregnant. Ezekiel would return to his family shortly after the baby was born and never have to leave them again. He'd been writing to a few guilds in the city about a job, though none of it had panned out yet.

Odd considering the Fairchild name held one of the best reputations in the country, but Ezekiel would figure it out. Harlan, however, had two years left on his tenure, and after that, he'd be re-enlisting. He had no one to go home to.

Which was another reason he wanted to make a difference here. He'd never leave the military, so why not make it successful? Why wait around for tragedy to strike?

He refused to allow another Ravenhelm under his watch. He was meant for something more. Why else would he have been the only survivor all those years ago?

Ezekiel dug his boot heel into the dirt, capturing Harlan's attention once more. He'd nearly forgotten his friend was still there.

"If I can find someone to hire me on, that is." Ezekiel's usual charming demeanor slipped with the admission. "My ideas are considered dangerous by the few people I've approached them with back in the city. A shame, really. Our ancestors soared through the stars, yet we're content sitting here in the mud."

It was a rare turn of events when Harlan was the one to encourage his friend out of a dour mood.

He placed a hand on his friend's shoulder and gave it a gentle squeeze. "Your ideas are brilliant, I'll admit, and you care. Not that my name is better than yours, but I'll happily write a letter of recommendation."

The music swelled and fell as the fiddler finished his song. A few soldiers called out requests, and after a minute or two, another melody began. Harlan recognized it as a song played in high society weddings, but by the words slurred on the wind, the men had turned it into some drunken bawdy shanty.

It wasn't hurting anything, not really, but it was yet another example of the military's poor management. No wonder he and Ezekiel were out here in the Nardens for months at a time without any reprieve. No wonder the Lord Kapitan refused to listen to Harlan's suggestions.

Why fix something the Lord Kapitan didn't consider broken?? Yet Harlan knew the rot that festered within, and if allowed to grow, it would spell the destruction of Jayde.

"However," Harlan said at last, trying to drown out his treasonous thoughts. "I do believe your experiments with electrical currents could prove deadly. Trying to harness the power of the skies is a dangerous game." He looked over at his friend, whose face was now drawn. "Your cauterization technique though with the Zuprium? That's brilliant. Maybe start there."

Ezekiel shrugged. "Maybe, but I think there's more to the metal than we think. I read a few books discussing the Yalven practices."

"The Yalvs?"

Ezekiel opened his mouth to respond, but an on-duty soldier appeared at the edge of Harlan's firelight. His boots kicked a few stray pebbles and dirt into the fire, causing it to sputter slightly.

The man halted, a messenger bag slung across his shoulder. He saluted both Harlan and Ezekiel. The fresh recruit was still round-faced and the light bright in his eyes. So hopeful. "I have a posted letter for you, Lieutenant Colonel."

Harlan stood and saluted before taking the folded parchment from the man's hand. He flipped it over, inspecting the wax seal. Maybe it was Carleton or the Lord Kapitan taking back their denial of his suggestions, but if that were the case, wouldn't the Colonel or even the Brigadier General set up a meeting to discuss the proposed changes?

The seal was simple, a sun with a single blade down the center. The Fairchild crest. Odd.

The boy saluted again before dashing off to his next assignment. Harlan flipped the letter over again. In elegant, swooping script on the bent and slightly battered parchment was his name, not Ezekiel's.

"I'll leave you to your post," Ezekiel said, draining the last of his ale and stretching. "Night."

Harlan didn't say much, only waved him off as he sat back down and cracked the seal.

What would Lady Rose or Celeste have to say to him? Why hadn't Ezekiel received a post? Making a grueling journey before reaching Harlan's worn and scarred hands, the parchment had been of the finest fiber. The ink was smudged in a few places, but the writing was still elegant and evenly spaced as if the writer took the utmost care in crafting each letter. He sat and began to read, the firelight scattering across the words, and the third verse of the nearby song in his ears.

Lieutenant Colonel,

I hope this letter finds you well and unharmed, but I doubt a few months on the front isn't nearly as troublesome as a night spent in the Fairchild household. We've only heard good news here in the capital in terms of the...disagreements between Jayde and Cerulene, so my hope is probably not misplaced.

I am aware a posted letter from myself was not expected, but I have come across a problem I believe you can solve, and while this letter has begun rather nonsensically, I must now move to graver tidings.

Lady Rose's pregnancy has taken a turn, and while we have been seeing the best medics the Fairchild name can afford, not one can decide how best to help her. With the advent of her final months, she finds herself ragged and most unwell. The medics are still analyzing her symptoms and believe the best answer is for her to deliver the child, but that's not to happen for at least two more months. While our ancestors might have performed cesarean surgeries with success, the medics believe doing so now will go poorly without more advanced technology.

She grows paler every day and sleeps well past breakfast only to wake and then require a nap after the noon meal. When she's awake, she oft complains of nausea and headaches, which only abate for a time after a meal. The medics are encouraging her to eat more, but she can only bear to eat a slim fare.

With Ezekiel being so close to the end of his service, Rose is unwilling to tell him the truth of her situation, which according to my own research might be rather dire as I believe it has something to do with her blood. Only one medic agrees with me, unfortunately, though he is at a loss to help other than rest and a balanced diet.

Rose is optimistic everything will be as it should soon, but I am quite worried. Someone must tell my brother what is happening, but I believe the news had best be delivered in person rather than with unfeeling ink and parchment.

*I shall deign to think better of you than my initial assessment
of your character if you would pass along the pertinent information
to Ezekiel. I appreciate your help in this endeavor.*

Warm regards,

Celeste Fairchild

The letter was full of the woman's tenacious and
persnickety character, yet despite the dark outlook and pleas,
his chest warmed a little at the thought that she believed it
best to write to him. It implied a level of trust in him he
hadn't expected to want from a woman he'd once gone tête-
à-tête with upon their first meeting. That feeling was
something he'd have to analyze later.

In the meantime, she'd given him a rather loathsome
task. As soon as Harlan told his friend of his wife's condition,
he would leave no matter what his assignment was.
Dishonorable discharge or absent without leave would
damage any hope of Ezekiel finding a steady income and
would force him to rely upon family money, which would
soon run out if not managed quite carefully. If Rose's
situation were in fact dire, Ezekiel would spend his entire
fortune to save her, money be blasted to the stars.

There was something honorable in that, yet it spelled
disaster.

What would Ezekiel do if he were in Harlan's shoes?
What would Harlan want his friend to say?

Moreover, what could Harlan do to protect his friend
and yet still honor the Lady Celeste's request?

He folded her letter and slipped it into the inside breast
pocket of his uniform. Though it was merely parchment, the
knowledge that it was so close to his heart—physically and
metaphorically—made his stomach churn, but not entirely in
a dread-like way.

He stepped into his tent and retrieved three pieces of
parchment, a quill, ink, and his seal set.

The first letter he penned was to Carleton, requesting he
use his influence to pressure the Colonel to move Ezekiel's
assignment to the capital. The second, to the Colonel himself
to commend his friend for a promotion to the city's Medic
Guild, stating family reasons and Ezekiel's own merit. Surely,
it would be enough, though with only a few months left in his
service, Harlan's requests might be denied.

The final letter—he wrote to Celeste.

Lady Fairchild,

I hope this letter finds you as well as yours did me, meaning for the most part, all is well. I cannot write more than that lest this letter be intercepted by those who wish our country ill, though I am not anyone with much importance and rarely correspond to anyone except Lady Shackley, and I admit, I am not the best of writers.

As to your other opening statement, I would be hesitant to compare my fare here with that of a night in your presence. As I recall, I not only intrigued you, but I also proved I am not a banal dining companion, because if I were, I would've not been invited back three nights hence after our first meeting and allowed to trade victories with you in cards. Though I must admit, my military academy days do me justice. You would've made out handsomely if given the opportunity to attend. Many of my contemporaries need the comeuppance.

I am sorry to hear of Lady Rose's misfortune and ill health. As Ezekiel's direct superior, I am requesting his reassignment to the capital. I feel it would be beneficial to all, but I am at the mercy of those above even me. I will speak with him regardless—because it is the right thing to do, not necessarily to stay in your good graces, though that is something I would not mind.

Tell me, have you been successful in finding examples of women controlling family estates? If not, I would wager you may find some in the collection at Shackley Manor. If you'd like, I shall write a letter of introduction on your behalf to my mother, though she would probably allow you anyway. She dearly loves to speak about her collection of both books and art. I'd personally rather be out in the open instead of stuck inside a dusty library. I do enjoy the legend of King Arthur, but what man wouldn't?

Warm regards,
Harlan Shackley

C H A P T E R 2 1

THE NEBULA

Kase

WITH HIS ONLY ACCESS TO the outside world being a notebook and pencil, Kase had no idea just how many days passed. Clara had visited twice more, but that and his meager rations delivered every few hours when he wasn't sleeping were his only indications the world kept moving. The only time he left his little tent prison was when his guards led him to the privy and back.

Not that exciting. But it was a little terrifying to do one's business hovering above a hole in the ground with only a rough bedlinen strung up to keep the prying eyes from watching. The line for the privy was always long, but whether it was the guard presence or Kase's scowl, most people ignored him.

The rest of the time in his tent was spent doodling in Clara's notebook and writing letters he'd never send. Most went a little like:

Hals,

Heard some good gossip today while waiting for the privy. Well, it wasn't gossip, necessarily. But I guess it would be now if I'm telling you? Whatever. Anyway, a woman is leaving her husband because he insulted someone important and got them booted from one of the nicer caverns (there is no such thing as a nicer cavern). She was telling her friend in line the whole ridiculous story that involved her calling her husband a clotpole. I think they're both clotpoles, but I thought you'd get a laugh either way. Seems you aren't the only one who loves Shakespeare.

Always,

Kase

He'd also told her about the arguments the neighbor couple had. He'd heard plenty in the short time he'd lived in these scant dwellings. Everyone was understandably on edge. It was too bad the tent walls were so thin, but at the same time, it kept him entertained. At night, though, when he was tired, he'd written a few more dramatic ones. Those went something like:

Hals,

You're not going to read this, but it makes me feel less stars-ridiculous if I pretend I'm writing to you than "exploring my emotions through journaling." That doesn't sound manly at all. And I'm extraordinarily manly and masculine and all those things, of course. So, apologies in advance for the rambling to come. I wish you were here so I could talk this through with you. You're much better than this journal and pencil. For one, they're not nearly as pretty as you. Don't let the compliment go to your head—even if it's obviously quite a feat to be more attractive than rough parchment and a stubby pencil.

Anyway, Clara came by with Samuel again today. Can't wait for you to meet the little tike. He's got some lungs on him, but he seems to like me well enough. Supposedly he can't smile yet, but I swear he did when he saw me today. Clara said he was simply relieved he burped and released the pressure that'd built up after his last feeding. I beg to differ. It was a real smile thrown at his Uncle Kase, his new favorite person in the world.

Actually, maybe you shouldn't meet him yet. He might like you better. Blast it.

Onto not so good things. There's still no news about Jove or Mother. In relation to my brother, something about the mechanism for something broke, and the crew is having to go above ground and get some supplies. Without electricity, it's been a more difficult rescue mission, and there are others who fell in a day or so after in a separate cave-in. And of course, the Cerls did another bombing run today. Not sure why they keep doing that. They've already pushed us underground. Maybe they're making sure we're all blasted to smithereens. Maybe they know we're underground and are attempting to make it all collapse on our heads. Either way, the supply retrieval team has to wait until nightfall to sneak back into Kyvena. I hate not being able to do anything to help at all. I've sent the Stradat Lord Kapitan a few strongly worded letters about letting me fly the hover, but they've been met with silence. Any other time, I'd count that as an improvement.

Shocks, will you just come back already? I miss you, and it's only been like a week. Or two. I've lost track.

Always,

Kase

He put on the finishing touches, signing the most recent letter with a flourish. Setting the pencil aside, he rubbed his eyes. With the fuel in his gas lantern getting low, it was high time he slept.

Hopefully he could.

He didn't feel nearly as heavy, not that he would admit to that. It was almost as if his emotions had bled out with the charcoal. Just a little. Maybe there was something to this journaling thing. Perhaps he might even enjoy writing books—he'd read enough of them to know how to tell a decent story. Hallie would understand, he was sure. He'd mention it in his next letter.

He tucked his pencil and journal underneath his pillow and turned down the lamp. Loud voices and some raucous laughter echoed in the cavern. Stars, couldn't his father have put him in his own little alcove somewhere? Wasn't he supposed to be in danger or something? Or was it that he was a danger to everyone else?

Still deserved his own alcove.

He stretched out on his back and stared at the ceiling. For once, he felt tired enough to fall asleep quickly. Most times he tried to sleep, his subconscious conjured nightmares where Jove and his mother were never found, and Kase was forced to step up and be a father figure in Samuel's life. It terrified him in a different way than before.

Mainly because now that he'd spent time with his new nephew, Kase felt responsible already. If anyone so much as looked at Samuel wrong, they would pay dearly. If Kase had lived a different life with the possibility of children in the future, would it feel like that if he had his own son?

Especially if the kid belonged to him and Hallie.

He rubbed his chest. He should really be used to the ache by then. It'd started when he'd left her in the caverns and had grown progressively worse. He needed to hold her if only to make sure he was still there. Writing her letters she'd never read couldn't replace that feeling.

Guess he wasn't going to get any sleep after all.

However, thoughts of Hallie always ended in him thinking about how she was off gallivanting somewhere with Niels. The man was supportive and loyal, Kase knew—but he'd apparently also told Stowe that Kase was rich and arrogant.

Oh Kase wanted to show him just how rich and arrogant his fists could be. He'd written one scathing letter about it the day before. It was one he'd promptly ripped out and thrown into the privy hole.

"Shackley," a brassy tenor voice said from the tent entrance.

The upper-class accent, tinged with the soft twang of the lower city, told him exactly who stood outside the tent. Eravin showing up at that moment made his jealousy vanish. The void was quickly filled with caution and a dash of anger. Sure, they had a truce, but that didn't erase the past. Kase sat up.

He had no idea what Eravin had been doing since he'd been brought in to speak with his father and subsequently put under house arrest. He also hadn't heard from Stowe, despite the note Kase had sent him. It worried him a little. What if he'd fallen into a collapsed hole like Jove? What would he tell Hallie then?

The tent flap opened, and Eravin's thin, gaunt face appeared. "Shackley."

Kase didn't get up from his place on the cot. "Not sure you're on the approved guest list."

"A small technicality." Eravin entered the tent, a cloak over one arm and a parchment held in the other. Kase glimpsed his own handwriting. The letter he'd written Stowe. "It seems you're desperate for my help."

That possibly explained the lack of response from

Hallie's father at least.

"I'd say not." Kase stared at the parchment. Had Stowe given it to him? Or sent Eravin in his place? That didn't feel like something Hallie's father would do. He seemed like a good judge of character, but Eravin was one of the only people he knew in Kyvena. Maybe he'd gone to Eravin for help. Maybe. Still showed a lack of good judgment he didn't associate with Stowe, but Kase couldn't blame him. Eravin was quite charming when he wanted to be—it had gotten them out of some close calls when they were younger.

He tossed Kase a gray cloak. "We're friends again, remember?"

On paper, the words seemed good-natured. It was the smirk that accompanied them that told him otherwise.

"We have a truce, sure, but that doesn't erase the fact you tried to blackmail me."

Eravin shrugged. "Successfully, I might add."

"You rigged the game."

"I promise I won't go back on my word." Eravin inspected his nails and after a second, chewed at a hangnail. "I didn't last time, either, even if it wasn't in your favor."

The cloak might've once been black, but it had since faded to a tired charcoal. Its frayed edges spoke of days and nights spent battling the weather. He had no reason to go with Eravin. He had every reason to stay. "I don't think this will be enough to slip past the guards."

But if it did, it might allow him to sneak about unrecognized.

Eravin shrugged again. "I have superior powers of persuasion."

Persuasion. Right. "What did you do?"

Eravin rolled his eyes. "Put on the cloak and pull up the hood."

"Why?"

Eravin opened the tent flap once more. "There's a good card game going on, and in light of everything, it should be a nice diversion."

Eravin looked little different than he had a few days prior. He still had that haunted look in his eyes, but Kase didn't know if that was because of the last few days or the last few years. Both had been horrific, and in both cases, Kase had abandoned him.

It hadn't been all his fault. He'd been so caught up in his own grief that when Eravin slammed the door physically and metaphorically in his face, he couldn't find it in himself to try.

Now Kase knew why. It was Kase's fault Eravin no longer had a mother, the only parent who had cared about him.

But could he trust Eravin now? The answer was probably no. Eravin *had* pointed a pistol at his head a few days ago.

But if his old friend was up for helping him escape this stupid tent, he should take advantage of the time outside. He might be able to do something about Jove, or at least go check on Stowe.

It was a gamble for sure, but it might be the best one he could make.

His decision made, he threw the cloak around his shoulders and tied the stays at his neck. It sat oddly atop the collar of his pilot's jacket underneath.

"Take off that blasted jacket."

"Not a chance."

Eravin sighed, and it was the first time Kase glimpsed his old friend hidden underneath the layer of metaphorical grime. Eravin jabbed his thumb at the front of the tent. "That jacket is like a beacon to the entire galaxy that you're the only pilot we have left."

"Maybe I shouldn't go, then."

Eravin stuffed his hands in his pockets. "Well, well, didn't realize you'd become quite the straight-lacer." Eravin half turned and looked back at Kase with a dash of his old mischief in his eyes, but only for a moment. "Fine. Stay locked up. I'll just have to blow my winnings on that sweetshop all by my lonesome."

Kase stared at him hard. At fancy dinners, they used to play cards with the other unfortunate children forced to attend with their parents. After the dinner was over and the adults headed to the parlor for drinks, the children would lock themselves away in the front drawing room. They never played with real money, but the joke was that if they were playing with real tenners, they'd use it to buy the sweetshop on the corner. The real fun was when Kase, Ana, and Eravin found ways to hustle the others—Ana being a superb actress even at age eight.

He grumbled under his breath, but he loosened the cloak and shed his leather jacket. Eravin grinned as Kase put the cloak back on and pulled up the hood. "What if someone recognizes me out there?"

Eravin chuckled. "I mean, what else could they possibly do to you?"

Kase couldn't help the snort that escaped. "I think that's exactly what they're trying to figure out."

If the Cerls hadn't invaded, he'd have been handed down a punishment harsher than house arrest, that was for sure. Funny that the Cerl attack might be the thing that saved Kase from corporal punishment. Not that he expected to survive the invasion. It was only a matter of time before the Cerls discovered their hiding place. In the stories of old, the royal family was the first to be executed, and while Kase didn't have the title of prince, he was the son of the only surviving Jaydian leader and the supreme military commander. It was why he'd known using himself as a trade for Hallie would result in an invitation to Fort Achilles when Hallie had been kidnapped.

Eravin stepped out of the tent. "Hurry now."

His guards were nowhere to be seen. A few other people milled about, but none paid too much attention. Kase raised a brow. "Not a bullet to the head this time, or have you already moved the bodies?"

He tried to appear confident and nonchalant, but he couldn't help the slight tremor in his voice on the last word. All he could think about was the Cerl from the Jayde Center. If the Cerl had truly destroyed the city as Eravin had said, he deserved the consequences for his choice, but a trial would've been more appropriate.

Eravin chuckled as he led Kase away from the tent prison. He didn't acknowledge Kase's anxiety, for which he was grateful, but he wasn't sure if it was purposeful or if it would come back to haunt him later. Kase barely heard his answer over the swell as they entered the tunnel proper. "Resorting to violence gets a little tiresome if it's my only recourse."

"One World not paying you enough? Or are you having to assassinate people on the side?"

"Why? You in the market for an assassin?"

"No."

Eravin sighed. "Don't get your knickers in a twist. Your little nanny guards were simply persuaded that they wanted a drink at one of the pop-up taverns someone's got going. They'll probably get their comeuppance once the Stradat Lord Kapitan finds they've shirked their responsibilities for alcohol."

"So you paid them off?"

"I cannot reveal all my secrets, Shackley."

They continued through the corridors and byways, past moss-choked crevices crawling up the walls like reaching hands and dozens of huddled groups, the oil lamps leaving a lingering metallic taste on the air.

Gas lanterns became more and more sporadic as the camps grew more and more desolate. Instead, small campfires began to take root, cloaking the smaller crypt-like caverns in a smell of thick smoke.

Not wise. But when Eravin led him around a crumbling hole in the floor, he looked up to see the night sky slipping through another crack in the ceiling above. It only made him feel moderately better about the situation.

A haunting song drifted from a tent they passed, a woman singing an old melody Kase remembered from his own childhood.

We come from the stars
Those who came here before
And we left all that is ours
In the wand'ring days of yore...

His mother used to sing it to him and Ana after the nanny had failed to put them to bed. Ana's fear of the dark always brought her to Kase's chamber sooner or later, and Kase's mother would sing them both to sleep.

Eravin led Kase to an alcove where two men sat, a lantern set on a small ledge above them. The light cast soft shadows upon their faces—too familiar, if haggard, and in desperate need of sleep.

The first was Neville Thatcher. In school, the girls had swooned over his chiseled jaw and warm brown eyes. They were no longer warm. The other was Waylan Peters, his light brown skin wan in the weak gaslamp light. He smiled at Kase first. "When Eravin said you were back in town, I didn't believe it, but I'd heard the rumors, of course." He stood and held out a hand for Kase to shake. "Neville here just lost a bet that you wouldn't show your face down here if you knew what was good for you."

Neville didn't say anything.

Kase took Waylan's outstretched hand and shook, but he felt a little awkward. Other than the few dinners or other inane social engagements Kase had been forced to attend over the years, he hadn't interacted with his old friends much. He hadn't tried, and they hadn't reached out. It had been a mutual thing, if unspoken. Kase gave him a forced, small smile. "Good to see you again."

Neville shuffled cards and dealt them out. Eravin and Waylan took seats on the ground, Kase following suit. He surveyed the tunnel alcove they'd found themselves in. It reminded him a little of the dungeon he and Hallie had been imprisoned in at Achilles, but Hallie wasn't there for him to kiss this time. He looked down at the cards. "I don't have any money to bet with."

He doubted they did either, judging by their states. Waylan grinned again and tossed out weary and crinkled parchment scraps. "We've been playing with these—and with secrets. Loser has to spill." He laughed a little. "The poor bloke who challenged us not ten minutes before you showed up hightailed it out of here when he lost his round. My guess is he knew his wife would find out what he had to hide."

Waylan distributed the parchment pieces, each torn in rough square shapes. One of Kase's five looked more like a grotesque diamond. Tiny, printed words marred both sides. He caught the name *Mondego*. Another had *Marseilles*.

He barely stopped himself from wincing. They'd ripped up *The Count of Monte Cristo* for their game.

Eravin scooped his up. "Whether because of the game or he's been spending too much time at the Houses, we'll never know, but he had that *look* about him."

Visiting the Houses was what lower-class men did when they realized that they would always be lower class no matter how many hours they put in at the forge, quarry, or shops. It was a way to forget your life for a bit and spend the life savings that wouldn't get you anywhere. The last few years of school, it'd been a big thing to sneak down to one of them. Kase had only gone once, just to see, but he hadn't partaken in the...festivities.

Regardless, Jove had been the one to light into him

about it, and Kase had felt guilty enough to never go again. As much as Jove drove him crazy, he did look up to his brother, and he'd felt properly ashamed after. It was a miracle that neither Harlan nor his mother ever found out.

He needed to find Jove.

Kase thumbed his nose and inspected the game. One game, then he'd figure out how to make his exit. He just needed to give Eravin the slip. Waylan took a swig of his flask and offered it to him. Kase shook his head. Waylan twisted the cap back on and set it beside him.

With the two cards dealt to each person, he guessed they were playing Hanged Man's Nebula. He hadn't played in years; he hadn't had the time or money to lose. He tugged the hood up more, casting his face further into shadow, and checked his hand.

Decent. A star and an empress.

Depending on the galley of cards laid in the middle to choose from, he might win the hand. If he could get a double sword, he could walk away easy. That would make his final card just extra insurance. Waylan started the betting round with three parchment squares.

Kase threw in the piece with *Mondego* on it, his eye on a card in the galley of four. Next betting round, he'd buy a blind card, unless someone ended the round before it got back to him. He tapped his cards on his knee, sitting back on his other hand. "Where'd Ellis end up?"

Ellis had been the one to lure Kase into the trap that led to him running from the city. For all he knew, Ellis was the reason they were here now. If Kase hadn't gone with him to meet One World, the city might've still been standing.

But if he hadn't, he might never have fallen in love with Hallie.

That was a sobering thought.

Eravin upped the bid. Neville passed with a quick tap of his finger. It was Waylan who finally answered, "He's dead."

Kase blinked, the tapping of his cards halting. "In the attack?"

No one said anything for a moment. Eravin chewed his thumbnail before saying, "Thanks to you, really."

"How?" Kase had run. He hadn't done a thing to Ellis.

Eravin gave a sardonic laugh. "Ellis took it upon himself to spread your secrets all over the city. But alas, he got too cocky and ended up in front of the High Council for his trouble. Perjury. Died when One World and the Cerls took out the Jayde Center."

Trying to process his thoughts, Kase stared at his cards, though he could no longer see them clearly. Anger started to build. "So you're saying that if you hadn't blackmailed me, Ellis would be alive?"

In Kase's peripheral, Waylan flipped through his hand. "Heard one of his sisters got out okay."

Kase's jaw ached with tension. Eravin didn't lower his gaze, only met Kase's fire with his own. "You dug your own grave." He held Kase's eyes for a moment more before gesturing to his cards. "But what's done is done. It's your play."

Finish the game. Finish the game, then we find Jove.

But he had to get rid of Eravin first.

Kase swiped Waylan's flask and signaled for a blind card. The whiskey burned all the way down. Kase screwed the cap back on and wiped his mouth with the back of his hand. He threw another book page square in the middle—the one with *revenge* inked on its fibers.

Maybe he could get the others drunk enough they wouldn't care if he wandered off. It was as good a Plan A as any.

The game continued with little conversation after that until someone lost. Kase won the first hand out of sheer luck. He'd only just edged out Eravin. Waylan came in last and regaled them with the tale of his first time at the Houses, when he'd overpaid extravagantly. Eravin laughed and said that the only good thing about the recent attack was that Waylan wouldn't make the same mistake a second time. Waylan took a swig of his flask and passed it to Eravin, who put the edge to his lips but didn't drink.

Blast. Kase needed him to drink.

He passed it to Kase. "The winner of our round needs a little boost, it seems."

Kase snatched it from him. Maybe if Eravin thought he was drunk enough, he'd follow suit.

The next two swigs burned less, but made his head swim a little more. He didn't drink whiskey often, and it would probably show. But for the first time in a while, the anxiety waiting at the edges of his consciousness faded. He could still read the cards in front of him, and no one had two heads. All positives.

Jove drinking to excess after Zeke died made sense. Kase had only ever been drunk three times in his life—that he remembered. The first was Ana's Burning, the second had been with Lavinia Richter, and the third...well, the third had been the night he and Hallie had decided to run away.

Not a great track record, if he was honest with himself.

He played a few more hands, each time managing to avoid spilling any secrets. He and Waylan passed the flask back and forth. Kase's muscles relaxed, and he found himself laughing at something the other man said. Shocks, he hadn't laughed in ages. Had it been with Hallie? Her face swam in front of his eyes. He took another go at the flask.

Maybe he wouldn't be able to sneak away and find Jove tonight, after all. Instead of rescuing him, he'd probably fall headfirst down one of the holes without meaning to.

If Hallie knew what he was doing, she'd scold him properly. He wished she would. He wished she were there to knock the cards from his hands and take him somewhere safe. Somewhere there wasn't a war going on. Somewhere they could be free. Somewhere they could hide away from the rest of the world and simply watch it burn.

He'd nearly done that the last time they'd been together.

He chewed on the edge of his lip and peeked at the cards Eravin dealt him. Not terrible, but he'd need more than luck to win.

Eravin laid out the six galley cards, and Neville started the bidding with three parchment squares. He'd won the last hand after losing the previous two and muttering two stories about the times he'd cheated on exams in lower school. Rather boring, if you asked Kase. Anyone worth their salt cheated at least twice in lower school.

The fact that he'd led with three squares didn't sit well with Kase. He looked at his own cards once more. He'd need a good blind card, and if the round continued past that, another. Risky. Maybe he could make an excuse to go to the privy and track down Saldr instead. He could probably use some of that dust to get rid of the alcohol in his blood. Then he could look for Jove.

A solid plan.

Except that the flask was empty, and Kase might've

broken his lucky streak.

He signaled for a blind card and threw out a single parchment square; he could no longer concentrate long enough to read what part of the book they were from. Eravin laid another card face down beside Kase. Eravin threw in two parchment squares. Kase had trouble focusing on the galley cards.

He should not have drunk the whiskey.

After a second or two more of squinting, he figured he could use the Priest and a Sevenser, but not if someone used one of those first. He ran a hand through his hair, knocking back the hood of his cloak. It would probably come down to his blind. He tapped his cards as Neville passed. Waylan deliberated his next move.

Kase did not want to lose. He had too many secrets. Why had he agreed to play this game anyway? Drink fogged his thoughts, and the flask was dry. He couldn't numb himself further. He needed to think, but that was near impossible. Waylan talked through what he wanted to do. Probably the whiskey rambling. Kase dragged a nail along the rim of the card, and when no one was paying close attention to him, he lifted the corner ever so slightly.

A Raven.

Blast.

It wouldn't throw him out, but it didn't help his situation, and he had a feeling he couldn't count on any galley card. If he went for another blind, he'd forfeit two bids, but if he didn't, he'd probably scrape out in third position, if not dead last.

Was chance on his side? Luck? If the second blind was the Hanged Man, he was done for.

Waylan nabbed a blind card, and it was Kase's turn at last.

"What you got left, Shackley? Anything good, or are you ready to spill?" Waylan teased, thrumming his fingers on his knee in a silent beat.

Eravin tapped the worn deck in front of him. "A blind for you? I haven't seen you look this nervous since you discovered that Lavinia Richter was, in fact, a woman."

Kase gritted his teeth to prevent him from spilling out something he'd regret. Waylan snorted. "That was a day for the books."

Kase looked at his cards again, as if they might've changed in the last two minutes. He shifted his weight. His left leg had fallen asleep. His head was heavy with drink. Should he risk the second blind? Neville's face hadn't changed across any of the rounds. No laughter, no anger—just numb. Eravin probably had a decent hand, based on his last bid. Waylan was the wild card. His bids had consistently gone up, but he'd drawn a blind. If Kase had to guess, Neville had the Nebula, the highest card in the game, but the big bid at the beginning could've been a ploy.

If Kase didn't take the second blind card, odds were he was losing with the Raven. The whiskey had messed with his head enough to know he hadn't hid his thoughts. They knew he was about to implode.

"Your guards change over in an hour, Shackley," Eravin said, tapping fingers on his knee. "I haven't had the chance to bribe them yet."

Kase had enough awareness to glare. Finally, he tapped the ground twice. Eravin smiled and passed him a blind card face down.

If I survive this round, I'm going to beg off to the privy.

With the second blind, Kase forfeited the next two bids, and that brought them to the end of the game. As the dealer, Eravin revealed his cards first, as well as his galley card choice. His blind card wasn't great, but if no one had the Nebula, he was winning this round.

Waylan revealed his cards: a flush, what could have been a winning hand if Eravin's hadn't been so good. He smiled and chose not to reveal any blinds.

Neville was slow and methodic about his hand reveal. The lantern light glinted off his respectable cards. Nothing too special, and if Kase had any luck left, not good enough to beat himself.

Then Neville turned over his blind.

The cards were old, faded, and probably filched from someone else, but the red eye was still bright against the brilliant blue grays surrounding it. The Nebula.

Blast it.

"Holding out on us, I see," Eravin said with a laugh. He turned to Kase. "Doubt you beat out anyone, so just get on with it."

Kase nearly threw the cards at him, but maybe he could

still scrape out something. He flipped his hand over. Waylan laughed. "Sorry about the Sevenser, mate."

Kase tapped the Priest card in the galley. Depending on his blind, the Priest put him over Waylan.

Eravin clicked his tongue. "As if you had a different choice."

Kase needed to choose a blind to flip. If he by some miracle got the Dagger, he'd tie with Eravin, and they'd go to a shootout. Flipping the Raven card on his right guaranteed a loss.

He chewed his lip and concentrated on the two cards in front of him. If he lost, he'd need to tell a secret. He played with the edge of the second blind with his thumb. But what would he tell about? Could he make something up about his childhood? He glanced at Eravin, who hovered on the line between bored and agitated. He'd pick out the lie in a heartbeat.

"I think I need to visit—" Kase started, but Waylan interrupted.

"Don't be a blasting dulkop. Flip your card." He punched Kase in the shoulder good-naturedly. "It's just a game."

Except Kase had too many secrets no one needed to know.

He closed his eyes as he flipped the second blind. He opened one eye a crack.

The straggly bearded man hung from the gallows, his blank eyes staring straight at him. Kase rubbed his hand down his face. The Hanged Man.

Waylan laughed too loudly again, drawing the attention of a nearby group of men passing around a pipe. "Sorry about that, mate."

A right sincere apology, of course.

Eravin gave Kase a slow clap. "A spectacular finish, really."

Kase rolled his eyes and set his cards in front of Eravin. "I'm done."

"Not yet, Shackley." Eravin gathered up the other cards and passed them to Neville.

"Didn't you say something about my guards changing? Probably should head back if I'm to make it."

"You lost. Pay up."

Kase shook his head. "The biggest secret I had, you

already spilled to the city—courtesy of Ellis Carrington."

Eravin's eyes went cold, and Kase knew he'd crossed a line. But his old friend no longer had the benefit of Kase's good will. What more could he expect from Kase?

"Exactly what was your relationship with Lavinia Richter?"

Neville asked the question slowly, as if he knew Kase wouldn't hear it properly with the tunnel noise and his wits scattered with drink. It was the first time all night the man had bothered to address him directly. Kase met his gaze.

"Doesn't matter."

Waylan nudged him with an elbow. "Come on, spill. It's not hurting anyone."

Neville spoke louder. "If we'd been playing with real sums, you'd be 200 gold tenners in the debts."

Kase fiddled with the ties of his borrowed cloak. "Nothing. She was nothing to me." He twisted Ana's ring around his finger and felt the shame burning his neck. "She was just a way to get back at my father."

"And Lucy Doyle. My mother, may her soul rest among the stars, was convinced you were the father of her child," Waylan said with a raised brow.

Skibs. Kase was going to be sick. He hadn't eaten much that day, only a portion or two of the rationed pork and hard tack. The whiskey was not settling well among such scant fare. He shook his head, and everything moved sluggishly with the drink. "No, not Lucy. I've only *been* with Lavinia, but she's dead, and it didn't matter because Loffler, not Richter, was the one the Cerls wanted—"

Waylan laughed sardonically and clapped him on the shoulder. Kase realized his mistake too late. Neville looked as if he were about to reach across and punch Kase's lights out. Eravin cleared his throat, "And the redhead? Hallie, is it? She your next conquest?"

Waylan stopped laughing for a moment. "Are you talking about Hallie Walker? Think Neville and I had a course with her last spring." He eyed Kase appreciatively. "Quite the looker for a lowborn if you ask me. A few of the guys had a bet on who'd be the first to sleep with—"

Kase lunged at Waylan and let his fist fly, knocking him squarely in the jaw. Pain like lightning lanced through his hand. Waylan flopped back from the force. Neville leapt up and shoved Kase off.

Kase grabbed Neville and tossed him to the ground. Neville recovered quickly and threw curses Kase had only heard in the Crews. Neville ran at him, but Kase dodged. Neville turned and gasped, "Lavinia deserved better than a pig like you."

Fueled by alcohol and the stress of the last few weeks, Kase shoved him. He breathed heavily. "Why'd she seek me out then? Huh?"

Neville growled and lunged at Kase again, but before he could make contact, Eravin grabbed him around the waist and threw him back. "No use fighting over a dead woman."

Neville's eyes were wild. "She's only dead because of *him!*"

"I wasn't even in the country when she died!" Kase glared. "Why don't you ask your buddy Eravin why she died?" He whirled toward Eravin. "You had a hand in that. You might've even done it. Weren't you saying the other day how a bloody smile is more your style?"

Eravin narrowed his eyes, not denying Kase's accusation, but not confirming it either. He held Neville back, who flung obscenities Kase's way, obviously not listening to a word Kase said. Waylan finally picked himself up from the ground, rubbing his red jaw. Kase hadn't realized he'd hit him that hard. He'd deserved it.

Kase didn't wait around to see what happened next. He did what he always did—he ran.

Knuckles aching, he stumbled through the throng of people. His hood was down. The roar of the refugees grew louder as they recognized him. Their voices buzzed in his ears, but he kept running, knocking into people and discarding them in the same breath.

His head was full and pounding. Too much whiskey. He swayed, caught himself on a man nearby, and shoved off him. Blackness encroached on the edges of his vision, oozing and spreading until Kase's knees hit the stony ground beneath him.

He was never drinking again. How did Jove stand it? His side ached, cramping. His stomach rocked like a stormy sea.

Hallie's voice echoed in his mind. "Focus on breathing...slow and steady. In and out."

He obeyed, but he was drunk, not having a panic attack.

The voices around him grew insistent. Hands snatched the back of his cloak, choking him. He fought them blindly. His head pounded.

An arm snaked around his back, a hand grabbing his own arm and tugging it onto his shoulders. Kase turned to the side and puked.

"Blast it, Shackley."

Eravin.

Kase tried to pull away, but his old friend only gripped him tighter. "You're no use to me drunk and beaten to a pulp, so let me rescue you—or would you rather me leave you to the bloodthirsty mob?"

The nausea receded having emptied the contents of his stomach. His head still pounded, but shapes and colors and sounds grew distinct. The sweat felt cold in the tunnel air. He blinked as his lungs expanded. The air was stained with sweat and sick.

Eravin shouted something to the crowd that had accumulated and dragged Kase forward. "Why did you drink so much whiskey?"

Kase focused on making sure he didn't stumble over the uneven ground beneath him. "Tasted good."

Eravin turned behind them and shouted something vulgar at one of the refugees who demanded Kase be left to them.

Kase couldn't help the snort that escaped. If Kase wasn't so certain he was, in fact, twenty-one years old, he would've sworn he was sixteen again, running through the lower city with his brother in everything but blood, acting like they were kings of the world.

A shiny trick of the whiskey. The years hadn't been kind to either of them, and Kase was certain he had vomit on his boots.

Eravin was silent the rest of their walk, but he didn't take Kase back to his tent with the missing guards. Instead, he led him to another one that looked only slightly less shoddy than its neighbors. Its edges weren't frayed, and it boasted no holes. Lamplight flickered within.

Eravin stopped just outside. Kase pulled out of his grip and stumbled, catching himself on the nearby wall. Eravin cleared his throat. "Stowe, you there?"

Kase went cold again. Hallie's father was the last person

he wanted to see him like this. He tried to back up but tripped over his own feet. Eravin caught him by the collar. "You need help, you dulkop."

The tent flap opened to reveal Stowe's face peeking out. He took one look at Eravin and Kase and opened it wider. "Bring him in."

Even in his current state, Kase flushed and put up his hands. "No, no, I'm fine, really."

Stowe furrowed his brow. "That would've been much more convincing if you weren't slurring something fierce, son."

Eravin still hadn't let go of Kase's collar. He pulled Kase along and shoved him into the tent in front of him, then stopped and spoke in low tones to Stowe.

The tent was small, with just enough room for two sleeping rolls and Stowe's assorted concoctions. Kase had to hunch over just to fit inside unless he stood in the exact middle.

He wasn't alone. A woman knelt in front of a pack, searching for something; upon Kase's entrance, she looked up, suspicion in her gaze. "And who might you be?"

Distrust arranged her dainty features in a fierce look, her green eyes bright against her dark graying hair braided and pulled into a tight bun in the back. She wore simple trousers and a green linen sash around her waist over a tucked white lace shirt. Unlike Kase, when she stood up, she didn't have to slouch. She only came up to the middle of Kase's chest.

He leaned a little too far to the right, but caught himself. "I'm...I'm Kase Shackley."

"Zelda Walker."

Hallie's mother. She was all right. Kase held out a hand so he could give hers the customary peck, but instead, she took it and shook it like a man would. Kase blinked at her firm grip. "Nice to...nice to meet you."

The more he tried to talk without slurring, the more his tongue felt too big for his mouth. Eravin left with a sharp look at Kase, and Stowe turned. "Let's get you some tonic, and you can sleep it off here. You can use my bedroll."

Kase waved his hands. "I'm fine. I don't want to be any trouble."

Zelda raised a brow. "Your knuckles say otherwise."

Stowe dragged his bedroll to the only open area of the tent and forced Kase to sit on top. He instructed Zelda to fetch a few things from his pack while he examined Kase's knuckles. "Tore these up something awful, but I got my salve with me." He grabbed Kase's chin and inspected his face. "Your jaw's gonna go purple and blue by dawn, but that can't be helped. That cut don't look too bad, though. Your other scar is healing nicely."

Kase brought a hand up to rub the place where the debris had fallen. He'd not looked in a mirror in weeks, so he had no idea how it looked. The skin was still raised and a little ropey. Zelda handed Stowe a small pot of his salve and threw a packet of something in a cup before pouring some water on top. She rummaged in her own pack and tossed in some flakes before handing it to him. "Drink this. I added some sugar to sweeten it, but this should sober you up soon."

Stowe thanked his wife and dabbed his homemade salve on Kase's knuckles. The relief was almost instant, the ache disappearing as soon as the tan goop made contact. Kase sighed in relief and took a sip of Zelda's concoction. The sickly sweetness warring with the taste of dirt choked him. He coughed and sputtered.

"What in the blazes did you just give me?"

Zelda gave him a waspish look. "Drink it or suffer tomorrow."

Stowe finished with the salve and wrapped Kase's knuckles with gauze. "Told you Hal got 'er tongue from her mama." Zelda hit her husband's shoulder good-naturedly. Stowe smiled as he pressed a bit on his knuckles. Kase winced. Stowe shook his head. "Don't think nothing's broken, but these'll be quite tender a few days more, I'd reckon."

Kase blinked. *Don't think nothing*...so did that mean something was broken or not? He really needed Hallie there to interpret the mountain slang. "So it's broken?"

"It's not. He thinks," Zelda said, arms crossed and watching him closely.

"Oh, I just..." He wasn't sure he'd remember all this the next morning, and when his father figured out he'd left the tent...old dread pooled in his stomach. "I need to go."

Zelda gave him a look. "And get mauled by the crowds? I think not, Kase Shackley." She stared pointedly at the cup in his uninjured hand. "Drink it now."

Kase gritted his teeth, but he took a deep breath before knocking back the rest of the sweet dirt liquid. It tasted even worse than the first sip. He coughed and tried his best not to throw the vile stuff back up. Zelda gave him a nod, and within minutes, Kase's limbs weighed twice as much as they usually did. His eyelids drooped. Stowe took off his mucky boots and helped him into the bedroll. He felt like a child, but whatever was in that concoction made his limbs too heavy and stuffed his head full of cotton.

As he fell into a deeper sleep, he got lost in the abyss. And he had to say...he didn't entirely mind it.

WITH OPEN ARMS

Kase

"GOOD OF YOU TO JOIN the living once more, Master Shackley."

The voice drove away the last remnants of sleep. Kase's hand ached, but his head didn't hurt, and that was saying something after a night of drinking straight whiskey. He wrenched his eyes open. The amount of effort that small motion took was rather embarrassing.

He blinked a few times to clear his vision. A woman stood above him, and his heart stopped. *Hallie.*

He hastily wiped away the dribble that had escaped the side of his mouth. Shocks, he'd slept hard. He winced at the pain in his hand. The woman held up a familiar jar. She came into focus, and Kase's heart dropped. Gray hair. Green eyes. Not Hallie.

It was the second time he'd made that mistake.

To say her daughter favored her was an understatement. Kase guessed Hallie inherited her coloring from her father, with his golden brown eyes and red hair, but that was pretty much it. Well, and the whole Yalven thing, of course.

"Try not to be too disappointed. I'm the reason you won't have a hangover today."

Warmth flooded his cheeks as he rubbed his face with his uninjured hand. "Thank you, Mrs. Walker."

Zelda only raised a brow before snatching his wrapped hand. Kase hissed at the movement. She unwrapped the gauze with expert efficiency and inspected Kase's angry, split knuckles. "Well, I'm still not convinced you didn't fracture anything, but the lack of intense swelling backs up my husband's diagnosis."

She dipped her fingers into the pot of salve and rubbed it on the broken skin. Kase thought it looked a little better, and he sagged with relief as the medicine took effect. Zelda looked up, her eyes searching. "And what might have caused you to do something so foolish as brawling?"

Kase opened his mouth to say something, but he didn't know what answer would be best. Would it make her like him more if he admitted he was protecting her daughter's honor? Or would it make her think less of him for associating with people who would insult it?

He cleared his throat. "Just a misunderstanding."

That was safe enough. For now.

She gave him a deadpanned look so reminiscent of Hallie, his chest physically hurt. Kase shrugged. "Thank you for helping."

Whether she believed him or not, she didn't say so either way. She wrapped his hand in new gauze and put away the salve. "Stowe tells me you and my daughter are involved."

Kase opened his mouth, but no sound came out. He didn't know exactly what he and Hallie were, but he'd rather have that conversation with her instead of her mother, who he was slowly realizing was much more intimidating than her father. It was probably a good thing she'd been on her way to Kyvena when Hallie had been kidnapped. She would've most definitely broken Kase's ankle instead of fixing it.

Zelda crossed her arms. Kase ran a hand through his hair. "I don't know if *involved* is the right word, necessarily..."

"Did you or did you not kiss her before you left the Stoneset caverns?"

"I did." He hesitated a little. "Look, Hallie is the—"

"You will address her as Miss Walker until you are betrothed—*if* I allow that to occur." Even though she was much shorter physically, she loomed miles above him. "I do not approve of my daughter running around with miscreants who involve themselves in drunken brawls."

Kase held up both hands. "That's not me, I swear...I just...Waylan just made a comment, and..."

The gauze wrapped around his injured hand made him a liar.

"So you have a short temper. Not a mark in your favor."

Kase's irritation rose with each word she said—which, honestly, might have proved her point. But he was not about to lose his temper at Hallie's mother of all people.

He ran his uninjured hand down his face, pushing himself to his feet to give him a little time to think of a response. Zelda Walker held her ground, though now Kase was at least two heads taller.

"Hal—Miss Walker is the reason I'm standing in front of you right now, and for that, I will always be grateful." Kase paused, and when he didn't get a tongue lashing in return, he continued, "She's the bravest, smartest, and most beautiful woman I've ever met. I love her, and there's nothing on this stars-forsaken planet that could change that."

The words hung in the air, and Kase's breath came in huffs. He hadn't meant to spill his feelings to Hallie's mother, but there they were, awaiting her judgment. Zelda held his stare, her arms still crossed. The silence bore down on him, but Kase didn't budge. Finally, Zelda pointed back to the bedroll Kase had used the previous night.

"Stowe says you're to stay here until he's happy with your healing." She bent down and fetched a jar and some bread out of her pack. She handed it to him. "Sit and eat. My husband will check you when he gets back. If he bothers the hospital medics enough, they usually let him help."

Kase took the food and sat. Somehow, he felt like he'd just passed some test. He twisted the lid on the jar off, the soft *pop* echoing in the stillness, and tore a piece of the bread, dipping it into the dark red goo. If Kase hadn't known it came from a simple glass jar and had been stashed in there for stars-knew how long, he would've guessed the berries had come straight from the bush. Flavor exploded on his tongue, just the right amount of tartness balanced by a caramel-like sweetness that had him dishing out more. The mazelberry jam tasted like heaven. "Thank you. Hallie was right. Your jam is truly the best."

Zelda turned from where she had been about to leave the tent. "I may have allowed you some of my jam, but I will remind you yet again that you have yet to earn the right to use my daughter's given name."

Kase choked on his next bite. When he'd recovered, he said, "Yes, Mrs. Walker. I apologize."

She stepped out of the tent only to pause and smile, though not at Kase. "Good morning, Mrs. Shackley."

Kase's organs leapt into his throat. He all but tossed the jar aside and lunged toward the tent flap. His mother. Somehow she was here, alive, not lost somewhere in the bombed-out capital buried under a heap of bodies and stone.

Zelda held the flap open, and instead of his mother, Clara appeared. Kase couldn't help his shoulders drooping slightly. Clara smiled at him before doing a double take. "Kase? What are you doing...why aren't you...?"

He opened his mouth and closed it again before saying, "I could ask you the same thing."

"Fair enough," Clara replied with a small laugh.

Kase moved aside so that she could enter the tent. Another woman followed. She was nearly Clara's twin, though her forehead was lined with age. Her dark eyes were just as bright. She held the bundle Kase recognized as Samuel.

The tent was hardly large enough for four adults and a baby. Kase quickly picked up his discarded breakfast and hid his bandaged hand behind his back. "I was just visiting."

Clara stared hard at him, but she didn't say anything. Kase wondered if anyone had realized he was no longer in his tent. Surely, someone had. Maybe Harlan thought it would be better if a refugee finished him off, after all. Then he wouldn't have to deal with the antics of his youngest son any longer.

Whether she accepted Kase's poor excuse or not, Clara still gave him a smile and turned to the unknown woman. "Kase, you may or may not remember, but this is my mother, Lady Miravel Davey. Mother, this is my brother-in-law, Master Kase Shackley."

"Call me Kase, Lady Davey, please." Kase took her proffered hand and gave it a quick peck. Lady Davey gave

Kase the once-over he was used to receiving by now, probably taking note of the bruises on his face and the hand still hidden behind his back.

"Yes, I remember you from the wedding. You look different."

Clara put a hand on her mother's shoulder. "It's been a few years, of course."

Lady Davey held herself like a queen, but when Samuel made a fussing noise from his bundle, she dropped her steely demeanor and shushed him while bouncing him in her arms. When he didn't calm down, she handed him to Clara. Once he recognized his mother, Samuel cooed in response. Lady Davey chuckled and smoothed the baby's hair. Clara smiled before turning back to Kase. "Now, what happened to your hand? The one you're trying to hide?"

"How do you know Mrs. Walker?" Kase countered.

Zelda fished out a few pastries and handed them to both Lady Davey and Clara. Clara shook her head, but Lady Davey took one with a murmured thanks.

Kase didn't get a pastry. His confidence fell a little.

Clara turned back to Kase. She swayed a little bit, keeping Samuel calm. "Zelda took pity on a new mother lost in the tunnels, and I'll be forever grateful for her help." She shot a smile to Zelda and said, "Mother didn't want to stay in her tent by herself with Samuel, and I'm going to help the men construct the ropes before they scale down into the hole. Could they stay with you, Zelda?"

Kase's ears perked up. "What?"

Clara chewed her lip and pulled Samuel closer to her chest. "They retrieved what they needed to go down into the hole where...where Jove supposedly fell. I...I want to help, but I don't..."

She faltered a little. Lady Davey clasped her daughter's shoulder, and Zelda found Clara's free hand. Kase stuffed his own into his pockets.

I cannot control other's actions, Kase thought hard to himself. Jove made a choice whether he meant to or not.

The silence waxed awkward, and Kase didn't quite know how to fix it. He wasn't sure he wanted to. Zelda might scold him for it.

Unfortunately, the universe had something else in mind.

Screams erupted from outside the tent, and the ground shook. Kase caught Lady Davey before she fell. Samuel cried. Clara and Zelda held onto each other. Shouts echoed down the tunnel. More screams.

His mind raced. Were they after him? Had his father sent soldiers to look for him? Was this the end? Could he throw the blame on Eravin?

Kase felt dirty just thinking about that possibility. Eravin had helped him last night, and not even twelve hours later, Kase plotted to repay him with accusations meant to save his own skin.

After making sure they weren't injured, Kase stepped up to the tent flap. Soldiers and civilians alike ran past. He caught a few words. Another collapse. The largest one yet. Cerl hovers were already in the area.

An attack. Had the Cerls caused the collapse? What reason could there be, except to look for survivors and finish them off?

Unless...unless they were looking for someone specific. Someone they needed. Like an Essence wielder. Like Loffler.

His chest squeezed.

If that was true, Kase had revealed that Loffler was the Essence wielder in the game last night. He hadn't meant to. It'd just come out. Someone had told. Was it Eravin? Neville and Waylan could have, too, he guessed. It had to have been Eravin.

Blast it. Kase knew he was part of One World, and he just—ugh, why did Kase keep screwing things up?

Maybe he did indeed deserve the metaphorical chains his father had placed around his wrists. Panic bloomed in his chest as more soldiers thundered by, not paying him any mind. He gripped the tent flap in his hand. He could barely hear Clara asking him what was happening.

A roaring boom shook the tunnel next. This time Kase fell over, but he launched himself to his feet quickly.

The tunnels were too exposed. The recent gaping holes had caused too much disruption, and now the Cerls knew where they'd been hiding. Without the Crews and hovers, the Jaydians were more akin to sitting ducks.

He ignored Samuel's cries and the women's questions as he stuffed everything he saw into the packs. Zelda seemed to understand without any words exchanged. She handed him salves and bandages and vials with stoppers. He tied up the pack and shoved it into her arms. "Take this and get to the lower tunnels. The Stradat Lord Kapitan's tent. Now."

Zelda pulled the pack on her back. Clara grabbed Kase's arm. "What is going on?"

"Attack."

Her eyes were wide, and her lip trembled. "Jove."

It was the first time since arriving in Kyvena that he saw the fear in her eyes. He needed to do something.

"If he's lasted this long, he can hold on for a few more hours." He was getting good at projecting confidence he didn't feel. He just hoped he wasn't lying.

Zelda grabbed Stowe's pack and gave it to Lady Davey. "Let's go."

Clara held Samuel tightly, her face tight with panic. Kase led them into the chaos. Refugees ran, their salvaged belongings gathered in their arms. Screams and the shouts of barked military orders echoed off the walls. Kase grabbed Clara's free hand and pulled her along. Zelda and Lady Davey followed close behind. Zelda glared at anyone who jostled them too hard.

They were trapped like rats, and they had no way of fighting back. What were the soldiers going to do? The swords were useless, and the electropistols were still dead. Was there a reserve of flashpistols anywhere? Though they wouldn't do much to the enemy hovers.

Helpless. It was a feeling Kase knew well, but as he dragged Clara, Samuel, Lady Davey, and Zelda through the crowds, he felt failure so hard it nearly made him collapse right then and there. There was no way out. There was no way to fight back.

If something happened to Clara or Samuel, Jove would never forgive him. *He* would never forgive himself.

Think. Think.

He had to do something. He could get them to safety, but how long would that last? How long would it be before the upper tunnels collapsed into the lower ones? How long would the bombardment go on? If he just had a hover, he could take out the enemy easily. But without electricity, any hovers that had survived the initial assault would be nearly as useless. He assumed they hadn't been refueled either, and he wouldn't have time to dig for more Yalvar fuel.

Then it clicked.

If he could just get to the surface, he could use the stolen hover. He whipped his head wildly around as he fought the river of refugees, searching for a ladder, another tunnel, anything that would lead him up.

People pressed against him. Screams and shouts rang through the air. His eyes scanned above their heads.

There. A ladder. Whatever guard who'd been manning it had disappeared into the fleeing populace.

He could make this right.

He pulled Clara close so she could hear what he said. "Find the Stradat Lord Kapitan. Stay safe. I'm going to help."

Clara's face was strained, and Samuel screamed, though his cries were lost to the cacophony around them. "Kase, no. Your mother would never forgive me."

"I have to, Clara. Please."

Zelda leaned close. "I'll take them."

Kase gave a nod of thanks as Zelda dragged the other two women back into the flow. Kase watched them disappear, ignoring the voice in the back of his head that said he was abandoning them only to die in the city above. Kase waited only one more second before fighting his way toward the nearest ladder. Shouts and screams bombarded him. Someone tried to pull him off the ladder. He kicked them, unsure if it was purposeful or accidental. He could apologize later.

He had to make this right. Especially if he was the reason it was all happening. He shouldn't have gone with Eravin. He shouldn't have drunk the whiskey. He was a stars-idiot.

His father was right. He was rubbish at decisions unless he was up in the sky.

The metal rungs chafed against his palms as he climbed. His forearms and calves burned with each step up to the next rung. The entire ladder shook. Whether that was from bombardment, cave-ins, or the general scrambling of refugees, Kase didn't know. He didn't look down, only climbed faster and faster until he reached a landing and a door cloaked in darkness, sunlight pushing through the infinitesimal crack to the right. Kase didn't see a knob or anything to open the door with. He wrenched himself up and pressed on the door. It was locked. Or coded. Or maybe even halfway sealed shut.

He felt along the edges, looking for hinges. He didn't find any, so the door had to open outward. A good sign. He didn't have much room to work with on the landing, but he'd have to make it work. He flung himself at the door; it gave only a little before bouncing him back. He caught himself on the rough stone wall to keep himself from falling back down the shaft.

"You have a death wish, Shackley?"

Kase glanced down toward the bottom of the ladder shaft to find the outline of Eravin Gray, sporting a busted lip. Of course.

Kase only felt slightly guilty, as he had a sneaking suspicion he'd been the one to give it to him. Kase rolled his shoulder, ignoring the pain; it was fading fast anyway. Maybe he should try kicking the door instead.

"Get out of here," Kase barked, turning back to the door. He lifted his right foot and placed it on the spot that would give him the best shot at kicking it open. He'd done it in the Narden Pass with a frozen lock and hadn't broken anything. Surely he could do it again here. If he didn't get to the hover, he would have more than a broken ankle to deal with.

The rumbling overhead was deafening. Kase jumped, covering his ears. He needed to get out there. He placed his foot against the door again.

"Stop, you're going to do something stupid," Eravin growled, crawling the rest of the way up. Kase pressed himself against the wall as Eravin joined him. His old friend pulled something Kase couldn't quite make out from his pocket and sliced it through the crack. "Simple locking mechanism, but it's not actually locked. Door's just jammed, I think. Easy fix if we do it together."

They lined their shoulders up against the door.

"On three?" Kase asked.

Eravin nodded.

Kase took a few steps back, and Eravin followed. "One…two…three!"

Both men surged forward, their shoulders leading the charge. They smacked against the door, pressing hard and fast. With a great groan, the door flew open, smacking the opposite wall.

Kase caught Eravin before he tumbled onto the stone walkway.

"Thanks," Eravin muttered as sunlight poured into the tiny space. Kase squinted painfully against the light and forced himself out into it, ducking instinctively when hovers roared over his head. His heart thumped in his ears louder than the hovers as he stumbled out onto the city wall. Eravin joined him moments later and cursed.

There were at least seven Cerl hovers flying in formation. They whipped over their heads. The force of wind knocked Kase into one of the battlements. Eravin hit the deck. Kase peeked around the stone monolith that had saved him from cascading off the wall. His heart sank. He was on the opposite side of the city from where he'd left the hover.

He cursed loudly, but not loud enough to drown out the quaking of stone as one of the hovers dropped some sort of electrobomb on a part of the outer city to the west. Holy shocks. He needed to get into that hover. He needed it faster than he could make it to the other side of the city. By the time he did, everyone below would be buried under rubble. His only chance had been taken from him, and he would never get to say goodbye to anyone. It was his curse to sit and watch as his world crumbled around him.

He turned and shoved Eravin. "This is your fault. If you hadn't told them about Loffler, we wouldn't be in this mess."

For once, Eravin's eyes were missing their cold undercurrent. He shook his head. "This wasn't the plan!"

His shouts got lost when another hover blazed directly over their heads. Kase dropped so hard on the top of the wall that he nearly knocked himself out. His head buzzed from the impact. Eravin landed beside him, the whites of his eyes showing and staring directly behind Kase.

Kase pushed himself to his knees, his body protesting the movement. He turned and nearly blacked out once again.

A Cerl airship. Guns out. Pointed directly at his heart.

He was about to die. How kind of the pilot to give him a chance to say his last rites.

He glared at the cockpit, determined to face his final moments with as much bravery as he could muster. Stubborn to the end.

Only the ship was...

Empty.

No one was flying the ship.

Kase's breath caught in his chest. It was *his* hover. The

one he'd stolen. How was that even possible? He laughed, the relief stealing away the panic. He lunged toward it, and miraculously, it popped open the top, hovering close enough to the wall for him to climb aboard. Kase patted the side almost like a hunter would his loyal hound. It was only slightly absurd, but after everything Kase had seen, he didn't question it. Eravin watched, shock elongating his features. Kase turned back and held out a hand. "Come on."

Eravin's face turned nasty. "How dare you accuse me of working with the Cerls when one of their machines welcomes you with open arms!"

Kase gritted his teeth before shouting, "Just trust me!"

It was a harsh echo from three years prior, when he'd stood outside Eravin's door...and his friend had shut it in his face.

Eravin didn't take Kase's proffered hand. Kase was unprepared for the sting of rejection it brought.

"I'm sorry," he croaked. "About your mother. It wasn't my intention, and if I could go back and change it, I would. But I'm trying to save the city and everyone in those tunnels now. I'm trying to do better. I'm sorry if you can't bring yourself to forgive me."

When Eravin shook his head, his jaw firm and unyielding, Kase closed the cockpit.

The truce might be over, but Kase had a job to do.

The ship rumbled, almost like a purring cat. It was pleased. Kase smirked. It was almost as if the hover had missed him. He was still struggling with the idea that the contraption had known Kase needed it and had come to find him. He filed that terrifying information away for later analysis. He strapped in and tugged the strange blanket across his legs.

The hover beeped a melody at him, and the steering control warmed under his palm. Kase gripped it tightly in response. The ship really was like a loyal pet. Maybe Eravin's hesitancy was justified. He shook his head to clear it. He needed to get the thing up and flying ten minutes ago.

He found the blaster trigger—just aim and squeeze—at the top of the steering control. Of course, it would be much easier if a second pilot was in control of that aspect, but alas, he had no choice. Kase flipped a switch, and the hover responded with a loud, comforting hum. With that, Kase was off, leaving Eravin on top of the wall, the gust from his take-off a parting gift.

Kase whipped through the skies after the other hovers, watching another drop a bomb onto a gaping maw in the landscape. He pressed hard on the pedals, his body going cold as he sped toward the threat. He squeezed the trigger twice as the bomb exploded.

Too late. Kase felt the punch in his gut.

His shots skewed wide, but whatever advantage he'd had before was gone. They now knew he was a rogue airship. Kase cursed and whipped the ship around as the other turned and fired. Without really meaning to, Kase rolled the ship left in a daring barrel roll. He'd thought about it, but he hadn't actually *done* it—he hadn't moved his hands. The shots missed, and Kase nearly puked from the pressure.

The ship. It had...it had just done what he'd thought.

Holy stars-blasted shocks.

Kase didn't have more time to analyze what had just happened as another hover joined the fray. Kase had spotted seven originally; the others wouldn't be far behind.

As a third joined, Kase stopped thinking through his actions and simply started doing, his instincts taking over, the ship responding with tenacious fervor. He veered right, then left, then flipped over a hover. He squeezed the trigger and fiery blue bolts lanced from his ship, spearing the enemy and bringing it down in a torrent of wind and fire.

Kase flew faster and higher than he ever had, his skin icy-hot, pressure bearing down on him as he climbed. But the hover sensed when he was about to black out from the gravitational forces thrust upon him and readjusted itself without him lifting a finger. They worked in perfect tandem as the ships below him teamed up to corner him in the sky.

Kase wouldn't have that.

He whipped around and fired. The enemy hover dodged but clipped its partner's wing. Kase's throat and lungs burned as he gasped for every breath. The enemy hover listed sideways, smoke leaking from the hit.

Got ya!

Kase took advantage and sent his blaster bolts into both. He didn't stop to see if they recovered or not. They would be on his tail in minutes, if not seconds, if they had—but three more hovers had appeared on the horizon, and Kase didn't have time to focus on potentially defeated foes.

The ensuing firefight was something out of the storybooks, Kase and his hover the poets of the skies. They whipped in and out, rose and dove, rolled and flipped. They fired when another hover was in range. It was as much a dance as it was a poem. They tangoed in the air, giving and taking. The rush of adrenaline was ablaze in his veins as he rolled and righted himself before firing at the tail of the final hover.

It erupted in flames, losing altitude in seconds and exploding on the city wall below.

Kase scanned the horizon, fear, exhaustion, and elation warring for a hold on his body and mind. Adrenaline still thrummed in his veins, and he was ready for anything they shot at him.

A blink on the horizon. Gold glittering in the midday sun.

Dragon.

Skibs.

Kase gripped his steering control. The hover hummed. He was ready. He could take on the dragon.

But could he fight Skibs?

He'd done it in the Gate chamber, and he'd lost. Hallie had been there to save him, but there was no one to save him now.

The beast's great wings thrust up and down. It lifted its great head into the air and roared. Kase winced and recoiled against the guttural, piercing cry. Fire exploded from its maw, devouring the clouds hundreds of feet above.

Kase nearly dropped himself out of the sky. The hover kept him steady.

He'd just gotten close enough to barely glimpse Skibs on its back when the dragon turned and flew back toward the horizon.

Sweat ran rivers down his face, soaking his collar. The hover's buttons sparkled and flashed in quick succession before humming once more.

With a shaking hand, Kase reached forward and patted the hover's dash. "Good boy. You scared him off."

Well, it did feel like a loyal dog. Kase had never had one before, but he thought he preferred a pet hover anyway—especially this one.

He searched below, lowering his hover to inspect the damage. Patches of blackened ground greeted him. Scraps of defeated hovers littered the road and caught city outbuildings on fire. Gaping, ravaged holes marred the surface. Bile rose in Kase's throat.

Near the tree line, a crowd began to amass, bubbling up from one of the holes. He drove his hover toward them. His hands shook harder as the adrenaline started fading, the strain and the terror catching up to him. The blanket had slid from his knees during the firefight. The hover had drained him.

By the time he set the ship down onto the grass, he was shaking all over. The shock of it all, of his *victory*, rocked him to his core.

Had he saved them? Had he been enough?

He swallowed as he switched off the ship. Cheers met his ears.

Too much. The wave of sound made it feel as if he'd plunged underwater. He fetched the blanket from the floor, warmth seeping back into his stiff, aching fingers. Kase looked out the cockpit window at the gathering, the muffled words of the Jaydian anthem sung loud and off-key, but full of hope and joy. He popped open the windshield and stood. They probably didn't realize for whom they cheered, that it was the criminal who had burned their homes three years prior. They didn't know that he was potentially the reason for today's attack, that those who'd died were on Kase's conscience.

But whether they knew or not, the triumphant joy was intoxicating. His eyes ached with unshed emotion. Regardless of whether the attack was his fault or not, he'd stopped it. He'd taken down at least seven hovers all on his own.

Maybe this was the start of his repentance. Maybe he could be forgiven.

CHAPTER 23

HUNG THE MOONS

Hallie

A RUMBLING SOUNDED IN THE distance, the ground shook, and the grass tasted like soot. Hallie had no clue why, or where she even was, but she prayed to Toro or whoever might hear her that she was in Kyvena. She couldn't handle anything less. A sob stuck in her throat, but it wouldn't release. She couldn't fall apart now.

She had Niels, Fely, and some answers. And a sword.

And she'd witnessed the Cerl King's death.

She hadn't expected that to hit her as hard as it had. All her life, she'd hated the shadow king she'd only heard horror stories about. She'd seen him kill Yarrow with his power, but in the end, he'd helped her.

She didn't know how to feel about that.

Unwittingly, he'd sacrificed himself to save Hallie and Niels, and she would never get to tell him thank you. That felt odd to even think.

Everything hurt.

She'd managed to get them somewhere, but for all she

knew, they were still in Myrrai, or trapped somewhere in Tev Rubika. She'd been screaming whatever she thought might work, thrusting power into empty stone. It could have taken them anywhere.

But they were no longer in the Gate chamber, so that had to be an improvement.

Pushing herself to her knees, she spit out dirt and grass. Pouring her power into the stone of the Gate chamber, she'd tried her best to focus on Kyvena, on the airfields, on Kase. But the use of her power made her feel alive and drained in the same breath. She was probably only still conscious because of Fely's help. Or the Gate's. She still wasn't sure what had happened.

Fely. Niels. His bloody wrist.

Hallie turned her head to find Niels lying face-down in the grass. He rolled over, clutching his arm. Blood stained his abdomen and sleeve and pretty much anything close to him. Hallie fumbled in her pack for something that could be used as a bandage. Niels groaned, "Just use the shirt in my pack. I don't care."

Hallie found the shirt in question. She hastily tied it around his wrist. Niels gritted his teeth.

Hallie looked over at Fely for help.

The Rubikan woman panted heavily on her other side and stared up at the sky. Sunlight made her dark hair shine like glass, though flecks of dirt and who knew what else decorated the strands. Whether or not the blood was hers or Filip's, Hallie wasn't sure. All she felt was relief, tinged with guilt.

"I can heal you," Hallie said, the sun burning her eyes as she looked up at the sky. "I just need to..."

Wait. It'd been night when they'd fought Loffler in the Gate chamber. Or maybe...

Hallie's head hurt.

"No," Fely said, rolling to her side and pushing herself to her knees. "You used too much power, and the only reason you didn't die was because you had the Gate to aid you." She sat back, pushing hair from her eyes. Her hand stumbled over the bandage still wrapped around her own head. "It's a miracle it worked, truly."

"But Niels—" Hallie started, "—and the King. And...and...the sun..."

Stars. She didn't even know what she was trying to say.

"I'll be fine, Hal." Niels looked too pale, but he sat up fully. "It's mostly numb now."

"That's not a good thing!" Did no one else realize that it was clearly midday?

"I can give him some Soul from the plant life here to get him through until we find help." Fely looked to the sky as if trying to gauge their location as well.

"What?" Hallie asked blankly. Stars, she needed some sleep. "But the King's dead."

"My unique ability to harvest plant Soul was the reason I was chosen as his bride and vessel. It complimented his Essence power, though I do not possess that myself." Placing her hand on the grass, Fely muttered something under her breath. Her hand glowed, and the grass browned and went brittle. Dead. "Not much, because spring is still trying to make its way here, but it will work for now."

"And the grass? You just...took its Soul?"

Chronals had abilities that were unique to themselves, and all could be used to defend the Gate. The embroidery on the ceremonial togas they wore were a way to showcase their specific skills. But she still didn't understand this one.

Fely siphoned more power. The brown grass surrounding her glowing hand was disconcerting. "It's best to use this sparingly. No grass or plants will grow here again."

Terrifying. And intriguing. Hallie wished she could ask more questions, but now was not the time.

Fely crawled over to Niels and pressed her glowing hand to his forearm, just above the shirt-wrapped wound. "We still have a mission. We need to find the General. He'll know what to do."

Like the *stars* would Hallie ever try to find Correa. She needed to find Kase.

"Thank you," Niels said, adjusting his bandage.

"Of course," Fely said. "It should stop the bleeding for now, but that is all I can spare."

Hallie felt a little relief. She shouldn't be thankful for the woman's terrifying power, but at this moment, she didn't care. It had worked, and she could debate the ramifications or ethics of it later.

Warmth radiated from Fely's touch on her shoulder. "It's not as potent as human Soul, but this should help a little."

With Fely's power bolstering her, Hallie's breathing slowed. They had a job to do. They had to find Kase—and Jove, hopefully. She'd even take the Stradat Lord Kapitan if he could help her make sense of what was to come.

"The General is unlikely to have made the journey so quickly unless he found a hover." Fely paused again and looked to the sky. "And if we are in Kyvena as you hoped, Asa will be here as well."

She couldn't worry about Correa or Filip's brother right now. She had more pressing matters on her mind.

A small copse of trees surrounded them, their branches beginning to show hints of spring, blossoms and green leaves finally sprouting. A few of the trees were fuller than others. Some were thicker. All cast shadows on her hands and arms as she stumbled toward them, searching between their close-knit trunks. The smoky scent floating on the air was still pungent, stinging her nose. Above the trees, she spotted black clouds.

"Something's on fire," Niels said, looking around.

Hallie nodded. But what? The city?

Just beyond the tree trunks, she spotted the outline of the capital. The trunks scratched the pads of her fingers as she brushed by them. It felt like a dream. She could make out the familiar stone city wall, and what should have been the airfields, except...

It was wrong. Everything was wrong.

Charred craters marred the hover runways. Twisted hunks of metal were barely recognizable from this distance, but with dawning horror, she realized exactly what they were: hovers.

What remained of them, anyway.

Huge swaths of the wall had been scattered as if kicked over by school children playing sport. Dark, ugly smoke rose like a horrible specter from the far side of the city. Some other blaze roared to the right.

She brought a shaking hand to her mouth.

It was Kyvena. Unmistakably.

She had to find Kase. He had to be here. She needed him to be here. That thought alone was enough to blot out her injuries and her exhaustion and her horror. She needed his arms around her, holding her tight, because only then would she know if she was all right.

Would he even have made it to the capital yet? How long had she been in Myrrai? Had it really only been five days since she'd said goodbye? Had the Gate shifted things somehow?

She needed him. But with another look at those decimated hovers, her heart dropped from her chest, stopping her breath.

She prayed he *hadn't* been here when that had happened. That none of those hovers hid...

She couldn't even think it.

"Fates and glory," Fely breathed.

Hallie's eyes stung with new tears.

What had once been a glittering capital made of whitewashed stone buildings with a mix of slate and thatched roofs was now a grotesque pit of despair. The longer she looked, the more ravaged it appeared, evident even from her distance.

It was as if a vengeful god had cast fire and brimstone from the heavens for forgotten sins.

She'd known that the city was under attack per the conversation with Correa and Filip in Achilles, but seeing it here in person was an entirely new horror. What were they dealing with? What weapons did the Cerls have at their disposal? Was there another Essence wielder that had caused this? Surely the destruction wasn't simply from hovers or those cannons. If so, Jayde didn't stand a chance. Nothing Hallie could do would fix the lives lost and nightmares written here.

"I didn't know," Fely said, her voice small. "I swear I didn't...I'm so sorry. I didn't know about the attack until that horrid display at Achilles."

Niels made his way slowly over and swore under his breath.

Hallie swallowed her emotion best she could, but it leaked into her words despite her effort. "Why?"

It was war. The Cerls had declared that when they'd attacked Stoneset and taken over Achilles. Only a small child at the time of the Great War, the only recollections she had were fleeting feelings of terror, dark corners of the basement, and the stories older villagers told her. Thankfully, the bulk of the fighting had been elsewhere, but Stoneset was no stranger to rogue Cerl bands.

Fely's only answer was silence. She'd lived through a civil war in her own country, and she knew the reality. But that didn't give Hallie any comfort.

The rumbling she'd been hearing grew louder. Hovers. Her heart pounded.

Maybe…maybe it was the Crews' pilots. Maybe it was a rescue team come to collect survivors, though almost a week had passed since the attack if King Filip's words at Achilles were to be believed.

She looked at her hands. She had power over time—could she do something to reset the city to the time before it was attacked? It would kill her, surely. But if it spared so many others—

"You shouldn't play with time," Fely said, as if reading her mind. "It's tempting, but the repercussions could be catastrophic."

Hallie opened her mouth to reply when something roared overhead, and the trio ducked, peeking up at the sky. Through the branches in the trees, a hover whizzed above their heads. Its passing whipped the branches and budding leaves into a whirlwind. Hallie's hair lashed her face.

Niels swore again.

The hover was flying so low it barely cleared the tree canopy, and it was going entirely too fast—inhumanly fast.

Holy blasting stars.

Three more hovers zoomed behind it. Hallie dropped to the ground, barely avoiding a large tree root, the sooty scent of grass filling her senses once more. The trees' protests were lost in the firefight as the hovers passed. Loud explosions echoed off the city walls, making it almost impossible to hear her own scream.

She untangled herself from her satchel and crawled to the edge of the trees. As terrifying as it sounded, the morbid fascination of it all took over. She needed to see what was happening.

The first hover she'd seen swooped in and out around the others, firing its blasters whenever another was in range. One hover screeched as it was hit square-on and crashed miles in the distance, an echoing boom and fiery cloud following.

That explained the other fires she'd seen earlier.

Hallie bit her lip to keep her terror from spilling out. She didn't understand. Those weren't Jaydian hovers. They were blue-tinged for one, but the one firing on them looked identical. Infighting? A traitor?

Fear froze her limbs as she watched the rogue hover take out the last two, rolling and weaving like a master of the air. Hallie couldn't help but gasp even as the rogue took out the final one after looping above and shooting it from behind The whole maneuver happened so quickly Hallie was dizzy just watching.

"Now *that's* a pilot." Niels' voice shook with awe.

"I'll say," Fely breathed.

The admiration in her voice was surprising. She had been betrothed to King Filip. Those were his men.

While Hallie still had no idea what was going on, she couldn't help the trickle of comradery she felt toward the other woman. She wasn't nearly as bad as Hallie had assumed.

Shouts and cheers erupted from her right, but she barely heard it over the explosion following the crash of the final hover into the city wall's remnants. They weren't alone.

Maybe they would find Cerl soldiers. Maybe they would find refugees.

No wonder the grass tasted like soot. The capital had been burning for days. She wondered if anyone had survived. She pushed herself to her knees.

The rogue hover pilot whipped his hover around and zoomed back toward Hallie, Fely, and Niels, flying just above the trees. She screamed, but it was lost in the wind tearing through her and blowing her sideways. She caught herself on a nearby trunk, the bark scraping her palms. With her pack and satchel on her shoulders, she followed the cheers punctuating the crackling of fire in the distance.

There was something familiar about the way the pilot flew, the loop at the end in particular.

Could it be Kase?

Her heart squeezed at the thought. She wanted it to be him so badly it hurt, but he could never have made it to the capital from the Nardens in such a short amount of time. Besides, how would he have gotten a hold of a Cerl hover?

But she couldn't help hoping for the impossible.

Just on the other side of the trees, the hover touched down in a small clearing encircling a gaping hole in the ground. It was as if someone had grabbed a chunk of earth and tossed it aside. Hallie tugged Fely behind a large oak. Niels followed suit.

People poured out of the hole and into the open, jostling one another for the best view of the pilot, who had yet to leave the hover. Their clothes were dusty, torn, looking as if they'd seen better days.

Jaydian refugees. They had to be.

Where had the hole come from, though? It wasn't natural. She'd been out here before, and she didn't remember it. Maybe bombs. Maybe…maybe…she didn't know what else, really.

When she saw a few soldiers with the Jaydian emblem on their breasts join the group, Hallie led Fely and Niels out from behind the trees.

"Just let me do the talking," Hallie whispered out the side of her mouth as they walked.

"Sure, Hal." Niels held his injured arm to his chest. He was being too nice. She guessed that was the best-case scenario after everything. Maybe she could figure out what else to say to him after a medic saw to his wrist. The makeshift bandage wasn't going to hold up much longer.

"I am perfectly capable of speaking for myself," Fely said firmly.

Hallie nodded. "Fine, if anyone asks, you're a Rubikan refugee." Her thick Rubikan accent wouldn't leave that to guesswork, anyway. "They've been pouring into the capital since the civil war. Just be smart about it."

"So I should not mention that my grandfather was the one who started that war?"

With everything that had happened in the last few days, Hallie shouldn't have been caught off guard—but there she was, gasping as they joined the group. She was about to whisper something back when she caught the sly grin on Fely's face. "Is that the truth?"

She just waved delicately. "No matter. Let us figure out who this skilled pilot is and scold them for scaring us half to death, shall we?"

No one glanced their way or questioned where they had come from. They were busy shouting about the pilot, who had finally popped open the windshield. While Hallie was tall, she still had to stand on her tiptoes to see anything at all.

A soldier or two tried to herd people back into the hole, but more kept climbing out of it.

Hiding underground? That would explain the empty streets of the capital, evident even from a mile or two away. Was it like the Stoneset caverns, hollowed out after the massacre at Ravenhelm?

Out in the open, they were sitting ducks for any other Cerl hovers that decided to fly over, but Hallie didn't think they cared. The smell of sweaty, unwashed bodies was nearly overwhelming. Fely's nose scrunched against the barrage. Niels didn't seem to care, just looked at the ground. Probably trying to keep his pain in check.

"Hey, that's my jacket."

Hallie jumped and turned to find someone standing at her other side, a man in his early twenties with jet-black hair and narrow obsidian eyes, like Petra's. She didn't know him.

When he grabbed her shoulder, Fely snatched his hand and shoved it away. "I'd suggest backing away."

A flawless Jaydian mountain accent poured out of Fely's mouth that time. Hallie's mouth dropped open, but she quickly shut it.

"I've been missing the jacket for a while," the man explained, flushing as he took his hand back. He pointed to Hallie's shoulder.

Hallie looked down at the name embroidered there. *Private Yolen.*

Oh, right. Kase had filched this one before they'd left Kyvena.

"Listen—" Hallie began, removing the jacket. She didn't take off her satchel, which made the entire action awkward in the enclosed space in the crowd. Finally extracting her other arm from the sleeve, she held it out to him. A nice breeze skittered across the back of her neck, now exposed without the jacket. "It's a long story, and I'm so sorry."

The man shook his head, pushing the jacket back to her. "No, it's fine. You probably saved my life." He held up a hand and gave her a quick smile. "Thanks for stealing it."

Huh?

Then he walked off, joining the rest of the crowd.

Fely gave the man a thoughtful look before turning back to her. "Jaydians are odd."

She huffed. "Just how many different accents can you

do?"

"A good amount," Fely said with a smile. "When you grow up in the home I did, you find ways to entertain yourself."

"I helped my parents run the inn. I've met dozens upon dozens of people from all parts of the planet, but I can't seem to replicate any of them so accurately."

"Didn't stop you from trying," Niels said, a small smile poking out.

Hallie raised her eyebrows. He must've been feeling better if he was bringing up old memories again. She remembered many a night entertaining the inn's guests with one of their plays. Those were some of her favorite memories with her brother and Niels. They were also some of the more painful.

She gave him a tentative smile back. If they could simply return to that friendship, everything would be all right, she thought.

But the emotion on his face disappeared as quickly as it had come about.

Enough of that, then.

"Well, it's only useful in the most ridiculous situations," Fely said, noticing Hallie's face and Niels' demeanor. "Good for party tricks. Estate dinners are quite a bore."

Hallie laughed a little at that, breaking the earlier tension. It was nice. The heaviness in her soul hesitantly lifted a little with it. This side of Fely, she found she liked. In a different world, they might have even been friends.

However, after everything they'd gone through in the last hour, from the fight with Loffler and her betrothed dying to the tumultuous trip to Kyvena, the woman looked...remarkably relaxed.

When she thought about it that way, it seemed clear something was off. She just couldn't pinpoint what, exactly. She glanced at Niels, but he hadn't seemed to notice. He was glaring toward the rogue hover.

She folded the jacket over her arms. It was getting warm anyway. She turned back toward the hover, where the pilot had finally stood and waved to the cheering crowd.

Fely gasped. "Wait, isn't that...of course, I cannot be certain, because I only saw him that one time with that horrid display of the General's...but then Achilles..."

But Hallie didn't hear a single word she said. She couldn't. Everything in her mind went silent—all the thoughts and misgivings about Fely and the underlying dread of what would happen now that King Filip was dead. Her ears rang with silence, like an explosion had gone off right next to her head. Tingles danced down her entire body and back up again, flashes of hot and cold taking turns flaring through her skin, like she had just used her power again.

The pilot's curly brown hair was more tousled than ever, made worse by his hand running through it as his eyes scanned the crowd. It had been a while since he'd shaved, a short beard decorating his cheeks. Her heart thumped harder.

How was he here? The timing didn't add up.

But she didn't care. She couldn't care.

The last time she'd seen him, he'd disappeared into the twisting corridors beneath the Nardens, the memory of his lips on hers was all she had left. She'd said goodbye with tears streaming down her face. A part of her had believed she'd never see him again. Never. She'd accepted her fate and prayed her fears would prove to be wrong.

He'd also been uncertain of what he would face when he reached Kyvena—whether he would be executed for his many crimes or locked in a dungeon cell. She hadn't realized until that moment just how much she'd dared to hope. The thought of him amidst the turmoil in the Gate chamber had brought her there, to this exact moment in time, to make this possible.

Kase Shackley stood in front of her, alive and well, against all odds.

And then his eyes found hers, and the impossible became real.

Trying to catch her breath was pointless. Her vision blurred. She blinked furiously, the emotions swirling within her heart fighting for attention: shock, joy, anguish, love—

Love.

She brought a shaking hand to her mouth. A single choked sob escaped her fingers. A few people turned toward her, their expressions skeptical, but she didn't care.

Kase.

She *had* recognized the pilot's flight patterns. Kase had taken down the enemy without any effort. He'd swept right over her head without her even knowing.

Tears flowed down her cheeks, and she didn't try to stop them. Her chest was going to explode.

She dropped the jacket. Fely said something, but she couldn't hear anything else, see anything else but the cocky pilot frozen on the hover wing, his hand raised mid-wave.

Another breeze rustled her wayward strands of dark auburn hair, wisps sticking to her damp cheeks. A watery smile split her face; it ached, but she couldn't relax it. Not when Kase was looking at her like she'd hung the moons in the sky, like the universe had finally given him a gift instead of a curse.

All she could see were those blue eyes and windswept hair, the teary smile meant for her. All she could feel was her pounding heart, the tingling having moved to her extremities. For that one moment, she could pretend she didn't carry the world on her shoulders.

Another moment of uncertainty passed, then Kase leaped down and landed with a dancer's grace, shoving through the crowd with his eyes anchored to her. She'd never seen him smile so broadly. He'd never had cause to. Not before.

He blurred in her vision once more, and she blinked the moisture away.

"Go." Fely shoved her forward, and Hallie dropped her pack.

Then she was running, and he was running, the crowd parting, and Hallie leapt, crashing into his arms, forgetting the onlookers. He held her so tightly his heart pounded beneath her chest. She buried her head in his neck. He smelled of leather and woodsmoke and...home. He smelled like home.

All the terror of the last few days fell away with a single touch.

After spinning her around in circles, her feet floating weightlessly with each twirl, he set her down and pulled back to look in her face. Tears budded in his eyes, his voice husky as he breathed, "It's *really* you."

All she could do was nod, because if she opened her mouth, she might start blubbering. She'd seen him not even a week ago, but she'd lived an eternity in those few days.

She hadn't expected to survive taking on and using her

power, but she had. And she'd been rewarded by finding him again. She refused to think that maybe it was a boon that would eventually lead to something worse—the calm before the storm.

Even if she only had this one moment, it was worth everything.

Another smile lit Kase's face like the sun as his hand tightened around her waist. He let his other hand trail down her cheek and rest, cupping the back of her neck, his thumb lazily tracing her jawline. He lowered his lips to hers.

Someone cleared their throat.

Hallie sucked in a breath and pulled back, her breathing heavy and her head lighter. Words wouldn't form—couldn't form. He was *here*. Her impossible hope had come true.

And she wasn't dreaming. This was real.

"As much as I hate to interrupt," Niels said, finally speaking.

The back of her neck prickled with annoyance as she turned slightly in Kase's arms.

"Yes?"

With each passing second, the sounds of the crowd came back, and the world unfroze. Fely winked at her, but then she subtly nodded in the direction of the soldiers, who were staring daggers at Kase.

Niels set down her pack, the sword sticking up and falling over from where it'd been hanging. "We have information that needs passing along."

Kase looked at Fely quizzically, his arms still wrapped around Hallie. "And you are? You look familiar."

"A friend," Fely said simply. She tucked a stray piece of midnight hair behind her ear and looked away, back toward the soldiers.

Kase held out one hand, the other not letting Hallie go. "I'm Kase."

Fely hesitated, but she allowed him to give it a quick peck. "Fely."

Kase then turned to Niels and shook his hand, though the exchange was cool at best. "Thank you for getting her back safely."

Niels nodded, his jaw steely. "It's what her father entrusted me to do."

"Of course."

Fely hesitated before stepping between the two men. "So, our information?"

Hallie tried to cover her unease with a smile. She only allowed herself to feel slightly guilty at Niels' tone. She'd told him how she'd felt, but maybe flaunting her choice in front of him was too much. However, with Kase's arms still around her, it was difficult to feel much pity for him. "Is there somewhere we can talk? And where is Papa?"

Kase looked like he wanted to forget about all his responsibilities and kiss her senseless, but he said, "He's with your mother. They're fine." He looked over at the pack and weapon on the ground. "I assume you have an explanation for the scary-looking sword?"

"Define explanation."

Kase raised his eyebrows. "Not sure if I should be nervous or not."

"Later." Hallie glanced at Fely, who shook her head and subtly gestured to the crowd still around them. With furtive glances at the sky, soldiers started herding people back into the hole in the ground.

"I didn't expect you to be here so soon," she said, squeezing his wrist. "How did you make it to the capital in only five days?"

Kase stared at her hard, his grip loosening a little. "Five days?"

"Give or take a few hours, I suppose, considering we're on a different continent," Hallie said, untangling herself and reaching for her pack. She made sure the sword was secure before pulling the straps onto her shoulders. "It felt like forever, though."

Kase looked at Niels, then at Fely before finally focusing on Hallie again. "Not sure I follow."

Hallie tilted her head. "Well, it should've taken you a few days to go through the tunnels in the Pass, I'd think." She looked to Niels for confirmation, but he only shrugged. "Which would mean you somehow made it from the Pass to Kyvena in two days. How?"

Kase stared at her, forehead wrinkled in confusion. She'd never seen him look at her like that before.

Her heart sank, heavy with unease. "Kase?"

He shook his head. "I, uh, stole that in Nar." He pointed at his hover. "It's quicker than most hovers. By a lot."

Both Hallie and Fely's mouths dropped open. Hallie recovered first. "You *stole* a Cerl hover?"

"Yeah, with your father." He took her hand and led her to his hover; Fely and Niels trailed behind them quietly. "But that's another story for another day. The point is, we did go faster because we had this, but it took us three days. Not two."

"Still quick!" Hallie said, still trying to figure out what was going on. Something didn't make sense. Maybe she'd lost track of the days? She truly was exhausted, though seeing Kase had injected some adrenaline into her veins.

Kase stared at her quizzically. Distractedly, he ran his hand along the airship's nose as if petting some sort of dog. A second later, the hover faded, replaced by the foliage behind it. She gasped. Kase jumped, but he quickly recovered. "That explains it."

"What?" Nothing was making sense. She thrust her hand out, her fingers colliding with the metal. It was still there—she just couldn't see it. Interesting. She spread her fingers out, marveling at the cool metal that she could no longer see. It was as if her hand pressed against solid air. "How?"

She nearly dug out her sketchbook to take a few notes, but it was not the time. She might persuade Kase to show it to her later. This was unbelievable.

As if invisible hoverships were much less believable than her ability to create a Passage with her magic and transport her thousands of miles in seconds. She shivered.

Kase shrugged. "Not really sure, but it's already saved me once or twice." He held his hand out for her pack, careful of the sword; he pulled the pack onto his own shoulders before helping Hallie into her jacket.

She thanked him and nodded toward Kyvena and the invisible hover. "That's how the Cerls took the city, isn't it?" She fiddled with the sleeve cuffs. "Do you know when the attack was?"

It was Fely who answered her question. "The day Achilles fell."

Kase gave her a look of suspicion. "Yes."

Hallie would have to tell him who Fely was—later. For now, she steered the conversation in a slightly different direction. "So five or six days. Why are the Cerls still bombing the city?"

Kase shook his head, concerned instead of confused

now. He pulled her closer, putting his palm against her forehead. "I think we should maybe get you looked at. You're not making sense.

"Excuse me, I am making perfect sense." But he *was* looking at her like she'd started speaking Yalven. "What are you talking about?

He turned slightly to look at her, searching her eyes and her face for some sort of answer, but he didn't seem to find it. "Hals, it's been nearly two weeks. I haven't seen you in about eleven days."

Impossible. Her calculations couldn't be off by *that* much, no matter how little sleep she'd gotten.

While she was doing the math again just to make sure, Kase cupped her cheek. "Are you hurt? Did something happen?"

Hallie could only stare blankly at him. It still wasn't adding up.

"No, it's only been five days. I'm almost positive." She pulled out of his grip and started counting on her fingers. "It was night when we left the Gate chamber. But it's midday here, and I'd guess it's only been a half hour, or an hour at most. Okay, so let's say six days. We spent yesterday hiking up to the city from the ruins. Before that, we were underneath the ruins, then in Ravenhelm, then Stoneset. And we spent three days there." She held up her fingers as if Kase couldn't see them clearly in front of her. "That's only five. Six at worst, considering the rotation of the planet, but that shouldn't have thrown us off all that much. Of course, maybe we were in the Gate chamber longer than I thought, though it couldn't have been more than late evening when…well, when everything—"

"Hals. Wait. You're confusing me." Kase held up his hand. "I swear to you that I haven't seen you in nearly two weeks. Let's get you to the hospital ward and let—"

Fely stepped up and put a hand on Hallie's shoulder. "We need to discuss this privately after we deliver our information."

"I don't understand," Hallie said. She couldn't get her brain to work right. Stars, she needed sleep. Had they stayed in Stoneset longer than she'd thought? Maybe she'd lost time when she'd used Navara's journals?

Maybe something had gone awry with the passage.

She'd lost control, she knew, but the Gate's remaining power had gotten them here. Fely had said that herself. She looked down at her hands.

Her power could reverse time in small increments. Other than creating or opening Passages, it'd been limited to healing that didn't hold, whatever she'd done to the beam in the Myrrai ruins, and...well, dissolving a man before her eyes, but she was desperately hoping that might prove to be an anomaly.

"Swear it's been that long?" Hallie asked, her stomach rebelling. Her skin flashed hot and cold.

Kase cupped her elbows and bent a little to look into her eyes. "Yes, I'm sure of it."

She didn't know how she'd done it, because it hadn't been intentional, but if her theory was correct...well, it was a miracle they'd only lost a week.

Her voice shook when she spoke again, so quietly Kase had to lean in to hear. "Then that means that I...somehow...sped up time."

OF YALVEN LORE

Niels

TO SAY NIELS WAS EXHAUSTED was an understatement.

In the last five days—that he remembered, at least—he'd been to the other side of the world and back because the girl he'd planned to marry had somehow acquired magic powers. Oh, and then she'd gone and healed his pistol wound with said magic. And now, apparently, she'd transported them a week or so into the future.

Magic. Sure, he'd known about her power ever since she'd woken after Achilles. He'd gone to the Yalven city knowing that. But he hadn't really grasped what that meant. It felt like a bad fairy tale, not reality.

He'd wondered more than once over this whole misadventure if he'd died when his family did, and this was all some bizarre afterlife.

He felt empty. Nothing quite registered any more. He didn't know if that was because he was losing everything that mattered—including the woman he loved—or because he'd possibly killed one of the leaders of Jayde by kicking him into a glowing archway, or if the numbness in his wrist had spread everywhere else, too.

He hoped it'd stopped bleeding, but he couldn't get it checked out yet.

It felt cold, though, which almost definitely wasn't good.

His feet dragged along the pebble strewn dirt tunnel floor beneath Kyvena on their way to see the Stradat Lord Kapitan, Kase's father. He'd always wanted to see the capital of Jayde. Every traveler he'd spoken to described it as a glittering city on a hill, something out of a dream.

He wondered what they would say if they saw the nightmare it'd become.

It almost felt as if he'd never left the Stoneset caverns.

He followed the soldiers and Hallie through tunnels that felt entirely too much like home, sans the familiar mountain accent. He heard a cocktail of dialects as they walked. He tried to focus on not getting caught up in the fray and staying on his feet. If he didn't look too far forward, he could pretend he couldn't see that Hallie kept brushing against Kase's hand.

Niels shouldn't have kissed her. That was a mistake. He'd just lost himself, lost control. She'd healed him, and in that moment of relief, he'd believed that they could go back to the way they'd been.

Maybe he could blame it on the Fogs if they ever got to really talk about it. Maybe she would change her mind. Maybe, maybe, maybe.

That was all his life would ever be: a ragtag bunch of maybes. A string of hopes and dreams, never anything more.

Just watching her walk beside Kase made his skin crawl.

They'd planned an excellent rescue for Hallie. They shared similar interests, like the desire to be out under the open sky. That didn't mean Niels didn't want to slug him every time he looked at Hallie the way he had when she'd leaped into his arms…like if he hadn't interrupted, Kase would've kissed her like she was the only woman in the world.

Maybe it was a good thing he felt numb all over. Otherwise, he might've done something he'd regret.

The tent they stopped at shouted *wealth* in the dimly lit cavern loud enough for Niels to hear the echoes. It looked like a miniature palace all stretched out across the back wall, its smaller sections jutting off each side of the taller one. The Stradat Lord Kapitan would've had the money and resources to commandeer something so grand while his citizens dealt with whatever they could scavenge.

A mix of gas lanterns and torches hung from the stone in intervals of ten feet or so. Tunnels branched off from the main thoroughfare, and the people here had begun to set up a market of sorts. He caught snippets of conversation every so often that suggested some people had stolen away to the capital and returned with bounty to sell.

It all left a bitter taste on his tongue. These people were in hiding. They'd been bombed not even an hour earlier. Yet, all they could think of was making a tenner.

Some of the coldness around his wound receded.

Niels finally looked over at Kase and noted his firm jaw and dead eyes, looking like he was ready for a Burning. The mutters he'd overheard on their hike down told him that the attack had taken out several sections of the tunnel. Maybe Kase was simply feeling for those lost.

"Kase?" Hallie prompted. "What's wrong?"

Apparently she'd noticed, too.

"Focus on what you need to report for now. I'll be with you the entire time." Kase put a hand to the small at Hallie's back and gestured her forward. Niels gritted his teeth and followed shortly after.

The inside of the tent was brighter than the outside tunnel. Three gas lanterns lit the space: one on a table that had clearly seen better days, judging by the suspicious darks stain on one side; one next to a cot, dimmer than the others; and the third atop a dilapidated desk holding neat stacks of parchment held in place by rock paperweights. The room felt sterile, in a weird way, even though the floor was packed with dirt and pebbles. Six chairs sat around the table, making the room feel much larger than it was.

A man in a military uniform sat at one end of the rectangular table. The man had a steely gray mustache and brushed back hair. A frown rested on his face, his arms crossed. If this was Kase's father, Niels was hard-pressed to find any similarities between the two.

The man gestured for them to sit, and Niels blinked out of his thoughts to pull out the nearest chair and offer it to Hallie. A few pebbles dislodged and skittered across the ground at the action. Kase cast him a fleeting glance before guiding her to the chair. She sank slowly into the seat, her gaze fixed upon the man at the other end. Kase sat heavily in the one between her and his father. Niels pulled another out for Fely before he sat on Hallie's left between them.

He kept his injured arm to his chest, though the wrapped shirt made it a little awkward. There wasn't much room between him and Hallie, but it felt like the chasm was only growing.

Hallie didn't look at him once. She kept her gaze trained on the Stradat Lord Kapitan, who finally spoke. "I was not expecting to see you, Miss Walker."

If Niels didn't know any better, he would've said that the words wore a coat of ice.

Her response came equally as cold. "And I, you."

Niels surreptitiously rubbed his hands together underneath the table. He'd thought it was merely an expression, but maybe Hallie's power could make him actually cold. His fingers felt stiff as they would've been if he eschewed gloves while clearing snow from the Metzinger farmhouse's path to town. Or maybe he'd lost more blood than he'd thought. The wound had hurt, and it'd been deep, but he'd thought they'd stopped the bleeding.

The man's stare hardened. "I only requested my son's presence, no one else's."

Niels caught the tightening of Hallie's fist where it sat upon the table. She moved it to her lap. Niels ignored his own discomfort and leaned forward. "Miss Walker and I have information for you."

Using his good arm, Niels leaned heavily on the tabletop. He hoped everyone took it as fervor, not that he needed it for support.

The man's hazel eyes narrowed in on him. "Who are you?"

Kase shifted in his seat. "This is Niels Metzinger. He...he helped me at Achilles."

"I appreciate the support, Kase." Niels straightened his shoulders and sat as tall as he could. He hoped he looked more confident than he felt. "However, I can answer for myself." He met the Stradat Lord Kapitan's gaze as steadily as he could. "Besides the information Miss Walker has for you, I have information for the High Council regarding the attack on Achilles in December."

"Then please begin," the Stradat Lord Kapitan said.

Kase tapped a few fingers on the table, seemingly to dispel nervous energy, but it only irritated Niels.

He nodded to Hallie. "I'll allow Miss Walker to speak first."

"The sooner we can get through this, the better. In case you didn't realize, we have been attacked once more, and my attention is needed elsewhere." The Stradat Lord Kapitan looked almost bored. Hallie's information was important, yet he acted like it was all a great inconvenience.

Kase stopped his light tapping and said, "Father, I promise this is worth your attention."

Niels sat back a little and saw Hallie's hand grabbing Kase's underneath the table. He clenched his jaw. She'd told him as much. He had bigger things to worry about than the relationship he didn't have.

The Stradat Lord Kapitan flicked a glance at his son. "We shall discuss your situation soon enough, so it would be prudent to keep silent."

A muscle fluttered in Kase's jaw. Some of Niels' jealousy ebbed. He wasn't sure what Kase had done to receive such treatment from his own father, but surely it wasn't warranted.

Hallie took a deep breath. Niels wanted to reach out and comfort her, but he couldn't, not when her hand was still in Kase's.

He was starting to feel foolish for agreeing to go along on Hallie's adventure. He hadn't done much to keep her safe. In fact, he'd probably done more to endanger her than anything else in his wounded state.

Hallie began, "General Correa is collecting Essences to defeat the ancient foe of Yalven lore called Jagamot. I'm unsure how much of this is fact and how much is fiction."

"This we already know."

Hallie shot a glance at Kase, and Niels shifted further back in his chair. The cold was back, climbing up his arm slowly. He caught Kase's hand letting go of hers and settling on her knee.

Niels would kill him.

He closed his eyes to calm himself. Where had that reaction come from? Blasted stars. It had to be the Fogs. The cold had reached his elbow but seemed to pause with the outburst of anger.

Kase mumbled, "I gave him my report. He knows you also have the Essence power."

Hallie was silent for a moment. Something in her jaw twitched ever so slightly. That was the only visible reaction she gave to the news. Niels wondered if she felt betrayed. It was her secret to tell, not anyone else's.

The woman Fely spoke up next before Hallie could respond. "I believe you know who I am, though we have not spoken face to face, Stradat Lord Kapitan."

Harlan's face didn't change as he finally looked up at her. "Yes, though I am uncertain as to why you're here."

Fely wet her lips. "After Glennar was killed by the General, I had no choice but to keep up appearances, and when the General and the King discovered Miss Walker attempting to use her power to create a Passage to the holy city, I went with her. The General believes me to be keeping tabs on her and is on his way to your capital in search of the second sword, Gate, and the final Essence."

"And your betrothed? Where is the King?"

Fely looked down at her entwined fingers set atop the table. "Dead. Killed by Abram Loffler."

Harlan stared at her hard, almost if he didn't quite understand what she'd said, before he swore.

Kase glanced quickly at Hallie, who nodded. The cold started creeping up Niels' other arm.

Harlan stood up from his chair and went over to his desk, scribbling something on a paper before handing it off to the guard outside the door. "Lord Stephenson. Now."

He then returned to the table, but he didn't sit, only leaned upon it. "Word of his death does not leave this tent." He glared each person in the eye. "To do so could bring even more of those bombs down on our heads. The Cerls will take it as an outright act of war, which gives us very little bargaining power in any negotiations. Lady Fely, do I have your word?"

Fely didn't seem to give any indication that she felt obliged to do anything at all. Her voice was steady. "As always, Stradat Lord Kapitan, my allegiance is to my people in the Isles. I will do nothing that betrays them, which means we are working toward the same goal."

Something seemed to finally click in Kase's brain,

because he burst out, "You're the one who killed Yarrow."

Niels wasn't sure who Yarrow was, but he was having more trouble concentrating on the conversation at hand.

"I did, but I did not relish it. Yarrow not only betrayed Miss Walker and King Filip, but also his brother, Glennar. If I had not gone along with appearances, he would have exposed me as a traitor. I was the one passing information through Glennar to Jayde."

Kase's thumb froze where he'd been stroking Hallie's knee. Niels clenched his teeth. He should stop watching them, but his anger was all that kept the cold at bay.

"You were the one the Stradat Lord Kapitan was meeting in the middle of the night," Kase rasped.

Hallie gave him an odd look. Fely shook her head. "My messengers. I am only the source of information."

Niels didn't understand anything at this point.

"And?" The Stradat Lord Kapitan folded his hands in front of him.

"It's much worse than you feared, Stradat Lord Kapitan." Fely leaned forward on the table, her long fingers splayed. "Stradat Loffler is not working with the General. He's gone rogue. And he's the reason Zalina, the end, is upon us. At least the General is trying to stop it."

No one spoke as the words weighed heavy in the air. Niels itched to pull Hallie into his arms and tell her that it was okay, but he never would be able to do that.

She wouldn't even look his way. Kase's hand was still on her knee. Niels tried to let go of the grief and anger building up within him. Hallie had rejected him. Niels knew he should have saved Jack. He knew he should've followed her to the capital.

But he hadn't, and she'd moved on.

He'd lost her and hadn't bothered to find her.

The Stradat Lord Kapitan rose and went to the tent entrance. "Sergeant Fisher, please fetch the Yalven emissary immediately. Tell him it's of the utmost urgency."

With the renewed silence, Niels looked at anything besides Kase and Hallie. He couldn't get the image of their reunion out of his head. It hurt. He also didn't want to make idle chat with the Stradat Lord Kapitan or Fely. He forced himself to inspect his bandage. It was only just starting to show the blood along one of the edges, but it definitely wasn't bleeding enough to cause this kind of chill.

So why did he feel so cold?

He was so focused on the chill creeping higher that he barely registered the man entering the tent a short time after. The numbness had started to feel blissful, but he noticed the man was extraordinarily tall with long braided hair. Someone gasped. He wasn't sure who. The man who'd entered looked quite ragged in his rumpled clothing—a long toga tucked underneath a thin cloak. Bags drooped under his red-veined eyes.

"Miss Walker—you're here." The man rushed over and bowed over her hand, saying something in a different language.

"And may they not fall when morning breaks," Hallie said back in Common with a tight smile. She went to say something else, but the man looked past her and froze.

"Lord Saldr," Fely said quietly. "I was not aware that you were…here."

Something happened, but Niels wasn't sure exactly what. One second the other man was there, and the next he sort of…flickered. He rubbed his eyes. Surely he was seeing things. He needed to sleep. That was it.

"Lady Felyra," the man, Saldr, breathed. "May the stars rise upon you."

The ice was creeping into his chest. It wasn't painful. Just cold. He was finally able to focus on something else besides Kase and Hallie, and with the encroaching chill, he barely minded that Kase had moved his hand from Hallie's knee to the back of her chair.

Fely finished the greeting and said, "It's been quite a while, hasn't it?"

"Indeed it has." The man took the vacant seat beside the woman but refused to look in her direction. He bowed his head slightly to the Stradat Lord Kapitan. "I understand why you called me here." He glanced over at Hallie. "It's true, isn't it?"

Who was this man, again? How did he know Hallie?

"I'm still unsure what it means. The only times I've used the power, I've lost control," she answered.

"And pray tell us, what does your supposed Essence power do?" The Stradat Lord Kapitan asked without inflection.

"I'm not entirely sure. I created a Passage here, for one, and...a few other things." Hallie played with the fingers in her lap.

Kase rubbed his thumb between her shoulder blades. Niels looked away.

"I don't know what I do, truly." Hallie wasn't being completely truthful. She chewed on the inside of her lip. There was something else, something she was scared to tell the Stradat Lord Kapitan. She'd messed something up in their journey here, leaving them lost in a void for a week without them realizing it.

She hadn't just lost control; something had gone very wrong. But to admit something like that to the most powerful man in Jayde would be ludicrous.

The other man in the room saved her from answering. "Your Essence manipulates time."

No one spoke. The words seemed to drown out sound outside the tent as well. They were heavy and laden with implications Niels didn't understand.

The Stradat Lord Kapitan looked thoughtful as if he'd expected the insanity. "If that is the case, using your power to restore the electricity to the city would go a long way to surviving this war." He pressed his fingers together and brought them to his lips in thought. "Yes, that would work quite well. We could scrounge up a few hovers, surely. We have three pilots, though my son is the only fully trained one, but a few of my own men could work in a pinch."

Silence permeated the air for a moment. Only the hawking of wares outside the tent interrupted it for a few loaded seconds.

"I don't know if...that is, I'm unsure if I can do something on that scale," Hallie said.

"You destroyed Achilles with your power," Fely added. "You used it on the structure itself. It's now a pile of rubble, almost as if it was thrust back to its beginning. I was lucky to escape the destruction, as were you."

Hallie shook her head. "But I was only trying to save Kase."

That hurt. Niels hadn't been able to explain the collapse of the fort from the outside. The flash bombs they'd levied at the gate were mere annoyances to the soldiers. They'd been meant only as a distraction. Then the fort began falling apart, even the stone catching fire, which Niels still couldn't entirely wrap his mind around.

But it had been Hallie's doing. All because she'd wanted to save Kase.

Not him. Kase.

Because Niels saved her instead of Jack. He'd saved himself instead of Jack.

And Hallie could never see him without seeing that day in her mind.

The conversation continued at a pace Niels had trouble keeping up with, the icy cold now affecting his toes. But he still heard the Stradat Lord Kapitan's next question.

"Now, if you would explain the sword?" Harlan asked, nodding at the blade still strapped to Hallie's pack. "Retrieve it for me, Kase."

Kase looked at Hallie, who nodded; he hesitated another moment before getting up. He unhooked it from her pack and set it lightly on the table.

Niels felt ill just looking at it lying there. It was almost as if the sword was a shadow. It'd cut him. It'd killed the Cerl King.

"It is one half of a pair," Fely said. "Like I mentioned earlier, the General seeks the second one, which they believe is here in Kyvena." She paused for a moment. "This is the one that killed the King. It holds his Essence power, Lord Saldr."

"If that is truly Kainadr, and it holds the Essence of Souls," Saldr said, voice shaking as he stared hard at the sword on the table, "then it would indicate the legends are indeed true, that the second Gate holds Xera."

Second Gate? What was that? No one else asked about it. It seemed like Niels was on the outside. What did this mean for him?

Everything sounded like he'd gotten stuck in a fantasy book. He remembered Jack loving one when they were younger about an epic black sword that spoke. The one on the table had yet to utter demands, thank the stars. The blade was still unnerving, though he wasn't sure why.

The Yalv, Saldr, held out his hands, "May I?"

He grabbed it from the table when no one objected and inspected it in silence.

The man whispered something before setting the sword back onto the table in front of him. "Many souls have lived on as keys, but none greater than Kainadr and Xera. How did you come across it?"

"The Gate." Hallie's voice shook a little. She glanced at Fely before continuing, "It showed it to me, and I took it."

The man muttered something in a different language vehemently under his breath. Kase leaned toward her, away from the sword. "I don't think I quite understand."

Hallie took a deep breath before saying, "Stradat Loffler stabbed King Filip with it. And then the chamber started coming apart at the seams. We escaped through the Passage...and ended up here."

No one else in the room moved. No one else spoke. It was as if the world around them had stopped.

"And where is the Essence of Spark?" Lord Saldr asked.

For the first time since they sat down, Hallie looked back at him. He shivered, more from the ice in his veins but her eyes asked the silent question. He ignored the unease in the room. "I...I only acted because..."

He didn't know what had happened. The man had killed the King of Cerulene. He was going to kill Hallie. Niels had acted on instinct.

But the man had still been a Stradat of Jayde.

"Go on, then," the Stradat Lord Kapitan said, his arms crossed.

Would he arrest Niels for what he'd done? It'd been self-defense. Niels cleared his throat to give himself another second. "He'd killed the Cerl King already. I tackled him before he swung that sword at Hallie or Lady Fely." He nodded to both. "And then I kicked him into whatever that archway thing was where Hal had gotten the sword."

A few painful beats before the Stradat Lord Kapitan said, "At least he can no longer cause issue here. He was working with the enemy, though I now think the enemy is no longer solely Cerulene."

"We must find the second Gate and restore both Kainadr and Xera with the powers infused into the swords." Fely smoothed back flyaway pieces of her dark hair. "Using that information, we might be able to bargain with the General to leave your city alone. He's bent on revenge, but in the end, you both aim for the same goal— to save Yalvara."

"I'll never give in to those blasted—" The Stradat Lord Kapitan used a word to describe them that wasn't polite for anyone's ears, much less the women in the room. Kase started to rise, but Hallie pulled him back down.

Niels just stared straight ahead. The cold had spread into his shoulders and his hips. He wanted to sleep.

"But what must we do? What will finding the swords accomplish?" Hallie sounded so much calmer than Niels would've figured possible, considering the circumstances.

It was Saldr that answered, "Some believe in combining the Essence powers, including the final sliver of Toro hidden within Valora, which would stop the destruction of the planet...for a time. No prophecy or ancient text tells us what will happen after."

"How would that work?" Niels asked, but everyone ignored him.

"There is a chance it all fails? That whatever we do will have no effect?" Hallie's freckles stood out starkly on her pale skin. Niels could've counted every single one. "Why wasn't this done earlier? When the Essences were together? And Loffler. He's somewhere in the Gate. He had an Essence power."

Saldr rubbed his jaw. "The secondary Gate—"

Saldr's answer was interrupted as one of the guards entered. The rush of noise from outside the tent physically hurt. Niels swayed. He gripped the edge of the table, but no one noticed, too focused on the guard.

"I'm sorry to interrupt, Stradat Lord Kapitan, but the Walkers are outside."

Hallie jerked her head toward the entrance and tried to stand, but the table was in the way. She cursed softly as her leg collided with it. She sat back down. Niels couldn't do anything to help. He was too numb.

"We are in a meeting," the Stradat Lord Kapitan said with irritation coloring the words. "I will not stand for petty interruptions."

Niels caught the feathering in Kase's jaw. Niels and his own father hadn't had the closest of relationships, but that didn't mean he hated him. Niels knew he hadn't been an easy child to raise, that he would never be as good as his brother, even if Niels had stayed to help provide for the family when Andre had left to sell furs in Nar. He'd failed and had returned home to help with the struggling farm.

But then they'd all died. Except for Niels.

Niels gripped the table even harder until it hurt. The pain kept the swaying at bay.

"They are quite insistent, Stradat Lord Kapitan."

"They will wait."

The soldier saluted and closed the flap behind him. The Stradat Lord Kapitan glared at Kase, "This is your doing, isn't it?"

"They're Hallie's parents." Kase crossed his arms. "They deserved to know when she returned." His voice was the fire to his father's ice.

Hallie stiffened. Niels' neck went cold.

The Stradat Lord Kapitan's eyes narrowed further as he opened his mouth to argue back. The tent flew open, interrupting the scathing remark he was sure to make.

Zelda Walker barged in, and for all her short stature, she looked about ten feet tall.

"I don't care who you are or that you could order my execution tomorrow." Zelda aimed her words at the Stradat Lord Kapitan. "But I will see my daughter."

Niels couldn't even muster up a smile at her audacity. It was like his face was frozen.

Hallie shot out of her seat. Kase stepped between his father and Zelda. Niels couldn't move. Hallie grabbed her mother by the hand and dragged her back to the tent entrance. "Mama, you need to wait."

Zelda did not like that one bit, but her dropped jaw and ready response got cut off by a rumble through the tunnels. Kase dove for Hallie, protecting her with his body. Something large and heavy crushed the sleeping cot.

Niels fell sideways onto the table and banged his head before tumbling out of his chair.

He barely felt it.

The other side of the tent collapsed around them, ripping it in two as the side with the Stradat Lord Kapitan's desk toppled into a growing, rattling crevice ripping open the stone floor. Both Fely and Saldr's chairs fell into the abyss. Fely screamed, scrambling for purchase along the giant crack that appeared in the floor. Saldr lunged, catching her by the wrists and pulling her up.

"What in the blazes?" Zelda asked as Stowe crawled over from where he'd fallen just outside the tent, only half of which remained. The loose pieces fluttered around them.

The soldiers, too, crawled along the ground.

Niels was able to get his body to move enough to push himself up onto his good elbow. He shivered harder. It was *so* cold.

Behind the Walkers, the cavern had broken into mass chaos. People screamed. Mothers shouted for their children. Half of the cavern had fallen into the gaping hole. Other soldiers clamored for order. Anyone who ran toward the Stradat Lord Kapitan's tent was thrust backward. One of the soldiers brandished his sword in one hand, a flashpistol in the other.

The rumbling ceased.

Out of breath, Saldr still managed to say, "That is why we must make peace with the Cerls, Stradat Lord Kapitan."

He pointed back toward the earthen maw marring the part of the tunnel that had collapsed down into the depths of the planet. In its place, a deep dark, congealed-looking gas oozed and seeped out of the center, floating in the air. It was almost like a grotesque mockery of smoke. That's when the scent hit him. It was almost as if his senses hadn't caught up with the chaos around him until that moment. The acrid burning smell stung his nostrils.

If you dug down deep enough, you could find it—yalvar fuel. As miners, they'd been warned to never touch it but to let the overseer know. Then a few of the more experienced miners were brought in to extract it for expedition to Achilles and Kyvena.

But why was Yalvar fuel floating up like that?

Why did Lord Saldr seem to think the Yalvar fuel was the reason they needed to ally with Correa? What had it to do with anything other than how Jayde fueled most of their engines?

Lord Saldr's voice was clear even with the surrounding turmoil. "Jagamot's corruption of the Zuprium crystals is complete."

Whatever emotion Niels was feeling barely registered in his brain. He shivered even harder. Something was wrong. He just couldn't say what. It wasn't that he didn't have the words. His lips were frozen shut. Blood loss. It had to be. Whatever help Lady Fely had given him earlier had worn off. Or maybe Hallie's other healing had failed again. He couldn't tell if it'd reopened.

He didn't hear anything, could barely see the shapes in front of him. He attempted to launch himself to his feet.

But he was frozen, the ice finally reaching his heart.

He needed to help Hallie.

He needed to win her...

He needed...

He...

And then he collapsed.

C H A P T E R 2 5

A LITTLE HAMLET

Jove

JOVE HAD NO IDEA HOW long they'd been trapped in that blasted room with the blasted crystal. His head ached, and his lips were chapped. With Kainadr's help, they'd found the origin of the stream, which gave them water and some odd-looking fish that made Jove's stomach turn at their sightless eyes.

It didn't help that his mother's cave plants were also slimy and not filling. He should be grateful they'd found anything to eat at all, but it was hard when you were just so blasted hungry.

Maybe Heddie had been right. He did need to find a new curse.

But his stomach grumbled too loudly for him to care.

Anderson still hadn't awoken. Every few hours, his mother would force water down his throat. Each day, he looked more and more as if he wouldn't wake up. It was only with Kainadr's magic dust they were able to do anything at all with him. It was only thanks to him falling in with them at all that they'd survived this long.

Terrible luck for the Yalv, really.

Or terrible luck for Jove, who'd learned far more about the chatty Yalven man than he cared to know, though it was interesting that the man could summon a sword out of his dust stuff. He kept talking about that.

Honestly, Jove privately worried the man was mad, though he refrained from telling him so. He wanted the man to keep purifying the cave water and making the creepy cave fish somewhat edible with his magic fire ball thing.

Thankfully, Kainadr was asleep now, and his mother was halfway between sleep and waking. Jove was on watch as he usually was. He didn't sleep much. Couldn't. Not with his thoughts to berate him when he closed his eyes. Those thoughts were usually of Clara and Samuel stuck in a hole like him, unable to climb their way out.

And Jove not being there to save them. Because he had gone off drinking.

"Why didn't you tell me about…about what your…" His mother spoke, her words choked and soft as if they kept getting caught in her throat. "Why didn't you tell me about what Harlan was doing to you?"

Jove ran a hand down his face. He'd been dreading this conversation. It was truly a miracle he'd avoided it thus far, but that still didn't mean he wanted to have it with his mother. It hardly seemed like an ideal time, though he was unsure if there would ever be. He'd already spilled his secrets to the High and City Councils. Was having to relive his most horrid memories penance for not telling anyone what happened?

He swallowed. "I'd rather not talk about it, Mother."

Les sniffed and wiped her face with the sleeve of her once fine gown. "I need to know."

Jove ran his fingers over his cracked and peeling lips. He took a few deep breaths. He worked his jaw. His mother waited patiently. He pinched the bridge of his nose.

"Please," his mother said quietly.

Jove didn't look at her. He hid his eyes behind his hand and stared at his filthy dress shoes. He could no longer tell what was dried blood and what was dirt. "It started the night Ana died."

The silence that followed was worse than Jove imagined.

It was only broken by the strange hissing coming from the corrupted crystal. Jove would've liked to move somewhere else, but of course, it was the only source of light, and Kainadr only had so much dust he could use to keep his light going.

"And those were the only times? Then and the night of the Rubikan estate dinner?" His mother's voice was hoarse. Whether it was from their situation or the conversation at hand, he didn't know. It was also pleading, as if she still hoped it had all been a horrible dream and they'd wake up twenty years ago.

He still didn't look over at her, content to hide behind the thin shield of his hand. "A few other times, but not many. Kase is usually the one who sets him off. Mostly he just shouts."

A few minutes more of silence, then, "I...I..."

Jove looked up, letting his hand fall from his eyes at last. His mother trembled, yet no tears fell. Her hands were clenched into fists. "I am sorry."

The words were tight and short as if she were holding her breath. Jove tentatively placed a hand over one of her fists. "You didn't know, and I can take care of myself. So can Kase."

She opened her mouth as if to say something, but she quickly shut it. For a moment, Jove wondered who she had to confide in besides his father. He knew she had friends, but they weren't close, and Jove wasn't sure if any of them survived the attack.

He squeezed her hand. She looked up at him, her blue eyes shadowed. "My job as a mother is to protect my children, and I failed."

"Mother..."

"I gave you the best life I possibly could, enrolled you in the best schools, read to you, loved you...but then Ana...Zeke...and now Kase. I can't fix it, and that thought alone might just kill me."

Jove scooted over and placed an arm around his mother's shoulders. It was odd to do so. For his entire life, she'd been the comforter, the one he went to when he scraped his knee. Was this what it was like to grow up? To go from the comforted to the comforter?

He felt differently about Harlan for obvious reasons. He was the sort of father who expected perfection, absolute blind obedience. Even before the abuse began, he'd been distant—both physically and emotionally. When he was home, he ran the household much like the army with cold indifference. His mother though...he didn't know if it was the situation, the fact he was an adult, or that he now had a son, but he'd never seen his mother as a mere human before—not before that very moment.

He was only twenty-five, yet for some reason, he was now discovering that truth. It was uncomfortable and even a little shocking. What would he face in his own life with Samuel? Would Jove turn into his father?

Was that to be his fate?

No. He refused to do so. How could anyone look into Samuel's small, cherub-like face and seek to do harm?

But he'd hit his father the night Kase ran.

Part of him had always known he had the capacity to become like Harlan. Jove tried to ignore those intrusive thoughts, the ones that made him think that he'd been dealt a hand he could never play, but it was always there. Sometimes, it felt like he was doomed to become Harlan merely because it was in his genes. That he couldn't escape his fate because it was part of him.

No alcohol could tamper the anger simmering just beneath the surface. That didn't change the fact that his fingers currently itched to have a mug of ale in hand.

Jove squeezed his mother's shoulder as a soft sob shook her body. When had it all fallen apart? How had someone as kindhearted as his mother fallen in love with someone as cold as Harlan Shackley? It didn't make sense.

His mother had told them the story when they were younger. They'd been introduced through her brother, Ezekiel, and then they'd written letters over the years his father had left in the military. They'd gotten married about two years after his uncle had left the service, but Harlan was still in it.

Four years later, they had Jove.

An uncomfortable truth surfaced in his mind. What if Harlan had thought the same when Jove was born? What if he'd promised to love and protect his children from anything, yet never dreamed the child who was a culmination of his and Les' love would need protecting from himself?

Maybe he couldn't have stopped the progression in his life. What if he was merely a product of circumstance or...or...what?

"Was Father always that way?"

What made him snap? Had he always been cruel?

Jove remembered his mother's words from before the sentencing, though now they seemed like light years away. Harlan had promised her happiness and a countryside escape, a life of fulfillment and joy. It didn't align with the father he'd always known.

His mother took a shaky breath. "No."

"Then what happened?"

His mother was so silent for so long, that he wasn't sure if she'd fallen asleep or merely had no desire to speak of what might've been only a dream. "I only have bits and pieces, but..."

"Tell me. Please."

His mother placed her hand on the one holding her shoulder and squeezed. She pulled out of his grip and let his hand fall. The Les Shackley he'd known in recent years had been a proud woman, holding herself high when hosting dinners and charity events or hunting down rare editions of her favorite books. Now, she sat starving in a cave with miraculously healed injuries, but no amount of magic dust could heal what was broken inside her. She still sat with her ankles crossed underneath her dirty skirt and her hands folded primly in her lap, though her shoulders sagged ever so slightly. She looked up again, the tears streaks still evident on her face, though her eyes were clear.

Her voice was thick, but it grew stronger the more words she spoke, "Your father was born in a small town on the other side of the Nardens, a little hamlet called Ravenhelm..."

IRKSOME LIZARD

Hallie

THE CHAOS OF THE CAVE in and black smoke that smelled and looked too much like Yalvar fuel with its stench of burned flesh was just another tick on Hallie's list of everything to go horribly wrong that day. After the conversation with the Stradat Lord Kapitan and Saldr, she hoped that this might be something she'd dreamed, because just about everything that had happened could very much be considered a nightmare.

Then Niels had collapsed from blood loss. Not only had his sword wound been spilling blood, but his leg wound had also reopened. Hallie was rubbish at using her power. Could she heal? Yes. Somehow. Could she transport people across the world? Also yes.

But she couldn't do any of it accurately.

Thankfully, Saldr had enough Vasa to stabilize him, but Niels hadn't woken up. He needed more blood, but that was something Saldr couldn't fix with his limited supply of dust.

His body would have to replenish on its own.

She tried not to blame herself. She'd done her best, but it wasn't enough.

After her father had done an initial assessment at the Stradat Lord Kapitan's tent and declared most everyone else stable, he insisted they all be further assessed at the hospital ward just in case he missed anything. He whispered something in her mother's ear, then helped Saldr carry Niels.

Hallie felt sick.

Kase took Hallie's pack onto his shoulders and took her hand. "I'll walk you down."

Zelda grabbed Hallie's other arm in her vice-like grip. Not only did it make for an awkward gait traversing the crowded tunnels, but it was also odd, because her mother hadn't seemed to care when Hallie had loaded herself up on the carriage heading for Kyvena.

She'd only received three letters from her parents in the time she'd been at the University. Maybe they would've written more if Hallie had put forth more effort, but now, it was like her mother was scared her daughter would simply vanish if she didn't keep a death grip on her.

Old Hallie would've wrenched away, annoyed at the gesture. Current Hallie only allowed her to continue because…well, if she was honest, she needed all the stability she could get.

The earthquakes had become more intense since Achilles. She'd merely thought it a coincidence, though she really had no reason to believe that other than she didn't want it to mean anything else. She hadn't expected the corrupted Zuprium crystals to be the reason, and she hadn't expected it to be the heralding of Jagamot.

How useless her studies on the Yalvs had been. She felt lost and unstable without her knowledge to rely upon. She felt like a bird with clipped wings.

The smell of the Yalvar fuel still penetrated her lungs with each step away from the cave in.

What did it all mean? How was the fuel going to do anything to them? It was corrosive. Was that what Saldr had meant? Was Jagamot the fuel?

That didn't make a lick of sense.

Hallie's head ached just thinking about it. As if he knew, her father turned around and kissed her forehead while they walked, promising one of his headache cures if the hospital ward was overloaded.

Her eyes started to burn. She looked at Kase to hide the tears from her father.

Kase didn't look much better. His eyes were narrowed as he inspected each person they passed. He was looking for someone, but Hallie didn't know who. Maybe his mother? Brother? Hallie would've expected them to be with the Stradat Lord Kapitan, unless...

Oh stars, had something happened to them? What about his sister-in-law, Clara? She'd been pregnant. Had they been able to escape the city during the attack?

It was Stoneset all over again. It was fighting Loffler in the Gate Chamber. It was King Filip, dead and sliding into the unnatural fissure.

It was losing Jack in the mines.

The pounding of her heart hurt, and every beat pierced her chest like that sword she'd discovered. The pain spiraled out from the wound like a spider's tangled web. She couldn't breathe. Ice and fire warred within her as her power tried to stop the panic, only to be beaten back in the next struggling breath.

She swayed. She was losing control.

Her vision narrowed, and the tunnels disappeared. Her mother and Kase vanished. All she could see was the ground beneath her. And then it bit into her knees, but the sensation was nothing compared to the vice grip on her chest.

"I'm here. Breathe with me. In for three, out for four."

That voice.

"In....out..."

Hallie tried to obey, but all she could get to was one. Panic attack. She was having a panic attack. She breathed again. Only got to one.

"The ground is rocky and packed with dirt. Feel it. Concentrate on it."

Pebbles and crags bit into her palms where she pressed them into the stone. The scent of woodsmoke and leather filled her nose. Her chest loosened a fraction.

"In for three...out for four..."

She couldn't. Everyone was going to die. There was no guesswork. There was no room for negotiation. She shivered from the chill of the tunnels and the ice warring inside her.

Her power had disappeared.

Hands on her face. Rough and calloused. Woodsmoke. Leather.

Kase.

"Focus on me. Focus on the ground. Imagine your lungs expanding with air. In for three…"

He was going to die. Like Jack. Except it was worse. It was Kase. There was no way for her to save him. It'd been clear as day in Saldr's eyes. Combining the Essences was impossible. Hallie didn't even know what it meant, only that Loffler was gone. He'd gone through the Gate. Correa had tortured her. He'd never agree to help them.

"Hals. Listen to my voice, focus on it. In for three, out for four." His voice was much closer and softer. His forehead pressed to her sweaty one. She didn't know how she could sweat when she felt so incredibly cold.

She breathed in for two. The tightness eased a little more.

"There you go. Feel the ground. Use me. Focus on me."

Two and a half.

"In for three…"

Three.

"…out for four."

Four.

She shivered. The oxygen flowed into her lungs again and out. In and out. Slow and steady. In and out. Her heart no longer pierced her chest.

Kase's lips met her forehead. "That's my girl."

Hallie blinked. Her eyesight finally expanded past the ground beneath her. The sound of the tunnels trickled back in. Kase's face came into view as he lifted her head—his short beard, his calm gaze, his perfectly formed lips.

"I'm not a girl."

He smiled, his hands still on her cheeks. "Irksome lizard, then."

Hallie gave him a shaky smile, even if the sweat and subtle quake of her hands negated it. "Thank you."

"You're the one who taught me how."

He pulled her into a hug, and for that moment, she melted into him. Engulfed in his scent and wrapped in his arms, the last vestiges of her panic attack receded more. The longer he held her, the more they faded. It had been years since her last one. Jack's death had brought them on. By the time she left for Kyvena, they'd been a thing of the past. It was how she'd been able to coach Kase through one, but apparently, she couldn't help herself anymore.

He was going to die.

She squeezed her eyes shut. Her breathing picked up.

Breathe in for three. Out for four.

It wasn't a nebulous something occurring someday in the far-flung future. It would happen. Soon. The world was falling apart. That was what the strange floating Yalvar fuel meant. They would all die, consumed by it.

In for three.

She only got to two.

"Hals," Kase whispered into her ear. He hadn't let her go, only kept holding her close. "If there's anyone who can figure out a way out of this, it's you."

"But Loffler and Niels and the...the...what Saldr said..."

She couldn't form a coherent sentence. Her thoughts were all a jumble, and she couldn't even determine what she wanted to say. Everything hurt. She needed sleep. Desperately.

"We'll do this together." He pulled back a little and hooked a finger underneath her chin. She opened her eyes and found his. He didn't blink. "You get a medic to look at you, since your father is busy helping Niels, and I'll be back before you're done, all right? I need to have a word with the Stradat Lord Kapitan."

In for three.

Hallie's words came out a little strained. "I'll go with you."

Her mother came back into sight then and interjected, "You need to rest. Now."

"I'll be fine." Hallie hadn't intended for the words to contain any bite, but they did. Her mother only raised a single brow. "Sorry, Mama."

Movement came from behind her. Hallie looked up to see her father conversing with a few medics. They directed him and Saldr to take Niels to the back of the ward. Fely followed behind.

"I'll stay until someone comes to check on you," Kase whispered in her ear.

According to a few people who scurried about with

supplies as they passed her, the hospital area had been moved due to the bombing. It would've been worse if Kase hadn't taken things into his own hands. Word must have spread at last, as several people who passed them by thanked him.

Not the sort of thing you said to the person who'd set the city on fire a few years ago. Did they not know? Or had saving their lives in a hover erased any ill will? At this point, Hallie didn't think she cared how it had happened, only that it did. Kase had messed up. Badly. But he'd grown in the years since, and the fact that he'd been willing to go back and face it head-on? That showed maturity.

Hallie could forgive him for telling the Stradat Lord Kapitar about her powers. It was foolish of her to feel betrayed over that anyway. He'd only wanted to win this horrible war. It still stung a little. But it was Kase. He only had her best interests at heart...she thought.

Stars. She hated that little seed of doubt. Why couldn't her brain just allow her a little bit of happiness, a little bit of sunlight on the dark horizon?

She tucked herself closer to Kase and tried to shove the thoughts away. The current situation at hand was enough to distract her. One of the nurses took Fely and Saldr back to one of the tents.

Like an ant hive, the hospital overflowed with people. Some constructed tents to house some patients or areas where surgery might be performed in relative privacy. Others were lying prone on the floor or in scavenged bed rolls. It was hard for Hallie to ignore the blood and frantic shouts of those waiting to be treated. Hallie looked down at her hands. It was better to focus there.

A pair of shoes came into view a few minutes later, but Hallie didn't look up. Her pulse had finally returned to normal.

"She's breathing and stable, but I'd like a medic to look her over, if you would," Kase told someone above her. He helped her stand and kept an arm around her. Hallie didn't hear the person's response, but Kase led her to the side where they could wait.

Once she was certain her daughter was not in any immediate danger, Zelda flagged down a passing nurse and asked what else could be done. Like always, her mother could never sit still. She always needed to feel useful—a blessing and a curse. They needed more bandages, so her mother went off to make some.

Hallie and Kase didn't talk as they waited for someone to come. Her brain was mostly blank. She barely held her intrusive thoughts at bay by trying to access a little bit of her power. It might help warm her up a little. She shivered. Kase's arm tightened around her shoulders.

Her power didn't respond to her prompting. It was as vacant as it had been before she'd taken it from the Lord Elder.

Hopefully it only meant she was tired. Her aching eyes supported that truth.

Hallie lost track of just how much time had passed. She and Kase had waited in near silence. She wished she could speak with him about what had happened before the planet had opened up, but with so many prying eyes and ears, she couldn't risk it. Everyone was so on edge after the bombing run and the newest cave-in that it would only make things worse if they believed anything Hallie said. Of course, they might simply think she was a raving lunatic, which Hallie wasn't entirely sure she would disagree with. Everything felt too unreal.

"Hello, I'm...*Hallie!*"

Hallie's head shot up. Petra. It was Petra. Her usually immaculate hair was tied back in a messy bun. Her eyes sported dark circles underneath, but that all disappeared with the smile gracing her friend's face.

Faster than Hallie could blink, Petra nearly tackled her. Hallie wrapped her own arms around her petite friend and held her tightly. It was nearly a minute before Petra extricated herself and gave Hallie a once-over.

"I've been worried sick." Petra dabbed her eyes with the edge of her ragged sleeve. She wore sensible trousers and a long-sleeved tunic that was at least one size too big underneath an apron of sorts. A roll of bandages peeked out of one of the pockets as well as a pair of dainty shears. "That note you left wasn't helpful at all, and then with everything..."

She then took notice of Kase standing to Hallie's side. He held out his hand. "Good to see you're okay, Miss Lieber."

Petra's face lost the joy it had held moments before. She stared at Kase's hand and didn't take it or offer her own for a kiss. "I've heard what you've done, Master Shackley, and the only reason I'm not kicking you out of this hospital ward right now is out of respect for my friend here."

"Petra." Hallie found Kase's hand. "If you've heard about—"

"I know all about the fire."

Hallie was taken back by her friend's interruption. It was very much unlike her to be rude to anyone at all—even if she didn't particularly care for the other person. She was sarcastic and a little petty, but this was different. Hallie tried to think back. Had Petra lost anyone in the fire? No, not that she knew of. But then again, it would have still affected her family in some capacity with her father's properties.

The awkwardness of the moment didn't thaw, but Kase ran the hand Petra didn't take through his hair before bending down to Hallie's ear. "I need to go meet with the Stradat Lord Kapitan."

To Petra, he said, "I apologize for any harm my actions have caused. They were unintentional, and I hope to make it better soon." He put a hand to Hallie's back. "I know you'll make sure Hallie is taken care of. I'll be back to check on her."

And then with a quick kiss to Hallie's temple, he left. She watched him go and resisted the urge to call him back. He needed to speak with his father, she knew, but she hated that he had to go alone. But she would only be a hindrance. The Stradat Lord Kapitan didn't trust her. The looks he'd given her during the meeting only confirmed it.

She just wished she knew why. Was it because she was unworthy of his son? Her Essence power? Both? Or something else?

"Let's get you out of the way and checked out, shall we?" Petra asked as she gestured for Hallie to follow her.

Hallie chewed on the inside of her cheek. So much had happened since she'd last seen her friend. She'd sent her a letter when she'd left for Stoneset. Before that, they'd gone out for afternoon tea. Now they were both trapped underground like rats with enough scars to fill the Lenara Canyon.

They passed by some of the tents and into an area where the injuries weren't quite so gruesome. Petra had Hallie take a seat on an upturned bucket. She pulled a few scraps of paper out of her other pocket, along with a pencil that was only but a nub. "Besides the fact you've clearly lost all your senses, what else brings you to this lovely hospital ward today?"

"Petra."

Her friend looked up, her dark eyes unamused. "He's half the reason we're here, right?"

Hallie took a deep breath, trying to figure out how to explain everything without encroaching on Kase's privacy, but Petra didn't wait for her to come up with her answer. "Ellis is dead."

Wait. What?

She must have heard incorrectly. Petra didn't even temper her voice. She just said, matter-of-factly, "He testified against Harlan and Kase Shackley, and now he's dead."

"Petra..." Hallie still couldn't comprehend the words. "Petra, how? How did that..."

Ellis. Not Ellis. She remembered what Kase had told her about his role in his flight from the capital with her, but he didn't deserve...oh stars. Hallie stood and pulled her friend into another hug. Petra didn't respond, only cried into Hallie's shoulder.

After another minute, Petra pulled back and wiped her eyes and nose with a wad of bandages from her pocket. She sighed. "I'm sorry. It's just been a lot, and with you missing on top of everything...and now I've ruined a roll of bandages when we're running low. They're already talking about forcing some of the lower-city citizens back to the surface. We can't continue supporting them down here. The spring planting was just starting outside the city, and those need people to tend them. It'll be a miracle if we survive this."

Hallie took her friend's hand. "What do you mean, they're going to send people back to the surface?"

Petra's cheeks pinked a shade darker. "Well, those who didn't have much before the attack have even less down here—whether that's supplies or influence. I've heard talk among some that the wealthier inhabitants are demanding that the 'load' down here be 'lightened.' Not sure where the information is coming from, but it doesn't seem too far-fetched. We're running out of supplies, but to go to the surface with the daily flyovers..." She took a deep breath. "I'm sorry, I'm supposed to be making sure you're okay and here I am just blabbering away."

Petra retrieved her parchment and pencil from where it had fallen to the floor. She wrote something down. "Now, you don't seem to be bleeding or missing any body parts, so how can I help you today?"

That was one way to change the subject.

Hallie gave her a tentative smile. The information made sense, but it still bothered her. Most of the wealthier families of Jayde had country estates they could escape to. Those who called the lower city home did not. She didn't really have a solution either other than to figure out a way to negotiate with the Cerls.

That brought her back to her power and the scary sword she'd brought with her to Kyvena, the one that Correa wanted. "I'm fine. Get back to your work, and we'll chat later?"

Petra stuffed her parchment away, as well as the soiled bandage. "Sure. Be careful of Shackley, would you? He's not good news."

Hallie wouldn't, and she wished she could tell her friend everything. But as Petra went back down the line checking on others, her tears only a memory, Hallie felt the gap between them grow. It'd been there since she'd returned from Myrrai, when she'd been forced to lie to her friends about everything that had happened to her.

And now it seemed she might never be able to repair it. She ran her hands down her face and went to find her mother. She needed to rest and process, and she couldn't very well do that in the hospital ward, the sights and smells remincing her of the fate she hadn't suffered...but Ellis had.

C H A P T E R 2 7

AS WERE THEY ALL

31 Years Ago

THE ONLY SOUNDS WERE THE crackling of the pyre and the soft tears of mourners.

The air still smelled damp from the rain earlier, yet the fire still burned behind Harlan's back. The mourning suit he wore was scratchy and ill fitting, but he'd not had time to get a new one tailored before the Burning. Neither the well-kept pyre plot nor those assembled noticed. Only Harlan. He tugged his bowler down his forehead, adjusting and hoped it shaded his eyes. The sunset was radiant above them, but Harlan refused to admire it.

It might've been a gift from the gods, but it was a cruel one at that. The Burnings of the Lady Rose Fairchild and her newborn daughter were nothing but tragedies.

To his left stood Carleton, his head bowed. Aurelia was tucked beside him in a demure black gown and veiled velvet-lined hat. The latter held a handkerchief to her mouth. His adoptive parents hadn't known Rose long, but after a note from Harlan upon Ezekiel's reassignment to the city, they'd taken the Fairchilds under their wing.

To Harlan's right, Les held herself together with pressed lips, her face pale, her curls pinned tightly, and her eyes wet. Admirable considering the circumstances. In the three months since their correspondence had begun, Harlan felt like he understood her, which was odd considering he'd discovered that by her letters. He'd received them weekly since that first one, and he'd looked forward to each.

While from very different origins, he'd found they both dreamed of acceptance. Harlan's looked a little different, but not since that tiny Ravenhelm schoolyard where he played groggon with his friends had he felt that someone truly saw him. Ezekiel had chipped the stone wall Harlan had surrounded himself with over the years, but Les had forced her way in with only inked words.

How different his outlook on life had changed since he'd met her. He'd not thought it possible to feel for someone in a way that a man cares about a woman. He never thought it would be for someone as ruined as he was. A boy from the mines never could've hoped for much more than a woman to cook his meals, keep his bed warm, and say his final rites when his time came too early.

That wasn't love. It was obligation and survival.

It was a way of life, and the only one Harlan had truly known. Carleton and Aurelia seemed to love each other in a deeper way, but that had very rarely been on display for Harlan. With Carleton's work, he wasn't at home often—even when he'd been promoted high enough to be stationed in the capital.

Ezekiel had been the first one he'd known to love his wife in a way that felt like more than just a rudimentary contract. He'd written religiously to her in the time Harlan had known him. He'd spoken about her constantly. He kept family portraits in his pocket.

And now, that was gone. Any revelation Harlan had over the last few months had been overshadowed by the last few weeks and the fire behind them.

Les' hand curled into a tight fist. The other was on her nephew Randall's shoulder. The boy stood stick straight, staring straight ahead, his face too calm for a boy who'd lost his mother and baby sister. The other boy, Sullivan, fidgeted with his tiny suit, his hand tucked tight within Rose's mother's grip. Her eyes were red, even evident from under her veil. Her husband, Rose's father, stood to her other side, his hands clasped in front of him, a tear sliding down his cheek.

Harlan's heart gave a painful twinge. The twins were so young. Younger than Harlan when he'd lost his entire family. Would losing your mother at such a tender age have as profound an impact on him as it had Harlan? Would they even remember the details? Or just the overwhelming darkness that hid deep inside one's soul?

Eyes shadowed and red, Ezekiel stood between them all. His mourning suit was neat and tidy, new and as dark as midnight. According to Les, he'd rarely slept since Rose and the baby passed, the tiny bundle her mother had named Emilia before she'd died, too.

Rose's parents moved into the Fairchild townhome to help with the boys. They and Les were the only reasons Ezekiel looked somewhat presentable.

His friend hadn't turned with the rest of the mourners. Some might say it disrespectful to the deceased, to watch them as their souls returned to the stars, but Harlan knew better. It was taking every bit of strength he had left to stay still instead of burning with his wife and child.

Sullivan, the little boy who'd been full of fire the day Harlan had met him, wailed. His grandfather picked him up, holding him to his chest. The boy didn't quiet. His twin at Les' side stayed silent. Ezekiel only flinched.

More tears spilled down.

Upon Harlan's return to the capital, he'd called upon Ezekiel to find him in the townhome study, an unopened bottle of gin upon the desk, his eyes unblinking. He hadn't changed out of his uniform since the day Rose went into labor—evidenced by its dishevelment and stains on the breast and once-shiny medals.

The medics said she'd bled out. They had no way to stop it, and none of their medical knowledge could have prevented it. Les had told him they believed in combination with her pre-labor issues and other evidences after birth, neither Rose nor the baby had a chance to survive.

Harlan had devoured every medical textbook he could get his hands on in the last weeks and found that nothing could have prevented it. On First Earth, they'd had the technology to not only detect placental abruption but also use life saving measures quickly to save both the baby and mother. Yet like spaceships, that technology had been lost to time.

"Go and find your place among the stars," the orator spoke.

Les' curled hand shook slightly at the words, tears slipping down her cheek at last. Ezekiel's shoulders shook. Harlan's own eyes stung. The effect this already had on his friend was terrifying, yet he couldn't blame him. All Harlan could remember from the Burning of Michael and the others at Ravenhelm was the heat. He'd blotted out and repressed everything else. It had affected him deeply and in ways he hadn't realized until years later.

What did that mean for Ezekiel? Would he ever return to the carefree man he'd been?

Les sniffed, and with only a second of hesitation, Harlan breached all society protocol and reached for her gloved hand. He wasn't sure he'd be received despite their intimate correspondence, but the gut reaction simply felt right. He wove his fingers through hers, the lace scratching against his own. She clung to him like someone drowning.

And she was. As were they all.

They were lost in a storm with no way of knowing if they'd weather it.

TUMBLING DOWN

Hallie

AFTER THREE DAYS OF SITTING in her parents' tent, Hallie was about ready to lose her mind.

For one, she'd only received three messages in those three days. One was from Kase saying that his father approved him to train the amateur pilots in preparation for the electricity being reinstated—once his house arrest ended. The second was from Saldr, saying that he and Fely would be training her starting the next morning. He'd needed to acquire more Zuprium dust first, as his own supply had been depleted.

The third was from the esteemed Stradat Lord Kapitan. Hallie was only vaguely impressed that he'd taken the time to seal it with wax engraved with his coat of arms, as if nothing was more important than sending missives to people properly in a time such as this. The contents of the note were brief and to the point. Hallie was to train with Saldr and use her power to restore the electricity. It was more of an official order than a personalized note.

It still seemed over the top to use the wax seal. It annoyed Hallie most because, unless he had the forethought to bring it with him to the Catacombs—which was unlikely, based on what she'd gleaned from her mother—then the man must have sent for them.

It really bothered her more than it should.

Hallie wasn't even sure she could restore the electricity. Even if she could, in the grand scheme of things, it was at the bottom of her list. She needed to find the second Gate, because finding it might be the way to get rid of this power to begin with. She just didn't know how she was to combine the Essence power with the others.

Both Fely and Saldr had been unwilling to tell her much. But she knew they still needed the other three Essences to show up in Kyvena. According to reports, Ben was still flying around on his dragon, more or less guarding the city. It hadn't attacked since the city fell, only watched. Hallie had yet to see it for herself and would have chalked it up to hearsay if Kase had not confirmed it in his note, as well.

Legends tended to grow the more fearful people were, but this one was plenty big on its own.

On top of all that, her power still hadn't resurfaced, and she was terrified that when it did, she'd bring the Catacombs down upon all their heads.

In the three days since she'd been back, she hadn't had the time or privacy to explore Navara's journals and enter her memories. Her mother hadn't left her alone, dragging her not only to the rations station to help prep for meals, which Hallie was rubbish at, but also to the hospital ward daily to help as needed. Niels still hadn't woken.

By the time Hallie returned to her parents' tent at night after consuming her meager rations, she was too exhausted to try much of anything. And she couldn't very well use the journal while her parents slept right next to her. Waking up to find their daughter in a trance or bleeding onto a journal would only terrify them and end with her herded off to get seen by a medic—after her father forced her to take some obscure medicinal herb solution he'd concocted first.

As relieved as she'd been to find them alive and relatively unharmed, she couldn't keep old resentment from creeping in. It probably made her a terrible daughter—well, scratch that, not probably—but she missed her time without someone looking over her shoulder. It almost made her long for the days when they'd all but ignored her existence after Jack died.

They might've all been wallowing in their grief, but at least it gave Hallie room to breathe.

It was a terrible and odd feeling, like trying to wear an old blouse that clearly no longer fit.

Hallie slipped the latest note, the one from the Stradat Lord Kapitan, away in her satchel with the others. She had one more day of ripping bedlinens into strips to prepare for use as makeshift bandages before her training with Saldr started. At least she got to chat with Petra during her shifts while they soaked each new strip in boiling water. It was nice to catch up, even if their conversations were overshadowed by past events. They shared tears over Ellis and the friends that hadn't been found yet. Thankfully, both Petra's parents made it through the attack, which Hallie was grateful for. None of it had changed her friend's view on Kase.

Hallie prayed he'd be released soon. The last few days with just a single solitary note in place of his company were agony enough without everything else going on. They'd finally reunited, and all she had of him was ink on paper.

Maybe she could visit him today. She'd have to be smart about it. He'd told her he wasn't allowed visitors—something about how that had led to his newest confinement. He hadn't clarified further than that. She didn't think she could pay off whoever had been tasked to guard him. Maybe there was an alternate way to his tent? Maybe she could just ask and use her feminine wiles.

That thought nearly made her laugh. It would make Kase laugh too.

Stars, she missed him. This was almost worse than when she was on the other side of the world. She was close enough to talk with him, see him, laugh with him, but still too far to reach him.

"Soon as they start releasing people back to the surface, we're headed home," Hallie's mother announced as she tied off her gray braid and pinned it into a bun at the base of her skull.

Hallie paused while tying off her own braid. It'd grown longer in her time away and needed a good trimming. She didn't tie it back into a bun, though, letting it fall down her back. "Home? To Stoneset?"

Her mother eyed her daughter's hair, but didn't comment, though Hallie could tell she wanted to. Dearly. "Yes."

She didn't elaborate, only tied on her matron belt before digging through the collection of tiny vials collected in one corner of the tent.

Hallie didn't know what to think. With her parents on their way back to Stoneset, she would be free again—but out on the open road, they'd be targets for any Cerls roaming the countryside. They were in an active war with Cerulene, and her parents wanted to go right to the border.

Despite wanting some freedom, Hallie didn't want them to leave.

She chewed the inside of her cheek as her mother pulled out a small vial tinged a light green—a headache cure of her father's. Zelda held it out to her. "Take this."

Hallie blanched. She'd always hated the taste of it—like molded mint leaves. Her mother shook it. "If you don't, you'll end up with another headache after today, and I'll need you at your best if you're to help us prepare to leave."

"So you're going to go back, just like that?" Hallie took the vial, but she didn't uncork it.

"My first purpose for coming to the capital was to get the word out about what happened to Achilles and Stoneset." Her mother straightened. "My second purpose was to find you and bring you home."

Hallie froze. Her mother expected her to go with them? Now? "I can't go back."

"You can, and you will."

Was she hearing her correctly? "Mama, there's no Stoneset to go back to."

With everything else that had happened, she'd pushed the attack to the back of her mind.

"Of course there is. I've seen it. Now drink up."

Hallie shook her head. "No, you don't understand. Soldiers found the cavern somehow, and—"

"We're survivors. We will rebuild."

Zelda packed her own little bag for her shifts that day. She had brought some extra sugar and spices and liked to add to the rations when she could. As a baker at heart, she couldn't help it. She'd garnered a little bit of a cult following in the last few days.

"Mama...we can't just leave."

"We're in a war we never asked to be a part of." Her mother crossed her arms. "I refuse to lose my daughter a second time. We will find a way to survive and help our neighbors rebuild."

Hallie shook her head. "I don't even know if there's anything to go back to. General Correa was looking for me, so I ran, and I left before I could check to see if anyone..."

She couldn't even finish that sentence.

"Like you left Niels behind before coming here?"

Hallie blinked. Because she wasn't sure if she heard her correctly. Where had that come from?

"That was three years ago." Hallie drew herself up to her full height. The other woman did not back down. Hallie mirrored her posture, arms crossed. "And it has nothing to do with what happened to Stoneset a few days ago."

This was why she needed her own tent. She loved her mother, but just three days under the same roof again was just long enough for them to be back at each other's throats for no real reason.

Whether or not her mother heard her words, she trudged forward without stopping or caring what grenades she hurled.

"You left him to go to University." Zelda wagged her finger in the air. "Now he's lying unconscious in the ward with no hope for tomorrow because he decided to chase you this time."

Hallie let out a frustrated noise. "What in the blazes does that have to do with me coming back with you to Stoneset? A place that I've established may no longer exist, by the way!"

"I have every right to let you know when you're throwing your life away." Zelda's ears were as red as Hallie's hair. "None of these people here care for you like your father and I do, like Niels does."

Hallie's skin prickled and her breath came in short bursts. Her mother no longer had a right to dictate her life. She'd lost that privilege when Hallie had been forced to grow up after her twin brother's death. "So this is about Kase? Is that it?"

She and the Stradat Lord Kapitan were quite the pair.

Blast them both.

"Did you know he stumbled into our tent the other night drunk, hand nearly broken, because he'd been fighting?" Zelda said it with such a superior tone that drove Hallie nuts. But before she could respond, her mother left with a parting, "You're coming home with us soon as we're clear to do so."

And then she closed the flap behind her and didn't look back.

Drunk? A fight? What in the blazes was her mother talking about? Kase had been under house arrest since he got to Kyvena. How could he have…wait. How had he gotten to the hover then?

Once out in the tunnel, Hallie pressed the heel of her palms to her eyes. Fighting with her mother was stupid, considering where they were and what was happening around them. But Hallie hadn't picked the fight. Zelda had.

It wasn't Hallie's fault her parents pushed her out the door three years ago because they couldn't deal with their own grief.

Her hand shook as she popped off the cork and downed the headache remedy. The moldy mint flavor didn't help her control her temper, and it would probably only dull her headache later. She needed to calm down before she headed to the hospital ward. Petra would want to know why she was out of sorts, and Hallie would only bite her head off. Her friend didn't deserve that—even if she was being hostile about Kase.

She needed to talk to him and get his side of the story. He would have an explanation, she was certain. Then she would find somewhere else to stay. Maybe Fely had room. Petra's tent was too crowded.

It'd only been a week, and her entire world had been rocked to the core and turned inside out all over again.

Well, maybe two weeks. Because Hallie had somehow lost control of the time or something.

No one could explain that.

If they didn't figure whatever puzzle or prophecy or legend out before the floating Yalvar fuel drowned them, there would be no more Yalvara. Even saying that in the privacy of her own thoughts sounded absolutely blasting ridiculous.

She needed to research, but Myrrai was out of the

question, as was the University library. Petra had said it'd been pretty much burned to the ground.

She elbowed and shouldered her way through the crowds. There were so many who had to suffer along the edges of the tunnels, and now with the threat of the cave-ins and the possible end of the world, Hallie didn't know what their fate would be. With each day that passed, it became clearer than ever that they couldn't stay forever. They needed to go back above. Soon.

The ones who'd been lucky enough to secure better lodgings probably would refuse until all threats were neutralized, but without the full might of the Crews, Jayde didn't stand a chance. It could be weeks or months before the Cerls gave up. Jayde couldn't last that long. The flyovers were an effective siege.

According to gossip, there'd been another one yesterday, but no bombs had been dropped. Probably just surveillance. Still made the more unsavory characters start taking bets on which tunnels would be hit next.

The closer she got to the central cavern, the further down into the planet she went. More and more people seemed to be milling about, which gave Hallie hope that the casualties weren't so terrible as first believed, that Kase had in fact made a difference.

Most of the cavern had been cleaned up, but the Stradat Lord Kapitan had been forced to move to another part of it, though he hadn't left the central cavern. The site of the latest cave-in had been roped off. Soldiers warned people away from the rift. Anyone with sense stayed far away from the bulbous black entity floating up like a specter from the hole. It didn't look like it had grown any in the days Hallie had been away, but it still lorded itself over the cavern...and smelled horrible.

The oddest part of it all was that Hallie seemed to be the only one who cared about the stench. Other people eyed it warily, but it looked as if most people hadn't bothered to move their temporary lodgings. The wealthier class of Kyvena stayed inside their carved-out homes lining the walls. Too proud to move to the sides of corridors or the lesser caverns it seemed, even if it smelled like burning flesh.

Hallie didn't know whether to give them credit for sticking it out or not.

More concerning were the new patients in the hospital ward Petra had attended to yesterday that claimed some of the Yalvar fuel had come up through another crack nearby. They said they hadn't touched it, and as their skin was still intact, the medics and Petra believed they'd just breathed in too many fumes. Why else would it make them feel sick?

A mystery to be solved soon, Hallie thought.

The only positive about the cave-in was that a portion of the ceiling had indeed collapsed on the Stradat Lord Kapitan's tent, which allowed the morning sun to shine through. Wasn't good for security's sake, but seeing the sun for the first time in three days did wonders for her spirit.

Maybe if Kase was released from house arrest, they could sneak out for an hour. She could smell the fresh air, hear the birds, and watch the wind blow the leaves in the trees. Hallie could also show him Navara's journal and see what he made of it.

Stars, she would be happy with five minutes.

Kase's note had said his tent was in a smaller cavern just off the larger one. Just which cavern was a mystery. Instead of giving more detailed directions, he'd drawn her a picture of what she assumed was both of them in a hover. She could only guess that because one of the rudimentary stick people in the oval shaped thing with wings had curly hair. She'd thought the other stick person had a braid, maybe. It hadn't been too clear.

He asked if she could give him sketching lessons and said he would keep sending her abysmal, rather frightful doodles until she did.

It'd made her smile at the very least, but he hadn't made good on that threat yet.

She passed by what appeared to be the Stradat Lord Kapitan's new tent. Soldiers armed with swords and flashpistols stood at the ready—all five of them. They were not taking any chances, it seemed. Besides a few City Council members, Harlan was the sole Jaydian leader who'd survived the attack on Kyvena, and if the rumors she'd heard passing amongst the populace was to be believed, he survived because he'd been in the dungeons awaiting his execution.

Hallie wasn't sure if that was good or bad fortune. How ironic one was to be killed in the morning only to wake as the sole leader of a country under fire. No wonder he had five guards. From what she'd gathered since her arrival, Harlan had admitted to covering up Kase's role in the Kyvena fire. She'd heard a few nastier rumors about abuse that she knew weren't hearsay.

None of it sat well with Hallie, and a small, vengeful part of her wished he hadn't survived the attack like the rest of the High Council.

Technically, they were at war with Cerulene at last, but if her memory served, she'd thought there was a system in place and votes from the City Council and City Governors. Maybe the Stradat Lord Kapitan had gotten the votes this time. She'd heard from Petra that they'd tried to declare it after the deaths of the Richter family, but the majority of the City Governors opposed the move. Maybe with the destruction of the capital, Harlan Shackley had taken it into his own hands. He had no fear anymore. What could they do to him? He was the only one left who had an inkling of how to run an entire country.

As much as Hallie despised him for his role as a father, she couldn't help but wonder if more guards might be necessary.

Hallie ducked into one of the side passages nearest the tent and was about to enter the first smaller cavern when someone called out from behind her.

"Hallie Walker! I haven't seen you in ages."

She paused just outside, allowing a small family with a screaming toddler to move past her. She turned to find three young men watching her—refugees as well, by the state of their dusty and torn dinner attire. The Catacombs had large bathing chambers making use of underground springs, but those had long lines and weren't to be used for clothing.

That one was an even longer line, and honestly, some of the stains would never be washed out no matter how hard anyone tried.

Hallie gave the men a cursory nod, unsure of what else to say because she only vaguely recognized the one who'd spoken. He had warm brown skin and darker hair that had a slight curl to it. The others were a mystery. The tallest of them looked rather like he'd always lived in the Catacombs with his sallow skin and sunken eyes. Something about him felt off, but she couldn't necessarily pinpoint why.

She had half a mind to ignore them, but the first one

spoke again. "Ancient Technologies of the First Settlers. Sheffield's course. The name's Waylan Peters."

She narrowed her eyes. She did remember that course, but per usual, she'd always sat in the very front of the auditorium and hardly paid attention to the other students. Why would she? Most of them were insufferable uppities who spent more time at the taverns than on coursework. And besides, the professor had been the premier researcher in all Yalvara on the subject of First Earth tech. She hadn't had time to play nice with the others. Both Petra and Ellis had taken it the semester before and had sung its praises.

"A pleasure." Hallie gave him a small smile. "I apologize, but I don't really have the time to chat at the moment."

The man in the back stepped forward, the one who resembled an animated skeleton. "I'm Mr. Gray, though unlike my mates here, I wasn't a student. And unless my eyes deceive me, you look rather lost."

"I'm not."

"My mistake," Mr. Gray said with a short bow. He looked back at the final member of their trio, who looked as if he'd rather be anywhere else but there. His dark eyes only glared at Hallie's feet. "Then you must be trying to rob the Stradat Lord Kapitan? From the way you eyed his new tent, that was my next guess."

The man, Waylan, gave him a pity laugh. The other moved his stare from her boots to the ground beneath them.

She wouldn't say they made her fearful, just uncomfortable. Mr. Gray had a look about him that screamed he'd been through something, though she wasn't sure if it was the way his eyes darted here and there looking for threats or the dark circles underneath them. The latter made his eyes look more like small hollows in his face.

Thankfully, the corridor had plenty of witnesses. She would just make sure she lost this trio before long. "Thank you, but I really must be going."

She went to go back to the larger cavern and find someone to help her. She might be able to ask one of the soldiers out in front of the Stradat Lord Kapitan's tent. If the three men were a danger to her, she couldn't fight them. Even if her power responded, which it still hadn't, she didn't want to do whatever she'd done to the Cerl soldiers to them. No one deserved that. She also didn't know if innocent bystanders would be safe from whatever power she would unleash. It was too much of a risk.

Mr. Gray caught her by the upper arm and gave her a warm smile. "Didn't mean to make you uneasy, but if you're looking for Kase, he's up the other way in the third cavern. Brown tent. Scary-looking soldier outside it. Looks more like his face was carved from marble."

Now the fear spiked, cold and sanguine, emanating from his hand.

She wrenched it out of his grasp. "If you lay a hand on me again, I will report you, sir."

Maybe too strong, but while she'd had a course with the other one, Waylan or something, this one really acted as if he *knew* her, though she couldn't remember him. Something was most definitely off.

Mr. Gray let his arm fall and shrugged. "We're only trying to help a friend out. Kase and I go way back, and I can see why you're his next conquest. He's always liked them fiery."

Waylan laughed at that, but Hallie narrowed her eyes. "You don't even know me."

She should have just left. She should have gone onto the hospital ward for her shift. This was a mistake. But his words dug a little too deeply for comfort, as much as she hated to admit it. Despite his appearance, he had that haughty air that most of the uppities held. If the other had been at the University, he most likely came from money. Very few were like Hallie, paying their own way through school.

Mr. Gray put his hands in his pockets as the surlier man and Waylan left the group, the latter distracted by someone else he supposedly knew. Mr. Gray leaned in, and Hallie edged away, but the wall was at her back.

"Played Hanged Man with Kase the other night, and when Kase lost, he told us Lavinia Richter was his way of getting back at his father—and that you, Miss Walker, were the latest iteration of that." He clucked his tongue, shaking his head. "Might've been Waylan who called you a conquest, but Kase didn't correct him."

Who did this person think he was? "I'd advise you to sober up and stop harassing women in the corridors."

Hallie finally turned on her heel and went back toward the Stradat Lord Kapitan's tent, leaving the odd Mr. Gray behind. She knew he was lying. Kase wasn't the type to play around with a girl's feelings. He had his flaws, but with everything they'd gone through, she knew Kase. She hadn't known the mysterious Mr. Gray existed until five minutes ago.

But there was that little voice in the back of her mind that wouldn't be quiet, the one that said she wasn't good enough for Kase. She didn't come from money. Kase hated his father, and someone like Hallie would be the perfect person to drive the wedge further between them.

Then there was what her mother had revealed—that Kase had shown up drunk and injured from a fight. Might've been unrelated, but her gut told her they were.

He *did* have a temper, and drinking would loosen any man's tongue. It was one of the reasons she herself refused to drink alcohol.

The man might have been lying about the game, but when Hallie crossed the larger cavern and found the one Mr. Gray had indicated held Kase's tent, she spotted exactly what he'd promised: a dark brown tent with an older soldier whose face did indeed look carved from marble.

Half of her wanted to ignore Mr. Gray's words. The other half wanted to confront Kase about it. She should do that. It was always better to get the worst part over with and have open communication. Hallie's morning had already been trying, and she was late for her shift.

She hesitated, her feet confused as to which way she wanted to go. If she went and talked to Kase right then, if she convinced the guard to let her in, then she could get answers...but then Petra would pry when Hallie finally arrived. She'd pry anyway, but what if her mother and Mr. Gray were right?

Kase wouldn't lie to her. He'd tell her what happened and wouldn't sugarcoat it. But could she handle the truth if it matched Mr. Gray's account?

If it'd only been his words, she could've easily dismissed them. But her mother's were harder to ignore.

She moved out of the way as a younger couple pushed past her and entered the tent next to Kase's, saying something about swiping more whiskey that night. Chewing on the inside of her cheek, she turned and left the cavern.

Maybe it was cowardly, but she wanted at least a few

more hours of believing the best in him before it all came tumbling down.

CHAPTER 29

A HANDSHAKE

JOVE WASN'T REALLY A SHACKLEY. His father had been adopted. The family legacy felt like a lie, so it was no wonder Jove was destined to fail. He'd risen to one of the highest offices in the land partly based on his merit and more importantly, though he wouldn't admit it out loud, his family name.

But that was a sham.

It was probably a good thing he'd thrown that all away.

However, that wasn't the most troubling part. Harlan had lost his entire family, had seen the massacre that had been Ravenhelm and had been the one to stop it at the mere age of twelve. It was a miracle he was as sane as he was. Cold and cruel, yes, but Jove didn't know if he would have survived at all if he'd been dealt his father's hand.

Jove had lost a sister to a fire his youngest brother started. He'd sent his best friend to die on the other side of the world, and he'd turned to alcohol to numb the pain.

Now what would become of Jove?

He had to find Clara. She was the only one who could keep him from spiraling. He just hoped that he survived long enough to get himself out of this hole, literally and figuratively.

But if he found that she and Samuel hadn't survived the attack on the capital...

He prayed to Clara's God and begged for her to be okay, because if she was gone, Jove hoped they never rescued him from the depths.

He prayed for days.

Maybe that was an answer. They'd been down here so long Jove was starting to question his sanity.

His mother had fallen into a fitful sleep, curled up on the jagged stone beside him. He'd made her take his jacket for a pillow. He shivered. Anderson still hadn't awoken, but at least he still had a pulse. Jove bit his nails. He'd worn down the ones on his right hand in the time they'd been down here without any cigarettes to calm his nerves. The lack of smokes only made him more anxious. It didn't help that one of his friends was probably dying before his eyes, and he couldn't do anything. If the Yalv with the magic healing powers couldn't fix him, then who could?

Kainadr sat on the other side of the cavern, murmuring to himself after throwing pinches of his dust in the air.

"I'd say you're wasting that dust of yours." Jove wasn't trying to be unkind, but he winced at the gruff tone. "Best to save it for light. I don't trust that crystal."

The malevolent-looking thing in the middle of the room writhed with darkness at that. Jove wasn't sure if it was coincidence or if the thing heard him. Turned out he was too cold and too worn down to care either way.

The Yalv turned slightly, his face a reflection of Jove's feelings—haggard and losing hope. "What good is being named after the greatest Yalven warrior only to be relegated to minor healings? I'm useless."

Not this again.

Jove looked over at his mother and then back at the other man. He did owe the man his life. Civility was the least he could muster. "I wouldn't say useless. You healed my mother and myself."

"But not the other one."

Jove glanced at his friend. He wasn't sure if it was the odd light from the crystal or his own imagination, but Anderson's skin had a grayish cast to it. Even though his chest rose and fell, Anderson appeared as good as dead. Jove felt helpless.

A loud clattering like rocks falling in one of the tunnels echoed and interrupted the conversation. His mother woke with a sharp inhale of breath. Jove rubbed where his head had hit the wall.

The rumbles weren't uncommon; they'd heard plenty in the time they'd been down there. More collapses. One of them sounded more like a bombing to his ears, but down as deep as they were, it was hard to tell the difference, if there even was one.

But this one definitely sounded different. Almost too close.

"Stay here," Jove said once the quakes had passed. "I'll see what's going on."

He inspected the small cavern they'd been holed up in for a sizable rock, but only found a few shards of the crystal that had somehow broken off. One was half the length of Jove's forearm. It would do.

"Dear, I'm sure it was another collapse." His mother folded his jacket over her arm and stood.

Jove shook his head. "If it is, then there might be others who need help."

"Then why do you need a weapon?"

"Might need it if it's a Cerl. Or Stradat Loffler."

He looked back at Anderson. The shard was a crude weapon, but hopefully it would be enough to finish Loffler...that is, if he didn't use that weird lightning power of his. Though without Anderson to complete the power, Jove might be okay.

He headed back the way they had come days ago, passing by the other tunnel to the underground stream they'd been using for water and cave fish for food. He tried not to grip the shard too tightly, lest he cut himself on the jagged edges. Being in the Watch meant he'd undergone some combat training after he'd graduated from the decoding department and before he took the role as Watch Captain of the upper quarter, but he was certain all that training had fallen to the wayside in the past year as High

Guardsman, much to Harlan's chagrin—only one of many disappointments.

He stepped through the opening and into the darker corridor beyond. Probably not the best call. He turned to go back and ask if Kainadr could lend him one of his magical fireballs when something caught in the corner of his eye. A light.

Jove whipped his head around. There it was. The visage was grainy and blurry at once. It wore a pristine soldier's jacket. Its hair was short on the sides, longer and smoothed back on top. A demure smile graced its lips.

Zeke. It was Zeke. A sob escaped Jove's lips. He stumbled forward just as his brother disappeared into the rock wall.

Jove let out a shuddering gasp, splaying his hands against the wall. No Zeke. No evidence that he'd been there. Just an unyielding rock wall layered with grime.

Why? Why couldn't Zeke stay? Why was he gone? Jove never got to say goodbye. Not really. He'd only given his brother a handshake and a muttered *good luck*.

Why had he done that? He'd known he was sending him on a mission that could very well have ended in him dying. He'd *known* that.

He hadn't embraced him. He hadn't said goodbye.

Jove should've gone instead. Zeke was the one who deserved to live. He'd always been the good one.

He let out a frustrated shout and slammed the fist with the shard into the wall. The water they'd been drinking must've been laced with something that caused hallucinations. Pain erupted in his hand, followed by warmth trickling down his wrist.

He leaned his head against the wall, watching the blood run down his forearm, disappearing into the dirty sleeves of his once-fine dress shirt. He pounded the wall again, tears flowing freely and uncontrollably. His palm was on fire.

Hands grabbed him from behind. Loffler.

Jove swung around, the now-bloody crystal shard with him, but the person ducked. The outline of a woman with bedraggled curly hair stood behind him.

His mother. Jove dropped the shard.

"Zeke. I saw Zeke," he gasped.

Hallucination or not, his body and mind couldn't handle it.

His mother didn't say anything, didn't call him crazy or remind him that it was impossible for her son to be there. Instead, she pulled him close and embraced him. She held him as she once did when he was a child, and that was the final straw.

His grief crashed in like a tidal wave, battering him senselessly. He clung to his mother and lost himself to the drowning abyss full of loss, frustration, and guilt. Jove didn't realize he had so many tears built up, but they flowed like a river through a burst dam.

His mother held him and stroked his hair. "I know. Just let it out."

His body was weak from lack of proper nutrition and sitting around waiting for rescue day after day. He no longer had the strength to do anything but sob.

He was nearly twenty-six, for stars-sake. He was a man. He shouldn't be spilling his emotions like this.

He couldn't help it. And now that it'd started, he couldn't seem to stop it.

Because at the end of the day, there was only one person he could blame. Himself.

He didn't know just how long they stood there, him soaking his mother's shoulder, but it was so long that he finally cried himself dry. His eyes physically hurt from producing so many tears.

His mother had stood there the entire time, holding him, rubbing his back, her own tears staining his shirt, though hers had been more subdued and ladylike.

She clasped his upper arms and pulled back. "It's going to be okay." Jove shook his head, but his mother squeezed his arms tight. "It will be. I refuse to let it not be."

"But—"

His mother shook her head back at him. "I've been a prisoner of grief before, and that blinded me to...things. I've learned my lesson, and I will not allow you to fall into the same trap I did...or your father."

She swallowed hard before giving his arms another squeeze and pressing her right hand to his cheek. "We'll get through this together."

More sounds came from around the corner, and Jove stood straight, wiping his eyes and nose on his already dirty sleeves. He didn't say anything, only retrieved the fallen shard and placed himself in front of his mother.

Could it really be Loffler? Someone else? A rescue? Or another hallucination?

Seconds later, a light appeared, followed by a man covered in dirt and dressed in a ragged military uniform underneath some sort of harness. He froze when he saw Jove and Les.

"Lady Shackley!" he exclaimed. "You're alive!" He turned back the way he'd come and shouted, "I found them! Bring the medic!"

Jove and his mother stood still. He was unsure whether he was seeing and hearing things correctly. He'd pretty much accepted the fact there was a very good chance they wouldn't be rescued, that they would die in the cave.

Jove's legs went weak. He'd prayed for this, to a deity he hadn't believed in, but he'd written it off almost within the same breath. Did that mean Clara was alive? Or was the god simply vengeful, wanting Jove to suffer even more?

The man smiled again. "Took some time to assemble the right team and tools, but the Stradat Lord Kapitan will be pleased. When we didn't find your bodies with the others, we were worried." He fiddled with the edge of his dirty uniform. "We also believed you, Lady Shackley, perished in the initial attack."

"Harlan?" Les choked. "Harlan organized this?"

"The Stradat Lord Kapitan would've been down here himself if it hadn't been for the flyovers this morning." He gave a small smile. "That trial really changed him, I think. He's been very involved in the recovery effort. Say what you want, but he's a dedicated leader." He held up the gas lantern and looked back the other way and shouted for his team to hurry. He turned back to Jove and Les, his face drawn and wan in the light from his gas lantern. "The Cerls hit us hard a few days ago. The cave-ins caused large holes and exposed our hiding place. Lost many good people in the days since, and then another cave-in exposed some Yalvar fuel. It's been a mess. Was glad that we were able to find a medic to help us. Granted, he's more of an herbalist from the Nardens, but he was willing to help when the others were needed in the ward this morning."

Jove swiped at his face again and gestured back toward the crystal chamber. "We have two others with us. One is unconscious."

Seconds later, a man with a little girth around his waist and a balding head of red hair appeared, a satchel at his shoulder. He looked worse than the other man, and that was saying something. Jove had a sinking suspicion he'd been attending to the other bodies of those who hadn't fared as well as Jove, his mother, and Kainadr. The expression on the man's face confirmed it. Closed and tight, a little red around the eyes.

"I'm Stowe," the man said, opening his satchel. He eyed Jove's hand. "Allow me to put some salve on that. It'll keep the bleeding down and numb the pain until we can patch it up real nice in the ward. We'll want to do that soon, because I can't clean it too good right now."

"Jove Shackley. This is my mother, Lady Celeste." He held out his damaged hand.

Stowe prodded the nasty-looking cut with a clean cloth he'd pulled from his satchel.

He wasn't sure how much an herbalist could do right then—especially if Kainadr could use that dust to patch it right up—but the man had come all the way down with the crew, so the least Jove could do was play along.

"You Kase's family?" The man paused in his inspection of Jove's hand. "They didn't tell me who we were going down for."

Jove was unsure if he wanted to answer in the positive. What if the man was one who'd lost his family in the fire and would take it out on Jove and his mother now?

His mother made the decision for him. "Yes. Do you know my youngest son?"

Stowe layered some sort of goop onto Jove's palm with the cloth, and the relief was almost instant. He sagged a little. The man gave a small chuckle despite the grim circumstances they'd found themselves in. "He's the reason I'm here in Kyvena." He paused for a second, as if deciding something. "Saved my life, actually. Glad I can repay the favor in a small way now."

His mother swayed a little, and Jove caught her with his good hand as she asked, "Is he all right? Where is he? Do you know?"

"Right as rain, far's I know." The medic gave Les a once-over. "You have any injuries, Lady Shackley?"

She gestured back toward the crystal chamber. "No, the kind Yalven man took care of the worst of them. Just rather hungry and in desperate need of a change of clothes." She grabbed Stowe's arm. "Where is my Kase?"

"He's here…well, above us, that is." Stowe wound a bandage around Jove's hand, tying it off with a quick knot. "He's the one who singlehandedly saved the rest of the tunnels from the bombing a few days ago."

Jove grabbed his mother to keep her from falling again. Kase was alive. Kase was here. Jove was unsure how he felt about it, but the good news was almost too much for his mother.

Jove cleared his throat. "Thank you. Stowe, was it?"

"Not sure I did all that much, but you're welcome all the same." He put away some of his tools and nodded to where Jove had pointed earlier. "There's two more, you say?"

"Yes," Jove answered, leading him toward where Kainadr and Anderson waited. "I know it's a long shot, but would you happen to have run across a woman named Clara Shackley? She's about this tall," Jove pointed to his shoulder, "and usually wears her hair in braids. And she'd have a little boy with her. A baby. Newborn."

Stowe stopped and smiled. "They're fine. Made friends with my wife. Very cute baby, too."

He caught Jove as he took his turn falling to his knees. They were okay. They were fine. Jove's eyes filled with tears again. He couldn't believe it.

He needed to get out of this stars-blasted hole. When he had his feet under him again, he hugged his mother and turned back to Stowe. "Thank you."

Everything was going to be okay. Kase was here. Clara and Samuel were fine. They were being rescued.

Though the circumstances were still quite grim, for the first time in months, Jove could see the light. It was small and dim, but it was there. He just needed to keep trudging toward it.

C H A P T E R   3 0

MELODRAMATIC DRIVEL

Kase

ANOTHER DAY, ANOTHER LETTER. MAYBE it was helping. Perhaps it wasn't, but Kase persisted.

Hals,

I've written you a real letter and sent it off…though I'll admit, it isn't quite as entertaining as the ones I'm never going to show you written in this here journal. However, I did enjoy attempting a sketch of my newest hover. Hopefully you could tell what it was. I had enough time to sit and perfect it, but I don't have that kind of patience.

But I digress. Today is the final day of my punishment. Seems like my stunt both annoyed and endeared me to the Stradat Lord Kapitan. Well, endeared is way too strong a word, but I only got moderately scolded for going off in the hover and taking out the Cerl bombers.

'Moderately' meaning I was called reckless yet again, though it didn't sting quite as much as usual. He didn't sound all that angry, anyway. It was more of a habit thing. Besides, reckless would mean my actions were irrational and unhelpful, and clearly, he's wrong.

Not to brag, but it was some of my best flying—especially being so new to the Cerl tech. And most people thanked me when I passed them in the corridor instead of spitting on me. A complete turnaround. Though I'll admit, I'd rather be spit upon than sucker-punched. That happened upon my arrival to the city—not sure if your father shared that with you or not. My stomach is still sore.

So in conclusion, the Stradat Lord Kapitan is incorrect as usual, and I'll be glad to get out of this tent. They brought me a chamber pot instead of allowing me to leave for the privy now, so all my lovely anecdotes from those invigorating outings won't be appearing in any more letters, sadly. You'll have to find out the latest gossip for yourself.

Guess that's on me, since I did technically violate my house arrest, but I didn't use my little break to find Jove like I'd planned. Got drunk and fought with another guy. Not my best moment. It did allow me to take out the Cerl hovers when they attacked, though, and that ended with you in my arms. So it was worth it.

My brain is entirely too tired to go into the ethics and logic of it all.

Come rescue me before I lose my mind or this letter devolves into senseless melodramatic drivel about how happy I am you're back.

Always,

Kase

Despite the lighter tone in his letter to Hallie, the only reason Kase allowed himself to be escorted back to his tent was that if he retaliated, he might end up worse off than he currently was. While his father might have lessened his sentence slightly, he still wasn't allowed full freedom after the final three days were done. After that, if he went anywhere, it needed to be a necessity and in the presence of a guard. "Necessity" really only referred to training the greenies.

Harlan said it was for his safety, but Kase wasn't so sure.

Even with all he'd learned upon his return and the fact that his father had yet to even come close to hitting him, the monster still lurked beneath the surface. It was just busy trying to keep the citizens under control. When this was all over, it would reemerge, and Kase didn't want to be anywhere close.

Granted, after all Kase had done, house arrest was the lightest sentence he could've expected. Maybe deep down, the Stradat Lord Kapitan knew the Cerls would return, and

Kase was their only hope of surviving. It might have even been a step toward respect.

Except his father would never be able to take back the words he'd spoken in that final argument before Kase had run, that he'd wished it'd been Kase instead of Zeke that died.

His breath sounded loud even to his own ears.

He rubbed his hands down his face as he sat on the cot in his tent. He needed Hallie. She was the only one who could talk him off this cliff. No number of letters he'd never send would help. She was the only one who could make sense of the guilt, confusion, and stress he was feeling. And she was back here with Niels, who was unconscious in the hospital ward. Jealousy reared its ugly head once more.

As if the man could make a move on her now. His presence still chafed at Kase.

Opening the tent flap, he met the eyes of his newest guard, a man who looked to be carved from the stone surrounding them. "I need you to escort me to the hospital ward."

The man kept a hand on his sword. "We've been warned about your ruses, Pilot Shackley."

"It's a necessity."

"You don't appear injured."

"I was in an airship battle. Surely that counts."

"Not if it's been three days since said battle."

Kase worked his jaw and looked around for something. The cavern was littered with rocks and other debris from the refugees. He just needed something sharp enough that wouldn't involve him stealing the sword off his nursemaid.

That would probably end rather badly.

Just outside the wall of his neighbor's tent, a long shard of brown glass caught his eye. Probably a piece of the liquor bottle he'd heard the neighbor bragging about sneaking back from the city the previous night. An hour or two ago, they'd returned from who knew where already planning on finding another.

Alcohol was one way to numb the pain.

"Pilot Shackley, I command—" the soldier started, but Kase didn't listen.

Kase lunged and grabbed it with his right hand and sliced his palm on the edge. He scrunched his face in pain. Probably stupid.

He forced himself to relax and hold the guard's gaze. "Take me to the hospital ward."

His hand stung even more. Yes, very much a stupid idea.

The man sighed and looked at his partner, who hadn't taken his eyes off the milling crowds. The partner said, "It'll be our necks on the line if he bleeds out from his own stupidity."

The first guard looked back at Kase. "Private Johns is right." He smoothed a hand over his blond stubble. "If you give us the slip, I will make sure you lose any privileges you may have earned. We're not like your guards from the other night."

These men weren't in Eravin's pocket, it seemed. That, or they were remarkable actors.

Kase's hand gave another twinge. Could one get any diseases from dirty glass? I mean, he was pretty sure it'd been from the liquor bottle, and they used alcohol to sanitize medical instruments. Cutting his hand with the stray bit of glass wasn't close to the dumbest decisions he'd ever made. He'd probably survive this little cut, though it would definitely be his luck to get some obscure incurable disease from it and die.

He smiled at the soldier. "I just need to go to the hospital ward, and I'll be a good prisoner and stay in my tent without complaining until afternoon training."

"I'll flag down someone who can bring us a medical kit."

"Please?" He sounded pathetic just then, but he was desperate—too desperate. Probably because he only wanted to talk to Hallie, but the longer he waited, the more anxious he got.

The man stared at him hard. "Then let's make it quick."

Kase scanned his little cell and grabbed a sock he'd thrown to the side while fishing around to see if he had an extra pencil somewhere at the bottom of his pack. He wrapped the sock around his bleeding palm. The blood had started to drip over the edge of his hand and down his fingers. "Lead on, soldier."

"Regrettably, it's Sergeant."

Kase's eyebrows rose.

"Got promoted three days ago."

Oof, the implications of that statement hit Kase like a ton of bricks. How many people had they lost in the attacks?

Sergeant rested his hand on his sword. "We're scant, and after the stunt you pulled the other night, I'm stuck here with you now."

Kase muttered, "If it makes you feel any better, I regret it."

"I don't get paid enough to deal with the cheekiness of a boy barely out of his adolescent years."

Kase bristled. The man must've been only five or six years Kase's senior, though Jove had more gray at his temples. But his brother worried too much. And was probably dead.

Kase swallowed his retort at the sobering thought. Maybe he did deserve a curmudgeon of a guard.

Sergeant turned to his partner and ordered, "No one comes in or out, or the Stradat Lord Kapitan will deal with you. We will be back shortly."

He put a lot of emphasis on that last word.

Whatever. Kase only needed a minute or two with Hallie.

The man saluted. Sergeant started off, leading the way. Kase scurried after him, afraid that if he waited too long, he'd be forced back into his tent. He tried not to be annoyed by his current predicament. He rubbed his neck as he walked. He was alive, and Hallie had returned to him. Most everything was better than he'd anticipated.

With the recent attack taking out a few of the larger upper corridors, the hospital ward had been moved even closer to Kase's area of the Catacombs. He caught a few bits of information as they walked down one corridor and through a cavern with carved out bunks and makeshift tents. They'd be at the hospital ward in the next cavern that looked nearly identical to the last. Really, the rocky scenery was getting monotonous. The addition of a few thousand skulls stacked along the walls might be an improvement, but alas, they were not on ancient First Earth, and using people's bones as grotesque decor would probably throw what little morale the people had left in the gutter.

With that disturbing thought, Kase made himself look forward to his training that afternoon instead. Hopefully, he could convince whoever he needed to let them outside. With the greenie Laurence Hixon still unable to use his legs, he only had two other greenies to train. He thought he could swing a little practice on the Cerl hover, if he was lucky. Maybe he could convince Hallie to come along. He wanted to show her more about the hover, and she'd probably want to sketch and study it. She was a scholar, after all.

He smiled to himself. How had he gotten so lucky?

They entered the next cavern and passed a group of soldiers chatting with a few medics, preparing to aid some of those in the upper tunnels for movement to the city.

The hospital ward looked the same as he'd left it three days prior, overflowing with the injured and overworked medics and nurses. He wasn't sure just how they were able to handle the swell in patients. The chorus of moans and curt instructions inundated his ears. He wove his way around the men and women and children laid out in varying states of distress. Medics and volunteers with sweaty faces and haunted eyes bustled from person to person trying to make sense of the mess they still found themselves in. Had there been another attack? A cave-in? Or something else?

He tried not to look too closely, but a few patients had what looked like black spider webs crawling up their arms. Not many, but enough for Kase to shift away from them. It was clearly contagious, and nothing Kase wanted to catch. He hated spiders.

Kase's own brow dampened in the compact quarters. The atmosphere wasn't ideal for him, nor the patients laid out in rows. He kept his eyes open for the pretty redheaded scholar. She'd told him she helped out here every day.

When he didn't see her anywhere, he began to lose hope that she was there at all. Surely that meant nothing sinister. He was about to give up when he spotted Zelda. She'd tied on a medic apron and was wrapping a man's ankle wound.

He shouldered his way past a few family members surrounding a young girl whose arm lay at an odd angle. Kase looked away hastily. At least it seemed to be the worst of her injuries. A broken arm could be fixed.

Zelda tied off the bandage on the man's ankle and looked up. Her eyes narrowed, and Kase itched to run a hand through his hair. He glanced back at the guard trailing him through the ward.

Zelda ignored Kase and spoke to her patient. "If you start running a fever in the next few hours, you come right back here."

The man mumbled something back, getting up off his makeshift chair of an overturned bucket and hobbled off. Zelda dusted her hands off on her apron.

"I'm in need of a salve," Kase said, holding up his wrapped hand. The sock was now a deep red from where he'd kept his fingers tight around it, but it looked like his hand had ceased bleeding.

Zelda stared at him hard. "We don't have time to deal with minor injuries."

Sergeant stood a short distance away, having fought his way through the crowds. He still looked ready to flay Kase alive if he did anything that would jeopardize his well-being with the Stradat Lord Kapitan. Kase flicked his gaze back to Zelda and leaned in. "Listen, I really need to speak with Hallie. It's urgent."

"Miss Walker, you mean?"

Kase clenched the sock bandage. "Yes, I mean, I'm looking for Miss Walker. I need to speak with her."

Zelda raised a brow and shot back, "Did you get into an argument?"

Confusion molded Kase's features. "Argument? No."

"Then why is she in such a foul mood?"

He hadn't said anything in his note to offend her. She'd replied, but it hadn't been anything special, just a note to say she would see him when he was done with his house arrest and that she was helping out where needed.

Granted, it was him. Kase was highly aware of his specific set of skills that riled her, but if he'd upset her somehow, it had been unintentional. He was certain if he had said something untoward, she would have called him out on it. Maybe it was because he hadn't sent another note? He probably should have. He'd written to her in the journal several times over the course of the last few days but had only sent the one.

"I'm not sure what you mean, Mrs. Walker. I haven't spoken to her in person since the other day."

"She's in the supply tent." Zelda fixed him with a steely stare so sharp it could've cut him open. "You may have won over my husband, but if you do anything to hurt my daughter before we leave..." She took the small set of shears from her apron and pointed them at him. "I know how to bake the most delicious pastries without anyone being the wiser as to what might be hiding in them."

"I'm sorry?"

It wasn't even the threat of poisoning him or the shears pointed at his chest that made him step back. Hallie was leaving?

"What do you mean, before you leave?" he pressed her again. "They're not supposed to let people above the surface until the day after tomorrow, and that's only an estimate."

Kase's trip to Kyvena only proved how dangerous it could be outside the city.

"I don't trust you one bit." Zelda started walking past him, but stopped at his shoulder, looking up, her face stone-like. She tapped his shoulder with the shears. "However, I'm giving you one chance to make it right, because you saved my life and my husband's. I'd advise you not waste it."

She left it at that and disappeared into the throng. What in the world had happened in the last few days? And how could he make anything better if he didn't even know what he'd supposedly done wrong?

He wound through the ward, asking one of the haggard nurses where he could find the supply tent. One patient, an elderly man who had a bandage over one eye, grabbed his hand. "Are you Kase Shackley?"

Kase paused. He wasn't sure which would be better, to not answer at all or say yes. The man was already in the hospital ward, possibly even missing an eye. Would anything Kase said make it better or worse?

He gave him the ghost of a smile. "Yes."

The man's dark eyes lit up. "Did you really take out those Cerl machines?"

"I did."

The man's chin wobbled. "Thank you."

Not sure what else to say, Kase gave the man a nod as his neck burned. How funny life was. A year ago, praise like that would've had Kase tugging on his jacket and puffing out his chest. It'd have him bragging to anyone who would listen that he was simply the best pilot Jayde had.

Now, he was the only pilot Jayde had. The only qualified one, at least.

A few other wounded cheered him as he passed. One man, a medic with blood staining his apron, stopped and actually saluted him. He weakly returned it. He hadn't realized how fickle the populace was. He hadn't gotten into the hover intending to change their minds—only wanting to save them. Honorable, he guessed, but he hadn't realized the effect it would have. The few days since also allowed the rumors to grow even more. The attention embarrassed him a little.

Kase of old would laugh at him now and call him weak.

Before he knew it, the supply tent stood before him in all its run-down glory. It was white and thin and could probably be described more accurately as what used to be a tent. The entrance fluttered in an unseen wind. His guard followed silently behind, though with an annoyed look on his face.

Kase took a minute to adjust the sock on his hand. No one had offered to clean and wrap it with a proper bandage. Too busy to notice the blood, he guessed. It stung when he moved his hand.

Still a stars-idiot move, though it'd gotten him here.

What would he say to Hallie? He'd come here to help him process everything, that her wisdom and advice was the one he valued most, but after his conversation with Zelda, his anxiety had ticked up at least two notches.

Maybe Hallie'd found out about the card game. Could he explain away his loose words? What excuse could he pull? None. But then again, how would she have found that out? Eravin wouldn't know who she was...wait, no, he did know. He'd known enough about her to threaten her before he'd left Kyvena. Waylan knew her from the University, and that red hair and those beautiful golden eyes would stand out amongst any crowd.

But would they run into one another down here? What were the odds? The Catacombs were crowded—too crowded. Besides, what reason would they have to tell her about what happened the other night?

He was being paranoid. His guilty conscience was simply getting the better of him. But he had no reason to even feel guilty, right? He'd defended her honor. She would appreciate that, wouldn't she? That is, if she ever found out.

And he wasn't planning on telling her anything. For now. She had enough on her plate.

Wait.

Zelda. Zelda must've told her. But her mother didn't

know everything. Only that Kase had showed up at her tent drunk and with busted knuckles.

Which was apparently enough to warrant telling her daughter he was trouble.

Kase wasn't sure he disagreed with her, but he would've liked to have been the one to explain to Hallie what happened…in a few months. When this was all over.

But what if he was wrong? What if it wasn't his fault at all? Plenty of other things could've happened in the past few days. They were in the middle of a war, hiding underground with no idea when everything would go back to normal. How self-centered was Kase to imagine only he could possibly frustrate her? He was just better at it than most…well, that, and Zelda seemed to think he was at fault.

"You're wasting my time, Pilot Shackley." Sergeant's gruff voice grated on his nerves.

Regrettably, he was right. It was pointless to just sit and stare while the entire world was literally crumbling around him.

Yet, he still stared.

A few more moments of indecision on his part gave enough time for Hallie to arrive, folded cloth bandages in her arms. She'd cleaned up and changed clothes since he'd last seen her. Her skirt was slightly shorter, more of her scuffed boots showing as she walked. Her shirt wasn't one of her lacy blouses but a plain one with simple buttons a quarter of the way down the front. It was tighter across her shoulders and chest. He had trouble focusing on her face.

She swept past him without even looking at him.

Yep. She was definitely angry at him.

Kase ran his good hand through his hair. Sergeant raised an eyebrow. Huh, maybe he did have a personality. Didn't help him now.

"Hallie, wait!" Kase said, reaching out.

She didn't, in fact, wait. Instead, she avoided his grasping hand. She wove her way through the throng, handing off a bandage to one of the medics. Kase followed, dread pooling in his core. She knew, and now he was going to pay for it.

I didn't mean to get into a fight. I didn't mean to get drunk. But I did.

"Hallie…" He caught up enough to grab her arm. She

didn't turn. "Hallie, could we talk?"

She yanked her arm out of his grip. Pausing to hand off another bandage, she still ignored him. Kase muttered a curse under his breath.

He trailed her back to the supply tent. She didn't look at him once and entered without turning back. With a deep breath, Kase straightened his shoulders and followed.

The space was small. Hallie stood in front of a makeshift table and gathered strips of cloth. Even with her anger permeating the air like the summer heat, Kase couldn't help but examine the line of her shoulders and the curve of her waist. Her long braid reached just past the middle of her back, and Kase had to resist the urge to reach forward and tug on it just to see how she'd react.

Probably a bad idea—tempting nonetheless.

He chewed on the inside of his cheek. Was he simply overthinking things because she was clearly mad at him? Women were confusing—Hallie especially.

She folded a strip of cloth around her hand and set it aside. "If you're going to ogle, then you can leave."

Nope. Not overthinking.

Kase swallowed. "I wanted to talk."

She folded another bandage and added it to her stack. "And if I don't want to?"

Blasted woman.

He stepped up to a pile of what looked like bedsheets. He grabbed the nearby knife and began cutting the sheet into strips and adding them to Hallie's pile to be folded. He was careful not to get his own blood onto the sheets. "Sorry I didn't write again, but I'm officially off house arrest now, though there are still some parameters."

Hallie focused on her work, not giving any indication that she'd heard him. His blood warmed—and not in a pleasant way. Kase's neck protested as he bent to avoid the tent's low ceiling, probably because he'd been sleeping at an odd angle in his cot every night. He paused his cutting and rubbed it. His injured hand twinged, and he sucked in a breath. Hallie shot him a quick glance before returning to her work. "So, the reason for the loaded flashpistol following you around?"

"Parameter."

She went silent once more. Kase rubbed his neck again

out of nervousness. Hallie turned and gestured to an empty bucket. "Sit on that and cut."

"Thanks."

He obliged, but even if his neck was no longer protesting at his positioning, the air still felt thick with tension. The only real sounds besides those of the hospital ward beyond the tent's canvas was the ripping of the old bedsheets. The soft yet piercing *scritch* of each tear only added to the tension. His cuts were imprecise and jagged, but he didn't think the people needing them would mind as long as they kept their wounds covered.

Kase finished the one he was working on and grabbed another. This one was the color of the night sky. It would hide blood better.

"You're angry with me," he said as he cut off another strip. *Scritch.* It was a little lopsided, but Kase didn't bother fixing it. He threw it on top of her pile.

Hallie's hands jerked with each movement of wrapping the next bandage.

Someone opened the tent flap. "You have another batch ready for sanitizing, Hal?"

It was the other woman, Petra. Hallie's friend looked much the same as she had when she'd been scolding Kase the other day—tired and overworked as everyone else. Her apron had a few more questionable stains than the last time.

Hallie set the current stack in her friends' arms. "I'll dry the other batch once I'm done here."

"Thank you." Petra turned to leave but not without a glare for Kase. "And you're not supposed to be here, Master Shackley. Especially after—"

"Thank you, Petra." Hallie said through gritted teeth.

Petra narrowed her eyes at Kase, but she left, the flap shooting a small breeze across Kase's damp skin.

Hallie turned back to her work. "Why are you here?"

"Because like I said before we were interrupted, you seem to be upset with me."

"Incredibly astute." She started on another pile of bandages. She wrapped another and threw it down onto the table. "What tipped you off?"

"Probably the fact that you're taking it out on bed linens."

She froze with the latest bandage wrapped around her

hand, which had begun to turn red from her vigorous wrapping. How was this same girl who'd run to him after he'd leapt off his hover? "Would you rather I take it out on you?"

Kase huffed. He tore another strip. "Actually, yes."

Scritch.

She still didn't turn. "Why do you care?"

"What?" He stopped, the knife hovering over the next section of the bed linen.

"You heard me."

It took every last ounce of self-control in that moment not to lose his cool. He would regret doing so if he did. He'd learned that lesson the hard way twelve too many times. "Stop being cryptic."

Hallie's shoulders tensed further. Well, he could've said worse.

"I am not being cryptic."

He stood then, leaving the linens and knife on the rocky ground. "Oh, I'm sorry. Just immature, then."

She twirled around then, her eyes blazing. "As if you're so high and mighty."

"At this moment?" He still had to stoop a little, but he crossed his arms. "I'm the one trying to talk to you about it, and you're acting like a petulant twelve-year-old."

She flinched only a little. "Why do you care? I'm merely a conquest to you, right?"

"What?"

She didn't drop her gaze. "Not to mention that you still can't control your temper."

All the anger and blood and anything remotely life-giving drained from Kase's face all the way down to his toes. "Hals, if this is about the card game, I can explain..."

"So it's all true?"

"How did you even find out?"

"Doesn't matter." Hallie threw the rest of the cloth strips down.

"It does."

Hallie played with a small hole in her blouse sleeve, her arms crossed, pinning them against her body as if keeping her from lashing out at Kase. "I thought I knew you. And it seems like I was wrong."

"I would've told you."

"When?"

That gave Kase pause. His eyes darted around the small tent, trying to think of any way to explain what he was thinking and how to say it in a way that made sense and calmed her down.

Probably expecting too much.

"Well, I'm not sure, but—"

Her face twisted. Oof, wrong thing to say. Really wrong thing to say.

Her voice was tight with anger. "You're telling me you would've continued dragging me along until you'd had your fun?"

"I would never do that to you."

"Then explain Lavinia Richter."

Kase opened his mouth and closed it again. He ran a hand through his hair. He wouldn't have any left if things kept up at this rate.

Hallie crossed her arms again, which was rather distracting even with her throwing daggers with her eyes. He forced his gaze to meet hers. "Listen, Eravin roped me into a game of Hanged Man's Nebula the other night, and...well, I wasn't planning on playing, not with everything...but I couldn't get out of it."

Hallie stayed silent, so he continued. "And I got to drinking, trying to get Eravin to lower his guard...losers had to spill secrets, which is ridiculous, but I was stuck." Kase fell back onto the bucket and rubbed a hand down his face. "I drank too much, and when I finally lost, Neville asked about Lavinia."

"Neville?"

"Old friend of mine. Or at least I'd thought he was." Kase stared at Hallie's boots. "Obviously, I was oblivious to how he felt, because he lit into me about her." He swallowed. "But he asked about her, and then..."

"Who is she?"

Kase looked up and instantly regretted it. He gritted his teeth. "She was Stradat Forrest Richter's eldest daughter."

"No." Hallie's voice held no trace of the tears threatening to fall. It was sharper than a knife and laced with frustration. "Who was she to you?"

Kase's eyes glazed over. He hadn't hit Neville hard enough, clearly. He briefly wondered if he could find him and do so. Shocks. But it wasn't Neville's fault. Kase was the one to blame. "We were involved a year or so back."

"And you used her to get back at your father?"

Kase's heart felt like someone was cutting it slowly, as if savoring the deed. "Yes."

He couldn't look at her. He didn't think he could bear the hurt in her gaze. Instead, he focused on her boots. Her feet seemed to make the decision for her, and she grabbed the piles of folded and unfolded bandages and made toward the entrance. Kase caught her hand. "Look...it was mutual. She was trying to get out of an arranged marriage to some dignitary from Tev Rubika. If given the chance, I'd do things differently. I'm...not proud of it."

"And am I just the next pretty face? The current pawn in your game?"

Kase shook his head, unable to believe that she could think that and also angry that he'd somehow allowed that line of thought to even enter her head. "How can you ask me that after everything we've been through?"

Hallie waited a moment, her arms full of crudely cut bandages, the tears in her eyes waiting in the wings. "And the fighting?"

Kase hesitated. He rubbed the back of his neck. "Waylan said something...crude. And well, I was drunk. I started the fight."

"Crude?"

He shook his head. "Doesn't matter now."

"It does if it makes you act like your father."

It turned out that being verbally sucker-punched by Hallie was much worse than actually being sucker-punched. She'd said it so calmly and quickly, as if she'd been prepared to use that line of attack. As if she'd just been waiting for the right moment. "What?"

"Lavinia Richter is one thing. I know I shouldn't be hurt. It was in the past. I was about to marry Niels, for stars-sake." She said the words as if in apology, but that couldn't make up for the other ones she'd needled at him. "If that's all it was, I could move past that. But...but..."

She took in a shaky breath, shutting the tent flap. "But if all it takes for you to lose your temper is some stupid words...if you think it's okay to get drunk and gamble away your money...or secrets, or whatever it might be, then I don't know if I can..."

Kase tried to control not only his temper, but also the urge to pull her into his arms—a true dichotomy. Because if she walked away now, he didn't know what he'd do. He'd already said goodbye to her once, and he'd hated every minute she was gone. He wet his lips to give him another moment to think and douse the anger warring for his attention.

She thought he was like his father.

The crushing realization she might be right was almost enough for him to run. If it was true, he might indeed lose her, and he wouldn't survive that.

He kept his words as measured as he could. "When you were at University, Waylan and a bunch of his friends had bets on who would sleep with you first. While yes, I wasn't in complete control of my faculties due to the amount of straight whiskey I drank, which was indeed a mistake, I did clock him for it. But I'd argue defending your honor doesn't make me Harlan Shackley."

Hallie's cheeks reddened at his words. "Oh."

She looked down. Kase played with his ring. She didn't say anything else, and the silence was deafening. She needed time to process his words, but the waiting for her reaction was agonizing. He chewed on the inside of his cheek.

"I kissed Niels."

Kase stiffened, his anger resurfacing. He tried to tamp it down—judging by her wince, he was unsuccessful. "What?"

A few tears managed to escape her hold at last. She brushed them away with a jerky movement. "I healed him from a bullet wound, and he kissed me."

"So you kissed him or he kissed you?" Blood roared in his ears. He could barely hear himself think. The man might already be comatose, but Kase would pummel him to dust anyway.

Which wouldn't help him with Hallie. But shocks, he wanted to.

"He kissed me," she said, burying her face in her hands. "I didn't kiss him back. After Jack died, I just up and left and never got closure with him, so...I didn't think I'd done anything to make him think he had a chance again, but obviously I was wrong."

Kase opened his mouth to respond, but nothing came out. He shut it again. All he could hear in his head was the pounding of his heart.

She pressed the heel of her hands into her eyes. "I just wanted to be honest with you."

He wasn't sure if those words were a dig at him or not. He had been honest. He should've told her about the card game before someone else had, but he hadn't lied. And who had told her about Lavinia? Surely not Zelda. How could she have known?

It was the comment about the conquest that bothered him. Yes, Lavinia had been a means to an end, and he regretted all of it. But Kase wasn't the type to use women as a counting stick of any sort. Not in that regard. Lavinia had been using him just as much.

Had Waylan said something? Eravin? Maybe Neville. They were the only ones who knew.

Before he could respond further, the tent flap opened again. Kase turned to ask Petra to let them have a few more minutes, but instead of Hallie's friend, it was Sergeant's face that appeared. "Sorry to interrupt, but Lord Jove and Lady Celeste are being brought to the ward. They'd both fallen in the same collapse."

Hallie's head whipped toward Kase. "Where have they been? I thought they were in another part of the Catacombs."

Kase shook his head, the rush of emotions in the last few minutes messing with his comprehension of Sergeant's words. "What do you mean?"

Jove—his mother. Had he heard the man correctly?

"They found them. They're alive."

C H A P T E R 3 1

ONE OF LIGHT

Kase

HEART POUNDING, KASE TOOK OFF into the fray. In the time they'd been in the supply tent, the chaos in the ward had only intensified. Hallie still held the bandages in her arms, and Kase still felt like his legs were too heavy and stiff. Sergeant led them both.

If it weren't for the fact that his mother and Jove had returned, he might've tracked down Waylan and given him another black eye. Of course, those actions would further cement in Hallie's mind that he was exactly like Harlan Shackley.

Hallie had been honest with him. He couldn't ask for more than that. Didn't mean it didn't sting worse than the cut on his hand still wrapped in a stupid sock.

He wished he could take it all back, but he couldn't undo the past. It only made him realize even more just how much he didn't want to lose the woman beside him. He'd do anything if it meant she'd stay.

And never, ever kiss Niels again.

He tried not to think about the last meeting with Saldr, that they were heading toward the end like a speeding hover unless Hallie did something. That only meant it was paramount he not lose her now when they didn't have much time left. He hardly understood anything about that meeting—only that Hallie was going to have to do things with her power and then lose it. But what did that entail? Or hadn't there been something about a second Gate?

It was all a mess to him.

He shot her a quick glance. Still stormy. She was squeezing the life out of those bed linen bandages.

Tension still flooded the tunnel air as Sergeant led them to where more dirt-streaked and battered refugees attempted to take care of one another, even though many had no experience doing so outside of the occasional cold remedy. There had to be a few certified medics or medical colonels like Zeke had been, or even village-trained like Stowe, but the volume of people needing attention must have overwhelmed their numbers.

He spotted Hallie's father first. He was covered in dust, dirt, and sweat, but he was holding up well. Was he simply there to help, or had he been the one to go down into the holes? Kase looked around. Probably the latter, as the hospital ward couldn't afford to spare anyone else with all the dead and dying sprawled across the cavern floor—especially as his mother and brother had been unlikely to survive such a fall. But they had. Somehow.

Behind Stowe stood a woman whose evening gown hung in tatters on her bruised and battered frame. Her silver-threaded dark hair fell limply down her back in familiar wayward curls. She argued with a female medic with tanned wrinkled skin and snow-white hair.

Kase froze, and Hallie bumped into him. He barely caught her. His heart stopped. His mother was there. Right there. She wasn't dead.

Hallie's hand slid into his and squeezed.

"I will be fine. Attend to my son, immediately. He needs the most help." His mother pointed at someone behind her.

"Yes, but the Stradat Lord Kapitan said—"

"I don't care what my husband said. You will see to my son first."

Kase caught sight of his brother slumped on a makeshift chair, hand crudely bandaged like his own, looking like he'd aged a few hundred years in Kase's absence. His eyes were red-rimmed and puffy, as if he'd been crying. He was saying something rather forceful to the soldier next to him. The soldier nodded, saluted, and hurried off.

Kase nearly choked on his joy.

"Mother!" He pushed past the guards, Stowe, and anyone else who got in his way. "Jove!"

They both looked up, his mother cutting off her next argument. Jove's eyes widened, and his mother's mouth dropped open in a silent gasp before bursting into tears. She lunged forward, slamming into him and gripping him with all the strength she had left. He returned it, tears budding in his eyes. She was okay. Jove was okay. They were here. They had survived.

"My Kase," his mother whispered. "I thought I'd never see you again."

A tear escaped and slipped down his nose. "I'm sorry."

They stayed like that for a few more moments, shedding a few more tears. After everything Kase had been through in his time away from the capital and upon his return, it was nice to feel safe in her arms once more, as if he were a child scared of the dark and she'd just turned on a nightlight. For a moment, there was peace. For a moment, there was nothing wrong with the world.

He was home.

His mother pulled back and wiped her eyes with one hand, the other still holding onto his arm. "Have you seen Clara? We've only heard she's alive."

Kase nodded. "Yes, I've also gotten to meet little Samuel. You made a cute kid, brother."

Jove just froze, his eyes immediately filling with tears. Eyes that were slightly, worrisomely crazed. "You're sure they're okay? They won't let me leave the hospital ward."

Kase nodded once more. "Yes, they're fine. Lady Davey is also here. She got stuck outside the city during the...riots." The riots he'd been responsible for.

His mother hugged him again, but she tugged Jove into it as well. "As long as we're all together again, it'll be okay." She sniffed, then pinched Kase's ear. "But if you *ever* pull a stunt like that again, I'll ground you for eternity."

Jove shrugged out of her hold and brushed a tear out of his eye. "Seeing as he's an adult, I doubt your threat is all that effective, Mother."

She brushed aside one of Kase's curls from his forehead. "My threats are always effective."

She stepped back, and after a moment's hesitation, Kase grasped Jove's good hand. "Glad you're okay, too."

But Jove wasn't happy with that. Instead, he pulled Kase in for a stiff hug. His brother smelled of dirt, sweat, and metal. He couldn't remember a time when his brother had hugged him, but Kase found he didn't mind. He'd been through a lot—he could be forgiven for such a sappy display.

Jove's words were full of steel, but tinged with emotion. "And if hers aren't, mine better be. If you even think of running again, I will hunt you down myself." He pulled back and squeezed Kase's shoulder. "Understood?"

Kase clenched his jaw but nodded. His mother then smiled, noticing someone behind Kase. "Miss Walker! Oh, it's so good to see you're all right as well."

Hallie had given away her bandages and had just finished speaking with her father, who waved and strode off with another one of the medics. She stepped up. "I'm happy to see you both."

His mother pulled her into a tight hug. Kase smiled at Hallie's surprised expression. After a second, Hallie hugged his mother back. When it looked as if his mother wouldn't release her, Kase tapped her on the shoulder. "She might like to breathe sometime soon."

His mother released her slowly and sniffed. "When we couldn't reach you during the riots, I was worried. And with my Kase gone...we feared the worst."

Hallie's cheeks pinked. "I'm sorry. That was my fault. I needed to get to Stoneset quickly, and well, Kase had a hover, and it just made sense he go with me, and I didn't realize what a problem that would cause and..." She trailed off. "Worrying you wasn't my intention at all."

A beat before Jove cleared his throat. "So you went to the mountains?"

Kase clasped his hands behind his back to keep himself from fiddling. "Sort of."

"Sort of?"

"Jay wouldn't allow a trip like that, and we needed to get

out quickly, and...well, at the time, it just made sense." It wouldn't do to go into the whole *blackmail* thing here. It would only make everything uncomfortable.

Jove snorted, the seriousness from earlier evaporating in an instant. He waved his hand—the injured one—then winced, as it hadn't been attended to quite yet. "That has to be the stupidest idea you've ever had—including the time you got that tattoo."

It was Kase's turn to flush scarlet. His mother glared at him, and Hallie looked between them before landing on Kase. "What tattoo?"

Kase shook his head. "Nothing. Jove's had too much morphine shot into his arm."

His brother just laughed. The stress and pain must've finally gotten to him. Kase glared.

A hush fell over the ward like water being thrown onto a campfire. For a moment, Kase thought it might've been the Cerls or Correa—or even Hallie, doing something with her power. She wasn't supposed to start training until the next day, but maybe she'd lost control. He glanced down at her and found his confusion reflected in her eyes. Guess not. He allowed himself a quick moment of relief.

"Les."

The word was spoken with authority, and while it wasn't loud, it echoed in the nearly silent ward.

The Stradat Lord Kapitan had arrived, his own guards in tow.

No one moved. It was as if everyone had frozen into place, silent and watching. Harlan strode forward. He looked no different than he had three days before. Kase subtly shifted in front of Hallie, hiding her from the Stradat Lord Kapitan's view.

"Harlan," Les said, finally breaking the silence.

She didn't move to hug him; in fact, it seemed like that stiff acknowledgment of his existence might be the beginning and end of their reunion. While Kase had never witnessed much affection between his parents, this interaction seemed abnormal, even for them. All he'd gleaned from his time back was that Harlan had taken the blame for getting Kase off after the fire, and the Cerls attacking had saved him from hanging. How had his mother felt about it all? What had she found out? What had she been through, to greet her husband in such a cold manner?

"Have you been treated for your injuries?" Harlan said, looking his wife over. He reached out as if to stroke her face, but she pulled away.

"I'm fine," she replied as his hand fell back to his side. "It was good we had Master Kainadr with us."

She gestured to a Yalven man behind the Stradat Lord Kapitan. He was tall like Saldr, yet he sported a short beard. He stepped up beside Kase's mother and bowed. "It is an honor, Stradat Lord Kapitan."

Harlan merely nodded at the man. Kase guessed that was an improvement. Old Harlan would've simply moved away without acknowledging him.

Les then said, "And Jove will be all right when someone is able to put more salve on his hand. Not that you asked, but your eldest son was down there with me."

Harlan glanced at Jove. "Good to see you're well."

His tone wasn't cold, but it wasn't exactly the tearful relief of a father reunited with his son, either. Harlan's eyes then landed on Kase. "I suppose their return is considered a necessity."

Tame, again. It wasn't warm, but it wasn't a reprimand. It was more than Kase could've anticipated. He hid his sock-bandaged hand behind his back.

Then Harlan turned back to his wife. "Make sure they run every test they can. I'll be back to check on you both soon."

Jove caught his father by the uniform sleeve. Harlan turned, his face a mask of calm Kase knew he didn't feel. Jove didn't seem to care whether or not he angered their father. He let go of Harlan. "Clara and Samuel."

The Stradat Lord Kapitan straightened his jacket and nodded. "They've been sent for."

Then he left, three soldiers following behind him.

Once he was out of sight, the ward released a collective breath. The noise started out small and inconsequential, but soon it was back to its chaotic mess. Hallie stepped past him and greeted the Yalven man who his mother had introduced to the Stradat Lord Kapitan. "May the stars shine upon you, Lord Kainadr."

Kainadr smiled in greeting, "And may they not fall when morning breaks. It is good to see you once more, Miss

Walker."

Kase didn't like the way the Yalv was looking at Hallie. Sure, she'd probably met him while she'd helped the Yalvs get acclimated a month or two ago, but still. He stepped up and held out his hand. "Kase Shackley. I understand you helped my mother and brother?"

He just caught Hallie's annoyed look, but his forthrightness also caught Kainadr off guard and broke his connection with Hallie, which Kase counted as a success.

Kainadr took Kase's hand and shook it tentatively. "I am Kainadr."

Les stepped up and put a hand on both their shoulders. "While I would never wish ill on anyone, it was quite fortunate for us that Lord Kainadr fell with us. His healing abilities saved your brother's life."

"You flatter me, Lady Shackley."

Kase was about to thank him when a haggard Saldr arrived. The woman, Fely, was nowhere to be seen. He tried not to worry too much about it. Surely she wouldn't go through all the trouble of passing information to his father and keeping Hallie safe to only betray them now, but as Kase had discovered with both Eravin and Ben, he wasn't the best judge of character.

Saldr ran to Hallie. "I've been told the man named Anderson Enright has been rescued?"

Kase furrowed his brow and looked around. He didn't see Anderson anywhere, and he was unsure why Saldr would care. Anderson was nice enough, but he wasn't anyone special.

After shooing off another medic who wanted to look at his hand, Jove said, "They took him back to one of the partitioned areas. They were worried he might make some uncomfortable."

Saldr bowed to Jove. "The stars definitely shine upon you, Master Shackley. Very good to know you are alive and mostly well." He nodded to Jove's hand. "Will you point me in his direction?"

Jove gestured for him to follow. Saldr turned to Hallie. "Miss Walker, please come with me as well. It is of great importance." He paused. "We might also need..." He looked to Kainadr. "Please send for Lady Fely Bessette. She should be with Jera, collecting more holy metal." Then he pointed to the pouch hanging from Kainadr's belt. "May I?"

Kainadr sighed, but he unattached the pouch. Kase wasn't sure why the pouch was important, but if the situation hadn't been so tense, he might've been amused by the exchange. Most of the time, the Yalvs were very respectful toward everyone, barely allowing any of their emotions to show on their face.

Kainadr coated his fingers with a little bit of dust before he handed the pouch over to Saldr. Saldr took it and said, "Please don't do—"

But it seemed Kainadr didn't care. With a snap of his dust-covered fingers and a murmur under his breath, the dust on his fingers congealed and rose into the air like a living flame. Those nearby gasped in varying shades of shock and terror. Kase might've been in their camp if he hadn't known what the Yalvs were capable of. Disappearing with a pop would've been worse.

And then Kainadr left, his glowing ball following him.

Saldr pinched the bridge of his nose. "Of course he would." He then looked to Jove. "Lead us to Master Anderson, please?"

A few of the people moved out of Jove's way as he led them through the ward. Kase didn't know if he was supposed to join their little band, but Saldr didn't say anything one way or the other. Hallie followed closely behind, as did Jove and his mother, who still had yet to be checked by a medic.

The Stradat Lord Kapitan wouldn't be happy about that, but then, he was never happy.

When they reached a more private part of the ward with little cells partitioned off with bedlinens and blankets rigged to hang from the rocky ceiling, a medic met them. She was the same one his mother had been arguing with earlier—the woman with the white hair.

"He hasn't been fully examined yet. We cannot allow any visitors at this time," the medic said when Saldr tried to move past her.

"Lord Saldr is an experienced healer among his people." Hallie interceded before anyone else could answer. She gave the woman a smile and asked, "Will you please fetch Petra Lieber? She's a volunteer here, but I don't see her at the moment."

"Miss Lieber?"

Hallie nodded. "She's this man's fiancée."

The woman sighed but walked off, grumbling under her breath. Kase held out his hand for Hallie to take, but she shook her head and followed Saldr inside the cell.

Kase stuffed his hands in his pockets to cover his embarrassment at her snub. They hadn't gotten to finish their conversation. He had no idea what time it was, but the pulsing behind his eyes meant he had a headache coming on. He needed to find the other greenies soon and start their training.

He didn't know quite what to do, but he knew he didn't want to leave Hallie, even if Sergeant was now glaring at him. Kase felt a little sorry for the man having to babysit all day, though obviously not enough to return to his tent without complaint. With a quick glance at Sergeant, he went inside the cell.

Kase, Jove, and his mother entered just as Saldr sprinkled some of his magic dust from the pouch he'd taken over Anderson's prone form. He hummed a little under his breath. The room was cramped, but Kase went to stand next to Hallie.

He looked back at the Yalven emissary and held in his gasp. Glowing symbols materialized in the air and floated above Anderson's prone form. No one else in the room seemed to react. His mother only looked on with a concerned look. Jove appeared on edge, his eyes inspecting the small cell. His hand was still in a makeshift bandage. Kase looked down at his own sock-wrapped injury.

If their looks didn't scream they were brothers, the matching injuries now cemented that fact.

Hallie stepped away from Kase to stand beside Saldr. "His soul?"

Saldr pointed to one of the glyphs. "This is the one that concerns me."

"But how do you repair a soul?"

Both Kase and Jove glanced at one another with confused expressions. No one was actually explaining anything. His mother didn't seem to notice anything odd at all. Why were they not reacting?

Without asking anyone for permission, Saldr lifted the hanging bedlinen to their right to reveal a sleeping Niels. He gestured for Kase to hold it back.

Kase obeyed, but he felt sick. It'd been only three days, and Niels looked much worse than he had the day he'd collapsed. His skin had a slight yellow sheen, almost like a corpse. If Kase hadn't noticed the subtle rise and fall of his chest, he would've assumed he was dead.

Saldr sprinkled some of his dust over Niels and repeated the humming and strange words. The dust flickered to life and hung in the air, coalescing into symbols.

Sweat glistened on Saldr's face. He'd been working too hard the last few days, clearly. Kase glanced around for a water pitcher. Nothing. He glanced at his mother, who seemed to know what he was thinking without him having to say it. She peeked her head out the entrance and whispered to someone standing outside. "Would you be a dear and find Lord Saldr some water?"

"I will see he gets something, Lady Shackley," came Sergeant's taut voice just outside. It was softer than before. Maybe because Kase's mother had been through an ordeal— or because Kase had run him ragged in the last hour.

Saldr rubbed his chin as he studied the floating symbols. Hallie leaned in close to the ones above Anderson before looking over at the ones above Niels. "They're the same."

The Yalven man nodded before dusting more Zuprium on each. It took a few minutes for this dust to form into more symbols. Kase guessed it was some sort of diagnostic spell, only because it made the most sense. It made him even more curious about the Yalven powers. If Hallie's could manipulate time...were there any limits on what was possible?

The final symbol snapped into place, flashing once before dimming down. Saldr's shoulders slumped. "It is as I feared."

The entrance to the cell opened, and Sergeant allowed the petite form of Petra inside. She carried a small canteen in her trembling hands, her wide eyes fixing on Anderson. "It's true, then? He's dead?"

Hallie rushed to her friend, taking her by the arm. "No, he's...well, I don't know. That's what Lord Saldr is trying to determine."

Taking the canteen from her, Hallie offered it to Saldr, but he put his hand up. His eyes stared at the symbols as if hoping they'd rearrange themselves into something he'd like better, but the lines continued to deepen on the man's face the longer he looked. Hallie clasped the canteen in her hand as Petra knelt by Anderson's side.

Right. Hallie had said something about Petra being Anderson's fiancée.

"What is it, Lord Saldr?" Hallie asked, her voice tired and strained.

Saldr sighed. "It is the same. This one," he pointed to Anderson, "no longer holds the Essence power. Stradat Loffler must have forced it from him, or he may have given it willingly. I do not know. But his soul is dying. I do not believe he will see another moonrise, but even if he defies the odds, he will live no better than a half-life."

"I'm not sure I understand." Jove's brow furrowed, his good hand playing with his frayed shirt collar. "What do you mean, his soul is dying? Wouldn't that just make him...you know, dead?"

"On Yalvara, souls are not only our lifeforce. They are also a source of energy, as the Cerls have discovered and utilized in their technology." Saldr knelt beside Anderson and felt along his wrist as if checking for a pulse. "Therefore, it can be siphoned off and used at will, if one has the knowledge and skill. But if the veil keeping the soul contained is rent, then your body will slowly leak the power over time, which in turn will lead to death."

Kase's mouth fell open slightly. Was that why he felt so cold when using the Cerl hover? Or one of their weapons? But the blanket in the hover had made him warm again. It seemed to counteract the cold. He looked at Anderson. Maybe bringing him the blanket would help. But would it heal the tear, or whatever Saldr was spouting on about? Or would it just keep him warm as he died?

Les looked thoughtful. "But you do have some legends that speak of soul sharing, do you not?"

Hallie looked over, surprise written all over her face—and intrigue. Yes, his mother and Hallie would indeed get along splendidly.

Saldr set Anderson's wrist aside and sat back. "The story of Kainadr and Xera is a favorite tale told around our feast tables. It is said when Kainadr sacrificed himself for Xera, their souls entwined, which allowed them to save Yalvara during the Dawn. We celebrate their victory over Jagamot every year...in fact, it would traditionally start tomorrow.

However, most of our scholars believe it to be a tale elaborated over the millennia since." Saldr sighed heavily, the burden of his exhaustion slumping his shoulders. "But what we do know for certain is that both Kainadr and Xera dedicated themselves to the Gates, going so far as to become their guardians in the form of two swords—one of which we have, thanks to the efforts of Miss Walker."

Kase would've thought exhaustion was making Saldr confuse fact with fairytale if Hallie hadn't indeed recovered that strange black sword from the Gate. The thing felt...off. There was no other way to describe it.

Even so, Kase drew the line at entwining souls. That was most definitely a story for starry-eyed dreamers. What he needed Saldr to tell him was what any of this meant for Hallie. She was a part of this grand mess, and he was going to get her out of it even if she hated him.

She still hadn't looked at him since they'd entered Anderson's little hospital cell.

Sergeant peered in again. "Apologies for the interruption, but Lady Clara Shackley has just—"

He didn't even finish the sentence before Jove pushed past him into the ward. Kase's mother hesitated, but Kase gestured with his head, still holding back the gray-and-brown striped bed linen that separated Niels from Anderson. "I'll fill you in on anything important."

She gave him a look that most definitely said, If you run off or do anything stupid, you will pay dearly for it.

It was one of the looks she'd perfected over the course of the last twenty-something years, and Kase had never appreciated it more than that moment, just happy she was there to make it.

Shocks, he'd been through it the last few days...no, months. And he still had more to go.

Once Jove and his mother were gone and the hanging sheet fell back in place, Hallie poked the floating symbols. They flashed in response, but they didn't seem to help her puzzle out whatever problem she was trying to solve in her head. "But Niels didn't have an Essence power."

"He has experienced the same type of injury, as he was cut with Kainadr's sword. Both Master Enright and your friend have hemorrhaging souls, which is the best way I can describe it in your language. With each passing moment, their souls lose more and more of their Spirits, and will continue to bleed until they become nothing but husks. Your friend is not so far gone as Master Enright, but I...I wish I had a better prognosis. Lady Fely was linked with the Cerl King, which makes her the vessel that holds Soul or Spirit when the Cerl King siphons the source from someone. It's a facet of time manipulation, like the other Essence powers. But without the King present..."

"So they'll both just wither away?" Kase asked, stepping up beside Hallie. She didn't move away. A good sign. "Lady Fely can't help them?"

"Even if she was able to give these two men Soul, it would only be a temporary fix. The veil wounds would not heal. Ancient writings speak of this being a relatively new phenomena, but others believe it to be an effect of the Dawn." The Yalv took a slow breath, composing himself. "I am uncertain as to their ultimate fates. Neither one has suffered a large ripping of their souls, according to the readings here." He waved at the floating symbols. They flickered a little as his hand passed through. "But even a little is enough..."

To kill them. Despite being left unspoken, the words rang through the hospital room like a gong.

Hallie's voice was heavy as she asked, "Is there anything that can possibly be done?"

"Not that I am aware of," Saldr said as he stepped back from the two unconscious men. He nodded at Kase, who let the makeshift curtain fall, hiding Niels from view once more. "I am sorry."

"So we just...wait for them to die?" Kase stared down at Anderson. He hadn't moved the entirety of the conversation. Miss Lieber looked a little too pale herself.

Saldr snapped his fingers, and the glowing symbols faded away. "We must wait. Whatever the outcome, it will be the will of Toro."

They were silent for a moment before Petra rose. "I will go inform his mother of his return. She will want to see him."

And then she left. Only Kase, Hallie, and Saldr remained. If Saldr said there was nothing, the blanket probably wouldn't do a thing. Right?

"But Kainadr—the original—was able to do it," Hallie said before he could ask, sliding down the wall and taking a seat. She looked just as tired as Kase felt, and it was only probably just after midday. He needed to go to training soon, but he didn't want to miss Saldr's response.

"Only the strongest Chronals are honored by the Sword, which is our way of living beyond death—we leave our soul in a sword created from the Gate. Yalven Chronals are gifted with magic, or as we say, a Calling." Saldr clasped his hands behind his back and turned away from Anderson. "I am a Chronal, as was my brother, Rodr—as is Lady Fely. Your Calling determines the sword you will become in death. My brother, Rodr..." Saldr paused for a moment, then continued, "His sword makes the wielder excellent at hunting and controlling prey. Others can make plants grow or transport people thousands of miles in the blink of an eye. Your friend Benjamin Reiss is the Essence of Keys, which allows him to manipulate the Gate's timelines, and with his possession of Rodr's sword when he entered the Gate, he was able to use it to bring back that terrifying beast, the dragonar, from a land we believed sealed off eons ago. But I digress...

"Kainadr and Xera were the greatest of us all. They lived in the time before the Dawn and were raised in Toro's light together. Inseparable until Kainadr was drawn into the darkness, joining the forces of Jagamot. He was an unmatched warrior with a sword forged by Toro himself. Xera was a fighter in her own right, but her particular gift was healing. She was also gifted a sword, one of light.

"Knowing that Kainadr was the pride of the Yalven nation, his betrayal stung, but to his wife, Xera, the wound was deeper. It drove her. Jagamot grew stronger as more and more of my ancient brethren joined his cause.

"In the Dawn, Xera and Kainadr met on the battlefield, their fighting fueled by rage, anguish, and betrayal. In the end, Kainadr wounded Xera. As she lay dying in the dirt, Kainadr gave up his allegiance to Jagamot, giving up his power and his sword. Losing his greatest asset, Jagamot took a near-fatal blow from Toro.

"Kainadr begged Xera to hold on, to live, but it was not only the physical wound. Kainadr was the one who dealt it. Her soul had been damaged beyond repair. Desperately, he pleaded with Toro to take his life instead of hers." Saldr wiped his brow with the sleeve of his robe. "The legend states that Kainadr's wish was granted, but as for the truth of it, we do not know. Only their swords remain, fueling the Gates for eternity—"

"Until the return of Jagamot," an accented voice said as the curtain was swept aside. Fely entered and looked down on Anderson. "The General has questionable methods, but he knows combining the five Essences into the swords and then giving them back to the Gate will allow Toro to vanquish the darkness once and for all."

Saldr shook his head. "What the Essence of Light doesn't know is a sliver of Toro still exists inside Valora. He cannot complete the ritual without it."

"The waiting place in the afterlife?" Hallie asked, her voice shaking a little. "But why did Correa not use the Lord Elder for this? Why make me take on his Essence? What was his intent?"

Kase ached to go to her, but he didn't know what he could do besides holding her. And after their argument, he wasn't sure if she wanted that. So instead, he tortured himself by standing by and watching as Saldr laid out her fate.

Fely looked at Saldr, eyes shadowed. Saldr took Hallie's hand in his. "Because we Yalven Chronals believe it best to reset the Aurora Gate in Myrrai, which would mean resetting time. The Lord Elder was waiting until it was known what the future held, what details the final battle would paint. And if all would be lost, he would use his power to reset the Gate. In the end, we would be better prepared to fight Jagamot. None of our prophecies or writings detail how to defeat Jagamot decisively—only theories."

"Without Kainadr's sword to take the Lord Elder's Essence power, the General needed someone else who would be weak enough in the power to manipulate into his own plan," Fely said. "And the Essence of Time can only be passed down a familial line."

"But Navara," Hallie said. "She was supposed to take the Essence power from him, but she ran to stop that from happening. Why do that if the Lord Elder was going to hold on to the power?"

Saldr chewed his lip. "Raern was never going to pass it to her. He'd always planned on letting her go."

"Then why did he pass it to me? What purpose did that serve in his grand plan?"

Both Saldr and Fely were silent. Kase didn't know what to think. He didn't understand much, only that it didn't sound good for Hallie. And his heart was breaking for her, for him, for the life they could have lived. For the future they might never have. Because, it seemed, she was always doomed to serve a higher purpose.

Still, a sliver of reckless hope stuck in him, some spark of determination to find a way out of this. He just needed to figure out how.

Saldr looked sadly at Hallie. "I do not know, but as the Essence of Time, he certainly had a reason. We must trust his judgment...and prepare you for the end."

CHAPTER 32

THE COLOR OF THE OCEAN

Clara

OF ALL THE DAYS TO be working the rations station instead of the hospital ward, it had to be *this* day. When the soldier delivered the message, Clara left without turning back. She'd apologize later.

She sprinted as fast as she could toward the ward, trying not to trample anyone or trip. Samuel bounced in the wrap she'd tied around crossways around her chest, her right arm keeping him tucked to her.

In her other hand, she clutched the Stradat Lord Kapitan's missive in her fist.

They have found Jove and Les and are taking them to the hospital ward. They are alive and relatively well.

It was a miracle she hadn't tripped on anything with the tears clouding her vision. Just one more tunnel. Just one more curve.

The air burned in her chest, but she only pressed on harder. He was alive. Alive. *Alive.* Her prayers had been answered. She dodged a few more refugees before she turned the corner and saw the crooked rows of pallets and hanging linens. She swiped at her tears with the back of her hand, still holding the missive. The proof she wasn't running to identify a body.

She whipped her head right, then left. Where was he? He should be there.

All she knew was that he was alive. And relatively well.

What did relatively mean in Harlan Shackley's estimation?

Where was *Jove*?

One of the men sent to fetch her raced ahead and spoke with another man, who nodded and wound his way to the back of the ward. Clara followed him, stepping around medics, nurses, and the injured.

The ward was loud as it usually was, the noise made worse by the Catacomb walls. Clara's eyes searched, her head on a swivel.

And then he was there, appearing as if from thin air.

Relatively well apparently meant *filthy and covered in blood.* Jove's face was haggard, his lips chapped. His days-old stubble clung in patches to his cheeks. His shirt was torn, bloody, and no longer white. One of his hands was swathed in bedlinen bandages. But his eyes burned in his face. They were still the color of the ocean she'd missed so dearly.

"Jove," she sobbed.

He couldn't have heard her, not over the noise in the ward, but it was still all the permission he needed. He sprinted toward her, clearing someone's pallet with one jump, not even clipping his shoe on the rail.

Then his arms wrapped around her, pulling her to his chest. Careful of Samuel, he cupped the back of her head, pressing his forehead to hers. Tears slid down his nose and hers. And then he kissed her.

"I love you, I'm sorry, I love you, I'm sorry..." he whispered against her lips.

She couldn't respond; she could only stretch to kiss him harder. He was there. He wasn't gone, and he'd returned to her, the torn and ragged edges of her bruised and aching heart fitting back together perfectly. They had much to discuss, but for a moment, it was enough just to love him. Just to have him.

He pulled back slightly to wipe the tears cascading down her face and pressed his lips to Samuel's head. His other arm didn't leave her waist, his fingers clutching her side as if she would disappear the moment he let go. He pressed his palm to her cheek and gave her a softer kiss.

"I'm…" His throat bobbed, and he shook his head. "I'm never going to let you…"

But his emotions got the better of him, choking the words he wanted to say.

She shook her head, her own emotions still clouding her mind. "I'll always be here, love. I promise."

With careful hands, she worked Samuel out of the wrap, mindful of his head. She laid him in her husband's arms, his hands trembling a little as he tucked their son close to his chest and brushed his fingers of his injured hand across the boy's face.

"Hello Sammy," Jove whispered as he kissed his son's forehead. Samuel squirmed and stuffed a fist into his mouth.

Clara wrapped her arm around Jove and laid her head on his shoulder. His presence was all she needed. Solid. Immovable. *Here.* "I'm sorry, too."

And she was. Leaving that note had been a moment of weakness, though one she needed to have in order to get to this moment. It hadn't been a mistake. It was a decision that might very well have saved her life and her son's.

She wasn't one to question providence. He was here, and so was she. They would get through this together.

He shook his head. "You have nothing to be sorry for. I'm the one who…" Jove's face crumpled again. "I don't know what I'd do without you."

She caressed his face with soft fingers. "We're together again, and that's all that matters now." He leaned into her touch.

He shifted a little, and Clara held him tighter. "You and me. And Sammy. We can do this."

He nodded, and even in the middle of a hospital ward with so much darkness surrounding them, Clara knew it was going to be okay.

C H A P T E R 3 3

A TORTURED WORM

Hallie

THE YALVEN QUARTERS IN THE Catacombs were quite nice for being underground. Fely had fetched Hallie from her parents' tent that morning and led her down several tunnels that traveled upward before dipping down again. It took nearly ten minutes of walking, but when she entered the first cavern, her already-aching lungs lost all the breath left inside them.

For one, everything was green—the ground, the trees, the walls. The cavern wasn't any larger than the others filled with tents and makeshift shelters, or the more developed ones with dwellings carved into the stone, but the Yalvs had made this place a home.

For another, the light felt more natural, and it made her realize how much she already missed the sun. Torch-like lanterns hung from the trees, casting a dawn-like glow over the cavern. Hallie's boots trod upon a worn path through ankle-high grasses, patches of clover, and speckled wildflowers—bee balm, asters, and daisies, plus others she didn't recognize. Even their tents looked like they'd been enchanted with their sparkling lights connecting them together like strings of fireflies.

Maybe Hallie could convince her parents to move their tent in here, though theirs would look quite dull in comparison.

"This is why we've had trouble finding enough Zuprium dust for you to practice with," Fely explained as she led her through the cavern, skirting around a bed of rose bushes and barely avoiding being barreled over by a gaggle of toga-clad children playing chase. "But I must admit, it's very nice to look at."

Hallie could only gawk as they wove in between the trees and tents, padding through soft meadow grass dotted with white and red clover. Fely nodded to several Yalvs as they passed by. A circle of women washed clothes in a water bucket outside a tent. Hallie recognized a few of them from her time before. She waved, and they tipped their heads in return.

The lazy scent of roasting chestnuts wafted past her nose, like sweet caramel and browned butter on sourdough bread. It mixed oddly with the perfume of the wildflowers, but it made the entire place feel rather cozy.

A few of the men gathered at a tent tucked further against a wall of kudzu. Saldr stood at the helm of the circle.

"We will not be able to fight if Jagamot gains a footing here," he was saying as they came near, gesturing around the rest of the cavern. "Our stores are running low."

She recognized the older man that spoke next; she had trouble remembering his name, but he'd worked with Saldr on getting the others settled in the capital. "We have enough stored away. You cannot deny our people the chance to make this place our own. We have suffered for months now."

"And the renewed plants only help me restore the Soul to those in the ward, Lord Saldr," Fely tacked on, joining the circle.

Hallie waited behind, her hands clasped in front of her. She itched to retrieve her satchel and take notes, but that might be rude. Instead, she squeezed her hands tightly together, lest she be tempted.

Saldr gave her a deadpan look. "Which is the only reason I have allowed so much Vasa to be used. But others have taken a seed and grown the entire garden." He looked pointedly at the older man who shrugged.

"I am only looking after the welfare of our people," the man said, gracefully bowing out of the circle. "We will send another mining crew shortly to retrieve more."

He and the other men left, bowing to both Fely and Hallie as well. Hallie curtsied back, murmuring the words of greeting.

"If we continue to use the Vasa at this rate, we can consider ourselves doomed," Saldr said under his breath as Hallie approached, gesturing to the large moss-covered stones set in a loose circle outside his tent. "Please, have a seat."

Hallie obeyed, easing herself down. The thick moss softened the seat, making it oddly comfortable.

A smirk flitted across Fely's face as she said, "I see you finally gave in."

Saldr's brow twitched. "Yramr complained daily about having to stand too long while I'm in meetings. Of course, he would be the only warrior Called we have with us, but I digress." He narrowed his eyes at Fely. "He does not easily accept being told no, and it was not a battle I wanted to continue fighting. Clearly, my approval led to other frivolity." He waved his hand at the kudzu wall behind him. "As if the subterranean grotto the others grew for you was not enough."

Fely's smug look spoke volumes. "I'm not sure if I like that I'm no longer the only one who can get under your skin."

Saldr didn't answer that; instead, he pulled a small pouch from the band at his waist and handed it over to Hallie.

She peeked inside the pouch. Glittering bronze-colored dust winked at her.

Vasa. She'd nearly forgotten the reason she was there in the first place. It was quite entertaining to watch Fely bring out the typically stoic Lord Saldr's jagged edges. They clearly had some sort of history, though she hadn't been bold enough to ask either about it. With her own argument with Kase, she would rather not pry, though part of her was dying to know the story.

"Once you master the basics, you should not need Vasa to aid you. Most would need to save it for more complex tasks, such as healing or summoning your sacred weapon—

however, with your power, you might not need to use the holy metal at all once you are fully trained. But that will take time."

He still wouldn't look at Fely. Hallie wondered if he knew the woman was smirking patiently, watching him like she was hoping for another chance to "get under his skin."

Saldr continued, "Yrea is the most basic spell a Chronal masters, so we will begin there. However, it still requires a good amount of control to perform it well. Coat your fingers with the dust and speak the word. The simplest spells need only a word or thought behind them. The more complex require song to guide the power." He gestured to her satchel. "I understand you have a Relic?"

Hallie nodded, tugging Kase's goggles out of her satchel before dipping her fingers into the pouch and coating them with the fine dust. It clung to her skin like granules of sand. She held it out, studying it with a hard swallow.

She had to learn control, but she didn't have it now— what if something went wrong while she was trying to learn? What if she accidentally ruined the timeline with an errant shift of her power? It was still a miracle she'd only lost a week in creating the Passage to Kyvena.

"What happens if I lose control?" Hallie asked, rubbing the dust between her fingers. "Will you be able to stop it? Reverse the time I speed up?"

Saldr hesitated, looking to Fely at last before turning back to Hallie. "I was not alive when the Lord Elder, Raern, took the power from his mother, but legend says he threw himself a hundred years into the past. He was able to figure out how to send himself back eventually, though I am told it took months. Of course, no one in the then-present day was aware until he returned."

Hallie's stomach dropped, and her blood ran cold. It must've shown on her face, because Fely groaned. "That was not the wisest story to share with us, *Sali.*" She clasped Hallie's hand in her own. "Mastering your power is the most important task to focus on at present. Without you to restore the Gates, we will lose the war. It is our highest honor and duty to teach you. If something goes awry, we will find a way to put it right. We will have no other choice."

Saldr cleared his throat. "I am not certain that was helpful either, *Lady Felyra.*"

Yep, definitely something going on, and something Hallie did not want to step into. With her own problems, she would be the worst person to do so.

Fely just shrugged and snapped her fingers; her lips didn't move until a soft golden fireball appeared above her hand; its undulating light lit up her satisfied grin. "Now you try. Focus on creating flames from the Vasa while speaking the word of power, Yrea. I would also suggest holding onto your Relic tightly."

Hallie pressed her lips together to keep herself from retorting. It wasn't going to work. The power within her was too unpredictable.

The world was going to end—supposedly—if she didn't master this. She had to try.

She played tug-of-war with her power, forcing it into her fingers. It balked against her force, but she pulled harder; for every inch it took back, she forced it to move two, clutching the goggles until they were coated in Vasa.

She might as well have been trying to bend one of the towering oaks above her to her will. But she kept trying.

Sweat beaded on her brow, but she kept her mental grip on one of the struggling tendrils of power as she cried, "Yrea!"

Nothing happened. Her fingers glittered with nothing but sweaty streaks of Vasa. Disappointment flooded through her

"*Yrea!*" she shouted, forcing more of the power into her palm and fingers. But when she tightened her grip on the goggles, her invisible hold slipped on the tendril.

A fireball erupted from her palm. Flames raged from her hand and funneled upward, consuming the tree above her.

Screams erupted around them as embers fled the scorched tree, catching its neighbors in her blaze. She dropped the goggles as her power winked out, going stone cold as she reached for the fire, trying to put it out with sheer force of will. Instead, the flames leapt out to her, scalding her skin, and she screamed through clenched teeth.

Fely leapt up, thrusting her hands into the ground. In seconds, the flames were gone as if they never were. Ash floated down like macabre snow, dressing the moss-covered stones and Kase's goggles with a light dusting. Hallie didn't have the courage to look up at the tree...or down at her burned hands.

"I'm so sorry," Hallie gasped as Saldr took her hands and pressed Vasa into them, singing softly as he healed her. When she finally got up the courage to look, she found they were more mild than when he'd healed her in the ruins. She still hissed through her teeth as they healed, her skin crawling as the magic restored it.

Saldr shook his head and continued his healing until he was satisfied with her condition. "The important thing is that you did not lose consciousness, which is one of the many reasons why I started with this skill."

Fely's locket caught Hallie's eye. An ethereal glow lit her from below, casting shadows across the angles of her face. Her Relic could've lit a moonless night. Fely eyed it carefully herself before clasping her hand around it. "This might actually be helpful to your friend in the ward. He's doing much better, but he requires replenishment at least once a day."

Hallie's stomach turned. That felt like her fault, too.

Saldr stood and paced in short bursts, his long robes hissing over the grass, scattering ash with each step. "You are clearly a strong wielder, but you have a severe lack of control, though we knew as much beforehand." He paused. "Did you try any particular technique to control it? You seemed to be doing well at first, but then it...escaped you."

Hallie shot a glance at Fely before saying, "King Filip and Fely taught me to visualize the power as tendrils of flame. I was holding onto one, but I lost hold of it the second time I said the word of power."

Shame coated her words, and she looked down at her healed hands.

Saldr nodded, taking up his pacing again. "Another method may suit you better. It might be helpful to observe others at tonight's celebration, as each Yalv will be performing the skill to light our traditional fire." He tapped his chin in thought. "I want you to practice finding your tendrils and holding onto them without pushing your power into a skill."

He then tugged out something from beneath his collar. A locket.

Hallie furrowed her brow. It looked very much like the one Fely had around her own throat. Saldr didn't quite make eye contact with her as he said, "Lady Felyra also informed me your Relic may need replacing, though it is nigh impossible to do so."

That seemed in keeping with everything else on her to-do list, at least. Master her power. Save the world. Replace an irreplaceable Relic.

As for the celebration, Hallie would've wanted to observe anyway from a scholarly standpoint, but it stung that he'd given up on this session so quickly. He'd made it sound like quite the simple feat. She'd failed only once—had failed spectacularly, yes, but still only once—and he'd already decided she couldn't do it.

All the more proof she wasn't good enough. Not good enough for this power. Not good enough to save the world. Not good enough for Kase.

"Why this spell?" she asked.

"It's not only useful, as you can observe by our light here," he said, gesturing to the hanging torches that looked like something more out of a fairy tale, "but it requires a certain level of control because the nature of this specific spell is fickle. Considering our time constraints, this might take longer to learn than some other spells, but I believe it will teach you control faster than a more gradual approach." Saldr tented his fingers and pressed them to his lips in thought. "It is also the basis for many of our fighting techniques, and despite you needing your power for the Gates, it might very well aid you in that quest. We do not know when the final fight will be, but the time for us to act may be upon us much sooner than we think. We must equip you in every way we can, as efficiently as we can."

No pressure, Hallie.

Saldr replaced the locket inside his collar. "I have a few things to finish up, but I will see you at the celebration tonight."

He left them with a bow, his robes scattering ash flakes with each step he took. Each soft swirl only reminded Hallie of her failure.

Fely stretched and gestured for Hallie to follow. "Don't let him fool you—he doesn't have a thing to do. He goes on walks when he needs to think."

Hallie retrieved the goggles and brushed them free of ash and Vasa. She still hadn't looked up at the tree. She tucked her useless Relic and the Vasa pouch into her satchel. Maybe she should go on a long walk, too; but doing so might mean running into Kase. He was officially off house arrest. It should have been good news.

She didn't think she could handle another argument on top of everything else.

Fely set a soft hand on her shoulder. "Don't fret. It's difficult for everyone at first, and you were given a worse start than most. I apologize for my hand in that." Hallie looked up to the woman's sad smile. "I used to believe that my lot was one of the worst, but alas, we all have our struggles and limits. Tonight is one of my favorite holidays... one I haven't been able to celebrate since my betrothal contract was signed." She took a moment to compose her features. "It is truly magical, in all senses of the word."

Hallie didn't really know how to respond to any of that. She would've argued that having a power thrust upon you and then being expected to save the world was the worse lot, but she couldn't speak for what the other woman had lived through.

Fely led her back through the meadow, pointing to a large circle of tents. "That's where we'll be celebrating tonight. Come by around dinner rations and spread the word to anyone you'd like to join. It would lift morale for everyone here, I'm certain." She paused and plucked a wildflower Hallie didn't recognize and tucked it behind her ear. "There will also be music and dancing. Maybe I'll find a decent partner." Fely winked. "Maybe you will, too."

Hallie only nodded. All she could think about was how badly she wished she could dance with Kase. She doubted he would want to, not after their argument.

As they left the Yalven cavern and entered the dark stone corridor beyond, a sense of loss flitted over her without the magic of the meadow to muffle it.

She could only hope the celebration would work its magic on her.

THE FIRE WAS ODD. IT neither smoked nor smelled like burned wood. Instead, it floated in the air like a shimmering, blazing ball of energy. It still burned like real fire on her skin, though.

Even with everything she'd seen in the last few months, this bonfire was an odd sight. Sure, Saldr and Fely had demonstrated the skill in a small way during her lesson, as had King Filip in Myrrai, but seeing so many of the Yalvs' powers melding together to create this smokeless, woodless bonfire was a little awe-inspiring.

Maybe Saldr had a point. Observing might help her. But the night was still young, and she privately feared she might still find a way to set the entire meadow alight.

The light orbs floated like graceful soap bubbles from Yalver fingertips to the center flame. Once joined with the others the effect of so many moving in harmony created a false flame, an illusion dancing like true fire against the high cavern walls and ceiling. The fire floated far enough away from the treetops to not catch the branches. Hallie refused to look where Saldr's tent sat underneath a scorched and dead tree further into the cavern.

A steady chorus of Yalvs chanting "Yrea" only added to the ambiance, making Hallie feel less like she was stuck underground in the middle of a war.

While she wasn't certain it would help her control her power, it certainly didn't hurt. If only the joy around her could help the whole Kase situation. After that fiasco of a first training session, their argument had replayed in her head over and over all day long.

He'd tried to talk to her again last evening after he'd finished working with the pilots, but his surly guard had dragged him back to his tent after she'd told him that she just wanted to sleep.

With everything, she'd needed time to think.

Logic told her what she felt for him was real, that their bond was deep enough to withstand anything life threw at them...but logic wasn't the one with hurt feelings. Maybe that was what scared her most.

Hallie had seen how Harlan treated his family and caught glimpses of his anger. Kase had told her more, and he did have a temper all his own. She'd been on the receiving end of it more than a few times during the *Eudora Jayde* mission. But she'd known that about him. It wasn't near the level of his father's.

Which meant there was only one real reason she'd been

angry: because she was terrified that she was going to lose him.

There were a hundred ways it could happen. Maybe his feelings didn't run nearly as deep as hers, or maybe he'd realize she wasn't good enough for him, or maybe he'd consider the kiss with Niels a betrayal he couldn't forgive her for. But for all the ways she could see herself losing him, she couldn't see a single way to keep him.

Maybe it would hurt less if she took herself out of the equation instead. Maybe that was why she'd lashed out, trying to stoke her anger enough to convince herself to walk away.

It hadn't worked. Even now, surrounded by magic, her feet ached to walk to wherever he was.

But even if they both stayed, what about the Yalven plan with the Gates? If she reset them, what would happen to her? To Kase? To time itself?

If her power undid everything that had led them to each other, would she find him again? Or would either of them—maybe both of them—cease to exist entirely?

She should just tell him how she felt, what she was thinking. They could talk it out. It was the mature thing to do. She was nearly twenty-two years old, for stars' sake—yet here she was, acting like an overemotional teenager. She clearly hadn't learned anything from how she'd handled things with Niels.

She couldn't walk away without saying goodbye this time. Not with Kase. They needed to talk...even if she didn't want to.

At least she'd told Kase about the kiss. That'd been healthy, right? She could have kept it quiet. Honesty was the right choice.

Even though it'd hurt him. His entire posture had changed, the light in his eyes completely doused.

Hallie had done that.

In front of her, the Yalvs continued adding more glowing balls of flame to the center fire. Each successive one grew smaller and smaller. Maybe they were trying to conserve Vasa now that the core of the fire was finished, though it still created a nice effect. Some Yalvs sang a soft, eloquent hymn in their native tongue, and the bonfire— which wasn't really a bonfire, but it was the only way Hallie could describe it—blazed a little brighter with each word. The wildflowers and grasses beneath it glowed, though they didn't catch.

Hallie hastily took notes in her sketchbook. She drew a few hurried images; they were nothing compared to the quality of her sketches before she'd lost her finger, but drawing still calmed her. It helped take her mind off of Kase and the lack of power thrumming through her veins. It reminded her of who she'd been before she'd lost her fingers before she'd become the Essence of Time.

A few Jaydians had joined the group, intrigued by the fire and the music—probably invited by Fely, who had spread the word on their way to the hospital ward earlier. The Yalvs welcomed them with open arms, inviting them to watch and join the dancing couples twirling before the bonfire. A few of the newcomers seemed wary of the strange fire without smoke or wood, but with everything else they'd gone through in the last few months, they soon proved too exhausted and heartsick to care.

The Yalvs seem to float as they wove in and out of the other couples dancing to the happy melodies. Hallie sketched one of them, then scribbled notes below:

To show thankfulness for Toro's strength in the Dawn, the Yalvs sing a mixture of traditional and modern songs while dancing around their Yazyrea, the eternal flame. The dancing became tradition about 1200 years after the Dawn (need to check the Yalven scholar, Hazrka, for the exact timing). It is not necessarily a religious celebration, only one of joy.

It is customary to eat certain dishes, including a roast goose, which is also not tied to a religious practice—it is a more recent tradition. According to Hazrka, the goose happened to be prevalent at one of the feasts about 100 years prior, so therefore, goose is now primarily served.

Noting here that this year's particular celebration is bittersweet, as the last year has been rife with death and the destruction of their ancestral home. Under the current circumstances, they have foregone many traditions and adapted others to the best of their ability.

There was no goose at this meal, only dried beef jerky and what looked to be some sort of fried fish. Hallie didn't want to know where they'd gotten the fish. They'd either found some underground river or created it with Vasa, and if it was the latter, Saldr probably wasn't happy about it. She took note of it regardless. Perhaps it would become part of the evolution of this holiday.

"Have you eaten?" Her mother sat beside her in the soft grass, a few cloth-wrapped pastries in hand. Hallie leaned back on another moss-covered stone. Seemed Saldr hadn't been able to stop anyone from making them, as many circled the bonfire.

"Yes."

Not a complete lie. She'd thought about eating, but the hardtack just hadn't appealed to her—especially with her failure this morning and all the emotions clouding her mind.

She hadn't truly spoken to her mother since their fight the day before. She'd been avoiding it, and Zelda often gave her time to "mull things over" after their fights. Hallie guessed her mother believed it would inevitably lead to Hallie agreeing with her.

She was wrong, but Hallie didn't feel like fighting about it again. Not yet.

Hallie had suffered a horrible few days in the relationships department.

Her mother leaned back against one of the moss stones and handed her a pastry. "Well, you look dead on your feet. Eat this."

"I'm fine, Mama." Hallie pulled back a corner of the purple-blotched cloth. Blackberry preserves. It would probably taste delicious to anyone but Hallie.

Her mother merely glared, and begrudgingly, Hallie took a bite. She felt ten again. At least her mother had managed to make the hardtack edible. Not everyone would know how to regrind and add flavor to something so dry and tasteless. It wasn't the first time Hallie wished she'd inherited her mother's talent for baking; even if she had the recipe right in front of her, she still managed to bungle something.

That was her talent.

Zelda gave her an appraising look as she finished off the snack. She swallowed. "Thank you."

A nod was all the praise she got. Of course. Hallie set aside her sketchbook and pencil and fetched the small pouch of Zuprium dust from her trouser pocket. She'd finally been able to clean her old clothes and change out of her mother's smaller skirt and blouse. The familiar lace at her throat and wrists was one comfort on this awful day.

She caught Saldr's gaze as he conversed with Fely on the other side of the fire. The firelight made the Yalv's golden eyes glow. He gestured toward the fire, and Hallie shook her head.

Saldr frowned, and Fely gave her an encouraging wave, but neither one could help her.

Her mother looked between the two, but wisely didn't comment—though by the tilt of her head and that look in her eyes, she very much wanted to. Hallie should give her more credit for her restraint.

Her father had been the one to explain to her mother what had happened to her at Achilles. It seemed Zelda didn't care that her daughter could now supposedly create fire with a word and a puff of the Zuprium dust that used to cling to the Stoneset cottages. Hallie hadn't spoken to her about it at all, but her advice here would be no help.

She needed to talk to Kase. She needed him so badly it hurt.

She'd been in the wrong. She just needed to talk to him about everything—about her feelings, about his. Because her feelings *were* deep. There would be no pushing him away. It was ridiculous of her to even think that.

That little voice in the back of her mind kept sowing doubt. It was only there to mock her, saying that she would never live up to who Kase needed her to be. Who the *world* needed her to be. The voice said Kase was merely marking time with her, that she was nothing but a nice diversion from the chaos at hand. She hated that Mr. Gray, whoever he was, had planted that in her head.

Kase had told her he loved her, but had he gotten swept up in the emotion of the moment? Had he truly meant it?

She'd given into her feelings when they'd been at Achilles, but now she felt as if she stood in the middle of a vast ocean, the only solid ground just wide enough for her feet. No matter which way she moved, she would drown. She needed Kase to pull her to safety, and—to continue with her slightly dramatic metaphor—to teach her to swim.

But maybe a simple literary device was all they were meant to be.

"Hal?"

Her father joined her mother, sitting on her other side.

He leaned across his wife and put a hand on his daughter's knee. "You all right?"

She chewed her lip as her mother also glanced at her. She felt like a lab specimen awaiting dissection. Not ideal. "I'm fine."

It was all she'd told her parents since she'd returned.

She was fine; she just needed sleep.

She was fine; she just needed to eat something.

She was fine; she was just thinking.

Nothing was ever going to be fine again.

At least if the world ended, she would no longer have to tell boldfaced lies about her current state of being.

"You know, I talked with Kase earlier today," her father said, taking his hand back and turning to watch the magical bonfire.

Hallie stiffened. Hopefully they couldn't tell. "That's good."

"What did he do?" Her mother's question was too pointed.

She'd never been a very good actress. "Nothing."

Her mother pursed her lips, but her father covered his wife's hand with his. "He came by the ward this morning to check on his family and give Niels a blanket from his hover. Said it might help. Asked after you."

She wasn't sure how she felt about any of that. The scholarly part of her brain latched onto the Niels bit, wondering why Kase thought that specific blanket might help. The hurt part of her began to complain—loudly—that he'd gone to see Niels instead of her…but the reasonable side reminded her it shouldn't have mattered, because she didn't want to see him anyway. She hated feeling so conflicted.

"How are Lady Les and Lord Jove? And Niels?"

If she kept her tone light, it would be fine.

"All are doing much better. The nurses think Niels will wake soon, and the Shackleys were leaving the ward this afternoon. The Yalv who was with them probably saved their lives." He gave a short, disbelieving snort. "To think Gran probably could do the same thing…"

Navara couldn't do much at all, according to her useless journals. Useless and…

Wait. Navara had been looking for a new way back to Myrrai, back to her people, so that the Lord Elder could heal her son.

Hallie's mind raced.

Navara might not ever have made it back to her people, but maybe her search had led her to clues as to the location of the Second Gate. If she couldn't use her power to reset the Gate, they would have to stop Jagamot with the swords—combining the Essences plus the sliver of Toro's soul that was in Valora.

It was the plan Hallie favored because it didn't need to use her power directly. She just had to put her power into a sword. What that entailed, she wasn't sure—she probably had to bleed onto the blade, but it seemed to be better on the outset. She'd be happy to give up the power forced upon her.

Supposedly, King Filip's power was in the sword. Hallie didn't quite understand why or how, but that was what Fely had said.

They'd also need to figure out the Loffler situation. He was still in the Gate somewhere. That certainly wouldn't help anything.

Saldr looked at her and gestured to the soft flames, but Hallie shook her head. He came over and, after bowing to her parents, took a seat on her other side.

"I can't," she said. "It won't work."

"If you approach the power with doubt, you will not succeed." Saldr smeared a little bit of dust between his index finger and thumb. Murmuring the word of power, the dust reacted, congealing into a sphere. It floated and emitted a glow that grew with each passing second. At his direction, the sphere floated from above his palm and joined the larger one a few feet away. "If you would like to practice, I will tell Fely to sit beside you just in case."

Hallie could feel her parents' stares burning into the side of her head. She wasn't sure if they were curious or terrified. She didn't like the idea of either.

"Will you give it another try?" Saldr asked. He slipped off his locket and set it in her hand. "Try it with my Relic. It will not offer the same control, but it is wholly constructed of Zuprium."

The weight and feel of it was the exact same as Fely's. She peeked at the lid, which was a match to hers, an intricate star pattern—like a decadent compass rose, delicate swirls hugging the edge. Interesting.

Hallie clutched it tightly and reached into her pouch. With the dust coating her fingers once more, she spoke the required word and, in her mind, concentrated on the product, on the glowing ball of fire made from dust all the while begging for her power to rise from her core. "Yrea."

Nothing. No heat. No spark. At least the trees were safe.

Was it because she wasn't fully Yalven? Was her blood mixed too much with those who didn't hold power?

She opened her eyes to see Saldr's small smile; he probably meant it to be encouraging, but to Hallie, it screamed disappointment. "I do not expect you to accomplish this task in one day, so do not be too hard on yourself. We will keep trying."

"We don't have time," she hissed through tight lips.

"We have no choice but to use however much we have left to us, whether it is enough or not." Saldr hesitated, but he put a gentle hand to her shoulder and squeezed. "We will work again tomorrow. Practice grounding yourself. Study."

To her, studying meant pouring over old texts in the library and taking copious notes, not people-watching. All she could grasp from watching the Yalvs use their power was that theirs worked and hers didn't. But she was too tired physically and emotionally to fight Saldr about it.

Besides, he was trying his best. She was the problem, not him.

She handed back his locket, and he draped it across his neck, tucking it away once more.

"I'll grab you some Pick Up. Gotta few bottles left." Hallie's father pushed himself to his feet. "Be back in a few minutes."

"No, Papa. I'm *fine*. I just—"

But of course, he was already leaving, never one to take no for an answer. Hallie told herself it was because he cared. Both her parents cared. It was why they were here...and why they insisted they would be taking her home with them soon.

Maybe if they'd decided to care sometime in the past three years instead, things would have been different.

The music picked up into a little jig, and with one last look and word of encouragement, Saldr rose to join the dancers, promising to check back in later.

Hallie tried not to dread it too much, going back to her sketchbook instead.

One of the moves in the dance was a small clap as you sashayed past your partner and back. Hallie took note. The details would matter if she wrote a book about the Yalven cultural background, something she'd once dreamed of doing. She'd wanted it to be more of a scholarly endeavor, but now it might feel more like an autobiography. She doodled a few of the wildflowers at the edges of the page. Some of the Yalvs had woven them into crowns, only enhancing their natural ethereal beauty.

She sketched and took more notes, ignoring her mother's inquiring gaze.

"About coming back home with us," Zelda finally started, her fingers tapping along with the beat of the song. The clapping one ended and another began. This one was just as jovial as the last and required a leap or two at the beginning. Hallie sketched harder, hoping that the pressure she placed on the pencil would signal to her mother she didn't want to speak about that now.

However, her mother wasn't one to be deterred either. Oh no, Zelda Walker would have blazed right through a snowstorm better than any wildfire. "Your father has had to take on more medic duties since Graham Fincher was killed in the attack, and I can't very well run the inn by myself. It's time for you to come home and help, and with everything here…" She gestured out among the dancers, but Hallie couldn't tell if she spoke about the celebration, the Yalvs, or the Catacombs in general. "It's dangerous. And you've had your fun. Your University training is admirable and will help with running the inn. But it's time you came home."

Hallie's pencil froze mid-stroke. She pulled it back in a hurry; if she kept it on the page, she might just rip a hole through the parchment. "Mama, have you even thought to ask what I want?"

That was the absolute wrong thing to say. She most definitely should have phrased that differently. Her mother's gaze turned…not quite murderous, but it was almost as bad as the time Hallie and Jack had snuck out in the middle of the night and ended up being returned home by the town patrolman.

Whether it was fortuitous timing or not, Hallie's father returned just then with a small vial in his hand. "Not as good as some of their concoctions here, but I've perfected my latest recipe." He handed off the vial; the liquid was littered with coffee shavings that hadn't quite dissolved into the fluid. She didn't really enjoy coffee so much. Her father then gestured behind him. "Found someone else loitering 'round our tent."

Beside one of the outer tents draped in woven flowers stood Kase, two bowls of rations in his hands, his surly guard with him. The entrancing fairy lights strung from tent to tent nearly caught in his curls. Hallie's mouth dropped open, but she quickly closed it and turned away.

Of course her father would've found Kase. If he hadn't brought his Pick Up concoction back with him, Hallie would've thought he'd gone off to find the pilot. To be honest, she suspected her father might've had the Pick Up in his pocket the entire time. He and Kase had clearly bonded over their trip to the capital.

Jealousy itched at her. Kase had seemingly found more common ground with her father in a matter of weeks than she had in her entire life. Unfair, it was.

A man entered the cavern behind Kase, bumping into his back. Kase stumbled, but managed to keep hold of the bowls as the man apologized, steadying Kase by the arm before moving on. He held up his fiddle as he greeted several of the Yalvs and Jaydians gathered around the fire and through the cavern. He was a small, petite man, the fiddle in his hands as beat up as most people looked.

Hallie recognized him. It was the fiddler from the Crowne Haven Inn.

She still hadn't seen or heard from Nole and Masie. Would the fiddler know what had befallen them? She'd told herself that the Catacombs were large, that Masie and Nole easily could be huddled in some cavern she'd never seen. But with each passing day, she grew less certain.

The current song ended, and Hallie did her best to ignore the bootsteps whispering toward her. The fiddler finished his greetings. One of the Yalvs held up a flute and played a few notes. The fiddler nodded and drew his bow across the strings, laughing a little at the discordant notes before working to tune it. Out of everything he owned, he'd chosen to save his fiddle. Now that was passion.

She wished she could feel his joy, the kindness evident in his smile as he started up a song, the flute following along.

She wanted to let go and spin around the bonfire, pretending the light came from the sun; instead, she danced through a storm, the rain filling her up and spilling out the cracks. Between the Essence power, the swords, Niels, and Kase, she was riddled with more branching fissures than she could fix.

Hallie kept her gaze pointedly away from Kase, though his eyes burned into the side of her face. A different rift snaked between them, its edges craggy and sharp. She did not know how to find her way across.

Kase spoke first. "Hey."

Hallie didn't look away from the fire. "Good to see you."

A *very* warm, friendly, and appropriate greeting for the man she loved, obviously. She could act when she tried hard enough.

Or maybe not, judging by Kase's grimace. She could only see it out of the corner of her eye, but guilt still needled at her.

The next song sounded familiar, a Jaydian melody rather than a Yalven one, perhaps to make their visitors feel more at home. The fiddler lit up, setting his bow to his instrument with a new stroke of boldness, adding his own flair to the music. A few of the Yalvs clapped along, the others a new dance, and smiles doubled in size around the fire. Laughter filtered through the magical meadow. Some of the Jaydians—and even a couple Yalvs—sang the words.

It was beautiful, but Hallie couldn't concentrate on them enough to take notes—not when Kase took a seat beside her. She cursed herself for taking a seat further from the others. He sat on the grass itself instead of the nearby moss stone. Saldr would appreciate the solidarity, she was sure, intentional or not.

Kase wobbled as he sat, more focused on balancing the rations in his hands than himself. He held out a bowl for Hallie. "Didn't know if you'd eaten yet."

Several Jaydians joined in the dancing at the behest of a few of the Yalvs. Saldr bowed to Fely, who blushed but nodded.

Yes, there was definitely something there, but it made Hallie question the woman's devotion to Filip. She'd given up her banked Soul just to heal him. Had that been merely an act? Or terror that without his Essence power, the world truly would end?

Regardless, the Rubikan woman was quite a graceful dancer; she knew the steps even better than Saldr. The latter wore a real, if reserved, smile on his face; it might've been one of the only times she'd ever seen him do that. Maybe his walk earlier that day had been the key…or perhaps it was the beautiful woman in his arms. They had matching Relics. That had to mean something.

But alas, she shouldn't pry. She didn't want anyone asking about her own love life.

Another of the Yalvs—the one that had been trapped with Jove—taught a few of the Jaydian children the dance steps a short distance away. Kainadr, she remembered—named after the warrior and sword of legend.

After a moment of hesitation, her father held out a hand to her mother. "Zelda?"

Her mother stiffened and looked at her daughter. "I don't know."

"Zelda."

Hallie still hadn't taken the rations: a mix of jerky, hard cheese, a variety of berries, an apple, and a thick slice of bread. Kase set the military-grade bowl on the ground. It was quite outclassed with its cheap metal next to the sparkling grasses of the meadow. At least the food wasn't hard tack.

Her mother sighed and stood, but not before throwing a waspish look Kase's way.

While Hallie had been on the receiving end of it more times than she could count—and had been again, moments earlier—she'd never appreciated her mother more than in that moment. It was nice to have someone take her side without question.

Hallie and Kase sat in silence, the only sound between them an occasional crunch as she finally gave in and took the apple out of her ration bowl. It was juicy, if a little soft. Probably something imported from the coast.

"Had to grease a few palms to get ahold of the fruit," Kase said, popping a dark pink mazelberry in his mouth. "Definitely worth it, though."

"Oh, thanks."

Part of her felt grateful. The food *was* nice. But then again, who would go without because she'd enjoyed a little more that night? She shouldn't let it bother her. The news had gone out a few hours before that those in certain sectors would start moving back into the city for cleanup the next day. The resources in the Catacombs wouldn't be so stretched after that.

Hopefully enough resources had survived the Cerl attack to keep those forced back to the surface fed, too.

She bit into the apple with another crunch, the juices skittering across her tongue. If she pretended the last day had never happened, she could almost believe things would be okay again. That she and Kase weren't fighting. That she could lean in and put her head on his shoulder, and maybe he would ask her to dance...

But she couldn't forget what she'd learned.

She swallowed and took another bite, still trying not to look too closely at the man sitting next to her like a silent mountain.

Wasn't it better that she knew more about his past? That she could understand more of who Kase was at his core? That she had the opportunity to accept him for who he was, to believe him when he said this was different?

But then there was the fight. He hadn't picked it for nothing. He'd been defending her honor. That was what all the damsels in fairytales dreamed of—men willing to go to war for their women. But did Hallie want that? The fairytales always ended just before the real story began. How did they fare afterward? Did they truly live *happily* ever after?

Did it even matter, when there might be no *ever after* for her and Kase at all?

They were in the middle of an actual war. If she couldn't master her power, the world would end. Even if she did, who knew what resetting the Gates might change about the reality they knew now?

All she needed to do was open her mouth and say something. That she forgave him. That they could forget it had ever happened.

Instead, she finished off the apple and started on the jerky.

Her thoughts were a muddled mess—because of the awkward tension between them, and because he wasn't wearing his pilot's jacket. Even in her current mood, she couldn't help it. In her periphery, she was highly aware of the muscles under his shirt, the sleeves clinging tightly to his biceps. Half of her wanted to run her fingers over the ridges.

The other half wanted to throw the apple core at his stupid face.

"Where did your parents learn to dance so well?" Kase asked, unscrewing the cap on the canteen and taking a swig. He leaned back on one arm.

His triceps contracted with the action and made it nearly impossible for Hallie to concentrate on her food. He might not have been nearly as built as the miners she'd grown up around, but with his broad shoulders and—

She forced the bite of jerky down her throat, turning back to the fire with a hard swallow. Every glimpse of him took a chisel to the wall she'd built around herself. If she didn't look at him, she'd be fine. "It's how they met."

"They didn't both grow up in Stoneset?"

Hallie shook her head, focusing on the distraction her parents provided. "Mama came from a family of tinkers. She was born in Jayde, but she spent a lot of time in Tev Rubika. Her family would stop in at Stoneset on their way to Kyvena for the summer markets. Papa says that Mama was the most beautiful woman he'd ever seen, and the first time he saw her, he simply *had* to ask her to dance." Hallie set aside her half-eaten food and pulled her knees to her chest. "Mama says she only said yes because Papa promised to buy one of her pastries, but it worked out for him in the end."

Hallie felt Kase's eyes on the side of her face again. "I like that story."

"Me too." It had made her believe, if only for a short while, that fairytale romance could exist in real life, too.

It was a relief when he finally looked back at the dancers. He tore off a chunk of bread and ate it. He leaned forward, forearms resting atop his knees. "Not many people know my parents were a love match, which is rare in our circles. Most are married for political or financial gains. Marriage is a contract."

Hallie's brows shot up. The second part didn't surprise her—Petra had been the intended victim of an arranged marriage—but how had someone as kind as Lady Les ended up with Harlan Shackley? Chosen him, even? "So what happened to make the Stradat Lord Kapitan..."

She waved her hand in the air instead of finishing the sentence. It didn't feel right for her to speak openly about the abuse, not without his permission or knowing who might be listening.

Kase shrugged, the fairy lights twinkling like stars in his pupils. "Not sure how he ended up being such a blasted *helviter*, but they met through my uncle. Mother told the story all the time when we were little because Ana would beg her. Time's blurred the details, and my sister stopped asking when she found out she'd be marrying for the good of the country."

The food weighed heavily in Hallie's stomach. Here she was wallowing in her own self-pity when Kase had lived a life of so little choice. Who was Hallie to judge him when she'd had the world at her feet without even realizing it?

Someone else had written Kase's future while she'd been able to choose her own—at least for a little while. No wonder he had a temper. She'd only recently had choice robbed from her, and look how angry she'd already become.

She shifted a little, the rocky ground uncomfortable. "So, Jove and Clara?"

"Clara's father is the Shield Marshal of southern Jayde, and she can trace her family's roots back to General Samuel McKenzie. The betrothal contract was drawn up when Jove was sixteen, when they met for the first time. Clara's a year younger, but the arrangement ended up working out quite well for them. He even went out of the way to propose when she turned eighteen as if it wasn't all prearranged. He married for love *and* political reasons." Kase rolled his eyes. "Always been lucky."

Hallie wanted to ask about Kase, but wasn't sure she wanted to know the answer. The Stradat Lord Kapitan had made it very clear at the estate dinner that Hallie wasn't worthy of his son. She never would be.

Wouldn't it be better to know the truth? Wasn't that what she'd learned with the Lavinia situation—or at least what she was trying to learn?

She picked at a fingernail. "What about you?"

She hoped the music and chatter from the others covered the fact that she didn't sound as nonchalant as she'd intended.

Kase took a little bit to respond. He tore the rest of his bread into pieces and tossed them into the bowl.

Blasted emotions. She'd pushed too far. It was none of her business. "You don't owe me an answer. I'm sorry. I just..."

Just what? Just wanted to know whether he believed the same as his father? That he wished he could've married Lavinia? That he regretted the last few months?

Kase shook his head. "If anyone deserves that answer, you do. My marriage *was* meant to be political, but...well, you heard the Stradat Lord Kapitan. I wasn't signed away at sixteen because he believed I needed to mature a little first." He rubbed the back of his neck. "Mother says she just wants me to be happy, even if she keeps dropping heavy-handed hints about grandchildren..." He coughed, blushing a little. "But Jove seems to have that covered.

"Up until now, I simply wanted to live my life and forget whatever societal obligations my family believes I have. But if I found...someone...who wouldn't mind spending an entire day discussing books, politics, or anything at all, I could see myself married." He twisted the ring around his finger. Ana's ring. After a long, hesitant pause, he glanced at her out of the corner of his eye. "You?"

Hallie weighed her answer. While hiking through the Narden Pass, they'd had a similar conversation about Niels being the one she'd been supposed to marry, but that had been different. Nothing had happened with Kase other than a few near-kisses. The conversation now was vastly different, and with the added pressure of their earlier fight, she didn't know how to respond. So much had happened. They were no longer dancing around one another, unsure of the other's feelings.

So she simply averted her eyes. "Not sure if it's an option now, with everything."

The music shifted to something slower, giving the dancers a little reprieve. Her father smiled before settling a hand on her mother's waist. Hallie caught her mother's eye roll, but her father merely chuckled and pulled her closer. Hallie chewed on her lip. Her parents were opposites in many ways, but they'd made it work. They complemented one another. It was nice—a perfect love story.

"Want to dance?" Kase asked softly.

She turned slightly. His earnest eyes sparkled in the light from the fire. He looked positively striking, laced with the golden light, the magical forest canopy twinkling above him. Her heart thumped painfully. She wanted to say yes so badly, but all she could think about was their fight earlier and the future they would never have, no matter if Hallie were a queen or a pauper. Even if his father decided to allow Hallie into Kase's life, she wasn't sure what the future held with the war and the need to combine Essence powers into the swords. He knew that. He knew they couldn't be anything more, because that would only lead to heartbreak.

"I don't know, Kase."

He waited a moment before digging into his pocket and pulled out a slightly flattened piece of candy wrapped in what used to be shiny blue paper. He held it out to Hallie. She raised an eyebrow. A caramel.

"I've been saving it for you."

She eyed it. Had he sat on it? "How long?"

Kase cocked his head and looked up, putting on a show of thinking about it. Playfulness tinged his tone when he said, "Oh, it's just the last one in the bag I picked up in Nar."

"Am I really supposed to believe you ate the rest of the bag all by yourself only to save the final one for me on the odd chance I returned to Kyvena?" Hallie relaxed a little at their banter. That was comfortable. That was safe.

"I don't know if you know this, but you're quite stubborn."

Hallie narrowed her eyes. "I'm not *that* stubborn."

"You are, and that's why I saved it for you. I knew you'd be back. And I knew you'd throttle me for taking the last caramel."

"You act like being stubborn is a bad thing."

"I would never say that." Kase had the audacity to look appalled by her accusation, though the twinkle in his eyes lessened the effect.

"You implied it."

"Well, if you weren't, you'd be out a delicious caramel now, wouldn't you?"

Hallie let out a small huff before shaking her head and reaching out to take the candy. "Fine."

She inspected the wrapper. The blue color had faded where it'd crinkled, though it still shone with the same shade as his eyes. It brought back the memory of the trapper cabin with Kase, what he'd said to her there...that it didn't matter who her ancestors were, only that she was Hallie Walker: intelligent, spirited, and stubborn as the stars.

"I'm sorry, Hals. I should've told you about Lavinia." His

voice was soft. "And I shouldn't have started the fight. I lost my temper, but I won't apologize for defending you." He paused. "But Niels...I'll apologize for that. I overreacted."

Hallie didn't look up, only used the edge of her fingernail to open the candy wrapper slightly. Heat crept into her cheeks, into her core.

He took a deep breath. "I don't know if you knew this, either, but I was a little bit of a stars-idiot before I stumbled into your bookshop. Still am sometimes. Ask Jove." Hesitantly, he reached over and took her hand. He rubbed his thumb across her knuckles. "I've learned that I must live with the past, and despite the fact I want to go pummel an unconscious Niels for making a move on you, I understand your need for closure. I've never been good at getting that, so I can't fault you for it."

Hallie only stared at their hands, her jumbled emotions making it impossible to figure out how she ought to react. Because he was right. She knew Kase was the one she wanted, not Niels. If Niels hadn't kissed her, she might never have known with such certainty.

"We both have pasts, and I've made more mistakes than I can count, but..." Kase laced his fingers through hers. She didn't stop him, and her heart picked up speed. "What you need to know now is that I love you, and I've...well...I've never, er, I've never told anyone that before." The places where their palms and fingers touched tingled almost painfully. He squeezed her hand. "You're the first."

How did she follow a speech like that? What had she done to deserve such a perfect confession?

But the little voice in her head wasn't to be deterred. It couldn't accept the words at face value; it needed logic. It needed proof. "But how do I know you're not just *saying* that?"

Kase blinked, looking perplexed. "Why would I just be saying that?"

"I don't know, because we're being pulled into some ancient war that could potentially spell death and destruction for all mankind?"

Kase hooked a finger underneath her chin. He was closer now, and she had trouble concentrating on their conversation and her anger and any arguments she had earlier. All she could think about was just how close his lips were to her own. At that moment, all her reservations vanished.

He grinned her favorite grin, the one where if she'd been standing, her knees might've given out. He murmured his next words so close, they danced across her lips. "We could be sitting in a library reading books, with nothing to bother us but the proper use of dinner forks, and I would still love you. And if you'll let me, I'll prove it."

Hallie held her breath as his lips teased hers, waiting for her to say yes. Part of her still wanted to push him away, to wallow in her hurt, but she couldn't. Because despite everything he'd done, she still wanted him.

"I...I..." Stars in heaven. She couldn't think.

Kase's smug grin widened further, knowing the exact effect he had on her. Oh stars, Hallie's entire body was about to combust right then and there. Every single last nerve tingled as if it'd been sprinkled with the brightest stardust. No matter how hard she fought it, even if they never found the peace they deserved, she was his, and he was hers.

A sparking sound exploded around them. Kase and Hallie sprang apart, looking for the source. It sounded just like an electrobolt firing, but many Yalvs laughed and cheered as the odd bonfire burned brighter.

Stars. At least they didn't bump heads that time.

"Yreava!" a few Yalvs shouted, continuing to dance. The frozen fiddler, also caught off guard, shook his head and started his tune again in sync with his Yalven counterpart.

"What did they say?" Kase asked.

Hallie unwrapped her caramel and popped it into her mouth. "Bless the day. Tonight's celebration is for Toro's victory over Jagamot the first time."

"Well, it's not been a terrible day, I guess." Kase said, standing and stretching. "Seems like it'll end well."

Hallie swallowed her candy and stood. Maybe she could wait to analyze their conversation later and determine what her next steps would be. She didn't think everything was ending in the next few hours. She could decide what to do about Kase tomorrow. For tonight, she could pretend it was all fine in the world. "Let's dance, Master Pilot."

Kase's entire face shone as he grabbed her hand and dragged her to where her parents and the others were still dancing.

The music was happy and bright, and Kase's arms were

around her as they spun around the fire, interweaving with the other couples. His laughter was full of the sunshine she hadn't properly seen in days, not a single shadow of his past to dim it. She hoped hers matched.

Music flitted around the dancers like wind through the forest trees, light and lilting, rich and dulcet. She sang half the words, not knowing them all or caring to remember them from her sketchbook notes. Even if she had, the dancing left her too out of breath to sing them all.

"Didn't realize you had a voice," Kase said, eyebrow raised as he spun her around with one hand holding hers tightly, the other lightly skimming her waist. "I'm disappointed this is my first time hearing you sing, even if I can't understand a single word."

"It's not nice to tease," she said with a laugh.

Kase wrapped his arm around her waist and dipped her low, and her breath left her chest. He whipped her back up and spun.

She panted. "That's not part of the dance!"

"Then teach me, birdy."

"Birdy?"

He turned the dance into a sort of ridiculously stiff tango, which did not go with the beat in the slightest. "For songbird. Not my best work, I'll admit."

"And why is that?"

He pulled her so close, she could scarcely breathe. He bent down, his lips close to her ear. "Well, I'm a bit distracted."

"Oh, really?" she asked, trying not to shiver as his lips didn't move from her ear.

"I'm dancing with the most beautiful woman I've ever seen. Distraction can't be helped."

Heat blazed from her core, causing her to stumble, but he already had her tight in his grip. "Whoa, whoa. You've already got me, birdy. No need to throw yourself at me."

She pulled back and swatted his shoulder. "Now you're just being cocky."

The heat dwindled to a simmer. Her power had come back—or maybe it was just the way Kase was looking at her.

At that moment, she didn't care which one it was.

Kase spun her out from him and back before the song ended. They broke apart briefly to clap. Hallie ignored the looks her mother threw her way from a few feet to the right. So much for being on her side.

The song slowed once more. This time, Fely stepped up to the fiddler and lent her voice to the performance, low and rich and a little sultry. Kase threaded his fingers through hers. "Dance with me again?" He gave her that stupid cocky grin again. "But I'll have you know, I'm not sharing you with anyone."

"That's a little selfish, don't you think?"

"Never."

His hands found the curve of her waist, and Hallie joined her fingers at the back of his neck. It was torment not to stand up on the tips of her toes and kiss him, but she didn't. Not yet. She didn't fancy a lecture from her mother about it later.

A few more Jaydians joined, including Jove and Clara. Samuel wasn't in sight. Probably off with Lady Davey, for it was rather late in the evening.

Hallie vaguely recognized a few of the other Jaydians from her days at the Crowne Haven Inn when they appeared with rations in their hands. They greeted the fiddler and a few of the Yalvs. It warmed Hallie's heart to see it. Seemed like her work before she'd left for the Nardens was finally paying off. Jove and Clara headed toward where Saldr stood conversing with a few other Yalven men.

A flash of blond caught her eye before her gaze turned back to Kase.

Niels. Her heart flew into her throat. He was awake and seemingly fine enough to leave the hospital ward.

Kase tightened his hands at her waist as he followed her line of sight. His eyebrows rose. "That's a little unexpected."

Hallie tried to shrug off the unease that entered her gut. She was relieved he was all right, at least for now. The ripped veil holding in his soul couldn't be repaired—Fely had warned them it was only a matter of time before he fell back into a comatose state. Seemed like the soul from her fire earlier in the day had done some good, though...even if a tree had to suffer for it.

Kase brushed her forearm. "Are you okay? We can go ask how he's...Hallie?"

She shook her head, forcing a smile to smooth out the awkwardness. "No, it's fine. I just...I wasn't expecting him to be up so quickly. It's a good thing."

It was the truth, so why didn't she feel better about it? The night had been going so well; there was no reason to let her misgivings derail it. Not that the guilt was helping, either, but that was understandable.

Looking at Niels now didn't spark anything in her chest but concern. She'd been as honest as she could've been back in the Gate chamber; with her piece said, he was free to move on, and she dearly hoped he would. He deserved someone who would be good to him and would help him grow, just as Kase had helped Hallie.

Maybe the final gift Hallie could give him was to solve the problem with the Gate and Essences. It would allow him to live free and find his own way in the world.

Kase reached up and gently took her hands from his neck, clasping them softly. "Hals, it's okay. Really. You can go talk with him if you'd like."

Deep down, she knew it grated at him, because it would've bothered her if their positions were reversed—as detailed by their earlier argument—but he was giving her the choice. He wasn't letting anger or jealousy control him. He was as steady as the stars in a clear night sky. His soft gaze was earnest and unwavering, like tempered steel.

It was honest, vulnerable, and full of deep love.

With that silent strength and even acceptance, she didn't know why she'd ever doubted his intentions. The lingering storm within her heart fizzled away, blooming into a thousand butterflies in her stomach. Sliding her hands out of his and back up his arms, tracing the muscles she'd noted earlier, she twisted a few of his curls at the nape of his neck around her finger. She met his eyes, and her heart thumped hard in her chest. Kase's eyes burned, and she almost didn't get the next part out. She took a deep breath and willed her heart and lungs to keep functioning normally. "I love you, Kase Shackley, and there is absolutely nothing I'd rather do right now than dance with you all night long."

His eyes widened, his mouth dropping open in a soft 'O' before a slow grin unfurled on his lips. It lit her from the inside out as he picked her up and swung her around, a few of the other dancers protesting as they nearly stumbled into them. Hallie just laughed and lowered her mouth to Kase's waiting lips.

A loud cough to her right pulled her away before she so much as brushed them. Kase set her down with a chuckle. Hallie turned to find her parents next to them. Her mother gave her a look, and Hallie's cheeks flushed.

Blasted stars.

Kase just tipped his head toward her parents before sliding his hands around Hallie's waist once more. Her father whispered something in her mother's ear before leading her in the other direction. Of course she would've been hovering nearby, watching like a hawk. Hallie gave an annoyed huff.

Kase tugged her back to him with a gentle finger on her chin. "Maybe one day, I'll get to kiss you again."

"Maybe." Hallie rolled her eyes, glad for the break in tension.

They lost themselves to the next dance, an upbeat jig. It was nice just to laugh and have fun and pretend the problems that awaited were far away. They wove through the others, spinning close to where Jove spoke with Saldr. The conversation seemed too serious for the moment, but Hallie couldn't hear them over the music, and it would be too obvious if they paused to eavesdrop.

The conversation ended shortly afterward, and Saldr gestured for him to join the festivities. The Yalv glanced over toward Fely, who was now speaking with Niels, and Hallie just caught the fleeting annoyance that spirited across Saldr's features.

Jove turned to Clara, who raised an eyebrow. Jove shrugged but pulled her into the dance, wearing a reserved smile even rarer than Saldr's as he looked into his wife's eyes.

Before she'd left for the Nardens, Hallie wasn't sure what was to become of them—not after that disastrous dinner where Jove had gone home drunk. It hadn't been a good night for anyone in attendance. But they seemed to be on the mend now.

Seeing Jove reminded her of something he'd said the previous day.

"So," Hallie said, playing with the empty buttonhole at Kase's shirt collar. "What was your brother saying about a tattoo?"

Kase nodded at Jove and Clara, the latter smiling slyly at Kase and Hallie. Kase spun her away from them. "A stupid idea."

"It was." Jove interrupted, apparently taking Kase's avoidance of him to heart—he sidled closer, pulling his wife along. "The artist wasn't exactly talent—"

Clara put a hand over his mouth. "Sorry, Kase."

Kase's grip on Hallie loosened as he glared at his brother. "Maybe you should turn in for the night. Jove seems a little out of sorts, though that's no surprise."

Jove narrowed his eyes and peeled his wife's hand off his mouth. "Listen, if you're trying to woo Miss Walker, surely she should know—"

Clara slapped her hand over his mouth again, but her eyes were full of laughter. "Excuse us, will you?" She turned to Jove. "Hallie is a lovely girl, and I'd hate for you to run her off."

Hallie laughed even as her cheeks burned. Kase glared daggers at his brother and sister-in-law as Clara pulled Jove away, but Kase's brother still managed to get in a: "I wouldn't say yes until you've seen his grammar school portrait!"

Kase's fingers tensed on her waist as Hallie asked, "Grammar school portrait?"

Kase slung a deadly look in his brother's direction. "The technology was rather new, and well, as we went to one of the wealthier schools in the city, they'd been testing out the newest flash portrait maker, something the First Settlers called a camera. I was eleven, and well...I may or may not have..."

"Spit it out."

"Eravin dared me. I swear."

"Kase, just tell me."

His face was bright red, but he ground out, "I may or may not have flashed the man taking the portrait."

"Kase Shackley!"

"I'm going to kill Jove."

She couldn't help it. She laughed so hard she could barely breathe. Kase was still blushing as dark as a mazelberry, but he joined in. They couldn't stop for a while, and a few people gave them strange looks. The laughter broke the last of the tension, and she caught her breath, wiping her tears when they finally calmed down enough to start dancing again. "The funniest part is that it doesn't even surprise me."

He shook his head, chuckling. "Mother was livid. Almost

as much as the time we broke the window playing cricket in the courtyard. Got Zeke to take the blame for that one, though.”

“Seems like you and Jack would’ve gotten along quite well. I only got him to take one flash portrait with me as a gift for Papa. Had to pinch him to get him to smile for it.”

Kase brushed a thumb over her cheek, wiping away one of the stray tears of laughter that had escaped her own fingers. “I’d have liked to meet him.”

The moment grew heavy, laden with everything they’d lost. Hallie wasn’t sure what to say, so she didn’t try; instead, she allowed Kase to lead her through the dance once more.

A few moments later, she remembered what they’d been talking about before Jove had interrupted. “But why?”

“Hmm?”

“Why was the tattoo a stupid idea?”

He spun her out and back in, almost to avoid answering because she knew that wasn’t the next dance step. “Told you I regret a lot of things.”

She wasn’t dissuaded. “Didn’t you say something earlier about proving you love me?”

“Yes.”

“This is your first test.”

“You’re rather frustrating. You know that, right?” He put his hand on her waist once more and guided them further away from Jove, who had spun his way back around the circle again, creeping ever closer. Hallie bit back a laugh.

“One of my many virtues.” Hallie said, allowing a smile to creep across her face.

“All right,” Kase said, a small roll of his eyes. “The one Jove referred to is a small dragon on my shoulder. Looks more like a tortured worm. Got it with Skibs after we graduated from the bikes.”

“Bikes?”

“Hoverbikes. New pilots ride them to learn the controls before they’re allowed real airships.”

Hallie tangled a few fingers of her right hand into the curls at the nape of his neck again. He moved his head a little, and Hallie laughed. “Like that, don’t you?”

“Feels nice, what can I say.”

They danced past a few Jaydians, who gave them appraising looks.

"You said the one Jove referred to." Hallie raised an eyebrow. "Does that mean there are more?"

He spun her out again, and she tripped. He caught her and brought her back smoothly. "Seems you don't know this dance very well."

"I've never heard this song."

"Maybe I should change your nickname to something more appropriate?"

"Birdy was a stupid one to begin with, and besides, you're being evasive, Master Pilot."

"Now that's an absolutely ridiculous nickname if I've ever heard one."

She placed a finger on his lips. "Tell me about your other tattoo."

He sighed. "The other one..." He kissed her finger before removing it with his other hand, kissing her knuckles instead. "It's one I got after the *Eudora* mission."

"And?"

"It might be worse than the dragon one. I was feeling poetic."

She laughed, imagining a floral pattern. "It's something frilly, isn't it?"

"Never."

Hallie thought for a moment. What would he have? She doubted it was another dragon. Maybe something from a book? *The Odyssey*? But what would be embarrassing about that? "It's my name."

He rolled his eyes. "Yes, I was so enamored by the only woman who dared spurn me that I got her name tattooed right above my—"

"If you finish that sentence, I will slap you for a third time."

Kase threw his head back and laughed again. Was that the third or fourth time that evening? She really liked this side of him. It was as if he'd finally let go. Whether that was from their honest discussion or the fact she'd told him she loved him, she didn't know, nor did she care. She never wanted him to stop.

"When I got back," he finally said, "I used reading as an escape for...everything. And a recent find of my mother's was the complete works of J.R.R. Tolkien, a First Earth fantasy author."

Oh no....oh no...surely not.

"So help me, if you have Tom Bombadil on your chest, I will never speak to you again."

"And of course, I wouldn't want that." She hit him lightly on the shoulder again, and he smiled, almost shy. "It's 'aurë entuluva.'"

She stared at him for a minute. Oh, that wasn't bad at all. "Day shall come again."

His eyebrows rose. "Impressive, Miss Walker."

"Tolkien created at least fifteen languages and dialects, including Quenya, so as a student of linguistics and etymology, I based one of my term papers on him."

His eyes sparkled in the firelight. "As one does."

"I got full marks."

"Well, I would've never given you the time of day if you'd received anything less."

He brushed a stray hair behind her ear. She leaned into his hand. "So only two?"

"Only two. The Elvish is on my upper inner arm." His fingers brushing the line of her jaw. Hallie shivered.

"Why?"

"I needed to do something besides spiral, and a very wise but frustrating scholar once told me I had to learn to keep on living."

"Quite pretty, too, I hear."

"And humble."

Hallie laughed. Kase pulled her even closer, the space between them almost nonexistent. He hooked his finger underneath her chin once more. She could feel the heat of his body, the smell of woodsmoke and leather filling her senses, and she was certain her heart was going to leap from her chest. Unfortunately, her father chose that moment to walk right past, leading her mother to a seat. Her mother glared at Kase. Heat pulsed in her core. Kase relaxed his grip, letting his finger fall and allowing more space than needed to come between them.

Why wouldn't he just kiss her already?

"I'm beginning to think they're doing that on purpose," Kase said dryly.

Her mother took a seat nearby and kept a sharp eye on their dance. Hallie blew out a sigh, turning her back on her mother. "I'm an adult, for stars-sake."

Kase pulled her into the next step, a little loop and spin together. "My mother and yours will get along splendidly, I think. All proper and such."

Hallie shot a glance behind her with the next twirl. Her mother's eyes didn't leave her, though her father tried to pull her into a conversation with Niels, who was pointedly not looking in their direction.

Kase's hand whispered over the curve of her waist. Her mother narrowed her eyes.

Hallie huffed and grumbled under her breath, "We ain't doing nothing wrong."

Kase missed a step and just caught himself. "I'm sorry. Did you just say *ain't?*"

Hallie's face caught fire. She'd worked very hard to hide her accent when she knew she'd be going to the capital. It'd taken her months to mask it enough. "I...well..."

Kase allowed a slow grin to curl across his face. "Normally, such an egregious breach of grammatical etiquette would be cause for ridicule, however, when you say it...well, it's rather attractive, if I do say so myself."

"Hush, you," Hallie managed to grind out even though her face probably rivaled her hair.

"And if I don't, are you going to bless my little heart? I'll let you."

Hallie swatted his shoulder. "That's not even the right context."

Kase just laughed. She willed her face to return to its normal color and cleared her throat. "As I was saying, we *weren't* doing *anything* wrong."

"Sure thing, darlin." Kase's eyes twinkled. He was proud of himself. Blasted man.

"I'm rolling my eyes at you."

"Of course you are." He pulled her closer. "Now, back to what I was saying...define wrong..."

Oh no.

"Kase..."

He glanced right and left, his smile listing more to the side and becoming a smirk. Hallie shook her head. "Whatever you think you're about to—"

He slid one hand into her hair, the other pulling her to him, cutting her off. And then his lips were on hers, no hesitation, no *what-ifs* or teasing. Her eyes fluttered shut as she melted into him, tangling her fingers in the front of his shirt. She'd most definitely get an earful later, but at that moment, she didn't care. She'd missed this so badly, it hurt.

He kissed her as if there hadn't been any before it. His thumb traced lazy circles at the tender spot beneath her ear, each stroke memorizing the skin beneath his featherlight touch. His lips were full of yearning and fear and passion. They were firm and desperate, as if he dared stop, she would simply disappear.

If every kiss was going to be like this, she might forgive him for just about anything. For this one moment, she could actually believe they'd have a future, even if it was a short one.

Someone whistled nearby. Another few followed.

Kase pulled back slowly, his arms still wound around her. She very pointedly did not look in her mother's direction. "That illegal...that be...." She took a breath. "Give me a moment."

"Told you my kisses were good," he whispered in her ear.

Hallie bit her lip. He wasn't wrong, but she refused to give him the satisfaction. Her fumbling words didn't help her case. "That might be against society rules. Just a little."

He gave her a short but sweet kiss that did not last long enough for her liking. His grin said he knew exactly what she was thinking. "You should know by now I never play by the rules."

She went to sleep that night knowing she would give him the world if he asked, and he would give her the stars. They just needed to figure out how to get there first.

C H A P T E R   3 4

TRUST ME

20 Years Ago

HARLAN FOUND A STEADY COMFORT in the old mechanical clock his adoptive mother, Aurelia, had given him. Family lore said the device had been crafted by one of the Shackley ancestors, though the stories disagreed on exactly whom. Whoever it was had been a master craftsman exemplified in the base's design alone. Three roses bloomed in the center, their leaves curling and scrolling outward, upward, and downward. Along the clock's trunk, thorn-cloaked vines crawled toward the clockface, twisting themselves around ionic columns until they kissed atop the twelfth hour.

Aurelia kept careful watch over the clock since she'd discovered it in the Manor's attic a year after she'd married. Over time, its upkeep helped her process the knowledge that she would never bear her own children. She hadn't stopped caring for it when they'd adopted Harlan, and it was her gift to him upon Jove's birth.

Harlan took care of it himself now it was in his new office at the Jayde Center, winding it each day, cleaning it weekly. It was as comforting as caring for his uniform, weapons, or medical equipment on the front. Now that he was in the capital as Brigadier General of the Medical Corps, he'd been deprived of his daily rhythms and found them again in the care of the old longcase clock.

He clung to those rhythms. He'd fall apart without them.

Les was to have their fourth child any day now, and the deep, earthy *tick-tock* echoing off the solid oak housing reminded him that time continued moving no matter how long the world held its breath. His clever wife had adjusted the hour chime to a three-note melody that reminded him of the song they'd danced to at their wedding feast—her idea, not his, but he didn't mind. It helped with the headaches, and the maintenance routine kept his life in order.

Everything was as it should be, yet it was only a matter of time before the house of matchsticks tumbled down.

The orderly had delivered the midday paper and laid it neatly on Harlan's desk a few hours earlier. With a moment to himself to listen to the clock, he allowed a quick reading of the day's most pressing stories.

The quick snapping as he opened it to the front page added a comforting ambiance at the end of a busy day full of meetings and posturing. The small amount of peace the paper supplied was much appreciated.

He had a military dinner to attend that evening. He'd rather go home to his wife and children and work in the Manor's study, but the dinner was to celebrate the anniversary of the Lord Kapitan's ascension. Les was determined to make it, though Harlan was wary. What if she went into labor during dinner? What if the midwife didn't make it in time in the event of a disaster?

What if, what if, what if?

And if he insisted she stay home, he'd get an earful. She knew it was an important dinner and only wanted Harlan to feel comfortable. With each promotion, he gained the ability to change the world for the better, and she insisted she be with him each step of the way. Her determination was one quality he admired most. He'd married the woman he'd needed even if he hadn't realized it upon their first meeting.

Maybe he was being paranoid about the dinner. She

would be fine. If she willed it, then it would happen.

He was only worried because while her last labor with Kase had been the quickest, it'd taken her longer to recover. Harlan wanted to stop having children at that point because of the stress that pregnancy and raising three boys took on her, but Les wanted *just* one more. He'd rarely been able to deny her anything, but it'd only been 18 months since Kase, and Les was nearing forty.

He rustled the newspaper again, and the sweet, dusty aroma soothed the stress of the day. The top story was about how the Cerl Queen made her first public appearance since losing her youngest son in infancy a year ago. Harlan didn't read that one too closely. It would only give way to his own fears.

He moved on to the next. Ezekiel's haggard face stared at him from near the center fold. The years since Rose and the newborn girl's death had carved shadows into his once full cheeks. The portrait was one of the only ones included in the paper due to the more labor-intensive process it took to recreate it. His brother-in-law's work with electricity and Zuprium might help in that regard, but it would be a while yet. His advancements were better suited to military uses at present.

The accompanying article detailed that Lord Ezekiel Fairchild, inventor and engineer, would be part of a diplomatic mission to Sol Adrid, the capital of Cerulene within the next few weeks to sign a trade negotiation. What the papers didn't detail was that Ezekiel had been working with the Cerl Engineering Corps for the last five years trying to ascertain their capabilities—all with a mask of civility and working for a better future.

It'd been the Lord Kapitan's idea—not Harlan's, though he was proud of Ezekiel's accomplishments. With electropistols now in mass production, a tentative peace grew between the nations of Yalvara. Jayde had the strength of advanced technology to keep their enemies in check.

It was the Yalvs who were giving them trouble—something about the misuse of Zuprium, but what they didn't realize was that Jayde's burgeoning military prowess was the only check against Cerulene. If Jayde didn't stand in their way, all Yalvara would resemble the ruins of Ravenhelm. The Yalvs—those that were left on this side of the world—would understand that in due time. They would feel the Cerl wrath unchecked. Only a few pockets of the Yalvs still lived in Cerulene.

Ezekiel's technology was indeed saving men on the front—misuse of Zuprium or not. Harlan just wished the friend he'd known over eleven years ago could've enjoyed the fruits of his accomplishments. Instead, he stayed buried in his work, his sons being his only assistants when they were not in school. The Fairchilds visited Shackley Manor for the odd dinner about every month or so. That was Les' doing, and their nephews, Sullivan and Randall, were teaching Jove to play cricket.

Harlan only allowed it because he'd been too busy to play groggon with his son the last few months. Temporary, he hoped. He also hoped Jove took more to his sport rather than his nephews', but that was only for selfish reasons.

Ezekiel merely sat eating silently at the dinner table, making a few remarks when questioned directly. Harlan wished he could do something, but he was powerless to the grief his friend knew intimately.

Grief was personal.

Sometimes it looked like buying too many dining room chairs after losing your husband of nearly 70 years like the woman in the manor down the street. Others, it was dozens of brown glass liquor bottles to numb the pain—deep, drowning, and desperate. With Ezekiel, it was pouring any life he had left into improving the world for others at his own expense.

For Harlan, it was in trying to forget the mountains he'd come from. It was in keeping Cerulene from hurting anyone else he loved again—no matter the cost. It was in the care of an old clock.

And Les. She was one of the few people who kept him from the darker side of himself.

He finished the article, which hadn't said much other than what was on the surface and was setting it aside when a terse knock came from his door.

He bit back a sigh. He'd been about to leave.

He had a distinct feeling it was a missive from the Kominder General about the supply budget argument they'd had in the midday meeting. Harlan had been right, and the Kominder General would realize they needed more money allotted to medical personnel soon.

The orderly opened the door a crack, making sure Harlan was available, before widening the gap further. He saluted. "Lord Fairchild here to see you, Brigadier General." The young man's obsidian eyes flicked toward the corridor behind him. "Said it's urgent, Sir."

A twinge of annoyance nipped at his emotions, but someone as familiar with military protocol as Ezekiel wouldn't do something as outrageous as demand to see someone as senior as Harlan without an appointment unless...unless...

Oh shocks. Les.

Harlan shoved back from his chair and leapt to his feet, a knee-jerk reaction, before straining to slow his galloping heart. The orderly recoiled with the sudden movement, his hand going to the sword at his waist.

Good instincts.

Harlan gripped the edge of the desk and willed himself to calm down. If something had happened to his wife, someone would've immediately sent word from the Manor or faced his wrath. They wouldn't have sent his brother-in-law. Ezekiel was hardly one to relay time-sensitive information these days. Randall and Sullivan were graduating from upper school soon, but the only reason Harlan was aware of the date and time was because of Les' contact with the headmaster.

"I apologize, Private Grantham." Harlan smoothed his mustache and found his seat once more. "Did Lord Fairchild give the reason for his visit?"

"No, Sir."

If it *had* been an issue with Les, he would've said so. Harlan cleared his throat. "Send him in, please, and ensure my motorcoach is ready. I'll be leaving shortly."

It would take several minutes to relay the request and crank the Yalvar fuel engine.

With another salute, Private Grantham left and moments later, the door opened once more.

Ezekiel Fairchild looked little different than the portrait in the papers. The ridges and valleys in his face were there, though more pronounced. Along with a gas lantern chandelier casting a soft glow upon the office, the golden sunlight of an early March sunset yawned across the mahogany desk and reflected off the clock face. It deepened the sadness in his brother-in-law's face.

The mostly gray curls hanging around Ezekiel's face were almost molten in the office light. It aged him nearly twenty years. His eyes had not dimmed, though they no longer lit with laughter.

Harlan rose and gestured to the leather seat in front of his desk. Ezekiel fell into the chair, but then straightened, perched on the edge. Elbows resting on his knees, his hands hung between them like the blooms of a bleeding heart. It'd been over a decade, but it still took Harlan back when Ezekiel didn't smile or make a quip at Harlan's stiff gestures and solemn demeanor.

"Good to see you," Harlan ventured, tapping a few fingers on his desk. It was free of clutter. The reassignments and memos he'd need to respond to tomorrow lay beneath a simple Zuprium paperweight engraved with the Jaydian emblem. Nothing else decorated his desk. Too much visual distraction would lead to lost details and focus. In his office, the only indulgence he allowed himself was the clock.

Ezekiel pressed his lips together and his fingers into the armrest until both were white. "I've come because..." His eyes flicked to the window, to the opposite corner, and the door before resting on Harlan. "I've needed to...I think..."

Harlan just waited. The *tick-tock* of the clock filled the silence. His chest was empty in such a way that it ached. A soft and subtle tingle like the zing of electricity under his skin started in his left small finger. The stirrings of a headache.

He tried to focus on the ticking of the clock. He wouldn't be able to make a poultice until he returned to the Manor. The herbal mix inside would help quell the worst pain, and he needed to be present that evening at the dinner. He prayed it was a manageable migraine.

Ezekiel rubbed a hand down his face. "I...I've discovered something, and I'm not sure how to..."

Even the way he spoke had changed. Instead of a steady, gentle fire, it'd become the lingering rain after a storm, sputtering and unstable.

"Your work?" Harlan prompted.

"I know how to save them."

Ezekiel didn't look at Harlan, only at his knotted fingers. Harlan blinked. "Save who?"

His brother-in-law and friend opened his mouth and closed it again, as if the words had withered on his tongue. Harlan pressed his nails into the desk until they hurt. The tingling like needles in a pincushion spread from his finger into his hand.

"Speak plainly, Ezekiel," Harlan said firmly. "What are you on about?"

The man fumbled with the neckline of his wrinkled collared shirt as if searching for something only to find it missing.

"Rose." Ezekiel's voice was hoarse. "Emilia. Asa."

It was Harlan's turn to be silent. What did he mean? Rose and the newborn girl, Emilia, had been Burned over a decade ago. There was no saving them. The tingling made it to Harlan's wrist.

He didn't know the third.

"What do you mean? Who is Asa?"

Ezekiel opened his mouth to respond, but nothing came out. He fidgeted and cleared his throat. His eyes swept the room again as if to assess if they had an audience.

"I...I had another...son, but he...didn't..."

Harlan could only stare at the man. It was like the words didn't quite make sense. Another son?

"Ezekiel, what do you mean?"

His brother-in-law didn't answer.

The tingling edged its way toward Harlan's elbow. Son. Another son. Asa. Who was the mother? Certainly not Rose. It wasn't possible that Ezekiel could've hidden another child for over a decade. He'd never seemed the type to take a mistress, though Harlan guessed it wasn't out of the realm of possibility. He just hadn't thought Ezekiel able to set aside his grief long enough to—

Oh shocks.

Harlan's eyes flicked to the newspaper he'd set down when his friend had entered the room. Ezekiel's haggard face stared into his soul. Right beneath the article about the Cerl Queen, her mourning period complete.

The consequences. The ramifications.

His heart hammered in his chest.

If it was true, it could very well be the spark that started the war waiting in the wings, the one Harlan had been working hard to prevent.

The gravity of that truth might just send the world into chaos. An emissary and spy having an affair with the enemy Queen? Surely, his brother-in-law hadn't been so careless. Surely, the man in front of him wouldn't have risked everything Harlan had stood for, that Jayde stood for.

"For the love of the stars, Ezekiel, if you have—"

The door slammed against the wall, rattling the clock. Harlan leapt to his feet, his hand ripping open the drawer where his flashpistol lay. The Cerls. They were here. They knew.

But instead of an attack, the orderly sprinted inside, his eyes wide.

"Apologies for the interruption." Private Grantham panted, parchment crumpled in his hand. "Your wife, Brigadier General. Lady Celeste. Water broke. Refusing to go to the Guild."

Harlan's headache flared. He squeezed his eyes shut and willed the pain to wait. He shut the weapons drawer.

Ezekiel could wait.

Harlan could only handle one crisis at a time.

"Is my motorcoach—" Harlan started, but the man interrupted.

"In the front drive, Sir."

"Thank you." Harlan walked briskly to the door and grabbed his hat. "Come with me, Ezekiel."

He nodded to the orderly. "Send my regrets to the Lord Kapitan."

Fear raced through Harlan's veins as he and his brother-in-law sped through the corridors and down the front staircase. Harlan saluted the men and women he passed, but he didn't take the time to do more than that. He couldn't.

Why Les would refuse to go to the Medic Guild, he didn't know, but he wasn't surprised. Last time, they hadn't allowed her to bring her books. She was probably being petty even if her medic had recommended going when the time came because of her age.

Stubborn woman. He loved her anyway.

And soon, he would be a father of four. A spark of hope threaded through the fear of loss—for his wife, his children, and Ezekiel.

THE LABOR LASTED HOURS, TOO long for a fourth birth.

Les was weak. Harlan was haggard, and yet, the baby had yet to arrive. All of Harlan's medical knowledge was useless. He'd researched many complications after Rose's death, but all he could remember in the time he held his wife through the pain was that Rose died.

They shouldn't have had another child. They had three strong, healthy boys. Ezekiel had gone to help the nanny attend to them. He wouldn't be much help in his state, but Harlan couldn't worry about his brother-in-law, not when the life leaked out of his wife.

Was this how Ezekiel felt? Helpless? Les was too pale. Her pulse was too weak.

Was there anything he could do to prevent the worst from happening? Would saving her mean sacrificing the babe she carried? Would Harlan do that? Would he wish that? If it would save his wife?

"One more push, my lady!" The midwife encouraged, her voice sounding ragged after hours of trying everything she could to help the labor progress.

Les whimpered, and Harlan smoothed her hair from her forehead and kissed the top of her head. "You can do this. It's almost done."

She squeezed his hand weakly as she cried out, pushing with all the strength she had left. Harlan never let her go.

"She's here! It's a girl!" the midwife cried. "She's..."

Harlan didn't hear the cry of life. All he heard was the midwife slapping the baby's skin.

Les' breathing was shallow. Harlan pushed himself up, his arm still around his wife. "Midwife?"

The woman's face was haggard and pale at the end of the bed. She met his eyes, panic clear in her gaze. "Brigadier General..."

Stars, no.

Had he wished it true? Had his thoughts about saving his wife over the baby made this happen? White hot fear and anger flooded his veins.

"Harlan?" Les asked, her voice barely above a whisper. "Where is...where is...she? Why can't I hear her?"

In that moment, the battlefield calm fell over him. He was no longer a husband and father. He was a medic on the front with soldiers who needed saving.

He pushed himself off the bed and went to the midwife. The baby girl in her arms was still wet and glistening, the birthing waters coating her blue skin. The woman tried to position the baby for better airway access. The baby wasn't moving or reacting to anything the woman did.

No.

Harlan took the girl from the midwife and ordered, "Fetch Lord Fairchild and warm blankets now!"

He needed his medic partner, and the baby needed warmth. There had to be a solution.

The midwife ran from the room, and Harlan didn't have enough knowledge of how to help a baby, but he looked toward his wife, whose blue eyes were wide with terror despite the exhaustion in the lines of her face. He placed the baby on her chest, grabbing whatever blankets he could find and bundling them both.

Les couldn't stop her tears as she clung to the girl. Neither could Harlan, though he was only vaguely aware of them cascading down his cheeks.

The baby's pulse. He couldn't feel it.

Her skin was too cold.

He could only feel his panic.

He couldn't lose someone else. His heart could not take it. He...he...

The door to the chamber burst open. The midwife sprinted in with more blankets. Ezekiel flew in behind her, his eyes and hair wild.

"The babe..." Harlan managed to get out.

His brother-in-law searched the room, his head whipping right and left. "Your locket, Lessie. Where is your locket? The one I gave you?"

Les was crying too hard to answer. Harlan tugged it over her head and handed it to Ezekiel. His friend pulled a pocketknife from his pocket.

Harlan paused, rubbing the girl's back as Ezekiel pressed the open knife to his finger and bled onto the locket in his hand.

"I need the baby's blood," Ezekiel commanded.

Harlan stopped him, pushing him away from his stillborn baby and his wife. "What are you doing?"

Ezekiel's eyes were filled with rage and anguish. "I can fix this."

Harlan still didn't move. Les cried harder.

Ezekiel growled. "Move or it will be too late." His blood coated the woodland scene and phoenix on the cover, making the Zuprium feathers turn red, noticeable even in the dim gas lantern light. "Just trust me, *please.*"

So, Harlan moved.

Despite all his medical expertise, the chaos of the moment, and the knowledge that Ezekiel was no longer the man he'd known, he still had a shred of stars-blasted, impossible hope.

Les held the baby tighter, her tears falling to the baby's skin. Ezekiel moved closer, taking the small, shriveled girl's foot, pressing the knife's blade to her heel. The girl didn't stir.

The midwife tried to intervene, but Harlan shook his head, watching as blood bubbled forth at last. Ezekiel smeared it onto the locket and clasped the necklace in his fist. He squeezed it so hard, his knuckles turned white. He panted as if the little blood leaving his body carried too much weight.

Opening his fist, the locket gave off a glow. A blue glow. Harlan could only stare, his mouth dropping open.

The gas lantern light was gold. The Zuprium was bronze. But the glow was distinctly blue, as blue as Les' eyes.

"Ezekiel, what..." but Harlan couldn't say more than that.

Ezekiel pressed the locket to the baby's silent heart. Her skin matched the glow. It bathed Les' wet, anguished face.

No one moved.

Harlan lost count of the heartbeats, but it wasn't until several minutes later that the glow abated, fading with the night and the silence.

The girl cried.

Ezekiel pulled his hand back. Les gasped, her sobs mixed with those of her now living daughter.

Ice as cold as a Narden winter inundated Harlan's veins. The baby was dead. Stillborn. More than likely from the prolonged labor. They couldn't predict complications during the birth itself—not like they were able to on First Earth.

What had Ezekiel done?

He met his friend's melancholy gaze. "What did—how did you—"

He couldn't even begin to understand what had happened, much less organize his own thoughts. Too much was happening at once, too much he didn't comprehend.

What Ezekiel had done was nothing short of a miracle.

It felt unnatural.

His brother-in-law had somehow brought back the dead.

"I know how to save them," Ezekiel whispered. "And it's too late."

Harlan stumbled over to Les and hugged them both. The baby was alive. Her skin's blueish tint had bled into red with each new cry.

He looked back at Ezekiel, "What did you do?"

Ezekiel walked toward the door, pausing just before he left. "What needed to be done."

"What is the cost?" Harlan choked over the emotions flooding his chest.

Ezekiel opened the door and looked back, his eyes once again shadowed and hollow at once. "The cost is worth it in the end."

And then he left Harlan with a deep sense of dread in his bones.

C H A P T E R   3 5

NEVER CHANGE

Kase

AFTER THE FIRE, KASE HAD given up smokes. He'd only started because he knew his father would hate it. But now, cigarettes only made him think of the fire that killed his sister and countless others. Quitting had been easy.

But every once in a while, the itch came back, the tingling in his fingertips that begged for release.

The tunnel wall scraped his shirt as he leaned against it, arms crossed. He'd found his way back to the scene where he'd played Hanged Man's Nebula. Sergeant had advised against it, but Kase didn't care. He had business with his old friends. His fingers twitched involuntarily. A quick puff or two would've smoothed away his anxiety.

Sergeant had followed him anyway, even if he'd disagreed. He'd probably make good back-up. Maybe having him watch his every move could be a blessing, not a bother.

Or a little bit of both, at least.

Sergeant hadn't interfered with his patrols yet, even if

Kase flew a little longer than necessary. He'd also been unsuccessful in convincing the other pilots to join him, and he hadn't had the courage to face or ask Laurence Hixon, the greenie Kase had dueled in the induction ritual months ago.

Well, there was a reason the others hadn't been called in when the Cerls attacked.

Kase needed to hurry with this little rendezvous, because he had things to do. Things like finding Hallie and seeing if she could beg off whatever she was doing for a few hours. He thought she'd said something about training with Saldr, but Kase hadn't been paying too much attention. He'd been too distracted by her lips.

Oh, and he also had a few patrols scheduled. Those were important.

But he had a purpose for being in this part of the Catacombs. Kase squatted next to an older gentleman wearing clothes that had seen better days. "The men who like to play Nebula over here. Have you seen them?"

"Not since two nights past." The man was missing a few teeth. He gestured to a few other fellow refugees. "Didn't like them much."

"Why?"

The man scratched his red-bearded chin. "There's two type of men who play the Nebula—the desperate and the idle. Most of us fit into the first. Those ones fit into the second."

Kase stood again. He looked back at his shadow. Sergeant inspected the surroundings and people, scanning for trouble with a hand on the sword at his waist. He was listening, but he didn't want to show it.

Kase chewed on the edge of his lip and made up his mind. "I think the men are part of One World. What have you heard of them?"

The old man coughed hard, his lung wheezing with each inhale. After he calmed down, he gave Kase a steely look. "Listened to some of them afore, and I would've agreed, but after they went ahead and betrayed us with those blasted Cerls..." He looked at a few of his fellow refugees, some which were leaning in. "It's probably best those boys never show their face in these parts again."

Well, at least Kase could agree with him on that. Still didn't help him find Eravin. He held out his hand for the man to shake. "Best of luck to you, then."

The man's equally shaggy eyebrows rose into his mussed hair, but he shook his hand. Kase bowed as he continued down another tunnel.

He asked around until his feet hurt. He couldn't check his pocket watch to see just how much time had passed, because he still hadn't bothered to find himself a new one, but he knew Hallie would be expecting him soon, and he wanted to clean up a little before he saw her next.

Picking up his pace, he turned down a new tunnel, losing count of just how many he'd traversed. The only difference between them all was the state of the refugees. The closer one got to the central cavern, the less bedraggled the refugees' clothing became—only because they'd started out looking much finer, though Kase was certain he'd spotted a lower-city councilman still donning his sleeping clothes.

Stopping a few times, he asked about Eravin and the others, but no one seemed to know who he was talking about. A few had spit when Kase mentioned his name rather than his description, though. Seemed as if Eravin's little stint with One World had backfired. Too late to save Kyvena, of course. He did wonder if the capital would've still fallen if One World hadn't taken root there.

If the people had known of the destruction to come, would they still have taken to the streets, protesting the Stradat Lord Kapitan and chanting for his death?

And Kase's.

Only one person gave him anything to work with, though she narrowed her eyes at his approach. Kase swallowed his exhaustion and uneasiness.

"Good morning," Kase greeted, giving her a tentative smile. The only indication she heard him was the subtle raise of her brow. "I'm looking for someone. Early twenties, close-cropped black hair, goes by Eravin. You seen him?"

The woman stared at him, eyes narrowing once more before she finally nodded. "Last night."

"Where?"

She pointed in the direction of the Stradat Lord Kapitan's tent. "Saw him sneaking round the central cavern while I was fetching rations. Listened to him preach a pretty sermon a few months back, but I didn't take the bait."

Kase started to thank her, but she interrupted him. "You

look mighty familiar yourself. What did you say your name was?"

She noticed his guard for the first time and tilted her head. He shook his. "Thank you for your time—"

She grabbed his wrist. "You're that Shackley boy. The one that burned the city, aren't you?"

He met her eyes and tried not to wrench his hand back. He didn't think she would punch him or curse him because her gaze wasn't filled with hate. That didn't mean she couldn't do anything or call on someone who would.

But he was done running. He'd gone through the caves and fought his way back to Kyvena to answer for his crimes—he'd been ready to take responsibility. He hadn't known he'd come back to find the city razed.

Besides, the world might be ending. What worse could this woman do if he answered the question truthfully?

Be honest, Hallie's voice said in his head.

Of course his subconscious now spoke with her voice. She'd be proud.

Kase placed his other hand over the woman's. "Yes. I can't even begin to tell you just how sorry…"

He clenched his jaw to prevent the emotion from leaking out as he trailed off. Kase tried to find his words again, but the woman shook her head before releasing him. "I'm praying for you, Master Shackley."

Well, that wasn't what he'd expected.

Kase swallowed, nodded, and turned back down the tunnel. He couldn't find any response to that.

He still didn't know what he believed in, and after the last few months, he wasn't sure what was real and what wasn't. His reality had been turned completely on its head. He blinked a few times as he wove between men and women who weren't Eravin. Maybe when he had time, he could ruminate more on the subject. Not that he knew when that would be, if ever.

Funny how time never did seem to be on his side, no matter how much he wished it would be.

"Pilot Shackley," Sergeant said, dismissing a runner who had just delivered a missive. He read the short note and handed it to Kase.

The parchment had been ripped from some other document, covered in print on the back that made no sense out of context. The writing on the front was firm, almost too neat.

You will report to the Command Tent at 1200 hours.

Kase recognized the Stradat Lord Kapitan's handwriting, but couldn't ascertain the motivation behind the summons. Maybe he wanted a report on his progress with the greenies? That wouldn't be a pleasant conversation. He'd been sending him daily scouting patrol reports through Sergeant. Maybe it was about those?

He'd kept the hover invisible on his recent patrols to escape attention, but he'd spied Skibs circling the city on his dragon more than once, including one incident where he'd been near the Jayde Center, inspecting the ruins. Kase had fired a few shots to warn him off, missing on purpose. He hadn't included *that* in his report.

Skibs was clearly searching for something, but Kase didn't know what. If it was the Catacombs, he could've inspected the gaping holes in the landscape created by bombs and cave-ins.

Whatever it was had to be important, and maybe he would lead them right to it. Then Kase could use it as leverage.

Maybe not the best plan, but as long as Skibs didn't threaten those hiding below, Kase would give him the chance to reveal his hand.

He eyed Sergeant and held up the paper, asking the unspoken question. Sergeant merely shrugged, indicating he knew nothing of what awaited Kase in roughly two hours. Of course.

Kase stuffed the parchment in his pocket and made to go further down the tunnel. Just when he thought he'd reached an understanding with his guard, he became the Stradat Lord Kapitan's pawn once more.

"Shackley! It's him!"

Kase whipped his head around to find a man pointing an arthritic finger at him. Others followed the man's finger and locked eyes with Kase.

Blast.

The crowd grew, pushing him to the side. The wall of bodies nearly swallowed him. Some screamed. He didn't have a pistol. He didn't have anything besides the missive with which to defend himself if someone sought to harm him, and a papercut wasn't going to scare anyone off.

"Back up!" Sergeant yelled. Kase caught sight of the man waving his sword about. Several people screamed. Another few stumbled away, tripping on others or refuse. "He is under the Stradat Lord Kapitan's protection, and any harm brought to him will be punished by the highest extent of Jaydian law."

A few shouted back something rather crude about nepotism. Kase felt the heat on his neck. They weren't wrong. Kase tried to speak, but Sergeant beat him to the punch.

"Pilot Kase Shackley is the only reason you lot aren't dead right now." Sergeant pointed his sword at one of the loudest offenders. "Don't give the Cerls the satisfaction of dividing us."

Kase swallowed. He hadn't expected such a defense from the man forced to guard him. Maybe he shouldn't be so hard on him.

Though a few onlookers looked like they had more to say, they clearly didn't like their odds. They might have had the numbers, but they were untrained and unwilling to test the Stradat Lord Kapitan's wrath, even if they didn't respect him as they once did.

"Thanks," Kase muttered as Sergeant returned to his side, sheathing his sword.

The guard only grunted. Back to holding a grudge about his assignment, then.

Kase dusted his shirt off. Better he just go back to his tent—obviously Eravin had run off somewhere, and he was risking too much trying to find him. He'd lost all his courage in the years since their split. The thought hurt Kase a little. He hadn't realized just how much he'd missed his friend until he'd blackmailed Kase. Ironic.

What was it about the people Kase befriended? Eravin had joined up with One World. Ben was working with the Cerls. Both had betrayed their people and everything they'd stood for. Was it Kase? Was he the problem? He was the common denominator.

Kase ran his tongue along his teeth as he strode down the corridor, ignoring the stares of those still dispersing. Hopefully his bad luck was up, and the same thing wouldn't happen to Hallie.

If he hurried, he could go fetch some rations and take them to Saldr's tent. She should be there training still. Maybe they could find a little privacy and continue what they'd started the previous night. Wouldn't leave them long if he had to be at the Stradat Lord Kapitan's tent at noon, but it was better than nothing.

"Heard you been asking 'round about me, Shackley."

Kase paused, and Sergeant's hand went back to his sword.

The tunnel he'd just entered was rather sparsely populated, a shortcut back to his tent. The only gas lantern hung at the end of it and offered shadows for those wishing to remain unidentified. Kase glanced at where the voice had come from. A man with a fisherman's cap tucked down over his forehead leaned against the wall. The man had a cigarette hanging from his lips, the smoldering tip casting a faint glow on the man's familiar features. His bottom lip sported a scab, as if it had been recently busted.

"Eravin."

Eravin took a puff and blew out, the smoke lazily snaking toward the ceiling. He pushed off the wall and nodded to a few women passing by the other way.

"So," he said casually, "have they decided if you're a traitor or not?"

Kase couldn't help the frustrated groan that escaped his lips. "Says the man who sold out his country to One World!"

Eravin gave a soft chuckle. "Really, that's the best you have?" He threw the cigarette down and ground it under the toe of his worn boot. "The High Council was corrupt, something I'm sure you'd agree with."

"Heddie Koppen isn't corrupt."

"Wasn't." Eravin stepped closer. "Heard she didn't make it out of the Jayde Center in time."

He'd already known, but the words were still like a punch in the gut. He'd liked the High Guardswoman, even if he hadn't spent too much time with her. Kase narrowed his eyes. "Your doing."

Eravin raised a brow. "Maybe, but like I said when we struck that truce, it wasn't part of my plan."

"Right." Kase rolled his eyes. "As if blackmailing people for state secrets wouldn't cause the government to collapse."

"Welcome to reality, Shackley." Eravin laughed mirthlessly. He glanced to the side where a pair of off-duty soldiers passed by. Sergeant nodded to them. "I'm doing my best to save our country. You have the audacity to fly a Cerl machine and call *me* the traitor?"

"If you would've let me explain, you would know I stole it and figured out how to use it against them."

"You've always been a good liar."

Kase balled his right hand into a fist. Despite the delivery, he tried to take that as a sort of twisted compliment. "That's not what I came to discuss."

Eravin stepped back and spread his arms to the dark tunnel. "And pray, what did you come to discuss? Come to thank me?"

"Stay away from Hallie."

Eravin's sardonic smile faltered. Lowering his arms, he furrowed his brow. "Hallie?"

"Don't play stupid."

"Well, seeing as I'm not..." He put his hands in his pockets and rocked back on his heels. "I'm just not sure why I would need to stay away from her, considering I haven't done anything to warrant such a directive."

"You're being a stars-blasted dulkop. Waylan and Neville, too."

"You never change."

Kase ignored the jab, though he eyed Sergeant standing a few feet away, his face half in shadow. Would he intervene if Kase decked Eravin? "Telling her about the card game was low. Even for you."

"How do you know it was me?"

Kase rolled his eyes. "I know your style."

"Telling the truth? You caught me."

"It was my story to tell, not yours."

Eravin ran a hand down his day-old stubble, rubbing his chin and going quiet when a group of women and a few children passed, their chatter echoing off the tunnel walls. "Why do you care so much? It's still difficult for me to believe you'd care so much about a girl so far below your station."

"Shut up."

"Surely, your father wouldn't approve. She's not much better than gutter scum. No money. No connections. Though I have to agree with Waylan...she *is* rather pretty." The corner of Eravin's mouth quirked up. His eyes caught on Kase's cheek. "Is that why you're sporting that new scar? Your father found out about your latest rebellion? Looks like Harlan's gotten sloppy."

For the third time in a week, Kase's rage boiled over, but instead of using his fists, he grabbed the front of Eravin's shirt and shoved him against the wall, his face so close, their noses nearly met. He wasn't certain Hallie would approve, but he would not back down. He would fight for her.

Sergeant moved closer as Kase shook his old friend. "Leave her out of this. That's all I came to say."

"Is that really all, or is there something else about her you aren't saying?"

Kase shoved him away. "Touch her, and you will regret it."

Eravin straightened his clothes and dusted off his shoulders. "Regret it? You must know that whenever I deal out, I'm never caught."

"I know you better than you know yourself. I'll catch you."

The other man chuckled darkly. "Doubt that."

And then he vanished as quickly as he had appeared.

His head spun, trying to unravel Eravin's shrewd smirk and double-meanings. Did Eravin know about Hallie being the Essence? Was that what he'd meant? Kase had been forced to tell the Stradat Lord Kapitan, but he refused to betray her trust like that again. It was only in the name of saving the country that he'd done it the first time. Still made him feel terrible.

He rubbed a hand down his face. Before he could come back to his senses enough to head for the more populated corridor, a voice echoed behind him: "Hey, Kase!"

Freezing, he looked to Sergeant, who wasn't reaching for his weapons. Friendly then. Besides, Eravin wouldn't call him by his given name.

The voice was one he recognized but had been avoiding for obvious reasons. He wasn't sure his anger from the encounter with Eravin had burned off, and he did not want to have it out with Niels there in the corridor.

He acted as if he hadn't heard his name and moved down the hallway instead, but a hand on his shoulder stopped him. Kase shrugged it off but turned. "May I help you, Mr. Metzinger?"

He'd accepted Hallie's explanation and had truly understood her need for closure, but that didn't mean Kase had to be friends with the guy. Niels stopped short. "Can we talk?"

Eyes narrowed, Kase shoved his hands into his pockets. It would keep him from lashing out, he hoped. Niels nodded toward one of the nearby cavern rooms. "In there?"

Kase shook his head. "No, I'd rather not."

A group of refugees shuffled by, giving them strange looks. Kase ignored them.

Once they'd passed, Niels said, "Listen, I just came to say—"

"That you'll stop messing with her head? I know about the kiss, and I should clock you for it." Kase clenched his teeth, nostrils flaring. "But I promised her I wouldn't, so you should be thanking her on bended knee you aren't back in that ward."

Niels threw up his hands. "Look, I was wrong. I shouldn't have done it. I was just acting on instinct, and I misread everything, I'll admit it. But that's not what I wanted to talk to you about."

Kase opened and closed his mouth, the wind dying in his sails. "Oh."

The other man held out his right wrist and plucked at a braided cord there. "I just wanted to thank you for the blanket. One of the nurses, Petra, helped me braid it into this cord so it'd be easier to lug around."

The bracelet sparkled softly in the dim cavern lighting. The tell-tale blue was only just discernible. Kase had to admit it was a good idea—one he wished he'd thought of earlier.

Niels continued, "So thank you for your help...I didn't expect any from you, especially with...well, me and Hal." He played with the braided cord. "And I heard...well, I overheard your conversation with that skeleton-looking fella. You did the right thing."

The use of his nickname for her grated on Kase's nerves, but he took a few deep breaths before remembering Stowe's words. "Thought you believed I was arrogant."

Niels' neck turned pink, and he rubbed it again. "That was before I knew what you'd done for her." He blew out a breath. "Just...thank you. I wouldn't be here without you...and..." Hesitantly, he stuck out his hand. "I'm grateful Hal's in good hands."

Kase chewed on the inside of his cheek. If anything, Kase

was in good hands with Hallie, but he accepted the handshake anyway. "Thanks."

And with a nod, Niels was off back down the tunnel, and Kase was left again with only his thoughts and Sergeant's watchful gaze.

C H A P T E R   3 6

A THOUSAND DEATHS

Hallie

SWEAT DRIPPED DOWN HALLIE'S FACE as she smudged the Vasa on her fingers.

Her core warmed as she concentrated harder, ignoring Saldr's narrowed eyes. The good news was that her power had begun to fill her once more. It made her feel calmer and anxious all at once.

The bad news: her own eyes stung from lack of sleep. Even though she and Kase had come to an agreement, she couldn't just let go of her feelings altogether. She needed time to work through them, and that had caused some tossing and turning. Still, she knew she'd get there. She couldn't imagine a life without their conversations, their banter, his sense of humor, and...well...and his lips.

"Yrea."

The dust on her fingers flared to life for one millisecond before sputtering out.

She cursed.

"You seem to be distracted, Miss Walker," Saldr said,

holding out the dust pouch again. "Though my tree thanks you for the control you have gained."

The tree above her was alive, no traces of trauma from the previous day. Saldr must've given in and allowed the use of Vasa to heal it.

Hallie grudgingly slipped her fingers in and pulled out another small pinch of the fine powder. She rubbed them together. "Yrea."

In her mind, she could see the flame, the fire, the heat in her core. She tugged at it and teased it past the barrier of her skin and out through her coated fingers.

Warmth danced at the edges and caught fire, but as soon as it happened, it went dark once more.

She wanted to scream, to hit something. But she couldn't. If she truly lost her temper, she might bring the entire city on their heads. Saldr's poor tree had been inconsequential compared to what she could possibly do. What she'd done before.

"Keep trying. You've made much progress in only one day," Saldr coaxed. "This is the first step to resetting the Gates. We cannot move forward until you master this. Were you observing the others last night like I suggested?"

Of course she had. She'd seen the spell performed dozens of times the night before. But she'd been distracted by her argument with Kase, and then their conversation, and then the dance, and that kiss...

She cursed as the light that had begun to radiate from her fingers went out as if doused with water.

"Don't I have a choice?" she asked, suddenly desperate. "What happens if I say no?"

Fely and Saldr looked at one another. It was the look you gave someone when there was something you didn't want to discuss, because it would only lead to something the other wouldn't like—something bad.

Hallie met Saldr's gaze. "What happens if I reset the Gate? What happens to me? To you? To Jayde?"

To Kase? She didn't say that last one aloud.

Fely left, and she didn't look at Hallie. She knew. She knew, and she didn't want to be the one to tell Hallie...or see her face when she found out the truth.

That hurt. Hallie had thought they'd started to form a friendship of sorts, especially after finding out she'd been working against Cerulene the entire time, but it seemed Hallie was wrong.

Saldr flickered the same way he had when the Cerls had attacked Myrrai last winter.

"Tell me, Saldr," Hallie said firmly.

He flickered again. "It is complicated, Miss Walker."

It was bad, then. Sinister, even. Something she wouldn't agree to if she knew the truth. According to Saldr, the only way to stop Jagamot and the inky black darkness that oozed out the holes in the ground at a growing pace was to do one thing—use her power to reset the Gate. Hallie had to assume that meant rewinding time to some point before, a point in the past where they could better prepare for Jagamot. It was meant to help them all.

But if all it took to defeat them was to combine the Essence powers into the swords, why didn't they just do that now? It was a surefire victory, and it didn't run the risk of failing in multiple ways.

"Saldr..."

He sighed and sat heavily on one of the stones, his knees bent to his chest, his head in his hands. "It is complicated, Miss Walker, because even I know not what will happen. Playing with time is dangerous, and without the Lord Elder's guidance, we are wandering through the dark. I only know what the goal was, not how it was to be accomplished."

"But if I reset time, does that mean we'll go back to the beginning of Yalvara? That the other peoples here might cease to exist? Time resetting would mean our ancestors have the opportunity to make different choices."

"Which is why it is complicated."

"But why go back to the beginning of the planet? Couldn't I choose a more recent point?"

As soon as she thought it, the plan seemed too good to be true. If she could reset time only about four years, she could save her brother. She could say no to the *Eudora* mission.

Her heart raced, thinking of the possibilities. She could save the Lord Elder and never have to take on this power at all.

Her fingertips tingled with heat.

But would that mean she'd never find Kase? Would that leave her stranded in Stoneset? She wouldn't know any differently, would she? Would she remember anything about the life she'd lived before?

Kase.

Saldr pressed his fingers together and tapped his chin. "Possible, yes, but still just as complicated." He met her eyes at last. "Truly, neither way of defeating Jagamot is easy."

"And combining the Essence powers?"

Saldr was silent.

Why had the Lord Elder been bent on resetting the Gate when the answer was right before them?

Hallie would gladly give up her power. She didn't even need the encouragement to save the world. She'd do it for free.

Then it hit her. It hit her so hard, she lost her breath. Her chest squeezed. Her heart drummed in her ears. Her eyesight narrowed to a single point, a red clover just beneath her boots.

No. How had she missed that part? How had she not put it together sooner?

"I'd die," she said slowly. "Filip didn't die from the fall or the sword wound. He..." Hallie's voice grew small as she'd finally realized what it all meant. "He died because ripping away the Essence power leads to the loss of your soul."

Anderson still hadn't awoken, despite Fely giving him fire soul and Kase's blanket. He'd had only a sliver of the Essence power. Hallie had the full power, as had King Filip. Fely was merely the vessel. She didn't actually hold the Essence power.

Hallie's stomach swirled sickeningly as she pieced together the rest. "And if I reset the Gate, we know how this would all end. We could combine all the first Essences, or even stop the Shattering of Toro in the Dawn..."

Saldr breathed deeply in and out. He no longer flickered. "And it means you and the others have the chance at life."

"Except that's not a guarantee."

Saldr nodded. "Correct, but it allows us to find the best way to save the most people. Combining the Essences into the swords will end Jagamot, but it could also destroy all Yalvara. The prophecies are inconclusive."

"So it's an impossible choice."

"Yes."

Too simple and quiet a word for the way it broke Hallie. It echoed in her head. It took up all the space she had left until she could no longer concentrate on anything else.

A buzzing started in her head, and she knew that if she stayed there any longer, she would lose it.

She threw the Zuprium pouch to the ground and left the circle of stones. She needed to be anywhere but where Saldr's eyes could bore into her, expecting her to make the choice to doom them all no matter what universe they found themselves in.

If she went with General Correa's plan, she died. If she went with Saldr and the Lord Elder's plan, everyone she knew might cease to exist. The only positive about the second option was the idea that they could all start over...but would people make the same choices? Would those choices inevitably lead her to this exact moment again? Would she be forced into a continuous time loop, never to escape? Wasn't that how it happened in books?

She sprinted through the meadow and out into the tunnels as people packed up their scant belongings. That was right. Today was the day some were heading back to the city. Hallie had been so caught up in her own life she'd forgotten people were returning to theirs.

Maybe she could go back to her apartment and hide away from anything and everything—or just leave entirely. Maybe she could create a portal to the other side of the world and hope for the best. She'd probably mess up time again, but it seemed she was doomed to do that anyway.

Could she sit and watch the world burn, knowing she could've done something to stop it? Was there truly no way out of this?

She hardly knew where she was going, but she somehow ended up in front of Kase's tent. After the beauty of the Yalvs' cavern, this one felt plain and cold. It was still better than Saldr's pitying look.

No guard waited outside his tent. Either the guard had finally been dismissed, or Kase was out training the new pilots. Her mind was so clouded, she couldn't remember where he was supposed to be or if he would be back soon. She assumed it was midday, but that meant nothing to her addled mind.

Hesitating for a moment and nodding awkwardly to the

couple next door who'd just finished packing up their tent, she went inside to wait. She couldn't go back to Saldr. She could maybe talk to Petra, but she doubted she would understand. Hallie hadn't told her what she was, and she didn't want to have to explain.

And who knew where Fely had gone off to.

Kase's tent was sparse and impersonal for the most part, but maybe it only felt that way because the tent she still shared with her parents was cramped with three adults. His held a cot with a green coverlet tossed haphazardly into a ball at the end, the pillow askew as if he'd slept nearly hanging his head off the side. His pilot jacket was folded neatly next to the pillow, and a shuttered gas lantern sat upon the ground. She flicked that on with a soft popping sound. His pack lay tucked under the cot, the mouth open, a few of his personal effects inside including a leatherbound book spilling out.

Hallie picked up the book. She couldn't help it. She had Frankenstein back in her parents' tent, tucked away in her pack. Sadly, she hadn't had the mind to read it lately, for it reminded her too much of her current situation. While she hadn't died and been stitched together with thread, the power within her certainly made her feel like a monster. She'd done monstrous things like killing and bringing down entire forts. She'd led Niels to what was likely to be his death.

Add Saldr's revelations to the pile, and she might deserve whatever fate awaited her.

She sat on the cot and inspected the leather book. Flipping to the first page, she expected typeface and the title. Instead, she found unfamiliar handwriting. The script was neat and evenly spaced. Each letter was formed with care. Hallie was jealous. Her writing was untidy at the best of times.

The first page went like:

Hals,

Heard some good gossip today while waiting for the privy. Well, it wasn't gossip, necessarily. But I guess it would be now if I'm telling you? Whatever...

She froze. It was written to her. She scanned the rest of the page and flipped through a few other pages. They were all letters, and each were signed 'Always, Kase.'

She fanned through the rest of the book, which was close to halfway full. All of them were addressed to her, but they varied in length and content. Had he meant to send them? Earlier, she'd wondered why he'd only sent her one message while under house arrest.

He'd only *sent* one. But he'd written dozens.

She couldn't help the smile that spread across her face. It helped thaw the ache in her heart. Just a little.

She read the first one about the lady in the privy line and laughed. She could hear his voice in her head, almost as if he was there telling her the story himself. She shouldn't read the rest. What if she was spoiling some surprise he had planned?

She partway closed the book, her finger keeping her place. Putting it back would be the kind thing to do. He probably hadn't meant for her to read them. It was an invasion of his privacy.

She bent to replace it, but hesitated.

Nevermind.

It was his fault he hadn't hidden the book better. She flipped the book back open and read greedily.

She turned to the next one, expecting more humor…only to find it hidden among more serious topics, like how he thought Jove and his mother dead. It was personal, and she realized in the second letter it was essentially his diary.

Except she couldn't stop reading. They were written to her, after all. Even if he'd never meant them as real letters, he'd obviously written them in such a way that they felt more like a conversation between them. It was the distraction she needed.

She read the first several, then read them again and again. Each word made her feel so much closer to him in a way she hadn't realized she could feel. She smiled at the lines at the end of one of the more serious ones.

I lay awake at night wishing I could see the moons and stars. Not because I want to comment on their beauty or how it still amazes me that our ancestors sped through them to find this planet. No, I want to see them because I know wherever you are, you're looking up at the same moons, the same stars, the same beautiful sky. And if I think of that, I don't feel so alone.

The corner of her eyes stung; out of love or sorrow, she wasn't sure which. Both, probably.

Because the reality was, he *would* be alone at the end of this. They would no longer be able to look up at the same sky.

All the love and warmth and glee over the words he'd written crashed into an ice-cold abyss inside her. No matter which decision she made, it would take her away from him.

"Let me grab my jacket, will you?" Kase's voice called from outside the tent.

Hallie sprang up, the journal falling to the floor. The tent flap opened as Hallie retrieved the book.

Kase froze in the entrance. "What're you doing?"

"Nothing." Hallie whipped the book behind her back.

He raised a brow, his mouth pulling up into a smirk. The scar on that side of his face creased a little with the movement. "Is that so? Because if I didn't know any better, I might say you were hiding something from me."

Hallie shook her head. "Nothing."

Well, she was hiding a lot of things, but nothing she wanted to discuss at that precise moment. He stepped fully into the tent, the canvas closing behind him. Stars, he was so tall. He must've recently finished a patrol on the hover, because his goggles were pushed into his hair—or maybe not, as he'd left his jacket here. Or maybe he was on his way there? Hallie cursed herself for not waiting outside for him to return. Her thoughts were all jumbled.

"Well, if I were a betting man, I'd say you've been reading that little book," Kase stepped close to her. "Shouldn't be surprised, bibliophile that you are."

Hallie backed up, but she stumbled at the edge of the cot. She would've fallen and probably hurt herself if Kase hadn't caught her around the waist and pulled her to him.

He used the opportunity to pluck the journal from her fingers. Without loosening his hold on her, he held it up with his free hand. "You weren't supposed to ever read these, you know."

Hallie's face burned, and she blurted, "I thought it might've been a novel or something and I was just waiting for you to come back and I'm sorry that I read them but I didn't read them all—well maybe most of them but I—"

He tossed the journal next to the balled-up blanket and bent his head down, his lips hovering just above hers. She trailed off. He chuckled, "Did your mother never teach you manners, Miss Walker?"

Hallie held her breath.

The tent flap opened again. "Hurry it up, will you?

Father's waiting."

Kase didn't even look, only tugged off his goggles and chucked them at the entrance. "Go away."

Hallie jumped, and Kase tightened his hold on her. Her face burned even more than it had moments ago when she'd blundered through her explanation of reading his journal. Kase turned a little to look at his brother. She half hid in Kase's arms, but she could still see Jove Shackley standing in the entrance, his arm propping the flap open.

He wore a smirk of his own—one so like Kase's it was uncanny. Jove held up Kase's goggles. "Probably shouldn't snog when you're needed at the command tent, but if you ask nicely, I could probably buy you five minutes." He tossed the goggles back. "But I'll call in a favor at a later date, of course."

Kase caught his goggles and tossed them on top of the journal. Hallie wanted to sink into the floor.

"Deal," Kase said, turning away from him. A grin split his face as Jove left. He touched his forehead to hers. Her stomach clenched, and her mind went completely blank. He slowly and deliberately brushed his nose against hers. "We can probably get away with ten minutes alone, depending on the excuse he comes up with. He's an overachiever."

Alone.

Alone...alone...

...And if I think of that, I don't feel so alone.

The letter. That line.

Kase had his brother. He had his mother. He had Clara and Samuel. He even had her father, maybe her mother. He would never be *alone* again.

But if she reset time, he just might be.

That was a sobering thought.

And it made her decision for her.

She would find Correa and collect the Essence powers. When they restored both Gates, Jagamot wouldn't be a threat, and Kase would be free.

It was the only way to save him with certainty.

Hallie couldn't help it. She started to cry, though that word was woefully inaccurate. It wasn't the pretty kind where she sniffled a little and a few tears trickled down her cheeks. No, it was the ugly kind that came with soul-spilling, heart-wringing tears and heaving shoulders and all the in-between. She just stood there going from calm and fluttery at his intimate touch to full-out sobs in seconds, her fingers curling into fists over his heart, clinging to his shirt. Her shoulders shook.

"Whoa, whoa, whoa, Hallie!" Kase clasped her upper arms, inspecting her with frantic eyes, looking for the injury or blood or anything to explain her meltdown. "What happened? Are you hurt? Did I squeeze you too hard?"

She shook her head, but she couldn't get out any words. She just did that awful gasping noise that meant she wasn't getting enough air, but she couldn't take a full breath. She just gasped harder.

Her death was inevitable if she wanted Kase to live the life he always deserved. She just wouldn't get to be a part of it. The only way to save him was to rid herself of her power.

It was cruel. It wasn't *fair*.

"Jove won't tell anyone about us in here or anything, and I was just kidding about the ten minutes and even the five. If you don't want to—we weren't doing anything wrong—"

A muttered voice came from the front of the tent, but Hallie was crying too hard to hear the exact words.

"We're fine. Just tell Jove I'll be late," Kase answered. Probably his guard.

The other man said something back, but she still couldn't tell what.

"I don't give a stars-blasted crap what the Stradat Lord Kapitan thinks. Tell him what you want."

She tugged out of his arms and sat heavily onto his cot, trembling harder with every sob. She hid her face in her hands. She couldn't get the crying to stop now that it was finally here. The cork keeping her emotions bottled up had finally popped, and she couldn't get the flood under control.

It was as if the last few weeks had finally caught up with her—the kidnapping and torture in Achilles, the Essence power, Ravenhelm, Myrrai, Filip, Niels, the fight with Kase, her parents wanting her to go home with them, the failed lessons, and now this. She was only one person. She was only twenty-one.

At her age, she wasn't supposed to do anything but live a happy life, finish University, get married, have a family, whatever she wanted. She wasn't supposed to save the world.

Despite her childish dreams, she'd never wanted to be the heroine.

Kase sat and wrapped his arms around her. He guided her head to his chest and held it there with the most tender touch. She hugged him back, hysteria wracking her chest with aching heat. Every time she felt herself calming down, a new wave of anguish rolled over her. Kase never let her go.

Would she even get to say goodbye? Or would she simply cease to be?

They held each other for stars-knew how long, Kase scratching her back softly and simply letting her cry. When she'd finally cried herself out to the point where she could breathe almost normally, Kase kissed the top of her head. He shifted himself out of her grip and helped her lay down. He untangled the blanket and drew it all the way to her chin. He unfolded his jacket and laid that on top for good measure. It was all so warm and smelled exactly like him. He smoothed back her hair.

"Rest here." He grabbed the journal from where it'd fallen and placed it near her head. "Feel free to read more. I'll bring back some food, and we can talk. All right?"

Hallie could only sniffle in response. She didn't want him to leave, but she also wanted to be alone so she could work out her thoughts. His white linen shirt was stained gray on half his chest, roughly in the shape of her face. She felt a little bad about that.

He rummaged in his pack for two more. He laid one on top of his jacket. "For you, if you want it."

He turned away, the other in his hand. "Don't be ogling, now."

He then tugged his shirt off over top his head. Hallie was only able to glimpse the muscles of his upper back bunching up for a second as well as the dragon tattoo he'd begrudgingly told her about before he tugged on the new shirt. It really did look like a tortured worm.

She hiccupped—then nearly died of embarrassment as he looked over his shoulder with that stupid smirk while pulling the hem down and straightening the collar. He buttoned up two of the four buttons at the top near his neck.

He threw his old shirt at his pack and squatted down next to Hallie. He leaned over and kissed the spot just above her ear. "I'll be back."

Hallie briefly wondered just how long he'd be gone and just how long Jove had needed to stall. The guilt ate away at her conscience. She might be the reason his father lost his temper yet again. She wondered if Saldr would be there, if he would tell them all how she'd failed and that they were all doomed and...

Before she allowed her mind to wander any further down that road, she pushed herself up and changed out of her dirty lace blouse. The thing was covered in spare Vasa she'd failed to light and streaks of dirt and trails of damp where she'd wiped her eyes.

She shrugged out of it and tugged on Kase's shirt. It was soft and a little too big. She buttoned all four buttons and rolled up the sleeves, the neckline dipping below the space between her collarbones. It was almost like she was back in that cave in the Nardens after the avalanche. Her mother would have a fit if she saw her wearing it.

Her heart leapt a little as she flicked off the lantern, settled herself back down onto his cot, the blanket and jacket pulled up to her chin.

They'd been through a lot the last few months—the last year, really—and to think that they'd started out hating each other was a little crazy to think about. How had he gone from rude bookshop patron to the man she loved so much she would die just to give him the chance to be happy?

She tucked herself further into the cocoon of his scent, thinking of anything but the grim future ahead of them. If she could just freeze time here, she might be content forever.

Hallie must've fallen asleep, because the next thing she knew, she woke to the back of Kase's head and the sound of pencil on parchment. He'd relit the lantern, its dim light gently illuminating his features.

Her eyes ached from her earlier crying. She rubbed them. It didn't help. Probably only made them look more swollen.

"You snore a little, you know?" Kase said, not turning. He sat with his back leaning on the edge of the cot, one knee propped up as he bent close to the journal atop it. "I've never heard a hibernating baby bear, but I'd wager you could compete."

Hallie slowly pushed herself up onto her elbow. It was more difficult than she cared to admit. All that crying and her nap had taken too much out of her; her body must've weighed a thousand pounds. She sniffled a little. "You know,

I could hear *you* all the way from our room on the *Eudora*."

Kase's pencil froze over the parchment. He'd been sketching what Hallie figured was a hover, but it needed a better shape to the nose, and the wing was way off. He grunted, "Wasn't me."

"No?" Hallie asked, sitting up completely and arranging herself so she could look over his shoulder better. She reached over and pointed to the lines that weren't right. "Keep your wrist straight. Use your whole arm. It'll help with the lines."

"It was Skibs, actually," he said, trying and failing to follow Hallie's advice. His attempt at smoothing out the bottom of the hover made it look like it tapered to a point. He tried again. This time he went too wide. "Kept me up all hours. Probably why I wasn't my usual perky self while we were on the mission."

"You? Perky?"

Kase held out his sketch and rotated it to the right. "How much would I have to pay you to fix this one for me?"

"At least a dozen gold tenners," Hallie said, pushing off his jacket and the blanket she'd slept under. She stretched until her back popped. Instant relief flooded through her.

He stuffed his pencil inside the book and pushed the whole thing into the pack under his bed. "Maybe later then. I'm out of gold."

He reached up behind him and grabbed her arm, pulling it down to press a soft kiss to the inside of her wrist. She couldn't help the voluntary shiver. Kase kissed it again. "Want something to eat?"

He let go of her wrist and grabbed a wrapped cloth bundle she hadn't noticed on the ground and handed it to her. "I was able to wrangle you a sandwich and was told explicitly by your mother that you were to be back at their tent before nightfall."

"Course you were."

He leaned on his elbow, his head resting on his fist. He laid his other hand on her closest knee and rubbed circles with his thumb. "That shirt looks nice on you, but I can't tell if it's the shirt itself or because it's mine and you're wearing it."

Her mouth went dry, and she couldn't think of a response. At all. Not even a sarcastic one.

Kase's slow grin told her everything she needed to know. He was quite aware of the effect he had on her. Blasted pilot with his perfect lips and jawline and sparkling blue eyes. He didn't stop tracing patterns on her knee, and she found it horribly difficult to concentrate on the roasted chicken sandwich she'd unwrapped. She took a bite to distract herself.

As if ignoring him had ever worked.

After weeks of subpar food, the richness of the sandwich nearly made her sick. The chicken was shredded and lukewarm, the bread slightly stale, but some sort of soft cheese was smeared on the bread's inside, and in that moment, it tasted like the best meal she'd ever had. She let out a soft moan. She couldn't help it.

"Glad you like it. Had to sell my soul to get it, but only the best for you, of course." He snagged a piece of chicken that had fallen out and popped it into his mouth. "Added a pinch of cinnamon. If I'd been able to toast the bread first, you would've thought this a gourmet meal, but just sneaking some cinnamon was a risk, and I value my head."

Hallie swallowed her bite. "Cinnamon?"

Now that she thought about it, there was a hint of sweet woodiness. It was a nice touch.

Kase snuck another piece. "A surprisingly good way to finish off many a dish."

Hallie took another few bites, savoring each one. Kase unscrewed the cap on his canteen and handed it to her. She washed down the food and set aside the rest of the sandwich. "Not sure I can finish it. Stomach's not used to it."

Kase scooped it up and took a bite. He nodded. "Delicious, but I'll pass the tip about the cinnamon along to your mother. Can't believe she didn't think of it first."

Hallie tilted her head slightly, the fingers twisting the cap back onto the canteen pausing for a moment. "You think it's wise to give my mother cooking advice?"

"Probably not." Kase let out a low laugh.

He took another bite and then lowered the sandwich. A few stray breadcrumbs clung to his beard. Without thinking, Hallie reached over and brushed them off, her fingertips lingering a beat too long. The coarse hair tickled her skin.

He swallowed his food and caught her hand before she could take it back. "I love you."

Stars, she'd thought she'd cried herself out, but the

stinging of her too-dry eyes proved otherwise. "I love you, too."

It was what made all of this so hard. Without him, she might not have cared that much.

His eyes moved to her lips.

And then he was pulling her hand, reeling her in. Time moved at a glacial pace. The gas lantern drew shadows along his jaw and over the scar interrupting his beard on the right side. His lids lowered halfway. He tugged her off the cot and into his lap. The cloth fluttered to the ground on top of the now-discarded sandwich. His other hand brushed a lock of hair that had escaped her braid and followed it behind her ear before tracing her jaw to her lips.

The moment fell upon them like new fallen snow, and a soft *something* zinged between them, raising goosebumps along her skin. His mouth formed itself into a half-smile, one that said he noticed and wanted to do it again. Her heart skipped and fluttered.

The Kase she'd met in that bookshop all those months ago and the one who looked at her now felt like night and day. He'd let down his walls, and she hers. She might not want to be a heroine in her story, but she wanted to be his. The space between them hung heavy with the past, the present, and the future they would never have. But she couldn't push him away now. Her eyes flicked to his lips, and he took that as a silent invitation.

His kiss was soft and hesitant, opposite to the one they'd shared the night of the bonfire. She closed her eyes, allowing herself to simply feel, to not overanalyze each action or consequence.

Love couldn't be quantified in lists, term papers, or crumbling artifacts. It couldn't be defined by ink on parchment.

Kase kissed her as if he'd never have enough of her. It deepened between breaths and heartbeats. The aching want in her chest only grew. She pressed herself against him.

He kissed her as she was, not desperate or needing or out of pain. She kissed him back, opening her mouth, inviting him in.

Her breath hitched, and her head spun. His hand tightened at her waist, the other tangled in her hair. He tasted faintly like cinnamon.

She felt *whole.*

Hallie couldn't remember the last time she'd felt that way.

He pulled back and lightly pressed his forehead to hers. "Feel better now?"

She leaned in and gave him a long, lingering kiss. "No," she said, breathless, "but it's okay if you keep trying."

He chuckled softly, brushing his thumb across her slightly swollen lips, smiling as she leaned into the touch. "I do like a challenge." He kissed her again, but he broke it before it could go any further than that. "But it's probably better if we talk, because I don't know if I..." He cleared his throat. "Let's go for a walk. Fresh Catacombs air can't fix a thing, but we might as well try."

He helped her stand, and Hallie's knees wobbled. Kase steadied her. He let her go only to help her into his jacket and put her satchel on her shoulder before taking her hand and leading her out into the cavern.

The air was colder out there, but it was warm and cozy wrapped in his pilot's jacket. They walked along, passing more and more people packing up to leave the Catacombs at last. With each person she passed, the reality she'd escaped from for the last half hour with Kase and his lips came crashing back down.

She wanted to go back to that place and never leave, but the noise around her cemented the fact that she couldn't. She never could.

His hand was a steady lifeline through the milling crowds. He led her right, then left, then left again. They traveled deeper and deeper until only the echoes of their footsteps followed them. Kase finally slowed at the last gas lantern hanging from a hook in the wall.

"Found this earlier." He nodded back the way they'd come. His guard waited about thirty feet or so away in the light of another lantern. To her left was almost complete darkness.

"And why were you looking for a secluded spot such as this?" Hallie asked, glancing around again. Now that her eyes had adjusted a little more, a soft glow came from far to her left in the darkness. Probably another lantern. All the corridors down here seemed to connect in some way. This was probably just one of the places yet to be used or already cleared out of refugees heading back into the city. "Wanted a good place to do unscrupulous things?"

"I love that you use big words like *unscrupulous*." He lightly kissed her nose. "I needed to clear my head the other day, and I stumbled across this and knew no one would be here now." He gestured back to his guard looking bored with a hand on his sword. "And you're safe from *unscrupulous things* as long as Sergeant stays with us."

Hallie rolled her eyes. Kase brought his other hand up and played with one of her stray hairs at the nape of her neck. "So talk to me. Please. I would rather not have you upset at me—especially after the other day with the whole card game and...well, you know."

Hallie wet her lips. Kase traced the movement with his eyes. She could tell he wanted to kiss her again, and besides Sergeant, there was no one there to stop them. Hallie almost pushed aside her fears and the things she needed to tell him and finished what they'd started back in his tent.

But she couldn't do that. She wouldn't do that to herself or to Kase. It wasn't fair.

She swallowed around the words aching in her throat. She might as well just say it. No matter what she said to soften the blow would make it any less cutting.

"I'm not going to reset the Gate."

Kase, who had been brushing his hand up and down her right arm, froze. "What does that mean?"

"My training isn't working, and I just...I just..."

His eyes narrowed in confusion. "Just tell me, Hallie. What does that mean?"

She looked down at her fingers just poking out of his jacket sleeve. "It means...I'm going to find Correa and use the swords to combine the Essence powers. Then I'm going to return the swords to the Gates. Of course, I need to find the second one first and its sword, and I think my great grandmother's journals might help with that, but regardless, it's the only sure way to defeat Jagamot."

Kase was quiet for a moment before he asked, "Does Saldr know?"

Hallie shook her head. "I made the decision a few hours ago after my session with him and Fely."

He tipped her chin up and made her look at him, his eyes searching. "And what happens when we combine the

Essence powers into those swords? There's something you're not telling me."

Hallie worked her jaw. She didn't want to cry again. It might break her resolve. No, not might. It would.

"Hals, you can tell me anything, I hope you know that," he said, his words soft and tender.

She licked her lips again and took a breath. His finger didn't leave her chin.

Her heart pounded against the cage in her chest. "It means...combining the swords means that I'll..."

The realization hit him without her having to say it out loud. His hand fell away. "You don't have to do that. You can't."

"I don't have a choice, Kase."

He shook his head. "Yes you do. You can go with Saldr's plan."

"I'm not going to do that."

"Why, Hallie?" He gripped her face in both hands, emotion tinging his words.

She put both of her hands on his and drew them away from her cheeks. "It's the only way to save you."

"I'm not worth saving," Kase said, his voice finally breaking all the way. "Not at that cost. I don't care what happens to me or to anyone else. I only care about you."

Arms clasped around her middle, Hallie turned away. She wouldn't cry anymore. She couldn't. She had to stay strong.

Kase grabbed her shoulders and forced her to face him. A tear trekked down his face.

She shook her head and tugged out of his arms. She walked down the corridor toward the other faint light. The warmth she'd forgotten over the last few hours awoke, rising to a simmer just beneath the surface of her skin. She stopped and looked at her hands, allowing the sleeves of Kase's jacket to fall back as she held them up. They looked normal. But she *felt* it.

Kase followed. "Hals..."

She looked toward the soft glow and frowned. There was no other lantern. There was no other side of the tunnel. It was coming from the ground, and it was familiar. "I thought the tunnels connected."

He stopped beside her. "Hallie, can we talk about this?

Really talk about it? Go through each option and decide together?"

She closed her eyes. "No."

"But why? Why do you get to go off and sacrifice yourself? Why do you get to make that choice?"

She threw up her hands. "Because I'm a Essence wielder! Because my great-grandmother decided she didn't want to do this. Because I fell for Correa's trap. Because I don't know, Kase. I don't know, but if I don't do this, if I follow Saldr's plan, there's a chance I never meet you. There's a chance I never kiss you. There's a chance I never fall in love with you. This way, I keep that. I keep that, and I know that you'll survive. I know that you'll be happy. My way guarantees that even if I never get to finish this life with you...I still *had* it."

Her throat burned with the words, and her hands shook.

"So that's why? You're scared that if you reset the Gate, you'll lose me?"

"Yes!" The confession broke her heart all over again.

He caught her wrist, tugging her to him, and crushed his mouth to hers. The heat within her rose to meet his passion, but before it bubbled over, he pulled back, hands cupping her face. He looked so deep into her eyes, she knew he saw her. The real her. The raw her. The one who wanted only to run away, but wouldn't. She would stay and fight and make sure that he lived.

His words were soft yet taut. "I will find you. I will find you in any and every timeline. I'd fight every dragon, find all the stars-blasted swords, die a thousand deaths if it meant I could be with you."

"But you can't *know* that." Hallie's voice broke.

"I do." He breathed heavily, and in the false twilight, his eyes were dark with emotion. "You're my fate, Hallie Walker, and I'm never letting you go."

Those words were what every girl dreamed of hearing. Hallie had. They were absolutely perfect, and if she'd read them in a book, she'd swoon. She'd cry. She'd dream about them forever.

But his words would not save her, the girl who was going to die for him. Nothing he said would change her mind.

And it broke her heart.

Heat flared in her core, and she stumbled back like she'd been pushed. Her vision clouded and darkened. Someone's hands encircled her wrists and dragged her back.

"Hallie!" A rough hand on her face. She was burning—with fever or fire or the sun itself, she didn't know. She couldn't open her eyes.

All she could do was burn.

C H A P T E R 3 7

HIS MISTAKES

Hallie

HALLIE'S BLOOD BURNED WITH SOMETHING worse than fire. Nothing she'd read about in any of her studies could've described it. She wished she'd passed out. It would've been less painful that way.

If not for the dirt-and-damp smell of the Catacombs and Saldr and Fely whispering above her, she would've thought her power had finally broken free and burned her to death. She couldn't even speak; when she tried, her raw throat ground it down into a wordless moan. Someone smoothed her hair; her head was cradled in someone's lap, but that was all she could figure out. She couldn't open her eyes.

"Her Relic isn't strong enough," Saldr was saying. "But why?"

There was a pause, broken only by the sound of objects bumping against one another, like someone was riffling through a bag. Fely finally said, "Her original Relic was lost in Achilles. These goggles were a replacement."

Saldr muttered Yalven curses under his breath. "That explains why her training hasn't progressed far."

Kase's voice rumbled above her. "Then how do we find her a new...whatever you said. Relic?"

"None of this would matter if we had the electricity," another voice said, harsher. The Stradat Lord Kapitan.

"With all due respect, Stradat Lord Kapitan," Saldr said tightly, as if that *due respect* took work for him to scrounge up, "Jagamot is here, and Miss Walker will be needed for the greater purpose of resetting the Gate. We cannot spend her power on any lesser pursuits."

Kase tensed, his leg muscles tightening beneath Hallie's head. "Neither of you are taking into account that Hallie has been tossed into this without her consent."

Hallie finally pried open her stinging eyes to find the world consumed by a strange golden haze. She blinked, but it didn't go away. She winced. It tingled so much worse than it had after Myrrai. Not pinpricks; more like being stabbed repeatedly with long, thin daggers.

"Hals," Kase said, resting his hand on her cheek. His head hung above her, his eyes widening a fraction. "You're awake."

He helped her sit up. Fely knelt beside her, taking her hand. It was warm to the touch, but Hallie allowed her to give her Soul. In a few seconds, the golden haze retreated, but only a little. It lingered in her periphery. The stabbing sensation faded back to prickles before disappearing completely.

"Thought you'd used most of your reserve," Hallie murmured—or tried to. Her throat wasn't cooperating. She had to repeat herself so that Fely could understand her.

Kase helped Hallie stand with a steadying hand on the small of her back. Hallie glanced around best she could, but she couldn't see much between the dim light and the golden haze at the edges of her sight. A little further down, where the tunnels still had gas lanterns, Kase's guard faced the opposite direction; though from what Hallie could tell, no one else was nearby. The tunnels must have been cleared out in the time since she and Kase had first come down here—either because they'd moved aboveground or because the Stradat Lord Kapitan ordered them out. She'd been in and out the last few minutes and could only recall bits and pieces as she fought to stay conscious.

Fely's face was drawn, but she offered a wan smile, touching her locket. "There are a few cave plants that have been sacrificed to aid your recovery."

Hallie could tell there was more to the story, but the Stradat Lord Kapitan didn't leave room for her to question further before he argued with Saldr again.

"Then what do you, Lord Saldr, suggest we do while Miss Walker continues to prepare?" He crossed his arms before him, his eyes hard. "I expect the Cerls will mount another full-blown attack soon, especially after Kase's stunt."

He said it like that *stunt* wasn't the reason they were all still alive. Kase's hand fell away from her back. Hallie peeked over at him. He didn't say anything; he simply stared at the ground, arms crossed. While his and his father's poses were similar the men themselves couldn't be more opposed. The tension between them was palpable.

Saldr, brave man that he was, merely said, "The Lord Elder's power is painful to wield and difficult to control. He had many years to prepare for his role; Miss Walker has had a few weeks. The fact that she's standing before us now is quite a feat in itself."

Kase turned his head toward Hallie, his eyes finding hers. Her heart leapt and warmed; her body swayed toward his like that look had some kind of magnetic pull. The heat in her chest grew, but it wasn't painful. The haze in her vision flared.

They still hadn't finished their conversation from earlier, and now it looked like they wouldn't get to for a while.

She should try to put some distance between them physically and emotionally, but she couldn't make herself do that. Not yet. Not after what he'd said before, about being his fate.

Her hand brushed his, and her skin heated at the brief touch. That wasn't her power.

"You said something about a Relic earlier. What is that?" Harlan asked, bringing Hallie back to the moment.

Saldr nodded. "A Relic is an object made of the holy metal. It helps the wielder control their power."

"So once you have that, she can restore the electricity?"

Kase opened his mouth to speak, but Hallie reached out

and set her hand on his arm. She stepped past him and held her shoulders high. "When I used the power without one, I destroyed Achilles, and it's only with the Gate's help that Niels, Fely, and I made it to Kyvena in one piece."

Saldr paled, and she didn't miss the way his gaze darted to Fely.

"But with the dragon and the rest of the Cerls still out there, the consequences might be worth it," she added reluctantly. "If the electricity will do that much good."

"Miss Walker," Saldr ventured, "using such power would take a toll."

"Yes. But it might be worth it," she repeated. Kase shifted uncomfortably.

It was at that moment that Jove Shackley spoke up. She hadn't noticed him leaning against the wall; the golden haze fizzing around her vision had hidden him until he'd stepped forward. "Perhaps. But what about Correa? We know he's coming here, and for all we know, he could have the rest of the army and air force at his back."

"Yet another reason we need to be ready for a fight," Harlan said gruffly. "I refuse to let them waltz in here again. We need Pilot Shackley and the others in the air as soon as possible."

Kase shook his head. "I can handle the Cerls."

"Not in one of their death machines." Harlan's voice was low and nearly as cold as it had been when Hallie had overheard them during the estate dinner months ago. "Your patrols are only a temporary solution."

Kase's voice only wavered slightly, but whether it was from fear, anger, or something else, Hallie couldn't decide. "I'd say my ability to work the hover is an asset, Stradat Lord Kapitan."

Jove stepped in between the two men. "Father's right, Kase. From the intelligence we have on the technology, it's dangerous."

"But—"

"And furthermore, we've lost the element of surprise with you taking out the last squadron." Jove turned to look at the Stradat Lord Kapitan. "It saved us, yes, but now Correa knows to look out for a rogue ship. They'll have new protocols in place to keep it from happening again."

Hallie wanted to argue on that front. She wasn't sure

where Correa was. She hadn't seen him since Ravenhelm. But then again, what was to say he wasn't already here in Kyvena, hidden among the refugees?

The soft golden glow winked in her vision. She turned toward it for a moment.

When she squinted, the golden fog narrowed to a point. It was unlike anything she'd experienced before...yet it also felt like a memory of some sort, or a dream that faded after waking.

Curious.

"But you don't understand," Kase said, gesturing with his hands. His words interrupted her thoughts, and she ducked just in time to avoid being accidentally hit as he pointed to his chest. "It's like the hover is a part of me. It knows what I want to do before I even do. It's the perfect weapon to fight them with. We'll never accomplish anything in one of our standard hovers unless your goal is for your last few pilots to go down in flames."

"Absolutely not."

"Why?" Kase shouted. "Just trust me! I can do this. I've already proven I can."

"You can't, Ezekiel! The cost is your *soul*!" The Stradat Lord Kapitan's shout rang off the walls so loudly, Hallie stumbled into Kase. His eyes were pits of darkness without much light in this part of the tunnels.

What?

Hallie narrowed her eyes, her gaze going between the Stradat Lord Kapitan—who clearly had lost his mind, if he thought he was talking to Zeke—to Kase, who looked ready to punch something or someone. Then to Jove, whose face had lost all color.

"As we've already established several times, I'm not Zeke," Kase spat, still raring for a fight.

"Sorry," Harlan said. His voice sounded like gravel. He didn't look at anyone, much less his sons. "I'm...sorry."

Kase curled his hands into fists. Jove was still pale, but he looked more intrigued now, as if his father had just spoken an entirely different language.

No one spoke for a few more seconds after that. In those moments, it was almost like they truly were in a place where they'd buried the dead. The air weighed heavy. All that surrounded them were the bones of secrets and memories left behind by beloved dead.

Zeke had died a hero, and his soul soared among the stars. That was something even someone like the Stradat Lord Kapitan could respect. So why would he connect the idea of losing a soul with his middle son?

There was something she was missing.

"The cost of what is his soul?" Hallie asked, not understanding what this had to do with his adamance that Kase not operate the Cerl hover. Was he somehow alluding to what King Filip's Essence power could do?

"Kase does look extraordinarily like him," Jove said quietly.

Both Hallie and Kase turned. "What do you mean?" Kase demanded.

She wanted to know, too. Kase looked far more like Jove than he had Zeke.

A sad smile flickered across Jove's face, but he didn't look at Kase; he still looked at Harlan. "That's why you're so hard on Kase, isn't it?"

Harlan finally looked up at his eldest son, his eyes hard. "You don't know what you're talking about."

Jove's stare stayed level. "I know everything. I've seen the files."

Harlan's jaw clenched. He looked away again. "Then you know I did what I had to do."

"Will one of you please explain what the blazes is going on?" Kase asked, his voice shaky.

"I barely remember him as it is, so I hadn't made the connection until now," Jove said, placing his hands behind his back. He looked right at Kase. "You're the spitting image of Uncle Ezekiel."

Ezekiel Fairchild. The man who betrayed all of Jayde.

Hallie sucked in a small breath. *Oh. Oh stars, this is…not where I need to be.*

Whatever was going on between the Shackley men, she didn't factor into it. But Kase's stance and the clench of his jaw told her if she left, he might lose it. She slipped her hand into his. It was cold, opposite to her heat.

"Explain." That was all Kase said. He tightened his hold on her hand.

The Stradat Lord Kapitan opened his mouth, then closed it again. Like he had to work to dredge up the words.

It'd been nearly fifteen years since the war ended, twenty since it'd begun. It was a long time to keep a secret.

"Tell us," Jove said quietly.

The Stradat Lord Kapitan crossed his arms and stared into the stone beneath his feet. "I met Ezekiel in the army. We were both medics, and we became friends…he even opened his home to me once or twice during the rare times we got leave together. That's how I met your mother." Harlan smoothed a hand over his mustache. "But near the end of his tenure, his wife gave birth to a baby girl. Both his wife and daughter died shortly after the birth. Complications stemming from the pregnancy. He joined the engineering corps, determined to stop the endless war no one would admit we were part of. He not only discovered a way to infuse Zuprium with electricity, giving us an advantage on the battlefield, but he…sold everything that made him human to do it. Even his sons joined, but they went too far."

Hallie's heart broke for a man she didn't know. What Hallie had been through in her short life had been bad, but it wasn't nearly as terrible as what had happened to Kase's uncle. She also had a feeling the Stradat Lord Kapitan couldn't tell the entire story. Grief could make you do horrible things, and with the amount of trauma Ezekiel Fairchild had experienced, it made sense he'd been lost to it.

But what went further than infusing Zuprium with electricity? That discovery alone changed the tide of the war. The electropistols and electrobombs allowed Jayde to gain an advantage and push Cerulene out of Jayde.

But what else was there? The Yalvs had their own powers, but she didn't think Ezekiel was Yalven, though she guessed it wasn't out of the realm of possibility—but no, that would have made Les part Yalven, which would have made *Kase* part Yalven, and nothing that had responded to Hallie's Yalven blood had never done the same for him.

What else was there? Was it another secret that had been buried with him?

Motion caught her attention, and she caught Fely playing with her locket, the one that held the Soul she took.

Soul.

Kase said only moments ago it felt like the Cerl hover was part of him. What if they didn't run on electricity and Yalvar fuel like she'd assumed? What if they ran on something else? The Cerl pistols had still worked in Myrrai when the electropistols had not. Kase's new hover worked despite the electricity not working in Kyvena.

What if the secret Ezekiel sold the Cerls wasn't about electricity at all?

"The Cerl weapons," Hallie whispered. "They work using Soul?"

Harlan simply nodded. Kase, still pale and perplexed, asked, "What do you mean?"

Jove said, "Uncle Ezekiel created Soul Technology, which is what the Cerl weapons and hovers use." Jove walked to the other side of the space, as if to leave. He paused and turned. "And in the end, he begged for death."

Hallie's heart thrummed in her ears. "So the story about him being a traitor?"

Surely it wasn't what she thought. Surely, there was another explanation, but Kase's father didn't offer much of one. "He wasn't in his right mind."

Hallie blinked. "Kind of like what happens to Zuprium miners?"

The Stradat Lord Kapitan cleared his throat. "Yes."

"So why sell the story that he committed treason?" Kase asked.

Hallie couldn't tell what his exact thoughts were, but he was still clutching her hand like he'd crumble if she let go. She leaned closer. The story of Ezekiel Fairchild was one of tragedy, certainly, but to beg for death...what exactly had he done to discover that you could use Soul, your very spirit, to fuel weapons? Hovers?

"He did commit treason." The Stradat Lord Kapitan pressed his thumb and forefinger to his eyes. "And we tried to cover up his tracks."

"The Queen." Hallie knew she was right even before she said it. It just made sense. Why else would the Jaydian government assassinate her? Whether or not they knew she was an Essence wielder, she had been the leader of the Cerl engineering corps, but that was it.

Harlan let out a shaky breath. "The war needed to end quickly, and the easiest way to do it was to kill the only Cerl who knew about Soul Tech."

"Why her? Was it because she was the Essence of Souls?" Hallie asked.

Harlan shook his head. If Hallie were to describe the moment she stood there, clinging to Kase as much as he did to her, it would be the breath one held before taking a plunge into a lake of ice. The air was no longer laden with the truth; it thinned as if they stood atop the highest peak in the Nardens. The world narrowed to a point.

"Because they were lovers. Killing her ended the war, but it also ended Ezekiel." Unsteadily, the Stradat Lord Kapitan straightened his uniform and arranged his features back into his mask of indifference tinged with what Hallie had always figured was anger. But it wasn't, not this time. This time, it was defeat. "And I have spent the last fifteen years trying to make up for his mistakes."

And then he left, leaving the rest of the group in stunned silence.

Kase

KASE DIDN'T REALLY KNOW WHAT to think. Everything he'd learned from his father in that tunnel was in the past, and it shouldn't have mattered any longer, but it was still a part of Kase. It was still his history; still his burden to bear, even fifteen years later.

Vaguely, Kase had known he resembled his Fairchild ancestors. He had gained nothing from the Shackley side except maybe his temper, which Hallie had pointed out. Funny the only thing he'd gotten from his father was the worst thing about him. Funny wasn't the right word at all, but when you lived the life he had, well, funny was the only word you could use.

Kase crushed Hallie's hand in his, but she didn't seem to mind. He dreaded the moment he'd have to let go.

He needed to get out of this tunnel.

Kase and Jove had demanded an answer, and for once, Harlan had given it; yet it made Kase feel even worse than before. It didn't solve anything at all. It only made him feel bitter. Bitter that it was his uncle's choices that had ruined Kase's life. It wasn't his fault. Ezekiel Fairchild had set him on this path, and Kase never had a chance to do anything to fix it.

Jove left shortly after. All he got from his eldest brother was, "Sorry, Kase."

Shocks, he needed to be up in the air. Immediately.

Hallie whispered something to Saldr and Fely before dragging Kase down the tunnel after his brother. He barely paid attention to where she led him. All he could think about was the hover.

It was siphoning off his *soul* to fly. He'd known something was different about it, he'd known it ran on something other than Yalvar fuel, but this…he hadn't imagined this.

To think the Cerls only had this technology because his uncle had discovered it and told his lover about it.

Now, it was Jayde's only defense—just Kase and a hover that his uncle had created and been executed for; an uncle who Kase took after in more ways than one. An uncle who had been drowning in grief; an uncle whose betrayal and death had changed his father for the worse.

The further he and Hallie traveled through the corridors, the more people they passed. Not everyone had been cleared to return to the surface yet—only those with essential jobs like clean up, which ended up being mostly lower-class folks.

While there hadn't been a full counterattack to Kase's feat days ago, they weren't safe. The flyovers weren't harmless; they merely confirmed that fact. After he'd destroyed all the hovers chasing him, they might be hesitant to send in more unless they were certain of what had occurred, but he doubted it. They were probably planning something even worse.

"Kase!"

He froze and half-turned. Hallie still looked pale as she tugged on his arm. She'd nearly blacked out with whatever happened in the tunnel, and that was after their wretched fight. He would never forget the desperation in her eyes as she pleaded with him, begging him to let her save him.

What a horrible day it had been.

He slowed down. "I'm so sorry. I didn't even think. Are you all right?"

She cupped his cheek with a slightly chilled hand. "Are *you* all right?"

He opened his mouth and closed it again. Of course he

wasn't, but if he admitted that, he wouldn't be able to put himself back together again. He needed to be up in a hover. "I have a patrol I'm late for, and one of the greenies is joining me finally."

"But Kase, your father…and your uncle…"

He shook his head. "I just need an hour in the hover."

His words were entirely too optimistic for what he felt. Hallie hadn't fallen for it, judging by the look on her face. "Are you sure? Especially after hearing…well…that?"

"I'll be okay." He brought her hand to his lips. "We can talk more later?"

She pursed her lips together but shrugged out of his jacket.

"No, you can keep it."

She shook her head. "You're not you without it."

That brought a small smile to his lips, It would make him feel a little better. At least on the surface. "But you'll fetch yours? I don't want you catching a cold."

She stood on tiptoe and gave him a chaste kiss. "I'm better now. I swear."

He leaned down and whispered in her ear. A few stray hairs tickled his lips. "Are you sure you'll be all right?"

She nodded.

"Then I'll see you at dinner."

She nodded again, and Kase gave her hand a soft squeeze before gesturing for Sergeant to follow. He let her hand fall as he turned and wove his way through the crowd.

His hand was cold without hers, but if he was to keep her safe and remain sane, he needed to be up in a hover. If he didn't get into the sky soon and escape the truths his father had just revealed, he wouldn't be able to think rationally when he talked with her about more important things later.

More important things, like her plan to *sacrifice* herself for him.

His stomach roiled.

He and Sergeant made their way past the central cavern, the chasm, and another three corridors before finding the correct one that would take them to the underground hangar. Just outside the door being manned by two stiff-backed soldiers, a young man leaned heavily on a cane, his legs in braces.

Kase would have bet everything he owned that this day

couldn't get any worse, but it seemed that was a bet he would've lost.

Today's greenie was Laurence Hixon, the one he'd been training before the bike accident. The man wore his gray training jacket, every button done up to his chin. His blond hair swept back from his temples, held in place by goggles.

Last Kase had heard, they hadn't thought Laurence would ever walk again. But the greenie stood before him now, a steely look on his face.

Kase now very much wished Hallie had come with him. Despite their argument and its consequences, she was his strength.

He ran a hand through his hair and stepped up to the younger man. He could deal with his emotions later. "Good to see you, Trainee Pilot Hixon."

He held out his hand, and while the greenie still leaned heavily on his cane, he took Kase's. "Pilot Shackley."

He couldn't tell if the boy was being hostile or just nervous. Last time the greenie had done anything remotely like this, he'd ended up on the brink of death.

Kase would've been scared out of his wits, yet Laurence Hixon stood—actually *stood*—before him, ready to fly again. Though with the braces factored in, he wasn't sure how he was going to get the man into the hover.

But he had to give credit where credit was due. The greenie had more guts than the others.

Kase let the boy's hand drop and nodded toward the hangar doors. "Hopefully this patrol will be uneventful, but it should get you used to the general sense of the hover in case we're able to...er, *when* we're able to get the others operational."

The other pilot gave him a quick nod. "Of course. I assume the functions and capabilities are similar to the standard military grade hovers?"

Hadn't lost a bit of that priggish nature, but Kase said, "Similar might be too strong a word, but it's all we've got."

Kase saluted the soldiers and moved past them as they wrenched the heavy metal doors open—yet another task made more difficult without the use of electricity.

They passed two hovers similar to the *Eudora* and three standard ones before they reached the Cerl machine. The others looked on like ghosts.

"Those hovers were the only ones?" Trainee Pilot Hixon asked; he was several steps behind Kase.

Kase slowed. "Those were here in the hangar and have never been flown. Once we're able to get them up in the air, one of them might be yours."

If Hallie attained some sort of mastery over her power before she rid herself of it, anyway.

Stars blast it.

Laurence followed him around slowly as Kase did his pre-flight checks. The metal was cool to the touch but warmed once it recognized him. He tried not to think too much about why. The ship hummed a little as he closed one of the panels.

The other pilot startled. Kase caught him before he could fall flat on his face. Laurence looked at Kase, then the hover. "I wasn't aware that...they told me the electricity hadn't been restored quite yet. I thought this was merely a demonstration on the use of the standard hovers."

Kase let go of the other pilot once he was sure he wouldn't fall over. He then ducked under the wing and checked the last panel. "This one is Cerl-made and doesn't need electricity to run. We'll be doing a short patrol in it today."

"Oh, I wasn't...I guess that's okay."

Kase shut the panel and searched for a ladder or anything that could help him into the cockpit. He wasn't sure if the other pilot would be able to climb up the wing. It depended on how much control Hixon had over his legs. If Kase could just get him onto the wing...well, then it would depend on the boy's upper arm strength. What if Kase got him onto the wing and then climbed up the other side before helping the greenie into the cockpit?

The ladder might be easiest.

Laurence seemed to understand his line of thinking. He gave Kase a rueful smile. "Truthfully, I cannot fly myself just yet. The feeling in my legs is only slowly returning, and while that is progress, I'm unable to press the pedals to move the craft at the speed required for it to be effective in an aerial engagement."

That was an awful lot of words just to say he couldn't operate the hover. Kase rubbed a hand over his chin. He still hadn't shaved, and it was no longer stubble. He spotted an equipment closet just off the side of one of the smaller sections with the nearest standard hover.

Dust blustered out as he opened the door. He coughed as his nose burned, but inside, he found a ladder with hooks at one end. He sneezed. Blasted dust. Grabbing the ladder, he carried it over to his hover and hooked it on the side of the airship. Tugging the rungs, it unfolded into a longer one. It wasn't a perfect fit, but the ladder was longer than needed, which made the incline less steep. That would make it a little easier for the man to make it up into the cockpit. Maybe.

"Well, Trainee Pilot Hixon," Kase said, standing back. "The good news is this hover is rather special." It beeped in response. Kase smiled a little. Despite its origins tangling with Kase's own, he couldn't help but like the ship. "I can't really go into the explanation right now, but I think you might enjoy this flight. And when the time comes, I'll need a weapons specialist, so the job is yours...if you want it."

Pilot Hixon nodded eagerly. "Thank you. I would be happy to join you in your quest to fight the Cerulene air force."

Kase was going to have to figure out a way to get the man to say what he needed in much fewer words. For now, he held out a hand to help the greenie up the ladder. The boy's hand was slick with sweat, but Kase held it tightly. One step at a time. The braces on the greenie's knees creaked, the movement straining them, but they held.

Laurence nearly fell twice, but with Kase's help, he made it into the cockpit.

After replacing the ladder, he went over to the hangar doors. Without electricity, he was forced to tug them open himself. He grunted and yanked bit by bit. The whining squeaks of the electrical components protesting the movement echoed throughout the mostly empty hangar. For some reason, opening them hadn't gotten any easier—his fingers burned as he pulled. The engineers building them relied too heavily on electricity, clearly, and hadn't thought they'd need to open it manually often enough to concern themselves with.

Blast them.

The spring air was a balm on his sweaty face as the doors finally gave and opened wide enough for Kase to fit the hover through.

He wiped the sweat away on the collar of his shirt, then jogged back over to the hover, his boots slapping the smooth rock floor. He scrambled up the wing and into the cockpit at last, nodding to the second seat. "Familiarize yourself with the weapons trigger over there and strap in. You'll be my eyes during patrol today."

The greenie dropped into his seat with a wince, setting his cane in the space between his seat and the side of the ship. The buckles latched with gentle, almost reverent clacks as he settled himself. Cautious movement—too cautious to be a pilot.

Kase's cheek stung; he kept absentmindedly chewing on the inside of it to keep him from saying something he'd regret.

With that kind of hesitation, the greenie wouldn't have made it through training even if he'd not suffered such a horrific injury—but he was here now, in a hover, ready to fly.

Kase had no choice but to train him. The other greenies weren't much better.

Kase finished a few more pre-flight checks before buckling himself in, and then they were off. The hover jerked forward, creeping along the hangar until the nose reflected sunlight.

"Ready?" Kase asked, settling his goggles into his hair. The familiar weight added a sense of normalcy he craved. "If you see anything that strikes you as even a little odd, speak up. We're looking for anything suspicious and will investigate as needed."

"What exactly qualifies as suspicious?"

"You'll know." He hoped. "Just trust your gut."

He pressed his fingers to the dash and sent a thought to the hover. *Invisible.*

The hover beeped in response.

For a moment, Kase's heart stopped. He'd expected it, and he'd known exactly what he was doing, but combined with the knowledge of his uncle...

Deep breaths.

Trying to quell the shaking in his hands, he gripped the steering control and refused to let his thoughts run wild. But he was beginning to think maybe the sky wouldn't provide the relief he needed.

"Head and shoulders back against your seat," Kase

instructed. "Tighten your core."

"Yes, sir!"

Kase smirked a little. He wasn't a *sir* for anyone, but he didn't correct him. "Then let's fly."

After pressing a few other buttons and flipping some switches, he raised the craft straight into the air, his stomach dropping with the sudden movement. He clenched his core and braced himself against the gravitational forces. He almost wished they didn't have the windshield. The cold air would've been nice on his skin. It would've distracted him even further from the revelations of the last hour.

But he also would've ended up eating at least a dozen insects. He didn't need a distraction *that* badly.

He slowed the craft, and the forces pressing against him abated. He clicked a few buttons to stabilize the pressure in the cockpit. Any other maneuvers he did in the air, the craft should combat it, a countermeasure that Jaydian hovers lacked.

This one was a test for the greenie. Kase peeked over at him, hoping he hadn't passed out.

Instead of finding a slumped form or a green face, he found the boy absolutely beaming.

Kase couldn't help the smile crossing his own face. He knew that joy.

"Wow," Hixon gasped as they rose at a more stable rate. The city shrunk with each yard they climbed until Kase leveled them out at about a mile or so above the capital. He pushed the craft forward. He'd do loops around the city, fanning outward and then back before doing a few lower-altitude sweeps above the trees and ruined buildings.

The familiar cold swept through his chest. He quickly retrieved the blanket from where he'd stashed it and set it behind his back. Warmth pulsed from where it touched, and he settled back. His theory about the blankets containing whatever made the hover run seemed to be mostly correct. Now that he knew the machine used his own Soul to power itself, so many things made more sense.

The question was, had the Cerls created the blankets because of what happened with his uncle? Or had Ezekiel already known about it?

Anderson still hadn't awoken even with the blanket's help. Clearly having an Essence power and then losing it was too much for even Cerl technology to help. That made him feel worse, because it'd been one of his ideas for keeping Hallie alive if she went through with her plan. It'd worked on Niels for now, but his injury hadn't been because he'd lost some otherworldly power.

A red button flashed at Kase, and he hurriedly directed his thoughts toward his flight. Thinking of the stupid stars-ridiculous mountain man only made Kase jealous, even if he knew Hallie was his. He couldn't help it.

Kase turned the craft southward, toward Crystalfell. He pointed to a display on the dash and said, "With the standard hovers, you'll need to keep your eye on the fuel gauge as they tend to eat it up quickly, which is why a fresh refuel before takeoff is vital." He pointed to the specific gauge that would've held the electrical input in a standard hover. This one was as blue as the sky, and now Kase knew why. He shook off his unease. "The larger, more advanced models rely more on electricity to power them in addition to what's needed to activate the hover capacities. Either way, keeping the gauge in the middle of your dash will allow you to maximize your flight and reserve enough fuel and energy in case of a firefight."

Hixon just nodded, his eyes still wide. A kernel of warmth—not from the blanket—skittered through his chest. There was just something about the sky that made everything more magical, and watching the greenie experience it for the first time was gratifying.

Kase explained a few more basic principles and tricks he'd learned over the years as they flew. With each passing mile of serene sky and rolling pasture or town cluster below, Hixon's shoulders relaxed. It reminded Kase of his first time in the sky. The day his world finally made sense.

For a moment, it was nice to pretend that the rest of the world and its problems didn't exist, and the only things that mattered were the clouds above and the ground below.

"I never dreamed it would be this beautiful," Hixon said, leaning to the right to inspect the village below.

They'd finished their outer circles and began their return to the city in lazy circuits. The ruined capital was just visible over the horizon. Nothing of note had happened. No Cerl hovers. No dragon. No Skibs.

That was all a relief, for certain, but something in Kase's

gut told him it wasn't reliable. The hovers could've been invisible like his own. There might've been something he missed. But he wouldn't worry about it just yet.

Hixon settled back into his seat, his fingers on the weapons trigger, ready to attack as needed. Kase could see why he'd been chosen to enter the Crews. The lad was intelligent and determined. He just needed to find his wings.

The words his father had slung at him the night of the induction ritual rang in his ears.

They put him with you for a reason, even if you just earned your jacket.

Yet the boy hadn't been given the chance because of the bike accident...until now. He wouldn't be able to work the accelerator or the foot controls. Not until he was fully healed, if ever.

Kase adjusted the blanket behind him. Could he do something with this hover? Would the hover allow the greenie to fly it if Kase still powered it with his own soul?

He tapped the side panel with his fingers and thought it to the craft. A trio of soft, happy beeps responded.

They sounded happy to his ear, at least.

Kase should have been more disturbed than he was, but he just smiled. "Hey greenie—want to fly?"

Hixon's mouth dropped open and he pointed to his legs. "What? I can't—I only know the basics and what's in the manual. I'm not—"

Kase let go of his controls. "Good luck, greenie. Better not crash us!"

The color drained out of the boy's face as the craft dropped a foot and listed to the right. He yanked his controls, and the hover responded with a few flashing lights. "Sir! *I cannot do this!*"

Kase reached over and grabbed his shoulder, giving it a squeeze. "Trust me. You steer. I'll control the speed. Got it?"

"I most definitely do not have it."

The craft stabilized under Kase's thought and the greenie's trembling hands. "You had the highest written examination score in history—even better than me—but the best way to learn is through doing, and you have what it takes. Just breathe and *feel.*"

"Feel *what?*"

"I already told you—follow your instincts. You know

what to do." He pointed to the dash, then to the horizon. "Don't worry about the fuel and the cabin pressure gauges. We'll add that next time. For today, you just keep us at a steady altitude." He tapped the greenie's steering control. "Do a few loops around the city...and have fun."

The boy's hands strangled the controls. "But what if we crash?"

"We won't."

"What if Cerls show up?"

"Then we'll deal with that when the time comes."

"But—"

Kase patted the greenie's head. "Let's fly, Pilot Hixon."

It was slow going at first, and Kase had to realign them in the sky a few times with the hover's help. But the closer they got to the capital, the less the greenie's hand shook. A smile even crept back across his face.

An hour or two later, Kase made him land the hover in a clearing just outside the hangar entrance. "Told you it's the best."

Hixon's face shone with sweat in the sunset light, but he grinned and looked over at Kase. "I never realized..." He took a few steadying breaths. "I never realized just how exhilarating that would be."

Still a lot of words, but fewer than before. Kase would take his wins where he could. "Welcome to the club."

They took off once more, and Kase guided the hover back into the hangar. After fumbling a little bit getting the greenie down from the cockpit, Kase finished off the post-flight checks with Hixon in tow, talking his ear off.

He didn't stop all the way to the rations station.

Oddly, Kase found he didn't mind. And when he returned to his tent that night, he found a small, wrapped package lay on his cot. Inside was a Zuprium dagger tucked inside an ornate red leather sheath embroidered with a sword mounted inside a stone, Arthurian-style. Under the dagger lay a small strip of parchment.

I never got to thank you for saving my life that night. Please accept this gift as my thanks. I've heard you are an avid reader, and I thought this would fit. Thank you.

Trainee Pilot Laurence Andrew Hixon

Kase could help the burning in his eyes, and despite the tempest of emotions and revelations of the day, he went to sleep feeling a little lighter.

PART III: SWORDS

Interlude II

NAVARA

Yet I know there is but one hope...love, which conquers all.

CHAPTER 38

THOSE CURLS

15 Years Ago

HARLAN'S HEADACHE BLAZED BRIGHTER THAN the sun shining on the beautiful summer day outside his chamber window.

The day was anything but warm.

Days like these made it nearly impossible to tell if his body was finally giving in to the Fogs or simply preparing him for the worst. Nothing seemed to help—not sleep, not food, not even the vintage wine in his glass. The wine, of course, had other uses. It helped dull the events of the morning to a mere memory, though he knew it would only be a short reprieve.

He would still wake up tomorrow as the man who'd executed his own brother-in-law and nephews.

It was what Ezekiel wanted, and with his crimes, it was what he deserved.

Outside his window in the manor courtyard, Harlan and Les' children were playing a game of tag. His adoptive mother, Aurelia, sat on a chair watching them, soaking in the joy that was her grandchildren. Carleton was cleaning up from the day's events, a kindness Harlan appreciated.

He focused on his children.

Ana, the youngest, was only four—and only four thanks to Ezekiel.

Harlan paused to take a steadying breath.

Ana's blonde hair, so like Michael's, blazed in the summer sunlight, unbound and swirling about her as she ran. Her tenacity often outpaced her ability to keep up; her giggly pursuit of her brothers ended with a scraped knee and heartbroken sobs after her feet got ahead of her. Kase skidded to a stop and awkwardly picked her up with his boyish strength, her feet dragging the ground. He took her to Aurelia, who pulled the girl into her ample lap. Once his sister was taken care of, Kase was off after Zeke, who'd ducked behind one of the trees. What Kase *didn't* see was Jove hiding in the branches above him. Jove pelted his youngest brother with a pinecone or something else of the sort. Kase barely dodged it and shouted something up to the other boy.

Despite being nearly six, Kase held his own against his two older brothers. He was quick, like Harlan had been at his age, and more than determined. His smile could light up any room, and if he continued to grow into those curls and that wicked sense of humor, he would be a perfect reflection of the man who'd hung from the gallows three hours before.

He hadn't seen Les since the execution. Once they'd returned in a silent carriage, she'd locked herself in her library. Of course, she'd been distant ever since her brother turned himself in, retreating further into herself with each passing day. He understood. He wouldn't want to be near himself, either.

How had they gotten here? How had they fallen so low? Harlan was Kominder General of Kyvena, the third-highest rank within the city, but the accolades on his military jacket felt more like a sham. His rank hadn't changed anything at all.

He'd still been forced to sit steely-eyed and firm-jawed as he watched the man he loved as his own brother hang for his crimes.

Ezekiel Fairchild betrayed the nation of his birth. Soul Technology had cost him everything good he had left after Rose died. That had been the turning point, that grief. Harlan knew it well.

Ezekiel—and eventually, Les—had brought him out of his own grief for one shining moment. The births of his four children proved how far he'd come from the man who'd sworn off the idea of having a family of his own. But now he faced a life where the consequences of Ezekiel's actions would haunt him and his family for eternity.

There was no going back to the sunny days of the past.

He looked over at the letter he'd penned to Les before they'd left for McKenzie Square, where the executions would take place. Being the wife of the Kominder General dictated she must attend the horrid event. She hadn't let go of a single tear, but Harlan saw her brokenness. Broken because she knew the truth; broken because she'd truly lost her brother years ago, and she would never have him back.

He'd hoped writing her a letter like their courting days would help ease the pain.

Dearest Les,

We'll be back in your countryside soon.

H

It wasn't much, but it was all he could manage. He hastily folded it and gave it to a servant waiting just outside the study. The man was off as soon as Harlan gave his curt directions.

He looked outside once again. Zeke pulled Jove up one of the rocks, and they shouted something at Kase, who threw a pinecone up at them. Not bad aim for a boy his age. He stomped off and sat beside Aurelia and Ana, who was now happily snuggled in her grandmother's lap, listening to the book Aurelia read out loud.

What would he do if any one of his children discovered the truth? Would they hate him? Would they despise their uncle? Jove was old enough to remember him, and Zeke. But the only Ezekiel they'd ever known was the ghost of the man who dared to smile, who dared to dream of a better world.

Where had Harlan gone wrong? Had they always been hurtling toward this end? This broken family legacy?

Harlan picked up his discarded wine glass and flung it at the fireplace.

It shattered into a thousand pieces.

His headache spiked, and Harlan fell into his armchair, hand across his eyes.

He'd never escape this life of horror.

CHAPTER 3 9

HEROES OF FIRST EARTH

Niels

WHEN NIELS HAD FIRST WOKEN up, he'd thought he was back in Stoneset.

But then he'd remembered the attack. Fleeing those caverns with Hallie and not looking back. Leaving the others to the mercy of the Cerls.

There might not be a Stoneset left to go back to anymore.

Part of him felt guilty. Another felt frustrated, and a third—a small third—felt relieved. He felt guilty for leaving them in chaos, but his only thought had been to get Hallie out of there. Still, he hated that he hadn't been able to help. Hallie had done far more than him, and it gnawed at him that he no longer needed to protect her. He was as useless as a creek flooding its banks during the rainy season.

The relief was something else entirely. No longer being trapped in the Stoneset caverns had allowed his mind to heal in a way it hadn't been able to in the months after the Cerl attack. Being around the people he'd known his entire life had only made it more clear that he no longer had a family.

He wasn't the only one who'd lost everyone. He knew that. But it was nice not to have constant reminders of his loss, even if the new caverns he found himself in were full of more war-torn refugees. This was different; these refugees, he could help. He no longer felt as if everyone was watching him with pity.

However, one could only go so long without seeing the sun without going stir-crazy, which was why the Yalven cavern had proven to be the perfect escape over the couple days since he'd woken. It was why he'd agreed to patrol duty in Stoneset.

He didn't belong underground trapped like a rat. He needed fresh air.

The cavern was still clearly burrow-deep with the jagged, dripping stalactites, but the Yalvs had used their powers to transform it into a meadow of sorts. Whether or not it was an illusion, Niels didn't care. Grass grew from the ground, and a worn pathway wound through the towering oaks. Wildflowers dotted the open spaces, and tents tucked themselves into crooks under trees. Children chased each other throughout, their laughter lightening the pall that hung in the air no matter where one went in the Catacombs.

It felt alive, and Niels no longer knew how much life he had left to live. He would use what he could of it and hope for another day.

He'd spent the previous afternoon helping several of the refugees prepare for their return to the surface. It was nice to feel useful, even with his limited capacity. He'd spent most of his time with a man who owned a woodworking shop. It was nice to be around someone who enjoyed the same hobby Niels did. It was something he hadn't gotten to do much besides occasionally whittling around the fire after suppers in recent months.

The man's apprentice had perished in the attack on Kyvena, and by the end of the night, he'd asked Niels if he'd like to stay on once everything was settled.

He'd told the man he'd think on it and get back with him the next day with his decision. Depending on the conversation he planned to have with Hallie that morning, he would hopefully say yes.

It was just nice to be needed, and the capital could offer him much more opportunity than Stoneset. It'd been Jack's dream, then Hallie's. Now it was his.

He wove his way through the grasses, nodding at the people he passed. The Yalvs were interesting, and they reminded him of his mother; stoic, but always willing to invite someone in. Fely had visited the day he'd woken and told him about the bonfire celebration, inviting him to come if he felt up to it.

He'd gone, but for some reason, he hadn't expected to see Hallie there.

Why he hadn't expected it, he wasn't sure, but when he'd walked into the celebration with a few other Jaydians, he had not expected or needed to see Hallie with Kase's hands on her waist.

Even two days later, the memory of their dancing alone poured the hot tang of jealousy down the back of his throat. But then he'd remember that Kase was the reason he was even standing there, thanks to the blanket he'd brought. Without it, Niels would still be trapped in that cold room with no way out.

Still, it'd taken everything in him to apologize to Kase for kissing her, and he probably wouldn't have done so if the *sterning* pilot hadn't forced his hand.

He rubbed the braided cord at his wrist.

The fibers were rough and threaded with blue. He wasn't sure he would've done the same for Kase if their positions had been reversed—especially not when it involved Hallie. That would've been selfish, but he didn't think he would've cared if it meant Hallie would look at him the way she looked at Kase.

Seeing them together, dancing, talking, and finally kissing in front of everyone...

Hallie had never looked at Niels that way, not even before Jack died.

That part hurt the most: his feelings for her were still there in his heart, yet he knew he would never have her.

He needed to move on. She'd told him as much. But how?

After a few more turns and nods to others, he found himself in a small meadow tucked up against the cavern wall covered in kudzu. A few trees enclosed the space, and a strange Yalven torch hung from a hook in one of the trunks, shining brighter than regular fire. It was almost like they'd mounted a small sun.

Against one of the trees sat Hallie, her sketchbook out, her pencil flying across the page. She didn't look up from her work, and Niels had to take a moment to simply admire her before her expression turned to one of displeasure or disappointment.

The grass bent under his boots, but his steps barely made a sound as he strode toward her. She still didn't look up, and it wasn't until he stopped a short distance away that she stopped writing.

Her eyes never left her page.

"Morning." That came out raspy. He cleared his throat. "Petra told me you like to come here when you're not busy."

She didn't answer, only stuck her pencil into her sketchbook and closed it.

But she didn't run away or curse him. He took that as a good sign and eased himself against the other side of the tree. Across the way, a few men sparred with Zuprium swords. The soft clangs didn't help his focus.

"Look," he tried again, "I didn't come here to argue or beg you to take me back. I heard what you said."

Even if I don't agree with it much.

He watched her out of the corner of his eye. She merely wet her lips, staring at the kudzu vines.

He continued, "I'm going to stay in the capital for a while yet, even after everything is set to rights, but I want you to know it's for myself, not...not because I'm going to keep chasing you. I'm not here to try again. I just wanted to apologize for my behavior."

She swallowed.

Niels hated that he was still aware of her every movement. It would be a long time yet before he could forget all her little mannerisms, but he would have to trust that it would fade. "If you don't want to forgive me, you don't have to. But just know that I only want you to be happy, and if he makes you happy, then so be it. I won't stand in your way."

The words felt more like gravel he forced through his teeth, but he'd said them. And he did mean them, or he would eventually.

He waited that time, hoping she would acknowledge

him in some inconsequential way, but she just chewed her lip.

Stars, she really had changed.

He pushed himself back to his feet and shoved his hands into his pockets. "That's really all I came to say. Good luck. I wish you all the best, truly."

He had just started back out of the meadow—feeling ridiculous, yet a little lighter at the same time—when she finally spoke. Her voice was small but clear.

"I'm glad you're okay."

He looked back and caught the tears in her eyes threatening to fall. She swiped at them before saying, "You saved us in the Gate chamber, and you saved me in the mine that day. Thank you."

Niels just smiled and tipped his head. "My pleasure."

Her words were the balm he needed, and his shoulders relaxed. Hallie packed away her sketchbook into her satchel and stood, gesturing for him to follow as she walked past. "What will you be doing in the city?"

He kept his gait slow so as not to outpace her. "Woodworking long as I'm able." He held up his bracelet. He didn't miss the shadow that crossed her face, but he forced himself not to reach out and smooth away the worry line in her brow. "Got an apprenticeship with a Woodwright soon as his shop is up and running again. Might've been a little desperate of him to hire me after helping him only for a few hours the other day, but I don't care."

Hallie tangled her hand in her satchel strap, a soft smile appearing. "I'm happy for you. I think you'll love the city."

They winded their way through the trees, chatting softly about nothing inconsequential before going their separate ways at the edge of the Yalven cavern. It burned him to say goodbye, but it was for the best. He had a mountain to climb...but with the whole world beyond it, he knew he could do it.

It was time he found that new dream.

Kase

CONSIDERING THE REVELATIONS ABOUT HIS uncle,

Kase needed to think more than ever. He needed to fly, and he'd convinced Hallie to join him the next day. The easy patrol with Laurence Hixon had been nice, but the greenie was no Hallie. Kase did keep his new dagger attached to his belt, though.

Besides, he needed to convince her to try resetting the Gate instead. Her diabolical plan to put herself into that sword wasn't going to work. He refused to allow her to do that. Not for him.

He'd meant it when he'd told her that he'd find her no matter where they ended up. They belonged together. It sounded insane, resetting time, but Kase would do anything to be with her. She was the only thing in his life that made sense.

Either way, he'd at least convinced her to study his hover. After the flight with the greenie the day prior, he wasn't sure he could trust the machine. Sure, he'd wanted Laurence to fly it, but he hadn't expected his idea to work. What if Kase had already given too much to it? What if he one day begged for death because too much of his soul had been taken or siphoned off or whatever the tech had done to his uncle?

But he wouldn't panic just yet.

If he could figure out how it worked, he could then convince Harlan to use that knowledge against the Cerls. Maybe Kase could figure out a way to turn their other machines against them, to commandeer them for Jayde instead. He had no idea how he would accomplish that, but he knew for certain negotiating a peace deal wasn't going to work. Correa wasn't the sort of man to bargain. Kase had nearly died at his hands. He wouldn't sit there and make peace with the man trying to kill Hallie.

Even if that's what she's trying to do.

Thankfully, Sergeant didn't run off to tattle on him when Kase led Hallie into the underground hangar. The guard followed but hung back a ways, one hand on his sword, the other on his flashpistol.

The man was so dutiful that Kase almost felt bad for dragging him along on this unscheduled outing—he wasn't due for patrol for at least three more hours. But he didn't feel bad enough to head back to his tent. Obviously. Kase wasn't that nice.

He walked Hallie to the edge of the hangar and opened the doors. The morning air was crisp and ruffled his hair. The fresh breeze was a nice change from the stale stench of the Catacombs, which made the day much better already.

Kase returned to Hallie and laced his fingers with hers. It was the perfect day for a foray into the skies. She just didn't know about that part yet.

"Are you sure it's okay to be out here?" Hallie asked, the apprehension in her voice evident as Kase led her to the Cerl craft. "I mean, I know you said I could study your machine, but..." She looked around the space as if waiting for someone to tell them off, but their only witnesses were the silent hovers—and Sergeant, who stood at attention near the hangar entrance. "...I also don't want to get thrown in the dungeons for breaking some sort of military protocol."

"Well, our outing today has been approved by Sergeant, who is my keeper," Kase said as he strode to the hover and placed a hand on the side. It hummed in response as Kase gave it a soft pat. "Granted, he thinks we're going to play nicely on the ground, and as long as we return within the hour, he won't go and tell the Stradat Lord Kapitan."

"What do you mean, he *thinks*?" Hallie practically squeaked.

Kase chuckled. "I promised to be a good boy. Just didn't elaborate on what 'good' meant."

He glanced back at the soldier, who hadn't moved from his post.

"No, no, not that part, though that brings up other concerns."

"Then what?"

Hallie pointed at the sky outside the underground hangar, exasperation in her voice. "That!"

"Not following?"

Hallie crossed her arms and frowned. "I did *not* sign up to fly today."

Kase ran his hand over the wing tip closest to him, and the ship warmed under his touch. He started his pre-flight systems checks. "You can't get all the research you need without seeing it in the air."

"But I can stay on the ground." Hallie backed up a little. "I can take notes just fine down here. Up against that tree out there. It looks like a nice one to lean against." She gestured to a pine not far from the hangar entrance.

Kase opened one of the panels and checked the wires. All good, though with everything he knew, he still wasn't entirely sure what they did. His uncle might've known. Good enough that they weren't frayed or anything, he guessed. The hover beeped at him softly as he closed the panel. "Nope, you're coming up with me."

"Absolutely not."

Kase paused in his inspection of the wing and put his hands on her shoulders, turning her toward him. "I promise not to let anything happen to you."

"Kase…" Her eyes were wide and full of fear. They sparkled like precious jewels in the early morning sun.

He blinked to focus himself. "Listen, I've learned a lot these last few months, and we can't let our fears control us."

"I wouldn't say it's controlling me, per se. I'd argue it's a very natural expression of my self-preservation instincts."

He gave her shoulders a squeeze. "Well, you refused to look out the window last time we flew over Kyvena, and you haven't lived until you've seen it from thousands of feet above."

"I didn't realize you were paying attention to me," Hallie said with suspicion in her gaze. A stray piece of auburn hair whisked across her face in the gentle breeze.

Kase hesitated a moment, leaning in closer. "Well, you're kind of difficult to ignore."

And then, with a flick to her nose, he let her go and returned to his pre-flight checks. Hallie made a disgruntled noise. "Why in the blazes did you do that?"

Kase laughed and half turned to find her holding her nose. "What?"

She let her hand fall. Annoyance painted her features. "Do you regularly go around flicking people's noses? Because in the world I live in, such behavior is considered odd, if not *outright* rude."

"Your nose is rather cute, and I don't necessarily think that about everyone's." Shocks, it felt so good just to be with her, tease her…and maybe later, kiss her. Combined with the fresh air and the promise of soaring through the skies, he could almost forget the rest of the world existed. He'd needed this. Badly. Tomorrow they could worry about the world ending.

Hallie rolled her eyes, though a light pink appeared on her cheeks. "Just don't do that again."

Kase opened another panel on the opposite side. "Yes, my lady."

Hallie walked toward the front of the ship, inspecting it. "Are you *certain* this is all right? Especially after what your father said? About your uncle?"

Kase closed the panel with a snap, and the machine beeped at him good-naturedly again. He ducked under the wing. "What the Stradat Lord Kapitan doesn't know won't hurt him, and besides, it's good to get out under the open sky."

"Still didn't answer my question." Hallie stepped up beside the ship's nose and rubbed her fingers against the blue-tinged metal. The ship hummed in response. She jumped. "Wait—did it—did I—?"

"I think it likes you," Kase whispered as he bent and kissed the soft spot beneath her ear. She shivered as Kase asked, "Got your sketchbook?"

The blush from earlier deepened on her cheeks, and she grinned, turning slightly in his arms. "By some miracle, I made it to the other side of the world and back with it this time." She patted her satchel. "For once, I'm actually excited to sketch."

"For once?" Kase straightened, but he kept one hand at her waist. "Those pencil strokes still haunt my nightmares."

Hallie smiled sadly. "Haven't really felt like it since the *Eudora*. Tried on our way to Stoneset, but it wasn't the same." She paused. "I did a little the other night during the bonfire, but I was quite rusty."

"Oh, I didn't realize..."

Well, that was one way to kill the mood.

Kase pulled her to his chest and wrapped his arms around her. She held him just as tightly. He rested his head on hers and breathed in her scent. The breeze tousled his curls. If only they could stay there forever. That thought came back to him, the one he'd had in Achilles before Hallie destroyed it—that *of course* he would find what he'd been looking for all this time right when he could no longer keep it. He squeezed her a little tighter.

If they figured some way out of this, he'd stay beside her until the end of his days. They'd discuss scholars, literature, and the benefits of obscure poetry. Maybe they'd even write about this adventure of theirs. She could teach him how to draw so they could illustrate it.

Kase would give anything to see that future. To make sure *Hallie* lived to see it.

After a moment more, Kase cleared the emotion from his throat. When had he become so soft? He pulled back and looked at her. "Then we should probably get into the air soon, though you can't include me in any sketches. I didn't do my hair this morning."

"Only if you swear not to do any mad loops or something else equally terrifying." She raised an eyebrow. "Been there, done that."

Kase laughed as he led her to the wing and knelt slightly, clasping his hands and creating a step-up for her to use. She slid her hand onto his shoulder, and even through the thick leather, heat spread at her touch. He wasn't sure if it was her power or simply the way she looked as she climbed up the wing and into the cockpit. He rather appreciated the way her trousers fit over her hips, as well as the maiden sash accentuating her curves. She threw her satchel into the co-pilot's seat and turned. When she noticed his glassy gaze, she rolled her eyes.

"If you don't stop gawking, I'll draw you like those Wanted posters in every sketch."

"Well, it's your fault, really." Kase pulled himself up onto the wing; Hallie stared at him, utterly deadpan, as he climbed into the cockpit and slid into his seat, smirking. "I'm only human."

He winked at her, then buckled himself in and performed the final pre-flight procedures, checking the power gauge and the oxygen levels. Muttering under her breath, Hallie took the seat beside him.

Kase looked over at her, lifting his eyebrow. Her soft pink lips tugged down at the corners, cheeks flushed with annoyance. It was a rather adorable scowl, made even more appealing by the fact he was the one who put it there. He resisted the urge to forget all his plans and spend the time kissing her instead. "Does my flirting displease you, my lady? Would you prefer I stop?" He pressed the button to warm up the engine. "My most sincere apologies if—"

The hover interrupted him with a spray of blue liquid

from the dash.

"*Blech*, you stars-ridiculous ship!" That was the second time the thing had doused him.

Hallie roared with laughter. "I guess Merlin doesn't appreciate your sarcasm."

He wiped his face with one of the blankets he'd tucked under his seat and laughed along with her. "Merlin?"

"All pets need a name, and this one needs a particularly noble one, seeing as it helped you save us all."

"Merlin was a wizard, not some dog."

"A wizard and companion to one of the most famous literary heroes of First Earth." Hallie patted the dashboard in front of her. The hover hummed in response.

Of course the machine would like her better.

She flashed him a victorious grin. "And as Merlin here has some sort of magical technology, well, it simply makes sense."

"So does that make me Arthur?"

Hallie thought for a moment. "Perhaps, but that would then make me Guinevere, and I'm not sure I'm okay with that."

"Feels appropriate to me. You certainly order people around as well as any queen."

"I feel like I should take offense to that."

"Well, Merlin and myself would be so grateful if you'd hold off on that and buckle your safety straps, Your Highness," Kase said, buckling his own.

"Technically, queens are addressed as *Majesty*." She clicked herself into her seat and pulled out her sketchpad and pencil.

Kase flipped the switch to turn the machine on completely. The hover purred in response. Maybe it was more like a pet than Kase realized. "Well, *Your Most Esteemed and Illustrious Royal Majesty*, we're about to take off, so hold on tight."

She clutched her sketching supplies in her lap, her nose scrunched and her eyes shut.

"Ready?"

She opened one eye. "No."

Smirking, Kase pressed lightly on the accelerator and pulled a lever to his left, turning on the hover ability. Cold started in his toes, but he pulled the blanket out and settled it over his legs. The cold stopped for the moment. He ignored his father's words about his uncle, that the reason this hover was here at all was because of his deadly discovery. Hallie didn't say anything about it again either. There was a chance she was being polite, though that wasn't necessarily her style, but more than likely, she probably thought if she pushed too much, she wouldn't get to study the machine.

He loved her curiosity and scholar's heart and the way she always found a way to make him laugh.

"So you just pulled that lever." Hallie leaned forward to look. "That's not like your old hover at all."

The night he'd taught Hallie how to fly his hover flashed in his mind. How he wished he could go back to that. Almost. He kind of liked how their story had played out, and despite the hardships they'd encountered, his love ran deeper than he could have ever imagined, the bond between them fire-forged.

She must've been thinking along the same lines, because she said, "This one doesn't have an electric gramophone hooked up to it, I assume?"

"Because I've had so much time to do so with my house arrest, of course." They rose higher at a steady rate, and Hallie's free hand clenched the arm rest. Kase eased back. "No, but a few of the bigger hovers we had used the same mechanism, so I'm familiar with it." His blanket slipped a little. "The lever usually releases a higher voltage of electricity to interact with the inner workings of the hover. I'm certain this does the same thing, except..."

The frosty sensation spread from his toes to the middle of his foot. He looked down to find the blanket had slid to the floor. Couldn't the Cerls have come up with a better way to keep it at bay? Maybe he should just make a bracelet like Niels had. Man was smarter than Kase gave him credit for. Well, to be fair, Niels had said it was Petra's idea. So she really deserved the credit. Yes, he liked that better.

With one hand still on the steering control, he grabbed the blanket with the other and tried to throw it over his shoulder.

The cold only receded a little but came back once the blanket fell once again. He stabilized the craft midair.

"Here, let me help you. Just don't crash." Hallie unbuckled herself and reached across. She tugged the blanket up over his shoulders.

With its replacement, warmth immediately flushed his system. "Thanks."

Buckling herself back in, she said, "What's the significance of the blanket, again?"

She grabbed her sketching supplies and flipped to a blank page. Kase eased the hover back into its ascent. "Something's woven into it that keeps me warm when I fly. The Soul Tech makes me cold." He nodded to her seat. "Should be another one under there, but I don't know if you'll feel the effects of the hover. Your father didn't."

Hallie pulled out the other blanket and assessed it. "Looks to be woven with the same metal as the ship. It's probably Zuprium, but why is it blue? I don't quite understand that."

Kase shrugged and slowed their climb further. They were about a mile above the city now, which would be the perfect view. "All I know is that it works, and that somehow this machine knows what I'm thinking. Haven't figured out how it can do that, but these days, I don't question things like that. Seen too much not to believe."

Hallie nodded and pulled something else out of her satchel. His old goggles. She clutched them in one hand, the pencil in the other.

Kase reached across and placed his hand over hers. "You're doing great, Hals. Now take a look below."

"But what if I fall?" She didn't look up.

"Then I'll catch you."

She shot him a half smile. "You make it sound so easy."

"Remember when we fell out of that tree? I could've made it to safety, but I grabbed you instead." Kase pulled his hand back and pressed the button to stabilize them further. A wave of cold swept over his hand, but it was gone in a second.

"And you didn't even like me then, did you?"

Kase cracked his neck. "I might've...had a small crush, but I was too stubborn to admit it." He pointed out the window again. "Now take a look before we fly a little to the west."

The smile didn't leave her face as she peeked over the edge of the hover. She gazed for a minute before sketching something quickly in her sketchbook. "Never realized the pattern the roads make leading up to McKenzie Square just before the Jayde Center. Looks like a starburst."

She sat back quickly before slowly edging toward the side again. He laughed. "Not so bad, isn't it?"

She laid a hand against her stomach. "Still feel a little nauseated, but it's pretty way up here."

"You're not so bad to look at either."

She raised a single brow, a soft flush brushing the tip of her nose and cheeks. "You're in a good mood."

"Everything is always better up in the sky." He pushed the craft forward at a slow pace. "Makes all the noise fall away."

They flew around in silence for several minutes. Hallie took notes or sketched in her book, and Kase took them in a wide circle above the capital city. From this angle, it almost looked as if the city was sleeping rather than lying in ruins. He could just make out a few specks below moving about. Slowly but surely, things were heading toward normalcy.

He glanced over at Hallie. She was intent on her sketch, her head bowed and her hand holding the pencil a little awkwardly. He couldn't really tell what she was drawing—being left-handed, she had to hold the book at a certain angle—but he noted the small smile on her face.

It might have been the calm before the storm, seeing as everything was certain to fall apart no matter what she decided. But it was still nice. He was here with her now, and he could simply take in the moment and enjoy it for what it was.

The ship beeped happily, and Hallie startled, her pencil shrieking over the paper. She cursed softly, and Kase grinned. "Told you it had a mind of its own."

Hallie rubbed the eraser down the side of the page where she'd scrawled across it. "Well, please tell Merlin that I would appreciate being able to draw without worrying we're about to drop out of the sky."

Kase patted the dash affectionately. "He wouldn't allow that. It's almost like he reads my thoughts. If it's really my Soul or something fueling him...well, it's a little creepy, but it at least means you're safe."

It should have been terrifying, but the technology only fascinated him. What else could they do with it? Could it save someone? Had that been Ezekiel's motivation after so much loss?

Had that been what his uncle had thought? Why had he told the Cerl Queen the secrets of Jaydian technology? Had she forced it out of him? Or had he told her in confidence only for her to betray him?

Maybe that was why he begged for death. Not because his soul had been damaged, but because losing just one more person he loved had been too much for him to take.

He looked over at Hallie again as she resumed her sketching. "Hals?"

She didn't look up. "Hmm?"

Kase flew them over the Jayde Center ruins. "Are you sure you won't reconsider your decision?"

He was impressed with how calm he sounded discussing something that drastic.

She paused, but she still didn't meet his eyes. "Decision?"

"About the Gate."

"We don't need to talk about this now."

"No guarantee now won't be the last chance we get to talk about it." He wasn't trying to be pushy; it was just true.

She looked up at last. "I lost a week getting us here, and I can't make that fireball. The very little healing I've done reverts in hours. I'm useless. Our only choice is combining the Essences."

"You're far from useless."

"You're just saying that."

"Hallie." He grabbed her hand and brushed his thumb over her knuckles. She peeked over at him through her lashes. "Your worth is not tied up in mastering the power that was thrust upon you weeks ago. Besides, aren't Fely and Saldr training you?"

"The only way I can fix this is if I don't have the power, and the only way to do that is to put it into that sword."

Kase gripped the steering control harder, and the ship beeped at him. He ignored the warning as he started them back toward the hangar. His time in the sky was probably finished until his patrol, but he hadn't noticed anything out of place. Two quiet flights in a row made him a little anxious, but if he didn't dwell too hard on it, he could accept the gift. "We can find another—"

BEEP! BEEP! SCREECH!

Kase only caught sight of the wall of flame just before it

hit the ship.

The windshield held under the blinding fire, but Kase's heart squeezed so tight, he thought it might actually burst. He could barely see anything at all. Too bright. Too hot.

Kase whipped them out of the onslaught. Hallie and the hover both screamed. Every indicator on the dash blinded him with flashing. A high-pitched squeal came from somewhere beneath or behind him. He couldn't tell. The metal of the ship's nose was tinged pink instead of blue.

The scent of hot metal burned his nose, and his eyes watered in the lingering pain from the flames.

"Hallie!" Kase shouted, looking over.

She pointed above them. "Dragon!"

His stomach dropped out. Fifty feet away was Skibs, riding atop his golden dragon. The beast opened its maw, a glowing ball of orange and gold sparking in the thing's throat.

The air rumbled and crackled with power.

I refuse to die today.

Locking his jaw, Kase let his instincts take over. He didn't know how he did it, exactly, but he pushed everything he had into the machine at his fingertips. His blood sang with each pounding, blistering heartbeat.

"Hold on and whatever you do, don't open your eyes!" he shouted.

And then they were off, Kase and his hover acting as one. They zoomed forward, rolling directly below the flames rocketing toward them. He wasn't sure if his hover could take another direct hit. Something flashed red on the dash, but Kase couldn't worry about that. Whatever it was probably was better than being burned alive by a dragon.

The ship righted itself, rolling back. On instinct, Kase pulled up on the steering control, completing a loop. He said a silent apology to Hallie, who would hopefully pull through this without passing out or puking. He'd promised her he wouldn't do exactly what he was doing, but he had no choice.

The dragon roared its fury as another flame jet missed its target.

Kase pressed down the trigger until his fingers ached, shooting at the beast. With immaculate precision, the dragon rolled in midair, the blazing Cerl bullet missing its massive wing by inches. Blast it.

The hover swerved as the dragon shot more flames at

Kase.

You will not win, he thought to the monster. Unshakable, he locked in, his hands squeezing the steering control.

Kase pressed the pedal, and the hover surged forward. He just needed to get out of the city. He needed to make sure they didn't fry anyone below. They'd already been through enough. They didn't deserve to suffer again.

But he wasn't sure if he could help it.

The dragon was hot on his heels. He swerved and banked. He glanced over at Hallie, who at least looked conscious, if rather green. Her pale, bloodless fingers gripped one armrest, his goggles strangled in her other hand. Her sketchbook and pencil were nowhere in sight, and her eyes were closed tight.

He needed to get her out of the hover. Could she eject? Would Skibs let her go? Or would that only kill her faster?

Kase's entire body went cold as he made his decision.

He wasn't sure if it was him flipping the hover again to face the dragon head on or the hover siphoning off his Soul, but his entire body hummed with arctic calm. Like ice ran through his veins.

Finger on the trigger, he shot three blasts in quick succession. The dragon dodged the first two, but the final one hit his tail.

Kase sped toward it head-on. He shot at it again and spun away just as he nearly collided with the beast's torso. Kase's ears popped, but he didn't suffer the g-force that would've normally accompanied such a move.

Whether it was because he was too focused or he was already dead, he didn't know, but by the time he realized it, he was already doing another loop and shooting at the dragon once more.

One, two, three.

This time, he hit the thing in the throat—right as he was about to shoot another blast of flames. All three shots hit their mark.

The sound turned back on.

The dragon screamed, its throat torn and raw from the fiery blue bullets Kase had stuffed down its throat. It writhed in midair, its wings freezing. Blood spurted and exploded in the air as the beast ripped at its wound with its clawed fingers.

And then it plummeted.

The figure on its back slid from the thing's shoulders. The dragon's thrashing wing nailed the rider in the back.

"Skibs!"

Kase didn't know what he was doing. He couldn't do anything, not really. He was in a hover. He didn't have any way of catching the man plunging thousands of feet to his death. That was, if he wasn't dead already.

Kase didn't think he'd hit him with a blast, but he'd been so focused on not being burnt alive he hadn't paid attention to the rider.

Kase pressed forward, all his focus riveted on Skibs. If he could slow Skibs' descent, the man might have a chance—but it might also crash Merlin directly into the ground. Skibs was falling too fast.

He shouldn't be trying to save him. Skibs had decimated the capital. He was half the reason Zeke was dead. But in the Gate Chamber, he'd been at war with himself, fighting whatever waited inside him.

Like Hallie was now.

And like Hallie could be saved—like Kase *had* to believe Hallie could be saved—maybe Skibs could, too.

A soft glow filled the cabin, and for a moment, everything slowed down to a glacial pace. Kase's vision faded in and out as he pushed himself further, allowing the hover to take whatever it needed from him. He couldn't tell if the blanket was still wrapped around his shoulders or not. He knew he was too cold, but he focused solely on the body clothed in that strange blue armor falling from the sky.

And then he was underneath Skibs. He held the craft steady, letting it descend, trying to match Skibs' rate of descent. He didn't know how far the ground was, only that he was playing a dangerous game.

Skibs cracked into the windshield above, but he didn't slide off. He stayed perfectly still—too still. The dash squealed at Kase.

The glow hadn't waned. Kase looked over to find Hallie bathed in light, her eyes still shut tight, her right hand squeezing his goggles. He hadn't realized she still had them. He blinked hard. Her power radiated off her being like a brilliant star in the night sky. It was blinding. She was a beacon—beautiful, alarming, and powerful.

The hover slowed, landing with a jolt. Without him

having to think about it.

Skibs slid off the windshield. Hallie collapsed in her seat, and his old goggles fell to the floor with a soft clunk.

"Hallie?" he asked, breathless; she didn't answer him. He went colder than the hover had ever made him. "*Hallie!*"

She'd done it. She'd done something to the ship or Skibs or—or *something*. It hadn't been his imagination, and now she was paying for it.

Kase fumbled with his safety buckles, which took entirely too long thanks to his stiff, frozen fingers. Blackness encroached on his vision. He'd given too much of himself to the ship.

He practically fell out of his seat. He didn't know where the dragon was or if Skibs was even alive. He didn't care.

Hallie's limp, gray form, held in place only by the safety straps, was all he could see.

CHAPTER 40

UNTIL THE STARS FALL

Hallie

THIS TIME, THE PAIN WAS different.

Her skin still burned, but not with heat—it burned like holding a fistful of snow without her gloves. The dark did not gleam with gold; instead, it pulsed with a halo that glowed faintly blue.

Under her skin, the fire remained. Its searing heat warred with the icy, piercing sting scraping over her skin, both only worsened by the caress of some kind of fabric. A blanket, maybe. Everywhere her skin was exposed, the fabric's touch only fanned the flames.

But once again, she knew she wasn't dead. Because she could hear familiar voices floating somewhere nearby...and because death would've been better than this.

The last thing she remembered was losing control of her power as Ben fell from the dragon's back. She'd been gripping both the goggles and a power tendril, but she'd lost hold of both. Heaviness thickened the blood in her veins at the memory of the giant reptile, its huge wings spread wide, maw open, flame building in its throat.

Kase.

Hallie jerked and pushed herself to her elbows, the pain receding with her panic. She winced still. The room was dark, lit only by a small gas lantern near her cot. Hanging linens surrounded her little cell. One was black as night but streaked with dust. Seemed she'd been given a more private room than most. She wasn't sure why; she wasn't anyone special.

The voices on the other side of the partition weren't concerned with waking the convalescing, clearly. Several shadows moved across the hanging linen in front of her. It felt like watching a strange show at Grieg's Theater, though not one she really wanted to see. One of the shadows—and the owner of the loudest voice—was Kase. His curly hair was slightly amorphous in shadow form, but she could tell it was him; the shadow he was arguing with was his father, straight-backed and lean as ever. The third shadow was more difficult for Hallie to distinguish, as he or she was only a bystander to the argument at hand.

Kase was okay.

Her vision blurred for a moment.

"If anything, I saved lives. *Again*," Kase shouted. "And now we have Skib—I mean, Ben—who could—"

"Who has been working with the *Cerls*," Harlan said, his voice quieter than Kase's but not without ringing authority. "I warned you about the dangers of using that machine!"

"I was doing a patrol."

"That you weren't scheduled to do for three more hours." When Kase failed to come up with an answer, Harlan scathingly added, "And you endangered Miss Walker, one of our greatest assets we have in this war."

"She's not just an *asset*," Kase growled.

"Yet another reason why I'm unsure as to why you risked her life in the hover."

Kase went silent again.

Hallie's heart ached for him. His father was right, though Hallie loathed to admit it— she'd had no business being up in the hover. If she was to do anything at all, she couldn't risk her life needlessly before she was able to restore the swords and the Essence powers to the Gates. Stupid.

But even if they'd made a mistake going up in the hover, Kase had defeated a dragon—the same monster that had destroyed much of Kyvena. Even if he'd been reckless, he'd proved he could take down the entire Cerl fleet with only his single ship, Merlin. Why couldn't his father see that? Was it solely because of his fear of the technology? Or was it something else?

Did he actually care for Kase in his own, if demented, way?

Another voice spoke up; the other shadow. "Miss Walker is stable," Jove Shackley said. "Kase got her to Saldr in time. No lasting damage was done." He paused, and neither his brother nor father filled the brief silence. "This may also prove she *can* restore the electricity. Saving Ben Reiss was quite the feat."

A few other voices joined the fray.

"Where is she?" Her mother's voice demanded, her shadow joining the others.

Her father followed, his silhouette thicker than the others. "Where is my daughter?"

Kase parted the sheet in front of her and allowed her parents inside. His eyes were rimmed in red, as if he hadn't slept in days. His curls were even more unkempt than usual, like he'd gone flying with the windshield down—or like he'd been dragging his fingers through them over and over.

How long had she been out?

When he made eye contact with her, his shoulders caved in. He broke eye contact almost immediately, ducking his head and pinching the bridge of his nose, expelling a harsh breath she could hear all the way on the cot.

She couldn't read that reaction. Frustration? Relief? Was he angry she'd used her power?

Her still-aching body protested as she sat up further. Her parents were both rather pale, but upon seeing her awake, they perked up. Her father hastened over and helped her. She winced.

"What hurts, Lark?" her father asked, eyes combing over her, trying to assess what he could do to fix whatever was broken.

Hallie shook her head, but that only made her wince more. Kase swiftly closed the sheet, staying outside rather than joining them. He said something low, and the other shadows moved away.

Nausea squirmed in Hallie's stomach for more than one

reason. She needed to speak with the Stradat Lord Kapitan. It wasn't all Kase's fault.

She was the one who'd chosen to use her power.

The pain in her head only sharpened the longer she sat up. Her father pulled a vial of Pick Up out of his pocket. He popped open the stopper and helped her drink it. "Last one."

She grimaced as the moldy taste slithered over her tongue but got it down. Her mother sat on the edge of the cot.

Hallie tried to give them a smile, but even those muscles hurt. Her mother's eyes watered, and she flung herself on top of Hallie and squeezed her. Hallie sucked in a breath at the pain. Her father tucked away the empty vial and put a hand on her head, stroking her hair. She bit her cheek to keep from crying outright.

Her mother released her and pulled back, kneeling on the rocky floor, hands on her daughter's shoulders. "What possessed you to do that?"

...And the reunion was over.

Guilt flooded Hallie's face with heat. Not the painful kind. "Mama, we were just on a patrol," she said, repeating Kase's excuse. Her mouth felt funny, like it was moving too slowly.

Her feeble protests weren't enough to dissuade Zelda Walker.

"After everything you went through," her mother hissed, squeezing her shoulders harder, "you went and made yourself a target?"

"Zelda." Hallie's father went around to her and pulled her to her feet. "Easy. She's still recovering."

"Mama, I appreciate the concern," Hallie said, trying to adjust her position. Her father hurried to take the pillow and prop it behind her. It only helped a little. "But just because you showed up in the capital doesn't mean you have any say over what I do."

The lines on her mother's face deepened, and Hallie knew she'd stepped over a line—even if she'd told the truth. She winced. Her parents simply cared, and Hallie had immediately become defensive. But this was one of the reasons she'd left Stoneset behind.

Her mother sat back a little more. Her father cleared his throat. "That's not fair, Lark."

"I know." Stars, Hallie's head hurt. She rubbed her eyes.

She'd just woken up from whatever had happened, and now she had to have it out with her parents. She was too tired to dig into the matter, and she didn't care to rehash the past. While she knew she wasn't being fair, that didn't repair the damage her own parents had done over three years prior. And it didn't change the fact that she could make her own choices.

Zelda sniffed. "I just want you to be safe." She crossed her arms and rubbed them as if she was cold. "A mother shouldn't have to Burn her child, much less two of them."

Hallie didn't have a response to that, not at all. She was the worst daughter on the planet. "I'm sorry, Mama."

It was all she could muster knowing what she planned to do.

Her mother would have no choice but to mourn her. It wasn't fair. Life never was. But she couldn't do anything about it.

"Don't be sorry. Just come home with us." Her mother's voice broke.

Hallie swallowed hard. "I can't."

"Why not?"

"Because I'm needed here." She scrubbed at her eyes, trying to stop the tears before they started. "I'm sorry. I'm sorry I've not been the daughter you needed or wanted, but I can't leave now. I'm the only one who can stop this madness."

Zelda shook her head, but her father pulled her to his chest and said, "What do you mean?"

Hallie's head was pounding. She really didn't want to go into it all, not with them. They wouldn't understand. But how else was she going to convince them to let her do what she needed to do? It'd been hard enough trying to convince Kase, and she hadn't even succeeded.

"I need to stay," she said lamely. "I need to use my power to stop what's coming, and...and when I do..."

Thankfully, someone else entered the room and saved her from some tense conversation that would only lead to hurt feelings and reopened wounds.

"Hals?"

Kase.

Hallie searched his face intently. No new scratches or evidence of harm other than the scar along his cheek. Under his eyes, dark circles were beginning to form, but Hallie was certain hers mirrored his. They looked a little redder, a little damp, but no tearstains gleamed on his cheeks. Still, her heart broke to see it.

But he was okay. He hadn't suffered any ill effects from the dragon battle nor the argument with his father.

"Oh, sorry, I'll just wait out here," he said as he spotted her parents, like he'd forgotten he'd let them in.

Her father shook his head. "No, it's all right, son. Come on in."

Before Hallie could respond, her parents walked toward the entrance. Her mother glared at Kase as she passed but held her tongue. Her father placed his hand along his wife's back. "We'll just be outside."

Hallie turned her eyes back to Kase once her parents' silhouettes appeared outside of her little cell. It was kind of nice to be given one of the more private ones, even if it meant the medics were unsure if her recovery was certain. She pushed herself up further, grimacing at the pain, and ran a hand over her hair. She must've looked a fright and was slightly embarrassed Kase had to see her in this state, but the look on his face drove away any of that.

"Saldr says Skibs is going to be okay," he said quietly as he sat on a crate that had been placed in there as a makeshift seat. He pulled it close to her cot, setting his hands on the blanket, hands folded as if in prayer. There wasn't a whole lot of room in her cell.

Hesitantly, she placed her hand over his. A little bit of warmth flushed over her at the touch. "That's good."

Kase didn't say anything, only took her hand and rubbed a thumb over her knuckles. He hid his face with his other hand. Her parents' shadows withdrew a little more.

"Why did you do that?" he asked, voice muffled in his palm.

Hallie tilted her head. "What do you mean?"

He looked at her then, his eyes dark. "Why would you risk yourself for him?"

Hallie opened her mouth and closed it again. She'd thought it obvious. Of course, she hadn't meant to overexert herself and lose control. It was just further proof the pilot goggles were not her Relic. "I couldn't let him die. Not even after everything he's done."

Kase clenched his jaw and looked down at their hands.

"Thank you." He took a breath and then said, "After what he did at Myrrai and what he did here, I didn't think I wanted him to survive, but now that he has, I…just thank you." He then took Hallie's face in his hands. "But if you ever do anything like that again, I will *never* forgive you."

Ouch.

She pulled back, and his hands fell away. She shook her head. Her headache was abating, but it still twinged a little at the motion. "Without me, he would've died."

"Yes, but…" He buried his face in his hands again. "I don't know what I'd do without you. When you wouldn't wake up, I thought…"

Chest aching, she reached out again, holding his wrists. "Kase."

He looked up, his eyes red-rimmed and miserable. He took his wrists away only to reach out and pin her hands between his instead. "Don't combine the Essences, Hals. Do what Saldr wants. Just stay with me, okay? Whatever happens, we'll be together. I know it."

She shook her head again. "You can't know that. You can't know anything about that."

"I do," he whispered. He released her to put a hand on his heart. "I feel it in here."

"It doesn't matter how badly I want to believe you. That's not a risk I want to take. Too many things could go wrong—not just never finding you," she said quietly.

What if resetting time only made it worse? What if she did it wrong?

"As if your way will work the way you want it to! Saldr said the prophecies or whatever were inconclusive. What if sacrificing yourself isn't the solution, and without your power, everyone dies?"

Her cheeks flushed. When he put it like that, maybe she was being selfish and childish. Of course that could happen. But something told her that her way was the right choice. She couldn't explain it. She couldn't make Kase understand the bone-deep feeling she had that if she followed through with her plan, everything would be okay.

She just wouldn't be a part of whatever future came after.

Her eyes burned. She looked anywhere but at him, tracing the gray veins on the rock ceiling above with her gaze to keep the tears at bay.

Her mother would have to mourn a second child, but she would learn what Hallie had: that while the puzzle would always be incomplete, there was beauty in the missing pieces. Kase would learn that too. He'd already begun to.

"I know it's the right thing to do," Hallie whispered. "I need to find the second Gate and restore the sword. All the Essence powers must return to the Gates. Otherwise, Jagamot will destroy the world." She tied her fingers into a knot in her lap. "I don't have a choice."

She wanted to say more, but she didn't know if she could find the words to express what she was really feeling—the depth of the emotions coursing through her, the urgency dogging her to keep moving toward her goal.

While she hated that it had taken Ben nearly dying for her power to resurface, its low heat still bubbled in her core alongside the bone-deep ache. She could feel it again, and she was afraid if she didn't find the sword soon, it would disappear.

Kase sat back, fiddling with the ring on his little finger. Ana's ring—a piece of his past he never let go of. Hallie unconsciously grabbed at her neckline for the pocket watch that no longer rested there and hadn't for months now. If she'd had it, maybe she wouldn't have nearly died saving Ben.

Kase had been amazing in the fight, as had Merlin. They'd taken down a dragon. That thought still seemed unbelievable. Say what you would about the Cerl technology, but the way the machine responded to Kase's mere thoughts was a phenomenon, something Hallie wished she had more time to study. But even if she'd had all the time in the world, she couldn't have asked him to keep using the hover more than necessary. That technology had led to his uncle's death.

His father was right—it was too dangerous.

Slowly, Kase took Hallie's hand again, loosely twining their fingers against the roughspun brown coverlet. He rubbed a thumb across her knuckles. "Hals...I..."

She chewed on the inside of her lip. She couldn't interpret his hesitation. Was he finally coming around to her plan? Would he allow her to save him?

"I've been thinking about something for a while now, and when I couldn't...uh, couldn't wake you up after Skibs fell..." His voice cracked; he paused to compose himself. "I was terrified the Soul Tech had done something. Interacted badly with your power or some other awful thing."

She could only imagine what he'd felt in that moment. She didn't know what she would have done if the roles had been reversed.

He played with each of her fingers as if trying to figure out just what else he wanted to say. His stare went glassy, distant. Haunted.

She had seen him vulnerable before—specifically in the hours after Zeke's death and then again in the dungeon, when he'd admitted to starting the Kyvena fire. But this...this was different. Vulnerable wasn't the right word. It was as if she was getting a glimpse of his very soul, deep and dark and bright all at once.

"It was my fault." She clung to his hand. "I lost control. Stop blaming yourself."

"You wouldn't have had to use your power if I'd been looking out for Skibs. I didn't see him and that dragon until it was too late."

"We wouldn't have been in the hover if I hadn't wanted to study it."

"I convinced you to come."

Hallie squeezed his hand softly. "If this is a contest of who's most at fault, I'd say we both win." She tried to smile, but he didn't return it. They'd both made mistakes, but if they were to keep score, they would only devolve into a pile of messy memories and regret. They had to move forward.

"I would've been in here when you woke if the Stradat Lord Kapitan hadn't come in and...well, you must've heard." He rubbed a hand down his face. "I ran you straight to the hospital ward, and they got Saldr, and the face he made when he saw..." His voice broke again on the last few words. "Stars, I thought I'd lost you. I never want to feel that way again, Hallie."

Her heart broke. While he might've been blaming himself, she was the one who chose to use her power. She was the one to lose control.

Yet, Ben would've died without her intervention. If he had, they would've lost the Essence power he possessed. Then Hallie would've been forced to reset the Gate and leave everything up to chance.

"I'm sorry," she whispered again, helpless. She couldn't

change what had happened. She couldn't fix how she'd frightened him.

Kase leaned forward on his free hand, his scent floating in the air between them. He still hadn't shaved properly, and his short beard had filled in even more. She resisted the urge to run her fingers along his jawline.

He spoke to their joined hands. "I know that we still have things to work through, even without the world falling apart." He rubbed her knuckles again. "I know I'm not going to convince you to reset the Gate instead of using the swords. You're too stubborn."

Her heart skittered at his touch. Where was he going with this?

"But if we do only have weeks, days, or even hours left, I want to—*need* to—spend every single last second with you."

So far, she didn't see any reason to argue. "I think my mother might have something to say about—"

"Let me finish." He brought her captured hand to his lips and kissed her knuckles, making her shiver. He met her gaze over their hands and said, low and husky, "Marry me, Hals. Right here. Right now."

Her eyes stung as air whooshed into her lungs. Letting go of her hand, Kase pulled Ana's ring off his little finger and held it out to her. The impossibility hit her like a raging storm. The emotions crowded in her chest, filling it to the brim. Her power added its heat. She brought a shaking hand to her mouth.

He wanted to marry her. A soft buzzing started in her ears, and her heart did a few funny flips in her chest.

The ring hadn't changed since she'd last inspected it, that day that felt like an eternity ago, the day the Cerls had kidnapped her. The Zuprium band was thin and dainty, its edges carved into miniature vines leading to a trio of roses, tiny Zuprium crystal chips—not diamonds, she realized— sparkling in the dim lantern light. Breathtaking.

Kase waited with his hand outstretched, the ring held before him between his index and thumb. "Please," he added, his strained, crooked grin melting her heart into a puddle.

When she was a little girl, she'd dreamed of the day a man would ask for her hand. For all their faults, she'd admired her parents and the relationship they had. They'd been a glowing example of what she herself had wanted.

When she'd fallen for Niels, she'd thought she'd live out her life as a miner's wife, running the inn and whiling away in a small mountain town, content—but then Jack had died.

Once she'd left for the capital, she'd never thought she'd find the sort of love one needed to marry someone. The University had given her purpose again, and she'd planned on teaching. That new dream hadn't left much room for romance, and she hadn't sought it out. She'd had a plan, and she'd thought she was content once more.

But then a cocky, stars-blasted pilot swept into her life like a maelstrom. She hadn't known love, *true* love, felt like soft, messy curls, tasted like caramel sweets, rustled like book pages, and smelled like wood smoke and leather.

Tears slipped down her cheeks, heavy and burning. She wanted to say yes so badly it physically hurt...but the reality was, Hallie was going to die. The world would end without her sacrifice.

She swiped at her eyes. "I can't." She looked down at the cot to avoid his gaze; if she saw the hurt and rejection well in his eyes, she'd break.

"Why not?"

Hallie could tell how carefully he was holding his emotions in check. He still hadn't let the hand with the ring drop. She shook her head. "With everything going on, it'd be selfish."

"I disagree."

"I don't want to marry you only because the world is ending." She finally looked up, and just like she'd feared, the hurt evident in his eyes crushed her. They loved each other. Kase had told her that she was his fate. And now she'd...what was she doing?

No, she couldn't take it back. Not now. Not yet. She wished she could give in to the desire and heat and everything, but the logical part of her brain wouldn't let her.

"I want to marry you because it's what we really want, not just as a last hurrah."

"I'm not asking because everything's falling apart." Kase took her hand again. She hadn't realized he'd let it go. Hallie could tell he was trying to keep himself calm, but the faint tremors in his fingers belied his emotions no matter how much he tried to hide it. "I know what I want. I've known for a while. I'm asking if you want it, too."

Just say yes. Just say yes and be happy. Just say yes and love him.

But she couldn't, and she was a stars-idiot.

Uncertainty crept into Kase's passionate gaze. The hand holding the ring dipped. "But if you don't, that's—"

"That's not what I'm saying." Of course she *wanted* to. But she'd told the truth. He was going to lose her. It would be selfish to make him mourn her not just as...whatever they were, exactly, but as a widower.

To grieve not Hallie Walker, but Hallie *Shackley*.

Her heart couldn't possibly break into more pieces than it already had. But it kept proving her so, so wrong.

"If you need proof I'm serious, take this as a promise." He placed the ring in her hand and closed her fingers around it. He stood. "I'll let you rest."

"Kase." Hallie clenched the ring so hard, it indented her palm. She looked back up at him, the words so thick she could barely spit them out. "It's not...I just...I'm sorry."

Kase smiled a small smile, a sad smile, one that nearly broke Hallie's resolve right then and there. He gave her a soft kiss atop her head before pausing at the entrance to her cell, one hand drawing the curtain aside. "I'll wait until the stars fall so long as I get to be with you in the end."

CHAPTER 41

BROKEN PEOPLE

Kase

HOT AND COLD. SWEAT AND shivers.

Kase didn't know what to feel. His body didn't know what to do. He raced away from the hospital ward like a coward, the empty space where Ana's ring once sat mocking him. At least he made it away from the ward before he lost control of his emotions.

He didn't know what had come over him. After fighting with Harlan and then with Hallie, it'd just hit him, and he hadn't been able to wait a second longer.

He'd known for a while he wanted to marry her, start a family with her, live the rest of their days in the shadow of the mountains—but he'd also known that was his delusional side talking. From the moment she'd brought down Achilles with whatever power she'd taken, he'd known it was impossible. He'd been in denial ever since.

He shouldn't have asked. What in the blazes had he been thinking?

And what was *she* thinking, with all that nonsense about

only marrying her because the world was ending?

Kase hadn't asked because of the tragedy they were all barreling toward. He would have asked even if Saldr had announced he'd found a new prophecy that stated Jagamot was going to take his sweet time, and they'd all be Burned long before the world met its end. All he knew was they were running out of time, and if everything was spiraling toward destruction, then why not have a little joy as they welcomed the end? Wasn't love enough? It always was in the stories.

Reality really was a two-blistered wench.

Some of the books Ana had loved to read were those sprawling romances with soulmates bound together by the universe, brought together against all odds in a bond that transcended time and space. It was a comforting notion, if unrealistic. Kase and Hallie weren't like that; they had been thrown together by fickle chance. Their decisions alone had led them to each other, not some otherworldly bond or something out of their grasp.

If he'd not taken the fall for the greenie that rainy night in late September or if he'd turned his brother down when asked to pilot the *Eudora* mission, he might never have met her. If she hadn't taken her family's savings and attended University, she wouldn't have become a scholar. If she hadn't needed the money, she would've told Jove no when asked to go on a mission from which she might never return. Maybe it had been something or someone guiding them unwittingly to each other, but Kase didn't think so. All his life he'd been told what to do, what to think, how to feel. He knew what having no choice felt like. Even his slight deviation into the Crews had only been possible with his father's begrudging blessing.

But it wasn't like that anymore. Kase *chose* Hallie. He would always choose her, whether it was just for a day or, by some miracle, the next fifty years.

He rubbed the spot where he'd worn Ana's ring. His sister would've been proud. Zeke, too. Maybe that was what they'd been trying to teach him all along, and he just hadn't wanted to listen.

What he'd said to her was true. He'd wait forever for her if he had to.

His breathing finally eased. He nodded to Saldr as he passed him in the corridor. Hopefully the perceptive Yalv couldn't see the desperation or despair or whatever it was Kase knew had to be showing in his eyes. The man nodded back, then greeted Sergeant, who followed close behind.

With it being the second day of reintegrating groups of people into the city for cleanup and normalcy, the corridors were less crowded than usual. The shouts and footsteps still echoed too loudly to concentrate on anything in particular, but it was nice to move at a steady pace without having to shoulder past people. Kase didn't know where his destination was. He just needed to think.

Before he knew it, he stood in front of the hangar.

Of course, even with the events of the day, he would end up here. He just hated that his safe space would now include the memory of Hallie's lifeless body replaying in his mind over and over again. He shouldn't trust the hover. Despite what she said, he wasn't sure the Soul Tech hadn't interfered with her power.

He wouldn't fly it again. Just being in the hangar might be enough to process everything. Then he could go back to the ward and check on Ben and...well, should he go see Hallie again? Would she want to talk with him again? Would it be too awkward?

He'd figure it out once he got there.

His first clue should have been the lack of guards, but alas, he wasn't entirely in his right mind as he tugged open the doors and stepped inside.

Sergeant tried to say something, but whatever he'd been about to say was drowned in the loud alarm that went off as soon as he walked past the first hover.

It was a screaming, whining whistle coming from Merlin, his hover. Kase jumped out of his skin and reached for his Cerl pistol, but it was missing. Blast it. Where had he left it? In the hover? He fumbled for the knife the greenie had given him. He wrenched it from its sheath and whirled around.

"Watch it, Shackley." Eravin stepped out of the shadow of the nearby hover. "Tell your pet to be quiet."

Merlin went silent, but Kase didn't know if that was because it had read his thoughts or not. He also wasn't sure if that was a good thing or a bad thing. He turned his attention back to Eravin.

His old friend looked even worse than the last time he'd

seen him in the corridor, the day Kase had threatened to end him if he laid a finger on Hallie.

How long had that been? A day? Two?

The hollows beneath his cheekbones had only sunk further. Maybe it was the dimly lit hangar, but stark black shadows lined his eyes. Eravin stopped a few paces away. "Just want to talk."

Kase didn't loosen his grip on his knife, but he also didn't throw it at the other man. Not yet.

A muffled yell came from behind him. Kase spun. A gagged Sergeant fought against an attacker—a man Kase had dreaded ever seeing again and had hoped had somehow died in Achilles, even though Hallie had told him otherwise. It'd been a pointless wish.

General Marcos Correa looked worse for wear, too. His skin had gone sallow, his hair unkempt. Shadows darkened his pale brown eyes to lightless pits. His clothing was dirty and torn. He had the same black lines around his eyes as Eravin. He finally wrangled Sergeant into a submissive position, though it took enough effort to keep Sergeant there that sweat beaded the Cerl general's brow. Sergeant still tugged and twisted best he could.

Kase took a step toward him, knife coming up to...to...to do what? He couldn't throw it at Correa. The Cerl would use Sergeant as a shield, and Kase wasn't skilled enough at knife throwing to avoid that outcome.

"Let him go," Kase demanded. "This doesn't involve him."

"We have a deal for you, Shackley," Eravin said, drawing Kase's attention. "Agree to help us, and we let your babysitter free."

Kase spat something foul at him. Eravin's eyebrows shot up. "Didn't realize you cared that much. Interesting."

Eravin nodded at Correa, who touched a finger to Sergeant's cheek. Sergeant screamed and collapsed into Correa's hold.

Kase flinched so hard, he nearly dropped his knife. He knew that pain. He'd lived it at Achilles. "Stop!"

Eravin walked back into his view. The lantern light hit him in such a way that his eyes were more visible. The veins in his eyes were black, not red—so numerous they nearly swallowed the whites entirely. Kase couldn't even find the voice to scream. Eravin was like a nightmare come to life.

"What—what are you?" Kase managed to choke and stumble away.

Eravin smirked, but it didn't look mischievous as it always had in the past. It spread nearly too wide for his face; his lips parted slightly, twitching, baring his teeth in a sinister slash that dragged chills down Kase's spine. "We are Jagamot."

"I don't understand." Kase's limbs turned cold. He could barely feel the knife in his hand. "You're not...Jagamot is something else. A god or something."

"Jagamot is darkness. He is inside all of us; you need only surrender to him for him to manifest. That stupid old man, Loffler, set it all off by destabilizing the planet enough to allow Jagamot's essence to filter throughout the atmosphere and enter every single person on this planet. Just inhaling the scent of the ashamox—the gaseous form of Yalvar fuel—allows him to take root. Particularly if you're broken enough." Eravin stepped closer. "And this city is rife with broken people."

Eravin was too close. Kase tried to raise his arm to stop him from doing anything else, from stepping closer, but his hand wouldn't work. His fingers refused to move; his knife slipped right out of them.

Eravin's smirk deepened. "Want this all to end? Hand over your girl. Give us Hallie Walker, the Essence of Time, and we'll allow you, your babysitter here, your mother, and your brother's family to live. Not many will get that gift. We'll even let the Stradat Lord Kapitan die. A gift for you. He was supposed to die weeks ago."

Kase still had enough in him to spit, "I already told you: touch her, and you die."

"Not really an option now. We can't have her combining the Essence powers or resetting the Gate, and she's very determined. She's got spunk." Eravin smiled, and Kase nearly puked. His gums were black. Darkness.

Jagamot.

Eravin was about to say something else when his eyes flicked up past his shoulder. "No! Don't—"

The right side of Kase's chest caught fire. But when he screamed, slapping at the flames, his hand met something wet and warm.

When he opened his eyes again, he was on the floor,

everything tipped at a sickening angle; above him, Eravin yanked the King Arthur knife out of its wielder's hand—Neville, whom Kase hadn't seen in the room until now.

In the blink of an eye, Eravin slit the man's throat.

Blood spurted from above him, splattering across Kase's cheek as Neville choked on a wet, bubbling gasp. He clawed at his throat and fell to his knees.

Neville. Kase blinked, trying to understand, trying to stay awake.

Neville had stabbed him with his own knife.

"Fool," Eravin shouted. "You let your petty revenge get the better of you, and now you'll die, just like Lavinia." He kicked Neville in the chest. He disappeared from Kase's line of sight. "Should've figured out I did that one in, too."

Kase couldn't move, and his brain couldn't comprehend his words, not fully. The pain in his chest grew with each passing second. But he couldn't let Eravin near Hallie. "Stay...away..."

Stay away from her.

But the crescendo of agony stole the breath he needed to finish the threat.

BANG.

The crack was like lightning in a storm. Kase's ears rang and warred with the pain flooding his system. Sergeant's flashpistol. He'd managed to get it off.

He'd done that despite being tortured by Correa. For Kase.

Kase could barely register that fact. Not with the fire consuming him.

The bullet screamed and sparked against the walls and the hovers. Merlin's screeches only fused with that of the stray bullet. Eravin ducked.

The echoes finally stopped. The bullet lay dead and near the end of the hangar, so close to the doors, so close to freedom, but not far enough. Sweat and who knew what else blurred Kase's vision.

Eravin leaned down. His eyes were completely black without the light to reflect off the white specks. It chilled Kase to his very core. "Tried to give you a chance to choose the right side of history, but looks like I'll have to do it myself." His smirk was cold and superior. "Things never change."

He looked up to Correa. "Kill him, and let's go. We have

a bit of a task ahead of us. This one deserves his pain."

Kase couldn't do anything as Sergeant yelled out, the note so anguished and full of torment, soul-rending. And then it went silent.

No.

Eravin disappeared. The pain in his side was so intense that he couldn't even scream. His lungs felt cased in iron; he could barely get them to lift enough to take in a breath. Pierced lung, maybe? He could barely concentrate with his vision going in and out.

He hadn't realized the alarm was going off again, but every few seconds or so, the Cerl hover's loud beeping interrupted the pain.

His next blink lasted too long; he only knew time had passed because Saldr stood over him when his vision returned next. Two Saldrs, actually, both blurry.

Fresh fire roared into his chest as golden light blinded him. What in the blazes was going on? Kase's body contorted with the pain, twisting him into knots of anguish. Maybe it wasn't Saldr. It had to be Correa; Kase had only felt this kind of pain being tortured by the Cerl general's lightning power. Kase clenched his teeth hard. He clawed at Correa. Someone held him down.

And then it was over.

"Rest now, Master Shackley. The Vasa needs time to do its work." Saldr. It was truly Saldr. Not Correa.

Kase couldn't rest. He didn't have time. *Hallie* didn't have time. Sweat poured down his face, but he pushed himself up. "Gotta get...need to find...Saldr, where's Hallie?"

"If you don't rest, the Vasa won't heal you—"

"I don't care!" Kase shouted. He pushed himself to his knees only to collapse. The pain spiked in his side again. Saldr said something. More golden light. And then darkness.

C H A P T E R 4 2

DAISIES

Hallie

HALLIE TURNED KASE'S RING OVER and over, staring at it for stars knew how long.

He'd asked her to marry him. Why hadn't she said yes? It would've been so easy; it had been so perfect, everything she'd never thought she'd have, and if everything wasn't going up in flames, she would've kissed him senseless for it.

After saying yes, of course.

That image was too much for her aching heart. She'd done the right thing, hadn't she? She thought so. But maybe she simply liked torturing herself. And Kase, while she was at it.

She'd said she wanted to put the Essence powers into the sword, sacrificing herself and the others in the process, to defeat Jagamot. That way she would be able to keep Kase in a small way...whereas the other way, the story might end differently.

So wouldn't marrying him now make sense, according to that logic?

But marriage—no matter how short or long—was too important to her. It was more than just agreeing to love someone until death parted them both. It was a commitment. The promise to live a life together.

How could she make that kind of promise, knowing she'd break it to save the world? What kind of partner would that make her?

But she had so little opportunity for happiness left to her. Why would she not say yes?

She pressed her palms to her eyes.

Unsure if it was the emotional turmoil within her making everything else feel less intense or just thanks to time passing, her pain had gently receded to a low hum over the past half hour or so, her power more like a pleasant warmth in the cold hospital ward. It helped her think more clearly, but no matter which path of thought she wandered down, her answer was still no.

Maybe she should've added a, 'Not right now.'

If she had, maybe he wouldn't have looked so heartbroken.

She lifted her face and looked at the ring again. It hadn't changed since Kase had pressed it into her palm. He'd said he'd wait for as long as it took.

He wouldn't have to wait long, if she followed through on her plan. Because she'd be gone, and there'd be no one left to wait for.

She pushed the thoughts to the side. She needed to figure this out. There had to be a way. They had to be missing something. What if restoring the swords didn't work? What if she wasted the chance to reset the Gates and it led to something worse? Or what if she did either one, but it made the ending of both much worse, like punting this duty off to someone else at some other time, when the hammer would fall even harder?

Should she feel responsible for people who had yet to live? What did it matter if she simply put off the inevitable? That was what Navara had done, what the Lord Elder had done. Why couldn't Hallie follow their example?

She shut her eyes, taking a breath. If she could figure something out, she could go find Kase right now, fall into his arms, and demand he marry her right then and there. Then she could truly give him the stars he'd asked for. She opened her eyes and grabbed the ring, slipping it on.

It was a good compromise.

To its left was only the memory of the little finger that had been there a few months ago. It was a reminder that life as she knew it could disappear in a breath. Ebba's life had moments before Hallie had lost her finger.

Oof. Ebba. What would she say? Would she call Hallie a *sterning* stars-idiot?

Probably. Hallie wished she was there to say anything at all.

The ring was in pristine condition—whether due to Kase's care or the nature of the Zuprium itself, she didn't know. The metal was mostly a mystery. Ezekiel Fairchild had discovered only two uses for it, one brilliant, the other terrifying.

The perfect fit to the ring was almost too much. What would happen if she did say yes? Would they be able to find something for her to wear? Did she even care? She looked down at her rumpled shirt that had seen much better days. There wasn't any blood on it—the only positive note. She could probably borrow another one of her mother's shirts, but they were a smidge too small. Kase could wear his pilot's jacket like soldiers in their uniform. Hallie's heart skipped a beat at that mental image. The back was stitched together sloppily, and they'd make quite the pair with their ramshackle wardrobes fit for a refugee camp, not a wedding. But it wouldn't matter. Not to Hallie.

She chewed the edge of her lip and twisted the ring around her finger. Would it be worth it? Even if they only had days left? A week or two at best?

She'd feel like a fraud unless she found a way to make it work.

What had she done wrong in her life to lead her here? Why did she, a scholar from Stoneset, have to make these difficult choices to save the world? Why her? Why now?

If she could simply find the other sword and Gate, they might be able to figure out some way forward. If she fixed both Gates, though she wasn't entirely sure what was wrong with them, maybe she could use them to do...something helpful. But what about the prophecies?

The heat in the core flared. She hissed and pressed her hand to her middle.

Stars.

What had caused that?

No answer came, of course.

But wasn't the way to repair the Gates to give them the swords full of Essence powers? Could she somehow figure out a way to repair souls first? Because as soon as she gave up her power, her soul would hemorrhage.

Anderson still hadn't woken up—even with the Cerl blanket. Niels was on borrowed time, though the bracelet he'd made out of the blanket fibers kept the worst of it at bay.

Maybe Hallie could somehow restore their lost Soul that had bled out? How much had they lost? How much did anyone start with? It wasn't something that could be measured like blood—at least, she didn't think so. Even if she could figure the biology out, if the Soul was no longer there, she would have to come up with a way to create it.

She could rewind and speed up time. She could heal. But could she combine that to create?

Something told her these thoughts bordered on dangerous. It felt too much like Soul Tech, toeing the line of ethics. Messing with that had led Ezekiel Fairchild and his sons to their deaths.

"Sorry to intrude, Miss Walker, but I have your satchel here."

Hallie looked up to find Clara peeking in. She tried to give the woman a warm smile. She'd only seen her in passing during hospital shifts. Hallie waved her in.

Clara stepped fully into the cell, Samuel wrapped in a cloth and tied crossways across her chest. She set the satchel on the edge of her cot.

Hallie pulled it into her lap. She hadn't even realized it was missing. "Thank you."

"You're welcome." Samuel made a small noise of discontent. His mother shushed him and rocked a little. "If he wasn't fighting a nap, I'd let him say hi. He seemed to like you last time."

Hallie smiled, hoping it would hide the pain she couldn't seem to avoid no matter which route she took. "I'd argue that he's perfect and can do no wrong, so if he doesn't want to nap, I wouldn't make him."

Clara laughed. "Except you will get to sleep somewhat soundly tonight regardless of whether he naps or not."

Not so soundly.

Her emotions must have played out on her face, because Clara took the seat Kase had vacated earlier. "I was relieved to hear you're going to be okay, but I can't imagine what you've gone through today."

Hallie shook her head. "Didn't you survive the first dragon attack on the city?"

Clara shrugged. "It was a little different. I was already at the wall, and the soldiers ushered me right into the Catacombs. I didn't experience much of the attack itself."

"I'm glad." Hallie brushed a stray hair behind her ear.

With the dragon fight earlier today, Hallie couldn't imagine being in the city during the initial attack. According to reports, much of the lower city had been heavily damaged by dragon fire and Cerl bombs. Would Hallie have made it to the Catacombs in time? Or would she have been caught in the destruction?

It was chilling to think about. It was even more disturbing to think her time in Achilles might've saved her the fate she would've suffered had she been in Kyvena.

"That's a pretty ring." Clara smoothed a hand over her son's fuzzy head.

Hallie hid her hand under her satchel, heart in her throat. "It's nothing."

Hallie had no mind to discuss all her problems with Kase's sister-in-law. She'd probably break her resolve.

Clara held one hand to her sleeping baby, the other to the cot as she pushed herself to her feet. "I can imagine why Kase might've given it to you, but since he's not here right now...well, just know that you won't have any judgment from me no matter what you choose. I'm just happy he trusts someone enough...we've all been through a lot, and I respect you very much, Miss Walker."

"Please, just Hallie is fine," she said, her cheeks burning all the more.

"I know I haven't known you long, Hallie, but..." Clara smiled and opened the curtain. "You deserve all the happiness in the world, as does Kase."

And then Hallie was left with her heavy satchel and heavier thoughts.

Now what was she going to do?

At least now, thanks to Clara, she had one distraction

available: a journal to inspect for what felt like the hundredth time. If she distracted herself enough, her mind might stumble upon a solution. She didn't know how to feel about Clara understanding the significance of the ring without Hallie having to tell her, but the woman was right about one thing.

Kase *did* deserve happiness. And he would find that. She would make sure of it.

She pulled Navara's worn leather journal and opened it to one of the last pages full of muddled Yalven. Without the proper lighting, she couldn't tell if the sparkle of Zuprium was present, but she had to assume it was.

But which memory to try and enter?

If she chose one of these last pages, she might see how the story ended. Maybe Navara had found a way back to Myrrai, and maybe that way had been the Second Gate. It might've been a long shot, but it was the only option she had. But then again, the journal was here in Hallie's hands, and Hallie's grandfather had died before she was born. The likelihood of Navara's success was slim, but she needed to explore that angle first before gathering her own data.

She needed her blood to make it work, but unless she fancied some splinters and a jagged scar from using the blunt side of the crate Kase and Clara had used as a seat, she needed to find something else. She would also rather not resort to papercutting herself repeatedly.

Granted, she was in the hospital ward. There had to be something *somewhere* that wouldn't be super painful.

Of course when she finally found herself alone long enough to use the journal, she had no way to slice herself properly. Just her luck.

Using the crate to aid her, she stood on shaky legs, but after a minute or two, she was able to stand without assistance. She pulled on her satchel and tucked the journal inside. Now to find shears or some sort of knife.

The hospital ward had both. The rations station might also have something she could borrow. She just wouldn't tell anyone why...and hopefully she wouldn't run into her mother in the meantime. That would infinitely complicate things.

She needed to have that conversation, the one they hadn't finished, but the hope that she might find a way to do this without sacrificing herself made her push it to the back of her mind. She would have time later.

But before she could make it further than her cell, Fely appeared.

Blast it.

Before Hallie could duck back into her little cell, Fely made eye contact with her and walked over. "How are you feeling?"

Blast. "Fine."

Even after adding a fake smile, Hallie could tell she hadn't fooled Fely, who raised one eyebrow in silent judgement. "And you're leaving the ward...why?"

Hallie tried to think of something that would work as an excuse, but she came up short. Maybe Fely would go along with Hallie's plan. It was worth a try. She'd once cared about King Filip, at least to an extent. Hallie's way might make certain his death had not been in vain.

"I need to go to the part of the tunnels from yesterday."

Fely narrowed her eyes. "Why?"

Hallie looked around. A few nurses entered two cells just a few down from hers. Another entered the area where the majority of those ill or injured lay in crooked rows out in the open, not afforded the privacy Hallie had been given. The gas lanterns tucked to the side of the strange cloth corridor made the shadows upon the ground longer. She tugged Fely into her cell.

"I know where the Second Gate is. Possibly. I just need to check it out."

Fely shook her head. "Saldr would have felt it."

Hallie held in the frustrated retort and said, "Maybe, but will you please just humor me? If it's nothing, it's nothing, and I'll move on to other ideas. But I need to check all possibilities...and I need something sharp."

"This is sounding less and less like a good idea," Fely said, crossing her arms. "I want no part of it. I was just on my way to see if Asa was showing any improvement."

"Asa?" Hallie wracked her brain for someone by that name. A Yalv? No, no, it wasn't that. "Wait, when you say Asa, are you talking about King Filip's brother?"

Fely, Filip, and Correa had mentioned him once or twice, and with everything going on, Hallie had forgotten about him. But why bring him up now?

Fely gave her an odd look. "What do you mean? Of course I'm talking about him."

Hallie was taken back by her tone. "I think I might be confused."

"You must know he's here. You saved his life. I was hoping to speak with him before any of the others had a chance to...coerce answers from him."

Hallie stared at her hard. "I saved his life? When?"

Who was she talking about? She couldn't be talking about Ben. There was no way. It had to be someone else, but he was the only one she remembered saving. Besides Niels. But it was absolutely impossible for it to be him.

Which left Ben.

"Today. Earlier. You used your power in the hover. You saved his life." Fely's annoyance turned to worry, and she reached out to lay a hand on Hallie's forehead as if testing for a fever. "Are you sure you're feeling well?"

Waves of heat and ice-chilling cold crashed into her body. She jerked away from Fely's touch. "I...I don't think I understand."

But she did—in a way. Ben had been working with the Cerls. He was an Essence wielder. But Hallie had only assumed he was a pawn, someone with Yalven blood they could manipulate, because the Ben she'd known was kind and Kase's best friend. Until he wasn't. Until the Essence power took control in the Gate chamber.

Her heart pounded. Every fiber of her being pulsed to its rhythm. "So you're telling me that Asa, brother to the King of Cerulene, is the man I know as Ben Reiss?"

"Ah." Understanding cleared the concern from Fely's gaze. "You know him by his false name. Yes, though I only learned of his false name myself this morning." Fely opened the curtain again. "It will take too long to explain now, and it's best if not many people know that—" she leaned over to whisper in Hallie's ear, "—the *only living heir* to the Cerl throne is in this hospital ward. In betraying Jayde in Myrrai, he was granted full heirship, though he was born illegitimate. I wasn't aware of that detail until after the fact, which only shows I was not as well-placed of a spy as the Stradat Lord Kapitan would have liked, but...what's done is done."

The shock was almost too overwhelming.

"I...I don't know what to say." How else was she supposed

to react to this sort of news? She needed to tell Kase, and Jove—probably their father, too. They needed to know exactly who she'd saved. It was dangerous to have him here for multiple reasons. What would happen if Correa found out where he was?

Though she hated to think it, Ben might make a valuable bargaining chip if the Stradat Lord Kapitan's plan was truly to negotiate for peace.

"I've collected Soul from a few plants to give to Asa to aid his recovery. If he wakes up while I'm there, that will be helpful. He needs to know about Filip and what his death now means, though they were not close. After, we can go inspect that site."

Fely led her around the corner and down an even more secluded area of the ward to a solitary cell with three guards glaring at any and all passersby. Made sense—Ben *was* a war criminal, after all—but three soldiers made it quite conspicuous that someone important was inside. Granted, the only Jaydian who knew his greater importance was Hallie.

She stood several feet away, unsure if she wanted to approach. Who knew what version of Ben waited inside?

She clutched the strap of her satchel. She expected the heat of her power to react to her feelings, as chaotic as they were, but it stayed at the same consistent, pleasant warmth instead.

It probably hadn't recovered from saving the stars-blasted new *King of Cerulene*.

Hallie still didn't quite comprehend it all. Part of her thought maybe she'd never awoken after saving him with her power, and that Kase's proposal and this revelation were all part of some elaborate dream.

She pinched herself to make sure. It hurt. Blast it.

Fely spoke softly to the guards, but they shook their heads. She said something else, something more forceful. The answer was the same.

The Rubikan woman walked away, jaw clenched. She reached Hallie and muttered, "On orders to not let anyone in except for the Stradat Lord Kapitan. I'll have a word with him and Saldr soon. Are you set on this plan of yours?"

Hallie nodded once. She could not be swayed.

Fely sighed. "Let's go and get this over with, shall we?"

Hallie followed her, taking one last look at the cell. The

soldiers stood unmoving, hands on their flashpistols.

Maybe if Hallie figured something out with the Gates, she could also free the man she'd known as Ben Reiss. Despite his duplicity, he hadn't acted like betraying them was strictly his desire—or even his choice. It was like the Essence power itself was controlling him. In the Gate chamber, the difference between Ben and his Essence-wielding self had been like night and day. The real Ben Reiss hadn't wanted to hurt Kase and Hallie.

Fely wove in between a few patients, nodding to medics and nurses alike. None of them stopped her or Hallie. They were too overworked to care. If she wasn't worried about her own well-being, then fine. They had fifty other injured or dying to worry about in her place.

She'd hoped the ward would've started emptying out as people filtered back to the surface. However, that didn't seem to be the case. Many of those she passed had inky black patterns like spider webs on their wrists or ankles. A few had it on their necks. One elderly woman had it near her temples. It took a second for Hallie to realize that they were veins. Black veins.

What had caused that? An elderly gentleman nearby had several of the veins going up his neck and one connecting to his eye.

Could these be the people affected by the Yalvar fuel exposure? Since her Essence power training began, she hadn't been in the ward much enough to study the effects and the patients, and she hadn't had much time to chat with Petra about it. These people weren't in any pain—visibly at least—but they did look rather tired. Made sense. Everyone was exhausted. Hopefully they would be moved to the surface soon.

She stopped by the supply tent and grabbed the pair of shears someone had been using to cut bandages. She stuffed them in her satchel and left the ward with Fely.

Walking the corridors, there didn't seem to be anything too crazy going on. The one that led toward the central cavern and hangar beyond was a little louder than the others, but that wasn't new. Hallie allowed her fingers to trail along the wall as she walked. Partly an unconscious habit, partly seeking the warmth of Essence power, hoping to find a Passage brick.

Her hopes fell flat when they finally reached the end of the Catacombs and no warmth found her fingers. Not that she'd expected it to be that easy. With a silent sigh, she grabbed the lantern from the hook and took it with them into the dark.

It was difficult to see much other than the crude stone floor, but the golden haze around Hallie's vision tipped her off. They were close.

She set down the lantern and fished out the journal and shears.

"Keep watch, if you don't mind. I need to use this for a moment," Hallie said with confidence she didn't feel. Her palms had healed considerably over the very little time it had been since she'd last used the journal. She'd lost track of just how much time it'd been, but not enough to fully heal the wounds.

Yet, all that was left of the previous cut was a thin white scar.

She tried not to think about how it was probably her power that had fixed it.

Chewing on the inside of her lip, she pressed the sharp edge of the shears against her palm along the faint white scar and winced against the pain. She tucked them back into her satchel and flipped the pages of the journal. She passed another sketch of something, but she didn't stop. The page she settled on was the messiest of all, nothing written in a straight line. Hopefully she wasn't about to make a fool of herself.

"And exactly what should I be looking for?" Fely asked, coming closer. "Because I'm not aware that using your blood here will do anything. Asa's, maybe, but not yours. Not in this case."

Right—because Asa was Ben, and Ben was the Essence wielder who had control over the Gates. Maybe they should've figured out a way around the guards and brought him down there, or at least a few drops of his blood. Probably would've been the smarter thing to do.

But going back would take too long, and while they were here, they might as well figure out a few things before enlisting Ben's help, if he was even capable of offering it...or allowed to do so. Hallie shook her head as she sat down against the wall. The golden haze had nearly occluded her vision entirely by now. "It would take too long to explain. Just stay here, and I'll be back soon."

"Stay here?"

Hallie didn't respond, only pressed her bleeding palm to the messy page. Fely would hopefully understand well enough soon.

She kept her palm pressed to the parchment.

Nothing happened. No suffocating darkness. Nothing.

"I am unsure how ruining your journal is meant to help locate the Gate," Fely said crossly, like she thought Hallie might be wasting her time or pulling some kind of prank.

Hallie stared at the page, her blood marring the words and staining the pages.

She pressed her hand to the parchment again and again, but there was no reaction, no memory. Had she imagined the earlier ones after all? Was Navara so far gone at the end that she'd forgotten to mix the ink with Zuprium dust?

She sliced her other palm and flipped to the page with the sketch. She barely registered it was an ornate sword before she pressed her hand to it, even though she knew it wouldn't work.

Nothing.

In a fit of madness, Hallie slammed the book shut and hurled it away from her. She had never done that to a book in her life, but she wasn't thinking straight. She'd spent the entire time since Achilles studying those stupid journals, thinking they held some secret that could help her understand her Essence power. But they were only ramblings of a mad woman fueled by grief, and the visions she'd had were simply her own mind trying to offer answers after being pushed to the brink of sanity.

Hallie was out of options. Without the second Gate, could she even restore it by combining the Essence powers into the swords? Or would she need to go all the way to Myrrai to reset that one? Would she be forced to follow Saldr's plan, after all?

Maybe Jagamot would win. Maybe every plan they had was always doomed to fail.

She had failed.

The book landed with a soft *thunk* and slid across the uneven floor, lost in the weird golden light that haloed her eyes. Another trick of a desperate mind, nothing more.

"Well, I'm not sure if that's what I was expecting, but—"

Fely was interrupted by an explosion of golden light streaming from the book.

Hallie's jaw dropped to the floor as she scrambled to her feet. Where the book lay, a long strand of fire grew like a vine from the center of the spine where the page lay open. It snaked its way into the air and into the ceiling above. The light was so bright, both Hallie and Fely shielded their eyes.

"Holy fates in heaven," Fely gasped.

Hallie scrambled toward it, grabbing the book. As soon as she pulled it toward her, the fire winked out.

"What?" Hallie breathed, inspecting the book for a clue as to what had happened. But the pages were unscathed except for her blood. She held it out again, closer to where the golden haze was in her vision.

Fire exploded again. Hallie dropped the book.

The book wasn't the Gate, but it revealed it. Whether it was because Hallie had put her own blood on it or the book was simply the key, she didn't know. Stars, she needed to sketch this.

"That has to be it!" Hallie exclaimed, fumbling through her satchel with shaking hands for her sketchbook and pencil. "Navara found it, and somehow...somehow the book is what triggers it. My guess is my blood on the pages, because I had the book last time I was down here, but that's probably why I lost control of my power. I stumbled into it with the book, but it didn't reveal itself until now because of that. Maybe. It's just a working theory."

Her fingers clasped around the stubby pencil as she flipped to the next blank page in her book. She hurriedly jotted down a few notes before making a quick sketch. "Do you think that this is only a part of it? Because it goes up toward the ceiling and...and...Fely?"

Fely didn't answer. Hallie looked up to see her staring awestruck at the Gate. It looked vastly different from the one in Myrrai, more akin to the Passage she and Kase had used on the *Eudora* mission to make it back to Kyvena.

Hallie stood, clutching her sketchpad to her chest. She walked over to the woman, careful not to look directly at the fiery archway. Inside it lay a flowering meadow, a little cottage in the background at the edge of a fairytale forest.

"Stars, what is that?" Hallie asked, leaning closer. Fely

grabbed her shoulder and pulled her back.

"Careful."

"What's on the other side? Is this not the Gate?" Disappointment laced the words. What if she'd merely created another Passage? The Gate in Myrrai had housed timelines flying by so fast that they were nothing but blurred images. This was perfectly clear and calm. Picturesque, even.

Fely shook her head. "I would assume that it would be much like the one in Myrrai, though I have only seen that one in books my family has in our library. This is different. It feels different, though I do not know why."

Hallie sketched out the base of it and looked toward the ceiling. Only half of the image was there, the flowers and the forest bleeding into the stone wall. "Not sure where we are in the city exactly, but if we could maybe find where this goes above us, we might have a better picture of what's on the other side?"

"Saldr needs to see this."

"But—" If Saldr came and inspected it, he might still want to go through with his plan.

Fely stuck a finger into the small pouch at her waist. When she took it out, it was covered in Zuprium dust. "I'll be back shortly. Stay here. Whatever you do, don't go through it."

"I think we should wait to tell him," she tried weakly. But Fely didn't answer, snapping her fingers instead. In the blink of an eye, she was gone.

Why couldn't Saldr have shown Hallie how to do that instead of pushing her so hard on the stupid fireball? She shook her head. This had to be the Gate. It didn't feel like the other Passages, though it looked like them. The other two had been characterized by a portal brick at the base. The only reason Hallie had thought to check out this area of the tunnels again was because her power had reacted to it when she was down here with Kase and the golden haze that had been present.

When Fely didn't return after a second or two, Hallie picked up the book, causing the Gate to disappear once more. She moved to the other side of the tunnel and held out the book.

Nothing.

She moved back toward the original point, holding out

the book at intervals. Five side steps forward brought the Gate into existence. And it continued to reappear until her right shoulder met the wall, though at that point, only the golden fire was visible—not the flower field.

That confirmed it wasn't the book itself. It was the area. But the book was the key.

Hallie set the journal down, allowing the center of the archway to appear. The flowers, faraway mountains, and little woodcutter's cottage painted a nice picture against the dimness of the Catacombs. She flipped the pages, careful not to touch the fiery outline herself. The images didn't waver. It didn't matter which page she was on, it seemed.

She flipped back to the sketch of the sword. It glowed in the light from the Gate. Quickly, she flipped to the next page in her sketchbook and copied it there. It looked so familiar, but she couldn't place it. Probably because it was similar to the shadow sword. This Gate wasn't angry like the other one, which might lend evidence to it only being a Passage.

It was still a good discovery, though. It might very well be one that had been closed decades ago with the Great War. She hoped not. She hoped that she'd stumbled across the one they needed.

She finished the sketch and tucked her book into her satchel. She took that off and set it to the side, rubbing her neck. Maybe she wasn't quite recovered from her ordeal earlier in the day. Stars, what time was it, even?

This had been one of the longest days of her life. Going up in the hover, saving Ben, almost dying herself, turning down Kase's proposal, finding out that Ben was really the heir to the Cerl throne, and now this.

Hopefully she could get some good sleep that night. She'd need it. Any rest she'd gotten after overextending her power with Ben had evaporated with the revelations and events of the last hour or so.

She stood and stretched a little more. Her back popped rather loudly. Where was Fely? Hadn't she been able to find Saldr? Surely they weren't coming the long way? Why use the Chronal power to flicker out of existence to fetch him only to walk all the way back?

She stretched her neck and was about to sit back down when a hand slid across her mouth and a knife pressed against her throat.

She froze.

"Found the other Gate, have we?"

That voice. She knew that voice. Hallie didn't respond. One wrong move or word would end with her throat sliced.

"Relax. I've been known to be merciful from time to time," the man whispered in her ear. "Instead of killing you outright, I'll let you go painlessly…because once you're on the other side, there's no returning for you. I'll tell Shackley you put up a fight."

She did the only thing she could do—reach for her power. If she could muster up enough, she might unravel the man who held her hostage. But it was for naught. She was too slow.

Before she could do anything else, the man shoved her into the flowery meadow. She screamed, falling to the ground, scrambling for purchase. Bright light assaulted her, but her fingers found purchase in Navara's journal. She yanked it. A ripping sound met her ears.

She squinted against the light burning her retinas to see Mr. Gray…and Correa behind him, torn journal pages in his hand.

"No!" She yelled, but it was too late. They were gone in a blink, the dark Catacombs disappearing as Fely had done earlier.

She thrust the book out in the same spot. She picked at her cuts that had begun to scab and bled onto the book, but nothing happened.

She scrambled around on her knees, holding the book out as a peace offering. Nothing appeared. Her only companions were the daisies.

C H A P T E R   4 3

OF OUTSTANDING CHARACTER

Les

BY NOW, LADY CELESTE SHACKLEY'S heart should have alchemized into solid stone.

The life she had been handed had been nothing but tragedy after tragedy. Every time she finally felt like she was above water, the depths dragged her down once more. It was an ocean, hitting her with wave after wave after wave. There would be a time when she rose no more. She just didn't know when that would be.

Would it be today?

Kase lay motionless on the cot beside her. They'd run out of space in the ward, and with Saldr needing to do all he could to fix her youngest son, they'd brought him here in his own tent. After using as much Vasa as he'd dared, Saldr bound Kase's chest in thick bandages, his wound carefully cleaned and dressed; traces of dried blood whorled over his exposed skin around the edges of the bandaged area. Saldr had to work fast. They'd missed a few spots while cleaning him up.

Les bent against the cot, wishing she could block the memory of seeing her father take up the very same position at her mother's bedside. It was one of her earliest memories.

Her father hadn't been the same since her mother took ill and passed when Les was only four years old. That was the day she'd lost her mother to the grave, but her father's heart had been buried with her. After that, he'd never given Les the time of day.

What became of a girl forced to grow up without a mother, without anyone to guide her in the world—a world on the brink of such tumultuous change, no less? Books and Ezekiel had gotten her through, though her brother was only five years her senior. Their father somehow clung to a half-life until Les was much older—in her early twenties. He'd become bitter with age and tired of her running off suitors. They'd never matched up to the heroes in the stories she loved so much.

Then Harlan had come into her life, and like fate had brought them together, she'd fallen deeper than she thought possible—so deep that she hadn't seen the warning signs until it was too late. She'd loved the broken man so deeply that she failed to see the shattered pieces of his heart had scattered before their children, putting them in harm's way.

Ezekiel's betrayal had nearly killed her, but it was her children who'd pulled her out of the suffocating sadness. Jove, Zeke, Kase, and Ana had needed her. They'd needed her just like she'd needed a mother all those years ago.

She refused to become her father. She refused to leave them alone in the world.

How ironic that in trying not to be like Lord Addison Fairchild, she'd become something worse. Her whole-minded focus on her children had blinded her to her husband's descent into abuse. She'd grown distant in the years since Ezekiel's and her nephew's deaths, and he had too. So distant she hadn't seen him become someone who would hurt the children they'd brought into the world with the greatest love she'd ever known.

How had something so wonderful and passionate rotted so thoroughly, its decayed visage was only recognizable by memories that faded each day?

She clung to her Kase's cold hand.

If he didn't wake, she feared this loss would be the one that dragged her under for good. He'd been on the brink of death, Saldr had said, but the magic dust that had saved her and Jove in the depths had finally taken root. Now, it was just a matter of his body using the power and speeding up the healing process.

If Kase hadn't been too far gone by the time Saldr reached him.

Between the pierced lung, chipped rib, and blood loss, it was a miracle her son was still alive at all; that she could count each of his steady, if shallow, breaths.

Kase was the lucky one. The other two gentlemen found with him had perished before Saldr could do anything at all.

Les wiped the tears from her eyes.

She'd thought losing her only daughter was insurmountable. The guilt and grief still haunted her nightmares. Many nights since, she'd woken and walked to Ana's room in a half-daze to check on her, only to realize it was never going to have a little blonde girl tucked beneath the covers again. Les would never sit holed up in the library with her daughter again, devouring romances and sipping tea, Ana reading all their favorite parts out loud.

She'd known the betrothal was a mistake, but she'd mistakenly trusted in her husband's wisdom. Jove had been happy, and Zeke had gone into the army, prolonging his eventual ties to an heiress in Tev Rubika, but Ana's had ended with her running away. Running directly into the flames.

Then Zeke hadn't returned from the mission with Kase. Her sweet, caring Zeke. Always the peacemaker between the brothers. The one who brought her flowers on each anniversary of Ezekiel's death. The one who'd constantly checked in on her after Ana's death, even with him being deployed most of the year in those early days.

She wasn't sure she had quite processed his death yet. It often hit her out of nowhere, and each blow brought her back to her knees.

The only good thing about experiencing so much loss was that she'd learned how to function normally on the outside, even if the inside was a raging storm.

Then the last few months happened, and she'd had no way to cope with the truth of the lies she'd been told. She'd been a broken shell the last few weeks, and she didn't know if anything could ever put her back together again.

She squeezed Kase's hand and willed him to be okay.

Beneath the cot lay a book. It was so like her son to have something to read on hand. He got that from her. Without letting go of his hand, she picked it up. She needed some way to keep her mind from spiraling further than it already had. Books had always been there even when no one else was.

She opened it to Kase's immaculate handwriting. Ah, a journal. She peeked at him. He hadn't moved. He did seem like the type to keep his thoughts somewhere secret like this. He might have worn his emotions on his sleeve—especially when it came to his brothers' teasing—but she never quite knew what he was *thinking*.

She shouldn't look. Not when he was fighting for his life.

But alas, Les read the first letter because it was addressed to *Hals*. She raised her eyebrows. Hals? She flipped through a few other pages. They were all addressed to Hals.

After picking up context clues here and there—including one atrocious, if adorable, stick figure doodle of a man and woman riding in what she thought was meant to be a hover—she guessed *Hals* was short for Hallie.

These were meant for Miss Walker.

She couldn't help the smile that graced her face despite everything going wrong. Her little boy had found someone to love, and if nothing else worked in their favor, at least Kase had found that.

She'd realized his feelings for the girl before she'd even met her. Kase would bring her up in conversations and make offhand remarks about how *Hallie* would love to see the first edition of Marisee's commentary of *Romeo and Juliet*. He'd mentioned girls in the past, but none brought the same sparkle to his eye like Miss Walker did.

She rubbed her thumb across his fingers and placed the journal back into its place. Miss Walker had been recovering from her own ordeal in the ward last Les heard. Did Kase know? Should she tell him once he woke up?

If he woke up.

She chewed on her tongue to keep her emotions in check. Kase would be fine. He would get through this. His body needed to replenish its energy and repair itself, that was all. If he'd survived the last fifteen years, he could survive almost anything.

Surely.

"I'm sorry," she whispered. "I'm so sorry I haven't protected you."

He didn't respond.

"I'll stay with you until you wake up. I promise."

Ana had always been the one scared of the dark, but it was Kase who'd refused sleep until he was certain both his sister and mother were taken care of. That was after the nanny had long since given up, of course. Those nights usually ended with Les singing them to sleep in his bed and tucking them in. He'd always been proud and curious and quick-witted, but he'd always been courteous…and quietly romantic, apparently, based on the journal letters.

He'd lost much of himself when Ana died, but he'd started to come back. Les suspected Hallie Walker had everything to do with that.

"Is she in there?" a feminine voice shouted from outside the tent.

Les jumped a little and rose, dropping Kase's hand. The tent had a few guards, but whoever had attacked Kase had murdered his last one. Bloodlessly, but the man was still dead, and she wouldn't allow the same to happen to her son.

It was difficult not to blame her husband for that oversight. She clenched her hands. Not yet. She wouldn't deal with that just yet. Not until Kase recovered.

She hadn't spoken to Harlan directly since being rescued. No matter what he said, she refused to listen. He didn't deserve it. She had a pile of unopened letters in her own tent, and she couldn't find the patience, grace, or love to read them. She wasn't certain she ever would.

One of the guards outside replied, but Les couldn't hear it. She moved toward the front of the tent.

"My daughter is missing, and Kase Shackley has something to do with it, so you'd best put that sword away before I snap it in half," the woman snapped.

Les opened the tent flap. A short woman with dark, graying hair pulled into a tight knot stood beside the medic who'd helped rescue her and Jove, Stowe. The woman looked like she could indeed snap a sword in half. Stowe looked dubious. "Zelda, I'm sure Hallie is just—"

"May I help you?" Les asked, stepping out of the tent and nodding to the three guards. "You must be Miss Walker's…?"

"I'm her mother," the woman said, crossing her arms. "And you are? Do you know where my daughter is?"

Les stood a little to the side. "Why don't you come inside? We can chat quietly without prying eyes and listening ears."

Most of the cavern housing Kase's tent had been cleared out by now; not entirely, but enough to give them space.

Stowe and Hallie's mother, Zelda, followed her inside. It was a little cramped but manageable. There were no other seats besides the little rocky outcropping Les herself had been using.

Zelda froze at the sight of Kase; Stowe's gaze locked on his wounds, widening in horror. Zelda took one step forward. "What—what happened?"

Les folded her hands in front of her and summoned the aristocratic lady she'd been raised to be. "My son was gravely injured during a skirmish not too long ago. I'm afraid no one witnessed the attack, so until he wakes up, we are at a loss as to what exactly occurred." She paused and glanced at him before turning back to the Walkers. "What is this about Miss Walker missing? The last I heard, she was in the ward. I was hoping to check in on her once I was certain my Kase would be fine."

Stowe gestured to Kase. "May I?"

Les nodded. "Lord Saldr is the reason he's even alive right now. Kase was going out to patrol, and someone tried to..." She took a moment to catch her breath, unable to speak past the terror gripping her throat. She couldn't say it, not without losing her composure. "We're uncertain as to who it was."

Stowe knelt next to her son and checked his vitals. Zelda crossed her arms. "Hallie ended up in the ward after *recklessly* going on patrol with your son. Kase came to speak with her, and now she's gone."

The words themselves were simply a list of events, but the emotion behind the words belied her feelings. Anger, grief, fear. She could have been holding a mirror to Les's heart.

"None of the medics saw where she went?"

"She wasn't supposed to leave." Zelda didn't change her tone. "And the last person she talked to was your son."

Uneasiness crept up Les' spine. Something wasn't right.

She pulled out her locket, the one that her brother had saved her daughter with only for her to die seventeen years later. She fiddled with the chain. Kase would've never done anything to willingly put Miss Walker in danger. She'd seen how he looked at her, and her him. She'd seen the letters. What if something had happened to her when Kase was attacked? Perhaps they'd left together. Had he tried to stop something from happening to her and nearly paid the ultimate price for it?

"Zelda, leave it. You saw how bad off he looked when we came to see Hallie—girl scared the life out of him as much as us. He wouldn't've taken her out of here before the medics cleared her, and even if he did, you think he's got any answers to give us right now? He's in a bad way, all right. Recovering and stable," he added when Les's hand flew to her chest, "but in no state for an interrogation."

Zelda's throat bobbed. Les understood; she couldn't rid herself of the lump in her throat, herself.

"There's plenty more caverns to check," Stowe insisted, laying a hand on his wife's shoulder. "'Sides, there's a very real chance she wandered to the public bathing springs to get cleaned up. She may've even returned to the ward in the time we've been away."

"And if she was with him?" If Les's heart had turned to stone, Zelda's voice shared the same fate.

"Then we'll owe him a heap of gratitude when we see him next, make no mistake. He'd set the fire for his own Burning 'fore he let anyone harm a hair on our girl's head. I know it. You know it too, stubborn as you are." There was no lack of affection in those words from Stowe. "If she was with him, I'd bet the clothes off my back he got himself in this state fighting to keep her safe."

Even if the man was voicing fears that had already passed through her head, she hoped it wasn't true. She couldn't bear the thought of something akin to what happened to Kase befalling Miss Walker.

"I'm sure she's all right," Les said. "She's a tough one, and I imagine that's because you raised her to be so."

Zelda uncrossed her arms. Stowe put one of his around her shoulders. "She's got some spunk, for certain."

Les smiled, and it lifted the sadness if only for a moment. "As much as I've failed as a mother, I am thankful my remaining sons have chosen women of outstanding character." Jove's was a betrothal at first, but in the end, he'd still had a final say. She looked at Kase for a moment before turning back to the Walkers. "Truly."

Zelda narrowed her eyes. "Remaining sons?"

"Our middle son perished on the same mission Kase and Miss Walker went on." Tears stung at the corners of Les' eyes. "And my daughter, Ana, passed in the fires that tore through the city some years ago. Kase and my eldest, Jove, are the only children I have left."

Zelda and Stowe looked at each other. Stowe said, "Kase mentioned something like that on our way to the capital. No details, but…"

The woman's steely demeanor finally thawed. "My son, Hallie's twin, passed three and a half years ago, so you can understand why I'm hesitant to let her out of my sight. It took me a while to find my way again."

Stowe rubbed his wife's shoulder, and Les held out her hand for the other woman to take. Hesitantly, she did. Les squeezed it. "I completely understand. More than most people."

Zelda gave her a shaky laugh, and Stowe said, "Which is another reason why I know that no matter what happens, both Hallie and Kase will be all right. I have faith."

Loud footsteps outside the tent interrupted the moment. "I have permission from the Stradat Lord Kapitan to enter this tent." A pause; the visitor's patience perished in that silence, and he barked, *Move aside!*"

Jove. Les gave Zelda's hand another squeeze, then opened the tent once more. Jove and Clara, panicked and searching, met the guards.

"Mother!" Jove's eyes were wide with nearly boyish terror. "We've only just heard, is he—tell me he's—"

"He's resting now. Come in." She gestured them in. With five grown adults—not including Kase outstretched on the cot—the tent was rather cramped. Jove nodded to Stowe, and Clara clasped Zelda's hand with surprising familiarity.

"How is he?" Jove demanded, leading Clara to sit on the little rocky outcropping. "What happened? Father only said he was gravely injured and told us where to find him."

Les would rather not delve into the fact that Harlan had yet to appear, so he'd likely shared the only information he had himself. She cleared her throat. "Lord Saldr took care of him best he could and believes he will recover, but he is uncertain of how long that will take."

The tent was silent before Clara tearfully asked, "Do we know what happened?"

Les hesitated. She wasn't sure if going into the few details she did know would be beneficial. She worried her lip for a moment before simply saying, "Kase was attacked in the hover hangar."

"Where was his *guard*? Sergeant Wiles was supposed to be with him at all times. Where is he now?" Jove settled Clara before lurching to Kase's bedside, halting just short of the cot; he stared down at his youngest brother, going a bit pale himself as his gaze settled on the blood, the bandages. "If he left Kase alone, I'll—"

Les shook her head. "He's...I'm afraid he...he was found deceased. As was another young man about Kase's age. Neville Thatcher, Lady Idell's son."

"Has anyone informed her?" Clara asked.

"From what I've heard, she didn't survive the initial attack on the city," Les said softly.

At least one mother would not have to bear the news of her child's death today.

The tent was silent after that.

Jove acted as if he was going to say something else, but he shut his mouth and pressed his thumb and forefinger to his eyes instead. "Father and I were afraid this would happen. We should have given him more guards...*I* should have stayed with him myself, I should have made sure he was safe. Stars-idiot."

No one said a word as Jove knuckled Kase's curls, a rough gesture she had to swallow a scolding for. He'd taken worse rough housing from his brothers over the years; it was how they'd always been, how they'd always bonded.

So Les bit her tongue as Jove rasped, voice coarse with unshed tears, "I should have...I'm sorry. I'm so sorry."

The silence had begun to wax awkward, the Walkers inching toward the tent's exit, when someone else entered the tent. Zelda and Stowe moved further inside instead, pressing Les closer to Clara, who rose.

In stepped her husband, the Stradat Lord Kapitan of Jayde, his fiery eyes taut at the corners. Ice-cold fury filled her veins. She pushed her way to him, standing between him and her children. Harlan surveyed the assembled group before laying eyes on his unconscious son. "He hasn't woken yet?"

It wouldn't do to reply snidely here, even if she wanted to. The others shouldn't be privy to her marital problems.

"I'm awake," Kase said weakly from the cot. Nearly everyone jumped; Jove snatched his hand back with a curse Clara smacked him on the arm for. Les tripped over someone's foot as she turned. Harlan caught her. She tugged out from his grip and fell to her knees beside the cot.

Those blue eyes of his peeked out from beneath heavy lids. He grimaced when he moved to readjust his position, but grinned feebly in Jove's direction. "Go on. You were saying something about being sorry?"

"I said you're a stars-idiot," Jove fumed. "A *blasted* stars-idiot."

"Forget it, then. I'm going back to sleep." Kase's eyes drifted shut again, his grin bending into a wince. "Maybe then you'll be nicer."

Jove growled—sniffled—then turned away, hand over his eyes. A gesture of exasperation, perhaps...or a sign he'd been overcome with emotion.

Had she been any kind of betting woman, she would have bet on the latter. Especially when Clara turned aside as well, rubbing her hand soothingly over his back and murmuring in his ear.

Les laid a hand on Kase's brow. It felt normal. No fever. "Baby, why didn't you say something sooner?"

"Hadn't slept that well in a while," he mumbled, fatigue slurring his words. His muscles quivered with each movement as he dragged himself up a bit on the pillow, groaning as he opened his eyes again. They were glazed, a little confused. He might not even remember what happened to him.

Never one for subtlety, Harlan held up a notebook not unlike the one Kase had been using to write letters. "Do you know what this book is?"

"Father, give him a moment," Jove snapped.

"If we're to find whoever did this, we need answers—now." Harlan's icy stare didn't crack. "Do you recognize it?"

Kase squinted up at his father. "I'm not sure what you..."

He stared at it for a moment more before his eyes widened. "Is that Hallie's? Where is she?"

Les detected a hint of desperation in his tone.

The Walkers pressed forward, but Harlan ignored them, flipping to a single page near the front and holding it up. "Do you recognize this?"

On the page was a rough sketch of a sword.

Les squeezed Kase's wrist. Jove leaned forward, scowl traded for intrigue. "Isn't that..."

"I don't care what it is," Kase choked. "I need to know where Hallie is. Now. Why isn't she here?"

Blunt. To the point. It broke Les' heart for the hundredth time.

"She left the ward," Stowe said, answering the question. "We were hoping you had an answer for us."

Kase tried to get up, but dropped back on his elbow, panting against the pain. Clara and Les both helped him sit up, but even that much effort poured sweat down his brow, his lungs heaving with every gasp. Maybe Saldr could give him more dust.

"Eravin Gray and General Marcos Correa are in the Catacombs. They're hunting her. I need to find her."

The muscle in Harlan's jaw feathered. "Lady Felyra Besette and Miss Walker were seeking the Gate in another portion of the Catacombs. They discovered and inspected it, and when Lady Besette went to fetch Lord Saldr, they returned to find her missing. Lady Besette believes Miss Walker went through the Gate, leaving behind this notebook. Now, how did she know about *this* sword?"

Les closed her eyes before opening them once more, this time finding her husband's hazel gaze. It used to be warm, if hesitant; in the years since Ezekiel's betrayal, it had frozen to ice.

"I don't know anything about the blasted sword!" Kase shouted; he doubled over, coughing. Fear stabbed Les's heart. She made him lie back, and the desperate way he looked up at her didn't break her heart. It ripped it out completely.

"We need to find her!" he shouted.

Her husband simply looked to Jove. "What about you?"

Les refused to let him keep pushing. She spoke the words so softly, she wasn't sure if anyone else would hear: "It's the Shackley sword."

The very one he had strapped to his hip.

Every eye in the tent glanced toward it. Harlan pulled it from its sheath for all to see. The runic pattern on the flat sides of the long blade winked in the lantern light as people moved out of the way. Les knew more runes lay beneath the worn brown leather wrapping the grip. Those were copied almost exactly on Hallie Walker's sketch. The very end was jagged, as if it had been broken. The blue sapphire in the pommel twinkled in the light.

It was the same sword Harlan had taken from the Cerl commander all those years ago in Ravenhelm, the one that Carleton had added to the family crest to make Harlan feel more a part of the Shackley legacy.

Harlan sheathed the sword again with quick efficiency.

Kase still did his best to push himself out of the cot, pushing himself even as agony doubled him up. He wasn't fully healed, and Les held him steady. Kase spat through gritted teeth, "I'm not sure why Hallie would have drawn it. She had no reason to."

He swayed a little, and Jove caught him on his other side. She slid her arm around Kase's waist, careful of the bandages.

That was when Saldr peeked in, another parchment in his hand. He held it up. "It's Xera's sword. I had one of our scholars confirm it."

On the parchment, the Shackley sword lay drawn in fading ink.

"I'm unsure what this means," Les said, trying to comprehend what her husband was getting at. What did it matter if Hallie had drawn the sword into her own book? Perhaps she'd seen it in the family crest or from that parchment and thought it would be good to add to her own sketchbook. Kase had mentioned ages ago that she enjoyed art. She didn't understand what the point was here.

And what did they mean, she'd gone through some gate? She hadn't seen any gates in the Catacombs.

"This sword is the key to the Gate." Harlan paused, a brief flash of uncertainty in his eyes before it disappeared. "Why she did not reveal this knowledge to us, we are not certain, which is why it is imperative you tell us everything you know, Kase. It might very well save her life."

Les still didn't understand, but Kase and Jove both seemed to. Kase turned white as a sheet. He no longer fought to stand. Jove frowned.

It was Zelda Walker who spoke up. "Where is she? What is this Gate?"

But no one was able to answer her, because a messenger interrupted. He gave a missive to the Stradat Lord Kapitan, who practically tore it open. He read the message, the line between his brows deepening with each word. He looked at Kase. "Ben Reiss is awake. He's requesting to speak with you immediately."

C H A P T E R 4 4

THE FRIEND HE'D KNOWN

Kase

HIS SIDE STILL BURNED LIKE the sun, but there was no way in the stars that he would just sit there in that thrice-blasted tent and wait until someone else found Hallie. Eravin and Correa needed her. They needed her dead.

The thought that Hallie had gone through the Gate on her own without telling anyone only worried him more. He didn't know what her plan was now. She didn't have the swords. His father had one—still unsure about how *that* had happened—and the other, Saldr had sheathed at his own waist. She couldn't sacrifice herself without them with her, which means she was either going to reset the Gates like Saldr wanted...or she had changed everything entirely and hadn't thought to tell him anything at all.

Or they were all wrong, and something worse had happened to her.

He just needed to see her, hold her, hear her say she was okay. If she'd come up with a new plan and gone through the Gate purposefully, he trusted she knew what she was doing, but that wasn't the problem. The problem was that Eravin and Correa were looking for her. And if they found her before he could...

Jove helped him into his last semi-clean shirt, the one Hallie had worn just yesterday. It still smelled faintly like her, like the crisp, clean mountain air. Shocks. He clenched his jaw and played it off as side pain instead of what it truly was when his mother gave him that waspish look of hers.

Then they left the tent, a crew of misfits.

His side twinged again, though the pain lessened the more he walked. He was too slow, only able to limp at a glacial pace through the slowly emptying Catacombs. Maybe Skibs could shed some light on the situation. Kase dearly hoped so. If he remembered correctly, he was supposed to have the Essence power that did something with the Gate in Myrrai.

But that was only if he intended to help Jayde, not hurt them. He'd once betrayed them. What was to say he wasn't still working for Correa?

As they walked in their mismatched group—Lord Saldr and the Stradat Lord Kapitan leading the entire party from his tent—Kase kept his head on a swivel. The last thing he remembered besides the threats to Hallie was Eravin's solid black glare.

Jagamot lived inside broken people. It sounded like some horror story from First Earth to him. But if anyone was broken, it was Kase. It was quite a feat he was still there, but he didn't feel like some other entity or...or...shadow was inside him. No one had said anything about black veins or eyes or anything to him.

Then again, he'd grown in the last few months, more than he even realized. Hallie had brought out only the best in him, and for that, he would be eternally grateful. She was his north star, guiding him to the life he was meant to lead.

Maybe he'd imagined the black veins. Wouldn't the same thing be happening in the other people in the Catacombs if it was true? Eravin had said the city was full of broken people.

Kase picked up his pace, ignoring the pain in his side.

The ward was still littered with patients. The more seriously sick or wounded wouldn't be moved until the Medic's Guildhouse was secure, which could take about a week, as his father had said in the meeting yesterday...the one he'd been late for because he'd been taking care of Hallie. He hadn't paid too much attention to what was said. His mind had been on the woman in his tent and the fact that the only reason he was in that meeting at all was because he was the most senior pilot Jayde had. They still hadn't received word from the bases further out. Without electricity, quick communication was nearly impossible. Any surviving pilots would've had to hire a horse or carriage to make it back to the capital, and that would take weeks depending on where they'd been stationed.

Unless they stole a Cerl hover and allowed it to siphon off their soul to fly. Like Kase had, if unwittingly.

He nodded to a few of the patients they passed, who all craned their necks to see why the large and rather bedraggled party was traipsing through. Kase glimpsed a few with the spiderwebbed black veins. Fear spiked in his chest. But they were all behaving relatively normally...sleeping or eating or chatting with medics. They didn't look broken or murderous. Some even smiled at him.

They didn't seem to be manifesting Jagamot. They'd probably head to the surface soon.

Saldr led them to the back of the ward where three guards waited in front of one of the little cells. Anderson was nearby, still comatose, still leaking Soul or whatever Saldr had said. Maybe Skibs would have answers regarding that as well.

He clenched his teeth against the sharp pain that spiked as he opened the curtain.

Sitting on the side of the little cot sat Ben Reiss, not looking at all like he'd fallen from a dragon hours earlier. Kase felt worse than he looked. It was a punch to the chest to see him not astride a dragon or about to stab him with a sword. He didn't have the crazed look he'd had at the end of the *Eudora* mission, nor did he look lost or out of it like he had after the crash in the Bay of Storms.

He looked like the man he'd met during pilot training nearly four years ago.

Skibs turned and smiled. It wasn't maniacal or spiteful. It was genuine and warm, if nervous. Like the friend he'd known. "Glad to see you showed up. Not sure if you were gonna."

"Skibs," Kase said cautiously, not sure Skibs wasn't going

to pull a sword out from underneath the cot and run him through with it.

Skibs pushed himself to his feet, grunting a little, and took a few steps forward before pulling Kase into a hug.

Kase froze. Skibs had never really been the hugging type. Neither had Kase, for that matter. He bit the inside of his cheek to keep himself from crying out as his side protested.

"I'm sorry," Skibs whispered before letting him go. He looked the same as ever. Same blond hair. Same sharp blue eyes, though there were a few lines around them. "I'm sorry for everything. I wasn't in my right mind, though it's not a good excuse. I just wanted to…I am sorry. So sorry. Especially for…Zeke." Skibs swallowed hard and crossed his arms. "I know…how hard that was for you."

Kase gritted his teeth. "If you hadn't attacked the city…"

Both cities, really.

Skibs looked away. "I don't expect you to ever forgive me for that, but I would like to explain."

"Let me see if I can guess first." Kase began counting off on his fingers, not bothering to keep his voice down. "You were working for the Cerls. You fulfilled whatever mission you were supposed to. And wait, I almost forgot—you were a *Yalven Essence wielder* the entire time, you blasted lying *dulkop*!"

Probably not the best choice of words. He needed Ben to help him with Hallie. He had to get his temper in check.

Skibs blew out a breath and sat on the edge of his cot. "Not by choice."

Kase didn't have time to talk about regrets or whoever had made Skibs' choices. "If you mean it, then prove it. Help us. I need you to tell me about the Gate here in Kyvena."

The other man jerked and looked up. "It's here? Truly? You know where it is?"

Too eager. Kase backtracked. "Why do you care?"

"Because that's why I'm here in Kyvena. It was the only reason I stayed in the capital after the attack. I've been searching above for any signs. The only hint I have is the layout of the city. Everything hinges on a singular point in McKenzie Square, but nothing I've done has triggered its opening." Skibs rubbed his stubbled chin. "I probably don't have the correct words of power, but my uncle assumed my

Essence power would reveal them to me when the time came.' He snorted. "Fates, I hate that man."

Fates. A Cerl curse. Kase didn't think he'd ever heard Skibs use it before, but he'd been pretending to be Jaydian for years. Now Kase knew the truth—that he was working with the enemy—it would make sense if the man he knew as Ben Reiss was actually from Cerulene. He narrowed his eyes in confusion. "Uncle? Did you...take your power from him?"

Maybe it was a situation like Hallie's.

Skibs froze. He looked as if someone had painted him into a portrait. He moved not a muscle.

When Skibs didn't answer, Kase leaned down. "How can we trust you? All you've done is betray us. You threw our friendship away. Is there anything you told me that wasn't a lie?"

Skibs just sat there, staring at the ground.

That was all the answer Kase needed. "I don't care what the truth is. I need your help with the Gate. If you do that, then I will put a good word in for you and do my best to make sure you at least get a trial. That's all I can promise. And it's the best deal you'll get."

Skibs still didn't speak. Kase just let out a frustrated growl He wasn't any closer to finding Hallie. If Skibs wouldn't help, he'd take one of the swords and go down to the tunnel himself. Maybe that would trigger something, if the swords were connected to the Gates somehow like Hallie and Saldr talked about. He would do whatever was needed to find her.

He reached for the curtain, but Skibs' voice stopped him.

"My name isn't Ben Reiss."

That revelation didn't necessarily surprise Kase, but the tone of the confession did. It came out strained, like Skibs was under duress. Like it was physically painful to say the words.

Kase let his hand drop. A few of the shadows on the other side moved, but no one came inside. He turned back to Skibs. Blond hair peeked out between the fingers pressed to his forehead, his face bowed and hidden.

"My real name is Asa aven d'Correa, crown prince of Cerulene," he said quietly. "I was the illegitimate son of the late Queen Astraea, but because I completed my mission, the one to Myrrai and opened the Gate, I was granted legitimacy.

"I ran away from home at seventeen and found myself in Kyvena two years later. However, I was recognized on one of the joint missions we had as pilots by a courtier friend of my uncle's. They blackmailed me into joining the Watch and then taking on the Essence power from Professor Owen Christie, who once was a Cerl asset during the Great War but had become more and more uncooperative in the years since. If I led a group of Cerls to Myrrai, activated the Gate, and subdued the Lord Elder, I would be granted full legitimacy. They'd found out about Lucy, too, and threatened her and our baby. That was what made me ultimately decide to go along with the plan."

Kase's mouth had fallen open near the beginning of the speech. It was still open. It was like Ben was reading out of some fantasy novel, not telling Kase his own life story. "So everything you told me *was* a lie."

Worse than that. His best friend was a Cerl Prince. Wait, no—Hallie'd said the King was dead, and if Skibs...blast it. If *Asa* was telling the truth about the legitimacy thing...

Kase couldn't think straight. Not knowing the man in front of him was now the King of Cerulene.

Holy stars, did that woman—Fely—did she know? She'd been Filip's betrothed. Had she known and not told anyone? Who was she really working for? Had they been duped?

If that was the case, had she lied about Hallie going through the Kyvena Gate? His chest tightened.

Skibs looked up, his eyes pink. "Not everything." He pressed his hands to his knees. "I tried to spare Hallie at the end. I knew what she'd translated in that notebook of hers was only possible with Yalven heritage. I didn't know what she was—whether she was Chronal or Chosen to take on an Essence power—but I tried to stop my uncle from finding out. I took it into the Aurora, or Myrrai Gate, with me."

Except Correa still found her. But Kase didn't point that out. Not yet.

"I was in control of the Essence power at the beginning, but hitting my head during that storm...broke me somehow. I wasn't able to control it well at all after that. Each power is different, and with the burden of the Gates, this particular Essence power requires immense control. It's more malignant than my brother's...or my uncle's, even. With the injuries sustained on the *Eudora* mission, I lost control."

Kase crossed his arms over his chest. "But if your mission was to lead the Cerls to Myrrai, why did you not go with us? Why did you disappear during the battle at the ruins?"

Kase had bargained with the Lord Elder to find him. He'd gone every day to the gatehouse to check on the scouting party's progress. Every single day.

A moment or two of silence passed, Ben looking anywhere but at Kase. Then it hit him like a hovership. Dread and anxiety built in his chest at the realization. "You tried to stop them, didn't you? But you lost control."

"And I've been trapped ever since. I couldn't—I never would've—I destroyed both the Yalven city and...and my home."

"Home?"

A beat or two before the choked word left his lips. "Kyvena."

Shocks. The hurt in his voice was very real. No one could fake that. Could it be that his friend was truly back? Kase chewed on the inside of his cheek again. It'd be raw by the end of the conversation.

"And now I've probably killed Lucy and our child, even if I wasn't in my right mind. So many dead." Ben covered his face, shuddering visibly. "So many."

He hadn't heard much about specific people since he returned, but he vaguely remembered hearing something before he'd left Kyvena with Hallie. He wet his lips. "Lucy wasn't in the city, to my knowledge. Rumor was she left for her family's country estate because of the pregnancy. Another rumor actually suggested *I* was the father." Kase rubbed a hand down his face. "She's probably the least traumatized out of all of us."

Skibs lifted his head, the blazing relief and stark sorrow in his eyes at odds with each other. "I should've just run away with her. We'd be destitute, but at least we'd be together. Now, with everything...it's probably better, I guess. This way, she's far away from me."

"We can find her after this is all done."

"Kase, this is the end, unless my uncle has found all the Essence wielders. We're still missing the Essence of Spark, who I think you know was Abram Loffler."

Kase felt like he'd missed a step on the stairs. That was

right. The card game. It was one of the things he'd revealed during that awful event. The bombing run had been the next day. Someone had told the Cerls. Probably Eravin, though he'd denied it.

It was then that the curtain opened to admit the Stradat Lord Kapitan, Fely, and Saldr. The Yalven man kept a hand on the shadow sword.

Kase cursed in his head. He was going to pay for that slip-up. Now they knew who had been the one to leak the information. He would never find Hallie.

It was Harlan who spoke, "You, Asa aven d'Correa, also known as Benjamin Reiss, are thereby under arrest by the power vested in me from the High Council of Jayde, as Stradat and Lord Kapitan. Any attempt to flee or use the Yalven power in your possession will result in your immediate execution."

He nodded toward Saldr, who unsheathed the shadow sword.

"I understand, and I deserve the punishment for my crimes." He stood and bowed to Harlan. "However, I do wish to help you, truly. My power is under control, and I fully intend to cooperate and share all the knowledge I possess."

It was Fely who spoke up next. "You are different, Asa."

"As are you, Lady Fely. Where is Filip?" Skibs looked around as if expecting the Cerl King to be hiding in plain sight. "Or Uncle? Have you abandoned them as well? I'll applaud you for it, if so. They deserved it."

Saldr shifted in front of her, the sword shimmering slightly in the light. "How do we know you are in full possession of your senses, that the Essence you wield is not controlling you? This sword will sever it, and you will die, your soul slipping away through a wound only Toro can fix. It is our only assurance. Can you offer a better one?"

Skibs looked a little puzzled by that. He shrugged. "All I know is that I woke without the weight that usually pushes my real self aside. That's the best way I can describe it. I feel like myself again, like I was before my uncle forced me to take the Essence power from Owen Christie."

Kase glanced at Saldr. He nodded, seemingly knowing exactly what Kase was thinking. Not only had Hallie slowed down time or whatever to save Skibs from falling to his death, but somehow...somehow, she'd healed him. No wonder she'd nearly burnt herself out. That was the only explanation. "Hallie's the one that saved you. She's the—"

He didn't finish the sentence. Screaming started in the ward. And Kase knew.

Eavin had arrived.

CHAPTER 45

FOR A CUPPA

Hallie

HALLIE CRUSHED THE DAISIES BETWEEN her fingers as she sat up. Deep green grass rolled out before her like a fine carpet, lush and well-cared for. The color threw her off. Kyvena was still on the outset of spring. Little patches of brown should've been woven into the more vibrant blades. This was somewhere entirely different.

The Myrrai Gate held numerous timelines. Was this one the same? Had she ended up in an entirely different time or world? Was she even still on Yalvara?

Her heart squeezed painfully, and she grabbed her chest. It didn't matter how beautiful the place she found herself in. The only thing that mattered was getting back to the Catacombs.

She pressed her hands into the ground and wrenched forth her power, thrusting it into the soft, loamy dirt. It came quicker this time—a cruel twist of fate. It'd failed only moments earlier in the Catacombs. *"Kyvena vreali Toro!"*

A smoky spark like lightning shot up from the ground

and twisted around her hands like yarn, but no Passage appeared. She tried again. And again. And again.

The strand of light thinned each successive attempt, and no Passage appeared.

"No, no, no." Her lungs were tight. "Please no."

Don't panic.

But holy stars, no matter how many times she told herself that, she couldn't help the dread settling into her bones

She switched up the words. Maybe those words of power were only good once.

"*Vrali Toro nah Kyvena!*" she screamed at her hands. She used a different variation of the word for Passage—and also added a *please.*

Her power didn't even bother to react.

Maybe she needed more Zuprium. She wouldn't find it so close to the surface, but she dug anyway. Dirt and grime and grass collected under her fingernails and in the cracks of her hands. She couldn't dig far. Not without a shovel.

Her hands, her fingers, even her nails ached with the effort of digging for the metal only to come up empty. She pressed her forehead to the muddy, disturbed ground and screamed in frustration.

She was so lost in her fury and desperation she didn't hear the footsteps behind her until a voice spoke.

"You're late."

Hallie tensed. It didn't sound like Mr. Gray or Correa.

"Could've predicted that. What I didn't figure was if I ever saw you again, you'd be throwing some sort of hissy fit." A pair of black boots stepped into her peripheral. "Nor would I have bet you'd be ruining my lawn." A soft scoff. "Probably why I was always rubbish at cards."

Hallie's heart stopped squeezing itself and flew into her throat. She choked on the air she'd breathed in. That voice. That accent. The lazy tilt to each vowel. But it was impossible. Absurd. Unless...unless...

This was what Mr. Gray had meant. It hadn't been physically painful, nor had her life flashed before her eyes, but somehow death had met her anyway.

Because the only way she would be hearing that exact voice was if she were dead.

She pushed herself to her knees, ignoring her aching

limbs, and looked up.

An older teenaged boy stood a few feet from her, a small pile of firewood in his arms. The little woodcutter's cottage she'd noticed earlier with Fely stood just behind him. The stone bricks were whiter than snow and gleamed in early evening light.

The boy himself was tall and lanky. Too skinny for his height, really, but that wasn't abnormal for him. His hair was red as fire, and his face was drowning in freckles. His eyes were a burnished bronze and full of mischief, a crooked smile to match.

A gasping sob was her only response. It couldn't be helped.

Jack hadn't changed one bit since the day he died.

"Now there ain't no reason for you to get all upset," Jack said, setting the wood in his arms onto the manicured grass Hallie hadn't torn up. "I ain't mad or nothing."

The sobs now came quickly. Soon, she was gasping for breath, tears pouring down her cheeks. She clenched her fingers, the dirt clogging further beneath her fingernails.

She'd thought she'd worked through most of the pain, but his presence before her now only ripped out the thread she'd used to sew up her damaged heart.

The pain was sharp and thick, lancing and stinging. It went as deep as the Josei Ocean and as high as First Earth's Mount Everest. On one hand, her twin stood before her, his work boots coming closer into her blurred view beyond the salty tears; on the other, somehow, she'd gained her brother back only to lose Kase.

The joy and anguish melded together, and she knew not where one ended and the other began. And at that moment, she didn't know which was loudest.

"I ain't about to complain—it's a little gratifying, if I'm being honest—but I'd reckon I don't deserve all that blubbering." Jack squatted down in front of her and held out a hand.

Hallie stared at it for a moment. Before his body had been Burned on the funeral pyre, that particular hand had been buried under the mine beam. After the mining crew recovered his body, Hallie couldn't bear to look at the rest of him—only his right hand. Mangled and flattened. She wouldn't forget it for as long as she lived.

Now it was whole and clean. No scars. No evidence of the mine collapse that had killed him. Nothing left to remind Hallie that Niels had pulled her away as the beam started falling, leaving Jack behind.

Like she'd been pushed here, leaving Kase behind.

Hallie grabbed his hand, pulling herself up. Her bones rattled with grief and shock. It ached. She clenched her teeth against it, but that only made her shake harder. Jack just raised a brow. It was a look she once would've throttled him for—one she hadn't realized she'd missed.

Her brother pulled her into a hug so crushing that the shakes ceased—not because she willed them to do so, but because he held her so tightly she physically couldn't manage it. She could finally smell the clean scent of linen that told her Jack was right there even if she didn't understand why.

That was when the dam broke loose. Sobs wracked her body instead of shakes, and her brother squeezed her harder. "I've missed you, Lark."

Three years. One year of darkness so deep she nearly wasted away. One year of finding the light. One year of hoping the light would keep shining.

And now this.

After a few more moments, she calmed herself enough to pull back and wipe her face with the edge of her sleeve. Kase's stolen military jacket had a few more knicks and scrapes on it from her recent ordeal. It stood in heavy contrast to Jack's pristine appearance.

"Is it really you?" Hallie stumbled through the question, her breathing still hitching with the aftermath of all the sobbing.

He gestured for her to follow him as he walked back toward his pile of wood. "Yeah, yeah, in the flesh—well, not flesh, but—aw, you know what I mean." She hadn't the faintest. "Before you start asking a bunch of questions, I can't answer all two hundred of them I know you got, so keep it to one at a time, will you?"

Hallie followed him, her boots scuffing on the dirt and well-kept lawn. "Where are we? Am I..."

"Ah-ah! That's two already! Still don't listen to a word I say." Jack stacked a few chunks of firewood into Hallie's arms and then loaded his own. "Are you dead? Probably. I like to call it Souls Meet, but Gran calls it something foreign." He nodded toward the cottage behind him. "Come on."

Hallie nearly tripped as he led her around to the back of the cottage. "Gran?"

Jack led her along the perfectly trimmed hedges that stood tall along the side, and the vesper flowers climbing up a wooden trellis. They leaned over like little pink and white prayers. They were her mother's favorites. She used the petals as a garnish for fancier inn dinners if someone special was visiting for the night. Otherwise, they weren't to be bothered, allowed to grow wild along the back fence.

"She'll be back soon. I sort of messed up one of the last Meetings, and I've been relegated to chores around the cottage and watching over the Nether Gate you came through until she deems me punished enough." Jack stopped in front of another pile of chopped wood, each one stacked neatly on a pallet before an arched side door. "She knows no one ever comes through that one. Except you, apparently."

Hallie set the wood down and ran her hand along the side of the cottage before looking back at him. "That didn't answer my question at all."

He picked up a bucket near the door and scooped out a handful of what looked like corn. He handed it to her. The kernels felt real, just like the daisies and the dirt still under her nails. But beneath the shock and the fear and the confusion, she felt warmth. It felt just like her power...but if she was dead, shouldn't her power be gone? Wouldn't it be reborn?

If the world hadn't ended when Mr. Gray had pushed her through the Gate, anyway.

Jack led her around the cottage to the far side, where chickens waited in a little fenced area and a tiny version of the cottage behind them. "I know you. No matter how many answers I throw at'cha, you'll just ask ten more questions, and Gran can answer them better than I ever could."

He dug in the bucket and fished out a handful of corn. He tossed it into the pen. The hens exploded with chatter and dove for the kernels. "Probably should throw that soon," he advised, nodding at her hand. "The ladies like their food, and if you don't throw it quick like, one of them is liable to peck you through the fence til you do."

He threw another handful in, and the hens descended on the food once more. One of the hens, one with feathers the color of the sunset, couldn't get close enough. Jack tsked at her. "Come here, Anne. You know you gotta be quicker than that." He gave her a few kernels.

She pecked his hand, and he drew it back with a snap, but no blood spotted his fingers. He laughed. "There's that spunk. Good girl. Now go lay me a good ole egg." He set the bucket on the ground and pointed to the various hens. "Now there's Jane and Lizzie. That one there? The one with the grayish brown and black feathers like a mockingbird's? Scout. Then there's Hester, Eowyn, Arwen, and Jo March. Thought she needed the full name. She's the one who's the most stubborn."

Hallie sprinkled her handful near Anne and the one she thought was Hester. They both clucked in approval. Maybe. It was hard to tell, but they snatched up the kernels rather quickly. "Jack, why are there chickens in the afterlife, and why in the stars are we feeding them if they're already dead?"

Because she was beginning to think this was all some horribly cruel and ridiculous dream her mind had drummed up to torture her. She hadn't taken anything besides Navara's journal through the Gate. She'd left her satchel on the ground.

Oh, stars, the journal! She'd left it.

"Wait! I'll be back. Just a moment." And then she hurried toward the other side of the cottage and into the little field beyond. The sky grew darker as the sun sank beyond the distant horizon. The golden light made the mountain tops glow.

There in the patch of ripped up daisies and messy dirt was the journal. She scooped it up and headed back toward Jack.

Jack nodded back toward the cottage. "Chickens die too, and they still need people to ferry them over. Just easier than people. Plus, I think Gran likes the company."

"Ferry them over?"

Jack hung the bucket on a hook by the door. "Like I said, *lots of times,* best to let Gran explain." He twisted the knob, putting on some terrible mimicry of an upper-crust Jaydian accent. "Come in for a cuppa, will you?"

Jack saw her hesitation and held out his hand. "No, really. It's about to be dark out, and it's best to be inside when that happens." His eyes looked beyond her at something only he could see.

Hallie looked back at the sunset. "What do you mean?" What could be dangerous about the dark when one was dead?

"Let's get you some tea. You still drink peppermint?"

Hallie turned back and narrowed her eyes. "Jack."

He rolled his eyes, but something about his smile twitched…resigned, maybe, or stubborn. Either way, it gave her the impression he either wouldn't or couldn't say anything else about it. "Come *in*, will you? Gran will be home soon, and then we can eat some of the stew I've had on the hearth all day. Made some bread, too."

Hallie chewed on the inside of her lip and stepped inside. "Fine."

The inside of the cottage looked very much like someone named Gran inhabited the place. The entire interior was two rooms with what Hallie assumed was a loft accessed by a ladder in the corner. The walls boasted various needlepoint landscapes. Hallie recognized both Stoneset and Myrrai in two of them. The others weren't familiar to her, but they were beautiful nonetheless with their great cedars and blue, misty mountains. A patchwork quilt lay folded on the back of a brown couch, and a wooden rocker sat near the generous brick hearth. On the other side, a little kitchen waited. A large farm sink with a Zuprium pump lay beneath a lace-curtained window facing the sunset mountains. A little wooden table was set with two places complete with placemats embroidered with bulbous red mazelberries and oak leaves along the edges.

Hallie sat on a small but sturdy wooden chair. Assorted dried herbs and flowers hung from the kitchen wall. Add a wall of shelves overflowing with books, and Hallie would be quite cozy in such a place.

Jack busied himself at the sink, pressing the lever down to dredge up water into a kettle. He set it on a tiny stove top before opening the grate below and adding a few smaller wood blocks to a dying fire. He used the final piece of wood to work up a few sparks before adding it to the pile inside. He shut the little door with a creak, twisting the handle and locking it in place.

"Welcome to my little corner of the world," Jack said, holding out his arms. "It really isn't much, but I do think the dried flowers and herbs add a nice touch."

Now that she had finally gotten over her shock, Hallie found the moment quite surreal. How was she with her brother right now? Was this truly the afterlife? It didn't feel quite right. Something about it simply felt...off. It all felt like a house of cards about to tumble down, but why that was, she couldn't pinpoint.

She laid the journal atop the table. Its cover was now streaked with dirt. She twisted her fingers together, holding them in her lap. For once, she felt like a proper uppity lady with stiff posture. Her mind, however, was still teeming. A paradox of sorts, really.

"You're no good at waiting," Jack chuckled. "Your foot's tapping something fierce."

A bit of frustration dredged itself up out of her general unease. "I don't like not having answers. I can't fear what I don't know."

"Plenty of people are terrified of the unknown—for good reason. You should join 'em."

Well, at least one thing hadn't changed in death. Jack still hated giving direct answers. "Quit being a sterning dulkop and tell me."

"*There* you are! With all that fancy city-folk talk, I was gettin' to think you might not be the real Hallie Walker."

"You're stalling."

She needed to understand something, *anything* about the strange world she found herself in. It was all chaos in her ordered mind, and if she didn't tidy it soon, she would lose hold of the barely-wrangled calm she'd scraped together.

Jack drummed his fingers on his elbows—also unscarred, also whole. Hallie glanced down at her lap to her tangled fingers. Her little finger was still missing. If she'd truly joined her brother in death, wouldn't her scars and maladies be healed? It gave her a sliver of hope, even if sorrow filled what was left—because if she wasn't dead, she would have to leave him once more.

She didn't know if she could do that again. And that terrified her.

Kase's ring still circled her finger. Her heart gave a painful throb. What would he do when he couldn't find her? Would it break him at last? Would he realize she hadn't left of her own free will?

He'd proposed to her, she'd said no, and now...now he

wouldn't know where she'd gone. What if he assumed he'd scared her off, or that she'd taken the coward's way out and run from her responsibility to sacrifice herself? It'd break his heart either way. He'd think she'd left him. Abandoned him.

Stop that, she scolded herself. *You might be dead. Get your priorities in order.*

Her twin chewed his thumbnail, a nervous habit he hadn't seemed to kick in death. "I don't know, Hallie, honest. All I know is that outta nowhere, bad stuff's started happening when the sun falls 'neath the horizon. Every night, some of us up and disappear. It's almost as if the night sky has a bit of a temper. Not even the stars shine no more."

Hallie resisted the urge to rub her eyes. Her brother would've been eaten alive at the University with that sort of dialect. She'd practiced for ages, using the sleepless nights after Jack's death to do so. It kept her mind busy and exhausted enough not to notice that he didn't knock messages on their shared wall in code when he couldn't sleep. She cleared her throat, "So you're saying something's going around at night and taking people? From *death*? Who else is here?"

"Not always taking people. We find them the next day, all gray and the like. It's something like out of a fairytale." He shivered. "Didn't start but recently...after I botched that Meeting. It's part of the reason Gran relegated me to the cottage. Thinks that particular soul wants his revenge for something or other."

Hallie leaned forward slightly, putting a few clues together. "So your purpose here is to meet with souls of the recently departed and ferry them? To what?"

"Dunno, not really, but I don't gotta worry about it. All I know is that I landed here some time ago and learned that I can still heal people by making sure they want to move on to the beyond. Souls Meet is more of a holding place. I think. It'll make more sense the longer you stay."

His offhand tone told her it wasn't a big deal, but the slight quiver of his hands belied how unsettled he really was. He busied himself by grabbing two teacups from his cupboard. He fished around in the back of the cabinet for a few tea bags.

Hallie found it all very odd and intriguing all at once. She wished she had her sketchbook with her. No one had written a book about the afterlife or anyplace called *Souls Meet*. Of course, anyone who would've known the full details would've needed to die and then return to life. Hallie was beginning to think that she hadn't found the second Gate at all, that it had been more of a Passage into death. But why was it in Kyvena?

And most importantly, was the woman Jack referred to as *Gran* actually Navara? She was the one who'd left the journal with the hints. She was the one who would've known enough about what both Stoneset and Myrrai looked like to recreate them with thread and hang them on her cottage walls.

Ignoring the fact that having such living comforts such as tea, chickens, thread, and old rocking chairs by the fireplace seemed entirely odd for death, this wasn't a bad place to be, not really. And maybe that was its purpose. Jack and Gran ferried souls to what lay next, but maybe the familiar comforts made the transition easier.

Jack set the tea supplies on the table, and Hallie grabbed the teacup first. The cup was plain white porcelain with finely painted pink roses on the side. A plump brown rabbit greeted her from the side of her brother's cup. "These are beautiful."

Jack smiled. "Gran. Probably where you got your art skills."

"So Gran is..."

"Pa's Gran, actually. She disappeared when he was little, but it's her story to tell, not mine." He got up to flick on the lanterns positioned around the cozy living area and close the shutters, locking them tight, and bolting the door. "Looks like she had to stay in the village for the night. Had a good influx of souls lately. Maybe she'll let me help her again soon. She's behind."

"Navara?" Hallie asked, though she was half distracted by the lanterns.

They looked like the ones she was familiar with, but instead of a small golden orange flame inside, the fire was tinted blue. Well, *fire* wasn't the right word. It was more akin to the Yalven fire she had never been able to conjure.

The tea kettle gave a little whistle before growing to an incessant whine. Jack jumped a little and grabbed a dishcloth from the side of the sink and pulled the kettle off. "Grab yourself a bag there and I'll pour."

Hallie inspected the little tags on the end of the bags and chose the one labeled 'Peppermint' in her brother's messy handwriting.

That simple sight nearly brought tears to her eyes, but she blinked them away and draped the bag into the cup and held it out.

Jack poured hot water into the cup, steam rising in little ghostly spirals. Hallie adjusted the bag and waited for the flavoring to settle and mix with the water. She took a small spoon and stirred it. "No sugar?"

Jack shook his head as he poured his own cup. "We're limited on sustenance here."

Hallie was still enamored by the fact that there was any food at all. "It's all right. I can drink it black."

Jack took an experimental sip of his before putting it back down. "Who are you and what have you done with my sister?"

Hallie laughed a little, the first since she'd arrived, and blew on her tea before taking a dainty sip. The hot liquid fanned across her tongue.

Mother of ash.

She blanched and resisted the urge to spit it back out. She tried not to gag as she forced herself to swallow. "Ugh, what kind of tea is this?"

Jack took another sip of his. "I'd wager this is my best batch. Made it about a week ago."

"You must be joking. This is at least years old." Hallie pushed the cup away. Jack picked it up and took a sip.

He swallowed and shrugged. "Tastes fine to me." He narrowed his eyes. "Or are you being ornery because I ain't let you ask all your questions?"

Well, then her brother had no taste at all. Hallie set her cup aside. "Tastes bad, but you've never had good taste." She tapped her fingernails on the side of the cup. "Never understood how you could stomach coffee."

Jack looked over with a grin before he noticed her hand.

He set his tea down and grabbed it before Hallie could hide it back under the table. "Two things. Where did your finger go, and why is there a ring on that one? A pretty one, at that. Expensive."

Hallie jerked her hand back and hid it. She played with the ring in question under the table. She'd been able to think about other things than Kase in the last few minutes, but now it was back, and it was about to break her heart. How could she explain it all? Could she even try? She shook her head. "It's been an eventful three years."

"Niels? Didn't think he could afford something uppity like that. Do I even want to know how he squirreled away enough to—"

Hallie shook her head. "Not Niels."

Jack's eyebrows rose. "Really? Poor man must've messed up something bad. Who then? So help me, if you up and married Willi Heinrich, I'm never speaking to you again."

Willi had been the mayor's son who always beat Jack in their mathematics assessments and in afternoon groggon matches. Hallie hadn't seen him since she'd left for Kyvena. He was more than likely one of the many who hadn't survived the initial Cerl attack.

"No, not Willi," Hallie sighed. "No one. I'm not married. Someone...asked, but I told him no."

"So you're wearing a ring on that finger because..."

Kase's last words echoed in her mind. I'll wait until the stars fall so long as I get to be with you in the end.

A tear slipped down her cheek. He'd get his chance to prove it—he'd be waiting forever now.

"Hal." Jack's voice lowered, mischief gone in a blink. "If he hurt you, I don't care who he is, I'll make sure he don't get ferried over. I have a lot of sway now, you know."

Hallie wiped the tear. "No."

"No, he didn't hurt you, or no, don't ferry him over? I'll tar an' feather him, just you watch—well, it'll be mud, and the girls don't shed awful much being dead and all, but I'll get creative. Hey, I know—corn. Roll him in mud, crust him in corn, toss him in the coop—"

"Jack!" In spite of herself, she laughed at the vision of poor Kase under attack by a handful of hens—then sobered. "No, he didn't hurt me. He would never, he...it's..."

Where did she even start?

"I love him," she confessed. "Kase, that is, but if...if I'm here, that means I..." She took a deep breath. "It's probably best if I start at the beginning. We'll be locked in here for the night, right?"

Jack got up and fetched two soup bowls and a loaf of bread from the cupboard. "You may as well go ahead and start, because the soup is ready, and I have a feeling this is gonna take a while. Not that I mind." He set a bowl before her and smiled. "I'm glad I'm here to listen."

C H A P T E R   4 6

I LOVE...

Kase

WITHOUT ANY HESITATION, KASE HURRIED behind Saldr and the Stradat Lord Kapitan out of Skibs' cell. Fely and Skibs followed, and not even his father tried to stop the man who had been under arrest not even five minutes ago.

Because they all knew the awful truth: they didn't have time. If they didn't stop whatever was causing the screaming, everyone would die.

Kase didn't have a weapon. He'd lost the King Arthur knife, and he hadn't had any time to figure out where his Cerl pistol went.

Jove ushered both their mother and Clara to the back of the ward. "Get out. Go into the city and hide. Now."

Clara grabbed his brother by the shirt and pulled him to her. "You come back to me, you hear? I won't lose you a second time."

He kissed her. "Keep Samuel safe. I love you."

"Jove!"

But he didn't turn around, only ran after the rest of

them. Kase thought he heard his mother call his name, but he didn't stop to find out. His side throbbed with agony as they sped through the little corridor with its hanging linen cells and gas lanterns dotted along the way.

People ran in all directions—medics, nurses, and patients alike all toward whatever exit they could find. Harlan unsheathed his sword. Its pale, almost-white Zuprium blade shone like a light in the darkness. The runes etched along it seemed to glow.

His father had a legendary sword. For some reason. It still hadn't sunk in.

They turned the corner.

General Marcos Correa's eyes weren't nearly as black as Eravin's, but black veins snaked down his temples and into his neck. He looked even worse than he had in the hangar.

He smiled, freezing in his tracks, and looked past Kase. "I've been looking for you."

Neither his father nor Saldr seemed to care that the man before them resembled some monster. They held their weapons out.

"Stop, Uncle." Skibs pushed past Kase, holding out his hands. "We must work together to save Yalvara. Jayde is not our enemy. Jagamot is."

Every breath was a knife to Kase's side and the brittle silence before them. The shadows on Correa's face were deeper, deadlier.

Correa spat onto the ground. "You would say that, wouldn't you?"

Ragged and worn, Zuprium streaks on her hands, Fely stepped up beside him, though Saldr reached out to hold her back. She sidestepped his hand. "Filip is dead. If we're to stop Jagamot, we need to work together."

Both Skibs and Correa froze. Skibs spoke first. "Dead? He's dead? How?"

Correa recovered quickly before his face contorted in one of rage. "Did *you* kill him?"

Fely shook her head. "No. Abram Loffler did, with Kainadr's sword. All isn't lost yet. We can still save Yalvara if you tell us where Hallie Walker is."

"Except your sole purpose was to make sure that he made it to Kyvena, you—" Correa took a threatening step toward Fely, and Saldr sidestepped in front of her.

Saldr lashed out with his ink dark blade, and Correa barely avoided it. The cold glare he fixed on Correa was almost more frightening than the soul-sundering blade in his hand.

"*Uncle!*" Skibs shouted, pushing past the Stradat Lord Kapitan and forming a fist with his hand. It started glowing. "Stop trying to—"

But Correa wouldn't be stopped. "I refuse to listen to the spawn of Jaydian filth! My sister was deceived, and look where it has led!"

Kase wasn't sure what the man was speaking about. He tensed, ready to move if Correa tried to use his Essence power on anyone, though he was nearly useless without a weapon. Besides, the man was tainted and working with Eravin. Maybe the General had gone mad.

"Kase." He recognized his mother's voice just before fingers closed around the back of his shirt, pulling him back. "Let them handle this. You are in no state."

He came by his own stubbornness quite honestly.

Kase half turned. "Go back to Clara. This isn't—"

"You've lost it, Uncle! I have no Jaydian blood—and even if I did, it wouldn't matter. If my brother is truly dead, as Lady Fely states, I am your king. You granted me legitimacy yourself."

Whether it was the power corrupting him or the black veins deteriorating his mind, Correa laughed and laughed like some kind of madman. It echoed in the near-empty tunnel. "You're wrong."

"My father was the stable master," Skibs spat. "You told me that yourself. Had him executed for it."

"Your father was Ezekiel Fairchild, the man who betrayed his own country and got your mother killed."

The words sucked up all the air in the room. His mother gasped. His father looked back, his grip on the sword wavering only a little. Kase could only stare forward. Saldr still stood in front of Lady Fely. The ward had emptied out, thankfully.

Skibs shook his head. "You're lying."

It was the Stradat Lord Kapitan's voice that spoke up next, a little hoarse. "He's not."

Everyone swung toward him. Kase's mother brought a hand to her mouth and shook her head. Harlan continued, "I knew Ezekiel had fathered a child with Queen Astraea, but I was told the child died in infancy."

"That doesn't make sense. My mother wouldn't have lied about that," Skibs said, looking lost. His fist had unclenched, and the golden light had vanished.

It was Kase's mother who stepped forward next. Harlan tried to grab her hand, but she yanked it out of his grip and pressed forward. She walked up to Skibs. He looked down at her, and she nodded. "I'd know those eyes anywhere. What the Stradat Lord Kapitan says is true."

Correa took the moment to attack and grabbed Les' arm. She screamed as the lightning pain shot through her.

Kase barreled forward with a shout—but his father was quicker. In a flash of snow-white steel, he cut in with the efficiency of a trained soldier and sheared Correa's arm off near the elbow. Correa's scream rocked the entire ward.

"You killed my brother. You tortured my son. You will not touch my wife!" Harlan yelled as he swung the sword around again and—before anyone, much less Correa, could react—stabbed the man through the heart.

Correa folded down over the blade, gasping, gurgling through blood; Harlan stepped closer, driving the sword through to the hilt. He leaned in face to face with the general, lips peeled back over gritted teeth, gaze bathed in hatred as he growled, "I've been waiting for this day a very long time. You have been a dead man walking since the day you spilled my brother's blood."

He wrenched the sword from the man's chest. Correa tipped sideways, eyes sightless, collapsing into a growing pool of his own blood. Kase couldn't tell if the blood looked black because of the lack of light, or...something more frightening.

The same clot-dark blood splattered on Harlan's military uniform. Breathing unevenly, the Stradat Lord Kapitan wiped the sword on his own trousers. The weapon glowed subtly in the darkness.

No one else moved. Kase and Skibs met each other's eyes. In the cast of silvery light, everything wavered around him like a moonlit dream; he could barely process it as reality.

Stowe moved first; Kase hadn't realized he was still there. He knelt beside Les, who had fallen beside Skibs, and dug around in his pack for one of his vials. Correa's hand still wrapped around his mother's arm. Harlan bent down and wrenched it off, flinging it down the corridor.

Black, tar-like blood grew in a puddle beneath the body. His eyes were no longer the color of midnight, but a soft, loamy brown.

"I...I—" Ben started, but the words wouldn't work.

Kase shook his head. His body fluctuated between hot and cold. His mouth was too dry. "I don't believe...I don't think...does that mean..."

Stowe helped his mother from the ground. Zelda sprinted over and held her other arm.

Harlan had a hand over his eyes.

Sheathing his sword, Saldr took Fely's hand. "Besides Master Kase's account, that man confirmed Jagamot is indeed here. We must find the second Gate and Miss Walker, though I fear it may already be too late."

The Stradat Lord Kapitan nodded, sheathing his own blade and strode past his wife, pausing only briefly to brush his fingers against her own before moving down the corridor. Everyone else made to follow, but his mother, though white and shaking, stopped Skibs. She clasped his arm and pulled him into a hug.

"Despite what his legacy became, my brother was the bravest man I've ever known. It takes courage to admit when you've done wrong and accept your consequences." Then she let go and followed her husband down the corridor.

Jove joined Kase and held out his hand to Skibs. "Cousins."

Skibs took it, but he still seemed out of sorts. His eyes were unfocused. Was he losing control? Was the Essence power taking over? Jove let his hand go and joined the others, who had also begun to follow.

Kase and Skibs were the only two left. It was Kase who finally said, "Does this mean that...I lose you again after this?"

Skibs rubbed a shaking hand down his face. He glanced toward his uncle's corpse and shook his head. "Honestly? I'm just ready for this all to end."

CORREA BEING DEAD WAS SOMETHING Kase's brain

couldn't quite accept. After what the man had done to Hallie, really, his end was poetic justice. Kase didn't grieve it, but he didn't understand why his father had executed judgment in a way that felt too personal. Kase had been the one tortured by him. But Harlan had mentioned something about a brother.

To Kase's knowledge, the only uncle he had was Ezekiel. Maybe that was what Harlan meant? Maybe Correa had something to do with Ezekiel's betrayal. That made sense with his uncle being involved with the Queen...and being Skibs' father.

Shocks.

To be honest, Kase didn't know if he'd ever be able to keep all these revelations straight. Not only was Skibs healed, but he was now the King of Cerulene. Furthermore, he was Kase's cousin.

And he couldn't reckon with even one of those new realities until he found Hallie.

Hopefully Fely was right and she'd found the Gate. Then Skibs could use his power to find her, right?

His fingers twitched as if he could reach out and grab her hand, but she wasn't there.

Of course, the only time he'd seen Skibs' power in use was in Myrrai, and he had created a sword out of the Yalv, Rodr.

He hoped that Hallie didn't have to be a sword for her to be free from the Gate.

His heart couldn't take it.

Eravin's absence made him uneasy. His side still ached, but his body seemed to be ignoring the worst pain thanks to the adrenaline still coursing through him...or maybe the Vasa was working well. He didn't care why it was—only that he was no longer favoring that side. He'd need to be at his best if and when he found Eravin.

As he followed the others through the corridors to the tunnel where Hallie and Fely had discovered the Gate, where Kase and Hallie had argued over what she was going to do, he kept his head on a swivel. There were very few people left in the tunnels now. Most had gone above ground, and the ward had cleared out with the arrival of Correa. Hopefully Clara made it to safety. He dearly hoped she'd not been caught up in any of it. Samuel had been with Lady Davey, well away from the chaos—that was a relief.

The group made it to the dark tunnel without much fanfare, but that quiet lack of confrontation was almost more jarring. He kept expecting enemies to jump out of every shadow.

Fely led Skibs over to a section of the tunnel as Saldr used his power to spark one of those little fireballs above his head. He joined Fely. "If the Nether Gate was here, I would have felt it, I'm certain. I can only detect the trace of Miss Walker's power like petrichor after a heavy mountain rain. It was much the same yesterday."

Fely gestured to the space just to the left of the wall. "All I know is that the book she had was what opened it. It looked different than the one in Myrrai. This one was all rope-like, and it only held one timeline. It resembled a Passage—a strong one. But if it was a Passage, there would be a brick."

Skibs bent down and rubbed his fingers over the stone floor. "It's definitely faint, but I sense something. The Aurora Gate in Myrrai was basically screaming at me by the time I got to the city. This one is more like a whisper, but it's there. Or...it was. Miss Walker entering it might've caused it to collapse, which would also account for no one else being able to sense it now."

Kase squatted next to him. "But you can open it?"

He needed it to open. He needed to find Hallie. If everything devolved into chaos, he needed to at least say goodbye. Surely, the universe wouldn't deny him that.

Skibs held out his hand. Slowly, a golden glow pulsed into existence around it, almost like he wore a translucent glove. He tapped it on the floor and muttered a few words Kase didn't recognize.

The glow disappeared, and Skibs let out a soft curse. "It might take a bit. I need to find the right words of power."

He tugged a delicate chain out of his collar. A familiar Zuprium pendant dangled on the end—a phoenix. Skibs had worn it since Kase had met him.

Les gasped and stumbled forward. "Is that..."

Skibs paused and looked up. Les knelt next to them both and held out a hand. "Do you mind? Just a moment?"

Shrugging it off over his head, he handed it over to her. "Mother gave it to me before she died. I was only seven."

Seven? Holy shocks.

Kase's father leaned over as well. His mother inspected the pendant with shaking fingers before she pulled her locket out and held it out to the light Saldr provided. Hers was engraved with a woodland scene; trees framed the center of the oblong pendant, but between them was…

A phoenix. The *same* phoenix.

"Isn't that…" the Stradat Lord Kapitan started, but he trailed off as if embarrassed he'd spoken.

Kase glanced up at him and caught the pain etched on his features a second before he schooled his face back into his typical mask.

His mother rubbed a thumb over the front of her locket before handing it back to Skibs. "That belonged to Ezekiel. He had the pair made the year he left for service. I didn't know what happened to it over the years…it saved…" she swallowed thickly. She couldn't continue.

Skibs replaced the pendant and squeezed it. "Thank you."

Kase looked back at Jove, but his brother only looked at his boots. What did his mother mean? Saved what? What was she talking about?

Jove didn't answer. No one explained.

After a few seconds, Jove cleared his throat. "Let's focus on finding Miss Walker, for the moment. I have this feeling that this isn't the end of…everything."

Jove was right. Hallie needed him.

Skibs nodded and closed his eyes, his hand starting to glow once more. He spoke a few different words.

Everyone waited with bated breath.

A soft golden mist floated like smoke from the floor and filled the tunnel. Saldr gasped, and Fely nodded. Skibs said a few other words, his hand glowing brighter, but the mist didn't change, only undulated in an invisible wind.

Kase ached to reach out and tear through it.

When nothing else happened, Skibs' hand went dark once more. "Still not right."

No one else spoke, only watched. But in the quiet, Kase found it impossible to quiet his curiosity any longer.

"Father," Kase said, standing and turning toward the Stradat Lord Kapitan, "what did you mean when you said Correa killed your brother? Did you mean Ezekiel?"

Jove's head shot up at that. Harlan merely looked at his

wife, who joined Jove at the side of the tunnel. Les didn't look at him.

"And while we're at it," Kase ventured further. Pushing his father was more reckless than any hover stunt he'd ever pulled, but it was something he was quite good at. "I still don't understand why you have a Yalven sword, or why it's part of the Shackley crest."

Harlan fiddled with the sleeves of his military jacket, speckled with drying blood. Correa's blood. He was stalling.

It reminded Kase of when they were down in these tunnels yesterday. He hadn't wanted to reveal the truth about Ezekiel. This was the same. There was a secret here that wanted to stay buried.

Kase's mother spoke up without looking at her husband. Staring directly at Kase, she clutched her locket in her hand. "There's no use hiding it from him. Not now."

A muscle in Harlan's jaw twitched. It was still several seconds before he spoke toward the ground. "Roughly fifty years ago, I took the sword from the Cerl commander in Ravenhelm when it was destroyed. Correa was his second-in-command."

What? Ravenhelm? Wasn't that the pile of ruins Hallie had explored so she could find the Passage to Myrrai?

Harlan would've been a child or even an early teen when the village was destroyed. It didn't make sense.

"Did Granddad and Nonna have a country estate there?" he asked.

They'd passed several years ago, and Kase only had vague memories of them, but he did remember Nonna always smelled of rose perfume. She also gave the best hugs.

Harlan heaved a heavy sigh. He pulled out his sword and inspected it as if waiting for it to tell its story. "No."

Kase glanced at Jove. His face was impassive and empty. He looked back at his father. "Then what in the stars are you talking about?"

It was Stowe that spoke up then, his voice quiet. Kase had forgotten he and Zelda were there. "You were the boy. The only one who survived."

The statement was met with silence before finally, Harlan said, "Yes."

Skibs continued to try and open the Gate, but each attempt failed. Every time the light sputtered, Kase's brain sputtered with it, struggling to put the pieces together. "I don't understand."

Any heat in the tunnel air bled away the longer they stood there. Finally, Harlan sheathed the sword once more. "Carleton Shackley, the Colonel of Achilles at the time, was the first on the scene of the Ravenhelm massacre. And as my entire family had been murdered—including my younger brother Michael, whom Marcos Correa personally killed—Carleton and Aurelia adopted me."

At this point, Kase didn't think he could take any more twists or turns. Over the last few hours, Hallie had gone missing, Skibs had been revealed as the next Cerl King *and* his cousin, and now this? There must be some mistake. It was too much. His father had to be lying.

He opened his mouth to tell him so, knowing it would lead to yet another argument. But the look in his mother's eyes had him swallowing his words because a ring of truth sounded in that name,

Michael.

Kase's middle name was Michael. He looked back up at his father; Harlan's eyes were dry, but for the first time in his life, Kase saw something else besides ice...there was rage, unadulterated fury, unlike anything he'd seen even when Kase was at his worst. It was a fire that'd been building for roughly half a century.

"I would do anything to keep the Cerls from winning. They've taken too much from me. My family. My friend. My very humanity, even," Harlan said, his voice still unnervingly calm. *"They will not win."*

Kase couldn't feel his fingers, his toes, or anything. He was entirely numb. But for some reason, one of the only things running through his mind was that if Harlan had come from the same mountains as Hallie, she and Kase were even more alike than they'd thought. She and Harlan were more alike.

He needed her. She would help make sense of the mess.

"Stradat Lord Kapitan, would you allow me to borrow Xera's sword? I think it might—" Skibs started to say.

"How kind of you all to gather in one place," a low voice interrupted from down the corridor, back the way they'd come.

Kase's heart flew into his throat, his hand going for a

phantom weapon.

Everyone tensed as Eravin Gray strode into the light. He walked right up to the group smiling, his black gums showing, his eyes gleaming like obsidian marbles. The veins now traced down his arms, poking out the sleeves of his dirty and rough spun jacket. "Someone killed the Cerl general? Annoying, but at the same time, it is appreciated. He's the one who wanted to decimate the capital. As the leader of One World, I wanted as many broken people as possible to *survive*, because how else was I supposed to raise an army of shadow soldiers? He and his second caused far too much chaos. Far more death than I would have liked. Messy. But it can't be helped now, can it?"

Jove met Kase's eyes, accusing him, but he just shook his head. How was he supposed to know when he'd struck that truce with Eravin in the Jayde Center that it would lead to this?

Eravin laughed. "I'm not one to belabor the point, however, because you're all here now, and I will need those two swords. I'll give you two options: a quick end, or you can join me."

Jove shielded their mother. Stowe pushed Zelda back toward Skibs, who hadn't stopped working.

Saldr unsheathed the shadow blade. "Jagamot."

Eravin might have rolled his eyes, but it was only discernible by the tilt of his eyebrows. "Thank you for stating the obvious. Now what will it be?"

Kase's father stepped up in front of the group. "You will not use us nor the people of Jayde." He unsheathed his sword, setting his stance. "And you will not get this sword."

Eravin scoffed. "Jayde? All of *Yalvara* is what I'll use. I've gotten rid of the Essence of Time. Now I simply need those swords, which won't be difficult at all. I'm giving you a choice because I do have a little bit of mercy. But I will make it for you if you will not."

"Where is she?" The cry tore him up from the inside out. Too much terror. Too much anger. He couldn't breathe.

Kase's heart plummeted to his toes. Eravin had said he would do something to Hallie. He knew it. She hadn't gone through the Gate.

"Don't worry...her end wasn't unpleasant, falling into Valora like that. The way she cried for you with that pretty ring on her finger, I just couldn't bring myself to make her suffer." Eravin's grin was pure cruelty. "But she would've been the key to my downfall. She had to go. You understand."

Kase lunged for him, but Harlan grabbed him, banding one arm over his chest and dropping his sword. Kase struggled against his father, but Harlan's grip held strong. His side twinged, but he fought harder still.

Eravin just laughed. Someone behind Kase let out a small cry. Zelda. Kase strained even more. He needed to end Eravin. Right there. Right now.

"Let me go!" Kase shouted. He twisted and kicked his father. Harlan released him.

Still without a real weapon, Kase wound his fist back to punch Eravin, but the man threw out his hand. Glittering black power spurted from it like water.

Something hit Kase hard in his shoulder. He landed on his wounded side, which lit up in agony. It was almost as if he'd been stabbed again. What had Eravin struck him with? The weight of someone pressed him into the stone. Only his side screamed. His vision blurred.

"Well, that was surprising. Who knew Harlan Shackley had a heart!" Eravin pulled his hand back, probably to shoot more of the power at Kase—but instead, a chain with a pendant locket that glowed blue wrapped itself around Eravin's throat. Kase could barely see anything through the haze of pain.

At the same moment, golden light burst into the tunnel, blinding everyone. It took a moment for Kase's pain to abate enough for him to see clearly. Eravin stumbled, trying and failing to rip the locket from his throat. He tripped over something, finally flinging the locket away, before falling headfirst into the golden light. The light cascaded over him like a waterfall, hiding him from view the further he fell.

And then he was just...gone.

The rest of them were left in the company of nothing but silence and light.

The person on top of him rolled off, and Kase, trying to control the pain in his side, pushed himself up with quaking arms. Sweat dampened his hairline.

His father's staccato breathing met his ears. Harlan's face was pale, which made the black veins only stand out in stark relief. His military jacket hung in tatters at his chest, where a wound was growing like a large spider, Harlan's blackened veins making up its legs. Too many legs. His father struggled to take each breath.

Kase scrambled over to him, as did his mother and Jove. Tears flooded his mother's cheeks. She gasped, "Harlan!"

Kase could only stare as the black poison spread further. The center of the wound turned gray, almost necrotic, like it was burning to ash.

Stowe, Zelda, Saldr, and Fely joined, all lending their hands to the task of trying to save Harlan's life. Kase barely understood what they did—could barely comprehend the sight before him. Their efforts were a waste—even that Zuprium dust Saldr threw at his father.

Kase opened his mouth and closed it. He did it again. Words wouldn't form. He breathed too heavily as the gray spread to the spider legs.

"Why?" Kase managed to choke out. "Why did you save me?"

His throat wasn't working properly. It was too tight.

His father looked at his mother, hand reaching out for hers. She clutched it to her chest. "I wasn't the husband..." He looked at Jove then at Kase, his gaze piercing all the way into his soul. "...or the father you needed. But even if I don't...deserve...your forgiveness...I can do this. I can do this for you." He took in a staggering breath. His mother squeezed her husband's hand with the strength she had left. Jove leaned forward, his hands pressed to the ground, the whites of his eyes showing. Harlan watched them all, the light in his eyes dimming.

"Harlan," his mother sobbed, "wait, please wait—"

Harlan's fingers closed weakly over hers; his mouth had gone stiff, losing function. But Kase had the senseless, impossible thought that his father might be trying to smile at her. "You are...have always been...formidable. But...no debating...with this." Harlan traced his fingertip over the curve of Les's chin. Wiping a tear. "I...I love..."

But his last breath ended before his last words did. One hand fell to his chest, limp; the other lost its grip on Les's fingers, but she clung on, kissing it with a strangled sob.

Jove wrapped his arms around her, murmuring in her ear, but Kase...

Kase could only stare.

All the times his father had shouted at Kase, demeaned him, hit him...all of the horrible memories he'd pushed to the back of his mind...each one replayed in his head as he watched, numb, waiting for his father to open his eyes and roar at him for being in the wrong place at the wrong time. For not seeing Eravin's blow coming.

He couldn't dredge up any good memories, nothing that suggested the man lying dead in front of him deserved his forgiveness.

There was no grief. No guilt. Just...numb.

After a moment, as if from a distance, he watched his own hand reach over and close his father's eyes. If not for the wound that had now gone entirely gray, his father might've only been sleeping.

But he was dead. Dead—and Kase was not.

He wrapped his arms around his mother as sobs wracked her body. She didn't release her husband's hand. Neither he nor Jove let go; if they didn't hold her together, she might very well fall apart. Kase would, if it was him, if it was Hallie with a colorless crater in her chest and lungs empty of breath.

When Ana had died, his mother had held him like this through her own tears.

The thought shook the icy stronghold of numbness keeping him together; he steadied it with a deep, forceful breath.

One he only drew thanks to his father.

He was going to be sick. He swallowed the bile that had risen in his throat. It tasted bitter.

Several minutes went by before Skibs finally spoke. "The Gate is here. If what he said was true, Hallie should be in it. But it's not like the others—it doesn't lead anywhere in this timeline, or any others. This Gate leads to Valora, the Realm of Souls."

Unable to aid Harlan further, Stowe stood and helped Zelda up. "Is there a way to bring her back?"

Skibs looked to Saldr and Fely. Saldr said, "It will become difficult for her to return here the longer she is present there. Time works differently in Valora. If she...if she passed first, then her soul will remain there until she chooses to move on. There will be no bringing her back."

Kase didn't let go of his mother, but he looked up,

clinging to that precious *if* with all his strength. "But there's a chance?"

"Jagamot's wording was vague, and he is deceptive—even if Miss Walker is not dead, it would serve his purposes to make us believe so. I would not give up hope until we see for ourselves." Despite the hopeful words, Saldr's quiet voice was heavy with dread. "Despite that demon entering the Gate, he will survive. He must be stopped. The last sliver of Toro's soul lay within. If he destroys it, no sword or anything Miss Walker might do will stop the end to come."

"I'll go," Skibs said, holding the sword Harlan had dropped. "When we kill him, I should be able to bring us back through the Gate to the right time and place."

"I'm going, too," Kase said. If there was even a chance Hallie could be saved, he would find her. He would bring her home. That had always been his promise.

"As will we," Stowe said, at the same time Zelda snapped, "I'm not leaving her alone with that monster."

Monster was too tame. Kase would end the helviter.

Kase tightened his hold on his mother before kissing her clammy cheek. "I love you."

His mother reached and squeezed his hand, but she couldn't get any words out. Kase understood.

It didn't feel right leaving her—not now. But Hallie needed him. If he didn't go, he would never forgive himself. He needed to know if she could be saved. If not, this might be his final goodbye.

He looked at his brother, whose eyes warred between sorrow and anger. Jove nodded. "Come back...or I'll track you down myself and make whatever Jagamot has planned for you look merciful."

Kase's jaw wobbled as he squeezed his brother's shoulder and then stepped up to the Gate. Skibs handed him his father's sword. "You take this one."

The leather grip was warm and the weight of the weapon was perfect. It felt right in his hands. Saldr reached out and handed Skibs the shadow sword. "I am needed here among my brethren."

Fely stepped around Kase and placed a hand on Skibs' shoulder. "If you see Filip, please tell him your uncle is gone. He can no longer hurt anyone else. I...I want him to know."

Skibs didn't react other than to say, "Of course."

She and Saldr passed by and waited on the other side of the corridor. Kase looked back one more time at his family. His mother watched him, her blue eyes red and swollen. His brother held her still, ever the eldest brother, the one who kept them all together. First Ana, then Zeke, now his father. Half his family was dead. Would Kase be next?

He gripped the sword tighter and tore himself away from the sight. The image through the Gate was beautiful and peaceful, unlike the one behind him. Flowers dotted the rolling hillside. A little cottage sat tucked into the trees. Majestic blue mountains stood like kings in the distance. "This the right one?"

Skibs nodded. "To the end, brother."

"To the end."

And then Kase stepped through, golden light blinding him once again.

I'm coming, Hals. Just hold on. For me.

C H A P T E R   4 7

JUST BEYOND

Hallie

THE NEXT DAY BROUGHT ON tired eyes and a need for something stronger than peppermint tea—and tasted much better than whatever Jack had in those tea bags. Wind howled and battered the cottage all night long, though Jack insisted it was normal. She'd told him most of her story, and sleep hadn't come easily afterward. The sleep she did get was much too light, thrust awake by every quake and quiver in the storm-ridden night.

Her brother let her have his bed while he slept in the loft, and at dawn, he yanked the covers away to wake her so they could go into the village to track down Gran—and some breakfast.

She still hadn't forgiven him for the rude awakening.

The early morning sunlight hitting the meadow daisies just right was exactly what Hallie needed. She ached to sketch the scene with the mountains in the background and the achingly cozy cottage tucked into the towering oaks. If this was truly dead, then maybe it wouldn't be so bad when it was actually her turn to stay.

Jack led her around the cottage and toward the chicken coop. "Need to check in on the girls before we go. They appreciate the doting, 'specially since Gran didn't greet 'em last night."

Hallie rolled her eyes, but she followed along. The nightmare of yesterday faded a little in the fresh morning air. Hopefully Gran—Navara—would know how she could get back to Kyvena and be able to help her get started.

If she could get back.

The serenity was only broken by the crunch of their shoes in the grass, the occasional chicken squawk, and Jack calling to them by name. The sweet aroma of pine shavings and nearby berries mixed with the damp, ashy smell that somehow the chickens hadn't lost in death met Hallie's nose as she approached the pen.

The chickens all huddled together toward the side of the fence, squawking and carrying on. Jack sped up. Had something killed one? Surely not. How could a chicken die twice? Maybe some other undead critter had gotten into the pen. She hadn't been around enough of them to know if they were naturally curious creatures or not. They seemed rather determined to peck whatever it was to death...or to death-er.

Hallie rubbed her head. She needed more sleep.

Jack opened the little gate and stepped inside. He shooed a few of the birds away, trying to determine what had them acting so strangely.

A chicken lay on the ground, gray and translucent, like a ghost from an old bedtime story. Jack stopped. "Oh, Hester. Course it'd be you."

Hallie stepped up to the fence. "Has she passed on?"

Jack shook his head. He stepped back and then left the pen, joining Hallie at the edge. "No. Not sure if there are others in the village, but it looks like Hester has suffered from whatever's causing souls to go missing in the night." He hung his head. "It's different when the souls have been ferried. We aren't sure why or where the souls who go all gray like that go. It's like they have one foot here and another somewhere else. Gran'll have to deal with it when she gets back." He checked their water trough and then headed off toward the trees, Hallie scurrying behind.

"I'm sorry." She walked fast to keep up with him. "But

chickens die all the time, so I'm sure another could replace her soon, right?"

A few orange and black butterflies fluttered by on the wind.

He led her along the path that wove around the edge of the trees and entered the woods further up from the cottage. Before he could answer, a glittering cloud of undulating dust popped up beside his head with a soft crack, almost like someone had popped their knuckles. Hallie gasped, but Jack just sighed. He waved the dust away with a swipe of his hand. He turned and looked past the cottage. Hallie turned too. She didn't see anything but the cottage and field of daisies.

Jack shrugged and moved on. "Probably just a glitch. That Gate hasn't worked right since Gran came through."

He started up the path again. Hallie looked back once more at where she'd arrived, but when nothing caught her attention, she hurried to catch up. Jack looked over. "And to answer your question, yes and no. Sure, bushels and pecks of chickens die every day—get it, *pecks*?—but not everyone comes to Souls Meet. Only those who weren't ready to move on. A good few still come here, but even among those, most souls accept death as soon as they arrive. The ones that don't? Those are the ones Gran helps."

"So when you die, you either arrive here or go wherever the final afterlife is?" Hallie asked, still confused. She desperately wished she had her sketchbook. "And Gran...helps them realize they died?"

The path twisted around an oak that must've been centuries old by its girth. The sunlight barely peeked through its branches above, but the bit that did created a lovely little pattern on the pathway.

A trio of field mice skittered across the roots intersecting their route ahead.

Jack stuck his hands in his pockets. "Mostly. I'm rubbish at explaining things properly, but she didn't come home last night, so it's her fault I'm picking up her slack right now." He threw her a crooked grin. "She's got a fancy title and everything. The Ever Soul. But she's overworked, and that's where I come in. Been helping her for a bit now. It's a good job. Keeps me busy."

Warmth pulsed in her core. Whether or not this was all in her imagination—which she was beginning to believe it was not—it looked like Jack might've still lived his dream in a way. Not even death could stop him.

A bit of the guilt she'd had over taking the funds to go to University after his death fell away. They'd both been able to pursue what they loved. Her power bubbled up again, but unlike before, it wasn't painful or overwhelming. It was comforting.

She welcomed it with open arms. It was one of the few things keeping her sane, and for once, she was grateful for its presence.

They walked the rest of the way to the little village in silence. As they turned the last corner and the path opened up onto a valley dotted with houses in the same style as Jack's cottage, he paused and swept his hands out before him.

"Welcome to the village. It's the only one, but the tavern's chef makes the absolute best bacon. Said he worked in the Sunken City's most expensive restaurant before he died. Said a grease fire burned the whole thing down with him in it. Awful way to go. But I'm selfish. I hope he stays a while longer here instead of moving on. Before he leaves, I need him to tell me his secret to the perfect crisp."

The ease with which her brother chatted about a man's violent end disturbed her. It also made her think of the Kyvena fire that Kase had accidentally started that had caused Ana's death. She pushed her unease away. Jack, here in Souls Meet, must have had a rough time adjusting too. He hadn't been ready to die, and he still hadn't accepted it. How could he? Maybe hearing of other people's more terrifying ends made his feel a little less daunting.

They walked through a small field of new sprouts. Someone must have planted them in the last few weeks. A few sprigs poked above the soil in neat rows. It all still felt otherworldly to Hallie. "Why is there a tavern? I feel like it's odd that people continue to live as if they never died. Wouldn't that make it harder to accept death?"

Jack shrugged. "It's not a bad place to be, sure. And those that don't want to move on quite yet end up helping out for a while. The tavern's barkeep's been here longest out of all of us barring Gran; even he don't remember how long he's been here. His ale is quite nice, but his fresh orange juice in the mornings is to die for."

He laughed at his own joke, but stopped when Hallie

didn't join. "Too soon? Anywho, he'll probably move on here in a bit. Longer you stay up here, the more memories you lose. Gran entered through the Nether, so she won't lose hers. As for me, Gran gives me a special elixir I gotta drink regular enough to keep mine intact. She came up with it herself, said I can only drink it every so often so I don't' run out too quickly because it takes some of her power to make. The ingredients are also sparse in here." He paused. "We usually don't tell anyone about the losing memories part, not until they refuse to move on. Sometimes the knowledge helps, but most times it doesn't."

"And the barkeep? Why hasn't he moved on?"

"Said he wouldn't mind losing some memories."

Hallie didn't have much to say to that. Would she begin to forget her life just like the other souls? If she stayed long enough, would she forget Kase? If she waited for him, would she even recognize him once he finally arrived, if he did at all?

She reached for the pocket watch around her neck, only to be reminded yet again that it was no longer there. Hopefully Jack wouldn't ask about it. He'd never known she had it, so the odds were probably not, but she'd conveniently left it out of her story from the night before for that reason. Vaguely, she wondered if it were somewhere here in Valora.

She dropped her hand and rotated Kase's ring around her finger instead.

She and Jack walked through the narrow village lanes, him nodding and waving to each person they passed. If Hallie didn't know they were in Souls Meet, she would've guessed they were somewhere in the Narden foothills. The charming village reminded her of a smaller version of Nar, where she'd busted Kase out of jail after crashing his hover.

There were no hovers here.

Jack opened the door to one of the little structures that felt and looked more like a cozy wooden lodge. Its beams were honey-brown, aged with years gone by. It was different from Jack's cottage but lacked none of its warmth.

Inside, more people milled about, sipping orange juice from glasses—an oddity in a tavern. The breakfast fare looked quite nice as they passed by a table of women eating the bacon with forks. High society in life, she guessed, and hadn't changed at all in death.

Hallie's heart flipped over as they approached the barkeep, a man who looked to be in his early fifties. She hadn't realized just how much she missed working at the Crowne Haven inn until that moment. She'd only gotten the job as a way to keep going after the trauma of the *Eudora* mission, but looking back, she could see that working there had been a very good thing. It'd kept her busy, had kept her from spiraling even after she'd dropped out of the University.

Jack shook the barkeep's hand. "We'll take the usual. Two this time. This here's my sister, Hallie."

The man looked up with kind yet haunting blue eyes, his face all angles and shadows. His curly hair was steely gray and slightly unkempt. "Addison, and it's a pleasure, my lady."

"And you. Jack says your chef has perfected the art of bacon frying. I'm eager to try it."

"Of course."

He left to go grab their food, and Jack led her to a table near one of the windows. When their food arrived, they bantered back and forth as they ate, laughing over some of their shared memories—like the time Hallie had beaten Jack in chess, and her brother had hounded her for a week straight afterward, insisting she'd cheated.

She had, but only that once.

It was nice to unwind a little after everything and enjoy having her brother back once more. The food still tasted stars-awful, but she gagged it down and convinced Jack that it was indeed the best thing she'd ever eaten. He probably didn't believe her, but she didn't want to take away his joy.

"Hey Addi, you seen Gran round this morning?" Jack shouted back at the barkeep.

He paused in his cleaning of a few of the glasses. He nodded out toward the door. "Left at first light. Said she was gonna be out at the Aurora for a bit and to tell you to hurry it up if you came by."

Jack rolled his eyes but grinned. "Thanks."

"Aurora?" Hallie asked.

Jack wiped his mouth with his blue-and-gold flannel sleeve. Some things hadn't changed. "The other Gate. It's been acting up as of late."

They finished up shortly, and Jack led her out of the village and toward the distant peaks. They reminded her of the Nardens with their snowy peaks and blue haze. It made her miss home even more. Before the *Eudora*, the mountains were one of the only things she'd missed. They were beautiful, if deadly, and their majestic power always took her breath away.

As they walked a well-trodden dirt path through more planting fields and past small copses of trees, Hallie said, "So tell me about the Gates. I thought only one existed until I found the...what did you call it? Nether Gate? And the one we're headed to now is called the Aurora?"

Jack nodded, picking a stray daisy and offering it to her. "For your hair, because it would annoy Mama the most."

Hallie rolled her eyes and plucked it from his fingers. She twirled it a few times before sticking it behind her ear. It was almost like having a pencil tucked away there. Almost.

Jack strode along, whistling a tune Hallie didn't recognize. Hallie caught his sleeve. A few people passed them, looking wan and tired, heading toward the village. Jack waved and smiled. "Good to see you this morning. Tell Addi at the tavern to give you some orange juice, it'll perk you right up!"

A woman with curly white hair, expensive yet ragged clothes, and a limp scowled at him, but kept walking nonetheless.

Once they'd passed out of earshot, Hallie hissed, "Jack, will you just answer my questions, please?"

He flashed her a mischievous grin before tugging his arm out of her grip. "Souls come through them. The Aurora and the Nether, though Gran says there was supposedly another that hasn't worked in ages. Gran don't know exactly what happened to it, but its ruins are up in the mountains." He gestured toward them with a flippant hand. "She's scared that whatever did that one in is doing the same to the Aurora, so she's been out trying to fix it since the Nether Gate is persnickety at the best of times."

The Aurora Gate must be the one from Myrrai. She wondered what Jack meant by it not working and when that had happened. Ben had done something to it, and then Hallie had taken the sword from it. Maybe the sword simply needed to be restored? That had been her plan, after all, to collect all the Essences into the sword and restore it to the Gate. It would destroy Jagamot and cost Hallie and the other

Essences their lives, but more would be saved.

She hoped.

But now she was here without the swords or the other Essences.

Maybe she should just accept her fate and live here with Jack and Gran. Maybe she could help ferry the souls. Though if Jagamot wasn't stopped, would this place cease to exist as well? Would he destroy the afterlife, too?

Birds chirped in the trees and chased each other overhead. The wind blew hair out of Hallie's face, which felt a little stiff and sensitive after basking so long in the sun. The serenity of it all calmed her nerves with each step they took.

About a quarter hour of walking later, a Zuprium-brick archway appeared from behind the trees. It served no purpose out in the open, no walls or ceiling to hold up, no entrance to anything beyond it; it was simply there. The space between flickered gold and brown and black and back again.

As they approached, Hallie saw people appear as if out of thin air once or twice. They spoke with a woman with jet black hair nearby. Sometimes she held their hand. Others, she hugged; but after speaking with her, they either vanished into thin air or—less frequently—trudged toward the path Jack and Hallie strolled down.

They had to get closer to the Gate before Hallie could read the symbols written on the bricks. *Anora Yas Ess Vanaktr.*

"Time is Powerful."

She hadn't been able to translate them before, but now the words shone as clearly in her head as the sunny day around them.

Jack looked back at her. "What?"

Hallie pointed to the Gate. "That's what the archway says."

He shrugged and went up to the woman helping the odd soul who came through. When she wasn't speaking or comforting someone, she poked and prodded the Gate. She even pulled Zuprium dust, Vasa, from a pouch at her waist and rubbed on the bricks. The dust glowed, then sank into the metal. Each time, she'd pause to write something down in her notebook.

The Gate looked calm on this side compared to the other, which had been a chaotic mess with the smoke leaking out and the incessant thumping of a heart in her ears.

"Hey Gran! Gotta visitor I'd like you to meet," her brother said, sidling up to the woman.

Her night-dark hair twisted in a tight bun at the base of her skull. She wore a dark blue petticoat and flowing skirt, a green matron belt wrapped around her waist. She was tall and willowy like other Yalvs. She was clearly where Hallie and Jack's father had gotten his height. A plain canvas satchel hung across her body.

A few people emerged from the Gate. An elderly couple and a young child. Hallie's heart hurt. Gran spoke quietly with them and then pointed them in the way of the village. "It will be about a fifteen-minute walk, but please feel free to have a look around on your way. Valora is a quaint and beautiful place." She stopped the little boy who couldn't have been older than seven. Tears streamed down his face. Gran handed Jack her notebook and bent down to his level. She gave him a hug and held him tightly. "It'll be all right, little one. You don't have to stay here. Do you have anyone else who has gone before you?"

The boy only nodded, too choked with his tears to say anything out loud. Gran pulled back and looked up at Jack. She looked younger than Hallie would have thought with a name like *Gran*. She had a gray-and-white streak of hair at the front that looped by her ears before being tucked into the bun. The lines around her mouth and her golden eyes weren't deep. Her nose was long and straight. "Will you look in the archives...." She turned back to the little boy. "What was their name, Liam?"

The boy, Liam, muttered something that Hallie couldn't quite hear. Gran nodded and repeated the name to Jack. "Brianka Veville, Tev Rubika"

Jack put his hand in a pouch at his waist and brought forth Vasa. He sprinkled it on the notebook in front of him. It didn't do anything for a minute or so before the glittering dust rose and coalesced in the form of parchment.

Hallie's mouth dropped open.

Jack checked the outside. "Yes, this should be the correct one." He squatted down next to the boy and Gran. "Hello, Liam. My name is Jack, and I know this is scary and confusing, but Gran and I are here to make you feel better. This letter is for you."

The boy took it with shaking hands. Gran rubbed the boy's arm. "Would you like me to read it to you?"

Her voice was melodic and soft but had an underbite of steel. It was so familiar to Hallie that she no longer had any doubt: the woman in front of her was Navara, the daughter of the Lord Elder. The woman who'd run away from her destiny…and had left Hallie to bear it instead.

Seemed she and Jack were *both* picking up the woman's slack. In two different worlds.

Her power responded to her frustration and resentment, but it was difficult to stay irritated with Navara when she opened the folded parchment and read:

"To my family who may come after me,
I love you, and I'm waiting for you just beyond.
Nana"

The boy gave Navara a watery smile before he faded away in the morning light as if he never was. Hallie gasped and reached out, but her fingers met only air, not even a hint of the corporeal boy who had been standing there with tears on his cheeks seconds before. It was as if he'd become the morning mist, only existing forevermore in her memory.

Jack stood and dusted off his hands. "Well, that was real easy."

Navara waved long fingers at the parchment, and as it had appeared, it vanished in a cloud of glittering dust. She stood and stretched a little. "Children usually are. That's why there aren't too many of them who come through Valora." She brushed off her skirts and then turned to Hallie at last.

Jack grabbed Hallie's hand, tugging her forward. "This is Hallie, my twin, though it's hard to tell now. I've been able to maintain my good looks. Poor girl wasn't so fortunate."

Hallie held out her hand to Navara so she wouldn't use it to slap Jack upside the head. "Pleasure to meet you, finally."

Maybe she should be cold toward the woman. She was half the reason Hallie was here now. She should retract her hand and demand answers.

But she might also be Hallie's way home.

Navara bypassed her hand and pulled her into a hug. She smelled of jasmine, mint, and a hint of cinnamon. It was a scent Hallie only knew from the memories stored in this woman's journal, though she hadn't realized it until then. It spoke of soft mornings and nights spent sewing beside a generous hearth. She couldn't help relaxing in the woman's grip and hugging her back.

"I'm sorry," the woman whispered in her ear. She pulled back and cupped Hallie's face. "You have done so well, my girl."

Despite reading her journals, Hallie had never interacted with the woman before her—she hadn't expected to be recognized in return. "I'm sorry…I'm not sure how you…"

Navara let go of her face and held out her hands for her notebook and golden quill. Jack handed it over, and Navara put both into the satchel at her side. "I did not take on my father's Essence power, but I can recognize it in you. You still radiate with it, which tells me you're not here to move on, but for another purpose. The prophecies foretold of a day such as this, and if the power has chosen you, then I am certain you will succeed." She glanced back at the Gate. "It also tells me the Aurora must be set back to rights soon, or we shall fade to nothing."

Hallie's stomach clenched. She knew. She knew what her father had planned with resetting the Gates. What did that mean? Did that mean she wouldn't allow Hallie to return?

The ground shook so hard that the only reason Hallie didn't fall over was because Jack caught her and Navara. The sun winked out, and the land plummeted into darkness. She thought she heard screaming, but before she could scream herself, it was over.

It had only been a moment, but it shook Hallie to her core. It reminded her of the quakes she'd experienced in Myrrai, but the darkness…that was new. Whether that was because she was in Valora or because something terrible was happening, she didn't know.

Once everything had stabilized, she looked back at the Gate. Maybe it had sensed Hallie's presence, like it seemingly had when she'd been in the Yalven city, and had reacted to it.

But it looked the same. Towering Zuprium bricks, a transparent, glassy center. It was entirely unaffected.

Jack gasped and pointed up toward the mountain. Thick, bulbous black smoke floated from one of the faraway peaks. Hallie's stomach roiled. It reminded her of the Yalvar fuel after the quake when she'd returned to Kyvena, the one that had hit while she stood in the Stradat Lord Kapitan's tent.

Saldr had said something about Jagamot then.

A knowing sort of terror shone in Navara's eyes. She turned to Jack. "Did anyone else come through the Nether Gate?"

Jack's ears turned pink. "I thought so, but when I checked, no one was there. You know how the Gate is."

Navara shook her head. "I'm afraid the Aurora is the least of our worries now. Let's get to the village and check the souls." She sighed. "I do not believe it is your fault, Jack, but I have a feeling that the man you tried to help the other day is the one causing the issues."

She started back toward the village. Hallie and Jack hurried behind her. Hallie asked, "Who was it? Do you know?"

Jack's face was missing some of its spunk, but he answered, "One awfully rude old man."

"What did he look like?"

Her twin eyed her oddly. "Why?"

"Just tell me, would you?"

He sighed and waved a hand. "Long beard. Brown-gold eyes. Thought he might be a bit like Gran here."

It was like a punch to the stomach. Loffler. It had been Loffler. He was trying to bring back Jagamot, and now he was here in Souls Meet. She was a little out of breath and also trying to keep the panic out of her voice, "That man, did he say anything? Like where he came from? Or how he died?"

Jack shook his head. "Refused to speak to me, but when I tried to lead him to the village, he ran off." Jack snorted. "Wish he'd come at night. Then Addi would've had to deal with him. He's better with the grumpier types."

Hallie hated to be the bearer of bad news, but she was the only one who might be able to stop whatever horror was heralded by that tarry smoke. "I believe the man was Abram Loffler, an Essence wielder who somehow brought back Jagamot."

Navara muttered something in Yalven. It was too quiet for Hallie to hear.

"Gran?" Jack asked uneasily.

They were almost back to the village. Navara took out her notebook and quill. She scribbled something before stuffing it all back in. She picked up her pace. "If he's up in the mountains, he's looking for the Chronal Gate and the remnant of Toro that resides in this place."

"Are we too late?" Hallie asked, pointing back at the smoke, dread starting to bleed to terror at the sight of it.

Navara shook her head. "If he was, we'd already be gone." She stopped and turned. "We need to combine the Essences into the swords. It is the only way. I'm not sure I can access either of them from this side, but you might could...you said you came through the Nether Gate? You didn't pass first?"

Hallie shook her head. "I don't...I'm not sure. I used your journals to get here. And somehow the last one opened it. I was pushed in...by someone, and I couldn't get back."

A new pang of terror struck when she reached for the memory and encountered only flashes among cloudy gray, like lightning flickering through a storm cloud. Hadn't those memories been crystal clear only hours ago?

Navara rubbed her chin in thought. "Maybe you could use your Essence power to work it. It would be difficult without the Essence of Keys, and it would be a gamble even with them, but with enough concentrated effort...it may be our best chance."

"I'm not certain where the Nether Gate sword is, but Kainadr, the one for the Aurora Gate, is in Kyvena. I...well, I took it from the Gate not too long ago. It sort of gave it to me? But I didn't have it with me when I went through the Nether Gate."

Navara touched the antique amber broach at her throat. "We might could send you back to Kyvena through the Aurora, but the timing would be tricky, and we are without the Essence of Keys. Time is a powerful yet unreliable friend. If you were to survive, you could very well end up thousands of years in the wrong direction, but attempting to send you back may very well be our only option."

They made it to the edge of the village before Hallie could muster a response. She didn't know if she could do that, risk that. The panic built with each step they took into the village. Souls milled about, abuzz with the events and the quaking. They reminded Hallie of a scattered ant hill.

While Navara spoke with a few of them, a golden dust cloud popped into existence in front of Jack. He waved it away. "Gran, more souls through the Nether Gate. Stars, I thought you said it was barely used."

Navara finished her conversation with a woman, squeezing her forearm softly, and looked over. "It is because I closed it, and the only person or people who would be able to open it would be whoever discovered the secrets of my journal or found the missing sword guardian. I was given the words of power by the Essence of Keys in my day, but that's another story altogether."

Jack paused a moment. "So you gave me the locked Gate because some old curmudgeon didn't want to talk to me?"

Navara sighed. "Not now, dear."

Jack grumbled something under his breath, but the older woman ignored him.

Navara led them into the center of the little village square and stood up onto the edge of the fountain. She was already quite tall, but now she towered well above everyone. Hallie estimated a few hundred souls assembled—not as many as Hallie would've thought. She vaguely wondered if there were more souls scattered throughout the realm, but she had to tamp down the scholarly part of her brain. Not everyone could've been in the village.

Once they figured out what to do with Loffler, she could satiate her burning curiosity.

Navara raised her hands and shouted above the din. "We are aware of the disturbance earlier, and I can understand that you might be frightened and confused. If you feel that you are ready to move forward to the beyond, Jack will record any last words you'd like to leave to anyone who comes after you. May Toro bless you all."

And then she got down and gave Jack her notebook and glowing Zuprium quill. "Prove yourself here, and we'll talk later."

Jack made a disbelieving noise. "Do you not want to watch over my shoulder just in case I unleash some sort of ancient power on the place? Seems like I have a track record, if you count Hal."

Navara just patted his cheek. "You have a line, dear."

She was right, about fifteen or so people had lined up in front of Jack. He saluted her and turned around. "Hello, Mrs. Cartwright. I see you're ready to leave Souls Meet, which is wonderful to hear, though I will miss your muffins, I'll say."

Navara took Hallie's arm and pulled her to the edge of the crowd. "You and I will see what souls might have entered through the Nether Gate, and after that, we need to head up into the mountains and assess the situation."

Should Hallie mention the Lord Elder and Saldr's plan? Should she admit to Navara that all she was good for was losing control of her power?

Instead, Hallie numbly nodded. Dread pooled in her stomach with each step she took away from her brother. It might very well be time to save the world, and she had no idea how to do it. She didn't have the swords. The Aurora Gate was dying, and supposedly, there was another one in the mountains housing what was left of a god.

Her lungs squeezed as she wove through the throng of people. If she could keep herself together long enough to make it back to the cottage, then she could fall apart before she went to her possible death. The air was taut with unease, yet Hallie couldn't understand a word of the murmurings as she passed. She couldn't focus on anything except putting one foot in front of the other. Each step she took was another whispered prayer lost in the storm of her heartbeat. She bumped into a few people, a soft apology on her lips before they even turned. She blindly followed the tall Yalven woman who towered above the rest.

She was going to reset the Gates.

It was the only thing she could do now, and now she would never get to tell Kase goodbye. Panic crawled up her throat.

"Hallie!"

Her heart stopped. The air in her lungs froze with such sudden ferocity that she wasn't certain they'd ever thaw.

That voice.

She whipped her head around, trying to find it. She needed that voice. Navara kept walking. Was it all in Hallie's mind?

"HALLIE!"

Palms sweating, she pushed through a few people, mumbling more apologies she wasn't sure they heard, but she didn't care. There were too many people barring her way from the edge of the square.

Like a breath of fresh mountain air, she made it out. She whirled frantically around, praying she wasn't dreaming. Surely, she'd been through enough in the last few days that her mind wouldn't choose a cruelty such as that.

There.

At the corner of the tavern stood Kase, his curls windswept and messy, his eyes shining so brightly they burned like new stars. Even with the thirty feet and people between them, he was the clearest thing she could see.

He was here.

She zagged in and out of the crowd, some joining the line to speak with her brother. She forgot about Navara and focused solely on reaching him.

And then she was in his arms. They crushed her to him. She still couldn't breathe, but she didn't care.

He'd found her. Even here in the realm of souls, he'd kept his promise.

C H A P T E R   4 8

TUCKED AWAY

Jove

JOVE'S CHEST WAS HEAVY, TOO heavy. He didn't know what to do with himself, but he needed to do something. If he stopped moving, he would drown.

The ropy, glowing Gate disappeared in a blink, and the tunnel was thrust into darkness. Kase had vanished as if he never was.

Harlan Shackley, the Stradat Lord Kapitan, his father, was dead.

He'd died.

The word sounded harsh even in Jove's head, so final, so cruel as if the word itself had dealt the killing blow. It tasted sour, like spoiled wine.

He half believed that any minute now, his father would stride around the corner and demand that they stop wasting time, or shout at him for doing nothing to stop his death or for not stopping Kase from leaving. But his father would never do any of that again.

The world felt muffled, like his ears were stuffed with

cotton. He held his mother tighter as her tears fell.

Formidable, his father had murmured among his final words—yet she felt so fragile and small in his arms, too light, a wisp that would scatter in the wind.

Now they very well might lose Kase too, and in the end, his father's sacrifice would be in vain.

Sacrifice. Would he have done it for Jove?

He stared at his father's closed, lifeless eyes, trying his best to not look at the grotesque wound in his chest.

He swallowed hard.

Jove needed to be strong. Whether he liked it or not, he was now the head of the Shackley family, and it was up to him to protect it.

While he'd never agreed with his father's methods, he could appreciate the strength he radiated. If Jove could admire one singular thing about his father, it was that Harlan hadn't broken despite his world crumbling for the third time in his life these past few months.

How would Jove have fared if he'd been in his father's shoes? Considering he'd barely felt alive these last few months in his own, he doubted he would've survived. How had his mother made it? How had she kept functioning through each heartache life dealt her?

What did true strength look like?

War was here, *had been* here for some time; in fact, he wasn't sure it had ever ended fifteen years ago. But he couldn't change that. They would lose today without whatever strength he could scrounge together.

Clara and Samuel's faces flashed in his mind's eye. They were somewhere above, and they needed his protection.

He needed to step into the shoes his father left behind. They wouldn't fit, but they didn't need to—Jove would make them his own.

"I need to speak with Lord Stephenson and the others," Jove whispered into his mother's hair. "This isn't over."

The weight on his chest never lifted, but he rose anyway.

His mother shook her head. "I can't...I can't leave him."

He helped her stand, and she clung to him. "I know."

"He's gone. I know he's not here, and that I...*hated* the person he became after all these years, but I knew the Harlan I loved was always tucked away, reaching. I just didn't search for him...I didn't reach back."

Jove didn't know what to say to that. He'd had a very complicated relationship with the man who'd fathered him; his grief felt infinitely more complex, so interwoven with anger and confusion he couldn't find a way to comfort her. Instead, he squeezed his mother tighter. "We'll figure this out."

His mother brushed away more tears.

Lady Fely edged forward, sword hanging by her side. "I will stay with her."

Saldr threw some dust over Harlan's body, murmuring a few words. A glow surrounded his father, and when it died down, his skin glistened, the hole in his chest covered by newly woven cloth.

Les jumped, but Jove held her tightly. "I swear I'll come back for you."

"When this is over, it would be my honor to burn him with the holy flames," Saldr said quietly. "A great honor to be bestowed on someone who is not of our race, but deserving of the man who sacrificed himself for another."

Jove's eyes stung. If Harlan hadn't knocked Kase out of the way, it would've been his brother lying before him, skin pale and chest unmoving. Jove had been frozen, unable to do anything but watch as his father shoved Kase to the ground, taking the blow for him.

His father did indeed have a heart hidden underneath the layers of ice, and the moment he'd revealed it, he'd died.

Neither Kase nor Jove would get to see the man Harlan Shackley could have been...the man he might have once been.

Once, when Jove was small, Harlan had played toy soldiers with him and Zeke. Once, his father had laughed at something his mother had said and drawn her close, kissing her softly to a chorus of groans from his children.

But those few memories had been buried beneath grief, pain, and abuse as if they never were. It was only now that Jove remembered, and it was too late. They would never return to a time such as that.

Jove refused to live like that. He'd allowed the alcohol to numb his pain, but it would no longer control him. He would do whatever it took to make sure Samuel could be proud of the man his father was. To make sure Samuel would know the man he'd become.

"Go," Les said, patting his cheek and waking him from

his thoughts. "Do what you were born to do."

Jove's chin wobbled, but he swallowed his emotion. He could grieve later. With one last squeeze of her hand, he strode away from his father's body.

C H A P T E R   4 9

I WILL BE

Kase

THE LAST HOUR'S WHIRLWIND OF emotions had picked up Kase's heart and tugged it every which way, but the moment he crushed Hallie in his arms, it settled into a steady rhythm again. She was okay—she was safe. He was safe.

"Kase," she mumbled. "Need to breathe."

He reluctantly set her down. He still didn't understand where they were, but that hardly mattered. He could be at the edge of the world or in some other dimension, but Hallie was with him. He'd found her.

"I'm never letting you out of my sight again," he whispered in her ear. "I'm sorry I wasn't there when Eravin...when he..."

Shocks, he couldn't even finish his sentence. Not when his mind whirred with shadowy power and his father's final breath and Eravin's cruel, mocking grin as he taunted him with Hallie's demise through bloodless lips.

Hallie blinked, eyes widening like she'd just remembered something; but instead of speaking, she stood on her tiptoes and gave him a quick kiss. Too quick. He needed it to last longer, but they had quite a large audience.

"That's a little extreme, don't you think?" She grabbed both his hands and threaded her fingers through his. Her tone was light and happy, and he wished he could share part of her optimism. She squeezed his hands. "But I'll allow it until we figure out if the world is going to end or not."

Kase furrowed his brow. "Eravin fell through the Gate...he's Jagamot."

Hallie blinked up at him. "I'm sorry, what?"

"Came through a few minutes before we did." Kase scanned the crowd milling about, looking for a man with voidless eyes and black veins. People wove in and out of each other like bees in a hive. Even so, Eravin would've stood out in such a crowd. The heads bobbed like sea waves, the soft murmur of fear running through them.

Eravin was nowhere to be found. How large was this place, that he could have vanished so quickly after falling through the gate? Could he be in the forest somewhere? Could he have reached the mountains by now?

They'd been wandering almost blind since they'd entered this realm. Skibs had knocked on the little woodcutter's cottage, and when no one answered, they'd gone toward the forest and found the path.

That had led them here. Maybe if they could stop Eravin from finding a way back to Kyvena, this could all be over. But if he broke back in and all of them were still stranded here...

His stomach clenched at that thought. Jove and his mother wouldn't be prepared for that. He was just about to tell Hallie when a gangly teenage boy with a shock of bright red hair separated himself from the milling crowd.

The boy stared Kase down. Kase looked behind him, thinking he mustn't be looking at him. He didn't know the bloke, but the boy didn't look dangerous, nor did he show any signs of being corrupted. Kase still put himself in between him and Hallie. He'd handed the sword off to Skibs when he'd spotted her, but he would use whatever was available—even if that was only his fists—to defend her.

Crossing his arms, the boy stopped before him and sized him up, a scowl on his face. A familiar scowl. "You must be the poor fool who stole my sister from my best friend. I gotta few questions for you, so you better answer them good or else."

Kase took a small step back, bumping into Hallie. *What?*

"Jack!" she hissed, stepping around Kase but keeping a hand on his arm. He could've sworn a hint of her mountain drawl bled through. He still couldn't say he hated it. "Leave him alone."

Jack didn't relax his stance. Even though he had to be a few years younger, he stood nearly as tall as Kase. "Hey now—dead or not, I gotta make sure you're taken care of. It's my duty as the older brother."

"By seven and a half minutes. Not years."

"Still counts."

Kase's mouth went dry as he looked at the boy again. No, it wasn't just the scowl. Though a shade darker than Hallie's, his bronze eyes were just as wide and curious with a hint of mischief in their depths. The way his lips turned up at the corners was exactly the same. Other than that, he could've been Stowe's twin instead of Hallie's.

Kase turned a little to her. "Is this..."

"Yes." She gestured to the boy. "Long story short, this is the realm where souls who aren't ready to pass on go, and this *dulkop* here helps ferry them over."

All the blood in his face fell to his toes before racing back up again. He swayed slightly with the dizzying rush. How was it even possible? More questions flew into his mind. If this was truly Jack, did that mean Ana was here? Zeke?

What about Harlan?

He wasn't sure how to ask, nor could he try with Jack still glaring at him, suspicion narrowing his eyes to slits. Kase didn't quite understand what implications they would face now that they were here, but so long as he got to stay with Hallie, he didn't care. He could worry about the rest later. He controlled his scurrying thoughts and held out a hand. "I'm Kase Shackley, and it's truly a pleasure to meet you."

Jack raised a brow but took his hand and shook. "Jack Walker. I'd say I've been dying to meet you, but I only found out you existed last night."

Jack's hand felt real—skin, bones, callouses—just as Hallie's had. But the boy was dead. He shouldn't feel like anything, right? He was just a memory, or a soul, or whatever.

Hallie groaned and covered her eyes. "You're impossible."

A grin crept across Kase's face that melted into a chuckle. So Hallie was the Jove in her family. Kase liked that—liked seeing this other side of her. But already his mind had hopped forward several steps to sadness, realizing that when they returned to Jayde, she'd go back to being an only child. This dynamic wouldn't last.

But at least they had this moment.

Jack seemed to appreciate his laughter and grinned. One test passed.

Someone gasped behind him. Kase slid his arm around Hallie's waist, tucking her close, but it was just Stowe and Zelda, finally catching up to him.

Jack froze before breaking into a smile. "Mama."

Zelda sprinted forward, crashing into her son. Her arms wrangled the boy into such a tight hug that Jack's face went red, his next breath more of a wheeze. It was a full minute before she pulled back, wiping her eyes with one hand and smoothing the boy's hair with the other. Kase's eyebrows rose. Seemed he would also get to see a different side of Zelda—one that didn't glare daggers at everyone she met.

Zelda cupped Jack's cheek. "My boy."

It wasn't until Stowe came over, clasping a hand on his son's shoulder and hugging him that Jack began to blink rapidly, holding back tears as he bumped his head into his father's shoulder. "Hey, Pa."

Kase shaded his eyes from the blistering sun. His shirt clung to his back underneath his jacket. He rubbed Hallie's shoulder, thinking. What would it be like if he saw Harlan now, after saving Kase's life? Would they have a similar reunion?

No, he knew better than that. But Kase would've liked to thank him. All he'd done at the end was question why his father had done what he did. He tightened his hold on Hallie.

She looked up at him, questioningly. He didn't answer. It wasn't the right time. He wouldn't spoil this happy moment for the Walkers. Kissing the top of her head, Kase nudged her toward them.

Her mother grabbed her hand and tugged her forward. Stowe pulled them all into a large family hug.

Kase stepped back, giving them their moment. He nodded at Skibs when he joined them, holding both swords. He subtly shook his head. No Eravin. Finding him so soon after they'd entered this strange realm would've been too easy, and Kase had never been that lucky.

Still, he looked around, hoping against hope until he realized he'd stopped looking for a man with dark veins and had started seeking a blonde girl, a tall soldier with hazel eyes...and a man with a steel gray mustache and pristine military uniform.

But among the people assembled, he still couldn't spot his family anywhere. Maybe they were in a different part? A darker part of him wondered if they didn't want to see him.

An older woman joined the group, dressed in something he was certain his grandmother had worn in her portraits in Shackley Manor. There were two of them, both hung in one of the lesser-used corridors near the solarium. This woman didn't look like her, though; she looked to be around his parents' ages.

No, *parent*. He no longer had two. It wouldn't be his parents' ages, his parents' home, his parents' motorcoach. It wouldn't be *his parents'* anything. They would be his mother's.

Kase clenched his teeth against the somewhat unexpected flare of grief. He'd hated Harlan. He'd never understood how someone could be so cruel to their own children, but now Kase had begun to understand. Harlan Shackley never stood a chance of being a good person, and that darkness lived inside Kase whether he wanted to admit it or not.

But even with that darkness, his father had still saved him.

Hallie was right. He was like his father. But did that mean he had to do the same terrible things? Or could he choose something nobler, like his father had in the end— even if Harlan had chosen too late to change anything?

He shook his head to dispel the unpleasant thoughts. Find Eravin. Stop him. Then deal with the consequences.

The older woman dusted off her blue skirts. "Jack, were you able to finish working with those souls?"

Jack pulled away from his family, only a little—and even that much distance made Zelda's white-knuckled grip tighten. "The ones that wanted to go. Took their letters, then asked them if they appreciated my service and if I could improve their experience in any way—you know, looking for feedback—and they said I did quite a *stars-blasted good job*.

Mrs. Cartwright's words, not mine."

The woman sighed. "Jack…"

"I can do this, Gran," the boy interrupted, suddenly serious. "I promise."

Stowe didn't take his hand off Jack's shoulder, but he looked over. "Gran?"

The woman smiled. "It's been a while, hasn't it?" She gave him a hug, even if he was still a little slack-jawed. Turning to Zelda, she held out her hand. "I'm Navara Walker. You must be Zelda. Jack has told me so much about you." She tipped her head in greeting. "You and Stowe have raised quite the young man, and he does you both proud here in Valora, though it grieves me you had to lose him so early."

Stowe put an arm around Zelda and pulled her close as the tears spilled forth once again.

It was Jack who broke the tension. "Well, that's the nicest thing you've ever said about me, Gran. I'm touched."

Navara laughed, as did the others. Hallie returned to Kase and wrapped an arm around his. Skibs stepped forward and handed Kase his father's sword. It felt heavier than it had earlier. Hallie held out her hand. He gave it to her, and she read the inscription on the blade. The early afternoon sun glinting off the metal nearly blinded him.

"Their specific runes mean *time, healing, soul*, and *love*." She twisted it to and fro, studying it with curiosity sparkling in her eyes. "Where did you find Xera's sword?"

"It's quite a long story," Kase said, taking it back and holding it loosely at his side. "but in short, my father had it."

Hallie looked at him questioningly.

"The important part is, I have it now, and Skibs helped us get here with it."

Hallie eyed him, and he knew she wanted to press him, but she only squeezed his arm softly before addressing Skibs. "I assume that this time, you aren't trying to kill us? Or should I take Kainadr's sword from you?"

Skibs rubbed the back of his neck. "Whatever you did when I was falling, it healed me. I thank you for that."

A soft rumbling began in the distance, slowly making its way toward the village square. Each successive quake swelled and surged until the ground itself shook in fury. Kase held onto Hallie and the sword until he couldn't hold both. He wrapped both arms around her, shielding and cushioning her as they collapsed. The sword slipped from his hand.

Then the quaking stopped just as quickly as it had begun.

"Are you okay?" Kase asked, untangling himself and assessing Hallie for any injuries. He ignored the twinge in his side. It wasn't nearly as horrible as it had been before—a testament to Saldr's healing.

Hallie's freckles stood out on her bloodless face, but she nodded. "You?"

"Yeah." As okay as he could be.

Navara helped them up. "We need to get to the mountain. Now. I daresay we have very little time left, if any."

"Mountain?" Kase asked, looking toward the peaks in the distance. A swollen black cloud hovered near one of them; it gave him the same feeling as seeing a hover with a smoking engine. Something was very, very wrong. "What is that?"

Hallie worried her lip with her teeth. "Loffler, we think. He's trying to kill the soul shard of Toro that resides within the ruined third Gate there. If he's successful, then it doesn't matter what we do—we can't stop Jagamot."

"Loffler? I thought you said he fell through the Gate in Myrrai!"

Hallie nodded. "He did—and he fell through it into here. If you have the swords, we just need his Essence power as well as Ben's and my own...wait, no, that's not right. Correa. Oh stars, it's not going to work after all!"

Kase and Skibs exchanged looks before Kase said, "His Essence power is in this sword. My father finished him off." He retrieved his father's sword from where he'd dropped it during the quake. "But I still think there's another way."

Hallie opened her mouth, and he readied himself for a different kind of battle—but instead, she just nodded. "Let's go."

Kase didn't like it. He knew her well enough to know that a non-answer didn't mean he'd won; it meant she was going to go through with her plan, but she didn't want to argue about it.

Fine. They wouldn't argue about it. Kase would just have to come up with his *own* plan to make sure *hers* didn't happen.

Navara turned to Jack and the rest of the Walkers. "Stay here and keep the peace. I have a feeling many people will need your aid soon."

"But Gran—" the boy started, but he was interrupted by the shake of the older woman's head.

"You are right—you can do this. And I trust you to do it well. You have learned much, and once I return, we can speak about rearranging your responsibilities." She turned to Stowe and Zelda. "Stay with your boy. I'm sure you have many stories to tell each other."

Zelda made a noise to argue, but Stowe held her back. "Our Lark can handle herself just fine. You seen what she can do—let her do it."

Jack himself accepted Navara's directive with a nod, but by the way his mouth quirked—much like his mother's had, *exactly* like Hallie's had—he wanted to.

Hallie hugged her family one more time. Zelda held her tightly and said something to her. Hallie said, "We'll fix this and then take the swords to the Gates. This is the last part, then we can go home."

She choked on the last part. Like the lie tasted foul, and she had to force it onto her tongue anyway.

Zelda kissed her daughter's cheek. "When we get back, it's...it's all right if you want to stay. Just promise you'll visit, will you?"

"Thank you, Mama." Hallie's chin wobbled. "I'll be back."

Kase wouldn't give away her lie. It was her choice to keep it from them, but if he'd had a say, he would have suggested she tell them the truth. Of course, if she did, they'd never let her leave; but wouldn't it be worse not to know, only to find out later that this goodbye was their last?

A wound sprouting crooked black veins. His father's rapid, shallow breaths. "I...I love..."

Kase shook the memory away, then shook Stowe's hand. "I won't leave her side."

The man surprised him by tugging him close and clapping his back much like he had Jack's.

Why did that make Kase's eyes prickle?

"You all right, son?" Stowe whispered in his ear.

"I will be." Of course he'd ask that—of course he could tell. He was a good father and an even better person. He could see the pain that only Kase could feel, the kind he had to keep buried until it was all done.

Why had Harlan saved Kase? Kase had tiptoed through

his own home, desperately avoiding the cracks in his father's temper, living in fear of accidentally falling through one and sending everything crumbling down.

Until he'd started jumping on the cracks instead, defiant and reckless. Not falling, but leaping.

The fear never saved him from falling. At least that way, the plunge was his choice.

Harlan had tormented Kase; Kase had infuriated Harlan. But in the end, his father had given everything for him—and Kase hadn't said a word as he died.

"Take care of her," Stowe said, releasing Kase's hand and stepping back to give his daughter a hug. "And yourself, you hear?"

"Yes, sir." The words didn't even begin to do his feelings in that regard justice.

He'd die for her, gladly—the *why* was no mystery. He just needed her to live. If his life was the price, he'd pay it a hundred times, a thousand times, however many times it took until she was safe. If he had to sacrifice himself in every timeline, he'd do it.

That was love, wasn't it? To want the best for someone even if you couldn't be a part of it?

Before he knew it, they were headed up the mountain toward the black smoke that hung like an ominous specter on the wind. Kase barely noticed the picturesque scenery around them. He could only focus on what wafted above.

They hiked mostly in silence, broken only by labored breathing or murmured directions. The climes they scaled melted away in the fear and anticipation of what waited for them. Hallie thought it was Loffler, and while that might be the case, Kase knew Eravin was there. He had to be. Thinking about him only brought back the events of the Catacomb tunnel the black pulsing wound on his father's chest, his mother's tears, his father's last rattling breath.

I love...

The smoke cloud billowed outward the closer they climbed, looming over their heads, and now they could smell it—yalvar fuel, hot, piercing, and potent. Kase vaguely remembered Eravin's words in the hangar, that everyone could succumb to Jagamot's power, that the Yalvar fuel was the key. When they finally gave in to the brokenness inside them, Jagamot would manifest within them. Eravin seemed to be the worst offender. Had this been his plan since the beginning? Had it been One World's?

Navara murmured something as they passed a large Zuprium crystal poking out of a crevice in the mountain side as they passed. Smoke leaked from it, its deadly shard-like spikes dark and empty. They kept hiking, faster than before. More sweat slid down Kase's neck and into the collar of his shirt. He should've left his jacket with the Walkers, but he was nothing without it.

Kase had hoped Eravin was softening, turning back to the boy he'd once known before everything fell apart. He'd helped Kase after the card game. When had he chosen to turn down the path of darkness? Or had he always been that way, and Kase just saw what he wanted to see?

Had his turn been Kase's fault, somehow?

His wrist burned against the weight of the sword. He shifted his grip.

A smudge of gray dust streaked across his wrist caught his eye. Absently, he rubbed it—

But it didn't budge.

Every muscle in his body turned to ice.

Not a smudge. Those were his veins doused in gray, like Hallie had sketched over them with her best charcoal.

They weren't black, but they weren't normal. He shifted his sleeve to cover it. Panicking would not help. He was tired and emotionally exhausted. It might very well be his imagination, his memory of his father's death playing tricks on his eyes. They weren't black like Eravin's or the other Jaydians in the ward. He wasn't soulless like Correa.

Shocks. The ward.

What would happen to all those people? Without Eravin in the city, would they go back to normal? Or would one of them seek to replace him?

He'd left Jove and his mother there. They'd just lost Harlan, and now they possibly had to defend themselves against an entity no one in the modern day could comprehend. The thoughts only added another layer of heavy guilt and grief to the wall he'd been building for years.

It seemed there was no limit.

His breathing thinned, his focus narrowed to a single point. He could do nothing about it now. He could only hope his brother could weather the storm at home. He had no choice but to keep his feet moving up the mountain.

Stray rocks skittered behind them, echoing in the unnatural stillness as the sun fell toward the horizon.

No one spoke—all too lost in their own thoughts. He found Hallie's hand again though his was slick with sweat, but he'd never held on tighter. She squeezed back, never loosening it, as if she'd drown without him to pull her to the surface.

His heart beat too fast, the exertion akin to barrel rolls in Merlin. They weren't going fast enough or slow enough. Everyone he knew would be dead as if they never existed soon. What chance did they have against a god?

Whether they'd been hiking minutes or hours, Kase didn't know, but despite the chill permeating the air, sweat never stopped rolling down his cheeks from his hairline.

"There," Navara said, her breaths heavy. She pointed to where the smoke rolled slowly out of a crevice in the side of the mountain as if it had all the time in the world. Mocking them.

With each step up the mountain, the sword had grown heavier as did the future ahead of him. But no matter how much or how little he prepared for what was to come, it was time.

C H A P T E R   5 0

ANYTHING AT ALL

Hallie

AFTER THE MOST GRUELING HIKE she'd ever done in her life, the smell of Yalvar fuel turned Hallie's stomach as they stepped inside the cave. The chasm in the tunnels where the Stradat Lord Kapitan's tent had been had boasted a good bit of it, and the smell hadn't been this strong.

This stench made her gag, forcing her to pull her jacket collar up over her nose as if that would help. She had to try something.

She wasn't sure what she was going to find inside. By the stench, she was expecting some sort of pool boiling with the stuff. It was odd to find the Yalvar fuel this high up in the mountains. You usually had to dig deep to find it.

The cave was pitch black, the only illumination coming from the late afternoon light streaming from behind them. They didn't have a lantern or torch, and she was uncertain if she wanted to continue to feel her way when the Yalvar fuel could've been anywhere. Dying from chemical burns would be a rather anticlimactic way to go while trying to save the world

Actual fire might not be the best idea with all these fumes...but maybe she could do something better.

Ben had said she'd healed him with her power. She'd suffered the consequence of losing control, of course, but she'd done it. Here in Valora, her power didn't feel so foreign and hostile. It felt like something that had always been a part of her, just waiting for her to realize it was there. She couldn't explain why she felt that way. It might very well have something to do with her brother. Just being with him, talking with him, teasing him—it healed her soul in ways she hadn't known were still missing.

Her power bobbed in her chest, a nudge of sorts. It wanted to be used.

If she tried what Saldr had taught her, could she summon that ball of Yalven fire? There were no trees to destroy in this cave. Just a gaseous entity that might explode.

But something in her knew she could do it right. And so she did.

"Yrea." She snapped her fingers softly.

A weak tongue of fire sparked to life above her fingers. It didn't go out. It didn't explode. Her hand didn't tingle.

She gasped.

It wasn't nearly as bright as anything the other Yalvs had made, nor did it mold itself into a ball, but it floated there above her fingers, shimmering with faint light.

"I knew you could do it," Kase said, putting a hand on the small of her back. She smiled up at him, the light just brushing the edges of his features. They made his eyes brighter and the shadows less severe. Something had happened after she'd been thrust into this strange reality. Something that would explain the sword clasped in his hand.

"Yrea." Skibs' flame was a little bigger and a little brighter.

Navara took the lead with her own. "Doing that without Zuprium is how I know all of you have passed into this realm the way I did, rather than through death."

"How do you stand it?" Skibs asked as he directed his to follow them down the tunnel. "Living in a place made for the dead?"

It took her a few moments to respond, the only sound being their footsteps on the stone beneath their feet. At last she sighed. "Truthfully, it hasn't been a terrible place to be...though I do miss the taste of real food."

Hallie let out a soft gasp. "So it tastes like ash because...it is the soul of food in the living realm?"

"The Soul it contains is enough to sustain a living person here, but that is its only good quality."

Hallie thought back to the journals. How far Navara had come—how far both of them had come. In the Stoneset cavern, she'd just figured out how to work the last journal, the one with the memories infused inside the ink. They were the last attempt of a woman who desperately wanted to save her son.

And it had led her here, to this place of souls.

"Why did you stay?" Hallie asked. "Why did you not use the Aurora Gate to go back to your people? Or back to Stoneset?"

Navara slowed, her skirts swishing against the silent stone. She looked at Hallie with those ageless eyes, the ones that Hallie had found in the Lord Elder. The only reason he'd given over his power to Hallie was because she'd told him about Navara. It was a destiny of a power that might very well doom them all.

Had he known? About Navara being here? Or that Hallie would one day join her in Valora?

He'd been the Essence of Time, the most powerful of all the Essences. Hallie had proven she could speed up time, and Saldr had told her the Lord Elder had thrown himself backward. What if he'd seen the future in those moments right before he'd given Hallie his power?

Had he always known it would end this way? Had he willingly given up his own life just so she could save the world? And in doing so, find the daughter he'd lost nearly a century ago?

She swallowed hard at the lump in her throat.

Her great grandmother smiled and rubbed a hand across Hallie's cheek. "Jack was right—you are full of questions."

Hallie blushed, grateful for the distraction. "It's just, in your journals, you were trying to find a way to cure the Fogs, and you thought the Lord Elder might have the answer. But...you're here, and you left the clues for me to find this place."

Navara took a deep breath. "To leave Valora, you must have the key. While the Aurora has dozens because of all the timelines it connects, the only way to leave Valora through the Nether Gate is for you to have the guardian. I was only given the words of power to enter by the man who was the Essence of Keys before your friend. I also did not have a key for the Aurora."

"That must have been difficult. You finally found the Gate only to realize you'd never leave, and..." Hallie left the other part unspoken: that her son had died, no matter how hard and far she'd searched for a way to cure him.

"It was, but I found a purpose here. And while I regret not spending the last days with my son, my journal served a purpose of its own. It eventually led you here, my dear. I trust in Toro's providence."

Ben spoke up, his voice echoing off the walls. "Would you return now that we have the guardian?"

"No," Navara said quietly. "Not now. There is nothing for me there."

Hallie squeezed Kase's hand.

She wasn't sure if she would have reacted so gracefully to what more or less amounted to imprisonment in Valora. She ached to return to the land of the living, though she also knew that would mean leaving her brother behind.

To have him back, only for him to be ripped away again? Unbearable.

Would it be so bad to stay here, as Navara had done? Kase could stay with her, and they could live out the rest of their lives here in the shadows of beautiful mountains and raise chickens and enjoy the peace Valora would bring once they figured out how to stop Loffler and Jagamot.

It was nice to think about. It distracted her from whatever might lay ahead.

The cave tunnel was oddly shaped; clearly manmade. It reminded Hallie a little of a mine, but instead of wood, the columns and beams were constructed of Zuprium. However, Hallie had never seen the metal in such disrepair. Whether it was blackened with time or maybe even the Yalvar fuel floating above their heads, she didn't know, but it added a heaviness, as if the cave itself held its breath. It was...inauspicious. Disquieting.

The further they hiked, the thicker the scent became. At

times, it burned her throat like fire. Hallie had to stop and cough multiple times. Her head swam as she was forced to take shallower and shallower breaths. Kase never left her side.

Navara turned and murmured something underneath her breath. In a moment, the air cleared; Hallie could breathe again, though her throat was still raw. "That spell works best with Vasa, but I'm trying to save what little I have. Do your best to breathe normally. Too quickly or deeply will make the spell dissipate faster. The *ashamox* is too strong."

"Ashamox?" Hallie asked.

Navara pointed at the smoke. "We must hurry."

Hallie could only nod, her throat still too sore to speak. Hopefully that would abate with the cleaner air.

Kase rubbed the back of her neck. "You going to be all right?"

She chewed on her lip, but nodded.

A few turns later, the tunnel opened into the largest cavern Hallie had ever seen. She couldn't see the top, but it was filled with the ashamox. She hadn't realized the tunnel they'd been walking through had been so tall. The smoke and darkness had masked the height.

The cavern wasn't really a cavern, though. It was the inside of some sort of structure, like a cathedral from First Earth. Crumbling archways soared into the smoke. Great windows stretched up and joined at a point, standing like ghosts in the walls, the swirled traceries empty of glass. Firelight flickered around the corner. The floor was covered in broken tile that had once been some sort of mosaic, so scattered and worn she could only wonder at what it might have once depicted.

If she'd had her satchel, she would've stopped and taken notes or sketched a bit of its otherworldly beauty. What had happened here in a place where souls rested before moving to whatever came next? What had wrought this destruction?

Something tickled the back of her mind. This place. It was familiar. She couldn't put a finger on it, though.

Partially collapsed beams blocked the view of the fire's origins. A statue missing its face stood to Hallie's right. It reminded her too much of the stone guardians from the forest on Tasava that had attacked the crew once she and Ben had done something in the temple to trigger them.

Maybe that was it—maybe it reminded her of the forest

temple. This one was free of swords.

She steered clear of the statue, but another without arms and a head replaced it a few feet away.

"Put your *yreasa* out," Navara whispered. She murmured something, her hand going into her pouch of Vasa at her side. She released the dust in the air, and as if by magic, a dazzling sword appeared in her hand. The Zuprium blade was unblemished, and the gemstone in the pommel sparkled with pure, crystalline gold. Navara gasped softly, as if startled by her own spell; but after a moment, she smiled sadly. "Raern."

Hallie stared hard at it while dismissing her small flame with a thought and wave of her hand. As if it was nothing. Saldr would have been elated—or as close to it as the stoic Yalv could get. "What? How did you do that?"

"With enough practice and the right words of power, you could as well," Navara said. "Let us hope there is time for learning later. I fear you may have to use your power past what you are ready for. Assess the state of the Chronal Gate and repair it." She looked to Ben. "You will need to combine your powers to do so." She glanced at Kase. Her golden eyes glowed, but Hallie couldn't tell if it was from the light or something more ethereal. "You and I will do what we can to distract him."

Hallie didn't like what that implied, but they didn't have a choice.

Then Navara put her own light out, and they were thrown into near-darkness, their only guide the flickering fire at the end of the cathedral past the broken arches and fallen beams.

"May the stars rise upon you," Navara whispered to them.

It was Ben who whispered, "And may they not fall when morning breaks."

Her heart was in her throat. She couldn't swallow. But then Kase squeezed her hand. She looked up to his steady gaze, ready for whatever might lay around the corner.

She could do this.

With Kase's hand in her own, Hallie strode forward, "Let's go."

Kase

LEAD FILLED KASE'S ENTIRE BODY as they wove through the ruins. He was partly curious as to how there were ruins in the spirit realm. Everyone in it was dead—barring himself, Skibs, Hallie, her parents, and apparently Navara. So how were there ruins? If something was already dead, it couldn't age. Jack was the shining example of that being eternally eighteen. That begged the question…what had happened in this place? What horrors had visited a world meant for those who were already dead?

Kase might not have died, but each step they took made him feel as if he had. He wasn't sure if it was the burning smell still making his sinuses ache, even with whatever Navara had done to help, or the fact that Eravin probably waited ahead. In the two times he'd faced the corrupted version of his friend, he hadn't ended with the upper hand. Only small mercies had allowed him to survive—Saldr arriving at the most opportune time, his father knocking him out of the way, and his mother using her locket to keep Eravin from finishing the job.

Shocks and bolts.

What was he doing? His hands were sweating—one around the hilt of the sword, the other around Hallie's icy fingers. He didn't know if he could do this. He didn't know if he could face him again. And what if Loffler was there? An Essence wielder with the power to take out electricity might not be much use here, but what did Kase know? Who knew what the old man could do that they hadn't witnessed?

Between him and Eravin, did they even stand a chance? Did they even have a choice?

They reached the largest archway yet, the firelight brighter without anything to block it. Kase squeezed Hallie's hand, trying desperately to keep himself grounded as he recognized the silhouette standing before a burning archway, another sprawled upon the floor.

Golden flames resembling the Yalven bonfire licked the furthest archway, ashamox billowing from the top and collecting above their heads.

"That's not Stradat Loffler," Hallie breathed. "That's…"

"Eravin Gray," Kase said in a voice that sounded entirely dead to his own ears.

His concerns about Loffler were quickly put to rest—because Loffler lay dead on the ground.

Navara breathed, "He's taken the Essence power."

Eravin paused his inspection of the burning archway, turning to observe them. His features looked even more sunken in with those obsidian eyes, his too-pale skin stretched over jutting cheekbones. His hands crackled with purple energy, Loffler unmoving at his feet. A black, pulsing spider wound nested in Stradat Loffler's chest.

I...I love...

Eravin was no longer the man Kase had known or the boy he'd grown up with. He was the monster who'd killed Harlan, who'd nearly killed Hallie and Kase himself. Who'd made the razing of Kyvena possible, whether he claimed to have wanted it or not.

He would pay.

Hallie's grip tightened on his own. He glanced down at her white face and clenched jaw. He didn't know what would happen, and he wasn't sure they'd both survive, but he would still fight.

"He's..." Hallie started, but it was too horrible for her to even voice.

Dark, sparkling power threaded with purple encompassed Eravin's right fist.

"Jagamot." Navara held her slim sword out before her with one hand and gripped a handful of Zuprium dust in the other.

Eravin took measured steps toward them. "You're too late."

It was the nudge Navara needed. She threw the Vasa into the air, yelling something in Yalven. A beam of light shot from that sword as she pointed it at Eravin, who dodged, deflecting it with his own power.

Hallie went to run, but Kase caught her by the wrist and pulled her back to him. He kissed her hard, desperation and the weight of what might happen crushing into her lips. "I love you."

"I love you."

And then she and Skibs took off to the side of the room, sprinting toward the burning archway.

He hefted his father's sword up and sprinted toward Eravin, who'd dodged Navara's second deadly beam. The far wall of the cathedral groaned with the impact.

He had no blasting idea how to use the sword and wished desperately for an electropistol or his hovership. Then he might've stood somewhat of a chance.

The flames painted Eravin's face in red and gold, rendering his dark eyes into bottomless pits, far more terrifying than they had been in the Catacombs full of shadowed tunnels and lightless voids. He shot that glittering darkness that had killed his father at the Yalven woman. Navara parried it with the sword in her hand, the darkness absorbed by the beaming blade. She winced, but didn't hesitate before twirling on her feet, slicing the sword across Eravin's middle, then slicing backhand when he sidestepped her first blow.

"Ah, a Chronal. Of course," Eravin spat as he dodged once more, throwing out his hand. Purple energy shot from his hands. Navara threw dust into the air that roared into a wall of flame mirrored almost exactly to her body, like a self-shaping shield.

Kase could only gape dumbly at the power. Could Hallie do that? He glanced at where she and Skibs knelt before the burning Gate. He needed to keep Eravin distracted, and he was just standing there slack-jawed.

Eravin ripped a familiar dagger from the sheath at his waist and cut his palm. His face barely twisted in pain, though the cut was deep. Black, bulbous blood spurted from the wound. *"Varkl drak!"*

It said something about who Kase was as a person, probably, that amidst all the terror and chaos around him, his first thought was, *That* helviter *stole my King Arthur dagger.*

Like he'd heard Kase's thoughts, Eravin dropped the dagger and held up his bleeding hand. The ashamox above him surged toward his fingers, coiling around them and solidifying into a blade of smoke, veined in red and gold like a fiery slab of marble.

The blade flashed in an arc, glittering power shooting out with the swipe. Both Kase and Navara dropped to avoid the wave. It whizzed over Kase's head, his curls rustling as if in the wind.

The smell of singed flesh burned his nose. Not his—at least, he hoped not.

He needed to do something, but what could he do

against *that*? He wasn't special. All he had was a borrowed sword and a past riddled with grief. He was useless as anything but bait.

His sword, his father's sword, might be able to do something if it truly was the Second Gate's guardian. That was what Hallie had been planning to do—kill herself by giving her power to it. Could Kase get close enough to cut Eravin? Would that be enough? Or would he have to stab him like his father had done Correa? And would that only take the Essence power from him, or would it also destroy Jagamot?

What if Kase was wrong about all of it?

Kase swung around the back side, hoping to catch him off guard while distracted by the rather impressive Yalven woman who had lived the last forty-odd years of her life in a place where souls came after death.

He glanced at Hallie and Skibs again, their shadowy silhouettes ablaze against the Gate. They hadn't moved. They had to fix it fast. He didn't know how much longer Navara could hold Eravin off. Whenever that pouch of dust ran out, she was doomed.

Eravin laughed, shooting another purple-laced beam at Navara. "It doesn't matter, Toro is dead."

"He will never die!" Navara shouted, charging forward and throwing all her weight behind the next thrust of her sword, the tang now dancing with fire like that of the archway behind her. "Not while we have the other Essences."

Eravin's sword met hers in a flurry of black and gold sparks, metal singing a high note that echoed through the cave. Navara was skilled, but she was no match for the man several decades her junior. He shoved her back, casting out a bolt of purple energy laced with glittering black.

She dodged, but the beam grazed her arm. She screamed but rolled back to her feet, grabbing a fistful of dust and ground it into her wound.

Would that blackness spread like it had in Harlan's wound? Would she too die in mere moments, leaving Kase as the only line of defense between Hallie and this monster?

The burning Gate crackled, and the ashamox roared in response, a booming rumble like thunder. Kase jumped. Everything was too loud in the chamber, the echoing making everything worse. The noise frayed his focus into tattered threads. He couldn't gather them all.

Eravin swaggered toward Navara, black fire consuming his sword, molten shadow shimmering at his sides. "Should I kill you now or let you suffer?"

He only waited one heartbeat before spinning his sword and cutting it through the air. He was too far away to cut her, but black flame flew from the blade, hurtling toward Navara. She heaved up a cloud of dust and cried, *"Yrea maxima!"*

The same firewall from earlier erupted from the dust particles, but it seemed weaker to Kase; the flames wavered at a glacial pace, not as bright or colorful. The wound was taking a toll on her. She couldn't hold out much longer.

Do something, you stars-idiot!

Eravin's fire collided with Navara's shield, shattering it, engulfing the woman's wounded arm. Her scream rang louder than the growl of the ashamox.

Kase had no choice. He had to move.

He threw himself forward, hefting the sword, and swung it with everything he had. A brutal, instinctive yell escaped his throat, but it was lost in the cacophony.

The blade soared for Eravin's neck. So close. So close—

At the last second, Eravin twisted around.

Metal impacted metal, rattling Kase's teeth so hard he saw stars. When his vision cleared, he saw why.

Eravin had caught his blade with his own.

"Good try," Eravin chuckled before kicking him in the chest, sending him flying.

Too fast. Too strong.

Impossible.

Kase tumbled in midair like he'd been taught during his pilot training, saving himself from a hard fall on his head; instead, he landed on his chest, skidding and rolling over the mosaic tile. A few loose pieces of tile cut the exposed areas of his skin. His scar from the Zuprium crystal chamber with Stowe stung.

Kase spit blood out of his mouth and pushed himself up, his chest screaming, but Eravin barely gave him a chance to recover. He flung a fiery ball of dark energy at him. Kase dropped, smacking his chin on the ground to avoid it. Another burst of stars thrown in his eyes. His head rang.

Another scream echoed in the chamber above the noise. Kase looked up to see Navara bring her sword down on her infected arm.

The blade cut through flesh and bone like they were nothing but mist.

Holy blasting shocks.

Kase's stomach roiled, but Eravin didn't care. He wrenched his sword up over his head and swung it down through Navara's weak defense.

"NO!" Kase screamed, but Navara, still shrieking through her own agony, managed to bring her sword up and block the death blow. The clang reverberated off the ancient stone walls. Blazes of darkness and light warred where the two swords met. Her single arm shook from holding the blow off. Her other bled freely onto the floor, marring any beauty the ancient tile had ever had.

Kase scrambled up, staggering forward with both hands wrapped around his sword's hilt. He hacked down, but Eravin was faster. He coated his hand in his power and kicked Navara. In the next moment, he deflected Kase's amateur strike with his sword and smashed his glowing fist into Kase's abdomen.

All the breath Kase had left whooshed out of him. He bent over, the pain like lightning lancing out from where he'd hit. "*Agh!*"

It burned. Fire ignited his veins. The gray streak on his wrist had darkened to pulsing black. It disappeared underneath his sleeve.

He could feel it in his heart.

He looked up through the haze of pain and darkness to see Eravin. The thing that had possessed him smiled, his teeth now stained black.

"You were always too reckless," Eravin spat. "Always needing to be saved."

He stalked closer. Kase couldn't move. Whatever power he'd hit him with wreaked havoc on his mind, his body. It hurt. Was this how his father had felt? Was Kase moments away from dying?

"You were never a hero."

Kase gripped the sword in his hand, falling backward. He ached. He couldn't stand.

"And you've never been able to protect those you love."

"*Srava krai!*" Navara croaked out. Soft golden flames erupted around Kase. Eravin paused, his grin wicked. It only slowed him for seconds. He swiped his hands, and the flames extinguished.

Kase froze, his heart pounding in his ears, his veins on fire.

But Eravin didn't finish Kase off. Instead, he swung his glittering black sword, heavy with dark power, straight at Hallie.

She didn't see it, didn't see the surge rocketing toward her. Her eyes were closed. She poured blue and gold lightning into Skibs' hand. She wasn't going to move in time. Even if he shouted her name, she'd look first to see what was coming.

He didn't have time to think. To come up with a plan.

But a pilot didn't fly with his head. A pilot flew by his instincts. His reflexes.

And he'd flown with the man next to Hallie long enough to know exactly which instinct would save them both.

"*Head down, Skibs*!" Kase bellowed through his anguish-addled haze.

And thanks to a reflex taught by flying with the best stars-blasted pilot the Crews ever saw, Skibs didn't hesitate for even a second before he ducked, yanking Hallie down with him.

The power collided with the glowing Gate instead. A clap loud as thunder rocked the cathedral. Hallie scrambled to her feet, her own fists glowing gold. She shouted something at him, but he couldn't hear it over the roaring in his ears.

Eravin swung his sword, more dark power surging out with the swing. Hallie held up her hands.

To Kase, just like every time he saw danger hurtling for Hallie, it all happened in slow motion. Was he doomed to repeat this same scenario until he finally died...or she did?

He watched in horror as the dark energy shattered the golden flaming shield Hallie erected around herself.

Ignoring the anguish in his veins, Kase launched himself forward, his sword swinging. "You *helviter*!"

Eravin caught his blade on his. Kase's face poured with sweat, pressing against the sword with all his strength. How was he so strong?

Eravin shoved him away. "*Ekzurel vilna*!"

The ground shook, and the ashamox writhed. Kase fell backward, immediately searching for Hallie; when he found her, she was pushing herself up to her elbows, breathing hard but seemingly unharmed.

She was okay.

His relief was short-lived. Gray, amorphous shapes rose from the cathedral floor and mixed with the ashamox from above, solidifying into...into...

People.

Screaming, tortured people.

The one closest to Kase was a man in his late forties, his eyes smelted black, his mouth open in a gut-wrenching wail. Kase shouted, stumbling back, swinging his sword out. It cut the man across his stomach, black ashamox leaking out the wound, but he kept coming.

Buzzing began in Kase's ears. What sort of nightmare was this? Was this merely something he'd conjured in his mind? Or was it a person? A soul? Something that mimicked one?

Despite his burning chest and stomach, he pushed himself to his feet. "Hallie!"

Whatever these creatures were, they weren't fighters; there were just too many of them. Hundreds of them. Maybe thousands. He swung awkwardly with his sword, gutting an elderly female ghost, black ichor spraying his jacket.

The substance scalded the leather. Yalvar fuel. Oh, shocks.

Yalven and guttural spells alike rebounded off the chamber walls, but all Kase could think was that he needed to get to Hallie.

He swung his sword blindly, clearing himself a path as he rammed through the mass of bodies, careful to dodge the corrosive fuel, though several droplets landed on his jacket.

The mass of wailing bodies thinned with each step he took, and finally, he saw her. Her hands blazed with power, her entire body radiant. Her hair whipped in an invisible wind. Each spirit that met her hands disintegrated in a flare of light, but more filled the gap. She was a force to be reckoned with—the Essence of Time.

"Hallie!"

He fought his way to her side. Skibs appeared at Kase's other side, the inky black sword like an extension of his own body as he fought his opponents. A natural.

But where was Eravin?

Dread filled his stomach like a pile of stones.

This wouldn't end if he escaped. Kase growled as he killed the soul of what looked like a young Jaydian soldier. "Back to back!"

Both Hallie and Skibs nodded, never letting their guard or strikes drop. Kase backed up until he met their shoulders. "Where's Eravin?"

"Navara," Hallie breathed. "He went for her."

"Hallie, you can return the souls," Skibs shouted above the wailing and his next swipe at another soul. "Reverse time on them."

"But that might only make them regenerate—"

"We'll figure it out!" Kase shouted, swinging at another soul and missing. The man grabbed Kase's wrist. Kase screamed. The man's fingers seared into his skin like fire.

Hallie's hand shot out, her fingers glowing. "*Anora van esque vral!*"

The soul in front of him puffed into golden mist. His sooty fingerprints encircled Kase's wrist, but whatever she'd done had worked.

Hallie thrust out her power, the words a chant. The trio worked their way toward where Navara had been.

"Try again, Hallie!" Skibs said. "Add *maxima!*"

"Anora van esque vral maxima!" Hallie shouted.

Golden light flared out from her hands, drowning the room in brilliance.

The souls vanished into glittering mist.

Hallie fell to her knees.

Kase dropped beside her.

"No! *Kase!*" Skibs screamed.

He looked up to see Eravin's glittering midnight sword arcing toward Hallie. Skibs swung the shadow sword. Missed. Kase fumbled for his own, raising it only a second before Eravin's sliced through Hallie's skull. The strike vibrated through his arm and shoulder, aching horribly.

He groaned against the strain. Skibs pulled Hallie away, but Kase couldn't get off his knees.

"Yrea va na tari!"

Golden fire blasted Eravin in the side, engulfing and knocking him sideways.

Hallie.

Kase's sword flew from his hands. He scrambled toward

it just as Eravin recovered enough to send more glittering black energy at her. Kase's fingers gripped his shining sword, and he flung himself to his feet, launching at Eravin.

"No!"

His father's sword, the one fabled to belong to a Yalven legend, blazed like lightning through the air, its arc aflame with searing white-gold.

In the second before the sword connected with his neck, Eravin turned, looking directly at Kase. His eyes were no longer solid black.

They were dark brown and unmarred.

Sad, anguished.

The shining sword sliced through muscle and sinew, bone and skin, black blood spraying Kase. It boiled. Kase screamed as it licked his skin like liquid flame. Eravin's head rolled off his shoulders and his body collapsed forward, his blood like a night sky without stars, spilling onto the ground.

Kase fell to his knees. He dropped the sword.

Everything burned.

Everything blurred.

He couldn't see. It had all happened so fast. His heart was going to beat out of his chest. Fire seared his insides like he'd drunk a gallon of acid. Whatever Eravin had punched him with earlier raged in his blood.

He was going to die just like his father.

A thousand memories, the worst ones, assaulted him as he knelt, his skin burning. The pain of breaking his arm when he was seven. The sickness that had taken both his grandparents. Each disappointed look from his father. A dozen near-death experiences with Eravin.

Just give in. Give in to the darkness.

The voice was small, soft, yet too familiar. He'd heard it before. It was the same one that always spoke to him in his darkest moments.

Ana's betrothal dinner ending in a plan to run away. His father nearly killing him when they'd tried. The fire, his aching lungs. Ana bleeding and burning in his arms. Her sweater melted into her skin. Eravin slamming the door in his face.

It's over. There is nothing you can do.

The *Eudora* mission, the storm, the stone statues, Ebba's death, Hallie's ruined hand, Zeke's blood. Another slamming door, his dying brother on the other side. Skibs' betrayal. Getting hit with the Cerl pistol in the Narden Pass. Hallie's kidnapping. Correa's torture. Achilles. Saying goodbye.

The weight of his failures bludgeoned him, crushing him into the stone beneath his knees. He couldn't see. It was too dark.

You're worthless, reckless, a waste.

Gray whimpered against black, a shadow puppet acting out every last thing that had chiseled cracks into his heart.

Hallie's trembling lips as she stared at his ring. "I don't want to marry you..."

Closing Harlan's sightless eyes. "I...I love..."

Eravin's black blood spurting from the place his head once sat. "We're friends again, remember?"

Kase didn't know if he was breathing. He couldn't feel his lungs filling and contracting. He could only feel the pain.

Just let go.

Hallie

THE FIRE WAS TOO BRIGHT to be natural. The ashamox was too thick. It was as if the Gate bled its life out into each burning gust. Hallie and Ben stood before it, unsure of anything but the improbability of what they needed to do.

"Do we put out the fire first?" Hallie asked, spinning Kase's ring around her finger. She purposefully did not look at him, wherever he was. She couldn't, not if she was going to do what she needed to do. One look at him would unravel any courage she managed to scrounge up.

Ben pressed his glowing hands to the ground a foot or two from the blazing archway. "It's this Gate's soul. It's too weak. I don't know if putting out the fire will do anything besides prolong its death. This one is unfamiliar. It doesn't feel like the other two Gates."

"What if I heal it? I don't know the first thing about doing that with a soul, but it's the only idea I have. Could you...I don't know...maybe..."

She was at a loss. It didn't make sense in her mind. Nothing did. It would just be easier to put the Essence powers into the swords and return them to their respective Gates, but according to Saldr, they needed the soul that was locked inside this one to even do that. Did they take the shadow sword Skibs had set aside and thrust it into the Gate? Hack at the carved Zuprium bricks with it?

Navara shouted something behind them, and Hallie peeked over to see a wall of flames colliding with shadowy power. The whole thing rocked and bowed when hit, but it held.

Stars, why had that woman run away from being the Essence of Time? With that kind of power and skill, she would've been a far better candidate than Hallie. Anyone would've been better than her.

Time was a thief and a liar.

"Pour your power into me," Ben said, holding out a glowing hand. "As if you're healing. If we join our power, we might be able to stop the complete destruction. Then we can reassess."

She didn't have a better idea, so she clutched his hand and funneled all the burning heat she could into the connection. He winced, but he pressed his hand into the flames anyway.

Holding a single tendril and letting the others loose into her hand, she fought the urge to let it all go. It was easier this time, though, than the other ones. She didn't have to fight as hard.

She opened one eye. How? How was she able to channel so much power into Ben without feeling the effects? Last time she'd slowed time and caught him after he'd fallen from the dragon, she'd felt herself falling deeper and deeper into the black hole, unable to pull herself out or even slow her descent.

This time was different. She wavered, but she kept a grip on reality, the power pouring out of her in a torrent. It was endless.

"Stop!" Ben said, releasing her hand.

She cut it off with barely a thought.

Stars. Was it because she was in Valora?

Hallie wiped the sweat rolling down her face. The fire had dimmed. Not enough. Ben cursed. "What are we missing? The other Essences? Maybe if we give it the swords and our own powers? But we'd need the one Jagamot took, and Kase's sword, too. It has Correa's."

Hallie pressed her palms to her eyes. She needed to think. Out of all her research and obsessive reading, she must have come across something, *anything* that could give her the answer.

She looked down at her hand, the one with Kase's ring. The band glowed subtly. Odd. Was it merely reflecting the firelight? Or was it coming from within?

The ring was pure Zuprium, the gemstones little chips from the crystal clusters themselves. Ever since Kase had pressed it into her hand, it'd felt right—even after her rejection.

Kase's goggles hadn't survived saving Ben, but they hadn't been her Relic to begin with. Her power craved freedom, but that would only lead to destruction—of what, whether that was herself or something else, she didn't know.

But this ring. It had been given out of pure love, with all the promise of forever.

She couldn't help the soft gasp that escaped her lips. It couldn't be.

Saldr had said replacing a Relic was nearly impossible—but not completely.

This was the Relic she'd needed all along.

She *would* finally find it right when she was about to give her power up to save the world. But what now? How could she use the Essence within her to fix the Gate before her?

To control her power, she needed a Relic. Before Kase had given her the ring, she'd been lost in that power, burning like this Gate. What was the Gate's Relic?

The swords. The other Gates needed those—the Nether and the Aurora. But this one? What had happened to its guardian? Had it ever had one?

She knew next to nothing about it, only that it had been ruined for as long as time immemorial. The state of the cathedral confirmed that.

"No!" Kase screamed.

Hallie looked up, heart in her throat, her hands filling with power. But that wall of flames Navara had thrown up earlier still held, keeping her and Ben from whatever was happening on the other side.

How long would it hold?

Could she get around it?

They needed to figure this out. Now.

What if the only way to fix the Gate and heal the soul of the god trapped inside was to give it a guardian, a Relic, whether that be find the original or create a new one? How did one do that? They didn't have time to search for the original—hunting it down could take years. Could Hallie do something about that? Could she somehow reverse time and find the sword?

Her fingers tingled with the thought.

What were the consequences of using her power on that scale? Would doing that cause some other horrific fallout now, making any sacrifice she made worthless?

Would it be the same as resetting the Gate? She'd been against the Lord Elder's plan because of the horrible ramifications it might cause. What if this did something worse?

"Hallie?" Ben asked, his voice interrupting her thought process.

But if she made a new sword...would the Gate even accept it?

"To fix this Gate, we have to recreate it, and we need a sword guardian! We don't have time to find the old one—we'll have to make one!" It was so loud in the cavern, she had to shout. The flames and energy and fight around them echoed off the walls.

Ben's face paled. "How?"

Hallie wet her lips. "I can create Passages and heal. You can control the Gates. We can combine our powers to create a Gate on top of this one, then create a sword guardian as the Gate's Relic. Like you did in Myrrai."

Ben swore loudly. "But we don't have all the Essence powers!"

"We have to try."

"It's not going to work!"

"Worst is we die trying. If we don't, we're dead anyway!"

Ben held up the sword, and Hallie flinched back. He pointed it at the Gate. "Can we use this one?"

Hallie shook her head. "It's connected to the Aurora Gate."

Nodding reluctantly and setting the sword aside, he held out a glowing hand. "What do we do about the guardian then? I can create the sword itself, but bonding it...we'll need a soul."

Her. Her sacrifice would save them all, would save Kase.

She would be the guardian, but first, they needed to create the Gate. "I don't know what to do, but I'll use the words of power and force my power into you again. You take it and...and..."

"I'll figure it out," he said firmly, still holding out his hand.

And oddly enough, she trusted that he would.

She grasped it and poured her power into him. *"Avali anora ess nah!"*

The Gate of the Essence.

"Another one!" Ben shouted.

"Ess anora ana kar vali!"

Essence Time, bring forth Gates.

Nothing.

"Again!"

"Avali crea ess, toro ano!"

The Essence of Creation Gate, Toro heal.

At this point, she was just going to throw all the possible words she could at it and hope one of the combinations worked.

What was she missing? She'd discovered that the words of power were often more literal, and the inflection had to be correct.

She wracked her brain for the answer, but in the chaos, it was difficult to do so. She didn't need to create fire. She needed something stronger, something powerful enough to create the center of timelines, a connection to the soul of the land and everyone who inhabited it.

Words of power combined with Vasa allowed Chronals to access their innate power. Hallie didn't have Vasa, and she barely had any words of power, yet something in her gut told her she was doing the right thing. Something told her that the ruin of this Chronal gate was the reason everything was happening. Without it, the melody—the song—was incomplete.

A song.

Singing.

Saldr had said that for more complex spells, singing was required.

That was it.

Without thinking much further than that, she put the words to one of the tunes from the bonfire celebration. *"Avali crea ess, Toro ano..."*

She didn't stop singing it, not until the light pouring from her tinged blue. Probably not good. She'd let her soul slip into it. Too much and she'd hemorrhage, but maybe that was the point. How could one not sacrifice their very essence to create something so powerful?

She was the Essence of Time. She could do this. She might very well be the *only* one who could.

"Head down, Skibs!"

She looked up to find a jet of black and purple power winnowing straight for her. The flame wall was gone.

Faster than she could have imagined, Ben tugged her down, and the power hit the Gate. A thunderous crash blasted her eardrums, made worse by the echoing in the cavern cathedral.

The Gate behind her raged, its flames climbing higher and mixing with the ashamox above, but Hallie pushed herself to her feet, her hands aglow.

"Kase!" He was hurt, his hand holding his stomach.

Mr. Gray swung a sword that looked too much like Kainadr's shadow sword, and power rushed out from its swing.

She didn't think. She just reacted.

"Yrea vas!"

The words simply came to her as if in a dream, and a shield of fire burst to life around her. She could do this. Kase's ring glowed gold, tempering the fallout from the Essence power raging within her.

The dark energy broke through, but she ducked, shooting her own at it and diverting it into the cathedral wall with a shuddering clap. A few stones rained down in its wake, but it held. She thrust her healing power at it, begging it not to collapse.

It worked.

She'd done that.

She could control the power.

"You helviter!"

Kase.

"Ekzurel vilna!" Mr. Gray shouted above the din.

Rumbling, the ground quaked like it had been ever since Achilles fell, keeping her pinned to the floor, her teeth and bones aching. She pushed herself to her elbows only to see the ashamox above surge into the gray souls rising from the floor. She leapt to her feet, more words of power echoing through her mind.

She whipped her hands out. "*Srav!*"

The soul beside her vanished in a spray of golden mist. They were the souls, the ones that had been missing, like Jack's chicken, Hester. It had to be. Bonded with the ashamox, they were corporeal. Would Hallie's power allow them to move on?

She didn't have time to think of the consequences as another soul swung at her.

Ben shouted, swinging Kainadr's Shadow sword and killing three. Black smoke poured from the wounds and sprayed the ground beneath his feet. Souls filled the space between them, closing in on Hallie.

Eravin gave her one look before heading toward Navara.

With glowing hands, Hallie fought the souls, working to find Kase, to find her grandmother, to end the suffering souls before her.

"Hallie!" Kase's voice shouted above the fray.

She looked, but she couldn't see him. She worked her way toward his voice, but there were countless souls in the way.

And then he was there. "Hallie!"

He bandied about Xera's Soul sword, ashamox eating away at his leather jacket. But he was okay. He was whole. Mostly. His shirt was shredded at his stomach, the skin beneath it purple.

He just looked relieved to see her. He eyed Ben, who'd fought his way to them. Kase growled and swung his sword at a soul who'd screamed, pressing in on them. "Back to back!"

Hallie nodded, and soon, her back was to both men, her hands out, her power ablaze. She felt powerful.

I can do this.

"Where's Eravin?" Kase asked above the din.

Hallie half turned. "Navara. He went for her."

"Hallie, you can return the souls," Skibs shouted. "Reverse time on them!"

True. She could do that, but what were the consequences? All she'd been doing was sending power through her hands at them, unsure of if she healed them or simply destroyed them, though with everything going on, she hadn't considered the consequences.

"But that might only make them regenerate!"

And even if it didn't, could she control her power enough to do it individually without hitting Kase or Skibs in her strikes?

"We'll figure it out!" Kase shouted, still fighting. He screamed as a soul grabbed his wrist, yanking him forward.

Blast the consequences.

"*Anora van esque vral!*" She whipped her hand out, her fingers glowing and sparkling gold like the sunset.

The soul, a man, unraveled and vanished into golden mist. Almost like the Cerl soldier in the Stoneset cavern. *Holy stars.*

It worked—for ill or not, she didn't care. They fought closer to where Navara had disappeared.

Ben pressed against her back. "Try again, Hallie! Add *maxima!*"

She did, and the entire room exploded into golden sunlight.

The souls glittered into nothing around them. She collapsed.

So tired. Too much power.

But not enough to knock her out. Her ring glowed brighter. Kase dropped beside her, his free arm coming around her.

"No! *Kase!*" Ben yelled above them.

The sword of darkness arced toward them, toward her. Her mouth fell open in a silent scream, but then Kase was there, his shining sword blocking the blow. Strong arms dragged her backward, as she scrambled to her knees, to her feet.

"*Yrea va na tari!*" Blazing golden flames shot from her fingers and blasted into Mr. Gray's side, knocking him sideways.

Kase's sword flew from his hands. Mr. Gray turned, his hands coming up and pushing crackling dark energy out of his palms.

No.

But then she glimpsed his eyes as he turned toward Kase's shout. They were no longer bottomless pits. Her stomach dropped out.

What?

Kase dropped, grabbing his sword and spinning. The Xera sword glowed like the sun as it swung in a graceful arc. In a flash, Mr. Gray's head tumbled from his body, his brown eyes wide in death, a silent, shocked gasp on his lips.

The body fell forward. Tripping backward, Hallie brought a shaking hand to her mouth. Kase stood behind him, chest heaving—but something was wrong.

He dropped the sword he'd used to kill Mr. Gray, a horrible scream erupting from his throat as he clawed at his arms and his legs and chest—anywhere Jagamot's black, glittering blood had landed. He collapsed, his face in his hands, screaming louder as he dragged his nails down his face, cutting bloody furrows into his skin.

Her heart pounded frantically in her chest. He needed her. Forget the Gate. Forget anything else. She slipped on the blood but kept her feet, skirting around Mr. Gray's legs. She fell beside Kase, grabbing his hands and tearing them from his eyes. She flung the sword away from her.

Those eyes were no longer the deep sapphire blue she loved. They were black. Solid black. Like Mr. Gray's.

"No, no, please no." Hallie grabbed Kase's face. "Kase!"

But he only stared sightlessly at her, his features suddenly slackening. Unnervingly blank.

"Kase!"

It couldn't be. Kase was strong. Kase had overcome so much. He couldn't...she needed to do something. She needed to stop him from...from whatever was happening. Jagamot. It was Jagamot. Killing Mr. Gray had caused this. Jagamot needed another host. Kase was becoming Jagamot.

Hallie yanked the heat left in her core to the surface and forced it into Kase with all the strength she had.

She could undo this. She had the power to rewind time.

She could heal him.

She could save him.

She'd evaporated hundreds of souls with a single spell.

She could do this. She *would* do this.

Dimly, she was aware of the light emitting from under her skin. It was like her power glowed within her very soul. Kase's dark eyes reflected the mix of gold and blue, but wouldn't absorb it. She couldn't push it into him. He refused to accept it.

A glittering black cloud of fire surrounded them—

almost like a dome. Her power raged at it uselessly.

"Come back to me! *Please!*" Desperately, she pressed her lips to his, begging him to fight, to not leave her.

One of his hands curled around hers, and her heart leapt, a sob of joyful relief escaping her lungs—

As Kase tore her hand away, his other hand found her throat and squeezed.

She gasped and choked, but his grip was too strong. She clawed at his hand. Her fingernails tore his flesh, but he didn't let go, didn't even flinch. Black blood ran in rivulets down Hallie's fingers, dripping like rain on the floor below.

"Please," she croaked. Her vision blurred, a dull haze creeping in. Even the golden light of her power couldn't push it back. "Kase...stop...s-stop...it's m...it's Hal..."

She couldn't do it. She couldn't speak.

She tried to force her power into him, anything, but he was like an impenetrable wall. His face contorted in rage. It made him look more like his father than he ever had.

What was the point of all this power if she couldn't use it to save the one she loved most?

Hallie couldn't breathe. Her throat swelled with pain, her lungs straining for breath that just wasn't there. She drew power up and into her hands, but all she could do was scratch weakly at his wrist. The nearly healed cut on her hand opened once more.

"Please," she mouthed with no voice.

She sensed someone come up behind her, but she couldn't see them, not really. Would Kase go after them next?

Not Kase. Jagamot. Kase was...

Kase was...

Tears welled in her eyes, pain and grief and abject, miserable *failure.*

She had done this to save him—and she had *failed.*

How did one die in Valora? Would her body fade away? Would she reappear beside her corpse, unable to rejoin it? Or would she simply move on to whatever awaited next? Loffler's hadn't disappeared. Neither had Mr. Gray's.

The darkness smothered her thoughts, a heaviness settling over her like a quilt. She could no longer see anything at all. Only one thing remained, a kernel of gold at the very end of a long, lightless tunnel.

"I...love...you."

And then she was gone.

C H A P T E R 5 1

WE'LL STAY

Kase

THE BATTLE RAGED IN KASE'S chest, his mind, his body, his very soul. All of him burned—from his skin to his soul, it was all ablaze.

It hurt so blasted much. He needed to give in, to make it all go away. He would no longer feel his pain and his sorrow and the agonizing darkness.

It would be a relief, a washing away, a new start.

Maybe it would kill him, whatever was happening to him. Maybe he could just let go and live in that beautiful meadow forever, the one filled with daisies, blue mountains in the background.

But Hallie wouldn't be there with him.

Her face swam before his eyes, crying and pleading with him. She glowed like the lights of a thousand stars. The last few months had been riddled with missteps and sorrow and mistakes, but she'd stood with him through it all. She was his truth, his forever, his very heart. He couldn't give up. Not when she still believed in him. Not when she still needed him.

The pain spiked as if he'd been the one decapitated with the sword. His head was going to explode.

Just give in. Give into the rage. Give into the agony. Embrace the void.

He teetered on the cliff, his fingers clinging to the edge. They ached. He gripped harder.

He'd fought for so long. He'd done his best—his best just wasn't good enough.

It had never been.

It never would be.

Sorrow and anguish had defined nearly every step of his existence. He'd never been given a chance in this life. Why should he even try to resist whatever this was? Jagamot? It couldn't be worse than the life he'd been handed. What did he have to fight for?

But if he gave in, he lost Hallie.

No.

Kase would not give in. Would not let go, not of her.

If he hadn't screamed for Skibs as Eravin shot power at Hallie, they would be dead. If Kase hadn't killed Eravin, he would've destroyed the world. If he hadn't been part of the induction ritual, he never would've saved Laurence Hixon's life.

Three things he had saved, not ruined.

The pain lessened.

If Zeke hadn't died, Kase never would have learned how to move on, that it was okay to do so. If Ana hadn't died, he would've never learned compassion. If Kase hadn't grown up in the Shackley family, he never would have learned strength.

Three things that could have broken him. Three ways they'd made him stronger instead.

The dark swirling power clouding his eyes lightened.

If he'd never been born, he would've never met Hallie.

Kase was more than a collection of screw-ups. He was more than his grief.

NO.

He would no longer allow it to dictate anything and everything he did. Kase Shackley would live, and he would live free.

The presence within him screamed, and the scorching pain of it nearly split his skull.

"I. Will. Not. Give. In."

The fire in his veins pressed harder.

"I...*refuse*...to bow...to you!"

And just like that, as if it had never been there at all...the pain evaporated.

He opened his eyes to a world clearer than any he'd seen in some time.

His vision was no longer clouded with shadows and pain and an endless abyss.

Ash drifted down; dying flames roared around him, above him. He looked down at his hands. Deep scratches crisscrossed his skin. Fresh blood—black and deep crimson—ran down his fingers. Had he done that? Or was it Eravin's blood? The ground beside him was coated in blood like black tar. The scratches on his hands were deep, jagged. The torn flesh stung.

His eyes travelled from his hands to the body lying in a pool of black blood, the flames surrounding them reflected in its depths. Her hair was like the deepest fire, the braid coming loose and soaking in the gore. A necklace of purple fingerprints hung around her throat. The hand bearing Ana's ring draped limply across her stomach. Her eyes were closed, light brown lashes dusting her freckled cheeks. Her pale lips parted slightly as if frozen in a soft sigh.

"Hallie?" The voice was so small, he almost didn't recognize it as his.

Nothing. She didn't move.

A fierce wave of nausea rocked him.

"Hal—Hallie? *Hallie*?"

The tingles began in his fingers and surged throughout his entire body. Pins and needles, hot and cold. The pins became knives. He couldn't work his throat or his voice or even his fingers right. Hands shaking, desperation stealing the breath from his lungs, he dragged himself to her side and scooped her up, clutching her limp body to his chest.

"Hal—" Her name broke on his lips. "Please no. Please, stars, no."

She wasn't breathing. He couldn't feel her breathing.

He cupped her cooling cheek. Panic whined in his head like an overheating hover, white-hot and wailing until he couldn't hear his own thoughts.

"Wake up," he begged. Like he'd begged her after Skibs

had fallen from the sky, but she'd been breathing then, she'd been warm then, and this... "Come on, Hals, wake up."

Her head only lolled to the side onto his arm. Too cold. If he'd had the blanket from his hover, he could've made her warm again. He didn't have it. He didn't have anything.

He couldn't fix this.

He hugged her to his chest and wept tears so hot, so heavy, he was going to drown in them. He pressed his forehead to hers.

"Sorry," he rambled, rocking back and forth. Half trying to rouse her, half afraid to break her in more ways than he already had. "I'm sorry, I'm...please?" She hated when he was rude, always had, couldn't stand it when he acted like an entitled *helviter*... "Sorry, please, Hallie. Please wake up."

Please, not her. Take me. Take my very soul—some of it, half of it, all of it. I don't blasting care.

He pressed her hand to his lips, kissing the ring he'd given her—the metal warm, as if stolen from her, his tears spilling over her too-cold fingers, and his blood dripping onto the band. Her blood from some unknown cut on her hand mixed with his. If his uncle could give his soul to cold, dead metal, why couldn't Kase give his to Hallie? He didn't care what it did to him. He'd go to the gallows for her. He'd do *anything*.

Please.

The fire wall surrounding them shattered into a million tiny dust particles.

"Kase!" someone yelled, trying to tug him away from her, but he resisted. He would not let her go. He would never let her go. "Kase! Let Navara help!"

Someone wrenched his arms away from Hallie, but she didn't fall; she slumped against another arm, one that guided her out of his lap. He fought with all his might, screaming or sobbing her name, he couldn't tell which—but he was too weak. He couldn't see clearly through the tears. Her weight was gone. It was too cold without her in his arms. They couldn't take her. He had to keep her warm.

"You didn't mean to. It was Jagamot. You didn't mean to," chanted Skibs in his ear. He, too, couldn't control his emotions. Tears choked his own words as he held Kase back.

The golden light flashing in front of his eyes helped clear them enough so he could see the woman before him.

Her mostly dark hair had come free, flowing down her back. She was bloody all over, and her arm was missing below the elbow, but she'd survived. Navara threw dust over Hallie, singing an almost familiar song. She was trying to save Hallie the way Kase could not. Trying to undo what Kase had done.

He'd done it. He'd killed her.

Those were *his* fingerprints on her neck.

He'd been fighting the invisible darkness. He'd won, but the cost had been too high.

Not her. Please.

He didn't know to whom he pleaded, to Jagamot or the Gate, to Clara's god or some other one, or to his own mind. He just needed her to be okay.

Skibs released him. He crawled over and took Hallie's hands, rubbing them, kissing them to warm them up. "I'm sorry. I'm so sorry."

Navara leaned over and kissed Hallie's brow. She pulled back. "She's alive, but not for much longer." She took a shuddering breath. "The damage...the damage from...I healed her windpipe. I cannot be sure of...her mind." Navara whispered another spell over Hallie. Kase could only stare at his hands, suddenly sickened by the sight of them strangling her fingers. But he couldn't bring himself to let go, either.

"But if you healed her, why—"

"There is also a rift in the veil that holds her soul," Navara interrupted gently. "It is too deep for me to heal, even with the renewal of the Chronal Gate."

Kase barely heard the words. He pulled Hallie back into his lap, holding her tightly. Her head lay on his shoulder, and tears slid down his face and into the collar of his blood-spattered shirt. She was warmer, a little. But she didn't wake.

He'd done that.

He'd promised to protect her, to take care of her.

He'd killed her.

How could he look Stowe in the eye ever again—how could he bring her back to her mother and brother like this?

Before him, golden and blue light sparkled around a glittering archway. Both colors danced on Hallie's blood-stained blouse. Her blood. His blood. Black blood.

"It needs a guardian," Skibs said from above him. "I can do it, but I'll need you to make sure..."

"No. *I* will become the guardian," Navara said, reaching

into her pocket and taking out a folded, slightly crumpled piece of parchment. "I've always known my destiny was not my own. I have run long enough. It is time I embrace it."

The air still burned with the scent of ashamox, and with each second, the dark entity closing in on the shimmering, blazing archway before them continued to expand.

"Give this to Jack Walker, please." Navara set the parchment in Skibs' hand. "We must finish this before Jagamot manifests once more."

Kase could barely focus on anything, the ice dripping through his blood making him want to shiver. But he could only hold Hallie tighter. Pray harder.

Please. Please.

Navara bent and kissed Hallie's head once more. "I am sorry, little one. You fought well."

She then walked to the Gate, the ashamox still writhing above them. Jagamot had failed to use Kase to manifest, but he awaited another opportunity to try. For all Kase knew, someone else in Kyvena was now fighting the same battle he had. The next second it could be Ben. It could be Kase again.

He didn't know if he would triumph a second time.

"I'm here, Hallie," he whispered into her hair, his voice shaking and uneven. "I will always be here. I'm not leaving you."

He kissed her hand again, noticing the odd blue sheen of Ana's ring. He held it closer to his face. It must've been a reflection from the Gate. Unless...maybe he'd been able to pour some of himself into it?

He looked at Hallie's face, analyzing the curves of her cheeks, the slope of her nose with the small knot in the center. He'd never gotten to ask how she'd broken it.

She was still pale. He couldn't tell if she was breathing yet. Navara had healed her windpipe, but had it been in time?

The anguish waged war on his soul, so potent it was like Jagamot had slunk back into his mind. His hands shook.

Resist. Don't give in.

I refuse to bow to you.

Navara stepped up to the center of the Gate, the light bathing her in a discordant glow. She placed a hand on the side and looked up into the rippling smoke that grew more furious the longer she waited. The two swords floated in the center, awaiting a third. "Raern knew, and now I do as well."

And then she walked through the center of the archway into the light.

Just like that. Without looking back.

Skibs stuck his hand in afterward, his fingers splayed between the swords of soul and shadow, saying something Kase couldn't hear. It struck him with déjà vu. It had been only a few months since he'd done the same thing to the Gate in Myrrai. He'd traded Saldr's brother for a sword. This time, it was Navara.

"Ka…Kase?"

Kase's heart stilled. Soft tufts of breath tickled the tiny hairs on his neck. Too soft. Too weak. But he felt them.

He shifted Hallie in his arms and tore his eyes away from the Gate. Slivers of golden brown peeked out at him from beneath heavy lids. Her skin still felt like ice against his. Or maybe he was cold, and he was just holding her too tightly to tell where he ended and she began.

Her lips, chapped and pale, tinted blue, barely moved. But they *moved*. "Kase."

He began to weep like a child. And he didn't even care.

"I'm here, oh stars, I'm here." *Thank you, thank you, thank you.* "Can you hear me?"

"I'm so…tired." Her voice was raspy and raw.

More tears slipped down his nose. He scrubbed them away with his sleeve. "Navara said it's your soul. It's bleeding out. Like Anderson's and Niels'. She said you're not going to…" He rubbed his wet cheek on the shoulder of his jacket. He wouldn't say it. He wouldn't believe it. "I'm sorry, I…I didn't know…I would never ever do anything to hurt…"

But he couldn't get the rest of it out. His jaw wobbled too much. It was a lie, anyway—his blasted fingerprints were bruised into her neck. How could he say he would never do anything to hurt her when he already had?

She blinked, sluggish, sleepy. He held his breath until her eyes opened again. "I know."

"But I…I can't…Hals, I'm so sorry, I'm so sorry." He was breathing too shallowly. Each inhale sounded like a hiccup, and he couldn't stop it.

Another blink, and a tear slipped down her pale cheek. "Y-yes."

"What?"

"Should've said…yes." Her chest shuddered, fighting for

every breath. "Marry...you."

His heart didn't crack this time—both sides wrenched apart, sundering completely from one another. Maybe his soul was bleeding, too. He shook his head. "No, you were right. You're always right."

She smiled, and her breathy laugh made him want to sob again. "Wh-who are you, and what did you—"

Her lungs seized up with a cough, wracking her frail body. He smoothed her hair with a shaking hand. "Shh. I'm going to get you home."

"No..."

"If I can get you to Saldr, maybe...maybe he can do something. Anything. Just let me take you home," Kase pleaded. "I did this, and I'm going to fix it. I promise I will."

Out of the corner of Kase's eye, Ben pulled a sword from the Gate. It was long and sturdy, the blade blindingly bright, the purest Zuprium Kase had ever seen. He held it out, the Gate's light setting his hair ablaze like a crown. The other two swords fell to the cathedral floor with a clatter.

"Kase..."

He turned his attention back to Hallie, rubbing his thumb along her cheekbone. Why was everything so cold? Were they both dying? He couldn't, not until he got her home, not until he saved her. He shivered, hard, holding her to him.

She struggled to swallow, but after a moment, she finally got the words out, though it was as if her throat wasn't working properly.

He'd done that. He tightened his hold on her waist. "What is it?"

"Already...home."

"No, you're not staying here, you're not dying—"

"Kase." A tear snake down her face. He kissed it away and pressed his forehead to hers. Her lips barely moved as she said, "*You*...are my...home."

His tears fell onto her face, mixing with her own.

"This is...good." Her lips tugged, almost smiling in spite of her tears. "Just...be here. Stay here. Please?"

He'd never leave her. But how could he just sit here while she was...

How could he let her go?

"Vrali anora ess kinl nah!" Skibs shouted.

Kase jerked his head up to see Skibs thrusting the new sword back into the Gate. Light burst from the center of the archway. Kase shielded Hallie from it, tucking her against his chest. A shockwave rocked the cavern cathedral, knocking them over. He cushioned her fall and took a knock on the head.

He gritted his teeth against the pain. A second and third shockwave rolled over them like the waves of a raging sea. He held Hallie so they wouldn't fall apart.

The quaking stopped.

Earsplitting screeches echoed in the cavern. It wasn't him, nor Hallie, nor Skibs.

It was the smoke.

Kase peeked up. The bulbous, foul-stenched mass roiled and writhed. It fought its fate, but the light was too strong. Another blinding flash burst from the Gate.

The ashamox screeched out one last death throe before silence fell.

Kase's head still ached from where he'd hit it, but he pushed himself to his elbow, still holding Hallie to him. The Gate's light faded to gold, the blue disappearing completely. Suspended in the center like an angelic wraith hung Navara's sword, its pommel gemstone a diamond.

Skibs stumbled over and fell to his knees beside Kase. "Are you all right? I think...I think we did it."

His breaths came heavy, and sweat dripped like rain down his face. It was as if he'd run miles, though he'd only walked fifteen feet. His eyes were awash with the Gate's glow, reminding Kase that Ben was more like himself than he'd known, yet so different at the same time.

Kase held Hallie's hand. The ring still had a soft blue glow. It wasn't the reflection from the Gate. Had he...?

No, surely not. He looked back at Skibs. "How? How did you do it? I thought it was the swords, or...or Hallie had to reset the Gate in Myrrai."

Skibs nodded to the woman in Kase's arms. "She figured it out. Creating a new Gate with my power and hers...it worked. Technically, we did combine all the Essence powers." He gestured back to where the two other swords lay, the Gate's light reflecting off their blades. "In a way." He laid a hand on Kase's shoulder. "You did well."

Not well at all. He'd defeated his own darkness, only to

find he'd hurt the person he loved most in the world.

Skibs pushed himself to his feet and walked to Eravin's corpse. Another victim of Kase's rage. He gritted his teeth against the wave of pain, terror, and relief warring within him.

Glaring down at the shell of the man, Skibs muttered, "For Kase, I'll give you a Yalven Burning. You don't deserve it for what you did to my home, my family, and nearly did to me." Skibs snapped his fingers. Tongues of fire leapt from them and encompassed the body and blood beneath it.

In moments, it was gone. But it didn't entirely feel different. The boy who had lost everything had been gone for a while. He'd died years ago, replaced with a bitter man who would never be able to overcome his grief. Kase hadn't really known that man.

Kase swallowed hard. That had almost been him.

Skibs did the same to Stradat Loffler, whom Kase had forgotten about in the fight.

"I'll be around the corner," Skibs said after he extinguished the flames from both pyres with another snap of his fingers. "Let me know if…let me know when you're ready."

Kase shook as Skibs walked away from them, another light at his fingertips. Hallie had healed him, he'd said. He'd been a prisoner in his own head for months, yet now, he was almost like the man he'd known before the *Eudora* mission. But even before he'd taken on the Essence, he'd had a light about him that no one could've given him. It came from within. Learning what Kase had in the past day or so, it was amazing Skibs could function at all. He'd grown up without a father, deemed illegitimate and treated as such. He'd lost his mother young, assassinated by Jayde for the sake of a secret.

And now? Now, he was King of Cerulene and had found a family he hadn't known he had—Kase, Les, and Jove.

If he could do it, so could Kase. Hadn't he been on that path before this?

It'd been Hallie who'd taught him how to fight. It'd been her strength and the light that pushed away the darkness.

If she died now, would he fall back into that all-encompassing grief?

She wouldn't want him to. She'd want him to live.

It was too hard. Impossible. But he would do it. He'd

never meet someone else with her fervor for life, her tenacity, her trust in him—but he'd have to be okay with that. He would have to learn to live with the guilt he was the reason she was no longer there.

But he would see her again in the ever after.

He wouldn't know when that would be, but he would wait for it.

He'd promised to find her in every timeline, and that included the end of all things.

She was his fate.

"All right," he whispered, even though it killed him. "We'll stay."

He barely got the words out.

It was still cold in the cavern cathedral, but with each minute that passed, feeling came back to his fingers and toes. The sword in the Gate flickered, but it didn't disappear. It was quiet. Hallie's labored breathing and the soft hum emanating from the Gate were the only sounds that met his ears.

He shut his eyes tight, setting his forehead against hers. Waiting, dread choking him, for her to draw her last breath.

He would hold her until he couldn't physically do so any longer. She wouldn't be alone. He clenched his teeth as another wave of grief rolled over him. She hadn't acknowledged him or responded at all since the Gate ritual had concluded. White hot fear burned through him, and he hugged her harder. He looked down. He expected to see her take her last rattling breath.

But instead, something changed.

Hallie stirred a little in his arms. He jumped, pulling back, focusing on her completely.

Her eyes were open again, their honey color on brilliant display. The corner of her lips quirked up. They were pink, not white, not blue.

He blinked. Her skin was no longer cold to the touch. A soft flush splashed across her cheeks. The bruises on her neck didn't stand out as much, almost like...

Almost like they were fading.

"Hals?"

Shaking, she brought her hand up to trace her fingers along the outline of his jaw, letting the catch on the stubble there. She brushed her thumb over his lips. "Looks like you saved me again, Master Pilot."

He shook his head, his eyes stinging. He couldn't get a full breath. "No, I killed you. I—" He choked on the emotions in his chest. "You're—I—"

She pressed her index finger to his lips before holding up her hand, the one with her ring. "You did this, didn't you?"

It still glowed a soft blue if smeared with blood. In the daylight, the light might not even be visible, but in this dusky cave, the only light coming from the Gate, it shone.

He opened his mouth and closed it again.

He'd said he'd give up his soul; some, half, all.

He'd thought the cold came from shock, from blood loss, from the horror of watching Hallie slip away…from anything besides what it was.

The ring had accepted the Soul he'd poured into it without him even knowing it. He'd never thought it'd actually work.

Hallie looked at him like he was the hero of a storybook tale. He'd defeated the dragon, the man bent on destroying the world, and had brought her back from the brink of death.

He stared at the ring. He wasn't sure how he'd done it. Desperately, he'd prayed, but he'd not expected it to work. Those prayers were the ramblings of a man clinging to what he could. But there was no denying the Soul Tech at work. Hallie lived and breathed in his arms. She was getting stronger, not weaker.

She smiled softly, slowly. "Guess we can thank your uncle for that. And that Gate."

"But I…I…I don't understand. I don't deserve…"

He couldn't even put a sentence together.

She brushed her fingers over his cheek again. "I forgive you, Kase. It wasn't you…" she trailed off for a moment. She paused as if rethinking her assessment and forgiveness. Kase's fingers shook. Then her eyes found his again. "You gave me your soul, part of it," Hallie said, her words choked. "Like the story, like Xera and Kainadr. It's true."

A few tears bubbled over the ledges of her eye and cascaded down her cheek. Kase wiped them away with his thumb.

"Whether you like it or not," Hallie whispered, "you're stuck with me. Maybe we'll even leave swords behind."

Kase didn't understand, not really, and maybe he never would. But he didn't care.

He'd accepted her death. He'd accepted he would live the rest of his days alone, but with the hope of finding her in the end.

Surely his brain was playing tricks on him. He'd scoffed about the story of the souls when Saldr had told it to them. Sharing souls only happened in stories.

But her fingers on his cheek were real.

She forgave him, and in time, he might be able to forgive himself.

He gazed deep into her eyes, and he was very much in danger of drowning in their depths. He wouldn't mind. He would stay there forever.

He wouldn't ever let her go. He'd never let her fall. He'd protect her to his last breath.

He drew her in and hooked one finger underneath her chin, tilting her face to his. He leaned forward, brushing his nose with hers.

Warmth. Tingling in his chest.

The pause was tense and one little breath could shatter it.

"I love you, Hallie Walker, and I'd do anything to keep you, even if you took my entire soul."

She could. It was hers to take.

"You are my forever, whether in this life or the next. I'm not perfect. I mess up more than most, but you've never given up on me. Not when we first met, not now."

He swallowed the lump that rose in his throat. Her breath trembled against his lips. "I want to cherish you, protect you, and start a family with you. I want to love you even when we find ourselves in the beyond."

Last time, he'd been sure. He'd known he wanted to be with her, had known she'd ruined every other woman for him. She was the sunshine to his summer day, the stars to his winter night...but the world had been on the brink, uncertain and braced for impact.

Now, there was nothing to hold them back, not even himself.

He teased her lips with his, brushing them softly as he whispered, "Marry me, Hals, please."

Her breath hitched, and she brushed his cheek with the back of her fingers. Her lips parted in a smile that teased him, begging for him to kiss her until she no longer remembered her name.

"Yes."

He'd kissed her before, but none of them compared to the feeling of her lips pressing to his right then. The storybooks always talked about sparks and fire, but this was an inferno, and he was consumed by the blaze. With it, the cracks in his heart welded back together. He'd never let her go. He didn't have to. She was his, he was hers. Forever.

Kase was finally free.

C H A P T E R   5 2

JOVE HARLAN SHACKLEY

Clara

EVEN THOUGH THEY HADN'T LEFT the capital, the landscape was utterly foreign to Clara after so much time spent in the Catacombs. It was almost as if she'd been living in another world, and the city that had been her home for the past five years was now a barely remembered dream. It took her too long to navigate the streets she'd once traversed by motorcoach. Debris littered the alleyways and lanes. Entire buildings had been blown apart, their white and wooden bones scattered like dead leaves across her path. As she guided her mother through the city and held her son close to her chest, she just wished it would all end.

It still didn't seem real that she'd survived the first attack; that the graves she now walked on could have been hers. Her son's. Her husband's.

She'd been fortunate not to Burn loved ones in the last weeks, but she wasn't sure if her luck would hold out much longer. Tragedy seemed to follow her like a hawk to its prey.

Adrenaline was the only thing keeping her on her feet

as her lips burned with the memory of the last kiss she'd given her husband. She hadn't wanted to leave him there amid such danger and uncertainty. She'd done that before, and it had nearly killed them both.

But even after everything, she trusted Jove with her whole heart. Samuel needed her, and she would protect him at all costs. She would deal with what came after as best she could, for everything would come together as it should—whether she were in the line of fire or not.

"Why are we leaving?" her mother asked, her skirts billowing around her as she ran through the streets behind her daughter. Even in the face of a refugee camp, her mother refused to wear more practical trousers.

Clara couldn't explain, not really. Her mother had been immensely helpful these last weeks while Clara searched for Jove or helped where needed, but that didn't mean she would understand the fear and dread thrumming through Clara's veins.

"I need to get Samuel out of the city—get *you* out of the city. Jove says something dangerous is coming. We need to go to Father."

Her words were true, but they still felt hollow.

"We won't find a carriage to take us anywhere," her mother pointed out, her breaths ragged. She'd been a proper lady before the attack on the capital. She wasn't alone in that description; Clara's lungs also burned with the effort of climbing toward the city gates, but at least she wasn't tangled in her skirts. The doors hung open, unrepaired from the destruction wrought weeks ago. Just past them, a green valley riddled with cave-ins and detritus from the bombing awaited.

Would they even survive if they left the city? Who knew what waited for them out there? Her father and her family estate were far to the south, but they could find a carriage in one of the outlying villages. She hoped.

Yes. They had no choice. They would survive. Her son would survive.

"If we can make it to one of the outlying villages before nightfall, then..." Clara trailed off as a bedraggled soldier stumbled into view out of the gatehouse, one arm reaching up to shield Samuel, the other out to stop her mother. She sent up a quick prayer for favor, for mercy.

She hadn't thought the gates would be manned. Not

now. There was too much going on, and something was happening down in the Catacombs—something Jove had gone to fight.

She'd left him.

Clara breathed through her nose, trying to calm her racing heart. They had both made logical decisions. They would find a way. Clara put her trust in a higher power. He was in control—not her.

There wasn't anything alarming about the man other than the state of his uniform, but she couldn't blame him for that. It was a miracle enough she could recognize the emblem on his chest.

"No one's to leave the city," the man's deteriorating voice ground out. It sounded as if he hadn't drunk water in weeks. His leg dragged behind him as he hobbled closer. "Word went out not two hours ago."

Clara tightened her hold on her son and blocked her mother from view best she could. She wasn't a fighter, but she would do whatever was needed to make sure her son was safe, and at the moment, that meant getting him out of the city. She would talk this soldier into letting her out. And if she couldn't talk, she'd fight—however she could.

She had no weapon.

Maybe she should find another way over the wall. She could certainly find her way back to the Catacombs and leave through another entrance or even one of the holes.

"Who gave those orders?" she asked.

It hadn't been Harlan. He'd been busy with Kase's attack and then interrogating Benjamin Reiss in the hospital ward. He'd been trying to solve the mystery of the sword in Hallie Walker's sketchbook.

The man limped closer, and Clara stepped back, turning to protect Samuel. Her eyes darted to the right and left, looking for anything to defend herself with. She wasn't sure if she should tell the man who she was. Using her husband's name might allow her passage, but there was something abnormal about the man's eyes. They seemed darker than they should be, but he was mostly shaded by the gatehouse.

His skin was too pale even for a white man. Possibly a byproduct of living underground the last few weeks, but something about the color reminded her of spoiled milk. Suspicion sent her stepping back as the man crept closer, his head tipped oddly.

"Orders from the top," was all the man said.

Clara's back met a wall. The brick pressed into her shoulder blades as the man approached, lurching like a drunkard. Her mother stepped in. "My name is Lady Miravel Davey, noble of this country, and my daughter is the wife of Jove Shackley, son of the Stradat Lord Kapitan. We have all the authority we need to leave this city."

Brave woman, but Clara gritted her teeth against the fear now flowing freely through her body.

The man sneered, sticking a hand inside his jacket. "Don't listen to him anymore."

Clara slid herself across the wall. To the right, the lane was mostly clear. To the left, blocked. Whether this man was a deserter or a traitor or simply out of his mind, she didn't know. All she knew was that they needed to either keep him talking long enough to distract him or run the other way, back to what semblance of civilization still existed. His leg injury would hinder any chase.

"Then who do you answer to, young sir?" her mother asked, not cowed one bit. "Because I don't believe harassing women for simply trying to find safety is approved by any surviving members of the City Council. I've read the decrees myself."

He didn't answer. He lunged, whipping out a dagger from his jacket. Clara screamed.

Her mother gasped as the knife bit into her side. "Run, Clara!"

But all she could do was stare as the blood blossomed on her mother's skirts. As she collapsed.

Then the man turned on her, his knife slick with blood. A spiderweb of blackened veins licked up and down his neck. One of the patients who'd encountered the Yalvar fuel. Clara's chest caved in on itself. Samuel's cries split the air. Blood pooled on the cracked cobblestones beneath her mother, whose eyes were shut tightly in pain, her hands holding in what life she had left.

"Run, love, run!" her mother gasped.

A sob escaped her lips, but Clara did.

She sprinted toward the open right, clutching her baby to her chest. Footsteps pounded behind her. The man's leg had been a ruse or he simply didn't care about pain. Maybe there'd been another assailant waiting in the shadows. It didn't matter.

She was too slow. She was too slow. *She was too slow.*

Her body screamed with the effort of sprinting, but she didn't stop.

Whipping to the right at the first opportunity, she careered down the other lane. More debris lay strewn across it, but people were ahead, cleaning it up.

Her throat was tight with tears and exertion, but she managed to scream, "Help!"

One young man nearby, his warm bronze skin lighter than her own, looked up. His dark eyes, one of which had been recently blackened—probably in one of the numerous fights that had broken out in the Catacombs with all the feelings running high—found her, hand going to his waistband.

Clara sprinted toward him. Footsteps still pounded behind her, and a hand grabbed her shoulder, tugging on the wrap holding Samuel to her. She screamed, but the young man flew past her, flash pistol out and pointed at the man behind her.

A sharp, deafening crack shattered the air, the burning smell of metal hot and heavy. The hand left her shoulder. Clara hunched over her screaming son.

Her ears ached with the echoes of the pistolshot. Tears cascaded down her face. Her hands and legs shook.

The young man came back, a hand out to help her up. "He's.."

His wrist. Black veins.

Clara shook her head, scrambling backward only for her hand to fall into the hot puddle of blood from her earlier assailant. She staggered to her feet, scrubbing her hand frantically on her trousers.

She turned and ran.

The city burst open with a roar, thundering chaos in the form of amorphous gray forms shuttering into existence to her right and left. Maybe she'd left the realm of the living and entered some sort of horrible nightmare, but she didn't stop. Each pounding footstep she took, she prayed harder. Her body obeyed, its primal instinct to flee overtaking any thought of stopping.

She needed Jove.

Her mother was dying or dead.

She couldn't get out of the city.

Her ankle twinged, the one that she'd twisted the night of the attack, and it sent her listing sideways into the nearest wall. She twisted just in time to keep Samuel from slamming into the charred whitewashed stone.

Her ankle throbbed, and her shoulder screamed, but she steadied herself against the wall. She couldn't stop. A flash of metal underneath an overturned crate caught her eye.

There were no gray shapes or people in the alley with her. She still limped toward the metal. It might be a weapon, and she prayed it was a flashpistol, something she could use if forced.

Her fingers clasped the handle. Blue. The metal was blue.

She aimed for the sky and fired it.

Blue fire, and immense cold flowed over her.

She dropped the Cerl weapon, her hand blazing from its icy touch.

Samuel wailed, and Clara thrust herself against the wall, but no one came around the corner. No one seemed to care that she'd foolishly given her position away. She breathed heavily as she assessed where she might be. She wasn't sure just how far she'd run, nor was she sure how many turns she'd taken.

No street signs were posted on the buildings, but a few of the shops still had their own signs hanging from doorways—those that had survived. There were a few with only a door, no sign. Most had neither.

The nearest one was missing half of it, but she read, *Beckh—Boo—*

For some reason, the name sounded familiar, though she wasn't certain as to why. She looked around some more. She looked inside the store only to find ashes and a few scattered book pages. She looked further down the street. A row of townhouses and apartments, most missing walls or roofs, lay tucked around the bend.

Zeke. This was the road Zeke had lived on.

She knew where she was.

If she could just make it back to the nearby marketplace, she could find her way to the Jayde Center and back down into the Catacombs.

She fetched the pistol, a grimace on her face.

She could do this.

She would not let her panic assault her now.

Kissing Samuel's head and shushing him best she could, she left the protection of the doorway.

Jove

THE CATACOMBS WERE TOO EMPTY. Many of the lower city citizens had returned to the surface, but Jove hadn't expected the tunnels to echo so much as they traveled up through the passage from where he, Saldr, and his father had entered weeks ago.

It felt more like an eternity.

He needed to plan with the remaining City Council members now that his father was dead. With all of their cooperation, they could organize the city and find a way to rebuild. He'd need to contact the City Governors and others like his father-in-law, the Shield Marshal of southern Jayde. With the entire High Council dead, they were running blind.

First, they needed to handle the Cerls. Kase's patrols had been helpful in keeping the flyovers minimal, and with Correa's death, maybe the others would surrender. But that was only a hope, not a certainty.

If only Hallie Walker had restored the electricity, they would've been in much better shape. His father, for all his faults, had been a competent leader. He put his country first—just to the detriment of his family, but apparently, that had been the only way he could cope after so much loss. Now it was Jove's job.

Hopefully Miss Walker and Kase returned soon.

And hopefully the world wouldn't fall apart before they did.

Jove lost count of each step as he scaled the winding stone stairs, his lungs and legs struggling the further up he went. Saldr's glowing orb guided them up the spiraling staircase. Jove touched the Cerl pistol holstered at his waist. Surely he wouldn't need it.

He didn't want to use it, not knowing the secret behind it—the secret his uncle had delivered to the Cerl queen—but he didn't have a choice. He was rubbish with a sword. He wasn't his father, nor was he Zeke.

He was Jove Harlan Shackley, and he would find a way to make this right. He would do what he could for his country and his family.

He had his family to protect and lead.

The closer to the surface they hiked, rumbling and thumping sounded above. Muffled clangs and distant roars leaked through the wall. Tremors rocked the door above. It was almost as if Jove's ears were submerged in water.

Saldr looked back, fear widening his eyes. "Jagamot has come."

Jove's blood ran cold. "But I thought...wasn't Eravin..."

Saldr nodded but said, "In the Dawn, he had many forms and an army of shadows. I fear..."

Clara was up there. And if those sounds were what he thought they were...

Jove charged past Saldr, drawing the pistol at his waist and cocking it with one smooth motion. He wrenched open the door at the top. Cold air, anguished screams, and the wet, hot smell of blood slammed into him like an ocean wave.

He caught himself on the doorframe as his eyes took in the destruction.

The city hadn't yet recovered from the first attack, but what little progress they'd made had been undone. The screams of the dying rang even louder than they had that first time. There was no dragon today, but the gray shadows fighting alongside those with black veins crawling up their necks scared him more. A few necks boasted a triple diamond tattoo.

The back of Jove's throat burned with bile, and a shudder rent his body. He couldn't move, only stare at the horror in front of him. Saldr joined him, breathless. One of the shadow specters clawed at an older gentleman bleeding from the head and a gash in his neck. Thrusting his hand in his pouch, Saldr slung dust in their direction, shouting in Yalven.

Golden light burst from his hand and shot toward the shadow creature.

It burst into mist, and the older man slumped, the relief and pain overwhelming him.

Jagamot's shadow army.

Jove sprinted into the fray, his pistol firing into the gray, but his bullets only grazed the demons. They worked on the black-veined men and women, though.

A soldier with solid black eyes like Eravin Gray's turned the corner, his bloody sword waving in the air. Jove didn't think, only took aim at him and fired. No time to grieve the necessity, to feel any guilt. He needed to find his wife and son.

Where would they have gone? The townhouse? If Clara had been thinking straight, she would've tried to leave the city. Could she have made it to the front city gates? Jove swung in and out of the chaos, focused solely on finding a woman with brown skin and braids and a baby in her arms.

With each person he passed who wasn't his wife, his panic heightened. Was she already dead? The city was too large. He would never find her.

He should be grateful he hadn't found her in the piles of the dead. But not knowing where she was? It was worse. His heart hammered, and his stomach roiled.

Losing track of just how many shadows or others he killed, he fought through the city. He stole a dying soldier's sword. He was rubbish at swordplay, but it still made him feel better with two weapons instead of one. With the pistol in one hand, the sword in the other, he leapt over rubble and shot another one of those shadows. Blue fire zinged out and blasted a hole in the specter. It slowed him enough for Jove to careen by.

Bursts of gold mist dusted his peripheral vision. The Yalvs were doing their best to beat back the invaders, but would they be enough? He hadn't seen Saldr since they'd reached the surface, and he hadn't seen the healer, Kainadr.

Jove fought his way underneath the towering gates to the lower city and down the streets until he found himself in one of the larger market squares. The trampled and blackened awnings were the only evidence it had once been a thriving center of trade and culture.

Jove sprinted over dead flowers and broken glass bottles. The marketplace was a chaotic mess with shadows and citizens alike. Those not infected with the Yalvar fuel were fighting best they could, but they were almost inconsequential compared to whatever demon ran in their enemies' veins.

"Jove!"

His heart stopped as he wiped blood and sweat from his brow. He whirled around, his sword flashing in the air. He scanned the massive crowd.

"JOVE!"

Where was she?

His arm stung as a woman with black blood leaking from her mouth clawed at him. Jove shoved her away. He swiped his sword at one of the shadows and followed it with a blast from his pistol.

His way was clear. He leapt on an overturned cart.

Finally, he saw her. Samuel was strapped to her chest, and she was covered in blood. His heart thumped in his ears.

"Clara!"

That blood was fresh.

Ice-cold rage encompassed him as he leapt down, pistol firing into the crowd, sword swinging.

Now he knew exactly how his father had felt when Correa had attacked his mother. He would mow down anyone in his path to reach his wife.

He only saw red. The blood on her face, on her clothing, on her hands.

He would kill whoever was responsible for shedding that blood.

Someone shouted his name, but it wasn't Clara, and he didn't care. He needed to get to her. He shouted his rage with each thrust and each blast.

Finally, she only stood a few strides away from him.

Her eyes met his, so beautiful yet terrified, relieved yet hollow. His name was on her lips.

A soldier stepped in front of her, a trio of diamonds tattooed on his neck, his blond hair braided back. Cerl. He swung his pistol toward Clara, his finger on the trigger. Black blood filled the man's veins.

Clara fell to her knees, her body turning to shield Samuel.

Jove bellowed his fury and terror. *"Get the stars away from her!"*

With a speed he hadn't even realized he possessed, Jove whipped his pistol up and fired at the man.

His aim struck true, the blue fire nailing the man in his chest, but the man's pistol still fired. The twin echoing cracks were buried by the chaos at hand, but in Jove's mind, the second one deafened him.

His heart didn't beat.

His lungs didn't fill with air.

"Clara!" He tried to scream her name. Instead, her name wheezed out on the winds of death.

The Cerl slumped forward, the impact of Jove's shot dropping him like a stone. Jove fell to his knees, clawing his way to the last place he'd seen his wife and son. He was too slow, too clumsy, his legs refused to work properly. His fingers clawed at the cobblestones, his sword and pistol forgotten. Nails ripped from their beds as he urged himself to move faster.

He shoved the Cerl soldier's dead weight off her. Blood leaked from her side.

"No no *no!*" Jove pleaded, cupping his hands over the wound. Clara's glassy eyes wandered over him, her lips weakly moving in a silent prayer.

His hands left bloody fingerprints on her face, her chest, on Samuel's blanket. His son. Screaming. Jove checked him for any injury. Nothing he could see. Clara had shielded him.

"Is he—" she whimpered.

"He's all right." Jove's hands shook too hard to take his son out of the sling. He didn't know what to do. He couldn't just sit there and watch her die. All of his training had utterly fled his mind. If he didn't do something, she would bleed out. He didn't know how deep the wound went. All he could see was blood.

"Help me, please!" Jove shouted into the void, unsure of just who would answer. "*Help me!*"

Clara shook her head, and Jove picked her and Samuel up, holding them both to this chest. He kissed her temple, tears streaming down both their faces. "Hang on. Just hang on."

He could not live without her. He had to find help.

A wink of blue caught his attention—the Cerl's pistol a few feet away, halfway tucked under his cooling body.

If Clara died, would he use it on himself?

His heart pounded in his chest. He could. He would be with her in whatever life awaited beyond this one. He'd nearly lost her to his own stupidity before the Kyvena attack, and he'd barely survived then.

He'd lost Ana, Zeke, and his father. He might've lost Kase. He could not lose his wife.

Samuel's cries reached a fever pitch, breaking Jove out of his thoughts. Clara's tears fell silently down her face, but she couldn't comfort their son. "Take him. Help him, please."

"Clara—"

"He needs his father."

"He needs *you*!" Jove's voice cracked, raw and pleading. "*I* need you!"

"Jove, please." Her voice broke. "Take him."

Jove set her down softly, trying not to jostle her wound. He unwound his son from the wrap, cradling him close to his chest.

The baby's mouth gaped open, his eyes scrunched in terror or displeasure or hunger. Blood not his own smeared his cheek. Jove's tears washed it away as he pressed a kiss to his head. "Shh, shh. I've got you. It'll be okay. "

It wouldn't, but Jove didn't know what else to say.

Clara fell back into her silent prayers, and Jove pressed Samuel's wrap to her wound, trying in vain to stop the flow.

"Master Jove!" a voice said above him. "Move aside."

He shook his head. He would not leave her.

"*Anoheme ana hoiseh li Valihanora!*" the voice shouted above him. Golden dust ignited around him. "*Jir dremu hiassa li grer mara.*"

Everything burned. His ears ceased working. He couldn't see.

It was like he stood on the surface of the sun. He could barely feel Samuel's weight against his chest or Clara's form beneath his hands. He nearly lost hold on his reality.

And then it was over. The noise around him returned, and then Kainadr's face appeared before his. Jove blinked.

"I healed your wife," he said, so casually calm it bordered on absurd. "You can let her go."

Jove looked down at Clara, whose eyes had cleared, losing their glassy luster. Relief hit him like a summer rainstorm, and he let out a restrained sob. "Thank you."

You can let her go. No, he couldn't. He'd never let her go again.

Clara pushed herself up and tugged him to her. He kissed her, her lips desperate and salty from tears.

"Have faith, my love," she whispered into the kiss.

Jove couldn't answer, only nodded, pressing his forehead to hers. It was okay. She was okay.

He needed to get her *out* of this city.

Kainadr helped them up, throwing some dust out again, and in seconds, a sword materialized in his outstretched hand. 'Got to use it once, but turns out I really am merely gifted with the healing arts. Take it—I'm as likely to slice my own head off as someone else's. It will help with the shadows. Get your wife out of here."

If the situation hadn't been so dire, he might've laughed. Instead, Jove took the sword from him and nodded. "Let's go."

Clara swathed Samuel in her bloodstained wrap and clasped Jove's hand. Her fingers were warm and alive, safe and snug in his own. She was alive.

They took off from the market square.

Jove's free hand clung to Kainadr's sword, ready to swing at anyone who dared come close. No one would touch his wife again. "Where is your mother? If you can make it to Windwick or one of the other nearby hamlets, you should be able to wait it out until..."

Clara let out a muffled sob. Jove stopped, dropping her hand. "What? What happened?"

Clara shook her head, her face and clothing still covered in blood. She brought a hand to her mouth, tears spilling onto her cheeks. "The soldier...I can't...I tried..."

Shouting echoed off the lanes behind him, but he ignored it.

Jove had just pulled her into his arms—unsure what happened but knowing it was bad—when white-hot pain struck him from behind. He cried out, careening forward. Clara screamed, catching him, holding him steady. His vision sputtered, flitting in and out, her face swimming before him. He fell to his knees

More shouting erupted behind him. Jove turned just enough to see Kainadr picking up the sword he'd just given Jove, swinging it with all the strength he had at one of the gray shadows, but the shadow was faster. It dodged the sword, and before Kainadr could recover, the shadow struck hard. Blood spurted from his stomach, and the Yalv went limp. The shadow wrenched its hand back out. Kainadr collapsed.

Clara screamed again. Jove fought against the lightning

pain in his back. He didn't know if Kainadr could survive that, but he would not let that thing kill his wife and child. The ground beneath him was slick with blood, too slick—his hands kept slipping as he tried to shove himself up.

Before he could fight his way to his feet, a rolling crack of thunder rent the air and threw him back to the ground. His head hit the cobblestones hard, and his head rang with the impact. Pain radiated through his skull and rattled his teeth. Another wave of energy crackled and blasted apart the shadow above him. A third wave had him heaving.

And then it was done.

He couldn't breathe deep enough, and Clara sobbed his name above him, trying to push him onto his side and stem the flow of the blood leaking out his back. His nerves sparked like loose wires, chills erupting over his feverish skin. Nausea rose in his stomach, and it took everything in him not to heave again. His body couldn't take it.

Weakness drifted through his limbs, and the thudding pulse in his ears slowed its rhythm. His vision sputtered and fizzed, gray at the edges.

Was this what it felt like to die?

He squeezed his eyes tight. No. Not like this. Not here, not now. Samuel and Clara needed him. He would not leave them here with no one to protect them. He refused to give in. Not yet.

He had more to live for.

Ironic he had to be dying to realize that.

He wrenched his eyes open and pressed hard against the nausea and weakness. The shapes above him were blurry and unfocused one second, snapped into clarity the next, then phased out again. Another face had joined Clara's in hovering over him, a man Jove vaguely recognized but couldn't place. The blond man had a gnarly cut above his eye, dark red blood mixed with clotted brown covering half his face, but his brown eyes were clear and free of black ink. "You Kase's brother?"

His ears felt full of water, and it took him a few extra seconds to realize what the man said.

Burning pain in his back had him silent save for the groan. A few more seconds and he gasped out, "Yes, but I don't know if that's a good or bad thing."

"Depends who you ask, I'd wager." The man's accent—

from the Nardens, he thought. It was hard to place with all the ringing in his ears. "What's hurt?"

Clara smoothed the hair back from his brow. "The shadow being hit him with something. I don't know how to…"

The blond man rummaged in a nearby pack. "Name's Niels Metzinger, and I owe Kase a favor." He pulled out bandages and a sewing kit. "I'll get you stitched up for now, and later, you can have a real medic take a look."

He fished out a flask and, without any preamble, splashed alcohol into the wound. Jove's vision went white, and he bucked against the pain.

"Sorry 'bout that," said the man, not sounding too sorry whatsoever, "but you oughta be just fine once you stop bleeding everywhere." The man rubbed some sort of cloth over the wound, and Jove nearly bit through his lip. This *Niels* claimed he owed Kase a favor, but this felt more like someone exacting vengeance meant for his brother out on Jove's flesh instead. Maybe he should have lied. "Not too deep, but enough to let you attend your own funeral if you can handle the pain."

Despite the man's odd assurances—at least, he thought they were supposed to be assurances—the damage felt like it went clean through his chest. The man handed him another cloth. "Bite down on this."

Jove was almost insulted, sure he could've handled the pain, but then—oh *stars and shocks*, this was worse than breaking his arm across Harlan's desk.

With each poke of the needle, Jove screamed into the cloth clenched between his teeth. Each jab sent a bolt of lightning throughout his entire body. Cold sweat gushed from his pores, but it did nothing to cool the jagged white fire pulsing from the stitching. Each pull-through and tightening of the thread was agony. His vision blanked again.

He must've passed out because the next thing he knew, the blond man—Niels—was gone, and Jove's head rested in Clara's lap. She stroked soaked hair at his temple, her fingertips both hot and cold at once.

"You're awake," she breathed.

The throbbing in his back promised him the pain wouldn't fade for a long while. It wasn't acute and all-consuming any longer, but any movement stretched the skin, creating a line of fire licking up his torso. He sucked in a breath and clenched his teeth.

"Love, you can rest for a while more. A few of the Yalvs are going around and helping those who are worse off. They'll help move you when you're ready," she said softly. Jove looked up at her, dazedly marveling at the sunset glowing in her midnight eyes. Samuel was quiet.

Was it truly over? Had they been victorious? Or was this battle only a precursor of something even worse to come?

Jove forced himself to rise, and even with Clara's help, the pain almost had him begging for a stiff drink. He ground his teeth until he was sitting up. Clara helped set his back against the cottage wall behind them. He gingerly tugged her under his arm and held her close to his uninjured side. Samuel squirmed, seemingly oblivious to the chaos he'd just survived.

If only Jove could be so carefree.

Maybe one day, he would be.

"I'll need to help them soon. They need someone to lead them," Jove said, his voice gruff from the trauma of the last few hours. "But for now, it's good to be here with you."

C H A P T E R   5 3

SEVEN AND A HALF MINUTES

Hallie

IN THE BRIGHT LIGHT OF day, the Nether Gate's opening was only visible by the dark Catacombs on the other side. The fiery outline that had nearly blinded her when she'd revealed it with Navara's journal was almost nonexistent on this side. Ben's hand still glowed from summoning it back into existence, his fingers wrapped tightly around the hilt of Xera's sword. It would be replaced once they were on the other side.

By the time she'd recovered enough to walk on her own, it'd been too dark to make the trip down the mountain even with the lights her and Ben's power would've provided. There was nothing in the night to spirit away souls with Jagamot defeated. Hallie hoped it was enough to signal to Jack and her parents that everything was okay.

She, Kase, and Ben spent the night bathed in the light of the Chronal Gate and a larger Yreasa. She'd said her goodbyes to Navara, pressing a bit of her Essence power into the arch. She was rewarded with a pleasant pulse of warmth in her core.

Navara's journals had gotten her here and allowed Jagamot to be defeated. The resentment she'd felt toward the woman for burdening her with the Essence power fell away. Their destinies had been intertwined, and without her, Hallie might have never gotten to see Jack again. It was bittersweet.

As the night went on, Ben and Kase—neither of whom seemed eager to sleep—entertained her with dozens of stories from their days as trainee pilots. The tales ranged from pulling pranks on other greenies to near-misses on missions to the full explanation of how they'd ended up with matching misshapen dragon tattoos.

They could have sat up all night trading jokes about hovers that flew straight over her head for all she cared. After the ordeal of the past few hours…days…months, really, it was just nice to sit tucked up next to Kase and laugh.

The dark cloud of the unknown that had hung over her head for so long dissipated with each inside joke and shared look.

When Ben fell asleep after making Kase swear he'd wake him in a few hours, the tone turned steeply somber as Hallie finally got the full story of why Kase had brought his father's sword through the Nether Gate. She curled against his chest and held him through the worst of it. His world had flipped completely upside down, and the hits hadn't stopped coming.

But she'd always seen Kase's inner strength, and now, he could see it too.

Hallie had waited to speak, letting him get it all out, but she'd wiped away the solitary tear that escaped his hold when he spoke about his father's final moments, his conflicting feelings, and the life he would now lead.

But now, in the afternoon light of the next day, it was time to say goodbye to Valora. They'd eaten an ashy late breakfast at the tavern, the bartender with the deep blue eyes and solemn voice whipping up orange juice and his best recreation of the old chef's bacon, egg, and cheese biscuit sandwich—the chef Jack loved had decided to move on after Jagamot's defeat. It'd been a decent first go, according to Jack, but Addi would need to practice.

Afterward, they walked back to the cottage as a group, Jack tucking Navara's parchment into his satchel with an uncharacteristically solemn expression. No one else would be able to tell, but Hallie was his sister, his twin—she knew the casual scrunch of his nose and the way he swatted at his eye and his vague mutters about *mosquito season* were part of a show to hide the tear he shed for the woman he'd called *Gran* with such disgruntled affection.

Hallie stalled as long as possible, but the waning daylight told her they needed to return to Kyvena. There were people who needed to know what had happened, and Ben, the lost heir to the Cerl throne, was needed to halt any future attacks on Jayde.

That Ben was not only the future king of Cerulene, but also Ezekiel's son—Kase's cousin—was still quite the shock. But that revelation could be handled more privately. Slowly. When it no longer felt like they might all die at any moment.

Kase kept his hand on the small of her back as they stood before the archway, staring out at the world they'd left behind. It was full of sorrow and pain and darkness, but it was where she belonged.

They all stood staring at it, no one wanting to be the first.

It was Jack who finally broke the silence. "Welp, guess it's time. I would say *hope to see you soon*, but I think that'd be in bad taste."

Her stoic, stern mother promptly burst into tears.

Jack groaned, wrapping his arms around her and patting her back, rolling his eyes over her shoulder where only Hallie could see. "Now, Ma, I ain't saying you're old, but if I had to guess, you might be showing up first. Don't worry. I ain't going nowhere, and I might even let you name one of my chickens."

"John Carl Walker, I know I raised you better than that," Zelda hissed, but her brother just laughed. Zelda obviously didn't appreciate his gallows humor, but she hugged him tightly anyway. Her father joined, and Hallie followed.

One last time, the Walker family was together again. It ached, but it was a good ache—a healing one. The scents of mint, coffee, and unsurprisingly, bacon, filled her. This was a gift she never thought she would get. She hugged her family tighter.

She wished Kase could've had the same.

He deserved it more than anyone.

Wait.

She hadn't seen Zeke or the girl she'd glimpsed in the

portrait in Shackley Manor, and Kase hadn't said he had either, but that didn't mean they weren't here—or had been here.

When the hug ended, Hallie stood on tiptoe to whisper in Jack's ear, "The letters. Could you find one or two for me? If you have them?"

She knew not everyone wrote them for loved ones, but if there was even a chance Ana or Zeke left something behind...

Jack raised a red brow. "Depends. They're technically only for people who need the motivation to pass on to the beyond."

"You owe me," Hallie quipped.

He narrowed his eyes, and she continued, "Mama still doesn't know you're the one who set fire to the begonias, and..."

She looked back at their parents. Her father was wiping away her mother's tears while not bothering to brush away his own. She kept her voice low. "If you let Kase read the letters his siblings might have left him, I will continue to keep your little secret."

"Why do I—hey. Look at me when I'm rolling my eyes at you. Why do I care if you tell her? I'm already dead."

Hallie glared at him until he finally sighed. "Fine, but if Gran ever found out, she'd scruff me and toss me right smack into the beyond."

Hallie kissed his cheek. "Thank you."

She turned back and waved Kase over as Jack dug out Navara's notebook and golden quill. "Now, what were their names?"

Kase looked at him questioningly. Hallie tapped the notebook impatiently. "Ezekiel, or Zeke, and Ana Shackley."

Kase shook his head. "What're you doing?"

Jack tapped the quill on the notebook, and after a moment, he frowned. "Ezekiel Shackley never came through. Probably was ready for his death. I'm sorry I can't help there."

Hallie's heart sank, though she wasn't entirely surprised. Zeke had chosen his end. And after getting to know him over the months they'd been on the *Eudora* mission, it made sense the steady, smiling man had been ready to move on.

Jack tapped the quill again. "Ana...Ana Shackley...that sounds awful familiar." He took a pinch of Zuprium dust out of the pouch at his waist and sprinkled it onto the parchment. "Ah, yup, here we go. Have several from her, and—oh, *right*, she's the one who called me a blasted stars-idiot my first day here. Lovely girl. But her letters were the first ones I ever took, so she came to her senses in the end."

Hallie groaned and smacked her brother on the back of the head. "That's because you are a blasted stars-idiot."

Jack glared at her before murmuring a few words and swirling the dust on the notebook around. In seconds, a pile of six letters appeared. He shuffled through them. "Here ya are. Kase."

With a trembling hand, Kase took the letter. "I don't understand."

Jack sprinkled more dust on the others and with another murmured word, they disappeared in a glittering *poof.* "Sometimes it's hard to move on, understandably so, but Gran started having souls write letters to their loved ones to help them and anyone else who died after them prepare to go beyond. Helps if they know they won't be alone, y'know?" He took a deep breath. "Stars above, I'm gonna miss her. The girls will too. She always had a way with them—especially Anne." He replaced his notebook in his satchel and pointed at the letter in Kase's hand. "That won't last long in the mortal realm. Best read it here. I'll make sure it stays all nice and new for ya if you do return someday."

Kase swallowed thickly and croaked, "Thank you."

He turned away to read his letter.

It was time.

And that was when the tears started. She'd known they would come, but she'd wanted to stay strong. It was one thing to think her brother was lost in the aether. It was another to *know* he was here waiting for them, never able to leave or change. Instead of feeling as if he was off in another dimension, pretending he was off having all the adventures they'd dreamed of having as kids, it'd feel like he was just on the other side of the door...unseen and out of reach despite being mere feet away.

Why did that feel so much harder to endure?

She tried to swallow, to regain her composure, but she couldn't get her throat to work. Then Jack pulled her into another hug, and she gave up, sobbing into his shoulder. The ugly kind, all snotty and soggy and awful. Nothing like the single graceful tear heroines shed in books.

"Aw, no, not you too, not the shirt," he moaned. "You know how hard it is to get new clothes here?"

She tried to laugh. Just sobbed harder instead.

"Aw, Hal." He got quiet, first—then a little shaky. "Shoulda told you sooner, but don't you feel guilty about all this, you hear? You tell Niels, too. If I'd gotten to choose who walked outta there, it'd'a gone the same way."

"I-I won't feel guilty." Every word emerged like a hiccup. "I pushed you, anyway. Don't tell Mama."

"I *knew* it," he gasped in false outrage, and she finally laughed, even if it sounded more like a whimper. "Always were jealous of me. Like it was my fault I got born the smarter twin, the better-looking—"

She leaned back, scowling. "*Jack.*"

"What? You started it." He crushed her against him again, and she let his gangly arms squeeze the life out of her. Metaphorically.

"Don't take this all wrong, but I hope I never see you again," he mumbled into her hair. "If you do end up in Souls Meet, though...I'll be here."

The soft summery breeze rustled her hair, and she squeezed her brother tighter. He was too skinny, always had been. It was almost as if he'd been doomed to break, but he never had. Not really. His body had been crushed by beams and stone in a faraway mine, but his spirit was where it needed to be.

He'd gotten to realize his own destiny here, just as Hallie had in Kyvena.

"Love you," Hallie sobbed.

"Love ya, Lark."

And then Jack pulled back, tears in his own eyes. "Get on, now, and don't you dare look back."

Stepping up beside Hallie and threading his arm around her waist, Kase held the letter out for her brother to take. "Thank you, Jack."

Jack took it and used more dust to make it disappear like the others. He smiled and held out his hand. Kase shook it. Jack used the motion to pull Kase in close and whisper something in his ear.

After a moment, Kase stepped back, nodding. "Promise."

Without a word or a look toward her, her brother turned and left to hug their parents again.

"What'd he say?" Hallie asked, glancing at her brother suspiciously, though still wiping a few stray tears from her eyes as she got her breathing under control.

Kase smiled, his eyes tinged pink. "To take care of you. And that if I didn't, I'd have to answer to him." Hallie groaned, and Kase let out a soft laugh. "Seems like we both have protective older brothers."

"Only by seven and a half minutes."

Kase merely laughed.

Hallie watched her parents and Jack a moment longer before facing where Ben waited at the Nether Gate's opening, his hand still glowing. She and Kase walked over.

Kase asked, "Do you know what happens to the Essence powers still in the guardian swords?"

Skibs had Kainadr's shadow sword in a sheath hanging off his belt. Xera's soul sword held the Gate open. Ben shook his head. "Dunno, but since we need to return the guardians to their respective Gates, I guess we'll find out? Let's just hope it doesn't cause the world to collapse or anything."

"Something for me to research when I go back to University in the autumn," Hallie said.

Kase smiled. "You're returning?"

Hallie nodded. "Yes. Only a semester and a half left before I can graduate, and I needed a few extra topics to add to my graduate thesis."

"I'm proud of you," Kase said, putting an arm around her shoulders and squeezing.

Ben rolled his eyes. "Listen, I put up with you both making eyes at each other all night last night, what with the near-death experiences and all. Please don't make me suffer the entire way back to the surface."

Kase laughed, but he didn't take his arm back. After another minute or two, her parents joined them. It was time.

First her parents went through, both looking over their shoulders at Jack one last time, Ben holding the Gate open with the guardian sword. Then it was Hallie and Kase's turn.

"Thank you. For getting me the letter," Kase said quietly.

She looked up at him, the golden afternoon sunlight illuminating his handsome features. "You're welcome. We'll see her again someday. And Zeke."

His jaw was firm, and teeth clenched. She rubbed his arm. "What did it say?"

He looked down at her, sliding his fingers into hers. "I forgive you."

Hallie squeezed his hand tighter, tears burning in her eyes. Kase blinked rapidly before putting on a small smile.

"I promised I'd get you home."

Then led her through the Nether Gate, and neither of them looked back.

LE MORTE D'ARTHUR

Ten Years Later

Jove

IN THE DECADE SINCE THE Gates War, the city of Kyvena had changed little. After months of repair, much of the city was back to its normal functionality, but it had taken years to dull the scars left behind in the minds of the citizens.

The leading scholars estimated nearly five thousand people were lost over the course of the war that had only lasted a few months, though some argued the Great War had never ended that day nearly twenty-five years ago when Ezekiel Fairchild had been executed, though all agreed that all conflict finally resolved on July 20, 4501, known as Gates Armistice Day, when Jove—reinstated as High Guardsman—the City Governors, and King Asa aven d'Correa signed the Armistice Treaty after a few months of negotiations. That was also the day Hallie Walker, now Shackley, restored electricity to Kyvena with the help of Felyra and Saldr.

The King himself financed the rebuilding of the city with the coffers General Marcos Correa had stockpiled in Sol Adrid. That was before Ben Reiss—an entirely separate man, of course—had been exiled for his war crimes.

Jove and the remaining Council members from across the country met and decided it best to let him live, as creating a power vacuum with their neighbor was hardly in their best interest. Thanks to the evidence presented by Saldr, Felyra, and the other Yalvs, it was proven Ben had not been in his right mind when attacking both Myrrai and Kyvena, courtesy of the malevolent power he wielded.

Didn't erase his crimes, but it allowed a more lenient sentence.

It'd taken Jove ten years to be able to walk the streets on Gates Armistice Day. It would take him a few more to make a speech on it. They asked him every year, but he'd always passed that duty to Saldr or Anderson Enright—healed once Hallie Walker and King Asa had forged the third Gate and who had most recently been elected Stradat. They had always been better with people, and Jove had no words that could describe what he'd felt that fateful day or in the ones that followed. He'd healed from them physically, but the emotional scars ran deep.

Clara, his sons, and their little one on the way were what got him through and kept him pushing forward trying to make Jayde the best it could possibly be while still respecting its shortcomings. With them and the nation depending on him, he hadn't had a drop of alcohol since the night the city fell.

A promise he'd finally kept.

Sammy and Jonathan ran ahead down the lane, racing toward the monument waiting at the end. Jonathan was three years Samuel's junior, but the boys were fast friends, and they always got into the most trouble whenever Arthur Jack tagged along.

The sight of the three boys together always brought tears to his eyes because all he could think about was another set of three boys traipsing through the city streets or in the Manor's courtyard.

Clara's hand slipped into his. "It's rather hot today." She

squeezed his fingers lightly. "Why don't we grab some ice cream on the way home?"

A parlor had recently opened in the market square near the Manor. Jove chuckled a little, breaking his melancholy. "When do you *not* want to stop for ice cream on the way home?"

Clara rubbed a hand over her swollen stomach and smiled. "If you want Miravel to like you, you'll buy her mama a chocolate sundae. Extra cherries."

"I still don't think it's a girl," Jove said, bringing her hand to his lips and giving it a soft kiss.

"Well, love, you're wrong, and you'll eat your words soon." She gave him a full-toothed grin. "And then you can bring me double the ice cream."

Jove wrapped an arm around her shoulder and squeezed. "I'll do that anyway."

With most people celebrating in the public squares, hearing speeches, and purchasing gifts for loved ones, the lane they walked down was mostly empty. The occasional bark of a dog or the soft echoes of the nearby square interrupted the solitude every few steps.

"Happy Gates!" a middle-aged woman greeted from where she decorated her shop door with bright yellow flowers looped together along the frame.

"Happy Gates to you," Clara said with a wave.

Jove tipped his bowler at the woman with a small smile. They walked a little further only greeting a few other stragglers who had yet to make their way to the celebrations. At the end stood the memorial his sons now chased each other around.

Jove and his family would be dining with Saldr, Felyra, and their children later that evening as was their yearly tradition. The Passages to the Yalven lands were open once more with the treaty signed.

Usually, Kase's family would join, but they'd recently returned from Cerulene and would be leaving on a trip to Crystalfell soon. They'd visit once the baby arrived. Newly postpartum, Clara would appreciate some painting time with Hallie.

"Sammy, Jon, come here, will you?" Clara said, slipping away from Jove and going to wrangle her children.

His mother was set to arrive soon to fetch the boys. With

the school year finishing and the baby due any day, it would be best if they stayed a few weeks out in the little hamlet of Windwick where his mother had taken up residence.

Once the baby came, she would come visit with the boys before staying a while to help them all settle in as a family of five.

His mother finally got to return to life in the countryside, though she split her time between the Manor, which now belonged to Jove, and her modest cottage. If Jove hadn't taken on his High Guardsman duties once more, he might've moved his family out there as well, but somehow he doubted it.

All his life, he'd been wary of his childhood home because the memories he'd lived there were quite painful. But now, with the life he and Clara had breathed into it, it finally felt like home. He felt a part of its history and couldn't imagine raising his family anywhere else.

Clara had also put the surviving oddly colored fruit paintings into storage and replaced them with her own works, which—in Jove's opinion—had made all the difference.

"Mama, Mama, Mama!" Jon cried, trying to climb up the fence surrounding the dark obelisk at the center of a small court. Benches dotted the outer edge, and red and blue flowers bloomed in the space between the fence and the monument.

"Yes, dearest?" Clara said, coming to stand beside him, putting a hand on his shoulder to keep him grounded.

"I wanna read the names. Sammy says Grandpa's name's there! And Grammy's!"

Clara smiled and pointed halfway up the pillar. "There, Miravel Davey. That's who baby Rav will be named after."

Her voice only strained once, but she swallowed hard. The years had made the loss easier to stand, but the ache would never truly leave. Jove stepped up beside her, giving the top of her head a soft kiss before setting a hand on Jon's other shoulder. Sammy came up beside him.

Jove pointed to a name near the bottom. "And that's Grandpa's. Can you read it?"

Jon's head bobbed. "Har...Har-lan *Shack*-ley."

Jove's stomach hardened at the sound of his father's name on his son's lips. He didn't think the guilt mixed with the relief and pride of his father's last actions in life would ever fade entirely. He'd hated the man, but in the end, he'd saved Kase. In the end, he'd tried, and it was enough for Jove to offer him a hint of respect all these years later. Because without that sacrifice, Jove's sons would have been reading their uncle's name engraved upon the polished black stone instead.

Jove squeezed his shoulder. "That's right. He and Grammy fought to keep us safe, and we're thankful for their sacrifice."

Jon still hadn't quite grasped that concept, but he nodded enthusiastically before dashing off around the court again.

Jove would fight any enemy, any battle for him to stay so carefree. That was why he agreed to step into the High Guardsman role at the end of the war, and he would stay as long as he was needed.

Samuel stayed a while longer, gazing up at it. "I was there, right?"

Jove knelt, taking his eldest son's hands in his. His blue eyes were just as bright as the day he'd been born, a light in the darkness. "You were, and you are the reason we're still here today."

"Really?" the boy asked, skeptical.

"Really," Jove said, reaching up and ruffling his tight curls. Samuel nodded and ran off after his brother, the serious slant of his brow gone with a game of their own making.

Jove rose, grimacing at the creak in his knees as he did so. Clara laughed at him, but he rolled his eyes and pulled her to his side. "I can't help it."

"At least you're not cramping all over," she chuckled, patting his chest as he led her from the court.

He gestured for his sons to follow. "Let's go get some ice cream, shall we?" She leaned her head against his shoulder as he said, "Unless you're trying to tell me our new little *boy* is on the way. Was that why you suggested we walk?"

She just laughed. "A lady never reveals her secrets."

His wife molded her body into his as they walked away from the memorial. So much had changed in the ten years since, and all of it for the better. When he felt the pull toward his vices and that deep, dark sadness that waited at the edge of his memory, he remembered all the good there was in the world and all the good that was to come. Many times he wished Zeke, Ana, and even Harlan were there to watch his children grow into adults, to see the families his siblings would have created and the grandfather Harlan might've been, but Jove was the man he was today because of both the light and the dark.

Time healed all wounds, but for the moment, he was thankful for scars.

Kase

KASE SET MERLIN, HIS HOVER, down at the edge of the meadow. He'd move him later. The way Hallie's eyes would light up when he surprised her coming home early was worth trudging back out to move it to the airfields. That was the only reason Merlin hadn't shot that blue liquid at him for leaving him in the wheat field. The machine had always liked Hallie more. Understandably. Hallie brought him a treat whenever they went on trips for her work in the form of new oil.

The needy thing still beeped sadly at him as he grabbed a small sack full to bursting with books he'd bought while on assignment in the city and climbed out of the cockpit. "I'll bring Hals with me when I move you later, deal?"

Merlin beeped at him a little worriedly. In the ten years since their meeting, Kase had learned how to interpret the different tones quite well. "Yes, I promise Jo will behave if she joins. Deal?"

Last time, the four-year-old had drawn stars and moons on the back of his seats. Merlin hadn't been pleased.

The hover flashed the headlights at him in agreement as Kase closed the windshield with a crisp snap. He patted its side. "Good boy."

Kase hopped off the wing and readjusted the sack on his back. He'd managed to find a copy of *Le Morte d'Arthur* at last. He'd thought they'd all been burned or otherwise destroyed during the war, but after some digging and his copilot Laurence Hixon's help, he'd discovered a small bookshop in Lenara had been hoarding the tome for nearly a millennium.

If Kase couldn't fly with Skibs, then Hix was the next best option.

Regardless, Hallie would probably bring the book on their upcoming trip to read to Merlin, which would only make him like her more.

Blast it.

But he guessed it couldn't be helped. He would also have to make sure his mother didn't sneak the copy out with her when she came over for tea the next day. He liked having her nearby, but he was beginning to suspect half the reason she'd wanted to move out to the countryside was because he and Hallie had all the books. Shackley Manor had been mostly restored, but she only stayed there when visiting with Clara and Jove for about a week or so every month.

The dying sunlight of the late July evening set the rippling waves of wheat aglow. This little hamlet on the east side of the Nardens, Windwick, hadn't been ravaged by the war. It was made up of a small smattering of houses and a few necessities such as a dry goods store, inn, and within the last five years or so, a school.

That'd been Hallie's doing. It'd been her first attempt at starting one outside Kyvena, and next week, she and Kase would be off to Crystalfell to open a third.

She'd also been in talks with King Asa's council in the Cerl capital of Sol Adrid. Skibs had started to turn the kingdom around, and a school like Hallie's was a popular idea among Cerl citizens. He and his wife, Queen Lucienne aven d'Fairchild, were planning on sending their children, Princess Lilian and Prince Ezekiel, there as soon as it was up and running the next year.

But while Hallie's dream grew from year to year, they never planned on moving from their cozy little two-story cottage filled with books, too many glass figurines, and love. They were only a half-hour Merlin flight to Kyvena and a simple Passage brick trip from Stoneset. Hallie had said unless the world needed saving, time didn't need any more manipulation, but she made an exception for her parents.

Problem was, once Arthur Jack had learned how to read and write, he'd started sending notes to Granna through it begging her to bring over cookies, cakes, and all sorts of confectionaries, and Zelda always obliged. He was also quite heavily influenced by his younger sisters. They particularly enjoyed Granna's lemon bars.

Kase didn't mind the extra sweets, and with Windwick being on a small lake, Stowe preferred fishing on this side of the Nardens. He, Kase, and Arthur Jack would regularly go out and catch a few, but they always had Zelda fry them up—safer that way.

Kase approached the cottage and its cobbled stone fence hugging the front garden. A little boy with bright red curls climbed up on top of the fence, a few wayward pebbles skittering in his wake.

Kase beamed, his chest light.

"Papa!" the boy shouted before leaping down, nearly tripping on the landing. He tumbled through the wheat and leapt into Kase's outstretched arms.

"See you've been placed on lookout duty, AJ?" Kase said with a laugh as he spun his son around. The boy was only seven, but he was growing like a wildfire. Kase had only been gone a week, and he could've sworn his son had grown another foot. The fault of Stowe's genes, and he'd blame him for it when AJ finally topped him in height.

Just like he could place the blame for AJ's garden-grubby hands digging into the sack on Kase's shoulder, going for the books, directly on Hallie's shoulders. Kase put him down. "Careful! These are for Mama. Besides, what'd we say about dirty hands around the books?"

"But that one has my name on it! And a sword!"

Kase laughed. "If Mama says yes, we can read that one tonight before bed."

AJ grumbled halfhearted complaints. Kase ruffled his curls. "I'll even see if Mama will read each character in her funny voices. Deal?"

The boy brightened at that, nodding and taking Kase's hand, pulling him toward the cottage. "Mama said Lolly's bringing back Sammy and Jon the day after tomorrow too because Auntie Clara is about to have the baby. Penny says it's a girl, but I hope it's another boy like me."

Penny, or Penelope, was the most opinionated and stubborn of his children. At only six, she was too bright for her own good.

"We won't know until the baby's here, but I'd wager Uncle Jove hopes it's a boy, too." Kase couldn't imagine what Jove would do with a girl. Never sleep soundly again, probably. Stars knew Kase hadn't. He kept a hand on his son's shoulder as they walked. "What do you think they should name it?"

AJ thought for a moment. "Aragorn."

Kase laughed. "Ah, Mama started reading *Lord of the Rings* to you?"

"Uh-huh."

"Aragorn is my favorite, too. Though I think Theoden is my second."

"Who?"

"Just wait." Kase squeezed his shoulder.

They'd just reached the gate when the cottage's front door opened, and two girls spilled out. "Papa!"

The smallest one, Jo, sprinted across the garden and threw herself at Kase's knees. Black curls flying, she knocked him off his feet. He fell backward into the wheat, his breath knocked out of him as she squealed, "*Papa!* You home!"

Her big blue eyes practically took up her entire face. She was only four, but there was no doubt that she was Kase's daughter...in looks and personality. He was in for it, that was for sure.

"Oof, Jo, I missed you too," Kase tugged her into his lap and squeezed her, tickling her sides.

She grunted and giggled, pushing against his chest. "Stop, Papa!"

"It's my turn," Penny whined, waiting with her arms crossed above them. She had her long brown hair pulled into a sensible, no-nonsense braid, her hazel eyes assessing. Jo turned around and stuck her tongue out at her sister. Penny returned it before also leaping onto Kase's chest as he tried to get up.

Penny kissed his cheek, then crawled over him to get to the sack of books that had fallen in the initial attack.

Kase groaned as one of the girls kneed him in the stomach. Probably Jo.

Laughter came from the cottage door. Kase shakily stood, brushing the dust and wheat and dirt off his trousers and pilot's jacket.

"You never stood a chance of making it to the door unscathed." Hallie stood in the cottage doorway, hand on the frame, a smile on her face. She was even more beautiful than the day he'd stumbled into the bookshop. Ten years hadn't felt long at all with her by his side. It didn't matter how many times he'd left for work and returned home; his heart still pounded in his chest every time he saw her, as if they were still newlyweds.

She ambled over, stopping by the sack of books their children had torn into. When she spotted the top book, she gasped and picked up *Le Morte d'Arthur*. "Where did you find this?"

"Lenara. Paid a pretty sum to get it for you, so you'd better be happy to eat only rice and beans on our trip next week."

Hallie hugged it to her chest. "Thank you."

Kase bent over, setting the sack right and handed it to AJ. "Go put them on the shelf. Carefully!"

"And alphabetically!" Hallie added.

"Hals, he's seven."

She waved impatiently. "He knows what to do."

AJ gasped excitedly and slung the bag onto his shoulder, sprinting toward the cottage, the books slapping against his back with each stride.

Penny skipped inside behind him, saying something about organizing them by color. Jo stomped in, whining, "I wanna touch the books too!"

Hallie blew a stray piece of hair that had fallen into her face. "I feel bad for my mother. She's going to have her hands full while we're gone."

Kase slid an arm around her waist and drew her to him. "Aren't you looking forward to some time with your dashing husband sans barbarians?"

"But they're *our* barbarians."

"True." He pressed a kiss to her lips. She grabbed his jacket and tugged him closer.

"Ew! Mama stop! Stop kissing Papa!" Jo shouted from the doorway. "EW!"

She really had only two volumes—loud and louder.

Hallie broke the kiss, a teasing smile on her face. "Still want to discuss having a fourth?"

Kase didn't let go of her waist as he led her toward the cottage. Jo scurried back inside, yelling something else at her siblings.

He rubbed his thumb across the bottom of Hallie's ribs, leaning in to whisper in her ear, "Why do you think I want some alone time with you on our trip?"

Her cheeks bloomed scarlet, and a grin curled across his face. He would never get tired of the way he could make her blush.

"Something wrong with that?" he teased.

"Not at all." Hallie turned to give him another lingering kiss. "We do have quite a few names left on our list."

Laughing, Kase followed her inside and closed the door behind him. He was home. He had a beautiful wife, three happy children, and all the books he could ask for. It was the life he'd always dreamed of, and he was grateful he got to live it.

L O V E   T H I S   B O O K ?

Consider leaving an honest review where you purchased this book and on social media.

ACKNOWLEDGMENTS

As always, I'm so thankful for my entire family and their encouragement—especially Jason and my children. Words can't really express just how thankful I am for you.

Thank you to my line editor, Cassidy Clarke. You're the reason this book sounds pretty, and I love that you loved Jack's chickens. Because they were also my favorite. Shoutout to my critique partners/early readers, Blake and Brittany. I'm sorry for the rollercoaster of "But what if I do this?" for the last year or so.

I also had some lovely beta readers this time around, whose feedback was just lovely: Jecoliah, Stephanie, Stevie, Emma, Alisha, Megan, Brenna, and Tristian. Thank you to Lauren for your filming the walk to your chicken coop so I could know what it smelled and sounded like. Jack's hens thank you, too.

I'd also like to thank my proofreader, Haven. I'm sorry I made you wait 40 chapters for a nose flick. Thank you also to Tiffany, who read my entire book in an incredibly short amount of time because I needed to know if I should add more scenes or not. This was all less than a month before release...and two weeks before upload day.

Deandra Scicluna, my cover artist, THANK YOU again for the amazing art!

And thank you to you, reader. I can't even begin to find a way to express my appreciation for all your support through this series. It's been my childhood dream to publish fantasy books, and it didn't really hit me until this last book was published. And that is all possible because you loved Kase and Hallie as much as I did (and still do). I also hope you loved Jack. He's one of my new favorites. Thank you.

GLOSSARY

Abram Loffler: oldest Stradat, known for taking naps
Anderson Enright [inn-RIGHT] Petra's betrothed, friend of Jove, vying for election to the City Council
Ana Shackley: youngest Shackley sibling, deceased
Asa aven d'Correa [AY-suh, AH-vin]: younger brother of Filip, illegitimate son of the late Queen
Astraea aven d'Soria: Queen of Cerulene during the Great War, mother of Filip and Asa
Aurora Gate: powerful magical archway that holds all timelines
Ben Reiss [RYSS]: Watch agent, best friend of Kase (known as Skibs), the Essence of Keys
Called: Chronals called to a higher purpose of protecting Yalvara and the Gate, most wield vasa in some capacity, some are more powerful or have more sophisticated purposes than others (ie: Saldr the only one of his purpose)
Cerulene [SIR-oo-LEEN]: powerful kingdom on Yalvara, ruled by King Filip
Chosen: Certain Chronals/Yalvs/those of Yalven ancestry chosen to wield an Essence power
Chronal [KROW-nul]: Yalv with the capacity to wield vasa or become an Essence, tasked with protecting the Gate
Clara Shackley [CLAHR-uh]: wife of Jove, mother of Samuel, painter
Dawn: beginning of time on Yalvara when Tovo was shattered to save humanity from Jagamot
Ebba Fleming [EBB-uh FLEM-ing]: mechanic
Ellis Carrington: Hallie's friend and classmate
Emilia Fairchild: daughter of Ezekiel and Rose, deceased

Engineer Corp: group of brilliant minds in Jayde tasked with developing new technology/recovering old technological secrets from First Earth

Eravin Gray [air-uh-VIN]: leader of One World's Kyvena group, ex-best friend of Kase

Essence: term used to describe the five splintered powers of Tovo (Essences of Keys, Time, Souls, Spark, and Light)

Eudora McKenzie [YOU-dor-UH]: wife of General Samuel McKenzie, founded Jayde's Engineer Corp

Ezekiel Fairchild: brother to Les, executed for selling hover secrets to Cerulene

Felyra Bessette [Fay-LEER-uh Buh-SET]: also known as Fely, hails from the Isles in Tev Rubika, Yalven, has a rare Chronal power that allows her to take Soul from living things such as plants, betrothed to King Filip aven d'Soria

Filip aven d'Soria [Fi-LIP, So-REE-uh]: King of Cerulene, Essence of Souls, betrothed to Lady Felyra Bessette

First Earth: third planet from the sun in the Milky Way solar system, destroyed over 1000 years prior to *Cities of Smoke & Starlight*

Fiver: denomination of Jaydian money, equal to 5 pieces

General Marcos Correa [COR-ray-UH]: supreme military leader of Cerl forces, Essence of Light

General Samuel McKenzie: man who led the Life Ships, established Jayde on Yalvara, husband of Eudora

Great War: began as a conflict over resources, world-wide, ended with the disappearance of the Yalvs

Hallie Walker [HAA-lee; 'Hallie' rhymes with 'valley']: Yalven scholar at the University, hails from Stoneset

Harlan Shackley: the Stradat Lord Kapitan of Jayde, father of Kase, Jove, Zeke, and Ana, husband of Les

Heddie Koppen: Head Guardswoman of the Watch

High Council: Jayde's governing body consisting of the Stradats, the Lord Kapitan, and the High Guardsmen

High Guardsman/woman: head of the Watch

Hover: general term for airship using hover technology

Hover Bike: motorcycle-like vehicle used by the Crews to train new pilots on hover controls, cheap

Hover Crews: sometimes called simply 'Crews', force of hover ships, an offshoot of the Jaydian military

Hunder [HUN-dur]: denomination of Jaydian money, equal to 100 pieces

Jack Walker: Hallie's twin brother, deceased

Jagamot [JAG-uh-mot]: great evil of Yalven lore

Jayde [JAYd]: nation ruled by an oligarchy called the High Council, founded by refugees of First Earth

Jove Shackley [JOHV]: oldest Shackley brother, married to Clara

Kase Shackley [KAEss SHACK-lee]: Senior Pilot, youngest son of the Stradat Lord Kapitan

Kyvena [Kigh-VIN-uh]: capital of Jayde

Laurent [luh-RAHNT]: small village between Kyvena and Narden Pass

Lavinia Richter [Luh-VIN-ee-uh RICK-ter] noble lady of Jayde, daughter of Stradat Forrest Richter, deceased, ex-love interest of Kase

Les Shackley [LESS]: mother of Kase, Jove, Zeke, and Ana, wife of Harlan, sister to Ezekiel Fairchild

Life Ships: enormous vessels that carried remnants of humanity from First Earth to Yalvara

Lord Elder: leader of the Yalven nations

Lord Kapitan [KAP-ih-TIN]: high commander of the military

Lucienne (Lucy) Doyle: Ben Reiss' sweetheart

Millicent Sarson: female Stradat and ex-military general, intent on taking down Harlan Shackley

Myrrai [muh-RAE]: Yalven city, known as the realm of starlight

Nar: large village at the entrance to the Narden Pass

Navara Walker [Nuh-VAR-uh]: great-grandmother of Hallie and Jack, daughter of the Lord Elder

Niels Metzinger [NEELS]: farmer turned miner from Stoneset, Hallie's ex-sweetheart, best friend of Jack

One World: group intent on uniting all Yalvara under one banner using whatever means necessary, considered anarchists

Owen Christie: Yalven professor at the University

Petra Lieber [Peh-TRAH Lee-BUR]: Hallie's friend and classmate, betrothed to Anderson Enright

Randall Fairchild: son of Ezekiel and Rose, twin brother to Sullivan, deceased

Relic: an item made from Zuprium to aid Essence wielders in controlling and focusing their power

Rose Fairchild: wife of Ezekiel, mother to Sullivan, Randall, and Emilia, deceased

Saldr [SAWL-der]: Yalven ambassador to Jayde, powerful Vasa wielder, Called

Silver Coast: small coastal nation, used to be a part of Jayde

Sol Adrid [SOL uh-DRID]: capital of Cerulene

Soul: life force, some can use this as a sort of magical power, Ezekiel Fairchild discovered how to harnass this

Stoneset: small mountain village in the Narden Range, on the other side of the Narden Pass

Stowe Walker: father of Hallie and Jack, husband of Zelda, village-trained medic, innkeeper

Stradat [straa-DIT]: highest elected official, three sit on the High Council

Sullivan Fairchild: son of Ezekiel and Rose, twin brother to Randall, deceased

Tenner: denomination of Jaydian money, equal to 10 pieces

Tev Rubika [TEV ROO-bih-KUH]: oldest non-Yalven nation, dealing with civil war aftermath

Toro [TOR-oh]: (known as Tovo by Jaydians) Yalven god, his powers were split in the Dawn during the great battle with Jagamot

Vasa [VAH-suh]: Zuprium dust used by Called Yalven for different purposes, used mainly to manipulate time

Watch: Jayde's intelligence and police force

Yalvar Fuel [YAAL-var]: caustic resource found beneath the surface Yalvara, used in engines, being fazed out by the introduction of electricity

Yalvara [YAAL-var-UH]: planet near the edge of the Milky Way

Yalvs [YAALvs]: people native to Yalvara

Yarrow Barbary: trapper working the Narden Range

Yrea [ee-RAY-uh]: basic skill all Called learn, creates a floating ball of energy that looks and acts like fire

Zalina [zuh-LEE-nuh]: end of time

Zeke Shackley [ZEEK]: Lieutenant Colonel, medical specialist, middle Shackley brother, deceased

Zelda Walker: mother of Hallie and Jack, wife of Stowe, renowned baker

Zuprium [Zuh-PREE-um]: metal found on Yalvara that doesn't rust, is difficult to destroy, and when combined with electricity, creates hover capabilities, sacred to Yalvs

ALLI EARNEST drinks way too much coffee and is obsessed with redwood candles, but growing up with two sisters, she's always been a tad overdramatic. It doesn't help that she enjoys books with dragons, wizards, and laser swords.

Graduating with a bachelor's degree in Middle Grades Education, Alli taught English Language Arts for five years and tried to convince thirteen-year-olds that Poe wasn't nearly as crazy as he sounded.

A present, Alli writes science-fiction and fantasy from an office filled with books and other collectibles. She lives in the southern US with her family.

www.alliearnest.com